Books by Thomas Williams

Ceremony of Love
Town Burning
The Night of Trees
A High New House
Whipple's Castle

WHIPPLE'S CASTLE

THOMAS WILLIAMS

WHIPPLE'S CASTLE

RANDOM HOUSE

NEW YORK

I would like to thank the people of the John Simon Guggenheim Memorial Foundation for their gift of a year's time to write. I would also like to thank all those responsible for the generous Roos/Atkins Literary Award of 1963.

PART I

How sweetly did they float upon the wings
Of silence, through the empty-vaulted night,
At every fall smoothing the Raven down
Of darkness till it smil'd . . .

John Milton: *Comus*

1

One evening in November of 1942, in the town of Leah, New Hampshire, the first real snow was falling. In the Town Square, at five o'clock, the big flakes fell slowly out of the darkness into the light from the store windows. They fell silently upon the bandstand, upon the long limbs of the elms, upon the few parked cars. Everything became bundled up and soft, and the snow still fell. Horace Whipple had just come out of Trask's Pharmacy, where he had been sent by his father to buy a bottle of aspirin, and he stood on the sidewalk in his leather-top boots. Where did the sidewalk end and the street begin? It was all so clean, it was all so cold. He was happy for the snow, and hoped that it would never stop. From Bank Street across the square came the dim lights of the plow truck, yellow as distant fires, the softened jangle and clank of tire chains, and the submerged boom of the plow.

As Horace walked away from the lights, the snow itself seemed to give him all the light he needed, and when he passed beneath a streetlight he was displeased by its brightness; the snow in the bright funnel swirled too quickly. As he left the streetlight he moved again into a dim limbo, where the world began again to glow with its own Christmas light. He was happy to be walking home in his warm mackinaw, with the bottle of aspirin safe in his deep pocket. There were reasons why he should not be happy, but the snow had somehow taken precedence over them, because the snow made this time all the times of snow, the first real snow of before Christmas, not just this year that he was fourteen.

All the families were warm and safe in their houses, and as he passed he saw across the round white hedges the orange windows, and inside were faces he knew, mouths smiling and moving. For a moment he thought: Are they talking about me? Are those smiles cruel? No. They were all smiling and saying words of love to each other, or deciding to make popcorn, and to have something sweet and hot to drink.

He was happy to see the snow build pure weightless epaulettes upon his mackinaw, to feel his body's heat come out of his collar and warm his chin. The snow had brought the families deep inside again, and told them it was white and deep and cold outside, all one whiteness without top or bottom to it, or sides. Infinity out there beyond the warm lights and the floor registers too hot, now, to walk upon in bare feet. When he got home he would enter a warmth like that, and shake off his snow as though it were proof of his bravery—proof of a journey the snow had made dramatic and hazardous; he had been outside, out in the world alone, and they would all look up at him and admire him. They would all be shivery and tender, chilled by the cold air that would breathe from his clothes into the warm house, and he would be swaggering and strong.

He strode along softly through the deep powder, and finally he came to High Street, where he would turn up the steep hill toward his family's house. The last streetlight stood on this corner, and he stopped just before he came into its light to look back downstreet toward the faint red glow of the Town Square. He looked down the long, silent street for a while, then climbed up into the hill that was smooth and strangely white even in its darkness, until he came like a traveler to the lights of his home.

Again he stopped, wishing his vision of welcome could be true. In order to prolong his journey he stepped off the pure blankness where he knew the front walk to be, onto the property of the lawn. The snow made everything the same beneath his feet, as though the high house were a rock towering out of the sea, and he moved slowly around it like a boat, breaking the even snow, leaving behind him only a temporary wake which would close perfectly again. A guilty feeling, to break the calm white and approach the bay window of the living room from the wrong side. He stopped ten yards away, now pretending to be a

tree rooted beneath the snow in solid earth, having a perfect right to stand forever outside the curved window. At first he saw only the flash of orange light crossed by the net of window sash, and then the sash disappeared as the walls inside, the tables and the lamps, his father's dangerous shoulders above the woven back of his wheelchair, sorted themselves out and became what they were.

Horace backed carefully away until a real tree touched him— a painful nudge that pushed his cap forward, and made him rub the back of his head. It was the white maple with faces in its burls, and arms that seemed always to strain horribly, yet now held up only the fine dim lace of snow. Above him the dark house rose away from the bay window to other lights in other windows that were dim because the light came down a hall, or through an empty room from an odd doorway that shouldn't have been left open. Somewhere in the house were his mother, his two brothers and his sister, each alone behind a door, or up a steep flight of open stairs in a private place. This was his home, and yet the huge house was not friendly to him. Its angles and alcoves were too sharp or deep for him. In it he had a room that was called his own, but strange shapes owned it, really; it had never been his. They let him sleep just outside the territory they claimed with shadow arms, only in the very center of his bed. One of his closets he could not enter except in the brightest daylight, and even then the light seemed reluctant to come into the room past the arched windows, as though fear dimmed it.

He would have to go back around to the tall front door and go inside, wanting to, loving to go inside near the hardwood fire, where his father might rule that he could stay and be warm. Yet as he moved back across the sifting white, it seemed as though the house itself slowly, ponderously turned to face him, to expect his entrance at the only proper place, and he would have to do some ritual of penance he should remember, but could not.

Harvey Whipple waited, imprisoned in his wheelchair, for his youngest son to come back with the aspirin. His pain was not sharp, but seemed to have behind it remorseless force, like an ocean liner's slow nudge against the pilings of its dock. His right

leg seemed to impale his hip, and that pressure grew and ebbed, grew and ebbed. He'd been trying to read the business section of the Sunday *Times,* and now his frustration at not having enough capital merged with the insistent push of pain in his leg and hip. The businessmen whose fortunes or promotions made them news smiled out of their gray photographs as though from another continent, another world. Harvey wanted to get rich too. What else was there to do now that he had to sit in a wheelchair and try to deal with pain that had a life—a personality, it seemed —of its own, with its own schedules of force and remission he could neither predict nor control? Only money, he had decided, lots of money, triumphant money, might act as a balm.

His leg had been crumpled, shredded, buckled, bent double in an automobile accident five years before. The accident had not been his fault, and the insurance settlement had been a good one, for New Hampshire; after all his medical bills had been paid he still had thirty-five thousand dollars. But he could hardly walk, and now seldom tried his crutches. When he wanted to go somewhere, his eldest son, Wood, had to drive him—an arrangement neither of them liked at all.

When Horace came in with the aspirin, he left the front inner door open, tipped over the elephant-leg umbrella stand and tracked snow all down the hall into the living room. Perhaps it was true that Horace intended to go back, shut the inner door and pick up the canes and marbles that had rolled out of the elephant leg; perhaps he hadn't waited to brush the snow off his boots because he hurried to give his father the aspirin. But by this time Harvey heard his own voice bellowing "God DAMN it, you clumsy IDIOT!" and saw the fear and disappointment on his son's face. It was real fear, the kind he never intended to invoke, and this infuriated him all the more, so that he yelled the words again, thinking how his son had no cause to fear him, because he was merely acting, that was all. And the pain could excuse whatever edge was in his voice—why wasn't it excused? Horace, the oaf who was always having accidents, who was in trouble at school, who was called "Horse," who was afraid of the dark but not of breaking his bones.

"Give me the goddam aspirin before you manage to break the bottle!"

Fear. Horace's hands wouldn't come out of his mittens; when they did, the change fell on the carpet and rolled perversely in all directions. In silence Harvey let the scattering of the change do its work—yet he didn't want his son to fear him, or anyone to fear him. He watched his son's broad young back, mackinaw skirts touching the floor as he grubbed for the change. Didn't they all know that he was only acting? While he yelled or swore at them he still thought clearly, and was just, even in his mock rage. But his children had never lived anywhere but in this madhouse; it was their only place to be. And so to them he was not the mad actor he considered himself to be, but a madman.

He had watched his own strange face in his bathroom mirror, and seen how it had grown white and slack about the cheeks while his eyes grew round and dark, like cripples' eyes. It was a quivering, frightening face, not really his. His crutches made his shoulders push his ears up. He'd seen that, and how in pain a tooth bared itself against his sick red lip. He would never believe that flab of body in the mirror to be his own, for once he had looked much like David, his middle son, who was now fifteen. He'd been as trim and lithe as that until he was forty years old.

When Horace had found the pennies and nickels, some in dangerous places near his father's feet, he bumped his head on the oak table next to his father's chair, and heard his father's gasp of anger and resignation. To Horace it was again the final judgment upon himself, the one repeated by his father, by everybody, by inanimate things; tables danced slyly out into his path, drawers slid out to catch him, trees had wicked elbows. These last things didn't talk or yell at him, or laugh at him, but they could be the meanest of all. His head hurt badly, and tears had come into his eyes, so that when he stood up he couldn't look at his father, but poured the change upon the table and ran for the dining-room archway.

"Horace!"

He couldn't stop; he would fall through the side of the house, hurt the house and himself and fall out into the snow.

"Horace come back here!"

He had to stop. He turned to see his father's face—white,

7

black across the eyes where the power was. The island of force that was his father in his chair was blurred by tears, prismatic and shattered.

"Shut the front door and pick up all that crap that came out of the umbrella stand!"

He had to do it.

When Horace came back through the living room, so obviously trying to be careful, to walk softly, Harvey tried to make himself smile at the boy, to do something like putting out a hand, or to thank him for getting the aspirin on a stormy night. But then he thought: Who could answer a smile, or any friendly thing, after having been treated like that? And so he watched as Horace went through the dining-room archway toward the kitchen. Then he took three aspirin dry and swallowed until they let go of the back of his tongue, leaving their little trail of taste.

When Horace came into the long, dark kitchen, he startled his mother. He always startled people; they always looked up at him with open, surprised faces that turned nervous and slightly shifty in the eyes, because they were thinking what was the matter with him. And how they could protect themselves.

"Horace, what's the matter?" his mother asked.

He had no answer, and she no longer expected one, although her eyes, behind her thick glasses for far-sightedness, were wide, and always seemed to be asking. They moved upon a different axis than the rest of her face; they moved too far each way, too quickly. Without her glasses her blue eyes were darker. She was small and strong, and when she took his arm to lead him safely around the table where plates and glasses were stacked, he knew she was thinking he might break them. She took off his mackinaw and hung it on the clothes bar over the black woodstove, and sat him down next to the heat. Drops of water fell and bounced furiously on the stove before they burned into vapor that had a dry, cisterny smell.

"Did you see anybody downstreet?" she asked.

8

He knew she thought of them seeing her son who had stolen the money from the school lockers.

"Mr. and Mrs. Trask, and Prudence."

"That's all?"

"Nobody else was in the store."

"Were the snowplows out?"

"Yeah."

"Oh, Horace!" she said, and put her dish-soaked warm hand on his neck. She had so often asked her son what the matter was that this question had become her standard greeting to him. Something was always the matter.

Nearly everyone in Leah knew something was wrong with Horace Whipple, but many of the theories about him were irreconcilable, mutually exclusive, paradoxical. He was too big for his age, but so were others. In school he pushed Mabel Andrews' head down on the drinking fountain and broke her tooth: why did he do it? "Why did you do it, Horace?" his mother had asked him, but he couldn't answer. When he became upset his long, rounded face turned dull and immobile, and his eyes grew so still she felt that no beating, no prodding of any kind could change his expression. He would just go farther and farther away, though his body might skittishly quiver, as it had one time she slapped him. His coarse blond hair quivered that time, and she would never forget the way he'd brought his head up again, as if to wait for the next blow.

When he was in first grade a little boy called him "Horse" because the little boy really thought his name was Horse, and the name remained with him—no one's choice; an accident. He broke windows with his elbows, but did he want to break them? His very desk in school, a desk made of cast iron and hardwood that had supported generations of violent children, broke. Miss Colchester, who had been his teacher in the fifth grade, said, "He has a way of leaning on things so that their very weakest places are under stress." He was not a stupid boy, nor was he mean, but after he broke Mabel Andrews' tooth, no one could blame her mother for calling it mean. Mabel knew it was love, and she had been scared, almost hysterical afterwards.

If Horace's brother Wood was making a model airplane, Horse was not allowed to enter Wood's room. If his brother David

9

was in his room, handloading black powder cartridges, it was the same. If his sister Kate had discovered a bolt of cloth in the attic and was transforming her room into an Arab tent, Horace was not allowed. In the kitchen he was carefully watched, and at the Whipples' round dining table, the chairs were always arranged so that Horace's arc of space was several degrees wider than the others'.

Was he simply awkward? He walked and ran with powerful grace. In school he was very good in mathematics and general science; things like leverage, gear directions, speeds and ratios, strangely enough, were transparently simple for him. Why, then, in laboratory period, did he break the wooden arm over the fulcrum?

He couldn't tell them because he had already acted, and the disaster had already occurred—the splintering, the always amazed groans and laughter of his classmates. But he had seen the pure, clean power of the lever, and acted upon it. He had perceived too quickly that he might lift the world; only afterwards, when it was too late, did he find that he had no place on which to stand.

Henrietta had been standing abstractedly, her hand still on Horace's neck. She felt the cords like ropes leading into his shoulders. When she was a little girl she had lived on a hill farm in Switches Corners—a place now all fallen in and grown up with trees—and she had a heifer she had to take care of. In a way she grew to love the gawky animal, yet it was always a terrible bother and responsibility. In it she had felt the same skittish strength that never seemed to yield willingly, yet did yield because of need. She could feel its brute push against the bucket when she fed it, and sometimes when it shied it would bang its bony head against a stanchion so hard, she feared it, and feared for it. Yet it never seemed to feel a blow.

"Will you get me some wood, dear?" she said. "And call them for supper?"

When he stood up she kept her hand on him, to guide him a little, and he knew it; she was afraid he would touch the stove.

"You've got a bad bump on the back of your head. Where did that come from?"

"I backed into a tree outside," he said. He had long ago given

up trying to explain his accidents in any rational way. He merely told the truth, or part of it.

"But why would you back into a tree?" She did care, he knew; her voice grew breathy, and her large eyes moved back and forth as though asking him "Why?"

He shrugged, wondering, now he thought of it, if he might have got that bump from the underside of his father's table.

"Oh, Horace," she said, and turned away.

He went out into the unheated shed to get the wood, an armful of split ash that he picked up all at once. He didn't bother to pile it a stick at a time into his arm, and so he skinned his knuckles, trying to worm his hand through the splintery pile. He came back into the heat and let the wood rumble into the woodbox.

"Don't shut the cover!" his mother said quickly, and then he saw that the wood came over the top of the woodbox so that the cover wouldn't have been able to close tight. But he wouldn't have broken the hinges; he knew he wouldn't have insisted that the cover close all the way.

"I wouldn't break it," he said, feeling self-pity clog his voice.

"I know you wouldn't mean to, dear. I know that." She turned her back to him and made precise adjustments of the pile of napkins and silverware.

"Tell them to get ready," his mother said.

He went up the narrow back stairs that turned so that his shoulders rubbed the wallpaper. This part of the house was dark and narrow, made originally for servants. Sometimes they had a sort of servant, Peggy Mudd, a girl Kate's age who lived most of the time with her mother in the old sugarhouse up in the woods. Sometimes Peggy stayed over with them, and Horace liked that, because he liked her very much. She was dark and bony, and his father said she was ugly as sin. He wished she were here now, so that he could knock on her door and ask her to get ready for supper, the way she usually knocked on his door and asked him to get ready for supper. She usually wore some dress he had seen on Kate, and on Peggy the dress would turn homely and easy.

He went through the empty servants' rooms, carefully turning on wall switches that let him go in light across a room or down

11

the hall; then, at the end, he turned on one switch at the same time he snapped off another, so that they made the same sound, and his path was lighted but his back trail dark. This part of the house was unheated, and beneath the old red carpeting, the floors creaked as he walked.

Then he came through a door into the part of the second floor where everything was larger, and the first door on the left was Kate's. She was thirteen, barely, but he had never said to her, "You're only thirteen, and I'm fourteen." Her door was closed, and he knocked.

"Who is it?" she said angrily from deep inside somewhere.

"It's Horace. Supper's nearly ready."

"Don't come in, Horsie! Do not enter!"

"Well, supper's nearly ready."

"Thanks for the great news. Now take a powder."

"I don't care what you're doing!" he shouted at the varnished door. She didn't answer, and he went on to David's door.

He hit the door with his fist, once, and yelled, "Supper's ready!"

David, as usual, surprised him. The door opened immediately and David's face was right next to his—on it a mock expression of horror and surprise.

"A horse. My God, a horse!" David said. And then he made his voice small and strangled as he shouted this news. He sounded far away. "There's a horse in the hall! Everybody! Believe me! Why don't you believe me?"

"Supper's ready," Horace said. He began to turn away, intending to go on to Wood's room, but his eyes began to sting, and suddenly, hardly knowing that he was doing it, he swung his arm back violently in a raking blow aimed at David, at the door and everything in general. Not really aimed; David couldn't be hit. His hand smashed into the doorframe, turned cold and dropped to his side.

"Hey!" David said seriously. "What the hell's the matter now?"

"Shut up!" His hand began to hurt badly, but he wouldn't try to flex it. He walked away, seeing pain in the form of little streaks of light, and beyond the pain he imagined David's smooth, confident face, his superior, aristocratic nose and neat blond hair, his square chin that was delicate without being weak. He admired

and sometimes feared David, the way a large animal might fear a smaller and more agile one. He could never keep David in focus, never knew quite what David's face signified, or where his hands were.

"Hey, Horse," David said, coming up behind him. "Hey, old Hoss, now. Didn't mean to get you all het up."

"Shut up. I hate you." Horace still walked away.

David said, "Aw, come on, now. Hey, Horace? Is the Whip going to eat with us?"

Horace wouldn't answer, and he heard David go back into his room.

When he knocked on Wood's door, Wood said "Come in," in a formal, deep voice. Horace opened the door to find him sitting at his desk, reading. Wood was eighteen, and he looked up with a bland, polite expression on his dark, handsome face.

"Come in, Horace," he said. Along the side of the long room hung some black, wooden airplane models he had made for the armed services, and hadn't yet given to the high-school shop teacher to send away. They would be used to teach servicemen aircraft identification. Wood had graduated from high school and was going into the Army anytime now.

"Please be careful," he said, then slowly frowned as he looked at Horace's face. He tapped his pipe on the heel of his hand and let the ashes slide neatly into his big ashtray. "That money business bothering you?"

Horace shook his head, then nodded. He loved Wood, and any expression of concern on Wood's austere face made him want to cry. Wood was bigger than his father, and he never got excited or made wisecracks. He thought carefully and spoke slowly. It was Wood Horace cried out for sometimes in the night, and it was Wood who, coming with strength and justice into Horace's room, could banish the dark shapes and let him be tired enough to sleep.

Wood looked at him steadily for a moment, and then said "Sit down," pointing to his deep easy chair.

"Supper's ready."

"Well, sit down for a minute anyway. Kate's got to set the table, hasn't she?"

"She hasn't set it yet."

"Is the Whip going to eat with us?"

13

"I don't know. I got the aspirin and he cursed me!" These words in a rush, with some tears.

"I know," Wood said.

"I tripped over the elephant leg, and all David's old marbles rolled out!"

"Why *do* you trip all the time, though?" Wood asked the old question as though he really wanted to know. This time he really seemed as though he wanted to know, and because Horace wanted to tell Wood, but had no answer, he felt the skin of his face congeal, his jaw stiffen with pain. He looked; his eyes received Wood, the room, Wood's trophies and pictures on the walls. His brother waited for an answer. "Uh," Horace said. "I. Oh!"

Wood waited calmly, but Horace couldn't speak. He tried, but from his frozen jaw came only another plugged, inhuman sound: "Ough!"

"They'll forget all about the money," Wood said. "You'll grow up and it will all be a thing that happened when you were a kid." Wood put his pipe in his circular rack and stood up, brushing off his sweater and straightening the open collar of his shirt. "Come on, we've got to wash up."

Horace went first. Wood, he knew, would follow to make sure he didn't knock anything over. Horace still couldn't speak, and for a crazy moment by the door he felt like reaching up with his painful hand and smashing the airplane model that hung so delicately on three black threads. But why? he asked himself. And who was he asking? He thought he knew who he was, but none of the others would be surprised at all if he broke Wood's airplane.

He had reached out for the doorknob with his hurt hand, which was still half numb, and it didn't do what he had commanded it to do—turn the big brass knob and push open the door. But his body still moved into the opening it believed would be there, and when he struck the door it felt as though someone had with vicious force slammed it against his face. His knees buckled for an instant, and then he caught himself and stood dazed, his hands flat in protest against the door panels.

Then he heard Wood's exclamation: "Oh, *God!*"

And heard in it, with the terrible precision of understanding he was always capable of, resignation and disgust that this had

happened so often and so predictably. Disgust. He scrabbled at the doorknob and got the door open, then ran down the hall to his room. As he entered the dark room and fell on the bed, the black shapes washed backwards in the force of his emotion, back into the closets, under the desk and into the odd shadows on the paneling. But they were not really dismayed; they would wait, and later, when they saw him get up to turn on the light, they would come out again.

Henrietta Whipple was forty years old. How old she looked, she had no idea. She had a son eighteen years old, two sons who were having growing pains and a daughter who had begun to menstruate—these seemed more a measure of her age than forty. Her life had been broken up into such different parts. First was her childhood on the farm at Switches Corners, which ended with the death of her grandfather, when everything fell apart in her family and her mother brought her into town. They lived here and there—in a tenement room, over a store. Her mother was sometimes a carder in the woolen mill, sometimes a waitress, and then, finally, housekeeper for a man she slept in bed with but wasn't married to. That was while Henrietta was in high school. Her father she could barely remember as a man who sat in the overheated kitchen at the farm in Switches Corners, who smelled bad because he had bandages, and couldn't heal. He'd fallen drunk into the pigpen and was partly eaten by the pigs. Part of an arm, part of a leg. When he died she was a stranger at his funeral, and only years later did she begin to remember little things about him, things he'd done for her when she was four and five years old. He made her a go-devil out of a wooden box and a sled runner, and she ran it down the crust through the buried kitchen garden, through the yellow stalks that stuck up through little round holes in the ice. Once he'd made her a willow whistle that blew like to pierce her eardrums, and a week later it was all dried up and split down past the hole.

Another part of her life began when she quit high school at sixteen and went to work in order to get out of the house her mother lived in. She didn't want to quit high school, but she had to get out of that house, and she would always do what she had to

do. It was an awful time. Because she wanted to stay in high school so badly she would put up with nearly anything.

They had lived with Harry Pedigree in his farmhouse on Back Hill, two miles out of town. He was always losing his cows when the TB inspector came, and the house was unpainted, nail-sprung, damp all the way through. It leaned. Harry Pedigree never changed his clothes, never paid his bills until the sheriff made him come to Petty Claims, where his foul mouth and shouting got him fined and talked about time and time again. His land was posted for taxes every year before he got around to redeeming it. He treated her mother like a breechy cow—like an animal that needed to be shown he was a man. Henrietta could still see his yellow teeth as he struck her mother; he seemed to want to hear the flat spank of his hand against her flesh.

Her mother seemed so old, such an old woman then, with her hair going gray and her belly sticking out as much in front as her behind did in back. Once Henrietta came home around ten at night and found them on the cot in the room off the kitchen, all their clothes on, her mother's black shoes with the straps, rolled blue stockings, legs blue-white like skim milk on each side of the cot, and his suspenders around his legs, his cracked ankle-high shoes with hay stuck between the heels and soles. Going it, his white hind end pumping on her mother, who just lay there with her dress up, taking it, rolling like a bladder under him.

She knew they did it, but knowing and seeing were different.

Sometimes her mother would agree with Henrietta that they should go away from there. But finally it became too obvious that her mother would never go away, and so she quit high school and went to work at Milledge & Cunningham, running a sewing machine. She lived at her father's cousin's house in Leah, and had her own room that she paid for. That was another time in her life, and lasted three years, until she was laid off when the orders didn't come in fast enough. She was nineteen.

Then came another time in her life, when Harvey Whipple was always after her. All he wanted to do was lay her, but she wouldn't, and then he began to take her to the Country Club, and he took her home with him, and he took her to the Winter Carnival at his college. Finally he had to have her, so he asked her to marry him. That's when she surprised him: she told him

straight out she'd marry him if he let her finish high school. By then his tongue was hanging so far out he'd have said yes to anything. She finished high school in one year, and that was a good thing, because by graduation time she was so big with Wood they wouldn't let her attend classes.

Henrietta laughed out loud, startling her husband. He had rolled his chair into the dining room to his place at the round table, and sat there reading his paper.

"What's so funny?" he said, looking around the paper at her. "If anything's funny around here, for Christ's sake tell me all about it."

"I was just thinking how big I was at high-school graduation. If it hadn't been for the robe, they wouldn't have let me go to it at all."

"You can tell Wood he graduated from high school twice," he said. She looked at him quickly, hoping to see some of his old humor in his face, but he grimaced as though he were embarrassed to be caught.

"Where in hell's Kate?" he said.

"I sent Horace up to tell her."

"Horace!"

"You ought to be nicer to him." As she spoke she watched Harvey carefully, expecting him to try to pump himself up into a rage. She didn't care if he did, and sometimes she caught herself deliberately goading him. Like poking a snake. But this time, in spite of his guilt, he merely looked sad and thoughtful, and said nothing. It made her sad to see him without even enough energy to yell; she knew what it meant to him to be a cripple—or part of it, anyway—because he used to be a man nobody could beat. He had to win whatever game he played, and win it fair, even giving away points. He'd been captain of the town baseball team, and co-captain of the Old Timers basketball team. When he got the ball he always did the right thing with it, smooth and quick. He'd taught her to play tennis and golf. Now he could hardly walk ten yards on crutches, and his body he'd been so proud of was getting whiter and softer. She had admired him for wanting to win, even if it did sometimes get awfully harsh before the end of the game, because she liked to win too. But he couldn't seem to win against his ruined leg.

17

He'd made good money, although he always said he didn't. Whatever money he made always sounded like a fortune to her, though, because she'd been brought up where there wasn't much cash money around at all, where a quarter seemed as big as a saucer. Right after they were married he sold siding, and then he bought into the insurance agency. Even after that he made a lot of money refereeing basketball and hockey games all over the state and sometimes out of it. Now he went down to his office no more than once a week, and took only his rare commissions and interest as salary. What he couldn't do best he hardly tried at all to do. He had to sit all day at home, and yell up a storm.

Kate appeared in the kitchen doorway, a bundle of silverware wrapped in a dishtowel swinging from her hands. *She hasn't been through what I've been through,* Henrietta thought. Kate was impervious to what could hurt Horace, to what could turn David silent and Wood cold with disdain. She was spoiled by her advantages. Yet with this thought came tenderness. When, and how, did you admit that your daughter was out of the ordinary? Like those mothers who could raise a deaf child and never quite know it was deaf, she had raised this almost too beautiful child without being able, most of the time, at least, to recognize its difference. Once she had heard a woman say that Kate Whipple was too pretty. There was an awe of Kate she was afraid might hurt her in some way, and it came from boys, from teachers, from mothers, from everybody. It might hurt her character. In a way it seemed monstrous that her father's rages made no impression upon Kate, that Kate felt her power too easily. She reminded Henrietta of the little bird called a water ouzel, that could hippity hop right under water in a brook and peck at its food with the white water pouring all over it, then hop out again dry as it hopped in. There were animals like that she'd read about—fish that lived among the poisonous stings of anemones and never got hurt, mosquitoes that were born and lived right in the throats of pitcher plants, and never got eaten.

"Hi, Hank. Hi, Whip," Kate said, letting the dishtowel unroll upon the table with a crash. She didn't care if this might make her father yell, just went about the setting of the table with the calm, professional look of a waitress. He didn't yell this time, but Kate wouldn't have cared at all if he did.

18

Henrietta looked for something of herself in Kate, her only daughter, and did find something—this self-confidence that bothered her because she couldn't find much that was similar in their experiences. And so she felt Kate's to be a little fraudulent, or at least mysterious. And how could one explain that perfection of skin and flesh? Clear and taut, stretched to its most youthful tenderness across her cheeks and hollows, every place on Kate was supple almost to breaking. Her hair was light brown like her father's, though so fine it gleamed gold. Her small hands were so clean and natural, so negligently, unconsciously graceful they could startle a person into that memory of a time when the human race did seem more beautiful than any other thing in creation. That ridiculous young belief came back again for a moment as she looked at Kate.

Henrietta knew she herself hadn't been bad-looking when she was a girl—wasn't now, for that matter, except for some iron in her dark hair, and the thick glasses that made her eyes seem as big as cows' eyes. In fact, she'd been called pretty too, but it was a more human and imperfect kind of good looks she'd had. Harvey Whipple had to chase her, and in the end had to have her, but she never scared him the way she'd seen young boys scared right out of words by Kate.

Now he was yelling again. Kate had touched him with her arm as she bent over to put his silver in order upon his napkin. Henrietta barely listened to the words. "Clumsy!" she heard, but it wasn't really a definition; Kate was anything but clumsy. It was as if, in the force of Kate's indifference, Harvey couldn't think of anything apt to say.

"Does it hurt to touch you anywhere?" Kate asked calmly, and this put out his rage entirely, for the moment.

"Just be careful, will you?" he said. His eyes were shiny things like mouses' eyes, but down in dark hollows, seeming to have lost all the little indicators—wrinkles, movements of his eyebrows— that used to let Henrietta understand him. Now there was only darkness there, and pale smooth skin everywhere else that spread smooth and white up underneath his brown hair.

He watched, or seemed to watch, intently as Kate finished setting the table, but when Wood appeared in the archway he said immediately, as though he'd been thinking of this all the

time, "Have you looked at the furnace lately? I mean within the last day or two?"

"The fire's all right," Wood said. "It's a cold night."

"Well, let's not have it a cold night *inside*."

"There's coal on it. Did you open the damper?" Wood went over to the two little chains just inside the archway and ran them up over their pulleys. From below came a dim clang. Then he ran them back again, and from below came a slightly different clang.

"It's open. You want me to build a fire in here?" Wood motioned with his head—leaned his head over in a rather haughty way toward the dining-room fireplace.

First was the pause, while Harvey's anger grew into his face, then into his voice. "God damn it! Don't you pull that superior business with me! I pay for the goddam coal and the goddam food and wood and everything else that gets burned around here, and if I'm cold I'm going to ask why!"

"Where's Horace?" Kate asked immediately, as though her father's shouting were something as loud, but harmless, as the sound of a train's passing, and now that it had passed one could resume a normal voice.

"God *damn* Horace!"

"Well!" Kate said, raising her eyebrows in mock indignation.

Wood had turned his back on his father even while he spoke, and had started into the living room.

"Come back here!"

Wood turned, half ignoring this command, and said in answer to Kate, "He went to his room."

"Was he upset?" Henrietta asked.

"When isn't he?" Kate said, but Henrietta noticed some worry in Kate. What had Kate done to him?

David had slipped into the room sometime during the shouting—materialized as easily as he could disappear if he wanted—and he looked somewhat guilty too.

"Let's eat supper!" Harvey said.

"You cursed him, of course," Wood said.

"That's enough out of you!"

"When he went out in this storm to get you your aspirin."

"*Enough!* Storm, *shit!* What storm? A little snow? And I

20

don't want any more sass from you! If I didn't have this leg you'd be over my knee right now, eighteen years old or not! You may think you're pretty big, but I'll tell you what you are! You're wet behind the ears! You're just a goddam pup, and don't forget it!"

Wood looked steadily at his father. "At least I'm getting out of here soon, but Horace can't."

"You can get the hell out of here right now!" His white skin rippled at his cheeks; it moved in waves, like dough rising too fast. Henrietta got up.

"Stop it," she said. "Kate, help me bring in the food."

"Do you want me to pack up right now?" Wood said.

"I don't give a damn what you do. You're lucky, that's all." This seemed milder, but then he began to think again, and his voice rose. "You're spoiled! You've had it too easy! You've had everything nice and none of the work! It's never hit you yet, so you think you're so goddam superior!"

"Do you want me—"

"Wood, *shut up!*" Henrietta said. "I'm not going to hear any more of it!"

Harvey began to speak, but she slapped her hand on the table, deliberately hard enough to make the silver jump and ring, and they were silent. She looked around at her family, seeing in each of them at that moment the qualities she disliked most: Kate's indifference, David's noncommitment, Wood's intolerance, and her husband's lack of the wit he once seemed to have. As if he thought a cripple's witless noise could substitute for strength.

"Now let's get the food," she said.

Kate got up to help her, and this new thing changed them all. It was Sunday night, and they were having macaroni and cheese, so there wasn't much to bring in. They took their places.

Like all the downstairs rooms, the round dining room was so high the ceiling remained in semidarkness. Now that they were silent, the room grew away from them, high above the cut-glass chandelier that hung down from a long brass rod. The brown walls were paneled, framed, then higher panels began up in the gloom. But the tablecloth was white and close, and the tall chair backs, except for Harvey's wheelchair, rose behind them just

up to the edge of the light, where glints from the colored glass of the chandelier shone red and blue upon the dark, varnished knobs.

For a while they ate in silence; only their forks clinked upon their plates. Then Harvey held his fork upright and said, "Did he say *why* he took the money?"

"How much did he take?" Kate said.

"He doesn't know," Wood said.

"You talked to him?"

Wood nodded. "Some."

"Why did he take it if he threw it away?" Harvey asked.

All this in voices quite calm, though precarious.

"He said he thought they shouldn't have it."

"Jesus Christ, why? We've got a Communist in the family?"

"It was what they were going to do with it," Wood said.

"So he went through all their lockers and took everybody's money?"

"Just some of them," Wood said. "He heard them talking about what they were going to do. Something about Susie Davis."

"Sam Davis' girl? Live out on the Northlee road? She's got a bad rep," Harvey said. "I've heard that."

"A bad *what?*" Kate said.

David laughed and said, "She's a hot sketch."

"Horace doesn't think so," Wood said.

"So he heard them planning something about Susie Davis?"

"I guess so. Chief Tuttle says he took about twenty-five dollars, in all. At least that's what they said was missing."

"That's a lot of goddam money," Harvey said. But he seemed so mild about it they all looked at him with surprise. Henrietta watched them reconsider their father, and in spite of all, she was pleased—just a spark of pleasure that he could stop shouting and surprise them.

"How come Tuttle hasn't come after me for it?"

"I paid it back," Wood said. He was visibly tense as he said this.

Harvey stared at him, and seemed about to speak, but then he didn't, and Henrietta felt her pulse in her temples. She grew short of breath. If only she could put words in Harvey's mouth,

now, when he needed the right ones. Strange how it was never too late. No, how it was always too late; but always there came a time when again, for a second or two, it was not too late.

Through hallways he knew not with affection but as maps of his indignities, up stairwells where he had tripped and hurt himself, Horace heard their angry voices like the hard clangor of bells. Be silent, be easy, he would have said if he dared. He was so careful even of what he thought. Once, long ago, in a time that seemed a different place, all the children had been told the story of the man who would find the treasure, providing he didn't think of a white bear. Now don't think of the room you are in, he thought. Hide from thinking of it. Don't think how it is exactly the same shape as Wood's room, with the same three tall windows at the end, and the same high ceiling, and the same small fireplace—Wood's warm as a friend who is alive, yours black and cold. In Wood's room the warm person of his brother owned the walls and corners where the light of his attention dared to go; this chamber was owned by things that were hollow and mean.

Like a fool he hadn't turned on the light when he came in—a stupid fool tricked by his anger into thinking it would last. Now he didn't dare move against the dark. If he turned his face out of his pillow and opened his eyes, the putty face of the madwoman would stare at him from the middle window, her eyes like blue coals, her fingers, brown as old bananas, reaching through the glass. If he moved his hand he would find that all this time it had been inside a wet mouth full of teeth like rusty nails, and a hot, slick tongue would lick along his palm before the teeth closed into his wrist. They were all cruel, and liked to laugh. Once he dreamed that they took a little puppy into the closet, all the time smirking and giggling. At first the puppy would wag his tail and be so confident they would pet him, and then with a quick snip and tear they flayed him alive, so that he ran skinless, in agony so great he couldn't even whine, and they threw him into the fire. As he writhed, beads of hot grease jumped out like BBs upon his naked sides.

In Wood's room the stern voice of his brother would have shamed them, and made justice. In this room empty of reason

and love, cruelty seeped out of cracks. Once he woke in the night, believing himself to be in Wood's room, where he was warm and could so easily go to sleep with his head out of the covers, and breathe long breaths. How wonderful it was to be tired, wrapped all around by his brother's rule! Then a cold hand had grabbed his ankle, and the madwoman had crept around on the drain gutter in triumph. Wood was dead. He had screamed until Wood was not dead, but shaking him awake, saying, "Horace! Horace! What's the matter?"

When he had stopped crying, his breath was still hydraulic and uncontrollable, but he said, "I dreamed you were dead!"

"I'm not dead. Here I am," Wood had said.

"They killed you in the closet!"

"You were dreaming. Just a nightmare. Now go on back to sleep."

But it wasn't a nightmare, because it could happen anytime. He couldn't not think of it asleep, he couldn't not think of it awake.

"I'll stay here a few minutes," Wood said that time.

"How long? How long exactly?"

"Ten minutes," Wood had said. But he stayed twelve minutes, sitting on Horace's bed, making the mattress slope down toward his strength. Twelve minutes the alarm clock ticked off like an eternity of rest; then, after Wood had left, the cold shapes washed back out of the crannies and he had to close himself up in the center of his bed, the smothering covers over his head, where he sometimes sweat so much he got into trouble with his mother, who thought he'd wet the bed a little.

Now the snow, in an occasional swirl of wind, brushed against the glass, and in the middle of his back a circle of cold grew like the print of a dead hand. He must get up and turn on the light. He had lived with the shapes for a long time, and knew some of the rules, some of the careful rituals he must follow if he were to make his way through their danger. One thing he must not do was to force them, for then they might not have time to get out of his way, and he might be touched by hair or claw. The madwoman was only at the window while he didn't look, and if he did look, he must turn very slowly, so that she had time to crouch down below the sill. Sometimes there was a great, sometimes

24

only a slight difference between seeing her crawly face in his mind, or in the flesh. If he looked, and knew he looked, and she was there, she would really be there.

The fear was cumulative, and he couldn't bear it much longer. How he had wished for a steady level of fear he might get used to! No, he had to move; how long had he been at their mercy? Had he slept? There was the hollow sense of loss, as though time had gone through him without his knowing it. No voices came up through the house. It was not the kind of fear that made him want to cry, because he knew they had no mercy. He could not pity himself now because the world in which he breathed, and his heart beat, had no pity. The fear was like pain, like a rock shot halfway through his chest. Shock, so that his very arms and legs, and his scrotum, wanted to retract into the center of him, to make their instinctive defense.

He must try to think his way out. Sometimes memory, if harsh enough in its own right, could buy him time from the fangs and cold hands. He would remember when Unk was hit on Bank Street in front of the Primer house near the high school. He was with Unk, knowing Unk was only a dog, but Unk had always more or less dominated him. But he was still responsible because Unk was only a dog, and dogs couldn't remember not to run straight across the street, directly in front of the cars that were always going too fast. Too fast!

Unk wouldn't pay any attention to him unless he wanted something, or wanted to be friendly. The only people he minded were his father, Wood, and especially David. Dogs were always aware of David. But Unk wouldn't pay any more attention to Horace, if he didn't want to, than he would to a butterfly.

Unk was in front of him, and ran out! The car hit him like a baseball bat hits a hard ball. Unk flew down the street like a brown and white rug, like a rug partly rolled up. His big springer ears rolled out and wrapped around his head, his front legs came stiffly around, upside down. He bounced on the street, slid against the curb and rolled over his stiff legs onto the worn earth they were always trying to make grass grow on in front of the high school. His hind legs were loose, going any which way. Horace must have run after him, because he stood over him as Unk opened his mouth but couldn't breathe. Unk's brown eyes were

wild with wanting air, white all around. His hind legs twitched like running, and loose gray dog stuff came out below his stumpy tail on the clean fur inside his legs. His front legs moved to crawl, but he couldn't. The big brown freckles in his front legs proved he was Unk. Blood began to come out of his hind end all over the gray dog stuff and his white legs. Then he coughed just like a person, and blood came out of his mouth. It dripped off the end of his tongue like sweat did when he was hot. Then Unk screamed and choked when he tried to breathe, and the blood came out faster. His eyes were alive.

Horace stood there, crying, until a warm body had him pressed close. He didn't know then that it was Susie Davis who cuddled him, her warm soft front against his face. She smelled of violets. She led him home. She seemed to know all about him, who he was, everything. How did she know his name, or care to know it? He never thought to ask her what hers was, she seemed so vast in her warmth, such a power then. Wood told him later who she was. Then ever after he watched for her, and they said hello whenever they passed. She had seemed so big and strong in her kindness then.

Suddenly he was back among the cold ones, in his room. That knowledge came with a breath of ice along his spine.

A mouth was at his ear, open, not breathing, waiting to trick him if he moved, yet he must turn his head against the chance of a scaly tongue in his ear, and the sudden stench of a cellar. He couldn't do it; he must do it. From his throat came a humming whine, and he heard it as the command the innards of his chest made to his brain: move. It is no longer tolerable for us. We will die.

Then came a real, light knock upon his door. So real he knew at once that it was the knock of someone alive. *Oh yes. Yes, please.*

"Come in," he said. A whimper because of pity, which had been permitted to return. It must be Wood, coming to give him a short reprieve from the dark.

As the door opened and a wedge of light crossed him, he could turn and look, raising himself from the bed into the now undangerous air, which was cold on his damp chest. But it was not Wood who entered his room, it was David, and the dark forces, though they had temporarily retreated into their holes, watched.

David turned on the wall switch, and in the light Horace gratefully closed his eyes. Then he had to watch his brother—a different sort of danger.

"Hey, Hoss," David said. "You all right?"

David's smooth face did betray some concern. Why was he here? Concern seemed to lie trapped behind David's confidence, and it was almost obscene to Horace that David could hold things back, and look straight at anything. There wasn't anything David couldn't look at, and keep looking at if he chose. Nothing ever seemed to scare him. He could leave any time, no matter what they had ever been playing at, and go away complete, taking his confidence with him as though he needed no one. Horace, when he was younger, had had accidents in his pants rather than leave a happy game to find a toilet, but David never seemed to care very much what he was doing. He could always drift away, calm and neat.

"Hey," David said as he came up to the bed. "Hey, boy."

"Yeah," Horace said, hearing the caution in his own voice.

"You all right?"

"What do you care?"

"I don't know exactly what."

"Well, never mind then." No, he didn't mean that; David might go away. "I've got a pain in my side." But David looked steadily at him, and seemed to see this lie.

"I'm sorry I kidded you," David said. He went to the mantel and leaned his back against it, his elbows propped so that his square hands hung relaxed and strong on each side of his chest. They showed no fear, no worry; they were dry and clean. It never seemed that David did a thing out of any need, or with any sense of danger.

"You hurt your hand on the doorframe," David said.

"What do you care?"

"I don't know, exactly. Except you were sort of aiming at me."

"I didn't hit you," Horace said.

"You only hit things you don't want to hit, Hoss."

"*Never mind!*" What a weak, stupid thing to say, Horace knew. He thought: I'm really stronger than he is; I can lift more, but when I lift it too high it comes down on me.

"Comes down on you?" David asked, and Horace realized he'd said that part aloud. David came over toward him.

"Hey, I don't want to screw you up all the time, Horace."

"You don't?"

"I don't mean to."

Someone else was at the door: Kate stood there in dungarees and a white sweat shirt, looking in.

"Horsie?" she said.

"Another guilty one," David said. "What did you do to old Hoss?"

"Button your lip," she said mildly, not even looking at David. She came up to Horace's bed and sat beside him. "I was changing my clothes, Horsie. That's why I said keep out."

But he thought: Then why didn't you say you were changing your clothes? I didn't want to see you undressed.

"I wouldn't come barging in on you," he said, knowing that he'd gone over the edge of self-pity, and couldn't speak again.

"You wouldn't mean to," Kate said. She put her hand on his arm and he pulled away. "Don't be skittish, Horace. We all love you. Don't we, Davy?"

"Love the bejesus out of you, Hoss," David said. "We got to stand firm against the Monster."

"Your *father*," Kate said.

"Our father who art," David said.

"He doesn't scare me. He doesn't mean anything when he yells." They seemed to have forgotten Horace, except that Kate's hand had captured his arm. He tried to pull it away, tentatively, but she squeezed and held on, as though she held a dog or a baby, paying no attention to its random wiggles. He couldn't speak, so he couldn't get away.

"Whipple the Cripple," David said.

"I don't think it's right to say that," Kate said, still mildly. Horace wouldn't have dared say that name, much less contradict David about it; that would be asking for the full force of David's sarcasm, and that would only lead to violence—his own ineffectual violence. *Don't ask me to move*, he would think, imploring anyone who teased him: *Don't make me answer in the only way I can.*

"It's what they call him," David said. "He knows it too."

28

"He's your father. 'Honor thy mother and father,'" Kate said.

"Oh, sure. I honor him by keeping out of his way."

"You're just a child," Kate said.

"And you're my little sister." David looked at her for a moment, and then said, "Hey, I saw Beggs downstreet today, and he said you were the prettiest girl in the eighth grade."

"Beggs can go to hell!" Suddenly Kate was really angry, even though she knew David had said this in order to upset her, and Horace could see her trying to take it in an easy way. But she couldn't manage it. David smiled at her, but Horace couldn't tell —couldn't ever tell—whether David's smile was cruel or not.

"H. Beggs, Jr., can go to hell," David said matter-of-factly, as though he were making a note of it.

"I'm sick—bored—with all that stuff," Kate said.

"You can't help it, little sister, if you're a freak." David said that, but he really admired her; Horace could see him looking her over proudly, appraising whatever it was that made her so pretty.

"You're a freak too!" Horace said, surprising himself. David thought this over, his eyebrows raised evenly above his calm eyes.

"How so, old Hoss?"

"Because you think you're so grown-up already."

"Maybe," David said.

"I know I'm a freak," Horace said.

"Everybody in this family's a freak," David said, "except maybe Wood and Hank."

Wood came into the room, and as he moved through the door with his solid step, David and Kate seemed all at once to shrink back, shrink down in size and force and become children again.

Kate said, seeming to be serious, "Wood, are you a freak too?"

"Nobody's a freak," Wood said. "It isn't a word you should use about people."

"Why not?" Horace asked, protected, he thought, by his own obvious freakishness.

"Say what's different about somebody, if you have to, but his differences aren't all of him."

Horace had seen David, at other times when Wood had made such statements, grin sardonically and try to catch Kate's eye. If he were behind Wood, where Wood couldn't see him, he'd put his

hands together in front of his face, like an angel praying, and look up at heaven.

"What about David?" Kate said. "Horace and I say he's a freak."

Wood looked down at her tolerantly, like a father in a movie. "David's very young," he said.

"That's what the Crip said about you, old gray-haired brother," David said. "So you've got two years on me, and maybe thirty pounds. Anyway, I've changed my mind. I say we're all freaks except Hank."

"Maybe she's a freak too," Kate said thoughtfully.

"You're talking about your mother," Wood said. His handsome face had turned genuinely stern and disapproving. His shoulders had squared. "Just how is your mother a freak?"

"I don't know. I just think she is. She doesn't do what other mothers do. She hardly even *knows* any other mothers!"

"She's always taken good care of us."

"Yes, but she just *does* it. You know what I mean, Wood? She doesn't do it like a mother."

"I've always found her maternal instincts perfectly adequate," Wood said.

David began to laugh, and because, in a way that hurt him in the throat, Horace wanted to laugh too, he heard himself shout, "She loves us!" The words came out of him in awkward, even shameful pieces, as though they were parts of something he had broken.

"Oh, Horace!" Kate said. She hugged him hard and kissed his cheek. "Of course she does!"

David said, "Yeah, Hoss. That wasn't what we were talking about."

Wood looked at his graduation wrist watch. "We've got to get up and shovel snow in the morning," he said.

They all looked, suddenly remembering the snow, to the three high windows. The snow still fell, passing down calmly through the light. It seemed impossible that the three boys would be able to affect it with their shovels; it would fall forever because it had paid no attention to them at all; through their small excitements and noises it had fallen steadily, at its own thick speed.

Henrietta came to the door. "Why, you're all here!" she said,

and it seemed to Horace that she was as surprised as she was pleased. Her eyes swerved back and forth, counting them all, before she looked more or less steadily at him, and frowned.

"Are you all right, Horace? You didn't eat supper."

"I'm all right," he said.

"Do you want something to eat? I left the macaroni and cheese on the oven door."

"I could make some popcorn," Kate said. "Anybody want some popcorn?"

"Gluh," David said.

"That would be nice," Henrietta said. "And we all could sit in the living room in front of the fire."

They all thought of Harvey Whipple. Father. Horace looked at each of their faces. Kate thought it might be a good idea. David showed no opinion one way or the other. Wood disapproved.

"I've got some reading to do," Wood said.

"Why can't you make an effort?" Henrietta said.

Wood was embarrassed; it was not like him to give excuses, and here he had been caught. Horace watched, with a sense of comfort, the inevitable triumph of Wood's duty. "All right," Wood said.

"Who could be hungry?" David said.

"Horace is hungry. He ought to come downstairs and be with the family. This is a family!" Henrietta was getting angry. She took off her glasses and wiped them on some loose cloth at her chest, and as she put them back to her dark face it seemed they were her eyes, and her eyes returned to her face.

"You do things because you ought to, for somebody else once in a while!"

They all thought of Harvey Whipple in his chair, down there in front of the fire, and of his white, violent face that would be the center of their attention, as though it were the center of light in the high room. They could look at the fire, but always they would be forced to turn away from the flames and to look at the cold light of that face. Pocked by his eyes, white like the moon.

"Your father," Henrietta said.

"Well, why doesn't he act like one?" Wood said.

"Only young people can act," Henrietta said, "because they don't have anything to lose. It's easy for them to be generous. Try

31

it when you see the end of your life coming up. He can't see any hope, don't you know that?"

Horace felt bad for his father, yet he believed the best thing was to stay away from him as long as possible, the way you rested when you were sick, so that you could heal better.

"He knows you avoid him," Henrietta said.

"Well, he ought to know why," Wood said.

"He knows why, but it doesn't help."

"He asks for trouble. He picks away until he finds some," Wood said.

"Oh, I don't like any of you when you're like this!" Henrietta took off her glasses and wiped them again, and they all stared at the brown hollows of her eyes, where tiny glints showed like pieces of glass. "Oh, oh!" she said. Wood stepped over and put his arm around her, but she jerked her shoulders and he dropped his arm. He remained next to her, though, leaning over almost as though he meant to threaten her.

She adjusted her glasses and stood with her shoulders squared, defiantly. No one said anything for too long a time. Horace's jaw ached, but he had no words he dared say. Kate still held his arm in her lap, and she squeezed it, as if she were asking him to say something. But he couldn't. He looked to Wood, who would know what to do, but Wood's face had grown stern and quiet. The snow, in a gust of wind around the eaves, ticked at the windows and then moved away. It was David who spoke first.

"Shall we go down?" David said. "Shall we descend, ladies and gentlemen?"

2

Harvey sat in his wheelchair, pretending for a moment that he was not its prisoner, and grasped the carved edge of his thick oak table. Firelight, reflected by the brass bowls and inflorescences of the chandelier, by the round mirror on the wall next to the dining room, by the curved lights of the bay window and other dark, polished surfaces, flickered warmly across the glassy oak. This was the place to sit—in this rich, ornate room he had always wanted to own, and now owned. But he was its prisoner. Ironic, like the wish in a child's tale; he was like Midas, who wanted flesh, surrounded by cold metal.

He knew his wife and children were upstairs together, and that their councils concerned him, their problem, the source of their quietness and tension. But what else could he be? Didn't they understand that a man like him, placed in this hellish position, was not going to be easy to get along with? But did they even understand what sort of man he was . . . had been? No, they had no idea. Henrietta, perhaps, because she had lived without him, and made a choice when she married him; but Wood and David and Horace and Kate? No, he was not a man at all, he was their father, whom they hadn't chosen. Everything he said to them, they took just a little wrong—just a degree beyond the force he meant it to have. They were all foreign to him, as though he spoke to people who could not quite grasp the exact meanings of his words. Even Henrietta now heard him through the dense, literal ears of her children, because she was worried about his effect on them. Often—always—they missed the hidden twinkle he meant to have in his eyes, behind his screaming. He imitated himself, and they saw only the fictional screamer he invented,

never the man inventing. The only one around who could see it, strangely enough, was Peggy Mudd. Kate was indifferent, but Peggy knew, and was not merely indifferent. So shy before the others she could hardly speak to them, she had no fear of him, even in those moments when he yelled so loud his ears popped, and he seemed to be hollering down inside the huge canyon of his head bones, playing with echoes and reverberations. That skinny, ugly, unfortunate girl would smile back at the joke he knew was almost invisible, as though she perceived it through the smoke and blast of an explosion.

As for the others, if they wanted to hate him or fear him, why couldn't they do it for the proper reasons? There they were, probably up in Horace's room, discussing the matter—a bunch of connivers, conniving for no reason, wanting peace when there wasn't any war in the first place. God damn it! Was this why he wanted this huge house, so he could sit in state like a monster king and scare everybody half to death?

But the house did give him pleasure. It was so generous it triumphed over its ugliness. Where it was cavernous and dark, it meant to be that way. No, it wasn't ugly—nothing made with such loving care could be ugly. It wasn't ugly any more than a lobster was ugly, or an alligator. He had been impressed, even scared, by this house ever since he was a little boy, when it had been the haunted house, and only an old, old lady—a De Oestris, Sally De Oestris' aunt—had lived alone in it with a crazy servant; a mad Swede who talked to himself on the street, who once, in Harvey's sight, ignored a stone that a boy bounced with an audible thunk off his cropped white head. The Swede went on, cursing at himself or to himself, never looking around.

When the old lady died, and the Swede had gone back to Sweden, the house stood empty for ten years, really haunted then by the bats that fled over the blackberry thicket that was the lawn, through windows broken by awed little boys. And then, just before Wood was born, Harvey bought it, thirty acres and twenty or more rooms, for five thousand dollars.

After her aunt's death, Sally De Oestris had taken away the things like silver and china and linen, but all the high, solid furniture remained. Even the harmonium, which sat like a monument below its own stained-glass window, still worked; the tile

roof and wide overhangs had protected the interior of the house in spite of broken windows. Harvey had come at night, with candles, before the electricity was connected, and wandered shivering with fear and pride through his dark castle.

The same architect had done Sally's father's house on Bank Street, which she still lived in, and she showed him the plans and letters the architect had left. She sat him down at her escritoire and moved her little gnome's body carefully, cane in one hand and a roll of thick yellow paper in the other, her round face crazed by twinkly little lines. She smiled nearly all the time, and her blue eyes were glittery.

"The man was more than eclectic," she said in her deep, playful voice, "he was a regular pack rat. A nut, an absolute nut. Nutty as a fruit cake. He thought he was creating his master-piece, but he was really trying to imitate the cathedral at Chartres." She giggled as she moved away, leaving him to unroll the yellow papers, and slowly poured two glasses of sherry from a crystal decanter.

"He says in one of his letters he had a dream of the cathedral," she said. "He certainly wasn't looking at a picture of it!"

It must have been a dream, she told him, in which strange lenses came across his mind—yes, something like lenses—to swell and wither the vision, leaving one area as blank as paper, while another bulged and squirmed like wall come alive. "Here, look," she said, pointing to the front elevation. "Here are the three arched doors, the three arched windows above them, and then the great round window with its twelve sets of spheres and sphe-roids—'oblate and prolate shapes,' he calls them. They look like eggs, or eyes." In her opinion, though this mad architect dreamed of Gothic, his imagination was essentially round—Romanesque and symmetrical. When he had conceived of one shape, his mind closed down upon his talent, and all he could do was to balance, in an utter void of inspiration, that shape with its mirror image. "He didn't know," Sally said triumphantly, "that Gothic is the triumph of asymmetry! Maybe nobody knew."

Another of the architect's troubles was that most of his raw material was wood, and another was that he built upon a steep, wooded hill in a small New Hampshire town among true Gothic structures made of pine and spruce that must have seemed to his

eyes only the result of material and spiritual poverty. His wood was cypress, sent by railroad from Florida; his moldings and parquetry, wooden imbrications and crenelations were none of them of local manufacture. His mind was cluttered with the vocabulary of his age—with quoin and groin, pantile and pilaster, pediment and parquet, trefoil and quatrefoil, marquee, mullion and modillion.

When the house was finished he wrote at the bottom of the front elevation sheets: *With this house I have cleaned my mind, so to speak. All I know of grandeur, the glory of all the ages of my art, has, as it were, been embodied here. This is the greatness of our time, that we embrace all styles, all fashions, and make them our own!*

"But who's to say whether this madman's masterpiece is supremely ugly, or supremely beautiful?" Sally asked. "You're obviously in love with it. I live in this one, although I'll admit it isn't half as big or quite as nutty. One thing I'll say for yours, it never looks the same twice. When I walked more, I used to go up High Street and look at it once in a while. Sometimes in the rain it looked like a toad. Sometimes, when the sun hit it right, in the late afternoon, it looked like a city in Tibet. If you take it by levels, or strata, you might say, it can look like the Paris of Villon. But then you look again and you can almost hear a muezzin singing from one of those four ridiculous minarets. You could get lost in the damned pile, but you'll never get bored with it."

And the house was beautifully made; where mansard met corbel, where corbel met Byzantine dome, there were no cracks or leaks. All of its cypress had been cured for five years in an open-walled shed, and periodically turned and restacked by Negroes before it had been sent north. Other wood had come from Burma and Africa and India; some was so dense it wouldn't float in water. Some had no perceptible grain at all, and was as smooth as yellow ivory.

"I always wanted to own that house," he said. "It's sort of like owning the Taj Mahal."

Sally bent backwards from her hips, to laugh, and tapped her cane on the floor. "Ho! Ho! Ho!" she laughed, her deep voice always strange, coming from such a little woman. He wondered where the room was, inside her, to cause such a deep

sound. "The Taj Mahal, Sterling Castle, the Shrine of the Three Buddhas in Nikko, the Medici Palace, Mount Vernon, and any Gothic cathedral seen through the wrong end of a telescope! That's why I sold it to you—you've got the proper sense of self-glorification. I don't care if you do get tired of it, or find it too expensive to heat. You're too easily obsessed, anyway, and you'll probably spin off somewhere else before you're through." She looked at him carefully. "I remember when you were a little boy. Your mother always said you had the shortest span of attention she'd ever seen, unless it was a sparrow."

She stood beside him as he sat before the unrolled papers, her head no higher than his. She had always reminded him of one of the objects she had brought home from her travels—a cloisonné vase, a jeweled hummingbird, or one of the little sake cups that whistled when wine was poured into it. She might have been incorporated whole into the decorative panel of a Chinese lacquer cabinet. Or perhaps she had even more in common with the small, gold-chased Samurai sword that hung over the dining-room archway.

"What does your wife think of it?" she asked, with some iron in her voice; she didn't approve of his marriage.

"She'll be back from the hospital in three days," he said.

"With your son. What did you name him? Wood Spencer?" she said, raising her painted eyebrows. "You mean to say you haven't told her about the house?"

"Not yet."

"Ho! Ho! Ho! Ho!" Sally laughed. "Well, it's going to be a surprise for the likes of Henrietta Sleeper!"

He felt resentment—the kind he always felt in the face of real authority. "You don't really know her," he said.

"Ah, well," she said with no resignation whatsoever in her voice, "I suppose things are changing more rapidly than an old woman like me can follow. In my day a Whipple didn't marry a Sleeper from Switches Corners—unless he had to."

"Had to?" he said. "It took me three years to get her to say yes."

"Tsk, tsk," she said. "And you the very hero of Leah? They tell me you can take a piece of wood and hit a round ball farther than anyone in three towns. Didn't that impress her?"

"I don't know." In spite of her sarcasm he was pleased that she knew about his skill at sports. "I don't think that impresses her as much as I'd like it to."

Sally raised her eyebrows again and pursed her crinkly little lips. Then, after a moment she said abruptly, "I'll have to meet this woman."

And their interview was over. "Take the plans with you—you'll most likely find a few rooms in the plans you don't even know are there. There's a secret room I used to play in, but I won't tell you where it is; it's not in the plans. One of your children might find it someday."

That interview had taken place nearly twenty years ago, and Sally De Oestris still hobbled about on her cane—sometimes two of them, now. She was a little more bent in the middle somewhere—she didn't seem to have any definable waist. Anyway, she got around a lot more easily than he did these days, and he was only forty-five. She must be very old. And he was never sure he'd found the secret room; he did find one that was fairly secret, but it might just have been a large closet that led off from another closet. There were so many different levels in the house it was almost impossible to discover extra space simply by measurement. By the time his fifty-foot tape traversed the width of the house it had been bent over too many short stairways, over balustrades and around too many angles. Maybe he hadn't found it at all.

Gradually, as if to prove to him that he was its captive, pain grew in his thigh, deep in the bone, like a hand turning a quiet and oily winch. He'd already had too many aspirin; he felt the beginnings of its aura, a kind of rigidity of the eyes, and knew that even one more would fill his head with tiny electric voices. The pain was, somehow, so personally administered that it seemed strange when it followed him precisely as he wheeled himself over to his desk. In the right-hand drawer was a bottle of P.M., which he took out and cradled in his lap for the return journey to the oak table.

"Henrietta!" he called. In the echo the little singing voices cried lightly and were silent again. "Henrietta!" God, he hated to be waited on. He wanted some ice in a glass, but the pain told him calmly that he couldn't make it to the kitchen and back. He took a swig of raw whiskey and followed its chemical burn to his

stomach, feeling it hit his shocked pyloric valve. "Ah," he said bitterly, "take that, take that crap," as if his body were his enemy, in cahoots with the ponderous hand that punished him. His hip was burning now, lightly, on the surface of his skin only. Playful little flames stabbed and stroked him, then moved on. He took another swig, retched and tasted water brash—cheese-flavored, alcohol-flavored—a chemical taste that made him feel like an inanimate object; a drain, a cloacal pipe, a vessel full of used crankcase drippings. No vomiting or catharsis of any kind would help, so with a will he controlled his throat, and sat very quietly.

They were coming down the curving staircase. Clump, clump, clump-clump. Saying nothing, but primed, no doubt, with artificial things to say. He didn't turn around, but when they approached him in phalanx, from behind, he mumbled "Don't make a wave. Don't make a wave"—the line from the joke about the room in hell. Only David laughed, and he had a quick twinge of love and envy for the boy.

"I'd like some ice in a tall glass, so I can take my medicine," he said. "A few ounces of old Post-Mortem."

Kate went out to get it, while the others, he knew, maneuvered for those chairs, or places on davenport and settee, that were just barely oblique to his vision. The power of his glance dismayed them. Dismayed them. Where am I? he thought. Am I underneath this pile of goop, or has Harvey Watson Whipple *become* goop? You can't think of yourself as being handsome and lithe for forty years, and then suddenly have to think of yourself as something so disgusting your children can't bear to look at you. In your own mind you remain, even for five rotting years, a man, not a melting marshmallow. But only when you don't have to read their eyes.

"You want another log on the fire?" Wood said, and Harvey could hear disapproval in his son's voice. All right, he thought, wait till you get pinned like a bug . . .

"Yes," he said. Wood strode out through the dining room.

"Don't make a wave," David said, and laughed. Harvey wanted to look around at him and at least smile, but remembered the power of his glance. He stared into the embers of the fire and saw an animal's head quivering in mute agony—a rhinoceros's head. Then the lower jaw flaked off as an ember fell.

"Kate's going to make some popcorn," Henrietta said. Wood came back with a piece of yellow birch and placed it carefully on the fire, obliterating the rest of the rhinoceros's head, and the flames quickly licked off the loose shreds of golden bark. Wood stood in front of the fire, watching to see if it were all right, then turned, meeting Harvey's eyes fleetingly, like a stranger, before he went back to his seat. Kate finally brought him a glass full of ice, and without meeting her eyes he poured some whiskey into it. She went back to the kitchen.

They were all silent for a while, and then Wood said, "It's still snowing hard."

In a while they heard popcorn popping, a soft splutter from the kitchen, and the shuffle of the popcorn basket across the stove. Harvey turned to Wood, not knowing exactly what attitude to assume, so that what he said came out rather badly, he thought. "Would you like a drink? You're going in the Army, so I suppose you're old enough."

Wood began to say no; then Harvey could see the gears working. "Yes, thanks," Wood said formally; he would have a social drink, and went out to get himself a glass. They both knew that Henrietta would approve of this. Harvey knew that David was the one who might have enjoyed drinking with him, but David was only fifteen, so the pretense that he didn't drink would have to be kept up. He was quite sure David didn't drink very much, but he knew he'd tried it. David was so much like him he'd be the first to try anything. But maybe that was a stupid idea. David *looked* like him all right, but in the last three years he'd grown away from all his children—or they from him. Kate was a girl, of course, and pretty as hell too; she'd have her problems. And Horace was—God knew what. Glandular, maybe. Where had he come from? He was just the kind of big, awkward person Harvey had always run circles around. No, not so much awkward as full of thoughts that got in his way and made him crash into things. You couldn't think while you acted—you had to trust the cerebellum.

Wood returned with a small juice glass, and Harvey poured whiskey over the one ice cube Wood had put in it. Wood thanked him again, irritatingly, and sat down.

"So you paid the money back," Harvey heard his voice say;

again he'd trapped himself into some kind of act, dammit. He leaned back against the dull, not painful now so much as solid, or congealed, feeling in his hip and thigh, and saw the darkened plaster dome of the ceiling above the heavy paneling. His castle hall: the upper paneling stood out a foot away from the wall to imitate a balcony, and this effect always gave him the creepy feeling that someone, perhaps in hauberk and casque, might be standing there looking down at him.

"Yes," Wood said, disapproving.

"You don't make that much, do you?" Wood had a job at Milledge & Cunningham, sweeping up after the cutters, and repairing things.

"I make thirty-two eighty a week," Wood said, "with double time on Saturdays."

"That's pretty good money, by God."

"Al Coutermarsh said I wasn't supposed to tell anybody down there how much I got. I get more than some of the girls on the sewing machines."

"I'll pay the money back!" Horace half shouted, half squeaked in his ragged, changing voice. It sounded like a yodel. They were all silent for a moment after this.

"Well, what did you do with the money you took?" Harvey asked, trying to be reasonably calm.

"I threw it away."

"Why?"

Horace didn't answer.

"Why in hell did you throw it away?" Harvey felt himself changing, going out of himself. He became in his own mind the monster their irrationality caused him to be. "Look," he said, turning his head like a turret to aim his eyes at Horace, "money isn't guilty. It isn't dirty. It isn't anything but the symbolic value of what it can buy. It doesn't breathe, think, eat, sleep or fart. Do you understand that?"

Horace didn't answer.

"Well, where did you throw it?"

"In the woods."

"Oh, great! Holy Jesus, that's great! I still can't figure out why you robbed the lockers in the first place, and now you throw

twenty-five bucks away in the woods! And where in hell do you think you're going to get twenty-five bucks to pay it back?"

"I'll get a job pretty soon," Horace said in a low voice.

"Sure! In a glass factory, I suppose."

"Harvey," Henrietta said.

"Well, for God's sake, what the hell am I supposed to say? Here I am, a goddam cripple, trying to make enough goddam money so I can support this goddam family, and they're busy as squirrels, throwing it away in the woods!"

Kate came in with a big bowl of popcorn and several smaller bowls. "Here," she said. "Fill your own. It's salted, buttered, and somewhat burned on the bottom. When are we going to get a decent stove?"

"You see what I mean? Three able-bodied boys and we can't even run a woodstove! First we had to have a refrigerator, because the ice was too heavy, or too cold or something, and now . . ." It was as though he had stopped listening to his own voice, or he had moved away, out of himself—perhaps to the fake balcony above, where he looked down at the fat white king jawing, jawing, saying what was nasty and always expected. How could he always believe that one more phrase, one more sentence, might turn his argument sound, triumph over his tone of voice by some logical point that always hovered just out of the reach of his mind? One more sentence, one more point, could totally vindicate him, but never quite did.

At last the voice that was not really his own subsided, and Wood was speaking.

"They were getting the money together so they could buy black-market gas coupons and liquor, and they were going to take her up to Donald Ramsey's father's camp, up on Back Lake, for a weekend. Seven of them. It was all over town."

"She was nice to me!" Horace shouted.

"She's too goddam nice to all the boys," Harvey said.

"It's just something you've heard," Henrietta said sternly. "You don't know."

"Well, I'm in no position to find out—dammit," Harvey said, and David chuckled.

"What's so funny?" Wood said to David. "Do you think it's funny to treat some poor girl that way?"

42

"That wasn't what I was laughing about," David said. "I kind of like Susie, myself . . ."

"Well, you stay away from her," Henrietta said, and David laughed.

"Listen," David said. "I'm not laughing at poor Susie Davis. She's a very kind person and all that. Next time I laugh, please believe that I'm not laughing at Susie. All right?"

"Don't be facetious," Wood said.

David turned, obviously trying to suppress more laughter, to Horace. He really seemed to be trying to be serious. "Look, Hoss, I mean it. I don't blame you a bit. I just can't help it!"

"I presume," Kate said, "that the reason I don't understand any of this is because I'm a lady."

"You're all sick," Wood said disgustedly.

Harvey heard the words of these strangers who had once been his children. He had to face it: he was jealous of them all, and not just because they could all run and walk. He understood them and they didn't care enough to know it. Or perhaps it was just more convenient for them to live with a monster than with a real person.

They ate their popcorn and watched the fire ember down. Harvey was silent, and deep inside his insulting body was a small ember of resentment, because he knew they all thought he was doing quite well by them this evening (for him). No really major fits at all—just one minor sort of skirmish. Maybe old Crip was mellowing a bit, eh? For a second he wanted to grab the huge brass and steel poker out of its holder and slam it beautifully down across the oak table. That would wake them up a little! But he'd have to back up, turn, wheel himself to the fire, and he'd probably fall flat on his face, as he had once before. Of course that time they'd been really terrified to see his smashed, fat, sluglike body writhing horribly all over the hearth. There was a certain satisfaction in that memory. That had been a fit to remember. A fit of lasting interest, you might say.

But he did nothing. He tried a few pieces of popcorn, and the texture of it—yielding, cottony yet crisp—the taste of the salted butter, was painfully nostalgic of a time of hopefulness. Popcorn. The very name of the stuff was wrong for what he was

now—as anachronistic as a continuing fondness for some frivolous food like Cracker Jack.

Outside the curved panes of the high bay window, the snow still fell, a bounteous, lovely, determined, unending fall. All his life he had loved the snow. He'd even liked to shovel it, to feel his shovel cut the cold, precise silence of it. He envied his sons the icy morning air, blue, white, cold enough to sear the nostrils, and the mist of crystals sifting off at each stroke of the light wooden shovels. And then in the afternoon maybe to take their langlauf skis up to the town reservoir, up a half-mile through the woods in back of the house, and ski down through the trees in snow so light and deep they'd never see their skis, just feel them flex through graceful, leaning turns.

Soon they could all make their excuses and go up to their rooms. Then poor Horace would have to go alone into his, where he was afraid of the dark. Horace was the only one who might have chosen to stay here in the monster's presence. Better the known than the unknown, perhaps. Perhaps. It all depended upon the known, however, and nobody knew this better than Harvey Watson Whipple.

Henrietta finished in the bathroom first, and lay on her back, staring up toward the ceiling. This was the front parlor, where they had to sleep now. A bathroom had been installed in the closet underneath the first landing of the stairs, and a window had been boarded and plastered over so there would be room for the head of the bed.

Was the ceiling there at all? Sometimes it was a cloud vaguely seen in the night sky, or a screen with all possible depths upon which she could project whatever had happened to her, or what might happen.

Her grandfather had an ax he had paid ten dollars for—a great deal of money in those days—and what had made the ax so expensive, she always remembered, and would always wonder why, was that it was made of *soft* steel. Why would anyone want steel to be soft? Soft steel. All her life, whenever she thought of steel, or even sometimes of trees, this little question hummed close to her mind and hummed away unanswered, and she knew

she would never really look for the real answer. *Soft steel.* Once she had a dream in which the ax, smooth as pearl, double-bitted, with one edge thin and sharp for cutting, the other thick for splitting—the ax slid not to cut, not to split, for her flesh had opened with sinful joy before the sliding blade. She knew the significance of the dream—that was obvious enough—but there were so many other dreams she had forgotten completely, and this one had been dreamed more than twenty-five years ago. There must be more to it, something she couldn't understand. And perhaps she added to it, in her memories, for it seemed there had been special words she'd either dreamed or made up, new words to describe what parts of her flesh were so wonderfully affected. *Lilipits.* Sloppy down there between her *filipupets*, sliding like a bone's end in its round socket, in thin oil that came from nowhere, and yet was there. That was all, just the ax sliding beautifully, dangerously, into its welcome.

She thought often, too, why she liked sex so much when she had seen so much of it as a girl, when it was so smelly and ugly she had almost desperately divided her daydreams into categories, and left sex blank—though she had left a space for it because she knew that it had to be. She dreamed of a nice house and nice clothes and a strong, handsome man she never had to take to bed during the dream. They never even kissed, just stood near each other in lovely rooms, gazing at each other. Now she wondered wherever she had got that idea about wordless understanding; had she ever done such a thing with any person? In any case, whatever happened between her and Harvey Whipple had been nothing like that. She never cared where they lived; this huge house was something his vanity needed, not hers.

He began to come out of the bathroom, wheezing a little, the leather grommets and packings of his crutches cracking like to break. *Bang* went one crutch against the door, then a moment of intense silence before he managed to pull the light cord. In darkness he lurched toward the bed, breathing hard, and let himself come down backwards upon it. His crutches fell together to the carpet, and the mattress changed its pressures as he leaned forward to help his leg into bed.

"Is the pain bad?" she asked.

"I took so many goddam aspirin my ears are ringing, but the pain's not so bad."

"I hope it isn't bad." The way she said it, she knew she'd given away her tenderness. They both held their breath for a moment.

"It's not the stupid pain that bothers me, anyway," he said.

"I know," she said.

"It's the . . . It's hard to do what I want to do, that's all." Then, surprising her a little, as he always could if he cared to, he chuckled and put his hand on her belly, then pulled up her nightgown and put his hand on her bare skin. His hand was warm from the hot water.

"We used to be a couple of rocks," he said. "Weren't we? Hard as a couple of goddam rocks."

"Yes. That's true."

"We used to wrestle all over the place. Right off the goddam bed."

"Sometimes I used to end up with shoes under me, and that wasn't comfortable."

"You never said anything about that!" Suddenly he laughed, pure and clear, and then stopped too quickly.

Although she wanted to, she wouldn't dare touch him. She knew how much he was bothered, not by the pain or by the idea of a useless leg; it was his softness, now, where he had been as tight as a green apple. She didn't care; it made no difference to her, but that would not satisfy him. After so many years of sleeping with him, that kind of physical beauty didn't matter, as though the man who slept with her was more the essence of him, and was not dependent upon good looks or moonbeams. But that would never help him at all.

The leg was ugly, bluish and darkened into red, with indentations where they shouldn't be, and streaks of bony pallor in it. She didn't seem to care. He knew she didn't care, but it didn't help his feelings at all to know it. A man was too conscious of what he was, of the picture he made. Even when he was deep in her he was still whole, still himself, but she was not. No, she was like . . . gas; like the sun, diffused and yet in the center so molten it was hotter by far than burning, and everything melted there and became her and him all at once for a long time

until she knew it was coming, when the sudden ice began to mount in him, and mount, more ice than the universe, and he stopped being able to breathe at all until in one cataclysm so awful it could never, ever possibly be repeated, the ice flowed into the very center of the sun.

And then she was herself, quenched, turned inside out, the way she wanted to be, and would be until he withdrew, cruelly, selfishly pulled away from her and turned her back into thinking and having parts and limbs, while he lay enclosed in himself, enclosed in his selfish sleep. Which she forgave before she breathed, before she thought of anything but the sorrow of his growing lightness and departure. And she knew, forgiving him, that it hadn't been anything like that to him. Oh yes, it was good. Yes, it was great. That was a good one, he might mumble, but she suspected that he had been thinking of her as Woman. Not even her, far less the losing of himself as himself. He was Harvey Whipple, and she was Woman, who, as was his right to expect, had before him lain back and taken. Oh, great honor! But she forgave him that.

"Tingalingaling," he said. "My goddam ears are ringing." His hand on her bare skin was dead to what it felt, she knew. Sometimes they tried, but now it was so much more than just the pain. He was beginning to see himself as a cripple, and even deep inside, where she knew he tried to protect what he used to be, he had begun to lose the idea of Harvey Whipple the God-given answer to women. Harvey Whipple the great stud and servicer of females, the great bull-deliverer of their allowances of pleasurable moans. Now he had begun to see, deep in there, what he saw in the mirror.

She reached over and touched his face, the skin soft, the whiskers in little holes now, where they used to stand hard as cactus. He didn't move; he would never accept a gesture of pity. Soon he was asleep, or pretending to sleep.

Harvey Watson Whipple. Whipple the Cripple. The nudge of pain was receding notch by notch, with just the slightest little increase before each notch, at his pulse, like an automobile jack being lowered. He was sure he could sleep, if he had anything

to sleep for. But why did he need the rest? The past, where his only happy thoughts could go, was no place for a man's thoughts, but if he didn't sleep, the past would come back to bother him, and tell him that all his triumphant memories were finished, because there was only the past. He would try to get rich, now, but what did that matter, really? What good was it to have money? No, he shouldn't jump to that conclusion; tomorrow those columns of figures would be as fascinating as ever. But now, at night, it was hot sun and bright days that he couldn't help remembering. Always in the daylight. That time: yes, here came a memory of not so long ago. The sun grew over him, over the baseball field, and the clean dust around home plate, the yells of his townspeople behind him, the tense Northlee players who had, for him, shifted their positions radically, and they knew that no matter what they did, he was dangerous. The outfield had gone deep, but the infield didn't know what to do. One player hollered to do this and the coach hollered to do that. Northlee had a new pitcher named Worthington, who had a fast ball, the fastest in the league, and he'd put two of them in a row just outside, and Harvey swung on both, and missed. Two strikes, and then he thought: He's going to do it again, because my bat's too light. I can see his pitches arc fast, and I swing too hard, and with this light bat I'm pulling in away from the ball. So he got George Fellows' great heavy bat that seemed to weigh as much as two ordinary bats. He slowly left the box and walked over and deliberately picked the monster out. How Northlee heckled him then! But they were worried. So was he. And on the next pitch Worthington put a fast ball down the outside and that was the last feel they got of it, because it hit a boxcar on the Cotter & Son siding, four hundred feet away. Northlee didn't say much as he loped around the bases, and how the Leah crowd roared when the batboy pretended he couldn't lift the big bat, and called to a friend of his to help him drag it off the field! The sun, how it pressed like a friend on his back!

3

A hundred yards away from the Whipples' house, through the falling snow, over an outcropping of ledge, its glacial tilt now masked and softened, through low, brushy hardwoods and a grove of tall white pine was the old sugarhouse, which once stood in the middle of a great forest of maples that extended all the way up to the town reservoir. Now only a few dying maples remained among the evergreens, gnarled, falling, split so their own offspring grew in the interstices of their squat trunks and further broke them down. The sugarhouse was rotten too, for its wood, deep beneath the pines, was always damp. Pine needles thatched the tarpaper-and-tin roof, and now the snow bundled and hushed the little building. The orange light of a kerosene lamp gleamed in a small window, one of whose lights was the outlet for a stovepipe which then turned, below the narrow eave, and cocked up at an angle, rusty and wet. Nearby, a dead 1927 Ford ton-and-a-half truck sank slowly into the earth—engine-less, tire-less, its grease licked clean by rain, with only a random wink of black paint against its general red rust. Its tires had been eaten to the wires by porcupines, and its wooden bed had wilted down among the axles. Near the dead truck was a small outhouse; all the other junk—pans with holes worn into their bottoms, a one-lunger saw engine with a crack in its water jacket, cans, barrel hoops, a barely recognizable mattress—all was now covered by the snow that still sifted through the pines.

The sugarhouse, and the short woods road that led to it, were owned by Harvey Whipple, and many people in Leah wondered why he let Bert Mudd squat on it and turn it into a typical squatter's junkyard. Harvey wasn't telling, however, so the ques-

tion had more or less faded out; Leah was full of such unanswered questions. Bert was now in the Army somewhere, with a San Francisco APO number. Harvey had received one letter from him saying that he was surely going to get killed, and wouldn't Harvey say that Bert worked on his "fram" and was needed at home in a civilian capacity to help produce needed and precious food for the war effort. Harvey had never answered the letter.

Bert's daughter, Peggy, who was now alone in the sugarhouse, reading by the oil lamp, had received a V-mail letter from him too:

> Dear Margaret you are my daugter and I want to say your father is in terrible danger they are shooting at me and shelling me something awful I cant tell you where I am at the censor would cut it out but it is just awful love your father,
>
> Pvt. Bertram H. Mudd

The lamp was smoking, a finger of yellow rising too high at one end of the wick, and Peggy turned it down. As the light dimmed, it was as if the room were a fist that closed upon her. She was afraid; she was too tender, all of a sudden, for a world in which people deliberately tried to kill, in which her father cried out like a baby. Every once in a while she would suddenly shiver with this fear, and feel for a while that she couldn't bear it. Once she had heard an ambulance scream down Bank Street, and burst into tears, not knowing who it was for, or what had happened, and said out loud "I don't want anybody to hurt!" before she realized what she had said; and then she'd thought: But that happens all the time, and I know it. I've even seen people hurt each other; I've seen men hurt my mother.

But she was not always so vulnerable, because she couldn't afford to be. At thirteen Peggy had come to realize that both her father and her mother could not remember things, or didn't bother to remember things. Neither of them ever finished anything. And then one day when she saw her mother forget that she was washing out a pair of rayons and throw them out with the water—that day the word "feeble-minded" flashed—she could see the letters spelling it in her mind: "Feeble-minded."

She could not afford to be weak. It was she who saw that the oil barrel was filled, and the oil stove kept reasonably clean and safe, and that some hot water was available in the morning to thaw and prime the pump, and that her mother gave her enough of her father's GI allotment check so they had food in the house, and little things like matches and towels and soap and dishcloths.

It was eleven o'clock, this Saturday night, and her mother hadn't come home. She'd come from work and then left at six with her blue dress on, Peggy's rain hat over her tightly kerchiefed hair, her overshoes buckled up around her rayons and her high heels in a paper bag under her coat. "See you later," she'd said. As she'd opened the tarpaper-covered door, a light swirl of snow came into the room like the cool touch of a hand. Peggy knew someone was probably waiting for her on High Street in a car.

The lamp continued to smoke, so Peggy lit another one, and let this one's chimney cool before she could trim the wick. The heavy smell of kerosene rose from the lamp, and just the slightest smell of maple syrup leaked from the damp walls of the room. Some of the metal troughs that had once held the syrup and sap had been flattened and nailed to two-by-four studs to make another room; her mother slept here in the kitchen part, which took up most of the little building, and Peggy slept in the small, cold room behind the nailed metal. Soon she would go back there and get into her cotton blankets, and blow out her lamp. She wished her mother would come home so she could put out both lamps and turn down the stove. She didn't trust her mother to do this, especially on a Saturday night.

In spite of her nervousness and fear, she was sleepy and wanted to go to bed. Not here, but in her room at the Whipples', that small, clean room with a window that slid up and down, and had a real window sill. It was always warm in that room because it was right over the kitchen, and she could look down through the little floor register and see the woodstove and the linoleum floor. And there she slept in sheets, on a bed with a carved wooden headboard, and all the Whipples slept in the same great house. She dreamed of being a Whipple herself: "Margaret Whipple," she said, and tried to make it seem possible, somehow, that perhaps Mr. Whipple was really her father. But then she

would look at the photograph her father had sent home from Camp Blanding, Florida, and there she was—the same dark skin, the thin, bony nose and heavy eyebrows, the face bones hard and shiny under the skin. Not that she'd want to look like Kate Whipple; that would frighten her. That would be too much.

Maybe if she went to bed she could pretend she was in the dry, warm bed in the room over the kitchen, with all those people, the Whipples, all of them bigger than life to her—handsome people—in the same house. They always seemed to have bigger things on their minds than any she could have, and even their problems were terribly important. They smiled at her, and were kind to her, and they would be in charge of the great house, so that she wouldn't have to worry about anything, and she could go to sleep so easily. She would pretend to be there, surrounded by their intelligence, in that room where everything worked; all hinges, drawer pulls, switches—everything fit, and everything was clean.

Sometimes in the night she would wake up hearing a harsh metallic clanging from below, from way below, and it was Wood, deep in the cellar, stoking the furnace, keeping them all safe and warm.

She turned the stove down just a little, thinking that if her mother came home and found the room too cold she would turn the stove up too high and forget it. If she could find just the right level to keep the dark orange flame, so dangerously boiling behind the dim isinglass window—not too high, not too low—her mother might not fool with the stove at all, and there wouldn't be too much danger. Once it had gone out because her mother turned it down too low, and it flooded, and then when her mother threw a match into it, it got so hot the enamel smoked and cracked, the wall behind it began to smoke, and they had to go outside and watch through the door while it decided not to burn the house down. The brown soap on the sink had melted, and the isinglass window turned so black Peggy had to buy some new stove mica, and cut it with a scissors so it would fit.

She trimmed the greasy wick of the lamp, wiped the carbon out of the chimney with a brown paper bag, then set it low for her mother, so she would be able to find a windowlight through the deep snow. It was still snowing, and in the morning she

would have to shovel a path to the outhouse and to the pump. When the Whipple boys had finished their driveway and walks they would come shoveling up the road, where she would meet them partway. They would joke and laugh and maybe have a mock snowball fight, and Wood might say, "Have you had breakfast? Come down with us and have some flapjacks—all that shoveling makes you hungry!" She would stick her shovel in the snow and follow them down the crisp path, marching, their shovels over their shoulders like guns, Wood calling out, "*Hup* two three four, *hup* two three four!" Then they would burst into the big, warm kitchen where Mrs. Whipple and Kate were pouring thick yellow batter on the hissing griddle, and the windows would be all steam. "Look what we found in the snow! It's little Peggy from the woods, come to have breakfast with us!" That might be David who said that, and Horace would be so pleased he'd smile at her, and Mrs. Whipple would wipe her hands on her apron and come over to her, smiling, and put her warm hands on Peggy's cold cheeks . . .

The flame wouldn't do what she wanted it to. She would have to clean the pipe that dripped oil into the pot. Tomorrow she would do this; she would take the copper wire and clean it out. Not tonight, because it would take too long for the stove to cool, and it was too cold a night. She was shivery anyway.

"I'm lonesome for the Whipples!" she said out loud, somewhat surprised to hear her own voice. Her eyes were suddenly wet. She recognized her self-pity, and named it. "But I am!" she said. "I don't care, I am!" She didn't even know why they let her stay in their house. She didn't do any more housework than Mrs. Whipple or Kate. She worked as hard as she could for them, but they didn't really need her. Last year when her mother had pneumonia she stayed in the Whipples' house for a whole week, and got up and went to school with Kate. To walk to school with Kate Whipple! There were girls who came up High Street, the long way, just in case they might meet Kate on the way to school, and arrive with her. If two others walked with Kate, Kate was always in the middle, and the other two always looked as if they were following her—in waiting upon her. Kate was never mean —she didn't have to be. Sometimes she hurt people, but she couldn't help it; everyone was a little frightened by her, and they

53

would do awkward, silly things. Boys would suddenly yell or throw stones at each other, or drop-kick their books, and girls would make horrible faces, or pretend to be imbeciles.

Peggy always wondered, even with a feeling of guilt, why Kate was so nice to her. Guilt because she could see no reason for it. She had done nothing to deserve it, had no talents, no good points about her. If anything, she was a total liability to Kate, and yet Kate always seemed to keep a protective eye on her. All of the Whipples did, for that matter. They might be nasty to each other sometimes, but they were kind to her. If they felt sorry for her, they never sounded quite the way other people did who were sorry for her. They were always kidding around, but not to hurt. Never really to hurt.

The snow swirled under the eave and hissed on the stovepipe at the window, where the pipe went through a hole in a flattened pork and beans can. What if the Whipples were not there at all, and the big house down on the road were empty and cold? She could not stand it. No matter how disorganized her own family became, or how heavy and unfair her own responsibilities, the Whipples were there, alive and warm. To think of that house dark, without their voices in its halls, made her stomach quiver, as if she were falling, and she turned cold with fear. Around her now were only the splattered, makeshift things that never had been finished and never would be repaired. Each damp board, and each half-tacked piece of tarpaper seemed to say to her how makeshift and valueless she and her mother and father were. Nothing in the house was worth a dollar, except maybe her father's old deer rifle that leaned, furry with dust, in the corner by the ice chest.

When would her mother get home? Maybe the snow was too deep, and had drifted in behind the plows. Or maybe whoever her mother went out with wouldn't give her a ride back to High Street.

The book she had been trying to read lay on the oilcloth as if it didn't belong there, seeming to float disdainfully above the cracked fabric. Kate had lent it to her, and told her she had to read it. It was a real book, bound in real cloth, its pages crisp and clean. *Wuthering Heights* was the title of it, and it was dark and scary in its pages, the people always doing mad, unhappy things

54

for reasons she couldn't understand, that she felt the author deliberately withheld from her. It was as if the author hated her, and wanted her to be afraid. She didn't want to go on reading it, because it didn't seem right that a book should make her even unhappier than she already was, but Kate had said she must. She wanted to go to bed, and she would take the book into her room with her. Unopened, it was a part of that other world of intelligence and reason. It was a book. She could look at the outside of it with pleasure, and feel its weight. It had cost nearly two dollars, and it proved there were people in the world somewhere who actually paid money for things like books. But she couldn't read it at night, when she was alone—not that dark story.

She adjusted the stove and lamp as well as she could, and got ready for bed, then took the book and carefully placed it on the chair inside her door before she blew out her lamp. It would sit there like magic, like a visitor, and protect her. All the time she thought this, as her blankets slowly warmed down toward her feet, she knew that her room and door meant nothing, because she had to be responsible for the whole house, for her mother who would probably come home drunk with her overshoes full of snow.

She wished for her room above the Whipples' kitchen; if only she could believe that she was there. Just to be able to go to sleep.

Then she was wide-awake, because the outer door had opened.

"Shhh!"

"Huh?"

"Shhh! You can't come in here!" Her mother's harsh whisper. "My kid's sleeping in there!"

Then the other voice, a man's, trying to whisper, but with a giggle underneath that forced out little oinks with the words: "I won't say nothing."

"No!"

"Chrissakes I spent more'n five bucks on you tonight."

"No! Now go on! Git!"

"Took you home through snow up to my ass."

"No! Now I mean it, Cal!"

"Aw, come on, honey."

55

"Quiet. You'll wake her up, now. Don't make any noise . . ."

But her mother's voice had turned from a whisper to a low, lazy, slow sound that purred and went down, down like something going away. Then it was close and startling again: "Jesus Christ! Wait a minute! Take it easy! Shhh!"

Then, "Phuh!" and the lamp in the other room went out.

The steel cords of her mother's bed slowly stretched, and lightened, and then complained loudly and were silent. And then began again to sing secret little words.

Peggy pushed the blanket up against her ears, and tried to make the singing of the bed into something else—a machine, or a bird calling over and over the same chirping call. If she were not here. If she were safe in the Whipples' house, in her safe room, it would be Wood, way down in the cellar, guarding them all in the night. Yes, it was Wood, so strong and big, down in the cellar shaking down the coals, building a fire to keep heat flowing through the great house.

4

Wood Spencer Whipple had decided, by the time he was twelve or thirteen years old, that though the governing principle of the world might not be evil, man's most powerful urges seemed to lie in that direction. He had been a boy scout and a preceptor of DeMolay, and of his family the only one who ever willingly went to church. He could not help observing how easily any moral law rode the arrogant or cringing shoulders of his contemporaries.

When he was twelve he saw the newsreels of the Japanese bombing raids on Shanghai, and of the aftermath, where, on paved streets as common as any in his experience, men picked up the still warm and flexible corpses and parts of corpses and

heaved them onto trucks. One sharp scene struck him, of the naked body of a girl, smooth belly and thighs and the soft veil between her legs—a slim and rubbery girl—just her lower body and pretty legs as they tossed her upon the other bodies; and then, on top of her, the similarly naked body of a thin young man landed and swayed upon the mass of legs and breasts and guts below, his penis lying aslant like a limp white finger. When the man's body swayed upon the woman's body, a sweet pleasure flowed through Wood's flesh, in the circumstances horrible, perverse, like the pleasure of grinding teeth. Once more he recognized his kinship.

But he didn't blame the Boy Scout Oath, or the Ten Commandments, for being untrue to man, and he never directed irony toward the mouthing of these commandments, even when he knew the preacher could never do as he preached.

That winter, while he waited for his induction notice, he worked in Milledge & Cunningham, sweeping up thread and cuttings, repairing push trucks, pulling and cutting nests of thread from their casters, and fixing V and flat belts on the humming shafts below the sewing tables—shafts that could never be stopped, because to stop one shaft would stop a dozen or more sewing machines. Each machine took power from a V belt and a flat belt, and these were always breaking. His boss, Al Coutermarsh, a thin, tall man of fifty with a blue-veined bald head, had lost his left index finger that fall on a sharp V-belt pulley, and he was glad to find that Wood could handle this job. It was for this that Wood had been given a raise to fifty-five cents an hour, but he told no one in his family the real reason.

During the noon half-hour he sat on paper-covered rolls of cloth in the basement near the shipping room and ate his lunch with Al Coutermarsh and Beady Palmer, the shipping clerk. Beady was twenty, and had married a woman who already had three children. He was 4-F because of his eyes.

"I've never seen the stars," he said. "I can look right up at them, but I can't see one goddam star. I can see pictures of stars, but I've never seen a real one. That's the truth." Beady was small and strong, with a red face hardened but not made ugly by acne. Whenever one of the girls came down to the shipping room for something or other, Beady would pleasantly ask for a quick one

("No harm in asking, is there?" he'd say). "No shit, Al, I can't get a driver's license. It's something about lights. Night vision. Something like that. Fow-eff," he said disgustedly, "and I can't even drive a car. How do you like that?"

"You'd rather go to war?" Al said mildly.

"Sure. Join the Marines. See the world."

"You'd like to be on Guadalcanal, shooting at the Japs, I suppose," Al said.

"Slap a Jap," Beady said. "Join the Marines. Boy, I'd like to strut into the Blue Moon some night with that old dress uniform on. Maybe sergeant stripes, couple of ribbons. Wow."

"How do you feel about it, Wood?" Al asked.

"I guess it's the only thing to do."

"Nothing else you one-A guys *can* do," Beady said.

"It's going to be a long war," Al said. "I wish you plenty of luck." He put his sandwich on the open cover of his lunch pail and rolled up one leg of his blue dress pants. Al was a supervisor, and always wore a shirt and tie at work. He held the cloth away from his leg, the stub of his left index finger cocked like a hammer. "Look at those," he said. In the bloodless ivory of his calf were two blue dents. "Kraut machine gun," he said.

"Wow!" Beady said. "You got a Purple Heart and everything?"

"I didn't mind that. The gas was the bad part. I've only got one lung." He looked strange to Wood now—rather dreamy and unlike himself. Wood realized that he had never considered Al as a man who had ever been different, who ever moved in time and once was younger. "Mustard, chlorine, lewisite . . . That was the hard part. I was glad to get stitched by that Kraut. That was the luckiest thing ever happened to me. Got me out of there with one lung left, anyway. I had a kind of TB, caused by the gas. We had gas masks, but they didn't work too good, and you couldn't see out of the things. I couldn't, anyway. So you were always getting whiffs. One kind smelled like garlic. Lewisite or phosgene. Mustard. I can't remember. Mustard would get on your skin, make it bubble, sort of. Guys went blind. Some went crazy."

"I just want those dress blues," Beady said. "Let's forget the war part. That old red stripe down the pants! Wow! I'd go through this town like physic through a goose. There's hundreds of women in this town ain't had it so long they're cross-eyed. I

58

can tell. It drives me crazy. I can smell it. Can't you smell it, Woodie?" Beady's little nose, on the red armor of his face, seemed to twitch. Al smiled tolerantly; he never joined in this kind of talk.

"Can't you smell it, Woodie?" Beady said slyly.

"What does it smell like?" Wood said.

"We got to get this boy laid," Beady said. "Suppose he goes out and gets himself killed, and never knew what it was? What a terrible tragedy! I can't bear to think of it. No, we got to do something, Al. Seriously."

Al stood up and closed his lunch pail. "Maybe he's got other things to think about," he said.

"Other things! What other things? I'll tell you what. I'll set it up with Martha. She's always good for a tumble in the inventory. A little long in the tooth, maybe, but good thighs. What do you think, Al?"

"I think your brain's gone soft," Al said.

"She's got a motion that can't be described. You ever get seasick, Woodie?"

Al shook his head disgustedly. "Don't believe a word he says," he said to Wood. "Martha kids around a lot, but that's as far as it goes."

"How the hell do you know?" Beady said.

"I know what goes on in my own shop," Al said.

Above them on the sewing floor, the huge electric motors began to turn up, and the rumble of the shafts came down through the wooden uprights. The air itself seemed to darken and grow heavy with the sound, and then the sewing machines began to stitch and drum upon the body of the steady sound, more and more of them, with a rhythm that was unpredictable and frantic.

"Is that what war sounds like?" Wood asked Al.

"What?"

Wood pointed at the ceiling, and his voice became accustomed to the noise, so Al could hear him. "Sound like war?"

"They aren't shooting at you," Al said. "That makes all the difference."

But the machines were dangerous to Wood, because he had to fix their belts when they broke. He had a wooden carpenter's

tray, with a wooden bail, and in it were staples for V belts, knuckles and pins for flat belts, extra sections of belting, crimping pliers and cutters. When a belt broke upstairs, a little red light would go on near the freight elevator, and a bell that sounded like a bicycle bell would continue to ring until he switched it off.

This afternoon he sat on a box near the elevator, next to the electric-saw table, fixing push trucks. After cleaning the thread from the casters he cut laths on the circular saw and nailed them diagonally onto the push-truck frames to try to stiffen them up a little. These never lasted too long, but anything else he could think of would have taken too much time. A row of ten leaning and half-collapsed trucks waited in line all the way to the scrap cloth bailer, a huge, medieval-looking machine he and Beady used once a week, crushing the scraps down by means of wooden windlasses.

When he looked up he could see through the open-sided elevator shaft into the shipping room, where Beady ratcheted blue steel bands around boxes of finished field jackets, the steel barrel of his felt marking pencil behind one red ear, his head moving slowly from side to side so the blank spaces of his vision would never cover one place too long. Beyond Beady, through the square windows toward the loading platform, the roofs of the railroad tenements were white and cold above their black, unpainted clapboards. The gray winter day seemed to push its drab glitter across the shipping room and into the basement, and when Wood looked down at his work again, the new laths were ghostly against the oily wood of the push truck. Then the overhead light made itself felt again, and he could see. The saw whined and bit as he cut four laths at a time; then it sighed back down again.

This building hummed and creaked for the war; it made no civilian clothes any more—only the green field jackets, some of which would later be sliced by metal fragments and soaked with blood. Perhaps a man would die in one of the jackets Beady just now sealed with steel tape in that big box. Wood, too, would probably wear one of those jackets soon. He had no desire to go into the war, although most of his friends were eager to get into uniform. But there was no alternative. Like this old factory, a five-story cliff of white clapboards, the whole world had changed to war. For a hundred years Milledge & Cunningham had made

60

nothing but work clothes, and now they made nothing but clothes for soldiers.

The war loomed ahead of Wood without glamour, because he knew that once in it he would have to tell other people what to do. It had always been this way with him—in his family because he was the oldest, in school, wherever he had worked—there had always been that short pause before any activity, and then all eyes had turned, evaluating, surreptitious, shirking, upon Wood. "You be captain," they always said. And half of any possible joy was gone, because he had to be captain, and to teach, and think, and be some kind of example.

He had few memories uncomplicated by responsibility; the fools were always so close to hurting, killing themselves. They always leaped with a weird stupid joy straight toward the machinery, and no one's arm but his own ever seemed to be there to pull them back.

The red light went on, and the little bell rang, as it would three or four times each day. He left the unfinished push truck and picked up his wooden tray. Because he had a repaired truck to bring upstairs, he would take the elevator. At the shaft he switched off the light and bell, then rang the elevator warning bell, waited a moment, and pulled the down rope. The big wheel at the bottom of the shaft turned slowly, and from three stories above, the elevator, big as a room, began to descend along its guides, moving from side to side in its ponderous, limited traverse. A thick wooden deck with its underbeams showing, it came slowly down, and as it moved past Wood's face he grasped the up rope, slowed it, and carefully pulled it into neutral at the level of the floor, where it became a strong but quickly stepped corridor into the shipping room.

He pushed the truck carefully ahead of him over the metal-bound crack onto the deck, rang the warning bell and pulled the up rope. A jerk, a falsetto squeak from below as the big wheel turned down there, and slowly he rose into the next floor, where the sewing machines rattled and stopped, rattled and stopped. Across the open room the rows of sewing tables, each with its single motor and shaft, jarred and hummed, and many of the girls looked up from their work as he stopped the elevator and looked around to see whose belt had broken. A woman stood up

and beckoned to him—a plump woman as old as his mother. She grinned as he came toward her. "Hurry up, sonny," she said, "I'm losing the war! Hurry up and fix my belt!"

The women nearby laughed, and still laughing turned their faces down toward the silver needles that hummed into the moving green cloth. This table sewed sleeves together, the one long seam on the inside-out sleeves, and beside each machine was a stack of flat, open sleeves with crisp, carved sides; these had come down by dumbwaiter from the cutting floor above.

As he knelt down to look under the table, the woman said, "Keep your eyes on the pulley, now. Not on Bessie's legs." The girl at the opposite machine cackled, and Wood looked up to see her peering at him through the arch of her machine—a pale, open, lewd face, with a splotch of red lipstick quivering ecstatically around one white, maloccluded tooth. The plump woman said, "Now, don't you give him no eyeful, Bessie. He don't want to lose a finger like Al!" Bessie giggled and shook her head.

Beneath the table the shaft hummed in its bearings, and the girl's round knees were pale balloons above her tightly rolled stockings. The pulleys ran silently; the one-inch flat belt had broken, and he brought it together over the shaft, cut its ragged edges straight, crimped on new knuckles, inserted the pin and got ready to snap it back on the moving pulley. The width of the knuckles, he hoped, would make up for the leather he had trimmed off. Guiding it toward the pulley with both hands, he let the force of the shaft begin to pull it along his palms until it was going almost as fast as the shaft and pulley, then firmly pressed it into place. Suddenly it was all the machine's; with a crack it resumed its strength and purpose, turning so fast and steady the knuckles disappeared, and it was all one taut, humming piece again. He got up.

"Did Bessie give you an eyeful?"

He shook his head.

"You're a nice boy," the woman said seriously. "Don't let us get you down. We don't mean nothing by it." She took her place again, and he went toward the elevator, where Al Coutermarsh waited for him.

"Be awful careful, Wood," Al said, holding up the stump of his finger. "This is a mighty dangerous place."

"I'm pretty careful," Wood said.

"I know you are." It was strange to see Al stopped, contemplative, not on his way somewhere. Now, for a moment he looked at Wood appraisingly. "I can't figure you out, Wood," he said. He paused, then spoke too softly, and Wood couldn't hear him.

"Can't hear you."

"I said you don't seem so damned innocent, somehow."

Suddenly Wood felt great tenderness for Al, and he put his hand on Al's shoulder. "You're a good man," he said, and Al actually blushed. It was like a dark light passing across his usually pale, bluish face and scalp—a dark color, not really red at all. Al patted him on the arm with his wounded hand, and turned to go. "I wish you weren't headed for the Army," he said. "But then I don't suspect we could keep you here anyway."

Back in the cellar at his push trucks, Wood wondered why he had felt it necessary at that moment to put his hand on Al's shoulder—why, without really thinking at all, he had done that little thing. It was almost as though he asked for the authority he didn't want. Perhaps it was because he wanted to say to Al, "Look, here's another one like you, living in a world of irresponsible children, never without the curse of responsibility." But that was to ask for duty, and he knew it.

At eighteen he seemed to have been an adult all his life—a grown man, even an old man. He resented the loss of his childhood, and for a moment remembered with nostalgia jumping from a barn beam twenty feet into hay—that feeling of being totally in the power of some higher force. Gravity. He could do nothing for twenty feet but fall, fall, and land in the hay that was infinitely soft and forgiving. And then to climb again up the sticks of ladder nailed to the heavy upright, and inch out on the beam where danger disappeared, where any fall was safe.

When he got up to cut more lath into struts, a girl stood next to the elevator, looking at him. Her face was in shadow, but she looked familiar to him—a big girl. Then she turned and went up the stairs, her blue skirt rippling above the flash of her leg. Beady immediately stuck his head around the corner by the stairwell and said, "Missed again, dammit!"

"Too bad," Wood said, and then asked, because it was always

something that had puzzled him, "Beady, how can you want it all the time, when you're married?"

"Ah, youth," Beady said, coming over. "I thought the same thing, once. 'Get married, and when it itches, scratch it.'"

"So?"

"There's a lot of different kinds of itches, Woodie."

"What do you mean?"

Beady looked at him and shook his head. He pulled the lobe of one ear, and his whole face seemed to tilt upon his stationary head, as if his hardened face were all one piece. "You really want an answer to that question?"

"Yes."

"You really do."

"Yes."

Beady took his marking pencil from behind his other ear and began, idly, to draw stripes on the white laths. "Woodie, I don't know why I want to do it, but I want . . . I really want to do it to every broad in Leah. There's something about a woman makes me think I have to do it to her. Does that explain it?"

"No."

"Even the ugly ones. I mean it. Sometimes it's like a holy place I've got to visit. I mean like a shrine. It's like religion to me. I really mean that, Woodie. I don't know why the hell I'm telling you. I never thought of it that way before. But I mean it. When a girl turns me down, hell, I laugh and make out it was a joke all the time, but I'll tell you I feel like God cast me out. I do. Cast me out into the everlasting darkness. Out of grace. *Out.*" Beady shook his head sadly. "I'm nuts, of course," he added. "And just now, hell. Susie Davis. I guess it's not my day."

"That was Susie Davis?"

"She's learning buttonhole machine. Al sent her down for some tape."

"I didn't know she'd quit high school."

"She's only seventeen, but man, oh, man!" Beady said reverently.

"It's too bad," Wood said, and was aware that Beady looked at him strangely.

"You mean that?" Beady said. "You think she ought to join the Rainbow Girls or something?" He giggled nervously.

64

"I like her," Wood said.

"I saw her standing there looking at you. I was going to throw some Gre-solvent at you through the elevator shaft. You really pissed me off for a minute. I'm a jealous son of a bitch. T.S. for old Beady. You and the whole Leah football team, God damn it, and she turns me down flat."

"You don't know about all that," Wood said.

"I know *you* probably never, but I'm pretty sure about the football team. After the Northlee game, in October sometime. They got her high on rum and took her out back of . . ."

"You don't really know what happened," Wood said, hearing a familiar steadiness enter his voice. Always unbidden, that sound of authority came between him and Beady now, and Beady shrugged his shoulders defensively.

"No, I'm not absolutely one hundred percent sure. I wasn't there. But I've heard some pretty convincing stories about it. Anyway, I've got a feeling she'd hand it to you on a platter. Here." He handed Wood a little square of paper, folded small like a secret high-school note. "She asked me to give you this."

Wood took it and put it in his shirt pocket.

"You going to read it?" Beady said.

"Sure."

"Well, don't worry about me, because I read it already."

Wood opened the thick little square and read the round, neat handwriting:

Dear Wood,
Don't believe everything you hear. Please.
                                   Sincerely,
                                        Susie D.
P.S.
Can I meet you after work today by the side door on Pleasant St. I want to tell you something.
                                        S.D.

"You want to borrow a couple rubbers?" Beady asked.

"No."

Beady looked a little exasperated. "Why don't you get mad at me? You trying to insult me to death? At least you could get slightly peed off. Don't you ever get mad?"

"Sure."

"Sure," Beady said, imitating him. "Jesus H. Baldheaded Christ, Woodie. You got to be seen to be believed."

Then Beady turned, shaking his head as hard as a dog with something stuck on his nose, and went back to the shipping room.

The afternoon went on; occasional flashes of the winter day, seen across the busy rooms, seemed at once more real and yet dead against the warm yellow lights on dark beams. The metal shafts and wheels seemed alive in their thin oil, almost as if they had skin. The pale sewing girls bent to their machines. Wood fixed another flat belt, the slim lines of a girl's legs in the corner of his eye, and later a V belt. On this one he didn't dare snap the belt on until he took a hammer and chisel and cut out a finger-deep notch in the wooden floor; the pulley came too close to the wood, and if his fingers slipped along with the belt they would have been crushed. Al saw him do this, and merely nodded.

Then back to the basement to fix the wobbly push trucks that really couldn't be fixed, and soon the old building began to sigh—a turning down of breath, little by little, as the machines slowed down and stopped. Above him he heard the small taps of heels as the girls left their tables to check out at the time clocks— dainty taps through the thick floor that no longer hummed. He washed with Beady at the shipping-room sink, Gre-solvent like cold Cream of Wheat between his fingers.

"You going to see her?" Beady asked.

"Yes."

"Why do you say 'Yes' like that? Why don't you say 'Yeah,' or 'Yup,' or something human, for Christ's sake?"

"Are you mad at me, Beady?"

"Why the hell should I be?"

"You just sound like it."

"Why the hell should I be? You're going in the Army, probably get your ass shot off."

"Probably not."

"You're a Whipple. I know why you look down on me. I ain't high society. You got your nose a mile in the air."

"I have?" Wood said.

Suddenly Beady was angry, and a mean look, surprising on Beady, turned his mouth white and shriveled.

"You think you're so goddam superior, don't you? So how about your brother? He learned how to be a thief up there in that mansion of yours, didn't he?"

Wood saw that Beady was astounded by what he was saying. Through Beady's angry face he saw Beady horrified by his own words.

"I could say a lot more, about every goddam one of you Whipples, buddy boy," Beady said, his voice high and cramped, desperation in his eyes. "Every goddam one of you. So don't play high and mighty with me! Understand?"

Wood meant to say something, and felt cruel in his silence, but he could think of nothing to say. He merely watched, sadly, what his silence did to Beady. Then Beady turned away and nearly ran to the cloak rack, where he jammed his feet into his overshoes, took his coat and scarf and again half ran to the stairwell and up, the wings of his open overshoes brushing together and hindering him, as though he waded through water.

Wood finished washing, got his coat and walked upstairs, past the empty tables and the silent machines. Without the solid noise, the bright gray winter day came more strongly through the high windows, and the room seemed cold. At the time clock he took his card from the in rack, placed it in the slot and pushed the lever that stamped it, then put it in the out rack. A hand touched his arm. Susie Davis stood close to him in the empty hallway.

"Oh, Wood!" she said, and smiled worriedly at him. She was a big girl, but this close to him she had turned smaller, and he realized that she was several inches shorter than he was. Her babushka was tied tightly over her brown hair and down under her wide cheeks. Skin of a warm color, creamy; she was the color of rich cream. A pretty girl, big and a little plump, mostly always smiling as if delighted. Now delight and worry appeared together, and her pinkish, big hand touched his sleeve again. "I was afraid you wouldn't wait to see me."

"I was going to, Susie," he said.

"Oh, Wood."

"Come on. I'll walk you downstreet."

They were looked at by the girls and men who waited at the door for their rides. Everybody knew about her. She walked along

beside him, bulky in her wool coat, taking delicate yet long steps in her rubber boots.

"You were nice to me once," she said. She looked at him quickly, and he saw that tears made her dark blue eyes shiny.

"I was?"

"Yes. In school. In hall, once. Junior Stevens was goosing me in hall, and you told him to cut it out."

He remembered her embarrassed smile when Junior Stevens put his fists together under her crotch, from behind, and lifted her up over the last step onto the second floor. At the time he wasn't sure she didn't like it, somehow. But he hadn't liked it, and he told Junior not to do it again.

"I remember telling him to stop," he said.

"You're the only one I care about knowing . . ." she said, and was silent.

"Knowing what?" They had reached the end of Pleasant Street, and turned onto Bank Street toward the Town Square. The sky above the bare elms was as white as the snow.

"The truth," she said.

"All right."

She touched him with her shoulder, lightly, deliberately, and he was flattered, and sorry for her. He considered her a casualty, in a way, of the war and its disruptions. This big, complaisant, creamy girl. Maybe he was wrong.

"When can I tell you? Can I see you sometime?" she said.

He felt a twinge of shameful caution. Her reputation . . . But her reputation was a prison, her prison, wasn't it? And beneath this kinder thought was the thrill of her offering—whatever it was she offered him. Shame because it was love, and he thought, saw, a sudden picture of her creamy long thighs. He stopped, and she turned quickly, frightened.

"What's the matter?" she asked. "Oh, I know. I'm sorry."

"No," he said quickly. "No, don't think—"

"Oh, what's the use," she said, more tears over her eyes. One went down her cheek and was absorbed in the rayon of her babushka. He saw it sucked in by the cloth. "Last year nobody thought anything about me, did they? I mean bad things?"

"All right," he said. He heard authority, that unwanted force, come into his voice. "All right, Susie. What's the truth you want

to tell me?" He heard authority and other things in his voice; responsibility, and a sweet, shameful martyrdom too. Part of him resented all this. Perhaps down there inside somewhere was a screech of laughter.

"Something," she said, and seemed coy all of a sudden. She lost value in his eyes, and the wind seemed to turn colder. He shivered, and wanted to turn and go home. "Can I tell you?" she asked. "Will you believe me?"

"I'll believe you if you want to tell me the truth," he said coldly.

"If you can get your father's car, I can get a T stamp from my father's tractor ration. He's got plenty of gas. We could go for a ride and talk. I'll tell you the truth." She seemed desperate. "Would you think of doing that, Wood?"

He was thinking about it. The truth, he thought. As if he didn't know the truth.

"Please," she said. "I can't talk to anybody else in Leah. There isn't anybody else. Even my father called me a whore." Her voice turned harsh. "Everybody else is after my big sweet ass."

He was cold. She smiled at him grimly, sarcastically, and it astounded him. "Is that all I've got to offer *you?*" she asked. "What did I do, scare you to death?"

"Yes," he said. "No, I scare myself to death. I don't want to treat you badly, Susie."

"You seem so much older. But just because I said 'sweet ass' you got all frozen. It's just something I heard. I don't know why I said it. Oh God, I hate this town!"

Then she turned and ran away from him. He watched her run down the sidewalk toward the Town Hall, a little hippily, yet graceful, one hand in a red knit mitten pressed to her face. Her father waited there in his pickup truck, and she opened the door and climbed into the seat. Immediately the truck started off. He felt that she and her father had exchanged no greetings. Her father was evidently ashamed to wait for her at Milledge & Cunningham, under the eyes of all those women.

After supper that evening he went to his room and saw only her stricken face. He saw her in her father's house, nobody saying a word. He went downstairs to the phone in the hall—his mother

69

and father were listening to Gabriel Heatter, so they wouldn't hear—and called her up. Her father answered.

"I'd like to speak to Susie," Wood said.

"Who the hell is this?"

"Wood Whipple. May I speak to Susie?"

"What do you want?"

"I want to speak to her."

"Don't get wise with me! I want to know what the hell she's got that you want!"

"Daddy!" he heard in the phone. "Daddy! Daddy! Please!"

A tinny thunk as the receiver hit the box, then crying, then loud breath. "Wood!" Susie said, and there was a man's harsh grunt as her voice fell away, crying. The line was dead.

He was shaking, and full of indignation. Something had to be done. In the living room Gabriel Heatter was over, and his mother had turned the volume down. He went up to his father, who looked up, surprised.

"I want to use the car. Can I?" His father looked at him carefully.

"What for?" his father said, and Wood saw, with surprise of his own, that his father was not going to use his urgency against him. For a moment he thought of this, and didn't speak.

"What for? We haven't many coupons left, you know."

It was almost as if Wood could see past the sick flesh of his father to the man he vaguely remembered, the man of years ago, to whom he remembered speaking without caution.

"It's important," Wood said. "I won't use a quarter of a gallon, I promise."

"Wood, you're in a state," his mother said. "What's the matter?"

Wood spoke to his father. "I want to go out to the Davis place and talk to Susie's father. I just called and I think he's beating her up."

"And you want to go there?"

"Yes."

"That's jailbait. You know that, don't you?"

"It's a girl that doesn't deserve to get beaten up just because I called her."

"Well, son of a bitch," his father said wonderingly. "You've

got more guts than brains, I'll say that. Sam Davis is a hell of a man to tangle asses with. Go ahead. We'll get the bandages ready."

"No! Wood!" his mother cried, but he was going. He grabbed his coat and ran out to the garage before his mother could say anything more. The Chevrolet started easily, thank God, and he eased down over the cinders of the shoveled driveway, between the white banks, and out onto High Street. The feeling of relief that he couldn't be stopped gave way to fear of this next absolute thing he had to do. He supposed the most the man could do would be to throw him off the side porch, but he was afraid of Sam Davis—not just the man, but the man in his anger, and what his anger was all about. His daughter more or less declared available. To groups. To conventions—like the sign over the banquet room of the hotel. To football teams. "Shut up," he said. The car went on toward the Davis farm. Such a short distance.

He turned into the Davis driveway. The dooryard was all bare earth and ice, and in the middle a rusty cultivator had been left out for the winter. A milk can shone silver next to the slanting porch. Plants grew in the kitchen window, olive-colored behind the greasy glass. He stopped, and though the lights were on in the kitchen and parlor, the house was hushed. His feet sounded aggressively heavy on the porch boards. Before he had a chance to knock, the kitchen storm door swung violently open and Sam Davis stood there in undershirt and overalls, a young-looking man with a fuzz of gray on his face, his bare white arms knobbed with short, hard muscles. He seemed ready to jump for Wood's throat, and his eyes actually glittered in the frosty air.

"Can I come in?" Wood said.

"What! What!" Sam Davis said. He almost fell forward, as though he had meant to jump, and changed his mind just too late.

"You the one called a while back?"

"Yes. I'm Wood Whipple."

Sam Davis moved back an inch or two, and Wood walked past him into the warm kitchen that smelled of supper and kerosene. A dark-haired woman, he couldn't tell her age, sat next to the oil stove in a straight chair. She was wrapped in what looked like a gray blanket—all except for her head and her fragile white

hands, which flashed and jerked, machinelike, over her knitting.

"Mrs. Davis?" Wood said. The woman didn't look up at him, but Sam Davis said harshly from behind him, "She ain't Mrs. Davis."

Wood turned to find a pump shotgun pointed right at the middle of him, right at his belly. He sucked in his breath involuntarily, and had a quick twinge of nausea. The hole in the end of the barrel looked enormous, and he believed for a second he would be shot.

The rigor of Sam Davis' face and hands grew, in that second, and his bumpy muscles grew larger. But the shot didn't come, the blue eyes flickered, and Wood knew that he wasn't about to do anything so foolish.

"You scared, sonny?" Sam Davis asked triumphantly, not knowing that his voice proved that there would be no shot.

"Yes," Wood said.

"Hah!" Sam Davis said. "I could kill you legal as hell."

"You have no reason to shoot me," Wood said.

"Maybe I'll just break a few of your bones for you!" Sam Davis put the shotgun in the corner and came back to stand a foot from Wood, his arms akimbo.

Wood looked down into Sam Davis' rigid, quivering face. Each gray bristle of his week-old beard seemed to point straight at Wood, and the blue eyes were lighter and colder than Susie's, dangerously flat. The man still looked like pure murder.

"I ought to . . ." he said without opening his teeth. "I ought to tear your balls off."

"I don't see why you ought to do anything," Wood said. "I mean no harm to you or Susie."

"What the hell's your name again?"

"Wood Whipple."

"You Harvey's boy?"

"Yes."

"You the one stole the money?"

"No, that was my brother Horace."

The danger of pure violence had lessened, as if each word were a counter for its lessening force. The yellow of the walls grew more distinct, and behind Wood the knitting needles clicked

on. It occurred to him that he was no longer afraid, but that he should be cautious.

Behind the wall a shallow-well pump began to clunk and hiss. A cow bawled in an outshed or barn. Then a nearer sound—the creak of a stair, and Sam Davis jumped past him into the door to the front hall, where there was violent breath and the hard sound of some thing, some animal, hurt—a short, desperate grunt. He came back pulling the big girl by the arm, and slammed her down in a kitchen chair. Her elbow hit the table like a board, and one of her legs swung away from the chair, a polka-dot pajama leg, bare foot, red toenail polish and calluses. She pulled her leg back and spread her faded blue bathrobe over her lap, then put her head on the table and hid her face in her brown hair. The back of her neck was red. She smelled of damp blankets and pillows—Wood smelled that child smell above the kitchen odors.

Sam Davis stood over her. "Listening, were you? Sneaking around listening? Well, you're going to hear a lot, and so am I! I didn't raise no daughter of mine for town pump!"

He turned to Wood. "How many times you had her ass?"

"Never."

"I bet! I could git you and about ten more in this town for statuary rape, sonny! Clap your ass in jail! You know that? She ain't at the age of consent! You know that?"

"I've never had sexual intercourse with your daughter," Wood said.

The words seemed to drive Sam Davis mad. Although he didn't come at Wood, he began to scream. "Sexual intercourse! Sexual intercourse! Sexual intercourse!" banging a chair down against the linoleum floor, picking it up like a post-hole digger and jabbing it down so hard Wood half expected it to go through linoleum, floorboards and all.

It was then Wood understood the man's powerlessness, and decided to do something. He never knew why he chose that moment to act. In another man's home, surrounded by that man's people and possessions, what right had he to take on authority? Why should he get away with it? These thoughts came later, when he and Sam Davis were sitting at the table, drinking hard cider. But perhaps at this moment he did perceive the real power of the phrase "sexual intercourse"—clinical words from a

vocabulary Sam Davis had always been led to fear and respect. "Statuary rape," Sam had said, and Wood thought of Susie as the Venus de Milo, or the Wingèd Victory of Samothrace. She was as still as a statue all through her father's destruction of the chair, which came apart in his hands.

What Wood did was to sit down at the table across from Susie. Sam Davis stared, pieces of the back of the chair in his hands.

"Sit down," Wood said, and the man did sit down in the one remaining chair, his sharp elbows on the table. The sticks of chair back lay on the table between them all, next to the sugar bowl and the salt and pepper shakers, each of these in the shape of a little outhouse. On one was written, "I'm fulla S.," and on the other, "I'm fulla P."

In this silence Susie raised her head and looked at them both, quickly, her face swollen and frightened. Then she hid again.

"Where's her mother?" Wood asked.

"Concord," Sam Davis said. "She's over to Concord." Said this way it meant the state mental institution. "Five years she's been over to Concord. Christ! How can a man raise a kid with no mother? I done the best I could."

"Has Susie told you what happened?"

"I got Chief Tuttle's version. He caught the bastards at it." Sam Davis seemed tired now and sad.

"And you didn't want to prosecute," Wood said.

"Bad enough already. What good's that?"

"But you were about to shoot me, or break my neck, or something."

Sam Davis looked at him. Now there were tears of self-pity in his eyes. "Christ, you can't blame a man for getting upset, can you?"

"But you never got Susie's version of what happened?"

"I couldn't git any more upset than I am right now." He wiped his eyes with a hand that seemed oversized on his naked arm.

"Susie," Wood said. She didn't move. "Susie?"

She made a raw, bawling sound into her hands, and in between hiccups and noisy breaths, tried to speak. *"Mine . . . brash!"* she said, and tried again. "Gordon nid it! Gordon!"

74

"That's the son of a bitch she went out with," Sam Davis said.

"I know," Wood said.

"Gordon Ward," Sam Davis said.

"Got me drunk," Susie said. Then she cried awhile.

"So they ended up in the cemetery behind the Congregational Church," Sam Davis said, calmly now. "Standing in line."

"Honest to God I don't remember!" Susie said clearly.

"Gordon would do that. I know him," Wood said.

"I loved him."

"So you dropped your pants," Sam Davis said.

Susie raised her disorganized face and shouted, "*Drunk!* He gave me a Coke, but it was mostly rum! I never—"

"I think that's the truth," Wood said.

They sat quietly, hearing only the click of the old woman's knitting needles and an occasional sniffle from Susie.

"At least she ain't knocked up," Sam Davis said.

"I had my period last week." Susie got up, her face averted, and went to the sink. She stood there, holding a wet dishcloth to her face for a minute. "They hurt me too. I was sore for a long time."

"Maybe they ought to go to jail," Wood said.

Sam Davis shrugged. "Oh, shit," he said. "You want a glass of cider?" Without waiting for Wood's answer he got a jug from beneath the sink. The dark woman, holding her blanket together with her elbows, got up and silently brought them two tumblers.

"Gordon Ward's in the Army now, anyways," Sam Davis said. "There ain't nothing much to do about it." He poured the light cider. "Listen. Why'd you come here tonight? What business is it of yours?"

"When I called I thought you were beating her up."

"No, I never."

"He never beat me," Susie said. "Even when he found out, he never beat me."

"How'd you get the nerve to come over here?"

"I wanted to do what was right," Wood said.

Sam Davis shook his head. "Well, you're a wonder," he said. They drank from the big tumblers of cider. Wood felt it im-

mediately, and drank slowly, but Sam Davis drank his in three or four gulps.

"I got to hit the hay," he said suddenly. "I'm glad to of met you, Wood. So I'll say good night. There's more cider in the jug if you want some." He turned to go, and the woman in the gray blanket got up to follow him. Wood never did see her face clearly. At the door Sam Davis turned and said, "Say hello to your Pa for me." Then the two of them were gone. Wood was astonished by this sudden disappearance, but Susie didn't seem to find it strange at all.

He sat across the table from her, under the bright overhead light, and she smiled at him. Her face was still puffy from the crying, and plain without lipstick. Her eyes were a deep, dull blue. She looked as though she had been beaten up, and she looked even younger than seventeen.

"Now you know," she said.

"You loved Gordon?"

"I used to. I don't any more." She looked down at the table, at her hands. "I love you."

He was shocked by these unanswerable words.

"I loved you for a long time before I loved Gordon," she said seriously. "The only reason I loved Gordon was I gave up on you. You never seemed to notice me. You always went out with that snooty Lois Potter. Do you love her, Wood?"

"I like Lois."

"But you don't love her? You don't? Really?"

"I don't know," he said, and she looked worried and unhappy.

"Don't love her, Wood! Please don't. She's not nice. She's pretty, but she's not nice. She's very selfish, did you know that? She's got a wonderful figure, I know. She's not fat like me . . . Do you think I'm fat? I'm not, really, I'm just bigger than her. I've got a lot to offer, I mean. I got as good marks in school as her too."

He didn't say anything, and she looked at him for a long time, her face as open as the moon. This woman. This girl; he felt her wanting him, a heavy, complicated force in her, convoluted and hot—all below that white face that hid nothing. But he could not understand why this need was so intense; what did he, or any man, have that was needed so badly? Looking deep into her face, he felt that what she wanted must be more than the electric

shock, quickly gone, of an orgasm, even as he had experienced them in the deep inside-out thrill of wet dreams. But what was the right thing to do for this girl?

"I love you," she said, nervous and soft. "I'll do anything for you. Anything. I love you so much I hurt."

"Susie—" he said.

"I don't care if you don't love me. I'll do anything you want me to."

"I've got to go, Susie." He got up and went to the door, and she followed him, now seeming shy, in her bare feet and red toenails. He opened the inner door and turned to say goodbye, but turned into her arms. She had moved so skillfully; it seemed a woman's knowledge. She was all up against him, and kissed him on the mouth. Her breath was sweet, and she smelled like blankets and pajamas, the moist warmth of sleeping children. Her eyes were shut, and he gently disengaged himself and went away.

5

The next night at supper, just after everyone had prepared his potatoes for gravy, Horace found his plate in his lap. It was right side up, and somehow neither his potatoes nor his carrots had spilled. For a while he sat there with the warm plate in his hands. No one seemed to have noticed that the plate had disappeared from the table, and he tried to figure out how to get it back on the table without anyone noticing. He knew this was impossible.

His father was looking at him. "Horace," he said, the white fat of his cheeks still, the dark eyes half closed, "are you going to eat out of your lap?"

Horace shook his head; his ears were hot.

"Then why don't you—carefully, with extreme care—lift your plate out of your lap and place it on the table?"

"Horace needs glasses," his mother said quickly. "He can't see the blackboard unless he sits in the front row."

Horace put his plate back on the table.

"I don't want to watch him pour the gravy," his father said.

"I've got to squint all the time," Horace said, grateful to his mother.

"Well, did you make him an appointment?"

"Yes," his mother said. "At the clinic in Northlee."

"It just happened this year," Horace said. "I can't see the little branches on the trees any more."

"He found an old pair of spectacles in the attic," his mother said quickly.

"And I could see the little branches! I could see every little branch!"

In a drawer of the old highboy—the one in the attic hall that led to Kate's tower—he'd found the leather box. Inside was a pair of gold-rimmed spectacles, their lenses as small as nickels. When he looked through them it felt as though his eyes were clamped in a vise, and he looked out one of the round hall windows to see each little tree branch, each shovel cut, each evergreen needle upon the snow. The world outside cut into his brain like little needles and knives.

"Well," his father said. "Maybe that's the trouble—"

"Let's eat supper," his mother said.

Horace tried to eat, but the potatoes tasted like paper. The gravy had no taste at all, and his arms felt huge and weak. He was afraid to put his hands over the table. He was thirsty, but didn't dare pick up his water glass. Everyone else seemed to be in a kind of shade—not of shadow, but of focus, and only he was bright and clear, with all his shameful faults exposed to them, like an animal in a cage.

They ate in silence, except for the clink of silverware on plates. Kate went to the kitchen and returned. He felt that he might fall out of his chair. Why not? He would just fall over sideways and crack his head on Wood's chair and crumple to the floor. Let them pick him up with a shovel.

Then his father looked at Wood and mentioned her name. He hadn't been listening until he heard her name. Susie Davis.

"What did old Sam do?"

"Nothing much," Wood said.

"That I find hard to believe."

"We talked it over. Susie told us what happened."

"Susie told you and her old man *exactly* what happened?" Horace watched his father's face grow long, and his mouth fall open.

"It wasn't her fault. Gordon Ward got her drunk and she never knew what was going on."

"Am I supposed to hear this?" Kate said.

"Oh, come off it," David said. "Listen to the little innocent."

"I *am* innocent," Kate said.

"As if you don't know exactly what happened," David said.

"Well, I'm not sure!" Kate said, getting angry.

"Shut up!" Horace's father shouted.

"Hush, Harvey," his mother said.

"I don't know why he didn't prefer charges against all of them," Wood said.

"I'll tell you why." Horace recognized his father's mean voice, the one used for conspiracies, the same voice he used when speaking about President Roosevelt, or the war. "Name off those little hotshots and you've named the sons of a lot of people Sam Davis owes his shirt to. Get it? Gordon's father could foreclose on Sam's farm tomorrow. Get it? I happen to know he's five months late on his payments. Someday you'll find out how the world works, sonny boy!" His father seemed triumphant, happy in this knowledge.

Wood didn't answer for a while, though his father sat staring at him, savoring his triumph.

"You don't have to tell me how filthy rotten the world is," Wood finally said. "I just don't think it's so funny. And I don't have to be that way myself."

"Hah! High and mighty! Oh, boy! Wait'll you get kissed by reality! You'll find yourself crawling around in the filth with the rest of them!"

Horace heard his own voice shouting, "Wood is good!"

79

"Wood the Good!" his father said, laughing. "Wood the Good! Hah! Hah! Hah! Wood the Sanctimonious!"

Wood looked steadily across the table, and at that moment Horace dropped a piece of carrot from his fork into his water glass. How did his glass get that close to his plate? The piece of carrot sank to the bottom of the glass, and butter scummed the water. If he drank all the water maybe he could drink the piece of carrot out.

Wood said, "Just because everybody else is cruel and dishonest, do I have to be?"

"Yes!"

"No!" Wood said. "At least I don't have to act that way. Even if I do feel that way, I keep it inside."

"I hope you kept something inside your pants last night, anyway," his father said, and laughed even louder.

"*Harvey!*" his mother said. "That's enough!"

"What did he mean?" Kate said.

"I'll tell you later," David said.

"You'll be *quiet!*" his mother said.

They had stewed prunes for dessert. Stewed prunes always made Horace nervous, because of the pits; but the argument, or whatever it was, simmered down, and they made it through dinner. Afterwards he followed Wood up to his room, and knocked on Wood's door.

"Come in, Horace," Wood's deep voice called.

Horace opened the big door. He couldn't explain why it always seemed heavier and warmer than his own. The warmth seemed to come from the air of this whole portion of the hall—Wood's territory. Inside Wood's room the light was golden and warm.

"Come in, Horace," Wood said again. "Sit down." He pointed to the leather armchair, and Horace sat down into it gratefully. As its thick arms surrounded him it seemed to him that for the first time that day his stomach and all his inner parts began to calm down and to work again, as they ought to. He sighed with pleasure. If only he could just stay here, out of Wood's way. He wouldn't say anything, or bother Wood at all . . .

"What's on your mind, Horace?" Wood sat at his desk, and began to fill a pipe.

"I . . ."

"Yes?"

"I like your room better than mine."

"They're exactly the same."

"No, they're not. Mine's . . ." He was going to say "evil," but didn't say it. "Mine's cold. I don't know."

"Horace," Wood said in a kindly voice. He seemed huge, a huge force. Horace thought of Atlas, from a picture of Radio City, the great constant strength of the wide shoulders. Not really straining, because the face was calm, and would last for eternity. "Horace, I'm going in the Army in a few weeks. Do you want to have my room then? We can trade."

"Yes!" Horace said. But Wood wouldn't be here then. "In a few *weeks?*" he said. "*Weeks?*"

"Probably. Maybe even sooner."

But what will I do then? Horace almost asked. Tears came to his eyes, and he wiped them off quickly.

"David and Kate and Mother and . . . Dad will be here," Wood said.

"I don't want you to go away."

"I've got to. That's all there is to it," Wood said, and even though Horace trusted Wood's affection, he heard Wood's desire to go.

"You want to go," he said accusingly.

"In a way, I do. I don't want to leave you, though. But Horace," Wood went on reasonably, "you've got to get along by yourself. You know that, don't you?"

"Yes. No. I know that. But I can't feel it. I don't believe it. What'll we do without you? What if David goes to Dexter-Benham next year, like Mother says?"

"You'll have to tend the furnace and mow the lawn, and shovel the driveways, and . . . change the storm windows." Horace saw his hesitation at the storm windows. "You'll be a year older . . ."

"I'm afraid of the cellar," Horace said, ashamed to say it but afraid not to say it—he had to get it on the record. "I can't go down there alone. I'm scared of it."

"There's nothing down there to be scared of."

"Everybody says things like that! But it doesn't help!" He

felt like a fool to have shouted, and now he was crying. He didn't have a handkerchief, and the backs of his hands were all wet and snotty. Wood went out of his blurry sight for a moment and came back with a clean, folded handkerchief. "I don't know . . ." Horace tried to say. His voice roared in his ears, but he knew it was not loud in the room. "I don't know what's wrong with me! What's the matter with me?"

"Nothing's the matter with you," Wood's calm voice said. "You're at an awkward age, that's all."

"*Awkward!*" He couldn't help giving a bark of laughter that turned into a sob so tangible he felt for a moment he'd have to swallow it to get rid of it. Wood's handsome face was still kind, concerned. Oh no, he thought as Wood's face revealed too much, I'll just bawl. I can't stand it.

Wood drew his desk chair over and sat next to him, then put both hands firmly on his arm. "Horace?" All he could do was nod, his free hand over his eyes. But he was not in pain; as long as he could stay in Wood's room, no matter how much of a baby and a fool he acted, part of him rested.

"Listen, Horace. You know I don't lie, don't you?"

He nodded.

"Well, I'll tell you. Everybody goes through something like you're going through. I did. You're finding out a lot of things you can't explain. Nobody can explain them, but later on you'll just get used to them."

"What am I finding out?" He thought of the banana-fingered woman outside his window, whose eyes were blue fire, her hair like rats' tails.

"Well, like how they treated Susie. I know how you feel about her, and I do too—"

"You do?" That was part of it, but they were not the ones who surrounded him at night and killed his rest, and looked at him, and breathed cellar cold into his ear.

"I think so," Wood said. "I mean I think I know how you feel."

"It was Gordon Ward. You said that." Gordon Ward, laughing fit to bust, his eyes cruel green pieces of ice. "What did he do to her?"

"They"—Wood hesitated, and Horace shivered—"took ad-

vantage of her. They had her drink rum and Coke, and they got her drunk."

Gordon Ward. Horace saw him in his tan, whipcord finger-tip coat, laughing, swaying, standing above the friends who always followed him. No, lurching, really, from side to side in a smoothly graceful, jivey way. Red hair the color of oxblood shoe polish. When he walked, his shoulders moved from side to side—a swagger. The girls said he was very handsome but awfully fast, stuck-up, loud; they talked about him all the time. His father was president of the Leah Savings Bank. There were parties in his home with no adults present. You ought to see him conga, tango, jitterbug. Secret language: "Yousa moooongusha! Do she?" Knowing laughter. Big as a man. Red. "I came I saw I con*quered!*" Conga line down the third-floor hall at school, stopped by Mr. Skelton. "Come on, Mr. S., grab ahold!" Nerve. Did he or didn't he go out with Miss Dube, the new teacher? 1936 Plymouth convertible coupé. Trojans in the glove compartment. Case of beer in the rumble seat. Girl's panties in his jacket pocket. "Ooops!" Laughter. Stories, rumors. A fight in the locker room, Donald Ramsey with sudden blood all over his undershirt, lower lip like a grape. Giants and their anger, frightening and remorseless.

And Susie Davis, so beautiful and fragile. How could she have resisted this power? Those hard eyes that chanced upon her, that cared no more about her than they would a cat on the road, or a snail on the sidewalk. Reducing her tender, immaculate body to their dirty use. A joke. Her kindness reduced to filth, having to do with excretions, ejaculations, liquids, oils, dirt. Laughter. The pink silk that covered her pulled down by whose red hands? "Don," he heard in the locker room, "got slimy seconds! Bruce got dirty thirds!" Laughter. Laughter. Now Gordon Ward had gone into the service, out of Leah. Only his lieutenants, his inferiors, who were maybe even crueler and dirtier but not as strong, remained.

Yet they were not, and never had been, the ones who crept out of the shadows at night and held their fangs against the quivering skin of his back. Without Wood he would be at the mercy of the ones who lived in his own darkness. If all the human power for evil or for good left Leah, he would be alone with *them*. When Wood left . . . But then, he thought, it would be a

long time before Wood left, and he wouldn't think of his going. Weeks and weeks before he would have to die into fright in a house—in a town—empty of his brother's justice.

6

One wall of David's room was nearly covered by *National Geographic* maps, held there by thumbtacks. The largest was a Mercator projection of the world, and during the last year he had placed pins with colored heads at the points of German and Japanese advances. For the first half of 1942 he had been more than queasy about the war. America was losing. And he remembered thinking that this was not the way the United States of America and its allies could be treated. America never lost; it couldn't lose. Every lesson he had ever learned had been of victory, and even while knowing it was a foolish idea, he had felt that time should turn back to 1941, so that America's part of the war could start all over again. For a moment this had seemed not only plausible, but inevitable; but of course that moment, which was nearly despair, had passed immediately, and left him again with the sheer reality of upset presuppositions.

Then came rumors of torpedoes that wouldn't explode, of obsolete equipment that turned upon our own soldiers and sailors. And even in the news he began to see reticence, even falsifications of the true state of the war. Were the Russians really holding at Stalingrad? How could those bumbling giants who had frozen stiff at the sight of the little Finns have turned into what *Life* magazine called "A great fighting team"? "MAGNIFICENT MEN AND WEAPONS GIVE RED ARMY AN UNCONQUERABLE WILL TO WIN," *Life* said.

And the landings in North Africa: "U.S. TAKES OVER NORTH

AFRICA," the headlines said. But some little things were wrong; there, for instance, was a photograph called "An American Landing Barge," but the barge wasn't American. Anyone could see that. It was a British LCM. If David Whipple could see that so easily, who was in charge? Was everybody else blind? And if Rommel had been defeated at El Alamein, where was he now? David had no places to put his pins. He could look from the fudgy, gray news pictures over to the colored ads full of P-38s triumphantly strafing tanks, the pilots' faces ruddy and clean. Budweiser beer was responsible for our having Diesel engines. Baby Ruth candy bars gave our soldiers energy, and Lucky Strike Green had gone to war. Van Heusen shirts "for the man behind the man in khaki" were somehow helping. But how many ships had we lost at Midway, or the battle of Savo Island? He wanted to believe, but little things were wrong. He wanted to believe that he could believe.

Everything was in flux; even definitions, positions, the whole reality of this war. Last fall, before Pearl Harbor, after the Germans had begun to roll through Russia, his father said with glee, "Well, I guess old Adolf's going to get old Joe!" And now *Life* said that the only place the war was really being fought, the major battles, the real surge of masses of men and materials, was in "Mother Russia," and that the Russian tanks were the best in the world, far superior to ours. Guadalcanal was small potatoes, and even in Africa only a small number of divisions were involved.

And now eighteen- and nineteen-year-olds were going to be drafted. Even Wood, who had lived with him in this house all his life, was being drafted into the war.

In Leah and the surrounding towns they had built tall platforms, towers manned constantly by men who watched for enemy planes, telephones handy. David would soon be sixteen, and even he would be eligible to take his turn on the Leah watchtower.

He had ten .22 Long Rifle cartridges he had saved, and would not shoot, and he saw himself leaning across the sill of his bedroom window as the enemy soldiers crept out of the woods and across the lawn, his Winchester Model 62 pump deadly in his hands, dropping those alien bodies with precise shots to the neck. When those shells ran out, he still had his muzzle-loading shotgun

and his underhammer percussion rifle—three deadly shots there—
and his old .32 caliber Iver Johnson revolver, ten real, commercially loaded cartridges and eighty rounds of handloaded black
powder cartridges. When the American infantry counterattacked
they would find David Whipple in charge, a company of dead
Germans or Japs littering the lawn and driveway.

He picked up his .22 and aimed at a rose on his wallpaper.
How could he miss? He could hit a squirrel in the head without
even thinking to aim; he seemed merely to think the bullet out
of the gun and into the heads of squirrels. They always fell dead—
a twitch or two and the last electric pulse of the tail. How could
he miss a target as big as a man?

A target as big as a man . . . For a moment he felt like the
hunter in the magic forest, to whom all the game suddenly gave
itself freely. Men! To be issued such a hunting license, and they
were being given by the millions now. Just for a moment, and
then he felt himself melting back into the tender child he knew
was still inside him. He had done cruel things, but not so cruel
as things he had seen his friends do. His little bullet would cause
rupture and terrible pain, and terror, but he had always been a
good shot, and if a squirrel tried to crawl away wounded, his second shot quieted him immediately. He skinned them and
stretched their skins over a board, and his mother cooked them.
Thus the having of them was more important than the killing—
or almost more important. But men, who cried and were sick
to death even without being shot; how would it be to add to that
general misery? All the sick and the dead stank up the world,
froze and thawed under the eyes of the living.

The only dead man he had ever seen outside of pictures was
the Negro janitor of the grammar school, who lay quiet in his
coffin in the Community Church among the heavy flowers and
the red velvet—all this more official and respectable than his life
among the brooms and cinder cans had ever seemed.

And there was his father, down in his wheelchair in the living
room, turned sick, nearly insane by the sudden lurch of a car. As
tender as gelatin, and he couldn't be put back together again.
David could remember when his father was funny, when he was
always running and jumping with the kind of lightness and energy

86

David found in himself. A little bullet could end all this, all the world. One little bullet.

He put his rifle back into its rack with the shotgun and the Hilliard, where it rested black and gleaming, like a reptile returned to bask in its nest.

He would grow older, and lose his childishness—this painful shift between toy and weapon—and live in a different kind of world. It would be in the city, among intelligence and music, where death would be in its proper place, dignified and ceremonial. And the first step toward that life would be his attendance at Dexter-Benham next fall. Leah High School had always struck him as a minor league sort of place, essentially unserious, even mindless, where he kept his mouth shut and only wrote for one or two teachers. The others were jailers; they had to be. The tone of the place was set by kids who had no brains but a kind of animal style—like Gordon Ward, Donald Ramsey and their younger underlings. Graceful morons, whose only charms were confidence and strength.

The teachers came and went, sometimes staying, now, only for a few weeks. In algebra he had taken the same test three times already this year, because of new teachers. One got married, and another, a man, went into the service. The third was rumored to have gone out with a senior, and she probably wouldn't last very long, either. She wore broomstick pleats, had lipstick on her teeth, and smiled so wide you thought she'd bite you in her joy. Once she came up beside his desk, and as she leaned down over him to mark his paper she slid the soft inner part of her arm along his cheek, giving him a hard-on he had to pray would go down before the bell rang. There was something demeaning in this too, because he would never have her, and he didn't like her, and she was too old.

He took his meerschaum pipe from his desk and filled it with Rum and Maple tobacco. As he lit it, the worldly fumes of the aromatic stuff made his teeth ache to bite down upon the stem —a kind of pleasurable pain.

Someone knocked loudly on his door, and he knew by the self-conscious insistence of the knocking that it was Kate.

"Enter," he said, and she opened the door.

"You busy, Davy?"

"No," he said. She still didn't come in, but stood there in her saddle shoes and bobbysocks, her knees small below her skirt. Her sweater fell in graceful rounds. Even though she was his sister, he saw why she stole the brains of his friends.

"Come in," he said, and motioned to his leather chair. "Want a butt?" He took an old pack of Chesterfields from his drawer.

"Yes," she said, but he knew she had something else on her mind. She came in and flopped down in his chair, then took a cigarette and was still and careful as he lit it for her. She didn't smoke in her own room because her mother would smell it.

"Ah," she said, letting the smoke dribble out in a thin line —an affectation of hers—as she shook her wheat-colored hair out from behind her head. Her nostrils seemed smaller and rounder than anyone else's. It seemed strange to remember, and yet he could, that he had seen her bawl and make ugly sounds. He had even caused her to make such noises.

"Have you ever gotten drunk, Davy?" she asked.

"Sure," he said.

"No, I mean it, now. Don't lie. Have you ever really been drunk?"

He could lie, and be quite convincing. He considered this, but then realized that he wished for more than any easy fantasy, that business of childhood. Kate was being very serious, for her, so he would be honest too.

"I tried, but I got sick before I really got drunk."

"Where was this?"

"Mike Spinelli got a bottle of Schenley's from Keith Joubert. He got it from Billy Muldrow, I guess. Billy bought it for him. And some of us chipped in on it and we went up above the Spinellis' garage."

"What was it like? What did it feel like?"

"I got a little dizzy. It felt kind of good for a while, and then all of a sudden I had to be sick."

"What did it feel like when it felt good?"

"Well . . ." What had it felt like? He'd taken four or five swigs from the bottle, as his turn came. It was cold on the lips, and the ice descended into the middle of his chest and began to fume and burn. "I liked the guys better. They seemed funnier than they were, and we laughed harder."

88

"I'd like to get drunk sometime."

"You mean like Susie?" he said.

She blushed and took a quick puff on her cigarette. "No. I'm just curious, Davy. Weren't you?"

"I still am, I guess," he said. "Anyway, Kenny Clark was sick before I was."

"Davy?" she said nervously, and flung her hair around so that it whipped her cheeks and then dropped lightly back, each strand softly in place again.

"What?" he said.

"Could we try it sometime? Just you and me? I think it might be a good idea—to see what it's like. I mean how it affects a person."

"Oh, I see," he said. "Forewarned and all that?" He saw that she was proud of her reason.

"You're the only one I know. Well enough, I mean. Everybody else . . . You know," she said.

He knew.

"How do you know it won't affect you like Susie Davis?" he said.

"That's just it. We could go up to my tower, maybe, and only you would be there, and you could tell me all about how I acted."

"It's too damn cold up there," he said, but it was the idea itself that gave him a funny sort of chill.

"But we couldn't have anybody barging in on us. That would be awful, wouldn't it? How about that old electric heater in the hall closet? Does it work?"

"The cord's all frayed." The heater was round, and grew copper-orange, like a big hot eye. His father used to sit in front of it and focus it on his leg. "Well, it's an idea," he said.

"And we could bring a basin in case we threw up."

"How about the booze?" he said.

She blushed again, guiltily. "I've been planning this, because I knew you'd go along. You have to, Davy. Who knows what I might do under the influence of alcohol? I might throw myself from the window. I knew you'd go along, Davy."

"You mean you've got the booze already?"

"I'm not usually sneaky, am I?" she asked, half proud of herself, but really worried about his opinion, he could see.

"No," he said. That was true. "No, Katie, you're pretty unsneaky. That's the truth. But how did you sneak the hooch? From Whip?"

"Yes. See, each time he wants a drink, or some ice in his glass or something, I try to be the one to get it. I've got a Mason jar—it's in back of the syrup jars, and it looks something like it from the outside." She was proud of herself now. "Anyway, each time I know he's had a drink I take just a little bit, and now I've got a whole Mason jar full, and Dad never seemed to notice. He gets confused, see, because he's got one bottle there in the drawer of his desk, and some others open in the kitchen, and I sort of switched them around once in a while, when nobody was home. He drinks a lot, did you know that? He drinks nearly a whole bottle a week."

"Okay, when do you want to make this experiment?" He surveyed its risks as he spoke.

"Tonight. We don't have to go to school tomorrow."

"How come you don't want to do this with one of your girl friends? Why me?" he asked.

"Oh, don't be like that, Davy!" she said, as if he'd betrayed her.

"I just wondered, that's all," he said.

"Girls aren't honest with each other, that's why. They're hypocrites. I don't know any girl as well as I know you. They're either all mushy over me, or they're sneaks. I don't talk to them much. I mean, to tell the truth. We gab all the time, but . . . Anyway, I don't like girls very much."

"But you trust me?" he asked, flattered but distrustful because it didn't seem anything he deserved.

"Stop that!" she said, looking at him sternly. "You're my favorite brother. We're just alike. We could be twins. We're the only people in this whole family that understand each other. I mean I don't care if you are nearly sixteen. Girls mature faster than boys. All the boys in my class still think they're cowboys and Indians—all a bunch of stupid little children shooting bent pins with rubber bands."

"But we've never told each other very much," he said, some-

what overawed, and not liking his cowardice. It seemed to him that he could be a betrayer.

"We've never had to, because we understand each other."

"Maybe you're right," he said.

"But you're still all embarrassed."

"Well, you shouldn't startle people, you know," he said.

"Huh."

"Okay, little sister . . ."

"Davy, don't pull that stuff with me."

"All right. All right. We'll get drunk and tell nothing but the truth," he said. "But you're just a kid, you know."

"Huh."

"We're both freaks, I guess," he said.

"Well, we don't have to tell *all*. There's no use going overboard, is there?"

"No," he said.

"You see? I understand you, don't I?" she said. "The main reason I like you is you don't blab your head off. Even if I got disgusting you probably wouldn't tell anybody about it, would you?"

"No, not about you. I'll tell you about it, though," he said. "You'll never hear the last of it, you know."

"Good. That's a chance I'm willing to take. I'll meet you in my tower at eleven o'clock sharp. It's now eight-thirty. I'll have everything else ready, but you bring the heater. Bring your ashtray and those Chesterfields, okay?"

"Right," he said, and couldn't help smiling.

"So it's sort of stupid, maybe. But I've got to find out."

"I'll take notes," he said, but he was nervous all the same.

Kate got up, brushing out her skirt as she went to the door. "I wonder if a person can be honest," she said thoughtfully. "But then, I don't have any real shameful secrets—I mean things that really happened. Do you, Davy?"

"You don't have to tell secrets just because you drink some whiskey," he said, and she studied him carefully. "I mean," he added, feeling guilty and wondering just why, "it's not like a Catholic confessing or anything like that." She still pondered him.

"I'd like to know your secrets, Davy," she said. "That would be interesting. I don't know anybody's secrets. Peggy tells me a

lot, but she doesn't seem to have any secrets. I like Peggy, don't you?"

"She's a girl. I thought you didn't like girls."

"She's different. She's so . . . unfortunate," Kate said.

"That's a good word for it," he said.

"Yes." She sighed. "Her mother is totally irresponsible."

"That's putting it mildly," he said. "You mean she's a prostitute."

"I know what that means. It's in the dictionary. I mean, in *general* I know what it means, but there're a lot of details that escape me."

He wondered if that were true, then realized that it was, because Kate never lied. No, she never did, and that was one of the things that always seemed to give her an advantage over him.

"Well!" she said briskly. "Are you game, David? Eleven sharp?"

"Okay, Katie," he said. She left, waving a thin hand, the last thing he saw as she closed the heavy door after her.

Suddenly his room was cold—or perhaps its sense of protection had faltered when that thin hand dematerialized as though it had gone like a ghost through the cypress door itself. This thought, too, occurred to him: it would have been better to have been born an only child, even an orphan, because then his essential coldness would not have cheated so many people. No, not coldness, really, but a feeling that he could not have a proper relationship with his own family. His feelings toward them were not familial. If he felt guilty about teasing Horace, or was somehow threatened by an eighth-grade girl, what did family have to do with his reactions? He felt no different about them than he did any other people he knew. They seemed no more vulnerable, or pitiful, and behind their eyes he felt the same yearnings he felt in strangers. They all claimed to be closer to his thoughts than they really were, and asked for his secrets. And his lack of curiosity about their secrets must be coldness in him. As he shivered, an icy wind seemed to come from his skin like the swirl of breath that had flowed down across the wooden shelves of the old icebox they used to have.

He opened his fireplace damper, started a small fire of just newspaper and kindling, and watched the bright flames crack.

As long as he could remember, this had been his room. Only a vague brightness, like a flash of blue, might have been the memory of another room he had slept in as a baby. That had been the nursery, a room next to his parents' old upstairs bedroom. Now both were empty except for bed frames and cardboard boxes. The nursery had bright blue wallpaper with white rabbits in diagonal rows, three slightly dissimilar rabbits repeated over and over from splashboard to picture molding. He hadn't looked into that room for a long time, but he would always remember the repetition of the three rabbits; the discovery of this small deception had always seemed to him an important step in his understanding of the ways of the world.

His own room had always been papered with the small, dark roses, most of them covered, now, by maps and pictures, by his pine gun rack and the back of his huge roll-top desk, a monster made of angry orange maple, with enough room in it for all his loading equipment, notebooks and papers.

He took a canister of black powder from one of its shelves and poured a thimbleful of the shiny grains into his palm, then tossed them into the fire. A soft whoosh, gray smoke in a solid, inside-out turning billow that the flue swallowed all at once in a silent gulp. Above the mantel, like a great nudge against the space of the room itself, hung the head of a bull moose with dusty staring eyes above its suitcase of a nose, and above them the spreading palmated antlers, where spiders lived. He'd found the moose head in the attic, shot long ago in Newfoundland by one of the hunting De Oestrises, combed and brushed it, painted in some of its mangy places and oiled the antlers. Now he hardly noticed it except when someone entered his room and looked above his head, quickly, as they always did. And yet that dark animal was up there, leaning anciently into the room.

He looked up at its pounds of nostrils; it seemed so much a thing of the past, so steady against this time of revolution and anxiety. The present was something tolerable mainly when it was possible to forget it, and his life itself either seemed over, so that he could look all the way back along its length, or not even begun. It would begin when he left Leah. Again he felt disloyal, this time toward all of his possessions. Of the four children's

bedrooms, his was the most cluttered, the most personal, and yet he would leave all these things so easily. The clutter seemed childish. Except for the old oil painting of Mt. Chocorua in a gilt frame, a picture full of dark browns, where even the green of the trees was brownish, most of the pictures had been clipped from magazines and crudely matted. One of Cézanne's views of L'Estaque was next to a long photograph of an engraved Winchester Model '76, and next to that a painting by Aaron Bohrod of a dark city street in winter, and next to that a map of Southeast Asia with yellow-headed pins representing Japanese advances.

All of his things were mixed, patternless, not quite what he really wanted. Because of the war he could no longer buy .22 shells or percussion caps, and sometimes the urge to shoot, to go out into the woods and deal with a reality that couldn't be denied, could not be called childish because there was the real blood, the real finality of the wild thing become still in his hand—sometimes the curtailment of this joy seemed to gray out his life, and a .22 Long Rifle hollow-point shell became as beautiful and meaningful an object as anything in the world.

And then, alternately, the joy of L'Estaque—what was that composed of, and was it more meaningful than a shell? Cézanne had made that bay, that sky, more powerful than any real view of any real place—a miracle. His own efforts, even though he sometimes worked on his own paintings so hard, and studied so hard he became bilious and fragile, never approached that clarity and power. His paintings were secret, and stood behind his desk, often painted out with white lead and begun again. His family knew he had paints, but after a while had never asked to see his work.

Last week, by accident, he had made a discovery that seemed so simple, afterwards, his excitement had been mixed with dread of his own blindness, as though in discovering light he had also discovered a congenital dimness of mind. He'd been scraping old paint from a canvas, and suddenly beneath his palette knife he found an impossible subtlety of color, then light, as though he were scraping paint from glass, and he looked through into sky. Not real sky with its artificial china-blue or dead flat gray, but a sky created, full of godlike power that flowed up through the knife into his hand. How could the opaque, garish paints in his tubes have been transmuted into such reality? But there it was,

an unpaintlike texture of tiny scrapes and flakes, variations, upon close examination, mostly of browns and greens—these last so faint, so mixed with whites and grays they had to be identified by a deliberate effort of the mind. That one patch of power was the only successful thing he'd ever done with paints, and he hadn't touched it again because he knew what would happen to it the second he put paint on a brush and touched its translucency with mud.

Things almost worked, but nothing really worked, and some of the things in his life that seemed almost to work, like that orphan patch of sky, were accidents he could not quite yet study hard enough to understand. He was a virgin, yet he could at night call up in his mind any girl in school and take her, carefully and slowly until his semen lay hot on his chest, heavy with strangeness and egg smell, and what had been the sacred deep vessel of her was only his hand, and she had never been with him at all.

He shivered, and stood up, turning his back on his little fire. Suddenly he was shaken by a profound emotion, at first unidentifiable. It was nostalgia, but for what? Loneliness, sad and terrible—but there seemed to be no object for this feeling. And then he realized the tears that threatened him were not caused by any hopeless love of any place or time he'd known. "I'm homesick," he said out loud, knowing now that his nostalgia was for no time in the past, but for the future. The alarm clock on his desk ticked and moved; he couldn't hasten the hands around. He couldn't go to sleep, that child's trick of Christmas Eve. He could only exist in this indefinite limbo. Bored, immobile, nervous, he must wait for time to turn.

7

Wood and Lois Potter came out of the Strand and stood for a moment on the cleared sidewalk, the moisture of the theater clammy on their skin. The December night was so clear the stars seemed to hang as if embedded in a black quilt just above the elm trees of the square. The town decorations had been set up—red, green and blue bulbs strung through the low blue spruce, and red boards had been nailed around the lampposts to make them look like Christmas candles. From the loudspeaker above the middle door of the Town Hall came "Silent Night," cold and dim, as if the orchestra that played it were miles away. All the people walked quickly away into the sharp cold, and those who were going to the second show had crowded, steamy and red-faced, into the right half of the lobby.

Lois put her furry mitten between his arm and his body and pressed his arm lightly against her as they walked toward Trask's Pharmacy, past the Town Hall and the green, slightly tilted statue of the Union soldier, past the old hotel and up the cement steps to the pharmacy. Red paper bells that folded out in honeycombs of tissue hung in the frosted windows.

They always stopped in Trask's after the movie, and long ago he had stopped bothering to suggest it. They would have a Coke, and speak to their friends, and then he would walk Lois the four blocks to her house, a high, white clapboard house, one of the oldest houses in Leah, where her mother and father would welcome him discreetly, trying not to show how pleased they were with him.

He steered Lois ahead of him through the big door, and she moved expertly at his direction. She was tall, slim and dark-

haired—aristocratic-looking, with fine-grained skin that never seemed to be affected by the cold air. In fact she was more or less an aristocrat in Leah. She was related to the De Oestrises— as he was, for that matter. They were distant cousins.

They sat in a booth below a great glass amphora full of red liquid, and smelled the syrups of the soda counter and the peppery chemicals from the prescription counter at the rear. One other couple was there—Foster Greenwood and Jean Welch, whose relationship had always been touched with romantic sadness because she was Catholic and he was not, and their parents were against them. Sometimes Foster would have Bob Contois pick Jean up at her house, and deliver her to him downstreet. They had always been slightly sad, star-crossed. The booths were too small for more than one couple, so Wood and Lois sat in a booth across from them. Prudence Trask brought their Cokes in paper cones set in metal holders. As she put them down she nodded toward Foster and Jean, then shook her head. Jean had been crying, and Foster held her hands.

At the counter Beady Palmer and Donald Ramsey were talking. Everyone knew that since the Susie Davis scandal, Donald's girl, Marilyn Jackson, a sophomore, wouldn't go out with him.

Lois looked across her Coke and exaggeratedly pursed her lips around her straw—an expression of concern for Jean, and Wood nodded. In these circumstances they wouldn't interrupt. They exchanged glances with Prudence, who had gone back behind the counter.

"Oh, Wood," Lois said softly. He nodded, and examined her long, thin nose, her perfectly symmetrical face, her almost garishly pretty eyes. In them green and brown mixed in bright splinters that flashed as she glanced up at him. She had always seemed just right for him, in every way. And then he thought: In every way outside of me. He was always pleased at the thought of the two of them, or at the vision of the two of them; he always seemed to be standing somewhere to the side, watching both the girl and the boy. Now, maybe because they sat next to Foster and Jean, who seemed mismatched in everything but their involvement with each other, he tried to bring himself back inside himself, and to look with his own eyes at this pretty girl everyone thought he

97

was to marry. And who, he knew, felt herself so lucky to have him. Again he felt several feet away from where he sat.

He imagined that Foster and Jean had no such problem. Foster was very tall, the center on the basketball team, and Jean was very short, so short it was awkward for them to dance together. When they walked together Foster would reach down and put his hand on the side of her neck. In fact Jean was so short she had a kind of midget look about her, or maybe even a dwarf look. She seemed almost to belong in another scale, especially when she stood next to Foster. She was always very sweet and even-tempered, and it did not seem strange to see her crying so silently and sadly. She had a freckled, Irish, kid-sister sort of face, and light brown hair that always looked as though it hadn't been out of curlers for the proper number of hours. Now she and Foster, by their whispering and sighs, still signaled to be left alone.

Beady, who hadn't spoken to Wood since his outburst at Milledge & Cunningham, had glanced over at him once or twice and looked away without admitting recognition. Wood knew he could have made up with Beady anytime, but had hesitated because he knew Beady felt guilty about it, and would feel better if he broke the silence himself. But now the silence had progressed too far, and Wood decided to do something about it Monday morning.

Beady swung around and went to the jukebox, put a coin in it, and as the arms and cams inside the glass chose his record he cocked his head like a dog, trying to see it all through his strange eyes. The song he had chosen was "That Old Black Magic." Once it began, he turned and went back to his stool, seeming to pay no more attention to it.

Jean had wiped her eyes with a paper napkin, and now looked up, abstractedly, and tapped her fingers on the table to the rhythm of the song. Foster hummed along.

> *That old black magic's got me in its spell,*
> *That old black magic that you weave so well . . .*

They were coming out of it, coming into public again. But aware, Wood thought, even in their sadness, of the dramatic

value of their predicament. For just a moment he felt jealous of their intensity. It seemed to him that all of his strongest feelings were a kind of resigned disgust at the way people acted—or sometimes anger, or pity.

"Where were you?" Lois said to him. She tapped him, quickly, on the hand with her sharp fingernail.

"Thinking, I guess."

"About?"

"Nothing."

"Sorry I asked."

"No, I can hardly remember what it was," he said.

"The Army?"

"No."

"I just think about you not being around," she said. "And me at college. College? Unh!"

"Don't you want to go?" he asked.

"I guess I have to. All Potters go to college, just like all Whipples—that don't get drafted, that is." Her eyes seemed to dim for a moment. "I wish we . . ." She shook her head, forbidding herself to go on.

"What do you wish, Lois?"

"Never mind."

Foster turned toward them. "You heard from the draft yet, Wood?"

"Not yet."

"Greetings!" Foster said, and made a surprised face. Jean laughed, and they all looked at her at once, which made her shy.

"I'm just waiting around," Wood said.

"I hope they wait till after Christmas, anyway," Lois said. She reached across and put both hands on his arm, holding it down on the table.

Jean poked Foster in the chest and said, "This jerk's been trying to enlist."

"You're not going to finish high school?" Wood asked him.

"They'd give me a diploma anyway," Foster said. "Anyway, all I want to be is a Navy pilot, and now I find out I'm too tall. You can't be over six-four. All they want is a bunch of shrimps."

"You can't fit in an airplane," Jean said. She turned to Lois,

pleased. "So he's not going to. He's going to graduate with his class in June. Aren't you, Foster?"

"I don't know. There's a war on out there."

"But you're only seventeen," Jean said. Foster frowned at her, and she ducked her head slightly.

"Old enough to join the Navy or the Marines," Foster said. This fact kept him from being more irritated by Jean's remark.

"That's true," Lois said, shaking her head. "My goodness, we've all . . . grown up!" She looked at Wood, still shaking her head. "We're men and women, aren't we."

Wood thought of Susie Davis, the big little girl, still soft with baby fat. Again, her having been known by all that raw sex, those brawling, howling red boys, seemed a part of the war.

"Where are you?" Lois asked him. "Where are you, Wood?"

He shook his head. "Just thinking."

"About?" Her hand came toward his, like a darting bird, and her cool finger tapped his hand, seeming to leave a little frozen spot just behind his knuckle. "Let's go to my house," she said, including Foster and Jean. "We can play the phonograph or something."

Foster and Jean, who had no place to go that wasn't dangerous, were happy with this idea. As they paid Prudence and left, Beady stared away, into the syrup pumps. Wood wondered what he saw, what fragments of light from the silvery spouts came into his brain. Monday he would have to make up with Beady.

They walked through the clear night on the shoveled sidewalks, between high banks of snow, the compressed snow beneath their feet hard and white as marble. Foster and Jean walked silently behind.

Wood thought how once, a year or two ago, this would have been exciting, because they would turn the lights down, and dance, and eventually each couple would retire into the darkness to mumble privately and neck—a funny word; it made him think of swans and ostriches. He did enjoy (what a word!) feeling Lois' pretty body next to him. When they kissed she seemed almost to lose consciousness, and he wondered how far she would really go. They had discussed this once, and had decided not to go all the way; that later, when they were older, or engaged (if they were to marry, and he knew that he was responsible for that "if" in

their agreement), they would. So he always went home from these sessions with a dull but almost intolerable ache in his testicles, and he would dream, not usually that night but the next, not of Lois but of some cheap faceless girl who shamelessly raised her skirt and invited him to take her standing up. He came as she laughed raucously, and he woke up, still seeing fragments of red lipstick and wide white teeth. There was no shame to this dream, only a kind of sadness because it was a dream of no one, with no love.

Yet he did believe that love existed. Foster and Jean were in love. They burned and froze in each other's sight. And Lois was in love with him—but he was in love with no one.

At the Potters' house Lois' mother and father greeted them pleasantly. A tall, wrinkled, friendly couple, worrying through their smiles, they soon retired to some other room in order to leave the young people alone. Wood rolled up the oriental rug in front of the embering living-room fireplace, and they danced to records. Lois had taught him to do all the popular steps, and he dutifully jitterbugged and fox-trotted. "String of Pearls," "Chattanooga Choo Choo," "If I Loved You"—it was something she liked very much to do. She hummed in his ear, and her dark hair, always clean and sweet smelling, touched his face. He seemed to feel her white bones twist in her sweet flesh. When they kissed she seemed so open and generous, he was sad that he didn't love her as much as he should.

Sometimes when he was alone in his room he would try to daydream of Lois, naked in his bed with him, but she always turned into that Lois Potter who had an address, parents, relatives, a class at school, possessions—a kind of social entity instead of a needful girl. She reminded him of responsibilities, and without the warmth and softness of her real presence she couldn't excite him the way the anonymous girl could.

After they had danced for a while Foster and Jean retired to a couch in a dark corner, and soon after that Lois turned off the phonograph and switched on the radio, low, to the long-distance station that came on in the night. First Wood sat beside her on the davenport, and then they lay down together. Lois moaned as they kissed.

"I love you," she whispered. "I love you so much." She kissed

his eyes and pulled his head against her. She was close to crying, and her lips grew soft as fleece, and silky. "I don't *want* you to go away. I want to . . . get married and sleep with you every night and have babies. You just don't have any idea how much I love you, do you?" Anger began, a hard, almost querulous edge. "I know you don't!" she whispered. "You don't know!"

"Yes, I love you, Lois," he said. "You've always been my girl."

"Yes, I'm your girl. But I'm more yours than you are mine. That's what makes me cry."

"That's not true," he whispered, knowing she recognized the lie; they always had to ignore it, or she would grow sad and tears would start. She pushed him up and got her arms under his sweater, hugging him as hard as she could. She spoke softly into his ear. "Sometimes I think when all this started it was like a devil or something got into me. I remember when we used to play together like a couple of boys. Remember? Five or six years ago? Remember my costume, with the big handlebar mustache, when I was the Duke of Venice and all that? I mean I always wanted to marry Wood Whipple someday, but I never cried over it. Sometimes I'd decide I didn't even like you, and I wasn't going to marry you after all. But damn you, you never really did anything nasty, or ugly, or mean enough so I could stop loving you. You always had the advantage. You're so much better than I ever was. I'm nasty sometimes, and I lie, and I used to steal things—"

"Shh. Everybody does things like that."

"But not *you*. Not Wood Whipple. God, sometimes I hate you. You're not even real sometimes. And then I think of you, no matter where I am. In school. Even during an exam, and I melt. Quickly she took his hand and put it on her breast. "Oh, God, I melt," she whispered. "I'm melting all over."

She moved against him, not rhythmically but as though she meant merely to shift position. He did this too, and in his eyes gold flashed. He saw whole mosaics of color. He could just stop himself from moving, moving against her.

Then they heard Jean cry out loud. "Oh no! Foster! You didn't!"

"Shh!" Foster said. "I'm sorry!"

"Oh no! No!" Jean sobbed.

Wood and Lois sat up. It was obviously not a private matter

with Jean, whatever it was. She was disconsolate. "No, I don't believe it! I do believe it!"

"What's the matter?" Lois said. "Jeannie?"

"He did!" Jean cried.

"Did what?"

"You know what! Foster Greenwood!" She turned on the bridge lamp next to their couch and sat under it, her lipstick spread lightly all over the lower part of her face. Foster loomed over her, the same amount of lipstick on his pale jaws.

"Now what will I do?" Jean cried.

"What did you do?" Lois said to Foster, who looked away, shrugging his shoulders.

"I guess I couldn't help it."

"He went all the way," Jean said. "He said he wouldn't. Now I'll have a baby . . ." She cried into her hands.

"Wait a minute, Jeannie," Wood said. "You don't always get one, you know."

"I couldn't stop myself," Foster said. "I guess I just lost my mind."

"Are you sure you . . . ?" Wood said.

"He did!" Jean said. "I asked him to stop. I said be careful, but he was just like a mad raving beast! I never saw you like that, Foster!"

"I lost my head, that's all."

"Are you sure you . . . ? Did you . . . come?" Wood said.

"I'm afraid so," Foster said.

Jean sat beside him, trembling, frozen. "Now I'm not a virgin," she said. "I can't confess that. I will not ever say that to Father Brangelli. I just couldn't!"

Suddenly Foster laughed. "What a mess!" he said. "What a mess! If you get pregnant! What a mess!"

"Lois!" Jean said. "Wood! You won't tell, will you?"

"Of course not," Wood said. "But anyway, Jeannie, it isn't that terrible, is it?"

"If she gets pregnant?" Foster said, raising his eyebrows incredulously.

"Oh, oh!" Jean cried, and threw herself across his lap. "It's all my fault! I couldn't expect him to have all the self-control. It's really all my fault."

"No, Jeannie," Foster said. "It was my responsibility." He looked at Wood. "Is there anything we can do about it now? To keep her from having a baby, I mean?" He looked at Lois, asking her too.

"It's kind of late to think about that," Wood said.

"What about . . . ?" Lois said. "Jeannie? Like in feminine hygiene, didn't it say . . . ?" She went over to Jean, who got up, and they moved away from the boys, whispering.

"Oh, I don't know," Jean said. "Miss Dube was pretty vague about that part."

"Can you do anything?" Foster called across the room to them. Lois gave him a blank look, which made him wince, and then she and Jean left the room. Wood and Foster looked at each other and shrugged.

"I know about nothing on that subject, to tell the truth," Foster said. "Even if I had a rubber I wouldn't have put it on, because I never intended to do it. You could have cut my left leg off and I wouldn't have given it a thought."

They stared morosely at the furniture.

"It's sort of embarrassing," Foster said. "I just couldn't stop. I tore the hell out of her panties. It was like . . ." He thought for a while. "I love her, you know," he said finally.

"You're kind of young to get married," Wood said.

"Thanks," Foster said. "Ow! And her family—a bunch of crazy harps. They think the Virgin Mary invented God. The time Jeannie took me to her house they looked at me like somebody'd laid a turd on the rug. If he knew I got her cherry he'd eat me up. Ow! Her old man. Look at that!" He held out his hands, and watched them tremble. "He's just a little banty rooster, but he'd eat me alive." He stared sadly at the radio, which uttered faint little chirps. "It was worth it, though," he said. "I'm going to do it again too, only next time I'll be prepared."

"Nothing's foolproof, though," Wood said. "I read that."

"Nothing ventured, nothing gained," Foster said, and then added in a smooth, thick voice, "I'll tell you somebody else who loved it too. While it was going on, Wood. I mean it. She grabbed me so hard you couldn't have pried her loose with a crowbar. Oh, Christ, I'm getting all horny again." He untangled his legs, got up

and turned away. "I guess I better join the Navy and get the hell out of this town."

When Lois brought Jean back to them, Jean was very shy again, and quiet. She went up to Foster and took his big hand. "I'm sorry," she said.

"The second show's going to be out soon," Foster said. "I'd better get you home before an Irish posse gets after me."

When they'd left, Lois tuned the radio in better. Johnny Mercer was singing "Sentimental Journey." She came and sat next to him. "It's amazing," she said.

"What's amazing?"

"They really did do it. Right over there." Lois was trembling. "I'm afraid to touch you," she said, and then added in a quick little mumbling voice, "I'd let you, you know that?"

"You shouldn't, Lois."

"Have you ever done it, Wood?"

"No, I haven't."

"Neither have I," she said, and giggled nervously. "Of course you know that."

"You're only seventeen," he said.

"Old enough to join the Navy or the Marines," she said, imitating Foster.

"But there are other things to think about. You know that," he said. He felt the old resentment, just its signal from a long way off, that he should always have to be the one to serve caution.

"Oh, I know," she said, and leaned back, sighing. She had washed her face, and now in the soft light she looked very young. A wave of love, like weakness, came over him, and he didn't move.

"Maybe after the war," he said. "Think about after all this is over, and we're older."

"It's never going to be over," she said bitterly. "Whatever it is. 'Victory.' That's all I ever hear. When's that going to be? Maybe you'll get killed. You!"

"I don't think I will," he said.

She grabbed his arm hard and held it against her side. "You'd be just the one to do something too brave. I know. Listen, I know all about you. I know everything you do. I've got my spies that tell me everything."

He laughed. "Who are your spies?"

"Never mind," she said. She wasn't smiling. "You know what I wish I had the power to do? I'd make you lose your mind. Jeannie—how can she have so much power?"

Suddenly he felt close to tears. It was pity for her, and disgust with whatever defect in him that had caused such a confession. He waited, hoping that this feeling would go away. Maybe, he thought, it was because that girl who came to him in his dream was really himself, only a creature of his imagination, that he could forget about responsibility and just go to it. She had no name, no past, no future to be jeopardized. But then a foreign little voice said, "Maybe you're afraid, Wood Whipple." What was that voice? Maybe he could not love Lois for her strangeness, her separateness, and if he became involved too closely he would no longer be free, and thus all his compulsive responsibility might be fraudulent.

"Lois?" he said. "Lois? We could lose our minds now . . ."

"I lost mine a long time ago," she said.

"But if we don't," he said, "you'll be grateful later on that we didn't. Who knows what's going to happen? You'll be so glad we didn't."

She pushed his arm away and turned toward him, her face in the soft shadow of her hair. Her eyes gleamed out of this shadow. "It's just the other way around," she said slowly and precisely. "It is just *opposite* to that."

"No," he said, knowing she was right. "Someday—"

" 'Someday my prince will come,' " she said, half singing the words, and laughed harshly. Then she put her hands over her face. "You're making me look so stupid! You'd better go home, or pretty soon I'll never be able to speak to you again."

She stood up, to show she really meant it. "And what did you tell Susie Davis last week when you went to her house? Did you tell her to be careful or something?" She went quickly to the hall closet and came back with his coat. "Sometimes you're so damned irritating," she said forgivingly.

He kissed her, and she leaned against him. "Why should I feel this way about a boy?" she said. "Somebody please tell me."

"You're so pretty," he said.

"So pretty you can hardly stand it."

"Now don't get like that again," he said, and tried to kiss

her, but she turned her face away. His lips touched her ear, and
it was cool and crisp. He ached down below; maybe the laughing,
abandoned girl with no name would come to him tonight and
relieve him of this care, this bottleneck. Lois kissed him and they
said good night. He walked out into the clear frozen air, zero,
windless. The snow cracked under his heels. Past several blocks
of the muffled houses, late lights in odd windows, he came to
High Street and climbed toward the huge house with its towers
and domes. As he approached he saw, high up in Kate's tower, a
yellow light that hollowed the little room. He stopped, wondering
if Kate had left the light on by mistake. But then a shadow grew
up the wall and disappeared. It must be cold up there, but Kate,
burning as she always was with some vivid project of her
imagination, probably wouldn't feel the cold at all. To be pretty—
too pretty—and not give the time to self-protection . . . what did
he fear for Kate? He was sad because they couldn't talk, and he
couldn't warn her of the bandits and thieves, the gross appetites
that would soon yawn for her.

8

When Kate came up the steep, narrow stairs—so steep they were
almost a ladder—the trap door was open and the old bridge lamp
was on. The electric heater was plugged in, and its copper eye
glowed warmly in the chilly room. She put down her pillow,
blanket and the basin and sat on the floor in front of the copper
light. It was almost eleven. Horace was asleep in his room with
the light on, and her mother and father had just gone to bed.
Wood wasn't home yet, and she considered his seeing the tower
light when he came up High Street, but then decided that it
didn't really matter if he did. He might at first think she had left

the light on by mistake, but if he came to the bottom of the stairs and heard any sort of noise, she was fairly sure he would go away and mind his own business.

The only furniture in the room besides the lamp was a doll-sized bureau she had once brought up, with David's help, from the old nursery. In the bottom drawer of this she had put the Mason jar of whiskey and two juice glasses. All right, she thought, here we go, three sheets to the wind! It was scary. What would this whiskey, this drug, do to her? Would she see with new sight? If she got terribly drunk, how would she get back down the stairs? She would have to sober off right here. With this thought, that she would be trapped by her addled brain on this high platform, she felt a twinge of vertigo, and put her palms flat on the varnished floor.

But David would be here to help her, if that became absolutely necessary. She heard him on the stairs, and soon his head appeared at the trap door. "Wood isn't home yet," he said.

"I don't think he'd butt in, though, do you?"

David hadn't climbed the rest of the way in, and now his head seemed to be sitting on the floor like a flowerpot. He looked quizzically at her. His blond hair, she thought, was cut like hers would be if she were a boy. If she had been a boy she would have been just like David, and if he had been a girl he would have been just like her. This was something she intended to suggest to him, even though she knew it might make him angry, because no boy wanted to be considered a girl in any way at all.

"I guess you're right," he said. He tossed the seat cushion from his easy chair up onto the floor and climbed in. "Your cigarettes, madame." He tossed the old pack of Chesterfields to her. "Your ashtray. Matches. I see you brought the emergency vomit basin." He shut the trap door and placed his cushion on it. He wore his old sheepskin jacket that had dried blood and grease all around the cuffs, and in that dirty, rough old thing his hands and face seemed almost too clean and bright.

"Wood wouldn't approve of this experiment, though," she said.

"Well, it's more or less in controlled circumstances. He might approve of that part."

"He's all right, though."

"Wood the Good," David said, smiling.

"I don't really know him very well, Davy. You know that?"

"Do you know anybody better?"

"You, Davy."

"Really?" he said. "You think so?" He didn't seem to be offended by this; he just sat there, wondering.

She lit one of the cigarettes and blew the smoke out of her mouth.

"Don't you inhale?" he said. "You know what F. P. Adams calls women who smoke but don't inhale? He calls them 'phoofs,' or something like that."

"I don't smoke in public," she said, which seemed to be the answer to that.

"I don't know anybody very well," he said, frowning. "Not that it bothers me too much. Hey, how about the experiment? You got your stolen booze up here?"

"I'm kind of scared," she admitted, but she reached over and got the Mason jar and juice glasses out of the dolls' bureau. Her hands were shaking. "I'm going to spill a little," she said as she pried open the wire clasp. "You want to pour?" He poured two glasses, spilling a little. Fumes filled the little room.

"Don't light a match," he said.

"Really?" She looked up at him, startled, and saw that he was kidding. "Don't do that, Davy. I'm nervous enough already." She showed him her cigarette. "I thought for a second we'd be blown to kingdom come."

"This'll just blow the back of your head off," he said. "Cheers!" He took a little sip, grimaced and shivered.

She put her mouth on the little glass, and it burned her lips. It smelled awful. "I wish it tasted better. I hate it," she said. It was sweetish, and as she tried to swallow, it seemed to eat her, to go right through the membranes of her throat and come out of her skin. "Agh!"

"It won't work until you've had at least a glass of it," David said. "Mark where the V basin is, just in case, and toss it down."

She did, and the chemicals boiled and burned inside her. Fumes even came out her nose. Finally she got a breath. "It's real, anyway," she said. "Now that's what I call *real*." She felt older, all of a sudden. A moment, or a year, or a whole age seemed

to go *click*, and she had passed a marker of some kind. "I can feel it already," she said. "Can you feel it, Davy?" She took her first long breath, and the air itself tasted sweetly chemical.

"Just the taste," he said.

"It's supposed to make you different, I know." She felt different, but she wasn't sure it was the alcohol. "Should I have some more yet?"

He poured her another glass. "I'll just nurse this first one along," he said, "in case you decide to throw yourself from the window."

"I don't think I will."

"Well, let me know if you decide to, so I can grab you by the foot or something." He laughed, took another sip and shivered again. "We ought to put the cover on the jar when we aren't pouring, so the alcohol won't evaporate." He did this.

Her cigarette tasted bad, so she put it out. When she moved her leg, the joint of her knee seemed to be full of molasses, and yet it was a lazy, pleasant feeling. Her elbows felt that way too. "I'm afraid I'm beginning to feel good," she said.

"Don't drink too fast or you'll get sick right away," David said. He sat across from her, perched on his cushion, looking at her interestedly.

"Oh me, oh my, oh me, oh my!" she said. "I can feel it, Davy. It's creeping all through my bones and up my nerves. Wow! The room looks different already."

"You know that alcohol is really a depressant?" he said.

"A what?"

"A depressant. It depresses you, I guess."

"It's not depressing me. I feel sort of good, except for the puky taste in my mouth."

"What I think it does," he said, "is depress your modesty or embarrassment or something like that, so you act freer. Something like that, anyway. Mr. Collins told us that in general science. He used another word for what it depresses, but I can't remember it."

"I wonder if it's depressing my modesty. I don't feel like doing a striptease, or anything," she said.

"Not in front of me, maybe, but—"

"Ridiculous!" She giggled, hearing the funny sounds come

from her own head. "I still don't know if I'm just thinking myself into feeling funny, though."

"That stuff you're drinking is the real McCoy, Katie. It's got to have some effect."

"'Old Post-Mortem,' Dad called it," she said. "What does that mean, Davy?"

"After death. In detective stories it means to examine the corpse after death, to see what it died of."

"That's a great name."

"Maybe they call it 'P.M.,' meaning afternoon, like you should start drinking it in the afternoon. I don't know."

"Dad doesn't start till around five."

"I think you're sobering off," David said, and poured some more of the whiskey into their juice glasses. Its very color, amber, seemed official and powerful. Adult. Not anything like the primary colors of childhood.

"I'm kind of filled up already," she said. The whiskey seemed to sit, steaming, right at the brim of her throat.

"Well, it ought to be working. You've had maybe four ounces."

She went to lean back against the wall, and bumped her head on the window sill. "Ow! That's dangerous. I didn't know the wall was that close. Now I am a little scared." She remembered that she had taken several sips without really thinking that it was whiskey, that ominous, experimental stuff. The brimming in her throat had gone down, and she was conscious of her spine, long and pearly, comfortable now in the warmth of her blood. Her whole lazy body was so friendly, so dependable and valuable. But then came a shiver, because she had bumped her head, hadn't she? Or had that really happened with enough importance to have really happened? She felt no pain; it seemed cancelable, theoretical, that she had bumped her head on the sill.

"I'm scared, Davy. But not really," she said. He looked at her calmly. "I'm in the grip of it. It's in my inside, holding onto me."

He nodded, and his bright face receded without moving, so that the room turned without turning into a huge hall, with a twenty-foot ceiling. Only David and the copper heater and she stayed the same size.

"Oh!" she said, and put her glass down carefully—her tiny glass.

"Do I look funny or something?" David asked. They were little children, sitting huddled and small in the great high room, with the frost creeping up the tall windows pane by pane.

"My tower," she said, looking up into its vastness. The rafters came together at the center of the peak, like the hub of a wheel big as the sky.

"Sally calls these things minarets," David said.

"No, they're not minarets. They're square," she said, impressed by her logic. "Do you ever go into yours, Davy?"

"Sometimes I shoot crows—shoot at crows, I mean—out the windows. I used to, I mean, when I could get CBs. Shorts make too much noise. And I can't even get shorts any more. You've got to go into the service to get ammunition these days."

"You?" Little David, who seemed her age.

"I'll be sixteen next week," he said. "In a year I could join the Navy. Maybe by then they'll be taking seventeen-year-olds in the Army, who knows?"

"Oh, a year." But as she said it, a year changed from forever to a very short time, no time at all.

"Wood, for instance," David said seriously. "He's just eighteen, and—"

"How can Wood go, Davy?"

"There's a war on," he said, and she saw him brace proudly, braggingly, to show her that he was a man. "Look at everybody we know who's gone into it. Peggy's father—"

"But he's grown-up."

"Gordon Ward, Eddie Kusacs—"

"Ugh. Gordon Ward. I hate him." The tower room had sneakily returned to its proper size. "Anyway, he's pretty old."

"Wood's age," David admitted.

"Did you ever know him very well, Davy?"

"Yeah, sort of. I think he kind of liked me, for some reason."

She reached down for her glass and spilled it onto the blanket, all of it. The whiskey ran lightly over the fuzz, as though it spurned the blanket, and then all at once it was sucked into the cloth.

"That's going to smell," David said. "What'll we do about that?"

"Oh, what the hell," she said. "If we're going to get drunk. I can leave this old blanket up here—Hank won't notice it's gone."

"You're feeling it, all right. Maybe you're getting too brave."

"I've always been pretty brave," she said. What the hell? It was true. David sat there pretending to be so calm, so neatly self-sufficient, and she wanted to use her bravery on him, to crack him open a little. Not to hurt him, but why should he sit there being so observant, and her like a little bug on a pin? A pug on a bin? Strange.

"Tell me a secret, Davy."

"What secret?" He smiled at her, a big-brother smile.

"Tell me about your secret love life. I know you've got a crush on Carol Oakes."

"Me?" He blushed a little. She saw that!

"What do you see in her, anyway? She's sort of rabbity. Sort of . . . mousery. All she has are those two big things in front." This shook him a little.

"This experiment's on you, not me," he said.

"I can tell by the way you danced with her. You didn't dare squeeze her. I could tell." She heard herself laughing, and listened carefully, interestedly.

"If you're going to laugh, laugh," David said.

"Fime gonna what?"

"Laugh."

"Don't change the subject. If you tell me exactly what you see in Carol Oakes, I'll tell you all about Wayne Facieux."

"Wayne Facieux?" he said incredulously, which she resented. "That meatball? That creep?"

"He's sensitive—"

"He's sort of a girl, if you ask me."

Now she saw that he really had a crush on Carol Oakes, who was dull and totally unworthy of him. Carol Oakes never said anything except to answer somebody else. She just washed herself carefully and brushed her hair and came to school to write the usual answers in nice round, soft, gooey handwriting. It was ridiculous. All she had was that fabulous set of jugs. But Wayne, with his pale thin arms, and bones sticking out behind his ears, and

113

the slight, distinguished stoop to his shoulders, and his gold-rimmed glasses—rimmed only around the tops. Among the other boys, he was delicate, like a prince. He used big words unashamedly, and wrote poetry for *The Quill.* "Garish," he said quite often. "That's really garish." About him a whole atmosphere moved, of culture and wit. He liked to talk to girls, and he had recommended her to be an editor of *The Quill* next year, when she would be in senior high.

"What do you see in him, anyway?" David asked. She blinked, and each time her eyes opened, his face had moved an inch to the left. It seemed a nasty trick on his part.

"All right!" she said, feeling anger. "I'll tell you! There's something sneaky about all you boys. You're bullies, and you're always trying to take advantage of a girl. You moon around, maybe, but once you get hold! Sneaky and smirky, and when you get a girl like Susie Davis the way you want her, you all . . . pile on . . . and then make your dirty jokes about her, and tell all about it as if you're great and she's just a piece of—"

"Hey! Whoa, Katie!"

"Whoa? What am I, some kind of a horse?"

"We already got a Horse."

"Oh, shut up!" Now, in her anger, the room grew intolerably small, and she was a big red creature, heated and cramped; her head pressed the ceiling and in a gulp she breathed all the air there was. "Oh!" she said.

"Don't get all upset, Katie," David said.

"Upset!"

"Yeah, huh?"

Then she was calmer, and David wasn't so bad. "Davy, I don't necessarily mean you, you know. But I suppose you're more or less the same as all of them." Oh, what the hell, she thought. "But all girls do is talk about boys. That's all we think about, do you know that? You don't have to settle for a little cuddlebunny like Carol Oakes, do you know that?"

"I'm not 'settling' for her, Katie. I hardly even talk to her. She's just—"

"A body."

"I guess so. Nice body," he said seriously. "To tell the truth,

it's her waist I like, for some reason, not the most obvious parts. She gets me."

She laughed, resenting this dissection of a girl. "What do boys talk about when they talk about girls? Things like that?"

"Yes. You wouldn't like it."

"Nobody's going to talk about me like that!"

"Well, you're pretty all over. You kind of stun them, if you want to know the truth."

"A freak."

"That doesn't please you, does it?" he said.

"It gets tiresome. I can't know anybody. Really." But she wondered how much it did displease her. She liked her body. She liked to look at herself in the mirror on her closet door. She had to admit that.

"What words do they use?" she said.

"Words?" he pretended to ask.

"You know what I mean. What words do they use for parts of girls? Come on, tell me."

"Well . . ." He blushed. "Tits. They talk about them quite a lot."

"What else?"

"The usual things."

"Look, Davy. If we can't be honest—"

"Well, you know them as well as I do," he said, beginning to get angry.

"What's for down there?" she said, and now he really blushed. Though she was nervous herself, she felt triumphant over him.

"There's a million words for that," he said. "But you probably know them as well as I do."

"No, maybe not. Girls don't talk the way boys do. They're different. They're ashamed."

"All right. *Cunt*," he said. "That's the usual one. Can we change the subject now?"

"My goodness. You're all embarrassed," she said.

"Well, you're a girl, after all. This whole conversation's unnatural." He took a sip of whiskey, and shook his head.

"We don't talk about boys' *parts* like that. You know that? We just say he's a real icky, he's handsome. Like that. He's sort

115

of all one piece. Like Wayne—he's not physical at all, really. Do you know what I mean, Davy? He doesn't have to be."

"He's not very physical. That I'll agree."

"A girl doesn't want some big, red, hairy boor of a muscle man like Gordon Ward, Davy."

"Well, some must."

"Maybe some, but not me." She thought of Gordon Ward, him leaning over her and breathing on her. He wouldn't let her go, and she began to suffocate. His big mouth latched onto her mouth and he forced her down against the greasy old seat cushions of his car. "Agh!"

"You sick?"

"I'm dizzy." With Wayne it was all blues and golds, fuzzy like a cloud, and the delicate tipping of his interesting face, and the way his long white hands expressed his thoughts about the meaning of style, how it shouldn't be garish. He meant something. Maybe he was kind of corny sometimes, but it went beyond all that too.

"I can't explain what I feel about Wayne, Davy."

"I can't explain what Carol has, either." Then David shook his head, as if to say "What the hell?" "I'll tell you a secret, though, if you'll keep your mouth shut."

She nodded.

"I mean it. Will you?"

"I promise, Davy."

"Because it's really juvenile, and I know it."

"Tell me."

"Well, sometimes I pretend my pillow is her. I hold it down next to me, around the middle. It's like it's full of electricity. And I've got a situation I think of—an imaginary situation. It's in a jungle, and she's . . . naked, lost, and I come swinging on a vine, like Tarzan. Only I'll tell you a little secret about that jungle. It's mine, and I had her taken there unconscious, and had all her clothes taken off just so I could come swinging in on that vine and land right beside her."

"What are you wearing?"

"Sort of a loincloth, something like that."

"Then what happens?"

116

"Well, she's scared, you know, but she just stands there, all naked, and I'm the boss. I can do anything I like with her."

"Do you?"

"Yes," he admitted.

"See? That's kind of cruel, isn't it?"

"But she likes it. It's such a strange situation she forgets all about not being supposed to, you see."

"You mean, you actually . . . ?"

"Well, it's only imaginary," he said. "Sometimes it's other girls."

"Which ones?"

"Other girls in my class. Some in other classes too."

"Who?"

"What difference does it make?" he said. "Just about all of them."

"Any girls in my class?"

"Maybe."

"Well, who?"

"Well, Gussie Contois, for instance."

"Gussie Contois! My goodness! How was she?"

"Oh, shut up!" he said, and began to laugh, leaning back against the wall. She laughed too, but a serious question remained.

"But haven't you ever been in love, Davy? I mean, wasn't there ever one girl that meant everything in the world to you, so you wouldn't go and think of seducing every girl in Leah High School?"

"That's funny. I used to, but not since . . ."

"Not since what?"

"Not since a couple of years ago." He seemed embarrassed, and yet prideful. "I became a man, more or less. I mean I got so I could be a father."

"Oh," she said. Now David seemed dangerously honest, and perhaps a little too composed. "That happened to me too," she said as a kind of counterattack.

"Really? You?" He was astonished.

"Girls begin earlier than boys."

"That's true," he said, and now she had him at a disadvantage. But he said, "We're growing up, Katie. We're getting to be

adults." The way he said this, with a kind of worldly resignation, evened things up again.

"I'm not drunk any more," she said, but then she leaned sideways and had to put a hand out quickly. "Oops!"

"Take it easy." He smiled at her.

"You hold yours pretty well," she said, and saw that this made him proud. He took a gentlemanly, or manly, sip.

"You haven't tried to throw yourself from the window, anyway," he said.

"You know, Davy, we can't really tell each other the truth, can we?" This was sad, all of a sudden.

"Cheer up," he said. "We're pretty honest."

"But if I can't be honest with you, who can I be honest with? We're brother and sister. You're a boy, yes, but you're my brother, so there isn't any of that business between us."

"No. It's been known to happen, though," he said.

"I can't see it. It just doesn't seem possible."

"Me, either," he said.

"We must be very normal," she said. "You know what I was going to tell you, Davy? I was going to say that if I'd been a boy I'd be just like you, and if you'd been a girl you'd be just like me. But I decided not to tell you because it might make you mad."

He thought for a while. "I'm not mad," he said. "I can't imagine what it would be like to be a girl. Anyway, I'm glad I'm not."

"I don't blame you one bit," she said. "It's just awfully *vague*, being a girl. You can't do anything but sort of wait around and gab and pretend, while the boys do everything."

"We do a lot of gabbing and pretending too," David said. "Waiting around. Waiting around." He yawned, and looked at his watch. "You know-ow," he said as his jaws sprung from the mammoth yawn, "this whiskey isn't driving either of us into hysterical fits of hilarity or anything."

"All it does is make me dizzy," she said. "We haven't actually drunk much of it." David's head still seemed to move sneakily sideways, now that she examined it closely again, and suddenly she realized that no effort of will could stop it. She was under another power, and with this knowledge she felt slightly sick. "Oh, God, I don't want to vomit," she said. "I hate to vomit." Vomiting

was like dying; that convulsive stretch had always frightened her. It seemed too final, as though her neck might split. But David's head kept moving and being in the same place, moving and being back, even in between the tiniest of little blinks.

"Stop your head," she said. He smiled, but at first it had seemed reasonable to her.

"Head is stopped," he said, as if answering an order.

"Oh, Davy! Everything's going haywire. Don't look!" She leaned over the basin, holding her hair out of the way with both hands, but nothing happened. "God, I'll fall in it, next," she said.

"Come on, Katie," David said, and touched her. "Let's get down the stairs. Moving around might help. I know it helped me. Come on."

"Okay," she said. A whisper of a belch fled past her teeth. "Ulg!" she heard from her throat, but it was nothing she had uttered.

"We'll go into the servants' quarters and walk up and down. Nobody'll hear us in there."

They made it down the stairs, David holding her by one arm-pit and more or less lowering her down, she thinking very deliberately which foot to put down next. Then she leaned against the cool woodwork while David went back to turn off the light and the copper heater. He came back lightly, quickly, and they slipped down the main upstairs hall and into the servants' quarters, where everything was a little smaller and plainer, where the old musty red carpets sometimes made her sneeze. David took her arm and walked her up and down the hall between Peggy's room and the hall door, back and forth until she stopped feeling like vomiting. Then she was very tired, and stopped to lean against the wallpaper, which felt grainy and warm against her forehead, like a book.

"Thanks, Davy," she said. "It was a great experiment."

"You all right now, Katie?"

"Yup, yup. You go on to bed. I'll be all right."

"In the morning you'll have the flapping hoo-hoos," he said, and turned to go. She turned her head and looked at him, one eye closed. He seemed to walk straight enough.

"Thanks for your secrets, Davy," she said.

"That's all right," he answered. "Good night."

"Good night, good night," she said, and he was gone. As the door closed at the end of the hall, her drunkenness changed again, and she wandered almost disembodied through the servants' quarters, through the ghosts of servants. There was Peggy's room, the bed made up neatly but nothing of Peggy's in the little room to show that she had ever slept there. A room poor Peggy didn't dare believe she could deserve.

Once she had been mean to Peggy—said something she couldn't even remember, that made Peggy cry and run home. Home? That awful wet shack up in the woods. That was where Peggy slept now, on that old cot with no sheets, among oil fumes and sour clothes smells, and the smell of feet, the smell of poor people. Maybe her mother wasn't even there, and Peggy slept alone in that grimy place. How could she stand it? Even here in this house Kate knew that a little eye of fear waited to wink at the back of her neck, because of the dark rooms yawning off the hallway. But why had she been mean to Peggy? She remembered only the tiny bite of pleasure it had given her. And then she felt terrible, and followed Peggy up through the woods, sneaked up and looked in the grayish window with the cracked pane and one pane filled with a flattened Campbell's Pork and Beans can. Peggy lay face down on her cot, and there was a little line of dirt on her leg in back of her knee—little dots and dashes of dirt where the skin folded when you knelt.

Now she felt so sorry for Peggy, who should have been in this neat room, she almost cried, then cut it off deliberately. If she were so damned sorry for Peggy she shouldn't stand around drunken and stupid, she ought to do something about it. But what?

"I am nice to Peggy," she said, and switched off the light. The sudden darkness, even though she had caused it herself, took on the authority of an event, an accident not accidental—a black answer to her voice. The eye of fear winked, and she ran silently down the hall and out of the servants' quarters. David had left one hall light on—the lamp on the marble-topped table. She went to her room, switched her lights on, came back to turn the hall lamp off, then ran softly back to her room.

Now her own room seemed strange, juvenile. The chintz frills on her dressing table, Jonquil the teddy bear, the carefully

arranged mirror system (closet door behind dressing-table mirror, hand mirror for profiles), the pink bows around the lamp bases, the baby-blue glass kitty cat with red collar and silver bell. It seemed years since she had enjoyed this room. Tomorrow she would go to another style. To hell with Veronica Lake.

She fell across her bed, partly as a dramatic gesture, but mostly from real weariness. Oh, God, she had to go to the bathroom, to enter the hall again in the witching hour; it was nearly three o'clock. She would have to. Click, she thought, click on the indifference to what is not clear, to what hides in puzzles and in the dark. Then it would be all right. It would be like David with dogs—he just held out his hand as if to say "Here, bite it if you want," and they never did. All right, move.

Later, when she lay in bed, her lights off, with no further reason not to enter sleep, she held sleep away. Or was she still under the power of another force? No, not really, but how could she be sure? Could she be sure in this darkness? She had been taken, under the influence of some powerful but harmless drug, by the impersonal hands of Punjab servants, eunuchs, Nubian slaves, to a dhow that sailed under warm foreign stars. They had prepared her, washed and anointed her naked body, and left her among the soft jungle ferns to wake. Would she be afraid to waken to the young god who came for her? Wayne? No. Wait a minute; this was David's jungle, now borrowed, because it couldn't be David. That would be a strange thing. That would be too weird, even in this warm trance, with the ferns like the fingers of hands smoothing her down. And yet David was a man now and could presumably make those brutish grinning motions she had seen dogs make, and do that on a girl. No, it would not be her who waited, afraid, grateful, a sacrifice to her brother. It would be Carol Oakes, with her rich auburn hair and full white breasts. She would wake before him. And now he lets fall his loincloth, and takes her all bare against him. He is *inside* her now, inside that soft white girl, his blood and skin deep in the dark middle of her. Then the business of the grinning dogs.

It all seemed so unsafe, so precarious. Not as though all of them—Wood, Horace, Hank, Whip, David, Peggy—were deliberately irresponsible. It was a force, and they couldn't stop it no matter how hard they tried. It was like a drug increasing tick by

tick as they left the time of her childhood, the happy Christmases before her father's accident, before the war that would now take Wood away, and maybe even David, and had taken Peggy's father. Tomorrow she would wake up hours more dangerous, more primed, and just as unready to lose her safety.

When Wood had gone, and David had gone, who would care for Horace, and who would talk to her? They had all kept a precarious balance among themselves. The Whipples. Her mother had to take care of her father. For years she had had no deeper energy than that. To take even one of them away would be like amputating a leg or an arm. The house would grow like a monster, too big, too hollow and cold. How much she had depended upon Wood's honor and duty, even when she joined David in smiling at him! Now she knew how much. She herself had somehow lost her neatness and her independence when her periods began, and now that messy schedule tied her to all women and told her of her common fate.

To sleep. Could she sleep with nothing but this small fear for her reward? Nothing moved now; her mind was clear once more, yet still she was in thrall. Deep in the register the coal fire shifted with a clink and a sigh of ashes, and the great hollow house slept into the dawn.

9

One morning that week Horace awoke feverish; all night he had hidden beneath the covers, and now he lay in a cold trough of his own sweat. They could get to him easily enough through the blankets and sheets, and he knew it was totally irrational to think that the bedclothes protected him in any way. But it was also irrational to think such monsters existed in their flesh and scales

in the first place. Irrational or not, they did exist; he could tell by the fluttering of his heart and the ice in the hollow of his back. It had only been recently that they had begun to have names, and to speak to him rather than to each other about him. The banana-fingered woman was Leverah. Though he never heard her voice as an actual sound, he knew when she spoke, and understood. Their cold voices echoed without sounding first. "Look! Look!" Leverah had commanded in the night. But he could still disobey.

Now it was daylight. A gray winter day. Tiny cracks of light crept down the interstices of his covers to his eyes. A dreary day that would come with its hesitant light to the walls of the house and stop, leaving off at the windows so the house still ruled its inner places. A cold day with the sky one chilly gray cloud. It was a particular day, he remembered now—it was the day his mother would take him on the bus to Northlee and have his eyes examined for glasses so he would be able to see all the tiny distant things again, and read the writing on the blackboard without having to sit in the front row in sight of everyone—even then squinting and pondering the chalky fragments of words upon the board.

Strange how he could see Leverah so clearly, even to the whiskers of her mustache, all down the length of his room—this without looking at her. It was another proof he didn't need that she was of his mind. Or rather a proof he couldn't use. The geometry of his fear was beyond his power to solve, but there must be a system to it, a way to make syllogisms out of it. Once in plain geometry Mr. Collins said they were using a system based upon logic rather than measurement. He would need an even more complicated system, and there must be one somewhere, either invented or waiting for invention, to solve Leverah and the others—the scaled ones, the hairless ones. There must be a solution, because he had never been told that he must die, and if he couldn't solve it he would not be able to go on living. Some night he would die of fear; their coldness and cruelty would enter his body like frost, and he would die.

He was not afraid so much of real bullies, though they did sometimes come after him, or waylay him—Keith Joubert, Junior Stevens and that bunch. With them he feared more what they

might make him do to them. He couldn't trust his strength because he broke even what he didn't want to break, and hurt those he loved. He saw Mabel Andrews' tooth lying in the water fountain, her very tooth, forever broken from her, a jewel not ever again to be part of her prettiness, and her howling, gapped face turned toward him, a reflection of his brutishness.

When they heard him think this, they smiled and moved stiff as puppets from his darkest closet. Now they dared him even in daylight. If only he had the warning system he had planned in such desperate detail. He would have a little contact switch on the end of a cord connected to a dry cell beneath his bed. Lamp cord would lead from it, beneath his door, beneath the hall carpet down to Wood's room. When they had him immobilized he would ring for Wood to come and banish them. He never dared suggest this to Wood, because in Wood's presence he was out of danger, and therefore somewhat ashamed of his fear. His whole life, his whole metabolism changed when Wood was there; his brain worked differently, his heart beat slower, and each breath seemed to take more oxygen from the air. Then, too, *they* had implied that they were his secret alone, that there was some certain danger not only to him but to his family if his knowledge of them were to be shared.

But there had to be some kind of accommodation with them. There had to be. And it was his responsibility to bring this about. Perhaps if he had an animal to keep him company . . . Or would they then kill it nightly, as they flayed and burned the little puppy? Each time he could not believe their cruelty; knowing in advance what they were going to do to the little dog, he could not believe it, and when they slyly took the friendly, wagging little animal by the loose skin of his back, made a quick slit and ripped down, the pain was bright and fresh each time. Suddenly to have no skin. No skin!

David skinned his squirrels on a board with a big nail in it. He impaled a squirrel's head on the nail, cut a slit around the back of the neck and pulled the gray lofted fur, the blue slick skin rolling inside out in the shape of a tube, right off the dark red muscle. He watched David do this with great wonder; it was so foreign to anything he expected of a person, a human, a brother. David might as well have been an armadillo, or an

aardvark. But then, why did he expect everyone to be unforeign to him? He was the strange one, battered by and battering all their arrangements, from tables and chairs to flesh and bones. Before the tomcat, Tom, had died or strayed or whatever had happened to him last spring—before he had disappeared, Horace had seen him be cruel beyond belief to chipmunks. David said that it was totally natural, and it would do no good at all to chase Tom, who ran away perplexed that Horace should object to his preparing and eating his food. The chipmunk in the cat's jaws didn't struggle, but his black eyes blazed with life. He knew he was in a mouth. When the cat let him go he braced, and arched his skimpy little tail, and defied the cat, who licked his pink chops fiercely and approved. If the chipmunk turned to run, a claw flicked into his side and pulled him back into the sharp teeth again. And again. And finally, after an eternity of hope and despair and little punctures, ate on him. If it was a mouse he'd caught, he ate him head first, crunch crunch, tail and all. Then found the sun and slept a natural sleep.

David was natural, of course. And Kate was natural, and Wood, and his father and mother. They were all natural. Even poor Peggy was natural. They all slid safely past the hard elbows and horrors of the world, slept deep and woke rested and dry. Even though his father's leg hurt, he could lie down without terror. Where he was was his property, and he ruled. His father owned oceans of cool air that he could breathe freely out of the dark.

He shivered in the cold oil of his sweat, and his thin bedclothes crept against his skin. Perhaps someone alive would come to wake him.

"We will wake you," sang their thin, gleeful voices. "We will wake you, Hoar-ass." How they laughed; they made sure to use their immeasurable power. Now they moved, still pretending to be puppets, back into the dark closet. One was Zoster, who always watched to see if Horace forgot and left a foot or a hand or an ear uncovered, then crept up with an expression of high glee on his metal-colored, shiny face, and put his great hollow mouth over whatever part Horace had left exposed. The triangular teeth, like sawteeth, came down just so as not to touch the skin, and Horace could not then snatch his flesh out of that mouth. If it

had him over his ear, he heard the click of swallowing and the damp creamy hiss of saliva. Around Zoster was always an aura, the cold earth of a cellar.

"Hoar-ass, Hoar-ass," they called. Some were little. The Herpes were nasty and tiny, nasty even to each other. They were the conductors and spectators of his nightmares. They brought him to that point in space, somewhere near the center of orbits, where the smooth roads ran radially from the point of responsibility, where the round tires ran down toward disaster. That dream was in color, and the roads were of smooth green and purple and red rubbery stuff, with fine black wires supporting them. The tires were pure white. And the disaster he was always about to cause would destroy the universe. The universe, all of it. "All because of Horace Sleeper Whipple, Horace Sleeper Whipple," the Herpes chirped at him, like a flock of evil sparrows. "It's all your fault, it's all your fault, your responsibility, your responsibility!" They cried this over and over, as if he didn't know it!

The Town Hall bell rang, and he tried to count, but the bells followed one another raggedly, fading or coming on a vagary of the atmosphere harsh and clear. He counted eight or nine clangs, or maybe only seven. He could risk leaving his damp bed for a different discomfort among the people downstairs, where he would become entangled again in all their complications and judgments. A world full of elbows and eyes. But Wood would be down there, maybe, if he hadn't already left for work. No, of course he would have left for work long ago, and Kate and David would be ready to go to school. A shiver of surprise and fear, and then he remembered that he hadn't been awakened because he was not going to school today, but to the eye clinic in Northlee. So his mother had let him sleep longer among his monsters.

Carefully he pulled his head around and uncovered his face to the chilly white air. His brown cold room, lighted down its length by the winter day, was empty, sinister and baldly innocent.

Henrietta stood in front of the woodstove, the black iron baking of its inner heat. She tipped a lid and looked into the firebox— fluffy gray ash like feathers around the embering center—and added two thin split sticks of maple. Harvey, who was, if any-

thing, merely irritated by the war, would defend this stove's economy for patriotic reasons. She really didn't mind too much, but did her part for the war effort with a strange sense of nostalgia. Most of the official directives on how to save and serve were no different from those she had learned as a child in Switches Corners. She saved grease and made lye soap, aged all store-bought toilet soap out of its wrappers to harden it so it would last longer, saved all trimmings of meat for stocks and gravies. Extra fat she saved in tin cans and sold to the butcher at the cash market. This fat was supposedly necessary for explosives, or maybe for greasing gun barrels, or something of that sort. In any case, she had never in her life thrown out perfectly good fat; most of these patriotic gestures were automatic.

Harvey would have periods when he demanded petty little savings in things, but not from interest in the war effort. One week he would watch the light bulbs, and everyone who left a light on, even to cross the room, would be told to come back and turn it off. Then something else would be the most important. Wood wasn't being economical with coal; he was using the fire door as an extra draft, or he wasn't running a big enough fire bed, or he wasn't keeping the ash pit clean enough. Or they were having meat too often. And then, for a week at a time, Harvey ignored economies, and demanded heat and light.

Burning coal instead of oil did save money, but she wondered how they were going to manage next winter, when Wood and David (if she could arrange David's living somewhere in Cascom, near Dexter-Benham) would both be gone. Horace could not be depended upon to take care of a coal fire. For one thing, he was afraid of the basement. She would do it, she supposed, but she sensed a hard little force of rebellion in her mind against such grimy duty. She might very well refuse; in fact, she predicted that she would refuse, and Harvey Whipple would have to think of some alternative. Period.

Harvey's alternative would be that David stay in Leah High School and take care of the furnace, but that was out. She was not a pushing, promoting, sacrificing mother, far from it, but David was loafing in Leah High School. He was bored, impatient, and tended more and more to leave the world and go into his private little hobbies and fantasies. Dexter-Benham seemed to be the

solution, so she would find the way. If he lived in Cascom, the day-student fee would not be too much, and Harvey would simply have to put up with it.

In the meantime she stood at the stove, saving vital war materials—in this case little bits of hand soap she had collected in a cup. Now she was melting these little chips down in a quart of water to make soap jelly for shampoo and for washing rayons and underthings. That would save Harvey Whipple twenty or thirty cents, anyway, and he could add that amount to the financial empire he was planning.

They had enlarged the old kitchen garden into a Victory Garden, and that summer and fall she and Peggy and Kate, with some help from David and Horace, had canned twenty-one quarts of green beans, twelve quarts of wax beans, thirteen quarts of Swiss chard, thirty-five quarts of tomatoes, twelve quarts of sour pickles, eight quarts of cucumber pickles, eight quarts of mustard relish, thirteen quarts of beets—ten sweet and three Harvard-style—fourteen quarts of carrots, five quarts of dandelion greens, ten quarts of raspberries and twenty-odd glasses of raspberry jelly, twenty-five quarts of apples and twenty-eight quarts of corn. And in cool storage in the cellar were cabbages, turnips and potatoes. Last March she had tapped all the maple trees around the house and grounds and boiled down five gallons of syrup. There were the figures, tacked to the bulletin board above the shelves for sugar and coffee ration coupons, bills and household notebooks. Harvey let her do all the household figuring, and he certainly had nothing to complain about. He knew she saved him a lot of money, and when his thrift tantrums came she always had in reserve a stern look that would calm him down considerably.

She stirred the soap emulsion with a long, enameled spoon, and when all the pieces had melted she set the pan on the sideboard to cool. Horace ought to be up by now. He hated to go to bed and he hated to get up. No one could understand him. He wasn't stupid; even Mr. Skelton said he wasn't stupid. And he wasn't unfeeling—he worshiped Wood. He was going to take Wood's leaving very hard, and she had explained this to David and Kate before they'd left for school. Both had looked away, perplexed, possibly a little ashamed of their indifference. But what could they do about it?

"We love Horace," Kate said. "He's our brother, after all. Don't we, Davy?" And David, pursing his lips judiciously, nodded.

"Oh, that's easy to say!" she said angrily, and when Kate's face fell she was sorry she'd said it. God knew, a girl Kate's age had enough problems without having to be responsible for a crazy brother. Crazy? She squeezed the dishtowel in her hands. Was he mental? Of course she'd thought about that, even though any child's eccentricities came on slowly over the years and tended to seem natural for him, and thus natural to his mother. But suddenly she really wondered if he were *certifiable* in any way. Stealing that money, not to have it but to punish those he stole it from, and throwing it away! And from men, really, not boys any longer. Gordon Ward was now a man, in the Army, and that was getting dangerous. The police had to speak to Wood about Horace, and thank God, Chief Tuttle was the DeMolay adviser and knew Wood so well. Sooner or later Horace would be too old to be protected as a child, and there wouldn't be anyone around to protect him.

She was afraid for him. This great house, in which they all lived like mice, not in its style, or with the money to impress its dark paneling and excessive spaces; it was no home to Horace. He was afraid of it. None of them really dominated its life, which seemed ancient, rich, made for De Oestrises. Of course Harvey's family was related, but his had been the poorer branch of the family, and they had all migrated to the cities to work for other people. All except Harvey. The Whipples and De Oestrises on that side had all moved away, and seldom came to Leah. And the only rich De Oestris left was Sally. Harvey's two brothers were in Boston and New York, and his sister lived in Pasadena, a continent away. But he had to live in this haunted castle and scheme like a miser while she worried about the plumbing freezing up, and saved scraps of hand soap, and Horace shivered with fear of the long hallways and the high ceilings occasionally hung with bats.

Before the accident Harvey used to amuse himself with the bats. He'd stand on a table, and as they swooped by he'd swat them out of the air with a rolled newspaper. Their mouse bodies would hit the wall and drop like little black cloths to the floor. They had weird, nasty little faces. God, you'd look at their

evil little faces and think about them for days. David used to shoot them off the moldings with his BB gun, and at least there weren't too many left.

There were mice too, of a lineage older than theirs, no doubt. Old Tom had kept them in check pretty well—at least he made them somewhat more cautious, so they hadn't crossed the corner of your eye like dim motes as they fled from one corner to another. They would have to get another cat. She would feed the first stray that came along, hoping for a good mouser.

She had been putting away the silverware, and now hung the dishtowel on its bar. The soap was cooling, but it wasn't cool enough for a glass jar yet.

Horace stood in the dining-room doorway. She tried to look at him slowly, unstartled. He had put on the clothes she had asked him to wear—a white shirt and his dark green gabardine pants—so she wouldn't have to chide him about that and send him back to his room to change. His head drooped, and he looked very tired, stooped in the shoulders.

"Are you hungry?" she asked.

"Sort of," he said.

"Didn't you sleep well?" When she put her hand on his forehead he submitted stolidly, his eyes downcast. His head was hard, wooden beneath her hand.

"I guess so," he said.

She knew better than to ask him what was the matter; he would say he didn't know. Once, just before Harvey's automobile accident—it must have been just about that time—Horace had tried to explain a nightmare. He must have been nine or ten, and he came screaming into their bedroom, which was then upstairs, next to his. He wanted to sleep with them, but they had both refused this. He cried and screamed and carried on about "the wires," and Harvey finally had to pry his fingers loose from the headboard of their bed. They had to insist that Horace was too big to sleep with them, and Harvey carried him back to his own bed. They let him keep his door open, and agreed to leave theirs open, but this wasn't enough. He came back, this time stealthily, and crept in beside his father. Then they really had to insist. Harvey gave him a sharp spank on his bottom. "Dammit!" Harvey said. "You've got to sleep in your own bed!"

"The wires!" Horace said. "They come down the wires!"

"What comes down the wires?"

"They do! And then they watch when the tires roll down. But the wires! The wires! They don't go anyplace! It's me, mine! I want to sleep in here with you!" He cried and whimpered, but they simply could not approve.

"I'll make you more scared of me than you are of the wires!" Harvey finally said, and spanked him hard until he was sullen in his fear, and submitted. In the morning his bed was wet, but it wasn't urine. He'd curled up into a ball under the covers, and the dampness was his sweat. She'd felt terrible, but punished him with her disapproval. He was simply too old to sleep with them. She explained to him that children don't sleep with their parents, thinking all the time how unfair it must seem to a child that his parents could sleep together, warm and safe all night, every night, while a child had to sleep all alone in an empty bed in an empty room. He had never asked to sleep with them again.

"Do you want hot cereal or eggs?" she asked. "How about some nice scrambled eggs?"

He grimaced. He had once said that eggs were dead chickens. Sometimes he would eat the white, but never the yolk.

"Wheaties," he said.

"That's all you ever have, Horace. Why don't you try something else for a change?"

He shrugged and looked down, sullenly. But he was not a sullen boy; she knew he didn't want to be. When he cared too much he burst out with it, and his words were exactly his thoughts. He was the strongest-looking of her children, the most . . . what? Peasant-looking. The crudest-looking, anyway, of all her children, and it was strange that he should have to be the one who suffered most from things inside his head. She would have thought Kate or David more likely to suffer this way, but they didn't seem to—at least not so that their troubles became known.

As Horace ate his Wheaties at the kitchen table, she watched him surreptitiously, seeing him eat with no real appetite. He was tired. A tremendous weight of tiredness seemed to press his arms to the table, and he lowered his head to his spoon. Something pressed down upon his broad shoulders, making the

strong body of her son listless and weak. She feared other things for him—the inevitable question of something physical—some tumor, or growth, or horrible thing in the brain. This thought was small, kept small, but it was the reason for going to the clinic today rather than to a mere optometrist in Leah. They were going to look very closely at more than his eyes.

Last June, when he'd broken the bone in his arm, Dr. Winston had looked him over carefully and made him do certain little test things with one eye closed and then the other, then both closed, and then both open, and tapped him here and there with a little rubber hammer. He told her he doubted very much if Horace had anything of that sort wrong with him at all.

"He's such a big, strapping boy," Dr. Winston said. "His restraint hasn't caught up with his momentum." That was Dr. Winston, though. Old Dr. Burnham could have told him that Horace had always had the same problems, even when he was a very little boy. She thought of the word "congenital." There had been something peculiar about Horace at birth, and she had almost forgotten about it, then remembered it years later when his odd behavior became too remarkable to ignore. When she got home from the hospital with him, and had a chance to look him over carefully, she found a little raw scar on his coccyx, at the base of his spine. When she asked old Dr. Burnham what it was, he tried to put her off. He was a gruff, even impolite old man who hated like sin to lie. Finally he told her that Horace had been born with a tail about two inches long. "Not prehensile," he said. "It's more common than you'd think—especially in this town!" And he laughed at her concern. "No, Henrietta, it's fairly common. A slight case of atavism—look that up and it'll just worry you. Never mind. Anyway, the doctor just snips it off and forgets it."

But even as a baby he was coarse of feature, and had thick, strong wrists. He weighed twelve pounds at birth. "There's a regular ploughboy for you," old Dr. Burnham said. "You done yourself proud this time, Henrietta!"

Horace finished his Wheaties and drank his orange juice. He jarred the table as he rose, and reached down quickly, with an apprehensive look, to steady it with his big hand. She wondered

if he thought it might continue to tip, to roll as if in slow motion across the kitchen and crash into smithereens against the pot and pan cupboards. He held it down for a moment, his head bent.

"We'll take the ten o'clock bus," she said. "We've got an hour before we have to leave."

Horace nodded, and went up the back stairs. She knew he chose the back stairs in order to avoid his father, who would now be up, sitting in his wheelchair, waiting for his morning coffee. It was true they had no words for each other.

The new coffee was ready, so she poured two mugs and put them on a tray with sugar and milk, spoons and napkins.

Harvey sat at his oak table before his ledgers and stock-market pages, tapping out numbers on his adding machine. His dark eyes gleamed above his soft white cheeks, and just for a moment she saw in his intensity the slim man who used to be his outward self.

"Ah," he said, peering at the coffee. She went to get a dining-room chair, and looked through the bars of its tall back as she carried it into the living room. As she sat down across from him, the heat from his floor register, dry heat with just a hint of coal fumes in it, fluttered her skirt around her legs.

He sipped his coffee in a way he would once have detested—greedily, his red lips smacking over its heat. Suddenly she was irritated by his incarceration in that wounded body. She thought of the farm, where such freakishness was not tolerated in animals, and of her father in his gray dressings and obvious stumps. She was irritated by such accidents, by the way Harvey's seemed to have hurt his children, and she wanted to ask him sarcastically if he was rich yet.

He tapped away on the keys, and pulled the handle down to total his figures—a gesture too expert and common, like a worker in a factory doing some mechanical operation he hardly understood but was an expert at in a flashy, moronic way. If it had been her with that leg she would have had it amputated and said to hell with it. To carry such an incubus of pain around seemed needless, even willful. She didn't care that much for parts that had gone wrong. Cut them off! Get rid of them! But she had read about a religion in which even the parings of fingernails

were saved because they were part of one, and therefore sacred to the body's unity. Yes, to lose a leg, a major part of one's living body, a leg with all its complicated muscles and veins and nerves running all down its length in miraculous ways—even the little patterns of hair, and the jointed bones, and the foot that had been so swift and sure in all its levers. No, she could see how he clung to the parts of himself. But still, she would not. She made bargains and compromises quickly, stuck to them and never welshed.

And she wouldn't welsh now, though the memory of him as a man was powerful. There had been too long a time when he was a man, and she would not abandon him in any way now. Heat flowed from his register along her thighs, even up around the table's edge to warm her elbows and arms.

With another expert motion his white hand pulled down the lever. He peered at the result, tore off the paper tape and inserted it in a manila folder.

"Humph!" he said, reaching for his coffee.

"Are we getting rich?" she asked.

He was wary, but took it mildly.

"What else is there to do?" he said. "It's going to cost money to send these kids to college. You'll find all this isn't just a game."

"David's going to Dexter-Benham," she said firmly.

"Leah High School's not that bad," he said.

"Leah High School is full of temporary teachers. A bunch of flibbertigibbets. There's very little there for David."

"Maybe I'd like some toast," he said.

"All right. I'll make you some toast. You ought to have a glass of orange juice too."

"Okay, Ma," he said, but he knew she meant it about David; she was certain of that.

10

David sat in study hall, in his homeroom. The dry dusty air was too warm, and chalk smell and girls' perfume, or powder, or whatever it was that surrounded them, smoothed away his resolve to finish a tense chart in French. The tenses of the verb *avoir* had to be looked up and then written down in the manner specified by old Mrs. Watson. He would have to do it, but he would do it with the sinking, lethargic feeling that not one of the words was being remembered by his brain. In and out; it was as if the information went no farther than the second knuckle of the index finger that pressed against his pen.

The pen was new, and still interesting. The cap was brass, and it was a thick, hefty pen with a new way to suck up the ink. Sally De Oestris had given it to him for his birthday. Inside was the same sort of rubber tube, but instead of the little cliplike lever on the side, you pulled out a cylinder, then pushed it in to create air pressure around the rubber tube, which collapsed. As the pressure leaked out through a little porthole, the tube grew round again and sucked up the ink. This process was much more interesting than French verbs he didn't even know how to pronounce. All they did in class was read and read and read *Les Misérables,* and translate it into English. They never pronounced a word of French.

The plunger of his pen came out slowly, as though it had great mass and momentum. Delayed by the physics of the atmosphere, it seemed to move with the calm dignity of natural law. The ink obediently moved in or out of the rubber bladder in the barrel, and the brass cap was as substantial as a part of a gun. He didn't want to use this pen on the French conjugation chart, and

when he made himself begin he found himself writing his name over and over in a bold hand. David Abbott Whipple. David Abbott Whipple. He wasn't very satisfied with the Whipple; better to have been named just David Abbott. That was a name with a dark New England sort of ring to it. It was his grandmother's maiden name—his mother's mother's name, but the best thing about it was that he didn't know another person in Leah named Abbott.

At the desk in front of him Mary Denney bent over her spiral notebook, her light brown hair frizzled over her white collar, her shoulders hunched studiously. She was a plain little girl, not ugly, just sort of standard. He'd never noticed her much until one time she sent him a note saying she loved him. That had been a funny feeling. He didn't know how to answer, and it had more or less passed off into silence. Now, as though she knew he was looking at her, she turned and gave him a quick glance. It was a small shock, and the sweet danger of her face remained in his eyes like a flash of light. Her light skin, her upper lip that protruded perhaps a little too much, her brown eyes looking clearly into him just for that tiny moment—these stayed with him as she turned. He seemed to be feeling her back through the cloth of her dress— her lean little sides, hard with ribs, and her shoulder blades, clavicles, the round muscles of her arms, the soft places where her little breasts were rooted. Even Mary Denney had those impossibly pink little nipples there beneath the fragile cloth, sacred to see, like Kate's he had seen once by accident in the bathroom. Though she was only Mary Denney, who was not too bright, who never talked very much at all, she was complete and terrible, like fainting, like an explosion.

But not like Carol Oakes, who sat two desks away, diagonally so he could see the rich curve and weight of her breast where it rested inside her fuzzy sweater, and the taut lean of her waist.

Think of something else, not of her thighs and the narrow waist leaning away above them, the miraculous strange swell of her hips around her dark secret entrance. Ten minutes till the bell would make him have to stand up and go to English class, and he'd better think of something else right away.

There was Ben Caswell, with his skinny blue-white face and thin, metal-colored hair, the brightest boy in school, his best

friend and worst enemy, doing his work perfectly as always. John Cotter sat dark and silent, motionlessly reading, and ahead of him was Michael Spinelli, who always got caught no matter what he did, who had been kicked out of school as recently as last week, who was at this moment bored into a coma. His long legs protruded slackly under Kenny Clark's seat, and he stared blindly at the region of the door.

In the front row, where he had been placed for disciplinary reasons, big Junior Stevens, bully, stupe, occasional tormentor of Horace, sat growing bristles on the back of his red neck. He, like Mike Spinelli, never read, never did homework, never did anything in school that had to do with learning anything. Separated from Junior by the two necessary aisles was his lieutenant, Keith Joubert, whom David had once wrestled to the ground and anointed with half-frozen mud. That had been sheer necessity. When Keith and Junior got together they seemed to feel the need of a victim. Alone, they were polite enough. Their most famous mistake was the time they chose Ben Caswell, their theory being that the smartest and skinniest boy in school would be a push-over. Ben was rather frightening, as David could have told them from experience. Anyway, it was beautiful to watch Ben transform himself immediately into a pure murderous madman and butt Junior in the chin with his head. Junior bit his tongue, bled all over, vomited from trying to swallow his own blood, and couldn't talk plainly for a week. Thereafter they let Ben Caswell alone.

The bell. At the end of this long day, Christmas vacation would start. Now he could stand up without embarrassment, gather his English book and notebook and go toward another kind of boredom.

Horace had not expected to be afraid of the examination. He was absolutely certain that the doctors would be trying to help him, that they would not hate him at all, in any way. And so he was surprised and frightened by the shock he felt as he followed his mother into the small waiting room. He began to tremble. His palms sweat so badly he had to keep wiping them on his shirt. Cold drops of sweat crawled down his sides, and he couldn't do anything about it.

A nurse who didn't quite look like a nurse—she looked more like a secretary who wore white—asked them to sit down, and they sat side by side on a cold, slippery couch with chrome legs and arms. Next to Horace a fragile floor lamp of turned wood, and a glass-topped table, stood ready to break. He kept his elbows rigidly to his sides, but tremors still came shaking down his arms and into his wrists. At the dentist's or at the doctor's he had never been this incontrollably nervous, even when he had been in pain. Pain he knew; he had grown up with it. But now they would be near his brain, at his eyes themselves. His mother had told him that it never hurt at all when she got her glasses, but she had been slightly evasive about that. Her eyes had moved away from his as she spoke.

Perhaps she didn't really believe him about what he had been able to see all of a sudden through the little gold-rimmed glasses. He had so many secrets anyway, maybe he didn't deserve to be believed. He couldn't tell anyone about Leverah and Zoster, or about any of the events of his nights, and yet he thought of them more and more during the daylight. Once they had been like dreams, forgotten soon after breakfast, but more and more the events of his days receded into thoughts and preparations for what would happen in the night. Now he dreaded any lessening of his concentration upon that ordeal. The examination might upset his balance, somehow, so that they would know where he'd been and what he'd done; they might so skillfully use his eyes against him.

"Horace?" his mother said. The air reeked of an odor like hollowness, as though part of the air were gone, one of its chemical components breathed out of it. Neon, hydrogen, oxygen . . .

"Horace?" She took his arm in her gloved hands. "You're rigid," she said. "You shouldn't be this nervous."

"I can't stop being nervous," he said.

"It's just an examination."

"I know it," he said. But he also knew that Leverah and Zoster were not real, and what good did that do? Reality was the shaking of his nerves, the stuttery little spasms in his arms. He would have to live through that first—except that he didn't ever see another side to it. There never seemed to be another

shore. Wood's room was like an island inhabited by friends, but there was no far happy shore.

The nurse, or the woman in white—she wore white shoes and stockings too, but had a corsage of little blue flowers as big as blueberries pinned to her blouse—came out of the door to the inner place and asked them to come in, smiling too briefly. Horace went first. He felt all wet, and had to sit in his own damp in a chair as machinelike as a dentist's chair. The doctor, who was young and wore pinkish-rimmed glasses, sternly took his head and shoved it back against leather rests, just at the angle Horace knew would soon cause a pain in his neck. Immediately a muscle fought itself below his ear, and the pain began. When he tried to move, the doctor's hands tightened, and his face grew stern. His eyes seemed to be looking through Horace's head to the rests. The black holes where his whiskers grew turned in the hundreds oval, then round again.

"There," the doctor said. But when he took his hands away, Horace's head moved with them. "Well," the doctor said.

"Sit up straight, Horace," his mother said anxiously.

"My neck hurts," he said, feeling that he had no right to say it. For the moment his neck muscle did relax, and the feeling was sweet because he knew how short a time he had bought.

The doctor pushed his head back against the rests. "Now, is that better?"

The muscle coiled again, and he looked to his mother. "I don't know *why* it hurts!"

"Well, we've got to find some sort of steady position," the doctor said, "so we can get on with the examination."

The doctor moved the rests forward. Horace hoped as hard as he could that the muscle would stop fighting, and this embarrassment would end. The doctor seemed by his impatience to think it was his fault, but he couldn't tell the doctor that he was all different parts—made of all different parts that did as they wanted, not as he wanted. Deep in the flesh and bone of his head, he had his own self with its reasonable desires, who desired to please and to make his mother calm. And for the moment, at least, nothing fought him openly. The doctor's face faded from Horace's left eye, and in his right all grew down into a tiny orange light. He looked out of his brain into the dark cave of his eyeball,

through that tunnel into the little orange light that flickered like a weak flashlight in a basement, peering around in that cobwebby cave as though the doctor, grown small as a little boy, were lost and apprehensive in there.

Then the light withdrew into daylight, and appeared, wavery and dim, at the tunnel of his other eye. After it had examined this entrance to his head, its flickering withdrew and the room came back clearly, though it had never quite gone out of sight. Its shapes and colors had hovered transparently before him all the time. One shape was now the doctor, who pivoted on his stool and moved a black machine around in front. Horace had noticed this complexity of black metal because it was attached to the chair, ready to work on whoever sat in the chair. As it came toward him he saw that it had a face of its own, black as an ape's, with staring, yet curiously impersonal frosted eyes. The doctor, or it— some confident smooth force—moved the black face toward his own, too close for any face to be until it actually pressed against his own, and pressed as it disappeared and became two frosted eyes against his eyes, his head against the rests in back so that he was its absolute prisoner.

He stared out through those other eyes, not his, and his flesh blended into its coldness—metal, but curved like a face inside out, not ungentle in its curves, but strong. Then he was it, and saw what it saw.

At first it was like looking down two gun barrels, except the rifling was a series of disks rather than a long spiral. With a smooth click the left eye went blank. Only the right was allowed to see, and at first it didn't really see, but was allowed only white light. Then came another click, and a knife-bright chart appeared. The doctor's voice asked him, through the machine, to read the letters of the chart. With sudden pride he read them all, his voice clear, not quite his—it came from below but was his voice, clearly and authoritatively reading the tiniest letters in the very bottom line.

The charts changed at the whim of the machine, became green and red, then changed and became tiny games with lines and colors, games he repeatedly solved with either eye. The machine helped him each time, and he grew calm behind it, or in it, or of it. It protected him, and grew warm. When it swung away,

suddenly, its mass and warmth gone away, his own face was damply cold and naked, almost as if it had been skinned.

"Now I'm going to put a little drop of this in each eye," the doctor said. He reached for a little eyedropper, and held it out like a magician, to prove that it was only what it seemed.

"What is it?" Horace asked.

"It's an eyedropper."

"I mean, what's in it?" A twinge of insult; he was not that stupid.

"It's an anesthetic. It's so you won't feel it when I test the pressure."

The bald statement froze him. "What pressure?"

"Horace," his mother said.

The doctor turned to her as though he'd given up trying to explain anything to someone as unreasonable as Horace. "It's just the standard test for glaucoma. A routine thing." He turned to Horace again. "I just put a little gauge against your eye—just for a moment, and it tells me if the pressure's normal or not. Okay?"

"What can I do about it?" Horace heard himself say. The doctor was startled, and so was he, but he could think of no way to apologize. He had done so well on the little visual games in the machine—he ought to get some credit for that.

"It won't hurt a bit," the doctor said.

Now, Horace thought, they are getting down to business. When they said that, they always got down to business.

On his right, past the black machine, was a small window surrounded by metal cabinets. Outside, the winter day was dim and cold. He shook as though he had been forced to lie naked on that crusted ice and snow. He could feel the crust cutting his skin, and the doctor's cold intentions gathering toward him. Stop it, he asked his shaking. This was fear without source, because there was no Leverah at that window, nothing, and probably it wouldn't hurt. But it hurt already, somewhere in the middle of his bones, because he was about to explode. What, exactly, am I afraid of? he asked himself. Where would I rather be? I couldn't even run to get there. I would stumble and let go of everything like a sick dog—like Unk when the car hit him on Bank Street.

Now was the time of no other choice. When he'd stepped on

141

a nail, Dr. Winston had to ream out the hole in his foot. That had hurt! And when the time had come to clean that nail hole, nothing else would do. It was the time, like all those other times that never seemed to end, but to be repeated in all sorts of varieties; like when it was necessary to set the ulna in his arm, or to put his dislocated finger back straight, or when his shoulder was dislocated, or when he pulled the tendons in his knee and it swelled up big as a cantaloupe, and it had to be moved in examination, or when the dentist said this would hurt a little bit. His parts did stupid things, went wrong all the time, and he paid in fear.

"All right," he said. But it was not just personal fear, either. He was afraid of what might be done by that doctor to that boy, just as he feared the moment the car hit Unk and threw his brown and white body down the sidewalk, his big spaniel ears flying. The sound of that blow. He heard the breath go like an ear popping, and the dog couldn't breathe to scream. That was nothing; it happened all the time. Men did worse things to men, to women and to little children. David shot bullets through the bodies of squirrels, and they kicked and kicked, unable to climb. In what pain. Gordon Ward and his big men, raping Susie on the grass, common as a toilet. None of them ever seemed to fear another's pain or fear. Never. They had appetites like the Herpes, all of them, until they had to scream themselves.

"I won't be able to hold my eyes open," he said to the doctor and to his mother. "If you want me to hold them open, I'm sorry."

"I'll hold them open," the doctor said.

11

One evening during the week before Christmas, Harvey sat in his wheelchair, alone before the embering fireplace. The owlhead andirons blinked coals at him through their amber eyes, and the dark panels and uprights of the tall room led his eyes upward to the false balcony. No one looked down at him; no De Oestris ghost-paced two dimensionally along that narrow ledge. He was alone in the big house, and even with his third drink in his hand he could not summon any pride in his possession of this great room. That had always been something to count upon, no matter how low he was; perhaps now he had worn out this gift. If he had, what had he left to enjoy? He had come against his will to believe that all men were leaky vessels whose enthusiasms, though they once seemed so bounteous and unending, died away in all the years, and when they were gone nothing could bring them back. Passion did not ever return, and the memory of passion was the most painful of all—much more painful than the memory of inadequacy or dishonor, or even of tragedy. His father's death had seemed, and still seemed, inevitable, sad but not wrong. But this slow death of desire!

Near the entrance to the dining room was a framed photograph of the family, taken before the accident. He could barely see it in this light, but he knew it well enough. Even from this distance he was a straight form in a white summer suit, suggesting energy and motion. Wood stood serious and tall, Horace, David and Kate were still children, and Hank was just a little slimmer and firmer, her bones more clearly defined. It was youth, just the last few years of it, that neither of them had known was slipping away. There was a stab of pain: the firm, clear-skinned

bodies of himself and his young wife, a flash, a confrontation naked and happy.

In the picture he was slightly apart from them, a little impatient, fond of them all, yes, and smiling, but ready to go elsewhere and come back almost before they knew he had gone. The very line of his hip, where the white jacket fell straight, and his foot on the rung of David's chair, predicted some smooth motion.

Fond of them, he had thought. How fond had he ever been of his children, really? He did remember their tenderness as babies, especially Wood, his first-born. But had he ever loved anyone in some way purified of his physical presence, his pride of creation or of ownership? How did he feel about them now? It was as though his own destruction had destroyed their worth. *Even I*, he thought, *even a self-centered son of a bitch like me can see how unnatural a father I am.* Horace, the difficult one; what had he ever done to help that child get through his darkest nights? Oh yes, he could remember times when he put his arm around those thick shoulders and tried to talk to the boy. But always, eventually, came the impasse, when his impatience won out. They had everything they needed, didn't they? Hadn't he managed to feed them and clothe them and give them what all the other children had (a great deal more than most, if they only knew; there were plenty of hungry kids in Leah)? Christ, if they didn't think so they only had to look at poor Peggy Mudd, with a moron for a father and a round-heeled mother.

Whenever he'd tried to find out what was bothering Horace he'd get frustrated and tell the boy how lucky he was. Sure. Count your blessings while a nightmare has you in its teeth. Be grateful! Be happy! Well, at least they'd found that he didn't have a brain tumor, only simple near-sightedness.

The fire creaked, and he threw his cigarette butt into it—carefully, so he wouldn't have to wheel himself over and push it off the rug with the poker. He watched it smoke and glow all over as the fire ate it. His drink was almost gone, and he wanted another, but he was alone in the house and couldn't yell for service. Too bad, he thought. That's just too bad.

David's main birthday present had been his driving license, so he had taken Hank and Kate Christmas shopping. Wood and

Horace were up in the woods, dragging in the tree they had picked out early in November, before snow.

He would have to wheel himself into the kitchen if he wanted any ice. His leg felt numb, but rather ominously so, and he would have to be careful. Lately, especially after the doctors' last prognostications—that he had a rather local but virulent form of arthritis in his hip and knee—he had begun to have an aura, a prediction of pain whose signals were at the same time certain and indistinct. If this were it, and he was doubtful and certain that it was, he would need the drink. Wood had long ago removed the doorsills between the downstairs rooms, so he could make it all right.

In the kitchen, just as he had twisted a few pieces of ice from the ice tray into his glass, a tapping came at the door.

"Come in!" he said. The inner door opened as the storm door shut, and Betty Mudd came shyly in and shut the door. She wore a light blue, belted, epauletted coat, and her long brown glamor-girl hair fell around her shoulders. She had on enough lipstick, it seemed to him, to choke a horse, but that was the style these days. She was very nervous, and her conventionally pretty but somewhat slack and stupid face was all set for some meaningful business. He could tell because she really looked as though she wanted a fight. Scared to death.

"You're lucky I was in the kitchen," he said. "I'd never have heard you from the living room. Want a drink?" He gestured with his glass, thinking that there had been a time when that offer might have meant something more than it did now.

"Well . . ." she said. "My ride's waiting."

"Ride to where?"

"Well, that's what I wanted to talk to you or Mrs. Whipple about."

He wheeled himself to the cupboard and got out a bottle of whiskey and another glass. "Get yourself some ice if you want it. Nobody's here but me." He poured himself some whiskey, and she quickly and expertly put the frozen tray under the faucet, loosened the ice cubes and fixed herself a drink. She was thirty-two now, approximately. He knew that she was nineteen when Peggy was born; he knew that, and he knew that at that time he was thirty-two. That was thirteen years ago. Hank was in

the hospital after having Kate, and he had dropped up to the sugarhouse to see the new baby, who was about eight weeks old. Bert Mudd was working in the woods up in Coos County, and wouldn't be home for a week. As a friendly gesture he'd brought along a bottle, in case she wanted a drink, which she did.

"It's about Peggy," she said, sitting down at the kitchen table. As she crossed her legs, her rayons gave a little electric squeak. With sadness he realized that she was still young and smooth. Sadness and affection, in a way, because she'd certainly never embarrassed him about those times long ago.

"You want her to stay here tonight? Is that it, Betty? You're all dolled up for a party, I can see that."

"Don't that bother you?" she asked.

"No, not the way you think. You mean about gallant Bertram Mudd out there in his foxhole? No, I'll tell you the truth. I'm a little jealous of that young buck out in the car, whoever he is."

She gazed at him affectionately for a second, during which time she looked exceedingly stupid and appealing. Maybe it was because she was almost the exact opposite of Hank that he'd occasionally lusted after her. She was one of those soft women who moved any way you wanted them to, who never seemed to need anything for themselves but a man on them, and whose softness after a while became an awful bore. But pretty, and made of warm flesh and blood.

"She could work for you, and I'll send money. I got a chance for a dollar an hour, see, in Worcester, Massachusetts, in a war plant. They teach me and all that. Plus overtime, time and a half." She ran out of facts, and looked at him worriedly.

"Are you sure you've got the job, Betty?"

"Sure I'm sure."

"It isn't just something he told you, you don't think?"

"Well, he told me about it, all right, but I'm sure it's true, Harvey. I seen ads in the paper they put in. Said you can make sixty dollars a week!"

"That's a lot of money. You going to be a Rosie the Riveter?"

"Maybe!"

"Have you told Peggy?"

Quickly she bit her lip and dropped her head. When she looked up, tears were pouring out of her big pale eyes. "I can't tell

her!" She bawled out loud, making sounds surprisingly like "boo-hoo!" In spite of his cold observation of these symptoms, he was touched.

"You could send for her," he said, feeling kind and rather inspired to have invented this lie. "When you get all settled you could send for her and Wood could put her on the train."

Suddenly she smiled. Did she know this was a lie? He didn't think she did. She smiled so wide he saw her pink gums, and noticed that one canine tooth had gone bad in these last years.

"Oh, Harvey! Thank you so much! I've just got to go now. I've really got to go." She took the rest of her drink in a gulp and went to the small mirror over the sink. "Shit, oh dear," she said evenly, "I'm a royal mess." She bent closer to fix her face, taking the necessary tools from her pocketbook with expert hands. With hard, professional motions that seemed to him impersonal, almost cruel, she fixed the face of a stern stranger.

"I'm no spring chicken," she muttered with her lips awry. "I've got to take care of my phiz."

"You're still a pretty girl, Betty," he said.

"Thank you, Harvey." She turned to him, all remade. "We had some fun too, didn't we?"

"Lots and lots of fun," he said.

"I'd kiss you, but I'd leave a big red raspberry glob on you."

"Good luck, Betty."

"Thanks again, Harvey. Bye now!" Gaily, off to the party. And she was gone.

"Now I know all about the war," he said out loud. "It's fun time for morons." And time for inflation that made his money lose value, God damn it. Sixty dollars a week! And also time for taxes and controls that kept him from making enough more. God damn Roosevelt, globaloney and alphabet soup. But he still had some irons in the fire.

He wheeled himself and his drink back through the dining room to his table before the fire, and stared into the coals. Ah, poor Betty Mudd! He could see her riveting all the boiler plates on inside out and upside down. No, her talents were more gentle and natural, and for a while she'd have a good time in the city. What the hell could he do about it, anyway? Could he make her

stay in Leah? When Wood and Horace came back he'd send them up to get Peggy and her things.

Peggy had been a little black-haired critter in a clothesbasket, back then. Betty had so much milk in her big breasts they were bluish and hard, and the milk was warm and sticky on his chest. Her pubic hair hadn't grown all the way out again since they'd shaved it off at the hospital, and it was furry and a little scratchy. She was nineteen, then, and youth firmed even the essential vacuousness of her face. She was a fine young animal full of red blood and heat, without regret. Without regret.

It was a strange night, for December—a thaw under an almost full moon. His new glasses had come just that afternoon, and Horace could see the face of the man in the moon. Then, with a blink to shift his mind a little, he could pick out what his mother called "the Gibson Girl." There she was, a dark cameo head against the ivory moon.

He and Wood rested, sitting on a log they had cleaned of the damp, crusted snow. When Wood lit his pipe his face gleamed in the match flame, and a puff of the rich smoke floated by, keeping the shape Wood had given it with his breath.

The heavy snow collected in the webbing of their snowshoes, so they'd had to stop often and tap them to free them up. The tree was a balsam fir he and Wood had found before snow, and they had marked its location so well they'd gone straight to it in the moonlight. Wood carried a flashlight and the pulp saw, and he carried the hatchet on his belt in its leather sheath. He chopped off the lowest branches so Wood could get the pulp saw in to the trunk, just at snow level. When the tree rolled softly over, as if with a sigh, they began the long drag back down the hill.

As they rested, sitting on the damp log, Horace felt his bones lying easy in his muscles. He breathed the cool air freely. He had sweat, and now, as his skin cooled, this rest was so easy, and the air was full of the sweet scent of spruce and pine. Wood was there, quietly resting too. Horace thought how good it would be if always he and Wood could be together and do some kind of work as hard and pleasant as this. This hill could last forever,

like the steep downturn of the world, and they could drag the tree down the snows of the world past hemlock and maple and birch trees in groves or standing like that rock maple, a giant singleton with its bare branches spread against the moon. Darkness turned to light at their approach, and the soft wind passed right through walls that weren't real blank walls but skeins of brush and branches. They, too, always found a passage through the darkest obstacles, and came down the long hill toward the bundled roofs and the orange windowlights of Leah.

When Wood puffed on his pipe, the coals inside the bowl lighted his finger and thumb as he cradled the small fire in his fist. When he spoke, at first Horace heard only the warm, fatherly sound of the voice, deep and calm, and his brain registered only that sound and his own feeling of gratitude. The tree, though; Wood had said something about the tree. He'd said that it was about the best one they'd ever found. It would stand nearly twelve feet tall in the high room, and they'd decorate the top of it from the stairs and with a stepladder.

Tonight Kate and his mother would get out the decorations that were packed lightly in their big boxes, Wood would test the strings of lights, and Kate would string popcorn on thread. He would watch them as they carefully, carefully hung the brilliant, beautiful, so fragile glass globes. Then at the last came the tin-foil icicles, and around the base the snow-white cotton batting. Then the tree would glow like a whole new universe of good intentions, rewards and love. While the tree stood, his life was different too, even in the dark. Other forces came into the house with the tree, and they were good.

Peggy came home from choir practice quite late. Because they were doing part of Handel's *Messiah*, they had long sessions. The note was half under the sugar bowl, in her mother's large round handwriting.

> Dearest Peggie—
> I have a chance to make good money and help the war—
> I am aranging with Mrs. Whipple about you for a wile

she will explain—I could not see you because of my ride
is waiting—I will write you soon—   always love—
                                                Your Ma

She sat down at the table and read the note again, then
went to the closet and pulled the curtain aside. Yes, her mother's
clothes had been picked over. Her best dresses and her blue coat
were gone. All her shoes were gone except the old pair of runover
fleece slippers, which sat there pigeon-toed and abandoned.

Her mother had gone away, and wasn't going to live here
any more at all. Her mother said in the note she was "aranging
with Mrs. Whipple," but what could her mother arrange? She'd
never arranged anything before, so how could she suddenly pretend to be responsible and arrange anything? She'd run off with
some man who had a car, who would probably turn insulting and
cruel. She'd be lost. She didn't know how Peggy and sometimes
the Whipples really took care of her. But hovering above this
concern was another person, a mother who was large and strong,
who gave everything that was ever given, who had cared for Peggy,
and who, still endowed with strength and immense warmth, had
gone away and left a child. Left a child alone in a house that
could no longer be used as a house at all, because the adult
person had gone. The small Christmas tree looked pitiful now,
at this news. With its few colored balls and crooked tinsel star,
it stood forlornly on the trunk, obviously the work of a child.

And at the same time, secretly at first, and then with total
loss of pride, her joy grew and grew and became, with a kind of
pulsing color, enormous. The colors of Christmas. To be a ward
of the Whipples and live (but would they let her?) in the Whipples' house! To have Christmas with them and their great tree
with its beautiful electric lights, with Wood there. This was what
she wanted more than anything in the world. Yes, more than anything. She wouldn't talk, she wouldn't speak unless spoken to.
She would work hard and do anything they asked, if she could
just sit in the shadows and be with them.

But why should they do this for her? There was no reason.
A girl whose own mother had abandoned her? Their Christmas
was their own, and they owed nothing of it to her. Christmas was
private, for each family. She had no presents for them, only the

compact she had saved up to buy for her mother, and the sewing kit Mrs. Andrews of the Red Cross had given her to send to her father. The compact was cheap and gaudy, with stars glued on it. Neither Mrs. Whipple nor Kate would want it.

Her mother had gone away for the men that wanted to go to bed with her. It was betrayal, because where was that love? Where was that love?

"Mother," she said sorrowfully, tentatively. "Mother." She heard her voice close up with self-pity, and thought of the choir, those full, open, joyful voices. She was listening to herself betrayed, to her own voice crying, and yet she was really inconsolable, and could not stop that retching sound.

The lamp was smoking. She must stop crying long enough to turn it down. Now, was that real sorrow? She carefully turned it down, because she had to. Or did she really have to? Yes, because she was not a baby, she was thirteen years old, and she couldn't let everything go crash, go black with soot. How was the fire in the oil stove? She had to look.

And then as she stood up to look at that fire, the word, as if to prove itself real, came unbidden as a hiccup and she was crying "Mother" in a voice so childish it frightened her.

David sat in the car outside Trotevale's Department Store, waiting for Kate and his mother. He was still a little hesitant about the clutch-accelerator-shift timing business, and now, because the car pressed forward against the curb, he practiced it with the motor off. Wood had taught him to drive without too much trouble, with very little anger on either side. For this he was grateful.

As everybody knew, the 1941 Chevrolet was a fine car—a very good year for Chevrolet. The '42 model, while more streamlined, had painted bumpers and drably painted trim, because of the chrome shortage. Even the grille of the '42 was painted. But the '41 stood light and high, and glittered nicely under its coat of simonize. It was miraculous the way the car went where he pointed it. Even though no one was supposed to go over thirty-five miles per hour, in order to conserve gas and tires, the wonder of that motion free of work and sweat—no pushing, no pedaling,

with the trees and turns going effortlessly by—was enough for him. It seemed that all at once, with his birthday and his driving license, time had suddenly moved, and he had advanced significantly toward real life.

He leaned back, conscious of his commanding presence before the dials and controls, and lit a Chesterfield. The night was warm, and both side windows were rolled down, so the smoke traveled right out the window.

Ben Caswell came along, skinny and whey-faced, always chilly-looking in a mackinaw that was inches too short in the sleeves. "Well," Ben said enviously, "are you driving or just sitting there?"

"Driving," David said. "I took Kate and my mother shopping, that's all."

"There's a war on," Ben said. "That's nonessential travel, isn't it?"

"Don't be a meatball," David said.

Ben leaned carefully against the fender and rubbed one long, grayish wrist. "Listen," he said. "You know why we're losing the war? I just read an article that says we ought to make cartridge cases out of gold. We've got plenty of gold, but we don't have enough copper."

"Sure."

"No, I'm telling the truth, Davy. What good is gold if you're losing the war?"

"I didn't think we were losing it."

"I didn't say we were going to lose it, eventually. I just said we're losing it now," Ben said. This was typical Ben Caswell hair-splitting—one of the reasons he and David quite often ended their arguments flat on the ground. That is, their arguments never really ended at all; after the bruises, bloody noses and recriminations had replaced them, they simply faded away.

"You know how the War Production Board classifies gold? 'Plentiful; to be substituted whenever possible for anything critical.' That's a direct quote."

And it would be too. With Ben, it never paid to get over on the shifty ground of fact. David thought awhile. Gold was too malleable for the pressures of military cartridges, and it would

weigh too much. "You mean make the cartridge cases out of gold, or the bullets? Or what?" he asked slyly.

But Ben, as usual, saw this feint and realized the counter-arguments, whether or not they had been in the magazine article. "Of course not," he said disgustedly. "I mean, to use it as an alloy in place of copper, to cut down corrosion and give the necessary malleability to the metal."

So he had known this all the time. Ben Caswell was, by common consent, the smartest boy in Leah High School, and he didn't mind proving it, ever. A slow red fog seemed to cover David's vision. As usual with Ben he felt maneuvered, like an experimental rat. Ben had deliberately exaggerated from the very beginning by saying that cartridge cases were to be made "out of gold," and while David sensed a fallacy here, he had no words to use in pointing it out. Ben was always doing these infuriating logical experiments on him, and would even occasionally give him patronizing compliments, as if to say "Your mind, though crude, is rather interesting." David couldn't remember how many fist fights they'd had in the last five years.

But here he sat, commandingly, negligently, authoritatively behind the wheel of a car, while skinny Ben stood in a frosty puddle, shivery in a mackinaw he'd outgrown, rubbing his gray-blue knuckles and no place to go. The fog of anger passed as he watched Ben, now hickish and vulnerable, jiggle in the puddle and look up and down the street. Mary Denney and her older sister came along, both carrying packages, and when Mary saw him sitting in the driver's seat and said "Hi," he answered and Ben didn't. Ben had always lived and acted as though girls didn't exist. If David ever talked about girls, he now realized, it was never with Ben Caswell. Although he supposed he spent more actual time with Ben than with anyone else, and therefore Ben was probably his best friend, they always talked about the war, or of technical, mechanical things, never about girls. He would never dare to ask Ben why this was so—which was a powerful and interesting thing in itself.

His mother and Kate came out of the wide, framed glass doors of Trotevale's, Mr. Hummington himself holding the door for them and wishing them Merry Christmas in his clipped, efficient way, his mauve-colored glasses glinting in the Christmas

lights. They carried their too easily identifiable packages in their arms—neckties, socks, shirts—all uninteresting items. Ben grew nervous as they approached, ducked his head, and backed into the side of the car parked in the next parking place.

"Hello, Ben," his mother said, and Ben said, "H'lo." To her only, not to Kate.

"Hello, Ben," Kate said directly to him, and Ben said, "Mmm-hmm."

Kate smiled at Ben rather humorously and cruelly, but with good nature. David couldn't help smiling. He felt Kate's power, and it was so much more powerful than Ben Caswell's brilliant mind.

"Have you done your tree yet, Ben?" his mother asked as she stowed the packages in the back seat. "We're doing ours tonight."

"Yes," Ben said. "Last night." Ben's father was a mailman, and they lived in a house that was almost miniature. It had many rooms in it, but they were all small. The Caswells always had a tree about four feet high, which Ben's mother covered with so many lights, balls, icicles, ropes of cellophane and tinsel that it looked like a big, glowing, icy hump. It was hard to tell if there was a real tree under there at all.

When the packages were all stowed away in the back seat, his mother got in back with them and Kate got in the front. Ben said, "You think about it, Davy."

"Think about what?" David said.

"The gold. The gold," Ben said with a kind of vague importance. He ambled back sideways, stepped up on the sidewalk and raised one thin arm rather significantly but still vaguely as he departed. He seemed to fade away, and David was grateful that he hadn't stayed to see him start the car and back out into the street, because sometimes, especially in reverse, he would let the clutch out too quickly and the car would buck and stall. This time it went all right. He backed up carefully, stopped without too much of a jerk, selected low, just remembered the function of the clutch in time, and they began to cruise slowly around the decorated square. He found second a little late, but that was all right, and they were finally safe in high on Bank Street. The hill at the beginning of High Street had been well sanded, so he didn't anticipate any trouble there, although a certain nervous stimulation made his left leg jump a little.

154

The engine hummed along smoothly, with that particular Chevy sound of friendly tappets tapping. On the road in the headlights, the slightly raised areas of compressed snow shone against the asphalt like maps of Baffin Land or Labrador before the wheels thumped lightly over them. The car had hardly warmed up before they reached High Street, where they would have to climb the hill in low. He glanced longingly at the wide street they had to leave. It went out of Leah and became Route 4, passed Cascom and Cascom Center and led south to all the states and cities. But he had to turn toward his home and the coziness of the ceremony of the tree.

He liked Christmas, although not as much as he used to. But what if the car were his, he had all the money and gas he wanted, and his suitcase was packed and safely in the trunk. He could cruise southward all through the warm December night. He would be twenty-six, a discharged veteran scarred not unhandsomely by shrapnel, wearing tweedy civilian clothes. Only in the bottom of his suitcase, in a plain flat box, would be his medals—the ones he showed nobody. In fact she would find them there by accident— the Purple Heart and the Silver Star. She would find them one night in her apartment in New York when she happened to look in his suitcase for a pack of cigarettes. Then, holding the medals before her suddenly glowing, understanding eyes, she would know why he hadn't answered the drunken sailor in the nightclub who had called him a shirker.

The headlights centered on the old stall at the rear of the garage, on cobwebs as thick as molasses between the rounded dark crossbars. He did think of the clutch, so the car didn't stall. He let it idle for a second and turned it off with the key. Kate and his mother bustled happily, gathering their presents, and the engine creaked as it cooled.

"You take these, David," his mother ordered. "I think one is yours, so don't squeeze."

After they'd come in from shopping and put the packages in one of the hall closets, Harvey said to Henrietta, "Betty Mudd was here."

"What was the matter?" she answered immediately, and he wondered if she knew about what had gone on up there in the

sugarhouse long ago. Not only up there, as a matter of fact, but in various other places as the opportunity had presented itself. They'd even had some close calls, and how Bertram Mudd ever managed not to know was an interesting problem in the psychology of cuckoldry. But then, maybe he did, and maybe Hank knew too, somewhere deep. Did he notice a slight extra keenness in her eye as he spoke of Betty?

"She left town," he said.

"Left town?"

"She thinks she has a job in Worcester at a dollar an hour, plus time and a half for overtime, whatever the hell that is. She's going to make sixty bucks a week. That's what she thinks, anyway. I wonder if they pay fifty cents an hour for undertime," he said, and laughed.

"What about Peggy?" she said, ignoring his laughter.

"We're to take care of Peggy until she gets settled, and then, if she happens to remember that she has a daughter, she's supposed to send for her."

"Oh, poor Peggy!" Hank's face went dark with concern, and her eyes blinked behind the magnifying glasses. "Just before Christmas."

"You know she'd be happy as hell to live here for a while."

"That isn't it!" Hank said angrily, surprising him. "You don't understand anything! Where is she now? Is she up there all alone and it's nearly ten o'clock? That woman ought to be—"

"Take it easy. I sent Wood and Horace up to get her."

"Sometimes I wonder about all you people," she said. "There's a callousness about you. Sometimes I think Horace—yes, Horace!—is the only one with any human understanding."

"Well," he said, "I don't mind having Peggy around. She's at least one poor soul I can feel sorry for."

Wood knocked on the tarpaper-covered door. Horace stood behind him, and he felt that Horace was greatly upset. He seemed to be hiding, because he didn't have to stand directly behind—there was room beside him where Peggy had shoveled around the door.

She opened the door and looked up at him with the dreamy

look of crying on her dim little face. Poor Peggy, he thought, poor little Peggy. She looked like a little woods animal just born and abandoned, frizzled and damp, with the last of its warmth going out. She was a few months older than Kate, but she looked younger and much more immature, as though the way she'd had to live, and the food she'd had to eat, had stunted her, and somehow kept her skin dark.

"Hello, Peggy," he said. His father had told him that she didn't know her mother had gone, but it looked as though she did.

"Hello, Wood," she said. Her always startling quality was strength. She saw Horace hulking behind him, and she said, "Hello, Horace."

Then he was startled again, because Horace pushed past him and lunged toward Peggy with a hoarse explosion of concern, like a deep cough or groan. It seemed primitive, troglodyte—the word came to his mind. Peggy was not startled at all, and put her dark hand on Horace's arm.

"Yes, yes," she said, patting him, and Horace backed up and stood quietly.

"You're going to come and live with us," Wood said. "We've come to get you and your things. Your mother's got a job in Worcester, Peggy, and she's going to send for you."

A small, ironic grimace flickered across her face—or perhaps he'd misread it. She stepped back and let them into the little shack with its close smell of old food, damp clothes and kerosene. The lamp's orange light couldn't quite define the far corners of the room, but he did see the small Christmas tree glinting in that semidarkness, and he felt the presence of the oil pot burner—a push of heat against his side.

"We'll have fun!" Horace said in his cracked voice. "We're going to put up the tree!"

"Why do you want me?" she asked from the shadow.

"We want you to have Christmas with us," Wood said.

"We love you!" Horace shouted, and Peggy started to cry. She sat down at the table and put her head on her arms. Horace went to her and put his hand on the back of her neck. Wood felt a surge of caution—would Horace hurt her neck? Horace patted the back of her neck, visibly moving her head. Her mouse-colored

hair seemed to absorb the lamplight, giving no highlights. She wore an old dress of Kate's, with short, puffed sleeves. The way the thread gathered the faded cotton around her thin arm seemed to him unsubstantial, haphazard, like her whole life. He felt that perhaps they ought to take her to a doctor, first, to see if she would live.

"I'm all packed," she said, getting up and rubbing her eyes in a businesslike manner. "I knew I'd have to go someplace else." She put on her overshoes and coat, and picked up her school books and loose-leaf notebook.

"You know, then," Wood said.

"My mother left me a note." She went to the oil stove and turned it off, then settled herself to watch it until the flame in the pot died out. "My trunk's over there," she said, pointing to the old tin trunk against the studs of the wall.

"You've got everything?" he asked.

"Everything that's mine," she said. Again he thought he heard irony in her voice.

"I'll carry the trunk!" Horace said. "I got it. I'll carry it!" He picked it up by the handle, like a suitcase. Of course the old strap broke, and the trunk crunched to the floor like a safe, shaking the whole building. "The handle broke," he said, looking from one of them to the other for judgment.

"It was old and rotten," Peggy said. "You'll have to carry it around the middle."

"All right!" Horace said, and picked it up in his arms. He went right out with it, and Wood followed him into the cool night, then turned just in time to see Peggy's face as she blew out the lamp. The orange light of the burning oil gave her face a high color, just for that second before she puffed the flame out, and her long, bony nose and dark eyebrows—the dark arches of her eyes—were defined by crisp black shadows, as were her wide lips and the cleft between chin and mouth. In that brilliant warm light her face was nearly handsome. Her lips formed an O, and then, in the immediate darkness, his eyes retained the image of her face. It seemed a moment struck with importance, as though he had seen a prediction of vivid form waiting in the young girl's bones.

12

In Leah, on Christmas Eve, it snowed all evening from the shut-
tered, windless dark. The hills seemed to close in, and the snow
sifted down upon the four main roads that led from the town,
softly crowding Leah in towards itself. Though the plow trucks
were busy, with their distant rumbles and dimly flashing lights,
they seemed insignificant and lonely in the measureless white. The
Cascom River was frozen over, and it, too, built up with snow,
except for black water splatting on black ice below the Cascom
Woolen Mill dam. The train from Concord, called "the Peanut,"
had stopped to let off passengers and mail, and now it huffed
its way down the slow grade along the Cascom River toward the
Connecticut River, where it would pass over a black iron bridge
into Vermont. The passengers it had let off were mostly soldiers
and sailors, and these took one look at the snow that hadn't even
been cleared from the small parking area beside the station,
shouldered their duffel bags and trudged off into the town, each
taking his own azimuth across the white. The other passengers
went quickly into the small waiting room and stood by the potbellied stove, thinking about what to do. Billy Grimes' taxi, the
stationmaster informed them, was following the plows to Northlee
with five people aboard, and wouldn't be back for at least an hour,
if then, because Billy had mentioned going home to have the
tree. "And so am I," the stationmaster said, putting on his overcoat and galoshes. His car had been put up for the war, he added,
or he'd give them a ride. And so they all trudged off, grunting
and leaning, toward their destinations.

The Town Square was deserted except for the green, red and
blue Christmas lights strung from the lampposts, and other lights

strung through the blue spruce. The loudspeaker over the Town Hall doorway had gone dead except for an occasional amplified crack of static; Mrs. Box, the town clerk's secretary, had gone home and left the phonograph amplifier on.

In their apartment over Trask's Pharmacy, across the hall from the Trasks themselves, Wayne Facieux and his mother looked at the tree Wayne had decorated. All the bulbs were blue, and the only other decorations Wayne had allowed this year were tin-foil icicles. He was pleased by the tree's cool, luminous deliberateness, its ethereal, un-Christmas purity. The whole room, filled as it was with his mother's tasteless gimcracks and cheap maple furniture, gleamed a stylish and original blue.

Across the hall, Mr. and Mrs. Trask and Prudence sat before their bright, conventionally various tree. The radio softly gave them carols, but something was wrong, because for long moments none of them moved, and their eyes were too grave and bright. The dinner dishes had been done too quickly, and though it was their custom to open presents on Christmas Eve, and they had opened them, no tissue paper, paper bells and red ribbon were scattered about on the flowered carpet. Mrs. Trask, who had just finished picking everything up, sat with the crushed tissue in her lap, wondering, with anxiety she could not control, or keep from inflicting upon her husband and daughter, upon what dark battlefield, among armed and violent men, her son's tender body lay in danger.

Across the square, where the great houses stood on their wide lawns, Mr. Gordon Ward, Sr., stood before a bowl of eggnog and shook into its creamy surface the last drop from a bottle of bourbon. "Whoopee!" he cheered softly to himself. "Whoopee doopee doo, and a twenty-three scaroo!" He was a big man, as violently red-haired and green-eyed as his son—who was enjoying Christmas at Camp Blanding, Florida, and thus, presumably, not in trouble. The Burtons had dropped over from next door, and everybody, even Mrs. Ward, had about the same glow on. Screeches of laughter came from the living room, and he was about to carry the silver bowl triumphantly to their waiting appetites.

A few blocks from the square, up Union Street, the Potters' high white house glowed cheerfully, with red electric candles in

all the front windows. In the living room was their wide-spreading tree, deep green and silver and red and blue. Lois and her parents sat in the handsome room before the lighted tree and a small fire of white birch logs. Her mother and father sipped dark sherry while they waited for the ceremonial Christmas visit of Sally De Oestris. Wood would be driving her around tonight, and Lois, looking bright and beautiful in a new knit dress, silk stockings and heels, waited for him.

Out on the flats toward Northlee, at Sam Davis' farm, Susie sat at the kitchen table, staring off into space somewhere above the sink. She had just come in from helping with the milking, having left her father as he lowered the heavy milk cans into the milk-house well. She could still smell the barn on her left shoulder, where she had pressed against the warm cows. Mrs. Garner sat in her chair with her black afghan over her shoulders, knitting, and the radio on its single-board shelf played, and had played, so many Christmas carols Susie had stopped identifying each one. The tree was in the parlor, but it was too cold in there to sit.

For long stretches she could forget about the scandal. People seemed to treat her about the same. The biggest change was leaving high school. Though she might have done that anyway, it seemed a direct result of what had happened that night. Most of the hurt was the betrayal. Before that Gordon had been so nice to her, and she'd really believed with all her heart, that first time she'd let him, that he loved her. And the second time, too, in his own house. But then he hadn't even looked at her for a month, and the next time he asked her out that thing happened. He had planned it. She couldn't seem to understand how anyone could lie like that. How could he have lied to her, straight to her face, when she had loved him? It made her into nothing.

In that part of the Whipples' barn that used to be the entrance to the horse stalls, and was now the garage, Wood jacked up the rear wheels of the car and put on the tire chains. David and Horace were just finishing up the shoveling, although the snow fell so thickly they'd have to do it all again, probably, after the presents in the morning. It would give them all good appetites for the turkey, anyway.

Sally De Oestris' old Filipino chauffeur had died two years ago, and since then it had been Wood's job to drive her around on Christmas Eve as she delivered presents to relatives, friends, old families she kept her eye on and poor families she kept her eye on—one of her kind, sarcastic, twinkly little ice-blue eyes. He'd fill the trunk and the back seat up with Sally's packages, then help her—in fact lift her—into the front seat, hand her her canes and wait while she arranged her fur coat, her fancy pocketbook, her hat and veil, and they would be off on their rounds.

When he got to her house this night, he had to bash through the bank the plow had raised, grind into her driveway and shovel a path from the car to her front entrance. All the lights in her house seemed to be on, and her uniformed maid, Sylvia Beaudette, a dark-haired young woman whose husband was in the Army Air Corps, was piling the packages in the front hall.

"Merry Christmas, Sylvia," Wood said.

"Merry Christmas, Wood. Sally'll be down in a minute, if the elevator works." Sally's elevator, a little seat that ran slowly up a slot in the stairwell, following the stairs, had never failed to work, as far as he knew, but nobody ever referred to it without this reservation.

Sylvia, evidently under orders, went out toward the dining room and came back with a glass of sherry on a salver. He took it, and Sylvia took away the salver. The dark, imported cream sherry was Sally's Christmas wine. No one knew how much of it she had left in her wine cellar, but it couldn't be bought any more. Her custom was to send a bottle of it to the houses where she intended to disembark from the car.

He sipped the smooth sherry and looked around at the trophies of Sally's travels. A brilliant Japanese wall hanging in silk, of a stylized woman in a red kimono, hung on the wall to the left of the dining-room arch. The woman played a small three-stringed instrument with a pick half as big as the instrument itself. It had always fascinated him that the tiny teeth in her delicately pouting little mouth were black. It occurred to him that he had known these objects from Japan—the lacquer bowls and tables, Samurai swords and sake sets—since he was a child, and had never, and couldn't quite even now, associate them with

the bucktoothed little caricatures of men he might be fighting soon. A shiver came at this thought.

A humming and clanking, such as an old cog railway might make, invaded the hall. It was the elevator, and soon, rounding the upper spiral of the stairs and descending slowly, came Sally, perched bright and glittering as a little bee queen. In a shimmery blue dress, twinkling and tinkling with bangles as bright as her bright blue eyes, she slowly descended.

"Merry Christmas! Merry Christmas!" she said in her deep voice. Her voice always astonished Wood, after not having heard it for a while, but after a few words he got used to it again. And every time he saw her she seemed a little smaller and more bent over, but just as bright and eager, always grinning in a fiercely pleased way, like the Cheshire cat in Tenniel's illustration.

Before they left, after he'd filled the car with packages, she gave him an A gas coupon. She rarely used her car any more, and when she did she hired a man to drive it. Her car was a 1937 Ford phaeton with a specially built, enclosed passenger compartment behind the open chauffeur's seat, and a little nautical porthole on each side. Sally had explained once that she liked the 1937 Ford's looks, and also its mechanical, rather than hydraulic, brakes. She was surprisingly technical-minded about things (although Wood disagreed about the Ford's cable brakes). Once, when she'd volunteered that she'd flown in an open-cockpit airplane from Paris to London in 1920, he asked her what kind of plane it was, and she explained without hesitation that it was a Bristol "Brisfit" two-seater fighter plane, and she'd sat in the gunner's seat. The gun had been removed, but the pilot had shown her patches in the wings that covered German bullet holes.

When they were cruising slowly down Bank Street in the quiet snow, with the tire chains gently thumping, Sally said, "I suppose you resent having to cart me around like this, but these little ceremonies are all we old women have left, you know."

"I don't mind," Wood said.

"Maybe you don't," she said, turning to look at him. Her neck didn't turn sideways, and if someone spoke to her from the side she had to move her whole body around. "We'll stop in at the Potters', and you won't mind that," she said cheerfully. "I've

explained to the rest that I can't get out of the car this year. This old body's too hard to manipulate these days."

He felt relieved.

"That pleased you, didn't it?" she said. "I don't have to imagine you'd rather fool with Lois Potter (my, isn't she getting to be a beauty?) than a seventy-year-old bag of bones like Sally De Oestris."

It was hard to see through the windshield and the constantly clogging wipers, but few other cars were out, so he didn't have to worry about them. He got stuck once down on Water Street, where one of Sally's poor families lived in a railroad tenement, but with a little shoveling got out again. Finally, after two hours, after explaining to everyone who wanted to give him a drink that Sally was out in the car, and after her friends, relatives and the people she kept an eye on had come out in the snow to greet her and kiss her through the car window, they had made all the calls except for the Potters'.

"It's quite a night," Sally said. "It's a night for a sleigh. I remember when we used sleighs all winter, nearly, when they didn't plow the snow at all."

"They didn't?"

"They rolled it down flat and hard. They used six-horse teams, and great rollers weighed down with cut granite blocks. That was exciting. I used to ride up on one of those rigs with Mr. Jason Campbell, captain-elect of the Cascom River Volunteer Fire Company."

The snow melted on the hood of the car, and the heater fan buzzed as they came back around the square. The Christmas lights were dim in the falling snow, and only one lane had been plowed on any street.

Mr. Potter had shoveled a two-shovel-wide corridor for Sally, and Wood crunched into the bank as far as he could, climbed around and repaired the corridor with his shovel before lifting Sally out. Mr. Potter, calling "Merry Christmas! Merry Christmas!" came out to guide Sally and her canes. Wood followed with the packages, his overshoes full of snow, and they all entered the suddenly warm, dim and cheerful house. Lois, her eyes bright, came and took the packages out of his arms so he could take off his coat and overshoes.

"Merry Christmas, Wood," she said shyly and softly. She came back to hang up his coat. As she turned, her soft black hair swirled, her slim legs flashed silk, and she was so pretty and dressed up, his legs grew weak. No, the weakness was because this lovely girl had made herself up just for his unworthy eyes.

They turned and entered the living room. Sally was enthroned in the sort of high, straight chair she found most comfortable, and Mr. Potter held her fur coat, melting crystals of snow gleaming on the long, dark tippets of fur. They had been laughing and chattering. "A white Christmas!" Mrs. Potter had just said. But now they turned, and were silent as they looked at Wood and Lois. Lois put her arm through his, and he felt her tremble. Sally's bright gaze narrowed as she smiled, and just perceptibly she nodded. Upon Mr. Potter's long, affable face was an expression almost of pain. But it was Mrs. Potter's face his eyes found and then jumped away from. She smiled, a speculative, encompassing smile, prideful and dark. He read everything in her naked face. She saw her virgin daughter with a man.

Peggy sat on a wicker stool next to the fireplace and stared at the lighted tree. The Whipples' tree was the grandest of all. At the very top, a delicate silver angel with real blond hair and a brilliant gold halo stood just below the ceiling, singing from a hymn book that was a real little leather-bound book, with real words in it. They were in a foreign language, though, and the letters were all so full of curlicues and bows she hadn't been able to read them. The angel had gone on the tree at the very last, and she had been the one to stand at the top of the stairs and hand it to Wood. He had stood on the stepladder, and she had put the fragile angel into his strong hand. He'd just been able to reach the top, and he stretched so far his shirt came out of his pants and she'd caught a glimpse of the blue band of his shorts. When he finally crimped the angel's wire holder with his fingers, to make it stand straight, he looked down at her and smiled so warm and triumphant a smile—just to her, because he and she had been the only ones to handle the angel—she became warm herself, and so happy she could name her happiness. Then she smiled, in turn, down at Horace, who had been allowed to steady

165

the ladder. She felt part of them all, being in that chain of warm regard.

Now it was Christmas Eve. The concert had been called off because of the snow, and instead the choir was to sing on the evening of the twenty-seventh in the Congregational Church. Wood hadn't come back with Sally De Oestris, David and Horace were still out shoveling snow, and Kate and Mrs. Whipple, with elaborate kindness and goodwill, had shooed her out of the kitchen and told her to go entertain Mr. Whipple. "He likes you, you know," Mrs. Whipple said.

She knew that was true. Mr. Whipple tended to yell a lot, and he pretended to start arguments with her, but she could see he didn't mean it in a bad way. He sat at his big table, drinking sherry. Mrs. Whipple had already told him twice not to drink it all before Sally De Oestris arrived.

"She's a good old bitch, and she'll understand," he'd answered.

Now he looked at her mock-fiercely and said, "So you're going to sing in the choir, eh?"

"Yup," she said, consciously impudent.

"All those yowling adenoids! Thank God I don't have to hear it!"

"You ought to come hear us. We're doing Handel's *Messiah*."

"Oh, God!" he said, "spare us poor sinners!"

Henrietta stood at the sink, where she and Kate were finishing up the last few odds and ends of pans, dishes and silverware. In a way she looked forward to Sally De Oestris' annual visit, although she hadn't liked Sally at all when she and Harvey were first married. She had sensed immediately that she was being patronized and "understood," that Sally was speaking to her as if to a hill farm girl. Of course she had always realized that Harvey belonged to a different class—she'd known that long before she seriously considered marrying him, when she began to learn the different vocabulary. But ever since she was a little girl she'd had a strange streak in her that made her quite unlike Sally's idea of a hill farm girl. She read odd books, and she was something of a scholar.

Harvey and Sally might laugh when she pronounced Dostoevsky "Dostóyvsky," but she had never heard anyone pronounce the name, even in high school. They knew how to pronounce the man's name, but she had read not only *Crime and Punishment* and *The Brothers Karamazov*, which they both vaguely allowed they'd read long ago in college, she'd read *The Idiot* and *Notes from Underground*. And she'd read all kinds of books. She'd read Ruskin and Cardinal Newman, Jerome K. Jerome, Stephen Leacock, Sir James Frazer and Bret Harte. She had no system, at first, only a dictionary and her curiosity. She read *A Tramp Abroad* as eagerly as *Tess of the d'Urbervilles*, and that as eagerly as *Anthony Adverse*. If books on economics and forestry and ornithology came to her hand, she took them home and read them. The two ladies who ran the Leah Public Library thought she was quite odd, but they would let her, at the ages of twelve and thirteen, take twice as many books home as they would the other children.

She still read a lot, but with a certain knowledge of categories now. She knew the difference between *Reader's Digest* and *The Atlantic*, or *The Virginian* and *The American*. It made her a little sad, this new knowledge, because she no longer read with that sense of unpredictable discovery.

Her politics were not Harvey's at all. She voted for Roosevelt in 1932, and she had in 1936 and 1940, and she would again too, if he ran for a fourth term. This drove Harvey mad, because he couldn't change her mind. And after Sally De Oestris had bumped into certain hard areas of knowledge and opinion in her, their attitudes toward each other changed very quickly. Sally was an odd character too—a rich girl who hadn't done what was expected of her, who had taken her freedom literally. She'd had lovers and never married. One of them had been a general in a revolution, and Sally had stood beside him and seen him order the death of a president. Later the general himself was taken and shot, and Sally took refuge in the American embassy. All this had happened before Henrietta was born, but she went to the college library in Northlee and found a history of those events. She found the general's name there, and with a sense of real shock, because she thought she'd believed Sally, found her name in a footnote: ". . . a wealthy American girl, Sally Destrous[?], friend of Gen-

eral Aranpo." Sally had told her about it with all the manifestations of truth Henrietta had always recognized and respected. It was simply the subject matter that could not, for all of Sally's authority, pass into Henrietta's mind as truth. And yet there it was. Sally Destrous; it could have been no one else, and she was shocked more by the discovery of her real disbelief than she was by the truth of the story.

Although it was not in Henrietta's nature to so casually mention things in her past, Sally would have found some of her experiences hard to believe too. That her father was partly eaten by pigs, for instance, or the winter they lived mostly on wild vegetables, tubers and johnnycake, when she had come down with what she now believed to have been either a vitamin deficiency or an allergy to some of that food—apples, pigweed, burdock, canned fiddleheads, dandelion greens, Jerusalem artichoke, hemlock tea and all the rest—and came out with sores and runny pus all over her body, so that she smelled awful, and most likely nearly died. The Overseer of the Poor brought them milk and flour. Their three cows had been condemned because of tuberculosis, and a bear had killed the two heifers in the orchard. They burned gray birch that winter, green and unsplit, and they were as close to the bone as most people ever got. They had no tree that Christmas because her grandfather was too tired to find one and drag it home. Her father sat in the kitchen, holding his soiled bandaged stumps with fearful care, and gave great breathless sobs because of his worthlessness and frustration. Of all the Christmases of her childhood, that was the one she remembered most clearly.

One miraculous thing happened on Christmas Eve, and at least one close shave. Tom came home after nearly a year of God knew where—that was the miracle. Kate heard a scrabbling, thumping noise at the back door and opened the inner door. There in the small window of the storm door was a cat's face staring at her, right into her eyes. Tom had climbed up the storm door by sheer claw, as he always did, and looked in. She opened the door and he dropped down, walked in, twitched his tail, thumped his head on her ankle as of old, jumped up on the stool and said "Miaow."

For a moment she was confused about his absence. Had he really been gone? There he was, looking no different. His eyes were as green, his gray tiger coat as smooth and neat as ever, his gums as pink. He licked a paw, combed his brow with it, and said "Miaow" again.

"Tom!" she said, and ran into the living room, where David, Horace, Peggy and her mother and father sat around the tree. "Tom's back!" To prove her point he followed her in, his tail up straight, each paw putting itself down with his old lion's authority, in which there always seemed to be some distaste for the texture of the carpet. He went straight to David, who sat in a high-backed oak and leather chair, jumped up on his lap and rolled over, exposing his fleecy white belly. When David scratched his stomach, Tom grabbed David's hand with his front paws and gently bit it as he went clawlessly through the gutting motions with his hind paws. There was no doubt that he was back, and that he didn't care to discuss his absence, or to allude to it by any way of strange behavior. He had been gone, they finally decided, about eight months.

"Where the hell have you been?" Harvey asked him. "Where the hell have you been, you murdering nightwalker?" Tom looked over at him and slowly closed his eyes.

"He's got one little souvenir of his travels," David said, rolling the fur away from a long scar on his flank. Tom batted his hand away and jumped down.

"He's been out on the tomcat trail," Harvey said. "He's lucky that's all he's got."

"When Wood and Sally come, let's not mention it," Kate said. "Let's see what Wood says!"

Tom walked over to where Horace was sitting on the floor with his back against the paneling. He sat down in front of Horace, looked at him and yawned fearsomely, exposing all his needle-like white teeth and the pink cavern of his throat.

Horace shivered and looked away from those weapons. He wished Wood were back. He had never understood the cat, never understood why the others all seemed to like it, and to kid with it, as his father just had, about its hunting prowess. "What a killer!" David had often said proudly.

The cat went to the dining-room archway and rubbed itself

in mock affection against the molding. "Miaow!" it said, and Kate rushed out to get it a saucer of milk.

Peggy sat next to the fire, licking a peppermint candy cane to make it last. She saw Horace shiver when the cat yawned at him, and she thought she knew how he felt. One night almost a year ago she woke up hearing the shrill death screams of a rabbit. Over and over the high "No! No!" broke out of the darkness, then died down, then was torn out again, pitiful and hopeless with terror. What could a rabbit call to for help? That cry was for no reason but pain and despair. It took a quarter of an hour before the cries came no more. In the morning by the outhouse she found a dead coney rabbit, its spine bare where a cat, or something, had eaten out its live backstrap muscles. The Whipples' fondness for Tom had always been a little strange to her too, and it made them all somehow larger than life, even somewhat frightening and heroic, as though they could look straight at death without even a shudder.

Wood and Sally De Oestris finally arrived, and Sally came slowly in on her canes, her deep voice merrily booming. Her fur coat was removed and she was ensconced in the high oak chair David vacated for her, and given a glass of sherry. She shook out her beads and adjusted herself and the brilliant folds of her blue dress, grinning all the while. She noticed Peggy and said, "Margaret Mudd! What's this? A little *Wandervogel* come for Christmas?"

Peggy nodded shyly, and Sally said, "I knew it. Wood told me in time to include something for you, Peggy Mudd. You'll find it under the tree in the morning." She looked fiercely about her and said, "Well!"

Wood and David had brought her packages in from the car, and now, as was their custom on Christmas Eve, they began with great mock secrecy, and lies as to which present was for whom, to put all the presents under the tree.

"A case of Lifebuoy for Kate!" David said, tucking a package far back under the tree. "Beee-oooh!" he said, imitating the radio.

"The keys to Davy's new Plymouth convertible!" Kate said as she came back from the hall closet with one tiny box in her hand.

Peggy sat basking in their energy. Mr. Whipple said something to Sally and she roared, though her white head barely moved.

Her carefully set white hair glinted all the colors of the tree. Mrs. Whipple took a glass of sherry and came to sit on another wicker stool next to Peggy.

"I saw another present for you in the hall closet," she whispered, and her hand came over to lie warmly on Peggy's arm.

Soon the presents were all partly hidden beneath the tree. Their shiny bows and flowered wrappings could be seen, precious and powerful shapes in there in the colorful dusk. Even she had bought presents for them all, because of Wood, who'd insisted on lending her five dollars. He'd ordered her to take the five dollars. When she said she couldn't, he said she must, and frowned at her from such a stern height she trembled, and couldn't refuse. She bought Wood a wallet, the most expensive thing, handkerchiefs for Kate and Mrs. Whipple, a boondoggle and steel key ring for David, a pair of knit gloves for Horace and, in consultation with Mrs. Whipple, a little pipe-reaming tool for Mr. Whipple, who occasionally smoked a pipe. All this came to four dollars and eighty-five cents. In spite of her happiness at having bought these things for all the Whipples, it seemed like such a lot of money she could never pay it back.

Just then Tom, evidently having finished his milk, stepped quietly into the center of the room, sat down, stuck one hind leg out straight as a Nazi saluting Hitler, and began to lick himself. Peggy watched Wood, and then, as Wood's eyes opened in surprise, she turned to Kate. Kate was bubbling inside and grinning —the only girl Peggy knew who could make faces and still look pretty.

"Look who came home for Christmas!" Kate said.

"It's Tom!" Wood said.

"Back from the wars, with a Purple Heart," David said.

Mrs. Whipple's hand tightened on Peggy's arm, and Peggy looked up at her. She was staring unhappily at Wood. Was it what David had said about the war? Wood was going into the Army soon, going away to danger. Suddenly her heart gave a great push, almost as if she'd lost her breath. How could he go from this house out there where her father was made sick with fear of the shells and bullets? It was more dangerous for Wood. Someone would take care of her father and tell him what to do, but Wood would choose to do what other people wouldn't dare to do. For him the

war would be too dangerous. He was too valuable, and somehow he shouldn't be allowed to go. With this thought, which seemed to carry in it all the truth in the world, she saw at once the horror and injustice of the war. Nothing could be done about it. Wood was not going of his own free will, even though he might give that impression because he was resigned to it. It was by force that he had to go, and that force came suddenly right into this room in spite of the beautiful tree and these Whipples who were being happy and good to each other. These moments of Christmas now became, in her new knowledge, infinitely pitiful and valuable.

Not hearing their talk, now, she began to make an accounting of this place in time, as if for future reference: the few pretty Christmas candies on waxed paper, Kate's beauty and grace, the angel singing its unknown hymn from the top of the tree, the dark strength of the high room looming over them, but now brushed gently with the kindly light of Christmas. There in the corner sat Horace with his blunt awkwardness, and in the middle of the room Sally De Oestris glittered like a funny little queen on her throne, while Mr. Whipple drank and joked like a slightly dangerous clown. Mrs. Whipple, who was always kind but sometimes distant, as if she'd been called away in her mind to some other place; David, who said quick things that might be funny yet might be cruel. And Wood, whom she loved with all her heart and because of this deeply feared. He reminded her of . . . God. From across the room his great warmth pressed against her with nearly as tangible a force as the fire at her side.

Horace watched Peggy through his crisp new glasses, seeing to his horror that tears were in her eyes. She was crying. He had to do something for her right now. Later, after all the excitement caused by this flash of need on his part had died down, he could not remember the idea of urgency at all; he merely acted. If only he could have made one intermediate step of some sort between the thought and its translation into action—if only he could learn to do this—such disasters might not always happen to him.

He did not remember getting up from the floor. As to what he intended to give Peggy, he was never certain; the nearest real object might possibly have been a candy cane hanging on a branch of the tree near a blue ball with a red light deeply re-

flected in its delicate, complicated panorama of reflections. But more than this, perhaps, was a kind of wonderful aura he crazily thought he might grasp out of the very air next to the tree—its calmness, its serenity before which they had all lost their cruelty—and bring this in his arms to Peggy. But then everything turned into slow motion; their horrified faces passed his dazed regard as slowly as great masses gather momentum. He had stepped on the cat, whose scream contained all kinds of judgments and bad information. He stepped off the cat into what seemed to be a slow yet irresistible wind. Their faces turned like moons, like the Herpes watching his total responsibility. He could make no explanations. His next step would, he realized, be upon a green-wrapped box he happened to know contained a present for his mother—a fragile lamp for her sewing table. So he did not take that step, and the wind, or whatever force it was, moved him toward the tree. Branches delicately touched his cheeks; lights and the glowing balls, icicles and strings of tinsel moved like galaxies toward and past his still wondering eyes as he passed remorselessly out of the room and into nightmare, the final, totally familiar crash and glassbreak of disaster.

Later, after Horace's groaning cries had stopped, the tree had been set straight again and the broken decorations picked up and swept up, they all sat quietly and listened to carols. Henrietta had her arm around Horace, and quieted him. Harvey searched for a way to make it less than it was, but could find no way to make it funny and small. The boy's sheer terror had even frightened him, and his first ironic comment now echoed cruelly in his ears. "God bless us, every one!" he'd said in the first shocked silence before Horace bawled.

Peggy sat on the other side of Horace and held his hand. David and Kate still looked rather stunned.

> Silent night, holy night,
> All is calm, all is bright . . .

the radio voices sang. After a while Kate made hot chocolate, and the disaster faded into less than tragedy. After a long time,

when Horace was even seen to smile, all their faces instantly imitated his.

There were few memories of Christmases, just memories of Christmas. In the Whipples' castle the great tree of one year faded into all the trees of all the years. But they would remember more clearly than most the Christmas Horace fell into the tree. The snow would stop, the roads would open out again from their house and from Leah, and the colors of Christmas, its familiar intimacies, its quality of truce, would change into the celebration of someone's return. In their memories this would be the last real Christmas of childhood.

PART II

Amerika, du hast es besser
Als unser Continent, das alte,
Hast keine verfallene Schlösser
Und keine Basalte.

Goethe: "Den Vereinigten Staaten"

13

Harvey learned in February that one of his out-of-town clients was planning to set up a new metal-working plant in Leah which would train and employ over two hundred workers. This, he foresaw, would change the whole economy of the town, and immediately he began to consider ways in which he might turn this development to his own profit. The factory was going to take over the complex of brick buildings that had been the home of the long defunct Leah Woolen Mills, and within walking distance was a large wooden tenement that had long been half-heartedly for sale. Of its nine apartments, four were vacant, and the others now rented for twelve dollars a month. The asking price was $8,500. Taxes on the building were at present $250 per year. With the advent of the factory and its wartime salaries, he figured he could rent eight of the apartments for $60 and give the other rent-free to a part-time janitor. This would give him an immediate return of $480 per month on an investment of $8,500, plus an outlay of $1,500 for needed repairs, which would constitute the down payment on the loan. Five-percent interest on $8,500 would amount to $425 per year. Say the total amount of his investment was $10,000—$8,500 of which he'd borrow from the Leah Savings Bank. His yearly income from rents would be $5,760. Deducting interest on the loan ($425), oil, electricity and water (about $480), taxes ($250), insurance and repairs, he'd make at least $3,000 to $4,000 a year, if he counted equity, on an initial cash investment of $1,500.

At first he thought of selling some common stocks and not dealing with the bank, but this would lose him 1 to 1½ percent in earnings. Gordon Ward, Sr., was, in dealings such as this, a fairly honest and very reasonable fellow, so he went ahead through Gordon's bank. The owner of the building was a rather senile old Jew who lived in Summersville and came to Leah once a month to collect his rents and have a shouting fit—his standard reaction to complaints about disrepair. Harvey knew most of this because he'd carried the insurance on the building for years.

Even if he could rent the apartments for only $50, or $45, he'd still be making money. Lots of money. In fact, there was another tenement nearby in better repair and thus more expensive, that he'd also decided to look into.

"Nothing ventured, nothing gained," he said thoughtfully. In a little while he got into the habit of saying this. He would hear the words echoing in his mind, just after having said them unconsciously. "Nothing ventured, nothing gained." In theory, at least, it seemed quite a good way to begin to get rich.

On Monday, March 15, Wood reported to Grenier Field, Manchester, New Hampshire, for his preinduction physical. His blood, bones, joints, heart, sight and hearing all seemed to be in order, and upon his avowal that sexually, he liked girls not boys, he passed. He was then directed to report to the Reception Center at Fort Devens, Massachusetts, for classification and assignment in fifteen days, on Tuesday, March 30, 1943. Transportation coupons were provided.

When Wood left on the Peanut for Manchester and his preinduction examinations, Horace began to believe that he might actually go away from their house and away from Leah. Horace couldn't go to the station with him because he had to be in school, and when Wood came back that night, saying that he had passed, Horace began to count the days. Fifteen days seemed at first a

long time. He couldn't divide it into weeks because it was longer than two weeks.

At dinner his father turned to Wood and said, "So he's going to be a doughboy."

Wood frowned slightly and nodded.

"They don't call them doughboys," David said. "They call them GIs now. 'Government Issue.'"

"Government Issue," Horace's father said. "The government issues about everything these days." He thought for a moment. "Well, it's a hell of a war, I'll say that." There seemed to be some grudging admiration in his voice. Usually he got impatient and even angry if anyone brought up the war.

"I don't want to talk about it!" Henrietta said.

"It's not something I want to do," Wood said. "I *have* to do it. Everybody has to do it."

"We can't lose the war," David said.

"I suppose you'll be wanting to go, next," Harvey said, looking straight at David. David shrugged proudly.

"You would," Harvey said. "I can see that."

They sat around the big table for a while after they were through eating. No one knew exactly what to say, but no one got up. It would be like leaving Wood to the war, now that he had to go. It was like a farewell party, or ceremony. Their regard of Wood chilled Horace, and went to prove that soon Wood would not be there.

Kate brought more coffee to her father and mother and Wood, and sat down again herself. She said to Wood in a low voice, "We'll miss you, Wood. We really will."

"Why shouldn't you?" Henrietta said.

"I didn't say we wouldn't!" Kate said, nearly crying.

"All right. All right," Henrietta said, patting Kate's shoulder.

Harvey suddenly rolled his chair back from the table, his white balloon face quivering from the effort. He snorted, swung his chair around and wheeled himself out into the living room. No one followed.

"David," Wood said. "You're going to have to take over the furnace altogether."

David groaned. "Until next fall, anyway," he said, and they all looked at Horace.

No, Horace thought. Impossible. Didn't they realize that he could hardly sleep? His head began to move from side to side. No, he was saying to them. Couldn't they see that he could not go alone into the cellar? He was afraid in the cellar even with Wood next to him. Even Wood couldn't surround him and protect him down there; one side was always exposed.

"We won't talk about that now," Henrietta said firmly.

Peggy, who hadn't said a word, although Horace had seen her not look at Wood when she wanted to, got up with Kate to take out the dishes.

Horace went into the living room and sat looking at *Life* for a long time, but just at one or two pages about the scientific explanation of radar, which could look through clouds and darkness. He was afraid to turn the pages indiscriminately and come upon the war and all the dead men. He was merely staring when Peggy came back. Her hand was soaked and spongy from dishwater, and when it touched his he looked up into her dark, skinny little face.

"Horace? If I'm still here I'll take care of the furnace," she said. She knelt down on one knee beside his chair.

He stared at her face. Her eyes were nearly black, they were such a dark brown—almost olive too. The lines of iris radiated out like the deep lines in agate. Her skin darkened where it folded around her eyelids, and each lash was a curved prong.

"I'm twice as big as you!" he said, and ducked slightly when his father stirred and for a moment looked around.

"It's all right," she said.

"You don't have to do it," he said.

"I didn't say I had to."

"Maybe I'll get so I can do it," he said, not believing this at all.

"Don't worry about it, though. All right?" Her little bony shoulders rose and then sank as she got up. The bones showed though the old red dress of Kate's that was still too big for Peggy, because her shoulders didn't come out wide enough to blend into the shoulder padding. The color of the dress was too bright for her, and unless he looked closely and deliberately at her face itself—at its little parts that made up its expressions—all he saw

was a dim presence behind the flash of red. But then he would look, and it was Peggy looking back at him.

His mother came in and asked him if he'd done his homework, but of course he had, in study hall. It kept him out of trouble in school to do his homework with complete concentration. Sometimes they forgot him, and didn't shoot him with rubber bands, or say anything about him. He couldn't hear them sometimes, and they forgot him.

Peggy had gone, and so had Wood and David and Kate, to the rooms that were theirs, where they wanted sometimes to be alone. He sat with his mother and father while they both read and the fire died down. He should have been in his room too, but it wasn't his room. Last night he had been badly scared. He hadn't slept well at all, and this night would probably be the same.

At ten o'clock he had to go to his room. Each step up the wide staircase was away from safety until he was halfway, and then it was toward safety again as he came near Wood's door—but that was a false safety now, like a warm, safe station a train had to pass, the warm lights receding in the night, because Wood had gone to bed. No light touched the carpet fuzz beneath Wood's door, so he had to proceed toward the black door of his room. He had left a light on, to make it a little easier, but he still had to open the door upon what might be inside. At the door he grunted and stumbled purposely, coughed and brushed the door with his elbow and sleeve to give them warning, to plead with them by this warning not to show themselves.

The next evening Lois Potter called Wood on the telephone and told him she'd heard. He could tell by the breath in her voice that she was very nervous. After all, he should have been the one to have told her. He could almost feel her breath moving against his ear, as though her mouth were right there.

"I knew you'd have to go," she said. "I knew there wasn't anything wrong with you, Wood."

"I guess not," he said, and then added, with some feeling of duty, "What are you doing? Anything?"

"Not a thing."

"I'll pick you up and we'll have a Coke," he said.

It was a cold, damp March night, the kind that felt colder than the coldest night in February. He shivered as he left the house and turned down High Street; his body felt tender and shockable. Even when he'd walked all the way to her house he was still a little chilly and sweaty. She was ready, and after he'd said hello to her father and mother, who didn't quite know whether to congratulate him or to commiserate with him, he and Lois went downstreet toward Trask's Pharmacy. She took his hand in her mittened one.

"When do you have to go? My spies didn't tell me that."

"In about two weeks."

"Oh!" She stopped suddenly and looked up at him. The knit tassel on her hat bounced, and her eyes glittered out of their shadows. "Two weeks! I thought they gave you thirty days, or something like that!"

"Well, I don't have many affairs to settle," he said.

"Affairs to settle," she said. "Are we an affair?"

"Not precisely," he said, and smiled down at her. She wouldn't turn to walk again, so he took her shoulders and turned her around toward the square. As they began to walk she took his arm in both her hands and pulled it against her.

"I know you don't like this—to walk this way," she said, "but I don't care any more. I've got to feel you." They walked along, somewhat awkwardly, and she said in a low voice, as if to herself, "We could be. We could be an affair." He was meant to hear it, however.

The first show hadn't let out yet, and no one was in Trask's except a couple of older people waiting at the prescription counter. Prudence got them their Cokes and sat down across from them.

"He's going in two weeks," Lois said.

"Oh!" Prudence said, her face turning sad. She was a very smart, handsome girl with straight lines and definite curves to all her features, and her sad expression seemed almost statuelike and sorrowful.

"Have you heard from John?" Lois asked.

"We had a letter last week, but he never says much. We're not even sure where he is. He says he's fine, but mother's upset about him all the time." Prudence sighed, and looked tired. She

put her hands on her thick auburn hair, cupping the rolled fringes above her shoulders as though to fold them into neater rolls. It occurred to Wood that it was strange she never went out with boys, but perhaps the answer was her rather statuesque, forbidding handsomeness. She had a strong, firm chin, and seemed much older than she was, although her skin was perfectly clear and her green eyes were kind and unforbidding. She seemed bigger than she was; in school plays she had always been somebody's mother.

Soon the first show let out at the Strand, and people they knew began to come in. Donald Ramsey came in with Marilyn Jackson, who had evidently forgiven him for his part in the Susie Davis affair. He was one of Gordon Ward's buddies, and had been in Wood's class until he stayed behind a year. He generally tried to keep up Gordon's old noise—the codelike words and the knowing yelps—but he was only an imitation. Whenever he laughed now he seemed a little lonely. Marilyn had fierce little brown eyes that always seemed to be looking for offense or triumph, and missed nothing.

Shortly after them, Keith Joubert, who was David's age, and a bully, came in by himself and sat at the counter. He was a rather stupid boy who said very little when alone, but in combination with others he could be extremely nasty. He had always been one of Horace's tormentors. He didn't take off his fingertip coat, but sat hunched up in order to make his shoulders look bigger. His blue gabardine pants were more than a little pegged, and lately his group affected jive talk. They were hepcats, and used words like "drape," "cape," and "lockit at the pockit"—these referred to clothes. Shoes were "garboes."

Others came in, and someone played "Praise the Lord and Pass the Ammunition" on the jukebox. Beneath that lively noise everyone seemed strangely hunched and secretive, too well aware of everyone else. Donald Ramsey, especially, seemed restless, as though he waited for a clue.

Beady Palmer came in and sat down by himself at the counter without seeming to see anyone. He would have preferred Futzie's Tavern, but he hadn't quite turned twenty-one yet, and Futzie had found out about it, so he had been banished. He and Wood had long ago made up their quarrel, but in Beady Wood still felt some reserve, and he suspected that Beady could not quite forgive

himself for having said what he had said. At work he never kidded Wood any more about girls, and there was a reserve that amounted to equality between them. Once Wood asked him why he never saw him out with his wife, and Beady said, "She's got three to take care of now, and another thing is she's knocked up higher than a kite." This seemed a strange thing to say about one's own wife—almost as though Beady had acknowledged Wood to be in some kind of league with him against women, and with these words had offered him something too intimate.

When Prudence served Beady his frappe he smiled at her with his head tilted. Wood was sure he hadn't asked Prudence his usual question.

"Well," Lois said, "your girl friend's here—didn't you see her?"

"Who?" Confused by her tone of voice, he looked around. He hadn't the slightest idea what she meant, and this was a strange thing to him. Then, behind the candy-display case, where one seat of a booth was partly hidden by the Fanny Farmer boxes, where the aisle at the rear was enclosed by another case displaying film and Brownie cameras, dark eyes were looking at him. It was Susie Davis, who looked at him with no recognition. Evidently his perplexed frown had caught her, and in that blank moment she stared past him and then turned her eyes back down. She sat alone. As she bent her head to her straw he saw only the blue babushka and her pale forehead. She didn't look up again, and he couldn't now signify that he had recognized her. It seemed a cold, inhuman moment, somehow typical of Leah. There was no ease, no freedom, only the short embarrassments of petty history.

But with Lois there, his loyalty was divided. One or the other must be hurt if he was kind, or simply real. As he turned back to Lois he detested himself for not knowing what to do. It seemed too large a problem for him, and it seemed so petty and stupid he felt himself shrinking, wrinkling somewhere inside.

Lois frowned unhappily. "What's the matter?" she asked him. "Wood?"

"Nothing," he said, and so she was quiet.

Bob Contois and Bruce Cotter came in. Bruce was short, dark and permanently cynical. He was rumored to be 4-F for some reason no one was sure about, and now he worked in his

father's lumberyard. He was one of the few who had a car, and for this reason he was fairly popular.

Foster Greenwood and Jean Welch came in after them. That is, Foster came to the door and saw who was there, then Jean appeared beside him, seeming to hide in his tall shadow as they went to the back and found one of the narrow booths. Foster's long legs would have to stick out into the aisle from that narrow place. Jean had not been made pregnant by what Foster called "that accident" at Lois' house. But he'd also told Wood that she wouldn't ever let him do it again. "Anyway," he'd said, "I've got something to remember when I jerk off."

Then Michael Spinelli came in with Carol Oakes. They were both in David's class. Mike was obviously proud, and a little awed by, his date with the class glamour girl. He was laughing as they came in—the first real laughter Wood had heard in that somber company. But Mike Spinelli laughed at anything. Carol smiled dimly and with care steered her large breasts toward the small table Mike selected in the middle of the store, then lowered herself undulantly onto the wire-backed chair, as though she were more than aware of the treasures she carried in breast and hip and thigh. Most faces turned toward her and then glanced away, dreamy and somewhat stunned behind facades of indifference, even of truculence.

The jukebox played "Der Führer's Face," and "Scatterbrain," then "Bei mir bist du schön," and those who spoke seemed secretive. Lois had been telling him in a carefully low voice about going to college, what she thought it would be like. Because she knew really nothing about what it would be like, and knew he didn't either, her questions began "I wonder . . ." and "Do you suppose . . . ?" She wasn't really interested, so he didn't have to think of answers.

The silence changed. That is, it seemed even amid the noise of the jukebox to have been a silence, almost a silence of intent among all the words they had all been speaking to each other. Bruce Cotter had gone over to Susie's booth. He bent over and spoke to her, and everyone turned around to look. Wood turned back quickly, seeing all those interested faces.

When the jukebox stopped playing they heard Susie's voice —polite, almost friendly. "No thanks, I don't want a ride home."

The faces, weighted with the one idea, turned away. Marilyn Jackson's sharp brown eye gleamed almost black, and Wood had the hallucinatory feeling that he could see images in her very mind. Donald's parts—he thought he saw that kind of mechanical awareness in her bright and practical eyes—shoved deep and against that creamy and alien girl. Marilyn's finger actually trembled as she took her straw in finger and thumb. Donald, enjoying both his reputation and Marilyn's knowledge, and also, Wood thought, Marilyn's capitulation, seemed pleased, although he didn't actually grin. He hadn't that much power over Marilyn yet. And Wood knew he would never have it, either. She was seventeen, Donald was eighteen, and Wood seemed to see with great weariness a relationship, going on and on through the years, of attempted domination, really of hatred. Why did she want to marry a boy so much less intelligent than herself? Whatever charm he had now in his exuberant youth would quickly fade when he had to produce something for the world. Then she would have him impaled by his own mediocrity, and maybe that was what those bright brown eyes wanted ever after to have done.

There seemed a tenseness emanating from Susie's corner, though the observing eyes were shy. Wood turned around, and as his head turned he found Bob Contois' eye upon him. *Keep out of it*, Bob seemed to say. Bruce had sat himself down across from Susie, and spoke now in a soft, private voice. "Oh, come on, Susie." Wood heard, and turned back.

Lois was caught staring at him—a hard look that made him think vaguely of Marilyn Jackson.

"Is it any of your business?" she said.

He wondered if it was.

"After all," Lois said coldly, "she does, doesn't she?"

He thought of asking Lois in a stern voice what exactly it was Susie did, but felt that would be unkind. No, not really; it would involve him with Lois too deeply in that question.

"She does it for boys," Lois said, conscious of her cruel words; she blushed a little.

"You don't know the whole story," he said.

"You mean how many?"

"Lois."

"Look," she said, "I can't lose any more pride with you.

What difference does it make what I say?" She made a noise like "urrr!" clenched her fists on the table and put her forehead down on them.

"No, thank you," Susie said again, just before the jukebox played and covered whatever else she and Bruce were saying. She had sounded firm, but she also sounded pleased, somehow, by Bruce Cotter's attention.

He wanted to protect Susie from her own loneliness, but that was impossible, because he could offer no alternative except himself, and that he wouldn't give. And he saw that his relationship with Lois was much the same. He would take no gifts because he could not deserve them. He wanted them, though. Sometimes he could think of neither Susie nor Lois except in postures of submission to him. Lace, silk, fresh skin of thigh and the tenderness of their acceptance. Didn't they know what a bad bargain that would be? They both seemed so childlike and defenseless, even suicidal in their generosity. They would give him everything, even in the knowledge that he was not ready to protect or support them. He seemed to see this irresponsibility everywhere; everyone he knew seemed in one way or another as essentially irresponsible as the two girls.

Lois raised her head and looked at him for a long time. "Are you going to marry me?" she said, finally.

"Lois," he said.

"Answer the question." Her mouth turned hard, and she trembled as if she were very much afraid of her recklessness.

"I don't know the answer," he said, recognizing in his voice a weariness that must have hurt her.

"Why are you so worried about Susie Davis?"

"I think she's a nice girl. She's been kind to Horace, for one thing." Into his voice crept force, which he couldn't stop. "And just because that cruel son of a bitch Gordon Ward raped her doesn't mean she's fair game for every horny little bastard in town. Do you see what I mean now?"

He had never spoken to her that way before, and her reaction surprised him. Her eyes glowed at him with pride, and she took his hands in hers. A little half-smile appeared on her lips for a moment. Then she turned sad again.

"You're always protecting somebody," she said. "You even

protect me. The only reason you came to get me tonight was to protect me, wasn't it?"

"No."

"Yes it was. You knew I'd be unhappy if I didn't see you, so you came."

"But I like to see you," he said.

"I'd let you do more than look. I'd let you see me all over." She blushed and looked away.

"Wait till I come back," he said.

"There's nothing else I can do," she said. "Is there? Is there anything else I can do? You'll just tell me I'm only seventeen. Only seventeen! How long am I supposed to wait? There's the boy I love, and he's alive and warm, and I'm alive and warm, and I don't want to wait for anything." She spoke in a low, intense voice, with her head down, hiding herself and her words from all the other people.

"Let's get out of here," he said, and reached for her coat. Obediently she slid out of the booth, though she was still dark with embarrassment. He helped her on with her coat, and she went to say hello to Foster and Jean. As he put on his coat he nodded to Foster, then turned toward Susie. He couldn't go to her booth because that would have been considered a flagrant insult to Lois, who was "pure." Even if Lois understood his reasons, she could not avoid being hurt by the opinions of the others. It was a stupid and inflexible rule.

Susie wouldn't let him catch her eye, but as he looked at her, her face grew sad. She muttered an answer to Bruce Cotter's question, and shook her head again and again. She had been smiling, but now she didn't smile. Then she turned and looked straight at Wood and away, so quickly he hadn't time to signal his recognition. But that look stayed with him for days, like an image cast into his optic nerves, so that he saw it sometimes reversed, like a negative in which Susie's hurt face was black, her eyes in that darkness gleaming white and blind as pearls.

14

The night before Wood left, Horace began to tremble so violently at dinner he had to excuse himself from the table. They were having meat that night too—pot roast, which he liked—and yet he had to go upstairs and be sick. He came back down and sat shivering in front of the fire while the rest finished dinner. Wood wasn't home—he was having dinner at the Potters'.

Kate came out of the dining room first, pulled up another wicker stool and sat beside him. "Are you okay now, Horsie?" she said. "Did you have to vomit?"

"Yes," he said. He could taste it, like a mouthful of cold metal.

"Ugh! I hate to vomit," she said, and took hold of his arm. "I hope you feel better now."

"Yeah," he said. She was small, though not so small as Peggy, yet she looked everything in the eye, like David. How could they be curious about what peered back at them?

"Is it Wood going?" she asked.

"I don't know," he said.

The fire warmed him on one side, but on his back a chill patch of sweat sucked cold into his skin. Flames quietly looped up around a maple log.

When the rest came in he went upstairs and entered Wood's room. This was against a rule they had made long ago about each other's rooms, but he remembered Wood's offer to exchange rooms, and this was his excuse. He had decided not to take Wood's offer; that would have been horrible, because then Wood's presence would be truly gone. He wanted the warm room to remain exactly as it was, smelling of Wood's pipes and tobacco. The air-

planes were already gone, but the pictures, the leather chair, the lamps and desk would remain. And Wood's clothes would still hang in the closet; his boots and shoes and his pack frame and canvas pack bag would still be there. The mounted brook trout would still stiffly arch upon the birch plaque. His scouting sash with all the merit badges would still hang on its peg, with the fishing rods horizontally across the top of the peg rack. All these things were perfectly Wood's, and he had used them and controlled them with his authority. His old pump shotgun stood in the corner, and even that weapon in Wood's control seemed a just power.

Yet how could anyone desire to own the agent of such power? Didn't it come anyway, unbidden, from the dark fissures that were everywhere? If he could see in his mind the Herpes tear the living skin from a puppy, wasn't he himself tearing the skin from that poor little animal? And if the monsters of his brain grew so powerful they owned his very room, wasn't that his doing? David, and even Wood, owned weapons that killed; didn't they then kill, maim, cause horrible pain, even when they merely fondled the black guns? No, maybe not really, but they did shoot and they did kill, because they wanted to. Even in Wood was that black desire.

The room was growing cold. Without permission he lit the fire Wood had prepared, and pulled the leather chair up closer to the fireplace. As the kindling blazed up and the hardwood sticks began to catch, he stretched out his legs and grew drowsy and numb. The desk lamp glowed warm orange over Wood's pipe rack and blotter and chair back. With the warm noises of the fire, Wood almost seemed to be somewhere in the room. He was coming; he would be home sooner or later, and this warm knowledge seeped into Horace's muscles and blood. He breathed easily, letting Wood's warmth fill all the spaces in him and around him.

At ten-thirty Wood left the Potters' and walked home through the melting night. Mr. and Mrs. Potter had been so proud of him, so solicitous, so sad and curious about his leaving for the Army, he had very little he could say at dinner. What could he say, anyway? He hadn't been in the Army yet, knew nothing about it except through hearsay, and most of that information had struck

him with the tinny sound of exaggeration. At the door Lois held onto him and cried a little, saying she would wait for him forever. He told her not to skip school in order to see him off on the train —an interruption of her vows he half meant to be cruel. Not cruel, really, but a sort of awakening of common sense. He had three or four months of training ahead of him, and he'd be back on furlough before going overseas. But her tears were real, and he experienced his usual mixture of pity and self-disgust. Lois wanted so badly to make him do something that would commit him irrevocably to her. She wanted this in all ways, and could barely keep from making sexual, copulatory motions against him as they'd stood in the foyer. Without motion at all, it was as though he felt the little nerve signals start through her body and then stop, waylayed by her embarrassment and restraint. As they'd kissed for the last time, her lips were soft, as they always were when she was near to crying. "I love you too," he'd said.

Now he felt free, relieved to be singular in the warm March night. Only a crusty fringe of damp snow—now really corned into soiled ice crystals—remained in certain depressions or behind houses and bushes. He smelled earth, strong for the first time.

"How were the Potters?" his mother asked when he got home. She and his father were alone in the living room, and they both looked at him closely. He didn't look directly at his father, but felt the dark eyes in the pale fat.

"Fine," he said. "They're all fine."

His father still looked at him, and he turned toward the wheelchair to acknowledge this attention.

"Have a drink," his father said, the moon face struggling against all past animosities. Could he smile back at his father, he wondered? They ought to try—he ought to try.

"Sure," he said, noticing exactly the tonal break of his false eagerness.

"Good. Get yourself some ice and a glass." This time his father did more successfully look pleased; Wood's counterfeit had been good enough. He went out to get a glass and some ice. "Get me some ice, too!" his father called.

"Okay," he answered. If they were to talk, they must use words constricted by their real voices. But it would be an attempt, at least.

When he came back from the kitchen his father said "Thanks," and he said "You're welcome," and sat where his father could see him. His mother looked up from her book, glanced from one to the other through her thick lenses, then turned back to her book.

"The nearest I ever got to the Army was R.O.T.C. in college," his father said.

An unanswerable statement.

"Well, I'll find out what it's like, I guess," Wood said.

"And you're on your way tomorrow."

"Yup."

They drank, saying other things Wood could not remember afterwards, because what they said were only those unrelated statements that are consciously composed. At eleven-thirty they said good night to each other like polite strangers. They did seem to be nothing but strangers, while they were polite. Only when they were saying unforgivable things to each other were they not. And Wood thought, of all the people he knew, his father was the strongest, the one who never asked him, even in the most hidden way, for guidance.

The light was on in his room, and Horace was asleep in the chair before a nearly dead fire, shivering in his sleep. Wood stood looking down at his unfortunate brother, at the coarse blond hair and the thick shoulders of the boy. Horace shivered and whimpered, his long legs drawn up against his body until he seemed to be crouched and hiding in the chair, yet his arms fell slackly and helplessly over the arms, palms up. The thick skin of his forehead was damp. Again his lip quivered in a silent whimper. His glasses had fallen off, and Wood picked them up and put them in his desk. He put some kindling on the fire, fanned it to make it flame up quickly, then got his old storm coat out of the closet and put it over Horace. Horace skipped a breath in his sleep.

Wood sat at his desk and filled a pipe. Horace still slept, but as the coat warmed him his face turned slack, and his legs slowly stretched out again. Wood decided to let him sleep awhile; he looked absolutely exhausted. As long as Horace slept, a shaming voice told him, he wouldn't have to face those problems of Horace's that had no solution. Horace was afraid of darkness, still air, and surrounded places—the ordinary hollows all men had to live in. He was afraid of what might wait around corners and

behind doors. The boy's whole world was turned inside out, because the walls and gates men made to protect themselves from the wild were to Horace the places where all horrors lived. But it wasn't really men that Horace feared, if Wood understood him, it was the creatures he imagined, as though he had abstracted what was evil in man, and made fleshed creatures out of qualities. He had even heard Horace mutter names, weird names for these creatures.

But he wondered why Horace found it necessary to make this substitution; certainly he had never found it necessary. Last night he'd been looking at an old *American Mercury*, the October issue, and in it he found this item:

QUESTION

I.H. writes: A. contends that the period of pregnancy in a Japanese woman is six months. B. says all races are alike —even the Nips. Who is right?

ANSWER

B. In spite of evidence to the contrary, the Japs belong to the human race and the gestation period is 280 days.

What evidence to the contrary? he had immediately asked himself. Just because they enjoyed rapine and, say, burying people alive, or placing a pistol to the back of a bound prisoner's head, as he'd seen in the newsreels, and touching off a round?

Beady had asked him the other day "What is mung?" and explained: "You take an eight-month-pregnant Jap, tie its legs together and get four husky buck niggers to beat it on the belly with baseball bats for five hours. Untie the rope and what comes out is mung."

Yet there were those prints of Sally's, by Hiroshige, and by others whose names he had forgotten, but had known so well in childhood. Those misty landscapes had taken him in, and even now they reminded him of childhood, order and nostalgia. Would he march across those graceful, moonlike bridges, through that mist? Dreamlike, he would fight in Sally's parlor, fading through mossy green and the deep veiled blues of air and delicate mountains. Then would come the sudden bite of gunfire. Planes would roar across that air, smelling of cordite and gasoline. He could

hardly believe it—as though Eddie Kusacs, who occasionally buzzed Leah in his Marine F4U Corsair, roared through Sally's parlor and set the china and silver rattling in their shelves, and the *kakemono* shaking on the walls.

First was the terror, as if he had been led into a trap, and awaited ambush. Horace didn't move; not even a finger. He looked out of his head through slits, his eyelashes down upon his hiding eyes like brush. No, he was in Wood's room, which was illegal, but a safe place. A scrape and a creak—what was that noise?

Then Wood's back obscured the fire as he bent to poke it. Wood was there, and he was safe. Someone had put a warm coat over him, and it must have been Wood. Wood had taken his storm coat and put it over him to keep him warm, and now his muscles fell loose, and he relaxed all over. His skin tingled with a great lazy feeling near to pain. He almost didn't have to pretend to be asleep, because he had no need at all to move. Even to open his eyes further—a fraction of a millimeter further—would have been an effort of delicious pain. He lay warm, descending not into sleep but into utter safety. The fire pressed gently against his face, and his legs seemed to glow in it below the storm coat. His hands lay wide apart down somewhere toward the floor, but he didn't care because no matter how extreme their positions, even with palms open, they were safe now.

He would not think, he would just feel, as though he were a baby again. He was a baby that was warm and could not fall—the center of gravity where there was no gravity, the center of the world where there was no weather, the center of all of the world's love and attention where there was no fear. He could not afford to waste such time in sleep.

Wood was aware that Horace was not asleep. Because he seemed to be resting, he let him hide his consciousness for a long time. But it was getting late, and Horace had to go to school tomorrow. "Horace?" he said.

"Yes?" Horace said immediately.

"It's getting pretty late."

"You're not mad at me for being here?"

"No."

Then an expression of anguish flashed across Horace's face and was gone. His face regained its usual guarded, almost beaten look, as if he were about to duck.

"You're going away tomorrow," Horace said, his voice thick.

"I'll write you letters," Wood said. "Would you like that?"

Horace shrugged off the letters. "Sure," he said.

"You know I've got to go," Wood said. "The war won't last forever, Horace. I'll be back. Besides, I'll be home on furlough after basic training." That's what he had told Lois, and his mother. It hadn't seemed to reassure anyone very much, but it was all he could think of to say. The reason he was being drafted was, presumably, to have him shoot enemy soldiers—who could shoot back —and somebody was bound to get killed.

Horace began to tremble, and his forehead was wet. That was fear; Wood knew he was looking at fear, at the pallor of it. The boy's face had turned leaden, as though he were suffering from shock. "Oh, oh," Horace said. "I'm shivering."

"Are you all right, Horace?"

"You can't go," Horace said. "You'll have to tell them."

"Horace?"

"You can tell them," Horace said in the higher register of his changing voice. "It's out of the question."

"I'm afraid it isn't out of the question, Horace." Wood smiled, but he was worried by the certainty he heard in that childish voice. Horace's blond bristles were so thick, his starved skin so tough yet defenseless. A victim, Wood thought; that skin was meant to be hurt. There was the long scar above his ear, that had taken fourteen stitches. A bicycle accident. That was the time he'd come down Pike Hill and his coaster brake burned out. He'd dislocated or cracked his shoulder then too and had to walk around for weeks with a wooden flying buttress coming from his waist to hold his arm out at the right angle. He'd crossed the Jenkins' lawn, hit their decorative windmill and demolished it. Scars upon scars. He would never, never understand why Horace was so foolhardy about what was real, and so frightened of what was not.

"Don't be silly, now, Horace. You know I've got to go. I've been drafted. We've been through all this before."

"I've tried everything," Horace said desperately. "Wood, I've *tried*. Everything you told me. But nothing works. I can't stand it!" Crying sounds came through his words.

"Come on, now," Wood said.

"I don't care any more because why should I care? I'm going to die anyway. I know it. I almost died already."

"Horace, for God's sake," he said, trying to sound calm.

Horace seemed to be in a state of rebellion now; prideless, with no dignity, what had he left to lose?

"I don't care!" Horace cried. "I can't help myself any more! I can't even remember all their rules!"

"Whose rules?"

"Their rules! Them!" Horace looked ravaged. His big lips were gummy, and a patch of watery snot shone below his nostrils. "You've never laughed at me before!"

"I'm not now. I'm not laughing at you, Horace."

"I'm dead."

"No, you're not."

"I'm as good as dead! They aren't kidding!" Horace stuttered and hiccuped. A thin whine underlay his breath.

"You've got Mother and Father to take care of you."

"They threw me away! They couldn't stand to look at me!"

"That's not true. You know very well that Mother and Father love you."

"You don't know! I'm just a *bother!*"

Wood thought of the little boy he'd known once, whose escapades were sometimes serious, sometimes funny. Now, in this new growth, with Horace nearly as big as he was, there was no possible lightness at all. A man agonized in that chair, and the ghosts of childhood were still in control.

Madness, of course. It was madness, yet Horace had always been reasonable. Wood had always been able to speak to reason in Horace, no matter how upset he was. Reason was there, and intelligence, no matter how small a flicker of it his fear allowed him to show.

With the word he felt anger toward Horace's monsters. If only they were real, he would smash them. If they were flesh and

blood, like Gordon Ward and his satellites, he would take care of them, just as he had effectively ended that sort of torment by dealing with Junior Stevens. If only he could corner them as he had cornered Junior in the basement of the Community Building. There, in his wrath, he'd made Junior afraid for his life—an emotion Junior had never experienced before. If only he could exorcise these monsters as easily . . .

Horace's red hand had moved, quick as a boxer's, and closed on Wood's wrist. "*Please* don't go, Wood!"

"Horace!"

"If you go I can't stand it! It's only you that keeps me!"

"Come on, Horace. Be reasonable."

"*Please!*"

"Horace. You know I have to go tomorrow. If I don't go they'll come and get me. I'm not a civilian any more. I can't go where I please and do what I please. You know that, don't you?"

"*Please!*"

The big hand had locked on. Wood felt the tingle of constriction in his fingers. He put his other hand on Horace's, first as a calming gesture, then to try to peel those thick fingers from his painful wrist.

"Horace, let go of my arm," he said. Then he looked at Horace's face and found no sign of reason. There was the flesh in the shape of a face—pores, mucous membrane, eyes that now seemed opaque. Now, for any gleam of recognition, it might have been the face of a horse, or a pig.

"Let go!" he said to that dense flesh. "Let go of my arm!"

No response, not even a tightening of the hand to show defiance of the order. He tried to pry Horace's fingers from his wrist, and though he was strong enough to do it, Horace's strength was unnatural. He was afraid he might break the fingers. They struggled silently. Horace's other hand came over and locked on too, and for an unreal moment it seemed to Wood that he was a spectator at this vicious contest between the wrestling hands.

The hands would not let him go, and suddenly they were every grasping needful human mess that wanted to, and somehow invariably did, lock onto him when he wanted to be free.

"Let *go!*" he said. When he pried two fingers loose, eight

others locked on harder. He could break, disjoint them—and he realized desperately that the only way to get loose was either to immobilize them one by one or to strike at the source of their strength.

"Let go," he said coldly. But the fingers wrapped him with insane strength. He began not to see clearly. The thing that had him would not let go. That force was too strong, and that was the end of it. The last choice had to come, came and was simultaneously acted upon. He hit the face and head of that other, unreasonable force, and each time it was like hammering nailed lumber apart. Little by little the strength ebbed, not in proportion to the force of the blows but, like nails coming out, bending into what held them, holding by their submerged friction until suddenly they let go and he was free. He raised his arms, looking at them free. The blood came back into his hand as it should, so that quickly he felt no more of the constriction or its effects, and he could move his fingers without that consciousness, with no unnatural feeling.

Then he had to turn toward the object he had disarmed, and Horace came back. His face was lumpy and discolored already. A thin line of blood rimmed his lower lip, and his tongue came out and licked it off.

"Horace!" Wood said. Yet he had known it was Horace. He tried to believe he hadn't known in his madness that it was Horace.

Horace stared at him with, it now seemed, the return of comprehension. *So that's how you really feel,* Wood read in that stare. *You too.* Horace got to his feet, and the storm coat fell to the floor. He turned and went out of the room. He'd forgotten his glasses, but he seemed to see all right.

He had the greatest power of anyone in the world to hurt Horace, and he had used it. No crime could be more monstrous than what he'd just done, and now Horace went back to those other monsters, somehow encompassing that betrayal.

But now, below his horror at himself, he felt the shameful symptoms of exultation. He was evil, as evil as any of the rest. Tomorrow he would leave them all to their needs, and from tomorrow on he would never reveal anything to anyone. Susie Davis, Horace, Lois, Beady, Al, Peggy Mudd, his mother, all the rest.

198

They would all be gone out of his regard, and he out of theirs. He would hide now until Leah was gone behind, and from then on he would hide within the business of the war.

15

One end of a small room called the teachers' lounge—a place where Kate had never seen a teacher lounge—had been set aside as *The Quill* office, with an old desk, a typewriter, a tall green filing cabinet and a cork bulletin board. Wayne Facieux had placed the filing cabinet out from the wall so that it formed a room divider. This, he explained, would give the editors of *The Quill* some smattering of privacy in case any teacher ever did have time to come in and lounge. One reason no teacher ever came there, Kate supposed, was that Mr. Skelton's office was right across the hall, and all doors were left open. Two Morris chairs and a maple table surrounded by straight chairs, and several metal ashtrays that stood on their own pedestals, were all the furniture in the lounge part. Long ago, by the looks of them, someone had hung some white faille curtains across the big institutional window at the end, and these looked out of place there, almost like filmy women's clothes. Everything was dusty in this room, and she wondered if it wasn't the pupils themselves, constantly sitting and rubbing and handling all the other furniture and objects in the school, that kept it reasonably dusted. Certainly Mr. Grand, the janitor, could be seen doing little except distributing chalk and erasers and emptying wastebaskets as he walked about with a flickering, hazy sort of smile on his face—this generally attributed to drink. David had shown her an actual revolver he'd bought from Mr. Grand for two dollars and fifty cents when Mr. Grand needed money for his liquor. That's what David had said,

anyway. The revolver was David's secret, and she'd really felt complimented when he confided in her about it.

Mr. Grand never came into the lounge at all, so the editors emptied their wastebasket into Mr. Skelton's secretary's wastebasket. His secretary was Mrs. Jarvis, a great big old lady who was supposed to have been there much longer than Mr. Skelton. When she went home they had to go home too. She would appear in the doorway—mountains and valleys of pleated, tucked and belted cloth, her hair like icy snow way up on top of her head, smile down at them and tell them that their labors in the vineyards of literature must cease for that day. Then, as they put things straight, she locked the principal's office and ushered them out the front door. This always happened about five o'clock, so they had about an hour and a half after school to work on *The Quill.*

Their advisor was Miss Palmer, who thought Wayne was a genius, so she didn't advise much; she mostly said "Oh!" and "Ah!" and "Isn't that beautiful!" Which was good, in a way, because Wayne had changed *The Quill* considerably during his editorship. He was awfully hard on girls who wrote stories about how a fluffy little chick feels when it first pecks its way out of its shell and views the great, wide, wonderful world. He could be positively mean. He'd put Carol Oakes into tears over her poem about the sun falling, falling, to the forest floor. The first thing he'd changed last fall, when he'd become editor in chief, was the cover, which had always had the same drawing of a quill pen on it.

"If we're going to have a silly, stereotyped name like *The Quill,* all we can do is try to use it as best we can," he said. Now his covers were different every issue. His first one was a caricature of a porcupine, and that was the one he was proudest of. The issue they were working on now would have a cover with one big rose on it. "The thorns," Wayne said. "That's our *motif—*beauty with a sting in it."

This afternoon Kate was typing on stencil some of Wayne's poems. She wasn't officially an editor yet, because she wouldn't be in ninth grade until the fall. She had turned fourteen, though, and Wayne called her his "editorial assistant."

Wayne sat across from her with several piles of manuscripts, alternately groaning and sighing judiciously. "My God," he

said, dropping his hand upon a pile of notebook paper. He resumed his reading. "Hmm. Listen to this: 'The sun stank up the sky like a big greasy fried egg.' Hmm. Some talent there. A squeak of talent. That is, providing the inelegance of that simile is altogether deliberate. Hmm."

She thought him handsome. His thin neck rose up out of the large open collar of his white shirt, then widened perceptibly just below his long, aristocratic ears. His dark hair, always worn long, partially covered the bows of his gold-rimmed glasses. Above his forehead, through the heavy dark hair, a narrow streak of white went up and over the top of his head. This was a strange natural mark that distinguished him from everyone else—the reason David and others sometimes called him "Skunkhead."

No one ever picked on Wayne, except to call him insulting names, and she sometimes wondered why they didn't torment him more, because Wayne made no concessions to the way they thought a boy should act. "You are simply being vulgar," he would say to them, give a haughty toss of his head and stride away on some business or other he considered important.

She turned back to her typing.

> Eld, coin-silver, gilt-medallion form,
> The deep fish drops through his fadings
> Down where flesh is wafer to bright
> Teeth . . .

Wayne came around and stood behind her, reading his poem over her shoulder.

"You don't, probably, see an admitted influence here. Gerard Manley Hopkins, to be brutally candid." He put a thin, cool finger through her hair and lightly touched her ear. "Ah, Veronica," he said. Sometimes he told her she looked like Veronica Lake. "No, let's put it this way," he'd said once, "Veronica Lake is privileged to resemble our Kate Whipple."

He drew his finger down to her shoulder, touched her lightly, and abruptly went back to his side of the desk. She shivered. There he sat, once more completely absorbed in his reading. She typed some more.

Waves no more the bright air push;
Hushed in iron deep the bleak teeth
Grind
Upon the needful bodies of the fish.
Oh! Dark Prince of fathoms down!
Where mariners dream from blind
White eyes,
Allow me power to look . . .
And then return!

She shivered again, full of admiration. Wayne's thin wrist and
hand rested across the disordered manuscripts, and his white
skin was clean. But *iron*, she thought, given a dark princely iron
value by the depths of his mind. He seemed ten times stronger
than any other boy. No, he didn't even live in the same world as
they. He was David's age, yet she couldn't conceive of him zoom-
ing around on a bike. He walked, always fast, always intently not
quite there, always unconscious of himself, always with his big
leather briefcase swinging. Sometimes his gestures, even his
walk, were delicately girlish, and when he crossed his legs he
never put his ankle on his knee, but crossed them completely.

Oh! There is fair vision yet
In such rueless dark
Where freak cracked forms must pulse neon
And sign their bones in that bleak dark!
Give me to look!

As far as she could understand it, the poet wanted, in a sort
of gruesomely cruel way, to look straight at a kind of hell. She
thought of poor Horace, who always tried not to look, but was
always finding monsters in every corner. As for herself, she didn't
want to look at such things either, but she wanted to be near
Wayne, and to listen to him. She had a real crush on him, all
right. She felt unworthy, because she couldn't write or say anything half as serious or clever as he could. She knew she was
pretty, but using this seemed the worst sort of cheating, and it
made her even more unworthy. At least she could work hard on
The Quill, and do more typing than any of the other editors.

Carol Oakes was supposed to be an editor, but she never did

anything any more, and Mary Denney ran around a lot, supposedly getting advertisements and looking for new material, but actually the same old advertisements appeared in each issue—Trask's Pharmacy, Trotevale's Department Store, the Thom McAn Shoe Store and the rest.

But even all this extra work was cheating, wasn't it? The only real qualifications one needed for Wayne's company—the company of wit and style and charm—were wit and style and charm. She could make a joke once in a while, but that was about it.

Oh well, back to work. Maybe Wayne would walk her home. If he didn't, she would think of an excuse to walk downstreet with him.

At five Mrs. Jarvis, in her kindly but ponderous fashion, shooed them out of the school. Mary Denney had come in just before, and the three of them stood on the front steps, looking at the four big piles of scrap iron for the war effort—one for each of the senior-high classes. The junior-class pile was much bigger than the others, mainly because of Junior Stevens' grandfather's farm truck, which Junior could drive. Also, Junior seemed to know where every old rusted cultivator or hay rake had been abandoned long ago. If this was a redeeming quality it was Junior's only one. He was a dull brute of a farm boy, and an imitator of Gordon Ward's. Ugh.

It was a warm day, with the new leaves green as lettuce, and the hard rusty iron seemed rather brutal itself the way it was piled among the hedges and young grass.

Without having to give a reason, she began walking downstreet with Mary and Wayne. Mary lived on the way, and she left them where she had to turn off, on Union Street. When they reached the square, Kate remembered that she had no money at all, so she couldn't go to Trask's as an excuse for this walk. She would leave Wayne there at the door to the stairs that led up to the apartments, then merely walk around the square and back home. But when they reached the sidewalk opposite the stairs Wayne said rather offhandedly, "Come up and I'll make you a cup of tea."

She considered this. To go up to the place where he lived. She would see his desk, his room, where he washed his face,

where he slept. Up the dark stairs were those rooms she had never seen.

"All right," she said. She was trembling, and her knees were a little weak as she climbed the long flight of wooden stairs. A smell of varnish and old cooking was in the hall, a smell that seemed as yellowish-brownish as the painted walls and moldings.

Wayne unlocked his door and moved her inside. "Here are our sumptuous quarters," he said. His hand slid around the doorframe and found a wall switch. They had entered a small kitchen-dining room. The overhead-light globe contained two moths and various flies, whose shadows fell upon the maple dinette table, where salt and pepper shakers and a sugar bowl stood centered upon a crocheted mat. Dimly, through a doorway, were the somnolent slits of dropped venetian blinds. The fat curve of an antimacassar predicted an overstuffed chair. The ceilings were very low, and the air was rich with the same varnishy smell of the hall. It all seemed very strange and exotic, and her heart was beating hard.

Wayne pulled out a kitchen chair and waved her to it, then quickly filled a teakettle and put it on the gas stove to boil. "There," he said. "As you can see, the place is sordid. Mother's taste in such matters is not mine, and I await the hour of my escape."

"Your father?" she asked.

"A good question. Yes, there generally is one of them around, isn't there?" He seemed completely unaffected by this question, his face calm. He leaned negligently against the counter. "I can barely remember him. Sometimes I don't think I actually remember him at all. I might be remembering the milkman or some other man who had to come to wherever we were living."

"But where's your mother?" Kate said.

"She works late today."

"Oh." She was alone with him in his apartment, and that was even more exciting.

"In any case, according to my mother he departed without warning. I sometimes wonder if there weren't warnings the poor old girl didn't happen to notice, but that's neither here nor there." He got down a brown teapot and spooned some black tea from a canister.

"We hardly ever have tea at home," she said.

He shrugged and peered at the kettle. "It whistles when the water boils. Come, I'll show you the rest of the place."

The living room, with its low ceiling, was so stuffed with furniture it seemed more a storage place than a room to live in. But she was used to the high ceilings of the castle ("Veronica of the High Castle," he'd called her). The wallpaper was alternate green and white vertical stripes, each about six inches wide, which gave her the feeling of being inside a Christmas box.

They skipped one door that must have been his mother's bedroom, and he opened another door. "My inner sanctum," he said. This room was different. The bed was a mattress that lay right on the floor, although it was neatly made up. Across one wall was a bookcase made of red bricks with boards running across them, and against the opposite wall was a kitchen table obviously used as a desk because there were papers and books and pencils on it. The one picture in the room, she recognized—the yellow-green portrait of a young man by Van Gogh.

"My ivory tower," he said.

In one way, at least, she was sorry for him. He had no friends. But who in Leah would he want for a friend? "Aren't you lonely sometimes?" she asked him.

He looked down at her and smiled benignly. "My feeling is that I'm in prison," he said. "My brain is imprisoned in this . . . adolescent body. At least I know that in two or three years I'll be able to go out of these doldrums into the real world."

"That's what David says!"

"David?" he said with distaste, his lip curling a little bit. "I doubt if we desire admittance to the same world."

"Maybe not," she said. It did seem sometimes that David was only a boy running around with toys, like his guns.

The teakettle in the kitchen began to whistle, so they moved back through the furniture. "That's the bathroom," he said, pointing to another door. "My mother's room is over there, and now you've seen the limits of my cage."

He set the tea to steeping and they sat down.

"I wonder," he said, looking steadily into her eyes. "I wonder if you know what you are."

"What do you mean?" No boy but Wayne, except for David,

maybe, had ever looked her straight in the eyes and spoken calmly.

"You know you're an extremely beautiful girl."

She would have resented that, but the way he said it—so calmly, with no cuteness or false sarcasm—took away her resentment. It was as though he were speaking to her about someone else, or about some objective quality she needn't blush about. He seemed to be inviting her honest opinion.

"All right, yes," she said, but she did blush, and her ears felt warm.

"A gift of the gods," he said. "A gift of the gods." He said this sadly, and rose to get the teacups and saucers from a cupboard. He poured the tea, and offered her sugar from the bowl. Each of his calm gestures seemed stranger and more grown-up than the last.

"There must be something wrong with you," he said. "Isn't there some little defect somewhere?" She thought of the mole down there, and shivered. "You're bright, you're not narcissistic . . ."

"What's that?"

"Narcissus so admired his reflection in the water he fell in and drowned."

"Sometimes I feel like a freak," she said.

"I'd ask you to be proud of it, but that might ruin you, Kate." He stood up. "May I ask you something?"

"Sure."

"It's a favor. Now don't get all worried."

She was, suddenly, frightened, but it was exciting. "What is it?" she said quickly.

"I'd like to comb your hair. Isn't that rather silly. But I'd like very much to comb your hair. I have a beautiful ivory comb. Wait, I'll show it to you." He went through the other room and in a minute came back with a wide yellow comb, very old and crazed with tiny hairlike cracks. One end was a handle, turned and carved with squares and little egg shapes.

"It's so old," she said. He picked it out of her fingers and moved behind her. It occurred to her that she hadn't given him permission. The teeth were like little fingers at first, that didn't seem to pull, but only to smooth. She wondered if he was using the toothed edge at all.

"Ah," he said. She felt him kneel behind her chair. "No, stand up," he said, getting up himself. She obeyed, and he moved her chair away. This time the comb drew deeper. A snarled strand cracked like a small electric shock, so small she wasn't sure she felt at all, it was such a small part of the massive gentle pull of the comb. Her chin rose, and the surface of her throat grew sensitive and at the same time languid. Each hair seemed to go deeper than her scalp. As he parted her hair it was like the cold slit of a knife, or a razor, and then the smoothness again. There was static, but those little snaps were nothing; they were like the tiniest little silverfish in a deep calm river. She loved to have her hair combed, and she began to feel all golden and ivory. The cups of dark tea grew darker, and incredibly round.

"Beautiful," he whispered.

She could so easily forget where she was. She wondered why she didn't simply forget. He seemed to be reaching with each long pull deep inside her, as though she were made all out of silk, and the comb had no teeth. She was endless, and the deep stroking was endless. Why not let him continue? Why want at all to think of not letting this go on? A boy was that close to her she felt his breath on her neck when he lifted—his hands on her and lifting—her hair from her nape. He bared her nape, and stroked her. Why shouldn't she let him, when she wanted him to?

"Ah," he said. The teeth icily began at her brow and combed back and over where they more deeply purchased, almost but not quite brutally, the thicker hair and wrung it smooth. It was a dry wringing, with the sound almost of liquid. She placed her hands on the chair back to steady her body against that pull, and the wood was cool as glass.

"Do you like it?" he asked in a low voice. His breath was shaky and warm.

"Yes," she said.

"Doesn't it feel good?"

"Yes," she said.

"What does it feel like?" He sounded almost in pain, and the pleasure she gave him seemed wrong. But why should it be wrong? She loved him, she knew, and wasn't that to want to give him pleasure? But this was getting to be wrong. His pleasure seemed to be what pulled and smoothed down through her skin,

where each strand flowed down into her and divided in an immensely complicated and forbidden way, and touched and enclosed her. With the ivory comb he seemed to be touching her where he shouldn't touch her at all, never, not now, because she was a child and shouldn't be made to feel this.

"What does it feel like?" he whispered.

"It feels wrong," she said.

"Isn't it a good feeling?"

"Yes, in a way," she said. She wondered if he were going to kiss her, to turn her around and put his mouth on her mouth. She would let him do things she shouldn't let him do. No, she wouldn't; there were places . . . things he was not supposed to do, but she wanted him to.

"Yes," he said, and then he said "No," and slouched down into a chair and crossed his legs. Carefully he removed two strands of her hair from the comb and wound them around and around the carved yellow handle. "This is sheer madness," he said. He seemed tired, and discouraged. In a sudden mood of pity and tenderness she bent over and kissed him on the cheek. Then she was embarrassed, and since he did nothing but stare morosely at the table, she said, "Well, I guess I'd better be going."

"Goodbye, Kate," he said, so she merely left.

She felt funny going down the long, grimy stairs. Furtive, somehow. At the bottom she would come out right next to the entrance to Trask's, where another world of hers—the only one, really, the legitimate one—existed. She had never been up these long dark stairs before, with their yellowish, eggy smells, but now she had, and what had happened up there seemed enormous. She felt all loose, as though she had been taken apart and not grown back all the way together again. She felt bigger in odd places.

She walked home in the balmy afternoon. Early evening, really, although the sun hadn't yet gone down and it slid yellow over toward Vermont. "I am Catherine Mary Whipple," she said out loud. "I'm fourteen years old, and I'm in the eighth grade of Leah Junior High School." She wondered how that could not seem completely true on this warm spring afternoon.

16

David, who had been working every day after school and on Saturdays as a clerk in Trotevale's Department Store, at twenty-five cents an hour, took over Wood's job at Milledge & Cunningham. Here he worked Tuesday and Wednesday afternoons after school and all day Saturday, at fifty cents an hour. Because he couldn't work as many hours as Wood had, and because of all the push trucks that needed repair, Al Coutermarsh hired Ben Caswell along with him.

Mr. Hummington, the manager of Trotevale's, never forgave him. Looking through his mauve-tinted glasses, Mr. Hummington said, "We offered you security. That job is strictly temporary. Money is far from everything." His sentences tended to be in telegraphic form.

"Jesus H. Christ!" David said later to Ben. He'd of course said nothing to Mr. Hummington. "Security! Can you imagine working in Trotevale's all your life? In twenty years you could work up to thirty-five a week!" The whole idea was crazy, even a little frightening, as though perhaps Mr. Hummington's evaluation of David Abbot Whipple were right, that the war really meant nothing, and all he'd ever amount to was a clerk in a store. "Son of a bitch," he said to Ben, who shrugged his shoulders.

"Does it bother you that much?" Ben had said, and David smelled what one of his English teachers would have called "a pejorative analysis" of his character coming up, so he changed the subject.

It was the war they usually spoke about—almost their only fairly neutral subject—because in many ways they were both in love with the war. To David, Ben didn't look much like a war

hero. He looked a great deal like his father, the mailman. In both of them, though, there was a kind of wheyish strength. They were both pale and thin, and they had a metallic hardness to their bodies, as though blood didn't run in their veins at all, but some sort of indestructible colorless fluid. He could never think of either one of them getting a tan, or blushing, because the warmth of color never appeared on their faces.

But the war was there, and its presence could be felt in Leah. One warm spring night not long after this, David stood on top of a crude tower made of pine logs. The tower was on top of Pike Hill, overlooking the town. He was armed, not with the anti-aircraft gun he would have chosen, but with his Winchester .22 pump. He owned ten shells—just ten—each a little jewel of power. At home in his room, he would play with them, line them up on their primer ends and shake each one at his ear to hear the smokeless powder whisper from inside. Now they were where they belonged, inside his rifle. Identical, anonymous, one in the chamber and nine in the tubular magazine, they gave to his rifle the proper weight of danger.

He was alone on the tower. The only light was from above, from the stars, and the soft darkness came in on him from the sides, as though he stood on a submerged rock in a warm lake. If it hadn't been for the war he might have been a little afraid. What nonhuman creatures might swim, with leathery flippers, out of the darkness to slide against his legs? But the war precluded such complicated, peacetime nightmares. The war was bright and official, like ballistics.

His duties were official too, and he carried his loaded rifle—half toy, half deadly weapon—because one part of him, at least, could believe in the possibility of an enemy invasion of New Hampshire. Witness all that adult effort with huge logs, a ladder and platform of dressed lumber, even a telephone line strung up through the pines and birches of Pike Hill. From eight until eleven that night, when Ben would relieve him, he was the air-raid watcher. If he saw or heard an airplane, he was to write it down in a little book that hung by the telephone, and describe its course and whatever else he could determine about it. If something really suspicious occurred—a sky full of parachutes, perhaps, or the drone of a hundred black Heinkel transports crossing, as they did in the

movies, a sky whose stars jerked ominously from side to side, he was to call Mr. Bemis, the Town Clerk, who was also chief air-raid warden.

What did happen that night was just outside the realm of any possibility he might have had in mind, and that may have been why it left him so emotionless. It was a very warm night, and the warmth gave it an odd depth and clarity, as though he could have heard someone talking over in Vermont. The dark pines below him seemed every so often to breathe out wind. He could hear them receiving the wind and moving with it, and then a slow gust would come folding up over him, gentle and warm as bath water. He leaned against the wooden rail and aimed his rifle at imaginary planes; he saw a meteor, and wished it were a burning Zero or Focke-Wulf. Below him, down the hill where the maples and elms began, the window lights of Leah were slowly going out.

Then he must have decided to get the binoculars from the telephone box. He had his rifle in his right hand, and he must have cocked it fully, so that the hammer wouldn't obscure the rear sight. He must have forgotten to set the hammer back on half cock.

Later he remembered a sort of instantaneous precision to that accident. It started and it was over, and there didn't seem to have been any middle part at all. There were sparks—the sky was full of sparks—but where was the explosion? He knew that he had been setting the rifle down, and then the explosion must have come, but it was like no shot he'd ever heard. It was more like one huge peal of a bell, a bell with no resonant aftertones to let him know that he had actually heard it, so that he wasn't quite sure that he had heard it at all. And all those sparks. He'd never shot a .22 at night before, and hadn't known how much fire came out with the bullet.

He just stood there for a moment, aware that his side itched —in the ribs on his right side. It never occurred to him that he might have been shot, and in fact he wasn't, but when he turned the flashlight on himself he found some interesting things. There was a burned hole about as big as a fifty-cent piece—only elongated somewhat—in his shirt. His undershirt was dark at that place but not burned through, and the slight burn he received

on his skin was no more than a vague red spot. He didn't find out until later that night when he was alone in his room that the bullet had actually gone through the folds of his shirt and come out near the breast pocket. Still, he didn't tremble, nor did his pulse increase because of that discovery. He did worry about his mother's ever missing that shirt and undershirt, which he put in the trash can, but if she did she never said anything about it.

When Ben came to relieve him—their DeMolay chapter had volunteered for this duty—they didn't make much of the accident. He told Ben about it, and showed him the hole in his shirt, but then they looked back at the sky, and soon David left for home. They were acting out bigger and better possibilities, and to have made too much of this little scrape with reality would have been to change the subject.

They knew, both of them, that an airborne invasion of Leah was fairly unlikely. They both had *National Geographic* maps on the walls of their bedrooms, and followed the war with little glass-headed pins. Sumatra, Java—the Battle of the Java Sea had been a frightening affair, even to David, because the Japanese seemed so invincible—Singapore, Dieppe. Gabriel Heatter's voice was as certain as God's, and proclaimed doom to the Axis. They had been worried, but by the spring of 1943 they had few doubts about winning. They could forget the war for hours at a time, but they didn't want to forget it. David was certain that it would be through the war that he would grow up, grow into a man who could have the experiences he wanted to have. How could he deserve the lovely girl he wanted until he had been to war and come back, like the heroes in the *Saturday Evening Post?* One had to have in one's eye that virile gleam that looked across a peaceful garden and saw in memory the deaths of comrades. There didn't seem to be any civilian love. "They're either too gray or too grassy green," sang the Andrews Sisters, and David believed it.

They didn't have to man the watchtower; it hadn't been taken seriously for a long time, and David was sure Mr. Bemis had no desire to be waked up in the middle of the night. Mr. Bemis couldn't say no to their patriotic gesture. He was a Mason, after all, and they were DeMolay. And this was a time when, upon the patriotic whim of Mr. Skelton, the whole high school might

suddenly, in the middle of any even mildly appropriate day, have to march all around town behind the band, singing "God Bless America."

There was Eddie Kusacs too, to remind them that they should have been at war. Every once in a while—it could be a quiet school afternoon, and they'd be in study hall—there would suddenly appear outside the windows Eddie Kusacs' great blue Marine F4U, its wicked radial engine screaming in their ears, its inverted gull wings wheeling down between the trees. Then up and back and around he'd come, lower than some of the school windows, as though he were following the cinder driveway down around in back to the boiler room. The huge airplane seemed to be going too fast and too slow at the same time—too fast for anything in Leah, too slow for the noise it made. After a few passes, during which they hardly breathed—David drank that sound; he was avid for that real noise—the airplane would come straight over the athletic field and drop a little yellow parachute about the size of a bushel basket. Then it was gone, flashing over a hill and out of sound, all that power suddenly gone out of the air.

But how real that airplane was, and how he wanted it! They would all be out of their desks and at the windows. Each time it happened he felt that he would never have to go back, that somehow his life had changed. When that violent machine hung in the air, he knew how inconsequential were the too familiar trees and streets of Leah. After it had gone, everything around him seemed tired; the dust in the sunlight of the brown study hall turned with a golden slowness. Then one of the teachers would go out and get the parachute, and they'd all file into the auditorium to hear what Eddie had written—usually best wishes to Mr. Skelton, Mrs. Watson and some of the other teachers, and come on, boys, join the Marines. And they'd all known Eddie. They'd known him when he came to school in a '35 Ford coupé, and here he was, godlike in his deadly blue Corsair.

The war was close enough to them; he and Ben were sixteen, and they could join the Navy at seventeen. But what were they to do in the meantime? It seemed they were living in a sort of limbo, a place where nothing much mattered, where he couldn't get hurt because he couldn't believe this limbo to be a place

where he was really mortal. This, he supposed, counted for his indifference to the tiny bullet that had so nearly entered his side. It was only a .22.

If anyone had asked him who his best friend was that year, he would have said Ben Caswell, yet he wondered how much they really liked each other. He had friends he thought he liked better, but didn't see as often. In some ways, he and Ben were too much alike. They were both rather independent, even a little bossy, so they were always a little irritated by each other. If David wanted to cross the street, or take a shortcut on his bike, chances were Ben wouldn't, and neither of them would change his mind. Quite often they would go to the same place by different routes.

Ben was tall and skinny and hard; he could knock a hole in you with his elbow, it seemed to David. His face was long and plain and slightly gray, like dishwater, and his hair, the color of gun metal, was flat and unhealthy looking. He'd had undulant fever for a long time, back in the third and fourth grades, and David remembered him bringing his special milk to school in Mason jars. He was strong enough, though. David could get him down, mainly because he was a little more compact than Ben, and thus quicker, but he always got bruised in the process, and once he had Ben pinned he was afraid to let him up. It could be very boring just holding someone down.

Ben got much better marks in school, of course, though David tried to discount the importance of this, feeling that he himself was just "mentally lazy," as Mr. Skelton had once called him. He didn't consider algebra, for instance, to be a discipline that could prove his brain unequal to Ben's. He considered those who were good at it to be slightly mad, and their concentration upon its rigid difficulties rather inhuman. But of course Ben was very good at that sort of thing; his homework was always done. Most of the boys in school that year didn't care much about homework, but Ben always did what he contracted to do. David considered this a lack of a sense of humor; the teachers themselves didn't seem to care as much as Ben did. Sometimes they would study their algebra or trigonometry together at the Whipples' house. These sessions were mostly for David's benefit, because, whatever the reason, David could hardly cope with things mathe-

214

matical. Ben was appalled at the shortness of his span of attention.

"Look," Ben would say. "You take the sine minus the cosine . . ." And with his words, so sober and knowledgeable, David would feel a weakness setting in, a strange, highly pleasant weakness in his legs and arms—euphoric, because everything became hilariously funny—and he'd look at an equation made of things called sines and cosines and see in it elaborate scansions. One, without its pluses and minuses, went, "Sine, cosine, cosine, sine=cosine, sosine, sine, sine." This David sang to the tune of "Yankee Doodle," while Ben looked stern and disgusted. David thought it hysterically funny, and his arms turned so weak from laughter he couldn't even hold a pencil. "Sine *minus* cosine!" Ben said, and David fell out of his chair onto the floor, screaming, "I'll sign! I'll sign anything! Just let me out of here!"

For some reason, he found it impossible to take those steps, those intermediate little steps, toward what he wanted to be. He wanted to be grown-up and powerful right now—to be part of the war, part of the world. Ben took each step as it came, and really mastered it. His head was full of equations and ways to factor them. David never took the time. But he was stronger than Ben; he could take him in a fight. He could get him down, but always he was fearfully aware of the difference between his mind and Ben's, and he knew that what he took down to the dirt and held there was somehow more intelligent, more valuable than he was.

Ben had many ways of being irritating. His bike, for instance, and his loyalty to that monster. It had thirty-inch wheels, and the tires were about as big around as a thumb. These were irreplaceable, of course, and not just because of the war—where could anyone have ever found such oddities? The rubber, in the few places where it showed through the friction tape, was very old, actually sticky to the touch. Nearly everybody else had balloon tires.

Between the girls' entrance and the boys' entrance to the high school was a cement sidewalk, and frost had heaved up one of the blocks so that it was canted at about a twenty-degree angle. Before school and after school, while the girls stood at their entrance and watched, the boys would get on their bikes, head down

the walk and hit that ramp. Pete Kelly had the record jump—a good fifteen feet, marked in chalk with his name. David's was nowhere near that, and Ben's was even less; his excuse was his giraffelike bike. David always tried to get Ben to use his, a pre-war Elgin, but Ben never would. Once when it was Ben's turn to go, he tried again. "Here, take mine," he said, in a rather unpleasant voice that was an insult to Ben's bike. The other jumpers were standing around impatiently, making airplane noises, and he didn't hear Ben's answer. He reached for Ben's bike and at the same time pushed the Elgin toward him by the center of the handlebars.

With a short, violent move, Ben shoved his hand away. "Mine!" he said. "I'll use mine!"

"Okay, hammerhead," David said.

It was Ben's loyalty to that bike, or perhaps the way he could bring up out of nowhere something that sounded like principle, that would enrage David. At the same time, he had to respect it, and that made it even more irritating. Here Ben was, with his narrow, washed-out face and lank, washed-out-looking hair, yet he could be as recalcitrant as a rock. David kept thinking he should have been more like his father, who looked like him but was a shy, friendly man who had to say hello a thousand times a day on his mail route and still seemed to enjoy it. For a moment he felt like kicking out a few of Ben's spokes, but he didn't, and Ben went ahead and made his usual short jump. David felt that Ben didn't really approve of the jumping, but they all had to do it. This was in lieu of being Eddie Kusacs in his Corsair, he supposed.

On the way home that afternoon he and Ben ended up fighting, their bikes in a pile on the sidewalk. He had Ben pinned, as usual, but in the process Ben had hit him in the nose, and it felt like a wedge driven between his eyes. His poor nose; he couldn't comfort it because he needed both hands and all his strength to hold Ben down. His cheekbones ached, and he seemed to taste the metal fillings in his teeth. He had Ben's head halfway under someone's barberry hedge, and one of the little thorns had come off its branch and was sticking in Ben's cheek.

"There's a thorn sticking in your cheek," he said. "I can see it sticking right in there."

Convulsive movements on Ben's part. His arm rose, and for the space of an inch it was invincible; David couldn't stop it. But Ben's strength was like a pump working upon David's tiny but real center of fear, and this forced strength into him so that he could push Ben back down again. His bony wrists gave David's fingers pain as he leaned on them.

"Sticking right into your flesh," he said. "Must be in a quarter of an inch."

Ben would never say a word while they were fighting. For him it was all beyond words, it was all power. He had no need to talk because what he wanted to do was clear enough. David had to talk. He was always talking at Ben's face, which was as unforgiving as a bird's. He'd talk and talk at that smooth, blank face while Ben despised his arguments.

"Will you give up? Will you give up? Can't you see I've got you pinned, you *bastard!* Hey, Ben, will you give up? I'll spit in your eyes, you bastard!"

He felt Ben waiting, letting his strength return. He was always just barely surprised by Ben's sudden strategies. Ben tried to butt his face with his forehead, and almost did. When David fought him, it was always to contain, to immobilize him. Though he may have bragged that he was deadly, any blow of Ben's that was really meant to hurt stayed with him for days, frightening yet admirable.

Even when Ben's father came along, David didn't dare let him up.

"What's going on here?" Mr. Caswell said mildly. He was smiling, which shocked David. He hardly dared look away from Ben, but he had to look up at Mr. Caswell's thin yet somehow droopy face.

Since Ben wouldn't talk, he had to answer. "We're wrestling," he said.

Mr. Caswell shifted his leather mailbag from one thin shoulder to another, then pulled his lapels straight. He just stood there in his baggy uniform, and it seemed strange to David to see a face so like Ben's yet so mild. "Why don't you come along home?"

"I don't want to let him up," David said.

Mr. Caswell understood why. "Ben," he said, "if David lets you up, will you stop fighting?"

Ben wouldn't answer; he tried to bridge and throw David off. David threw his weight on him hard and flattened him out again. Then he tried to butt David with his forehead, but he'd tried that before.

"You boys are friends," Mr. Caswell said. "Why do you have to fight so much?"

"He wouldn't use my bike!" David said. He was very angry, and sorry for himself, even afraid that he might cry.

"Ben wouldn't use your bike?"

"He wouldn't use it!"

"My goodness!" Mr. Caswell said, trying to be funny. He was a funny man, actually. One time he told them he had a cold in his elbow, and he said it in such a serious, surprised sort of voice even Ben laughed. "Heavens to Betsy! It's like I tried to give a man five dollars and he wouldn't take it so I hit him!"

Neither Ben nor David thought this was very funny.

"Well, what are you going to do when it comes suppertime? Can we send out some food for you?" Mr. Caswell asked.

"I don't want to keep him down!" David burst out, regretting it immediately, because he saw a flicker of satisfaction on Ben's face. "I wish I had another arm," he said through his teeth. "I'd bash your face in!"

"Well, boys," Mr. Caswell said, "are you going to hurt yourselves?"

"I don't want to hurt him!" David said, still feeling sorry for himself. After all, hadn't he won this fight?

"Ben?" Mr. Caswell said.

Ben wouldn't answer.

"Ben," Mr. Caswell said. David sensed pride and resignation in the word. Mr. Caswell thought for a moment, then said, "Well, I'm not going to butt in. Seems you're both old enough so it wouldn't help anyway. I'd stop and chat awhile, but I've got to finish my route."

Before he left them, he reached down and with gentle fingers brushed the thorn from Ben's cheek. It was just in the skin, and Ben's cheek didn't even bleed. Then he was off, ambling along in his casual, mailman's stride, leaving them with their problem.

It was now late in the afternoon. Although on these spring evenings it stayed light until nearly nine o'clock, the quality of

the light changed just perceptibly, and the edges and colors of the barberry hedge grew sharp with the slanting light. To David they seemed to have been prisoners of that small place for hours, and he began to recognize each tuft of grass. A few inches from Ben's white hand was a crushed dandelion stem, split and bent so that he could see the silver inside of it, and he saw it again, with recognition, noting that it hadn't changed. Ben strained against his weight, and each time David could summon just enough strength to overpower him.

How long were they held in that deadlock? Ben's face flickered in the new light as David's eyes moved, and the small twigs faded upward into Ben's hair. David knew Ben would never give up. Once Ben actually spoke. "Will you give up?" Ben asked. It was like a dream in which logic turns crazy. Was Ben the one who held him down? Once Ben caught him off guard, and for a violent moment they scrabbled, sobbing, into the barberry hedge. He fought Ben back down again, and brought him gasping into the dirt alongside the hedge. He hadn't known he had such strength; he'd bent Ben's arms where he had no leverage, where pain alone seemed to be his strength. His fingers seemed to have gone right through Ben's wrists between tendon and bone. Ben cursed him in a high, strangely babyish voice, half bawling—one long little scream. He sobbed his own curses back at Ben, crying because it wasn't fair that his greater strength hadn't won this fight. Then there were long periods of silence, almost of relaxation, as he listened to cars pass along the street. Suddenly they both knew it must be long past suppertime.

And somehow their fight ended, not necessarily because of the time and its official demand upon them. Their fights always had to end in some sort of truce, which could be forgotten, so that they could fight again the next time. Neither of them ever won. On this occasion, he would have to meet Ben the next day, Saturday, because of their jobs at Milledge & Cunningham. And Sunday night Ben would be relieving him again on the air-raid tower. They couldn't get away from each other if they tried.

When he got home there was the matter of missing supper, and his soiled clothes. Also, about fourteen people had seen the fight, including Horace and Kate. It was decided that after supper and a bath he would go to the Caswells' and apologize. This was his mother's decision; she took a totally unreasonable attitude

toward what was to him an ordinary occurrence. His arguments against this were useless.

He didn't mind facing Ben or his father, but Mrs. Caswell was another thing. She usually affected a richly ironic tone that left him speechless—even, he sometimes felt, armless and legless. He couldn't cope with it. "To what honor do we owe your illustrious presence, Sir David?" That sort of thing. Mr. Caswell was hardly ever in sight. He'd be down in the basement or out in the garage.

He rode his bike the two blocks to Ben's house. It was nearly ten o'clock, and he didn't have a light. There was only one streetlight in between, at the bottom of High Street, but they always rode right on through the darkness. Ben's little house was always strange, after the Whipples' huge house. The Atwater Kent radio touched the living-room sofa on one side and the matching chair on the other. He frequently bumped his head when he went upstairs. Ben was an only child, so they didn't need much room, but to see him stooping around in the halls and in his own narrow, low-ceilinged room made David want to get outside. The place was like a doll's house, and Mrs. Caswell was the doll—she was round and short. The rest of them should have been outside, sticking their hands in through the windows. Nothing inside ever seemed to change, to get used; the lace antimacassars on the sofa arms never got dirty, never were pushed askew.

When he reached the house, he dropped his bike on the grass and went up to the little porch as quietly as he could. Finally he knocked, and Mrs. Caswell came to the door. Her skin had tiny striations on it, like a McIntosh apple; in some kinds of light she looked as though she had a rash all over. She was full of pressure, and she made him nervous.

"David, David, David," she said, sighing with weary tolerance, as though he'd been there too often. Which he certainly hadn't. She smiled—she always smiled—and he thought it hurt her to smile, because that constant irony seemed to be the result of pain.

She put her hand on his arm and drew him inside; she was always touching him. "Our postman is in his hobby shop," she said, "and our good boy is in his books."

She sat him down, too deeply, into the sofa. He never knew where to sit on it, in that last moment when there was still a little

choice, because the cushions tilted and shifted. This time he sat next to the arm, too deep, but he hooked an elbow over the arm to hold himself up.

"Shouldn't you allow Benjamin to do his homework?" she asked. "I suppose yours is all done, neat as pie?"

"No," he said. Already he was going into a mild, classroom-like coma. Nothing that was going to happen was anything he wanted to happen.

"But David," she said, affecting a reasonable tone, "how can our Benjamin be valedictorian if we don't let him study?"

This was ridiculous. Nothing in the world could keep Ben from being valedictorian. Usually a girl was, because they took easy subjects like home economics or typing, but Ben's only rival, Joan Warren, had moved to Northlee. Who cared, anyway? He didn't think Ben cared; Ben just had the habit of doing all his work. Nothing like that could ever really be pinned on Ben. But he thought: Why is she trying to ruin her son's reputation? His own mother would have more sense than that.

Ben had heard them, and came stooping down the stairs, no opinion visible on his sallow face.

"Hi, Dave," he said. His eyes were blank, as though he were still thinking equations.

It was then that David confessed, lying, and trying to make little of it. "We were just wrestling," he said.

"My little boys were wrestling!" Mrs. Caswell said. "My little cubs, trying out their new muscles!"

"Yeah," David said. "Just wrestling a little." He got up to go, but as he turned toward the door she came up to him and took him fiercely by the arm. He looked down into her hard face.

"Don't you realize that Benjamin is a genius?" she said. There was a lot of hissing in her voice; she really meant it. He didn't really doubt it himself. But she scared him. She scared him by saying such a crazy thing. He jerked his arm away from her hand and ran out of the house.

A few days later, just before school let out, Eddie Kusacs buzzed them all again. He came five times that spring, and each time would remain distinct in David's memory. He never knew where Eddie came from, or what he was doing in a Marine Corsair so far from the sea. But there he was, fracturing the blue

sky above the high school, fracturing their attention, fracturing the school, the teachers, telling them all how they were prisoners of their little town. Then he was gone.

The bicycle jumping that afternoon was more daring than usual. Pete Kelly established a new record. David beat his old mark by one foot. The sunlight made him sneeze as it bounced off the sidewalk, and beneath him was the familiar noise of sprockets and spokes, the little stressful twangs and creaks of his bike—then the lift and belly thrill of the flight. No one went very high in the air, but when he landed there was a dense, hard push through his elbows, and his handlebars squeaked down an inch or two. Then the slewing in the dry dirt beyond the walk, and for a moment all the girls' eyes were upon him.

As Ben came up to take his ritual jump, David said, "Come on, genius." This was a bit like poking a snake, and he didn't say it very loudly. He never knew if Ben heard it or not. But afterwards he would still see him clearly as he swung his long leg up over his bike—his blue sock and a section of white, hairless leg, thin and uniform as a length of two-inch pipe. He pushed off and began to pump hard. His long, limp hair came down over his forehead, and the wind pushed it aside, parted it in the middle. His mouth was set, made into a little slit by effort—the same expression he wore when he was mad at David—as he hunched over those strange handlebars that bent down and around like rams' horns. There he went, his chain grinding, and he hit the ramp. David always thought his tire blew then and his wheel buckled later, when he landed, but others said no, everything went haywire at once.

David saw Ben in the air, swimming, parallel to his bike, on his face still that same determined, closed look. Then he and the bike came down together. They all got to him pretty quickly; David was proud that he was the first to get there, and they tried to untangle him. It was serious, he knew—no mere scrape case. Ben's head didn't want to come off the handlebars. They all knew enough to leave it alone while the girls' screams brought authority from inside the school.

Dr. Winston was there in ten minutes. When he and the school nurse removed Ben from his bike, Ben's long hands spread and contracted as though he were rubbing coins between his

thumbs and fingers. They took him off to Northlee to the hospital, and by the next day the janitor had put bleach on the cement where Ben had bled, and a sawhorse over the canted block of sidewalk.

How were they all affected by this? It was shocking enough, but it was only a bicycle accident. That hex nut, for instance, that dented Ben's skull—he'd turned it with a wrench while Ben held the handlebars straight. It was too familiar, not the instrument for the drama they all wanted in their lives—not with the shadow of a Corsair in their minds and that huge radial engine still roaring in their ears.

When he met Mr. Caswell on the street a few days after the accident—he had called at the house earlier—he asked again how Ben was getting along.

"Ben is still very sick, David," he said. "He's very, very sick."

"Is he going to be out of school long?"

"We don't know how long." Mr. Caswell's voice was calm and exact. "He hasn't come to yet, you see."

Later, when David found out the truth—that the part of Ben's brain that governed consciousness had been damaged—he wondered if Mr. Caswell really knew it then. His voice was calm, but his eyes were glittery—not really wet, but they looked as if they had been polished.

"I hope he gets well soon," David said.

"Thank you. Thank you, David," Mr. Caswell said.

David didn't know what to do, so he stared at Mr. Caswell for a moment, not able to share his feelings, though he knew immediately that Ben was in very grave danger and that Mr. Caswell was grieving for his son. Already grieving—that he knew. He told Mr. Caswell that Mr. Skelton had announced in assembly that Ben would get full credit for the spring term and become a senior in the fall.

"Yes, he told us," Mr. Caswell said.

And then a strange thing happened to Mr. Caswell's mouth. As he drew in a long breath, his teeth clicked together, hard, about ten times. Nothing else happened, except that David suddenly felt that grief behind his own eyes, and his throat hurt badly. For a moment Mr. Caswell looked straight at him, seeing what David was embarrassed to be caught at. David thought: It

isn't certain that Ben won't get well again. But he knew, and he felt himself begin to burn with an indignation inexpressible any other way.

"It was that lousy bike!" he shouted. "That stupid bike!"

Mr. Caswell was surprised. His mouth opened and closed upon the colorless, uniform rows of his dentures. He made a motion with his arm, and because David thought he meant to put his mailbag down, so that he could comfort him, he turned quickly from Mr. Caswell and walked away without looking back.

17

As Wood fell exhaustedly to sleep, or as he woke sometimes for moments in the sleeping barracks, after a day of marching, running, or the nervous fondling of the new weapons, from the long Georgia hill to the west came the stutter and *pah* of machine guns. If he looked from the window beside the head of his bunk, the tracers arched into the hill and then, erratic after their impact, rose slowly in fountains, in single aberrant parabolas into the black sky before they burned dull red and out. In between each tracer were four dark bullets, invisible as planets among stars, but though they trailed no fire, they were there. The Georgia sky was sewn with copper and lead.

On farther ranges howitzers lofted their shells, and the deeper bark and cough of these, the 105s, grew louder and closer if the wind were right. The men snored and complained in their sleep, and the rumble, the faraway crush of concussion, was always there, day and night.

Men? Wood lay awake in the heat of the July night. About him the children slept. It was a wonder they could hold grenades in their trembling hands, throw them and move forward into

the red dust raised by the explosions. But they did. He wondered
if the war were being fought by children such as Talley and
Pickett, Stallings, Scarpone, Warfield, Shoup and the others.
Even Sergeant Garbanks, behind his rehearsed sarcasm, peered
at his effect with a pleased surprise he could only conceal as a
child might, with a cartoon scowl. But then it was only children
he warned and frightened, and perhaps he knew that.

Lieutenant Knobloch, who had been on Guadalcanal, took
joy in telling how he had stepped from the jungle and shot twenty
Japanese sailors who had come from a sinking ship. They tried to
run back into the waves, and he had potted them one by one with
his carbine. It had taken three magazines of ammunition before he
got them all. He had recurring malaria, and wasn't with them too
often. Captain Harry T. Jones led the company on marches, but
rarely spoke. He was a tall, rangy man of twenty-four, who had
been wounded in the leg in North Africa. It was generally believed that he made them march and run so much because he
thought it was good exercise for his leg. Sergeant Garbanks, who
was with the platoon all the time, was really in charge of their
training. A Corporal Hughes was listed on the platoon roster, but
he was A.W.O.L., and had been A.W.O.L. no one knew how
long. It was said that he held the Congressional Medal of Honor,
and thus could get away with anything, could quit the Army
any time he liked.

But it was the men of his platoon, with one or two exceptions,
who dismayed Wood. Poor little Pickett, who looked like a sick
chicken, who couldn't really read or write; when they were first
assigned to the 3rd Battalion Pickett had been sent to the dentist's, and he came back that afternoon with half his teeth gone
from his pink ragged gums. It was hard to see how they could
have pulled the splintery stumps from his white formless jaws
without tearing everything into rags. His flesh didn't seem strong
enough to take such wrenching. He'd weighed 125, and before he
got his false teeth he lost ten pounds. He managed to keep up
with them on marches, but Wood could never understand how he
did it. Then there was Talley, who remained so distant from the
rest, frozen by some inner defect, maybe fear, who would never
answer "Ho!" like the other Southerners when his name was
called, the joke of his name freezing him still deeper into some

private world or other. But Wood suspected there was no real world there at all, and the boy's dull eyes didn't look to any inner resources, just more dully at the fading outer world. To fight alongside him? Or Thompson, whose neck and head were a thick pillar leaning over always to the right, a pillar with colorless, slatey hair on top—he was another semiliterate. Or fat Smallers, who always lagged behind, sometimes a company or two behind, who could be seen to cry during ten-minute breaks, his pants dropped, his paper bag of talcum powder in hand as he tenderly smeared his incandescent thighs.

Most of the men in his platoon were Southerners, who had sounded strange only at first. Soon they had revealed themselves, and they might just as well have been from Leah.

But it was Stefan who caused him more than dismay. Stefan was older than any of them—twenty-six. He was married, and had a child. They called him "Pop," and he was always slightly abstracted; his wide gray eyes peered seriously and somewhat askew at any problem. Quite often he put his leggings on the wrong legs, so that the lacings and buckles were on the insides. Here they could catch and trip him up, but mainly they sent Sergeant Garbanks into screaming fits; half hysterical with anger and laughter, he'd send poor Pop Stefan to all-night K.P. or guard duty. Stefan needed his sleep very badly. He was thin and always croupy, and one bony shoulder curved toward the front more than the other, as though he were pointing with it. His sternum was depressed into a cavity in his chest the size of a baseball. His voice itself came out slightly exhausted, an old man's voice that was thin above the sudden barrel-deep and reverberant explosions of croup.

Wood began to keep an eye on him, and managed to save him quite a bit of sleep by telling him when only one side of his canteen hanger was hooked to his webbed belt, or when he'd left the gas-cylinder lock screw out of his rifle, and such small things. He couldn't protect him from M-1 thumb, a condition caused by the spring-laden closure of the Garand rifle's bolt. Stefan could never learn to take his thumb out of the way in time. That is, he could never learn a consistent way of doing it, and naturally he handled his rifle as though it were a dangerous and moody animal. At inspection he dropped it, a crime so heinous the whole

platoon had lost its breath. He just stood there, sucking his inflamed thumb, and though the incredulous Sergeant Garbanks couldn't swear in front of Captain Jones, later on his voice ricocheted from all the barracks in the battalion quadrangle.

Now, in the night, the distant machine guns rattled in hesitant spurts, and the tracers climbed slowly into the black sky. It was three in the morning, and Wood knew he would pay tomorrow for every minute of sleep he lost now. He leaned on his elbow and watched the long hill to the west, where the tracers grew like bright worms. From beyond the hill somewhere, on one of the interlocking ranges, shell bursts lit the clouds with hot red flashes, and the sound rolled slowly toward and over him.

His mother had written, asking him to write more letters to Horace, but what could he say to Horace? The world was full of Horaces; he was in a whole platoon of Horaces. An incident at the gas area had somehow proven the prevalence of Horaces—how, he didn't quite know, but it had been profoundly depressing. After going into the tear-gas chamber, removing their gas masks and giving their name, rank and serial number to a masked cadre sergeant, they were assembled outside and given a lecture on gases, how each one smelled and so on. He had thought of Al Coutermarsh, and wondered which kind of gas had injured his lung. After the lecture small charges were exploded, of lewisite, mustard, phosgene and chlorine, and they had to smell the faint wisps of smoke and fill out a little mimeographed quiz on the subject. Some of the men were whispering the answers to each other when a lieutenant said sarcastically, "Don't bother to cheat, men. You won't flunk out of the infantry."

Wood had found himself nodding with satisfaction. Good, this was where he belonged. But soon he was depressed. Poor Horaces, all of them, responding in senseless ways to what was immaterial, habitual, stupid, irrelevant. Was that it? The incident didn't seem to warrant such depression. But that wasn't the only cause of it, of course. One of the Horaces of the world was his flesh and blood, his brother, whom he had badly hurt, and perhaps even more depressing than that, today Sergeant Garbanks had ordered him to report to Captain Harry T. Jones, who had practically ordered him to appear before the Officer Candidate Board a week from now.

He couldn't think of a way to say no to the captain, who had looked at him carefully, looked away, and then looked more closely at him. A strangely familiar thing had happened; he had been recognized, as Al Coutermarsh had recognized him in Milledge & Cunningham. There was that look of recognition and equality.

But he must sleep now, to the distant mumble of the guns. He must sleep. What could he do, go around with his lower lip hanging out, and a pendulum of drool on his chin? No, they would still find him out. The captain had said, "Whipple? At ease." He pronounced it Whey-pul? like a question, drawling it easily and slowly as if it had several syllables in it. "Sergeant Garbanks allows you have officer potential?"

"I don't know, sir," Wood said, but the captain didn't choose at first to let him mean what he really meant. The captain's eyes widened for just a second and became clear and cold. He went on in his relaxed, soft yet ominous drawl. "The Officer Candidate Board meets next week at battalion headquarters, and I would like for you to be there."

"Well, sir—" Wood said, but the captain interrupted him.

"It's a bad war over there. You know that, don't you? And we do what we ought to do, if we can do it? Now, we have a terrible need of infantry officers, and them that have the potential, why I feel it is no less than their duty. Whey-pul? To take on that responsibility."

"Yes sir," Wood said. "But—"

"You going to tell me you don't think you have officer potential?" The captain smiled coolly. "You just take a careful look around this company. How we going to take these misfits into combat and bring some of 'em back whole? Can you answer that? Some of us got to wipe their noses and tell 'em which way to run. We got to tell 'em what to do, because they sure not going to figure it out for themselves."

"Yes sir," Wood said, but he hadn't given in, and the captain knew it.

"You think it over a few days more, and I'm going to ask you one more time. Dismissed."

He must sleep. All around him the sleeping men huffed and puffed, snored and sighed. Down the row of bunks someone squeaked loudly in complaint against his dream.

His mother's letters were always short and nongossipy:

Dear Wood,

We are all fine & hope you are. Dad's leg doesn't seem any worse & he is quite cheerful about the new ball bearing factory & his two tenements. He didn't get the rent he thought from each apt. but good money & you know how much that means to him now. Gordon Ward Sr. foreclosed Sam Davis' farm & Sam is working in the new factory & being janitor to the two tenements. Seems to be working out all right as he is on the night shift & does his janitor work days.

Saw Lois & she says she writes to you. She is so pretty. She is going to Smith College in the fall but I suppose you know that.

One favor I would like. Will you write to Horace? Your letters mean so much to him, Wood. He has been different since you left & not better at all. Last Wed. he woke us all up screaming he was so scared of those things he imagines. I do hate to bother you with these troubles & I know you have your own life to live in the Army, but Horace needs to know you think of him. Kate misses you, & Peggy most of all. You sure have an admirer there! David says Al Coutermarsh & Beady (?) send you their best. So do we all.

Love,
Mother

When he'd read the words about Horace screaming he trembled with fear for Horace, and felt the boy's desperation; tears came to his eyes. Horace would hate so much to have to scream for help. The monsters must have been doing something awful to him.

But sleep, he must sleep. Once his mother had told him to think of a tall pine, rising, rising slowly up toward the sky, branches and trunk, needles, branches and smooth trunk growing forever upwards, smoothly rising. He would see this calm tree clear, and think of nothing.

That Saturday Stefan took him on pass into Macon to meet his wife and child, who were living in a two-room apartment on the third floor of a wooden tenement. The rent was too high, the

cockroaches passed along the mopboards in convoys, and when it rained, Stefan had told him, the punky plaster walls turned damp, and the flowered wallpaper changed color, like litmus paper. The small rooms—kitchen-living room and bedroom—smelled of damp paper and glue. Not even the smells of cooking could compete with that smell, and the apartment, hastily partitioned from what had been a larger one, did not seem whole—seemed not sure, somehow, of its walls. The kitchen was obviously not a kitchen, but a room into which a stove, an icebox and a sink had been placed. An overstuffed sofa and a bridge lamp formed the living-room side of it. The bathroom was communal, down a short hall-way with a tilted, linoleum floor. The frame of one window was flush against a partitioning wall, behind which a radio played at that low, constant volume, its occasional voices not quite under-standable, that indicates it is always on, from waking until sleep and perhaps beyond.

Lenore Stefan was a thin, homely girl not much older than Wood. Her chief asset and chief vanity was a mane of long black undulating hair, silky and soft and well kept. Her narrow face was slashed with lipstick, and between the vivid red and the luxuriant black, Lenore herself seemed to peer out shyly. She was very shy of him; when she smiled she was always in the process of looking away, so that she continued to smile at a window or a wall. Her nose was long, and gave the impression of lumpiness, yet when he looked closely Wood saw that it was an ordinary sort of nose, just too long, and indecisive toward its end.

She seemed too fragile—she and Stefan both—to have been taken from Delaware, Ohio, and made to come to this soldier town. She could see Stefan only on Sunday or an occasional weekend, and few of them because of his tendency to get guard duty and K.P.

She knelt at the icebox and got them each a bottle of beer, and when she put the bottles on the table to open them, Stefan noticed a Band-Aid on her thumb.

"What happened?" he said worriedly, taking her hand.

"Oh, I just cut myself on a can."

"You must be more careful," Stefan said.

"Now, George. I'm the one that's careful," she said, pleased. A flash of her smile was directed at Wood, to show him how silly

and nice was her husband's concern. "It's just a little tiny cut. You want to see?" Stefan nodded gravely, and she peeled back the tape and let him see. He gazed at her thumb, holding her hand in both of his—that strange, seal-like stare, slightly walleyed, as though he looked at infinity. Finally he nodded, and she pressed the tape back smooth and opened the two bottles.

"You want a glass, Wood?" she asked.

"No, thanks," he said. The baby uttered a plaintive, questioning sound from the other room, and she went quickly after it. She came back with a large baby, pink and white, in blue pajamas, with a fat fist in its eye.

"Georgie woke up," she said to the baby, "Little Georgie just woke up!"

The way she stood, her skinny but womanly hips forward, with the clear small bulge of her belly showing through the shiny rayon of her print dress, seemed pathetic to Wood. Her pelvis seemed open, canted toward openness, generous though skimpy in a childish way. Pop Stefan looked at her and at his child as though he were a child acting the part of a father. Yet this was real, and these two children had managed somehow, God knew how, to come together, to have made this child, even to have arrived here in this slum. Below on the streets the soldiers prowled. The whole city seemed dark, a jungle of olive drab, whiskey, fighting and vomit. The Negroes here seemed darker, blacker than any he had ever seen, and they prowled too, frightened and dangerous. The mattresses of the cheap hotels were full of bedbugs and lice, the women of venereal disease. Waitresses slugged the dregs of the soldiers' glasses, and the officers who had to walk on the sidewalks tried to miss the soldiers' eyes in order to save their tired arms from the constant saluting. It was a city of strangers, where the military police cruised along the alleys in jeeps, and areas of whole blocks were off limits.

Stefan coughed deeply, his hand over his mouth, the uneven bones of his shoulders turning. It was as if Wood could see a diagram of his awkwardly cantilevered bones.

Lenore was heating Georgie's bottle in a pan of water, and Stefan held Georgie, who cried, then stared, his face wrinkling and unwrinkling, in focus and out.

"He was born with an enlarged thymus gland," Stefan

said. "And Lenore didn't make enough milk, she's so little up there. We had quite a time of it, didn't we, Georgie?" He chuckled and crooned into Georgie's damp pink ear. "He's fine now, though. He's a healthy baby now, isn't he, Georgie? Isn't he?"

Georgie stared from his olive-colored eyes, and hit the table a miniature blow with his fist.

After a while, Wood said goodbye to Pop Stefan and Lenore. "See you Monday morning," he said. When Stefan's face grew stiff, almost ashy at this prospect, he wished he hadn't said it.

"You won't have supper with us?" Lenore said.

"I said I'd meet Perrone and Quillen," Wood said. This was almost a lie—there had been only a vague sort of arrangement. He knew the Stefans had no time for company, and hardly any money. What he really meant to do was to go by the hotel and if Perrone and Quillen weren't in its bar—called "The Boiler Room"—he'd buy a magazine, eat while reading it in some restaurant, then take an early bus back to camp. This seemed a pleasant enough prospect. The city depressed him; it felt invaded, and in the eyes of the civilians he found a mixture of greed and disgust that amounted to disease. At least the Army camp was free of this. On a weekend when the company was on pass it would be free of about everything, in fact.

As he walked back downtown, keeping an eye out for officers he would have to salute, he thought of the pleasantness of an evening by himself. He preferred this emptiness. He would not think of the Stefans, would not pity them, would not tremble for them. Macon was full of such people, some of them doomed— maybe all of them. He could see the thin girl-mother, the unhealthy scraped color of her legs. Did she and Stefan take each other seriously? Could they believe in their own future, and if so what did they foresee? He saw her having her periods, her headaches, babies, sniffles, bowel movements, intercourse with her frail and awkward husband. On and on, so real because it would go on for a while, and yet not real. If for some reason he went back to the Stefans' apartment, would they still be there? It was as if the Stefans were made of cardboard and weren't aware of it. They thought they were real, but the damp would creep in and they would grow spongy and disintegrate, and no one would ever really be called upon to care very much.

Stefan had gone to Ohio Wesleyan for two years, then lost interest in college, then sold advertising for the local newspaper, but didn't sell much. He'd tried to sell other things, he'd told Wood with as little interest in the telling as there had been in the doing. Selling was always there for a while, for those who couldn't do it. What Stefan really wanted was to be home with Lenore, where they could play, and she could get him his dinner. He was color-blind, and was amazed that the Army took him. He hadn't got over that amazement yet, and if he didn't it might kill him.

Wood cursed himself and kept walking. He saluted a captain with a service forces patch on his shoulder, a harried-looking captain whose garrison cap wasn't on straight, an obvious civilian type. Somewhere down a side street an MP's whistle blew, shrill as a scream, and in the corner of his eye, in the corner of his head, was the feeling of running and of fear.

Perrone and Quillen were in The Boiler Room, and saw him as he stood in the door. The big room was full of the khaki of the summer uniforms.

"Hey, Whip!" Perrone yelled, standing up and motioning him over. It always gave Wood the feeling, when he was called this name, that he was impersonating his father. Perrone's square, dark face split and there was the flash of his huge grin. Wood sometimes found himself counting Perrone's teeth. "Hey, you Yankee bastard!" The word came out "basstid." Perrone came from what he called "Goombahdaville—Seconanyeh." This meant Second Avenue, in Manhattan. But soon Wood understood Perrone's language clearly enough, even when, for ironic and sometimes crazy reasons of his own, he spoke half in Italian. These Italian phrases he translated in the same breath. "*Mangia qualunque cosa mangefran*'—he eats anything." This about poor fat Smallers in the mess hall.

Quillen grinned good-naturedly, with perhaps an icy glint in his eye. He was a tall Georgia boy with dark curly hair, always cheerful. Wood had always thought he'd detected a warning of violence in Quillen, and then he'd seen Quillen in a fight behind the PX one night. The violence was there, all right. He'd cold-cocked a soldier from the 2nd Battalion, and that with a left, which seemed to Wood, and most likely to the soldier from the

2nd Battalion, as being so skillfully professional it was almost unfair. He came from Gum Log. "That's a real place, Whipple," he'd explained. "I wouldn't shit you, even if you are a damyankee."

The three of them had become more than merely acquainted because they had been assigned by Sergeant Garbanks as acting squad leaders. The other squad, the first, was led by a boy named Tate who came from a military school, knew all about military matters, spoke always in tones of command and was, by common consent, a flaming asshole.

"Where you been?" Quillen said, signaling for beer.

"At Pop Stefan's place."

"The left-footed titmouse," Quillen said, shaking his head.

"Well, you got Smallers in your squad," Perrone said.

"And you got Pickett, Thompson and, my God, Whetzel," Quillen said. "Let's face it. What we plainly ought to do is let these poor li'l rabbity bastards go back home where they belong."

"Have a beer," Perrone said. "You nervous in the service, Gum Log?"

"Did you know when we got back from the range Friday that dumb-ass Philpotts had a live round-chambered in his goddam rifle? And I got to walk ahead of him?"

Perrone's eyes widened at this enormity. "Grabass find out?"

"Hell, no. He would've strung that boy up by his puckerstring and plucked him clean. He got enough trouble in this man's army. Hoo!"

Wood sipped his beer and listened to their talk. In spite of their bitching they were really unconcerned, even cheerful. The stupidity or the awkwardness of the men amused them. And yet within a few months—three at the most—they would be in combat. People would be shooting at them and very sincerely trying to kill them. They ordered more beer, and the afternoon passed. Once a young soldier was sick on the way to the men's room, and his friends cleaned him up and took him away.

"Oh, ah," Quillen said, "I would surely like a little clean, white poontang."

"If it's poontang it ain't clean," Perrone said.

"Some pretty girls in Macon."

"If there is any they got 'em locked up for the duration."

"I come here to play basketball once, met this pretty girl name of Anna Mae Mingledorf."

"Sure."

"No, I ain't shittin' you, Perrone. That was her name, Anna Mae Mingledorf. Just as *pretty*. Big blue eyes and a little bitty butt on her. I mean she was pretty." Quillen's voice had turned smooth and easy, and then he shook his head as if to wake himself. "She don't live here inny more."

"Anna doesn't live here any more," Perrone sang.

"That's a sad, sad song, Perrone. But the time will come. Just we sit and wait and don't git it caught in the gears."

"Or shot off, maybe." Perrone turned to Wood. "What you think, Whip? Say something. You gonna be an officer like Captain Harry T. Jones wants?"

"I don't know."

"Now, that's the kind of decisive, pee-positive man we need to lead us into the blood and glory of combat," Perrone said.

Quillen laughed. "Oh my!" he said.

"Anyway," Perrone said, "it'd get you out of this crummy outfit."

"I'll tell you a awful secret," Quillen said. "This is the best outfit in the whole U.S. of A. Army."

"So we lose the war," Perrone said, shrugging his shoulders.

"Ain't it a shame, though."

"It'll be a hell of a disappointment to the folks on the home front."

"Hell, Perrone, ain't you on Mussolini's side anyways?"

The afternoon passed in their bantering, and they seemed to like Wood for an audience. He rarely joined in. Soldiers came and went, from the bar at one moment came the signals of a near-fight—breath and silence. They watched and turned away. Perrone and Quillen decided that after they ate they'd buy a pint of Green Mule and go to the USO dance. Wood ate with them in the restaurant—thin steaks and French fries—and afterwards bade them luck and took a nearly empty bus back to camp.

He would be alone in the barracks, where he could write the letters he had to write, to Horace and Lois and his mother. The prospect seemed like an examination, one of the bad kinds you weren't quite prepared for. As he sat in the jiggling bus, holding

the chrome rail of the empty seat ahead of him, the first easy words appeared.

Dear Horace,
How are you? I'm fine . . .

Lights passed. Ahead he could see the glow in the sky made by the lights of all the battalion areas. After the letters, inadequate as they would be, he would crawl into his hard sack and listen to the machine guns, which stuttered out their lead day and night, weekends and all. There was a war on. Stefan would be in the frail arms of his little girl, his deformed chest and scraggly hairs against her deprived nipples, and at least for a while they would be convinced of their happiness.

On Sunday afternoon Sergeant Garbanks came into the barracks and found Wood on his bunk reading.

"What's the Fourth General Order?" he said in order to engage in conversation.

"To repeat all calls from posts more distant from the guardhouse than my own."

"The Fifth."

"To quit my post only when properly relieved."

"How come you ain't in town?"

"That town gives me the creeps," Wood said.

"Give you the crabs is more likely." Sergeant Garbanks did want to talk, but beneath his suddenly mild, conversational tone was the pressure of anger.

"Captain Jones says you don't want to go to OCS." Wonder was in his voice, that anyone could say such a thing to Captain Jones.

"I told him I wasn't sure about it."

"Jesus Christ!"

"Why don't you go to OCS?" Wood said, aware of the danger of such an interjection.

"I ain't officer material. I'm a noncom and proud of it."

He seemed to be saying that it wasn't a matter of ability, but of something like species. "You ain't noncom material, Whipple. You're either a buck-ass private or an officer, and Captain Jones wants you to go for an officer." He said this sternly, yet with some diffidence. He stood straight, the neat creases of his uniform too spick and span, as though he were being observed by an officer. "Let me tell you something, and you can take it any way you like. I ain't chickenshit and I ain't no boy scout, but I highly recommend you don't give Captain Jones no more of this 'I don't know, sir' crap." He stared into Wood's eyes for a moment, and then said, "What's the Seventh?"

"To talk to no one except in the line of duty."

"It ain't something you got a choice about. Captain Jones *asks* you to do something, you do it. It might not sound like an order, Whipple, but you let me tell you, when Captain Jones says 'Shit,' you squat and strain. You ain't no civilian no more."

He waited for an answer, and when one didn't come he said, "What's the Second?"

"To walk my post in a military manner, keeping always on the alert and observing everything that takes place within sight or hearing."

"Okay." Sergeant Garbanks turned stiffly and walked to the stairs and down.

Wood had always wondered about the reverence in Sergeant Garbanks' voice when he spoke of Captain Jones. At first he'd thought it had something to do with the training of the troops —purposely exaggerated so they would be awed by any officer's authority. Then he thought it might have been the result of some personal thing. Had the gallant captain, wounded in chest and thigh, carried his unconscious sergeant across minefields under deadly fire? No, Sergeant Garbanks hadn't yet been in combat. It was neither of these; this reverence was real—a delusion familiar to Wood.

By nine o'clock on Monday morning, D Company had marched to the booby-trap area, where they stood at ease around

a large dirt quadrangle. Unoccupied barracks and outbuildings surrounded the quadrangle, their windows cracked or gone, doors splintered or canted on sprung hinges. In the center, on the turned and blasted red earth, a strange lieutenant placed a steel helmet over a lighted two-inch firecracker and stepped back. *Thuh.* The helmet rose, and kept on rising—they couldn't believe it—until it was tiny against the blue; then it fell the long way back, turning slowly until it hit the dirt with a loud clang.

"That's just to show you we're not playing around with ladyfingers," the lieutenant said. "These little bastards'll take your fingers off. They'll blow dirt in your eyes and blind you—that's happened. So don't get careless or cocky. If one of these goes off within six feet of you, in combat it'd be a Jap or German mine, so consider yourself dead. You've got to find them, figure out which type of detonator's used, and disarm them." He turned toward a building at the side. "At ease! Look over there." They all turned, and he must have given a signal. An explosion blew the porch and door into fragments. The wind pushed their faces, and splinters of wood, boards, dirt and oddly soft-shaped, suggestive things climbed above them and fell rattling and thudding on their helmet liners. Some of the men had fallen to the ground; they couldn't believe the nearness and violence of the explosion, or that an officer, the Army, whoever was in charge of their welfare, could have allowed it to happen.

Wood turned toward the men of his platoon and saw that they were afraid.

"That was the real thing," the lieutenant said. "That was a mine rigged to the door." He seemed angry at them, at their ignorance and surprise. "Open a door like that and there's a new face in hell!"

The word came whispered through the ranks: this was the Mad Bomber. It's him. Grabass said so. The sun made ovens of their helmet liners, and their rifles were slippery in their hands. Talley took off his metal-rimmed GI glasses and attempted to wipe them on his fatigues. The depressions they left on the bridge of his thin nose glowed waxy and cruel. He winced as he strung the wire bows back over his ears. Pickett, Stefan, Shoup, Thompson, Stainback, Spradlin, Whetzel—they all stood sweating, superficially alike in their green fatigues.

The lieutenant's black bushy chest hair puffed out of the neck of his fatigues. As he walked purposefully toward the 3rd Platoon they saw water flow down his face and chin and disappear into the black hair. Above his red, angry face, his name, WARM-BUCK, flickered in their eyes, where it was stenciled on his helmet liner. They looked from the letters of the name to the face, and in the sun the white letters flickered.

The platoons were separated. While the others went through the booby-trapped barracks, Sergeant Garbanks entrusted the 3rd Platoon to the Mad Bomber, who marched them down to a small grandstand. They climbed onto the wooden planks and waited. In front of them the Mad Bomber stood, grinning now, behind a big table piled with dangerous-looking tubes, wires, fuses, recognizable grenades and mines. At his back the ground dropped ten feet into a swamp—a sheer drop down to the reeds and marshy tangle. Before he spoke at all he took an olive-drab grenade—the real kind, not the black of practice nor the blue that is fused but not loaded—pulled the ring and let the fuse handle fly off. They heard the pop as the fuse began, and the wisp of smoke circled his hairy hand. By the time they thought to count the seven seconds of the fuse, they knew it was too late, but he kept the smoking grenade in his hand, smiling at them, until it must have been much too late, and when they had begun to think it was all a trick and the grenade was not loaded, with a negligent flip of his fingers he sent it over the edge of the bank and it blew, right then. Steel fragments zicked through the top of the mulberry tree beside his table. A leaf came floating down, slowly, rocking, like any leaf falling.

The Mad Bomber smiled. He hadn't moved, hadn't paid any attention to the explosion. Now he picked another O.D. grenade from the table and tossed it in his hand without looking at it. His smile seemed more vindictive now, as though his anger at them had cooled into a more lasting hatred.

"I'm going to show you dogfaces some of the toys you'll be playing around with in combat," he said. "I know you've thrown a few grenades, but you haven't learned to live with them and love them." He smiled. "Now listen closely, and if any one of you can't remember what I show you, get out your little notebook and pencil and write your last will and testament, because sure

as hell one of these"—he pointed to the collection of dangerous-looking objects on the table—"one of these little toys will surely kill you."

He tossed the O.D. grenade in his hand; they saw him pull its ring, and watched the fusing handle spring away from the dull body of the grenade. The fuse popped, and he tossed the grenade the wrong way. He tossed it toward them. It made a short, unbelievable arc, trailing white smoke, and fell into Talley's lap. Talley looked down at it, where it rested in his hands. Or he seemed to look down at it, but Wood saw that he wasn't there; Talley had departed toward some interior destination. His round, simple mouth, at the bottom of his long face, turned down like a sucker's, as though it were meant to move along the bottom. Now it pointed, suckerlike, sweet and vacant, at the hissing grenade.

The lieutenant was yelling orders at Talley, and Wood moved across the suddenly empty planks. The 3rd Platoon had opened out like a huge green flower, leaving Talley alone at its center. Wood took the grenade from Talley's lap and threw it over the bank, where it blew. Dirt, sticks and brown muddy water geysered up and fell back.

The lieutenant was out of his mind. He stared, screaming, at Talley. "You're dead! You're dead! Soldier, you're a dead man! Get down here, you dumb shit! Get down here! Jesus Christ Almighty get *down* here!" He pointed to the ground in front of him. Talley didn't move, so Wood punched him in the back and pushed him up. Talley stood up and walked down the planks toward the lieutenant. The butt of his rifle hit the bottom plank, and for a moment it tilted forward and pointed at the lieutenant, who gave out a deep, hoarse bellow before he regained his speech.

"Give me your bayonet! Your bayonet!" Finally Talley seemed to understand. With some difficulty he drew his bayonet from its scabbard. The lieutenant grabbed it and Talley's rifle, fixed the bayonet to the rifle, walked a few yards along the bank and jammed the rifle, bayonet first, into the dirt. "You know what that means?" Talley looked at him through his GI lenses. "That's you!" The lieutenant pointed to the ground. Water poured down his face, and the whole chest of his fatigues was dark and wet. "You're dead! You're in the ground! There's dirt up your ass!"

Talley seemed to watch.

"Now I'll tell you what you're going to do." The lieutenant marched back and stood in front of Talley. "See that shed over there?" He pointed to a small, unpainted shed not ten yards away. "Do you see it? Can you find it?" Talley seemed to nod. "In that shed is a spade. I want you to go to that shed, open the door, get that spade and bring it back here. Is that clear?" Talley's long face seemed to signify that he'd understood. He turned toward the shed.

The 3rd Platoon had reassembled on the grandstand, and the lieutenant turned toward them. "Welcome back. Welcome back."

Talley had reached the shed. The door was held by a padlock hasp with a stick jammed through it. Talley studied this. Then he seemed to have figured it out, and to Wood it seemed a good sign, somehow, that Talley, a soldier in his squad, could figure out the business of the stick; if he pulled it out, the hasp could then open. Perhaps some memory of childhood came to help him, but he did pull out the stick, open the hasp and pull the door open.

The roof and back of the shed blew off. When the smoke and dust drifted away, Talley stood there holding the door.

"You're dead!" the lieutenant yelled. "You're dead! Your guts are strung around your neck!"

Talley turned slowly and began to come back.

"Soldier, I gave you an order! I believe I told you there was a spade in that building. I want you to turn around and get that spade, and then I want you to go to the place over there where your rifle is stuck in the ground, and I want you to dig your grave. You are a casualty. You are dead! You are a zombie!"

Talley got the spade from the ruins of the shed and began to dig his grave. It was to be six feet long, two feet wide, and keep going down. He wasn't to pay any attention to any small noises he might hear while he was at it, either, because he was dead.

There were noises. Dynamite caps, nitrostarch, percussion grenades, antitank grenades, Bangalore torpedoes, a mine that caused the air in the gulley to change to solid matter that rose slowly up and over. The ground beneath the stand trembled, and mud came down to splotch their helmet liners. Sixty-millimeter mortar shells could double as grenades if they were armed by

pounding their rear ends down on the table hard enough. The Mad Bomber spaced and mounted his explosions as though he conducted some mad, apocalyptic orchestra, and his joy in his crescendoes registered on his face; it softened toward them in their appreciation of his virtuosity. They breathed the exciting fumes of cordite and fear. Pickett vomited, thinly, without losing his teeth, on his legging and shoe, and was too excited to be ashamed.

And yet the explosions were too close to have any depth in their reverberations. They were only deafening and mean in the final snap, and produced only smoke and dirt. The Mad Bomber grew arm-weary at last, and almost disconsolately gave them a ten-minute break so they might stretch and smoke. They were still incredulous; it seemed possible to get used to the noise. This was what they could hardly believe. Pop Stefan gazed, scratching the poison oak on his skinny ribs, his eyes as always slightly askew. Even Talley was given a ten-minute break in the digging of his grave, and he sat on the pile of dirt he'd made, staring at nothing that caused any movement of his dull eyes.

Perrone and Quillen admired the way Wood had plucked the grenade from Talley's lap. "You sure enough saved old Talley's ass," Quillen said.

"*Marrone!*" Perrone said. "I was taking care of Number One, man. I flew through the blue like a big-ass bird."

Wood thought: If I hadn't done it, nobody would have done it. Nobody at all. That grenade would have cleaned the meat off Talley's pelvis, and Talley would be dead.

So Talley would be dead, and his little mouth with its sweet, hurt, vacant expression, his grayish fingers that were always a little grubby at the knuckles, as though his mother had never shown him how to wash his hands properly—all would become the weird gray meat that is a corpse. It would be too much like the snuffing out of some small, patient animal, like a mouse or even a toad, the sort of animal he always seemed to come upon when it was in the clutches of a cat or a snake, in that most important, dramatic process of dying. Yet it died with a calm face, almost as though it were used to dying. It seemed to care less than the observer.

Soon Sergeant Garbanks came to get them, and the Mad

Bomber told him what Talley had done. Talley's grave was about two feet deep, and the Mad Bomber told him to lie down in it. Talley slowly and obediently lay down into the red dirt.

"God!" the Mad Bomber said to Sergeant Garbanks. "Why don't we just cover him up and save all the trouble later?"

The platoon gathered around to see Talley in his grave. Sergeant Garbanks kicked some dirt in on Talley, who looked up at him with a dim expression.

"Save a hell of a lot of time and money, sir," Sergeant Garbanks said.

A tear was seen to crawl down Talley's temple toward his ear.

"What do you say, soldier?" the Mad Bomber said. "Aren't you all comfy in that nice warm hole? The big, bad grenades can't get you, and the nasty machine guns, and the naughty eighty-eights. Wouldn't you rather just say your prayers now and go beddie-bye?"

Wood felt hatred, just a twinge of it; it was not a common emotion in him, he knew, and he discovered that it was almost exhilarating.

"Cat got your tongue?" the Mad Bomber asked. "Oh, maybe you're just making up your mind? Now, over on the table I've got a forty-five, and if you take my advice and call it quits and no harm done, I'll go get my pistol belt and I'll just quick as a wink put you out of your misery. How about it?"

"No," Talley said faintly.

"What did you say, soldier?"

"No."

"No, *what?*"

"No sir."

The Mad Bomber looked at heaven. "Holy God Almighty," he said, "be on our side, 'cause we'll need You!"

Wood examined the Mad Bomber, and Sergeant Garbanks, who would always act as foil for the insignia of authority. This, he saw clearly, was the only humor of power.

Talley was induced to rise from the dead, and they left the Mad Bomber. They were taken through a booby-trapped barracks where, statistically, they were all killed. The only real casualty was, satisfyingly, Sergeant Garbanks, who got a blood blister as

big as a dime on the palm of his hand when one firecracker went off as he probed for another one's detonator.

They had learned very little, it seemed to Wood, but perhaps it was a hard subject to teach to people who were that scared.

The next day, on the rifle range, Pop Stefan went mad and broke his rifle stock. Wood didn't see it because the squad had been separated and he was in the butts, raising and lowering targets and taping bullet holes. He got the story from several witnesses, including Pop Stefan a few days later when he was allowed to visit him in the violent ward. The other witnesses said Pop Stefan had, in front of Lieutenant Knobloch, picked up his rifle by the barrel and smashed it down on the ground, breaking the stock at the pistol grip.

"Lieutenant Knobloch shit," Perrone said.

Stefan told him more of the details. They sat on a wooden bench in a narrow dirt courtyard between the one-story violent ward and a high fence with several strands of barbed wire along its top. From narrow windows just below the eaves of the violent ward came violent sounds—screams, moans and laughter.

"I can't stand it much longer, Wood," Stefan said. "I can't eat, I can't sleep. I'm the only one in there who isn't a raving maniac." He did look tired and sick. His skin was grayish, and his chin and neck, the only parts that had tanned, because of the shade of his helmet liner, looked leatherish and sickly. His gray eyes were bloodshot, and those smears of red were the brightest places on his face.

"I have to do everything," he said. "Those medics make me do everything. I have to feed and shave those crazy people, and they spit at me and try to grab the razor. There's one that always tries to grab me by the testicles, even."

There weren't any wooden seats on the toilets, Stefan told him, just the cold ceramic stone, because the men would tear them up to use them for weapons. One of them had pried loose a tile from the latrine floor and cut his wrists and throat. Stefan had to clean up all the blood. Some befouled their beds, and some

tried to make ropes out of their blankets. One sneaked up and urinated on Stefan's bunk.

"I told the medics I wasn't crazy, so they make me do everything," Stefan said plaintively. "Wood, I've got to get out of here soon."

But what had happened on the range? Wood asked. Stefan told him in his dry, matter-of-fact, old man's voice. He seemed unaware, as always, of what might be ludicrous, and he made no special effort to convince.

"I forgot my gas-cylinder plug again. Jeeze, Wood, I don't know what it is about that gas-plug thing, but I can't seem to remember to screw it back in there."

He'd gone on the range without his gas-cylinder lock screw, and discovered its absence the first time he fired; the sound was funny, hollow, and a great cloud of blue smoke came out of the rifle. A range officer came running along behind the firing line, chewed him out and sent him back two hundred yards to the ordnance shack to get a gas-cylinder lock screw. The ordnance shack didn't have a spare gas-cylinder lock screw, so he came back to find Lieutenant Knobloch, who was yellow-faced and perhaps dizzy in the head from Atabrine. Lieutenant Knobloch told him to get down on his belly and finish that target. "But," Stefan said, and Lieutenant Knobloch said, "Listen, soldier, give me no buts." Then Lieutenant Knobloch left. Thus began what seemed no comedy of orders to Stefan. He fired blue smoke, and back came the range officer.

"You tell those ordnance people they better goddam well give you a gas-cylinder lock screw or they'll hear from me! Now git!"

But Stefan was, of course, unfit to carry any such threat, so he returned from the ordnance shack without a gas-cylinder lock screw. He found Lieutenant Knobloch, yellower in the face than ever. "Shoot that goddam rahfle," Lieutenant Knobloch said, "or I'll have your ass." Then he left. Stefan shot, and the range officer saw the cloud.

Could this have happened so many times? Wood wondered. Yes, it could, of course it could. Stefan remembered speaking to the extremely unfriendly ordnance sergeant three, maybe even four times. When he returned from what was to be his last trip to the ordnance shack, Lieutenant Knobloch abused him for the

last time, saying that this time it would be a summary court-martial, and Stefan broke his rifle in two.

"I'm not crazy, Wood," he said. "I'm really not. I saw a doctor but he wouldn't let me tell what happened. He said he knew all about it already. My shoulder kept twitching, and that was all he was interested in. He asked me why it twitched—you know how it does sometimes. I said I didn't know why, and all he did was nod."

Wood had to leave because it was time for Stefan to feed the patients. Before he left, Stefan gave him a letter for Lenore and made him promise to see her and reinforce the lie in the letter—that he'd sprained his back and was in the hospital. "I think I did sprain it a little," he said seriously.

"I'll do what I can, but I don't know just what I can do," Wood said.

"Please hurry," Stefan said. "Please, Wood. Hurry up and do something."

Wood hitched a ride on a ton-and-a-half back to the 3rd Battalion area. While waiting for the mess hall to open he read the bulletin board, then turned to find Captain Harry T. Jones standing beside him. The captain returned his salute and asked him to come into the orderly room.

"Well?" he said. "Have you made up your mind?"

"Yes sir. I've decided not to take the OCS Boards."

"*Not to?*"

"Yes sir."

"Listen, Whipple. I want you should change your mind."

Wood started to speak, but the captain braced and said, "At ease!" He stared at Wood for a moment, controlling his anger. "All right, then. Why not?"

"I don't want the responsibility, sir."

"Don't give me that crap! You take to responsibility like a goddam duck takes to water. You think we're all blind? You've been mothering that squad of yours—that collection of hind-tit, bad-luck yardbirds—like you were their goddam fairy godfather. Lieutenant Warmbuck told me, for Christ's sake, you even saved Talley's life. You thought you were, anyway—that grenade was fake. You thought fast and you acted. You know your men, such

as they are. You knew Talley'd never get that grenade away. Don't tell me you don't want responsibility."

"I'm tired of it," Wood said. "I've been responsible all my life, it seems like, and I don't want any more of it than I've got."

"You're yellow."

"Maybe I am, sir."

"Shut up! I know and you know you're not yellow. You think I'd of recommended you for OCS if I thought for one goddam minute you were yellow? Now listen close. I'm going to try and explain one more time. In fact, I'll give you an example that's much too close to home, and it's something I surely should not do. How'd you like to go into combat, your platoon led by Lieutenant Knobloch?"

Wood considered his answer. Before he could speak, the captain said, "That's what I thought. You bet your sweet ass you wouldn't. How'd you like to have your men at the mercy of that stupid shit? Why, he's so goddam dumb he couldn't pour piss out of a boot. I know it and you know it."

The captain fumed for a moment.

"Now I really am mad," he said, " 'cause you made me to say that about an officer in front of an enlisted man. Hear? I am now highly pissed off!"

The captain walked up and down the orderly room, past the first sergeant's desk and back. He snapped his cap against his leg and looked out a window onto the dusty parade ground and its islands of starved grass. "Private Stefan's in your squad, isn't he?" he said.

"Yes sir. I'd like to ask you about him."

"Ask what?"

"If you could get him out of that place, and back in the company. Evidently the medics think he's a good thing. They make him do all the dirty work."

"How do you know?" The captain looked at him closely.

"I saw him just now."

"You saw him just now. You took it upon yourself to go see him, and now you, a buck private, want to get him out of the funny farm. Did you tell him you'd take care of it?"

"I told him I'd do what I could, sir."

"I'll tell you exactly what you can do, Private. You can take

the matter up with Sergeant Garbanks, who can, if he so chooses, take it up with Lieutenant Knobloch, who, if he gives a shit, might come to me with it. If we were up to our full T.O., of course, you'd go through your squad leader, who'd be a sergeant, who'd go through his section leader, who'd be a staff sergeant, who'd go through Lieutenant Knobloch, who'd go through the executive officer, who might possibly mention it to me. In the meanwhile those medics have found a cheap orderly. But I'll tell you what I'll do. If you happen to get any ideas about how you might implement some sort of decision in the case of Private Stefan, I give you permission to come straight to me instead of through channels. There's mess call. Dismissed."

Wood had taken his tray to the table before he realized, or perhaps let himself realize, the captain's threat. He ate his pale porkchops, sauerkraut and boiled potatoes. Someone spoke, or began to speak to him, and must have noticed his preoccupied mood. It was Seabolt, one of the small, usually quiet ones, and as Wood got up he put his hand on Seabolt's thin shoulder to show he knew he'd been spoken to. Seabolt, gravely pleased by this, nodded toward his tray. Wood resented Seabolt's pleasure as much as he despised his own preoccupation with Stefan and his fate. Everything seemed to make him come out fake, and he despised his patronizing gesture toward Seabolt.

He dumped his garbage in the GI can and went back to the barracks. Tomorrow was Saturday, and those men who could remember their general orders, provided they weren't on Sergeant Garbanks' shit list and on guard or K.P., could go on weekend pass. Perrone and Quillen had reserved a hotel room, where they planned to have an "orgy," if possible. He'd been invited to drop in anytime. He did have some curiosity about what they considered an orgy to be, and in any case he wondered how they would go about getting the girls. They had been disconcerted at least once when two semiprofessional whores in their middle or late twenties had directed motherly smiles at them and told them they were too young to commence a life of sin just yet. In their training, in the warp of explosions, when they skewered the bayonet dummies with steel, they prepared for real war, but Perrone was eighteen and Quillen was nineteen, and they risked

being patronized by the V girls. This was demoralizing, to say the least.

"You git to be an officer," Quillen said, "you git all the nooky you want."

Perrone looked at Wood—the slightly abstracted look that meant he was thinking basic thoughts about Wood's character.

"Neither of us can figure you out, Whip," he said.

"Well, I can't either," Wood said.

"Don't you want to get laid?" Perrone said.

"I don't know. I figure I've got a lot of that to do later, and I don't want to get dosed up now because of some prostitute."

"Maybe later if you don't get your ass shot off first," Perrone said.

"It's more than that, I suppose," Wood said.

"What's more than that?"

"Love," Wood said. They were startled, but didn't laugh, as he'd half expected them to. Their looks were somewhat skeptical, ironic but thoughtful.

"I've got to go see Lenore Stefan and tell her some lies about Pop," he said. He'd thought of the Stefans' precarious little nest, and that was real.

"Oh my," Quillen said. "How about that?"

Perrone grinned, then seemed to think better of that line of thought.

"What I meant," Wood said, hearing sternness in his voice, "was that they love each other. It's real. That's all I meant."

"Okay, okay," Perrone said. "If it was anybody else I'd laugh my ass off, but you're too good to be true."

"Maybe you're right," Wood said.

Perrone looked at him. "I don't mean to say you can't be a pain in the ass sometimes." A little bit of steel had entered Perrone's voice; he was worried about Wood's reaction, but prepared for anything.

"I know," Wood said. He liked them, and wanted to tell them what he really thought, but of course he didn't know what he really thought. "Look," he said. "I don't want to be anybody's nursemaid. I don't want to be an officer, or even a goddam squad leader. But every time I open my eyes some pitiful little creep is about to get in trouble. What am I supposed to do? I don't want

to take care of Stefan. Do you understand? I'm younger than Stefan, for one thing. Why do I have to take charge? Captain Jones more or less told me, just before chow, he'd let Stefan rot in the violent ward if I don't go through with this OCS business."

"Hey, hey!" Perrone said.

"Yeah, Whip," Quillen said. "Don't you git all upset."

"Well, God damn it!" Wood said. They were concerned. Their rugged faces were full of sympathy. He had startled them very much; but wasn't the whole thing futile? Why blow off to Perrone and Quillen? They couldn't do anything about it. He turned quickly, afraid of their concern, and left the barracks.

Yesterday he'd heard from Horace, and on the bus into town he read the letter again. Somehow he couldn't make it out; he could hardly see the big boy, and found it hard even to remember what had happened that last night. Had he actually lost his temper and hit Horace? How many times had he hit him? They had never mentioned it again—not the next morning, or in any of their letters. Horace's cracked lip had been noticed, but that was not too strange a wound for him to carry around. The tough skin of his face had recovered quickly. Perhaps Horace had been as much ashamed of his panic as Wood was of his. For a moment on that last night their weaknesses had combined to cause that violence. Sure. The real fact was that he had hit that fragile person who loved him, and done it to get him off, to get away from him.

Dear Wood,

Things are going pretty good here, and hope you are having a good time down south. I guess it is warm in Georgia now. I mean too hot, but it is not too bad here. I have been mowing lawns and make a quarter an hour. Not bad. When are you coming home on your furlow(?)?

Bob Pacquette dove in the scrape and cracked his head on a rock. He was not hurt bad but Dr. Winston had to put two clips in the top of his head.

Ben Caswell is still in the hospital, and he is uncontious. They feed him through a tube. Peggy got a letter

from her mother saying she is fine and saving up to send for her. Peggy cries sometimes. She looks like it, any way.

Everybody sends you their love.

Love, Horace

P.S. Peggy does not want to go with her mother. That is what she cries about. Can't we keep her?

H.

The low sun shone across the tired, dark city, and in the long shadows the soldiers walked toward nothing, away from nothing. In their walking were those qualities, dangerous and enervating to watch, of boredom, of the true hatred of themselves and their possibilities that came from not wanting to be where they were.

He walked toward the Stefans' apartment. Pop Stefan had once told him that he ached for his wife. Ached for her. Wood had felt such a pang of jealousy for that pain, he'd turned away from Stefan to hide his face. He tried to imagine aching for Lois, but the fact was he didn't ache for Lois at all. They signed their letters "Love," but the word was not magic, and caused no pain.

He came to the wooden fire-escape stairs that climbed toward the Stefans' apartment. The unpainted stairs and platforms listed dangerously, so much that he thought of the whole staircase sliding out and down away from the punky wood of the building, and he had a moment of vertigo. It seemed hardly any safer when he stood at the door. If the stairs began to bend and slide downward he could grab the doorsill, but he then had a vision of the sill crumbling off, and then the clapboards, and finally the whole building would crumble down into dust and disaster.

Lenore came to the door with Georgie in her arm, his bottle in his mouth. She knew Wood was coming, and she was all dressed up in a flowered print dress of shiny material, summery and pathetically gay, silk stockings and thin low shoes with little white tassels on the lacings.

"George's letter says he's all right. Is he all right, Wood?" She let him in and made him sit down.

"He's fine," Wood said.

"Oh, good! That's wonderful!" she said, and only then turned shy. "It's so nice of you to come see us. You don't know . . ." At that moment Georgie came to some impasse with the bottle he gripped in both pudgy hands, and a dribble of white appeared on his cheek. She wiped his face with his bib, and held the bottle up. "Georgie's got to burp," she said, expertly put him over her shoulder and patted his back. He burped throatily, and she took him and the remainder of the bottle into the other room. He complained once, and then Wood heard the sucking again, the avid valving of the baby's mouth. Lenore came back, smiled widely and shyly, her lips so big and red she seemed all black hair and bright red, like a flag.

"I just wanted to let you know he's fine," Wood said.

"Oh no! Don't go yet, Wood!" she said. "Do you want a beer?" She knelt at the icebox, and he knew that she was all dressed up just for him, for the formality of his visit. Playing grown-up, she maintained the Stefan hospitality. She blushed and said she'd join him in a beer. As she stood up he saw that she was conscious of her body, that she made some attempt at grace in her posture. Through the sheer material of her dress he could see the lines of the little hems and straps that circled her, that pretended to be necessary.

She poured the beer, expertly tilting the glasses so they wouldn't foam over, then sat down across the wooden kitchen table from him. She took a small sip, left a vague smudge of lipstick on her glass, and offered him a cigarette from a crushed pack of Camels. He took it, and as he held a lighted match to her cigarette she started to take his hand, to steady it, then took her hand away and placed it in her lap, out of sight, as though it had done something wrong and should be hidden.

"Oh, poor George," she said. "You saw him?"

"Yes, I saw him."

"And he's going to be fine? He has this trick thing in his back, you know. Every once in a while, it doesn't matter what he's doing, it goes out somehow or other and he can't do a blessed thing until it gets better."

He had wondered at first if it might not be a good thing for Stefan to remain in the violent ward—at least he wouldn't have to go into combat. That was before he'd seen the terrible exhaustion in Stefan's face. It was a dangerous place for him, and the danger was certain; they would keep him as long as he was sane and could do their work for them, because Stefan would never have the talent or the authority to convince a doctor over the medics' recommendations. What would happen was that Stefan would really break down. By the time they got around to giving him a section-eight discharge it might really be too late for him.

Lenore was telling him again how glad she was he could come to see them.

"I don't know anybody down here and I'm so lonely, Wood. Sometimes I wish so much Georgie was old enough to talk. Sometimes I talk and talk to him anyway even though he can't understand a blessed word of what I'm saying." She blushed. "My, how I go on! Do you mind if I talk and talk, Wood?"

"I don't mind," he said.

"It's so nice of you. You've been a good friend to George, I know. He never talked much, but I know. Oh, I'm getting to know you too now. It's so nice to have someone to talk to!"

She stood up and smoothed her dress down over her hips. "It's like a prison sometimes." She walked to the window and moved the oilcloth curtains aside. "This town seems so old, like it was always full of soldiers and soldiers. There was a terrible fight in the alley last night. I heard bottles breaking, and cursing —you never heard such a sound. Like a lion roaring, right down in the alley. When I went out with Georgie to get the beer and groceries this morning there was blood on the cement, there, and later on, somebody, I don't know who, came and threw a bucket of water on it. I was scared silly. I'm still scared, except that you're here now."

He had no answer because he had the same fears for her, and even worse ones. Now she wouldn't let him go, yet she kept herself ill at ease with him. This tension grew with each gesture; she faced him and put her hands beneath her hair and lifted it from her shoulders.

"Oh, dear." She sighed. "How I wish the war was over and George had a good job, so he wouldn't worry." And yet her

actions didn't seem to say this. She preened before him, and seemed languorous, as though she felt some inner joy. Perhaps she didn't know how to act in any other way. She was embarrassed to be alone in this room with him, the baby asleep in its crib in the dark bedroom, yet she was afraid he might go away.

"Then we'll be back in Ohio, in a real house. I try to keep this place clean, but I told George it's just like scrubbing a cardboard box. The more you scrub, the more it sort of peels off. The paint, that Beaverboard, the wallpaper—it all sort of gets spongy and peels off." She looked at him, worried that he didn't speak, and he saw her eyes. Their eyes held for the smallest moment, then shied off, full of knowledge they could not decipher. Outside, the dark orange of the sunset faded from the railings, and the room grew dim.

"Don't go yet, Wood," she said. "Georgie'll sleep for another hour or more. I don't know why, but this is the worst time." She opened two more bottles of beer and turned on the bridge lamp beside the sofa. "Sit here. It's more comfortable. George said you never get to sit in soft chairs. Come and sit here."

He sat deep into the sofa, which breathed its musty, used smell around him. Lenore brought him an ashtray and his beer. "There," she said. "Isn't that more comfortable?" Suddenly she looked unhappy, and her thin hands came together as though she were praying. "Oh, I suppose you want to go do something more interesting than keep me company. I don't blame you. I guess I'm not very entertaining, am I."

"I'll stay with you if you want," he said. "I'd just go drink beer somewhere else."

She still looked sad. "It's just to have somebody to talk to. Just being lonely is all. I suppose it must seem funny to you, but you know we're not used to having friends. We never really had any. Hardly anybody ever came to our house, and then they didn't ever seem to stay very long. I guess we sort of bored people." She arranged a kitchen chair for their glasses and the ashtray, then sat down on the sofa herself. The sofa moved, and breathed out its history of use. Her perfume, or powder, or whatever it was, moved around him, and beneath it another odor, her deeper one, he supposed, a pleasant warmth with hints of . . . what? Calluses, shaving soap, skin—alive and nervous.

She was telling him about her family. She was a farm girl. Her father was killed by a Fordson tractor when she was seventeen . . .

He no longer listened to her words. He watched her. Her little voice with its hesitations and certainties was part of what he perceived of her, yet he no longer followed any strand of meaning. She was forgetting herself, part of herself, and grew calm and even happy. She smiled often, and occasionally laughed, red lips quivering over the bright teeth, her eyes unself-consciously meeting his. It all seemed familiar, and with a small shock he identified the painted lips. How different she was, really, from the girl in his recurring dream. Her dress had moved above her knees, and the round of beginning thigh hovered like a sharp light, though it was soft and dim—a light he hardly dared to glance upon. He was alone with this woman, in a far country hardly less foreign than the violent world of his dreams. Should he object to such a fantasy, or not? He was still here, this was no dream, and he was in control. She had asked him to stay and listen, and he would pretend to listen. In the dream she raised her dress to reveal a darkness he had never actually experienced awake. There was the connection, like warm water in the dark, and the flash, but the actual mechanics remained vague, always separated from the diagrams in books —that kind of knowledge. She was here, complete, and so was he. He had grown enormous, and he held his arm on his lap to shield it from her. She mustn't see that opinion, how it had crudely overtaken him. If she saw it, everything he really meant to feel towards her would be wiped out, and that engorged imperative would define her, though it was not really him.

She had asked him a question, and her words came slowly back, as though they had remained in the air where he could read them.

"How old are you, Wood?"

"Eighteen."

"Is that all? Really? My goodness, I thought you were older than that!" She laughed. "Eighteen! You know how old I am, Wood? Twenty-three!"

Suddenly she was looking at him differently. Her voice had changed too. It took on the confidence of those years, and was deeper, more knowing—a voice that might even presume to ad-

vise. "Eighteen," she said. "I thought you were at least my age. You seem to be more—experienced, in a way. I don't know."

"Well, I'm not," he said. "I'm just a kid."

"I thought maybe you'd even been married or something. Really. Isn't that strange. Eighteen." She looked at him searchingly, as if to find evidence of his absurd youth.

"Nope," he said.

"And you have to go fight in the war." Her face darkened and her hand moved toward him, quickly, really, but with each smooth inch of its light thrust documented in his mind. Her hand rested on his arm, light but firm, on the arm that shielded him. Each of her fingers seemed to go deep into his arm, deep as the heavy nonfeeling of a needle. She pressed his arm down upon that evidence with what seemed to be concern, and at that moment he came to believe that she was aware of it. She knew all about it, he was certain; but he was not quite certain. He was not certain, but whatever she said or did now was changed. She rose to look in on Georgie, and then turned back toward him, her eyes gleaming in the lamplight.

"He's sound asleep," she said, and he seemed to look into her mind, where his rigid tuberant sex had printed itself. She knew what it wanted, else why had it grown? But she might not even be aware of it. His intelligence, what little he could still command, seemed rooted down there. He could not command that center; it disobeyed all orders, and pulsed against the taut cloth. Tiny diamonds and triangles of light shimmered at the periphery of the room. She stood for a moment, her thin hips tilted, her dark hair falling along her cheek. With a little-girl strut, somehow an imitation, she came back and sat beside him again. She pulled her legs up beneath her, aware or not aware. The dusky hairs on her forearm were golden-tipped.

"But you must have a girl at home, Wood. Haven't you?"

"Yes," he said.

"Are you planning to get married someday?"

"I'm not sure," he said.

"Oh, you'll get married. George and I've been married three years. George's family wondered whether something was wrong because I didn't get pregnant, but there was nothing wrong, we just wanted to wait awhile. Actually we wanted to wait even

longer but one time George ran out of those things, and the drug-store was closed, and so we had Georgie. That was all right, because we wanted Georgie and all, but now George keeps those things all over the place."

She laughed, and touched his arm. "But don't worry, Wood, you'll get married. A man has to live with a woman, and a woman has to live with a man. It's not natural to live alone. It's awful to be alone. I think it's very wrong—I mean even for a little while."

She looked at him seriously, wisely.

"Well, I've managed," he said.

"But isn't it hard? How can you stand it?"

"I guess because I never . . ." His voice trembled slightly as the word, whatever it was, or ought to have been, didn't come. "I guess because I never began," he said. "I mean I've never been married."

She looked at him wonderingly, no longer shy. "I know you've never been married, but you mean you've never slept with a girl?"

"Not really," he said.

"But surely you could have, Wood."

"Yes, I guess so."

"I mean, didn't you want to?"

"Yes, in one way."

"What way didn't you?" She seemed nothing but curious.

"I didn't want to get the girl all . . . involved. It was because of the girl . . ."

"Oh," she said. Her hand rested lightly on his arm again, as if to detain him while she thought. "But it isn't really that important, in that way, is it? I mean it doesn't mean the end of the world, Wood. Two people are alive and warm, and it doesn't hurt anybody."

He groaned at his knowledge. Like a snake, it had pushed against the cloth, as if it owned him.

"It's just that I think," she said in a low voice. "I think if it ever wasn't. I mean, if I asked, and it wouldn't . . ."

"What?" he asked. His heels trembled lightly on the rug.

"I mean if I asked someone, and they didn't. Would you? Wouldn't you?"

She leaned toward him, on her knees, her black hair floating over his face. He breathed her, and his blood seemed to thicken in his lips; all his senses diffused in her warmth. All was moisture, the taste of water, and that gentle merging seemed to prove her right of insistence. When she was sure of him she touched the monstrous part of him, shyly, for reassurance, as if a small bird had landed and quickly flown. She removed herself and drew the curtains across the door, then turned out the light. She could be heard stepping out of her clothes—the slippery tick of silk.

"Take off all your clothes," she whispered from the dark.

"I didn't come here to . . ." he said.

"Won't you?"

He wondered why Stefan did not seem to be hurt at all, why he wasn't there at all. "Yes," he said, and she was there, helping to make him naked.

She was of a smoothness he could hardly believe, like eels, silken, like cool water. He could, was allowed, was welcomed against her smoothness. With shy delicacy she moved beneath him, he amazed that the hugeness of him could be so welcomed into her slender body. She sighed and pulled him into her, giving little warbles and mews of pleasure.

She stiffened, suddenly. "Oh, wait, Wood! We forgot!"

But it was too late. From the waist down he melted, as though his hips and thighs had turned to liquid and gallons of him poured upward into her.

After a moment he pulled away, exhausted, empty, full of remorse.

"Oh, dear," she said. "We forgot to use a rubber thing. And you came so quick. My goodness!"

He moved off her and sat on the couch, his feet on the floor. She knelt beside him and put her arms around him. "Don't worry, darling," she said. "Dearest, my darling." The words seemed out of a foreign language. They meant betrayal of her husband, whom she seemed to have forgotten entirely. "Oh, my big man," she said with a kind of innocent, uncomplicated joy.

Miraculously his sadness began to change, then was gone. He turned, seeming to fall lightly until they were in that position again. So easily. "Oh, oh, that's right," she cried softly. "This time it'll be so much better, darling!"

When she next fed Georgie he waited, a madman staring at the remains of a family, this bit of destruction he had caused. He lay naked, waiting for her.

At dawn, after sleep, she said she was actually a little sore. The baby was quiet, and he took her again. Afterwards in the dismal light she held him in her thin arms and told him she loved him so much she was crazy, that she would do anything for him, anything in the world. She called him by so many names of endearment he had to stop listening, saying to himself that he must never come back to this place, never.

But during the next week, leaning against his pack in the dust during ten-minute breaks, he felt her warble of pleasure in his ears, like a voice from childhood—from somewhere when touch was more important than breath. As soon as he could get a pass his feet carried him back, up the leaning wooden stairs, where she greeted him with smiles and kisses.

18

The summer lost its breath, and the maple leaves grew enormous about the house, so that only the four towers rose above the leaves for a view of the undulant green cloud that Leah had become. In only two months all the gray bones had fleshed out in green and darker green. Kate stood at her tower window and gazed across the soft town. From below the strata of leaves came the scything whirr of the lawn mower, a dry sound muted now by the rich grass. A hungry sound, as though those teeth were famished for all the moist green, and no matter how long they cut the swathes they were still bright and eager. She could almost see them down deep in there, Horace grimly leaning them forward, the steel blades coated by the mint-green blood of the dark

grass. The heavy air was furry, velvety with the smells of summer, and from an eave paper wasps shot like bullets, out and away. Those coming in suddenly appeared, stopped, as though they had hit an invisible target, then turned to prove they were alive and had an intense purpose. They knew exactly what to do, and she was full of respect for their authority and knowledge. The summer was thick, night and day, with such insistent business. The robins' stiff ceremonies were only jaunty and impertinent until you saw the cold knowing eye, and the colder green eyes of Tom the cat, watching from the top step.

Wood was away, and they all felt incomplete. With her it was a slight breathlessness, as if she were about to call to someone who wasn't there. Wood had always been there, or at least somewhere not too far. He was part of them, almost as if with all their arguing and fighting and independence they were one, really. One organism, and you couldn't take a part away. Someone else had said that. Was it Peggy? But Peggy missed Wood so much, with such tender nervousness. She said she was writing him a letter, but she seemed to be having a hard time of it. She had a funny little habit of biting her lower lip when she sat down to write, as if that helped force the words off the end of her pen, or forced her hand to write, and her dark little face squinched down upon the task. Right now she was in her room, writing to Wood, but could she say what she wanted to say? Wood was Peggy's hero. Once she had said, in a sudden outburst, that Wood was the best person in the world.

Poor Peggy, she thought guiltily, to have only us. Several times she had found Peggy crumpled over, hiding her face. She had heard from her mother, from Worcester, and she missed her mother because she was her mother, but she didn't want to go down there.

"My mother's a whore," Peggy had said, shrugging her shoulders, tears on her face.

"Peggy!" she'd said. They had been in Kate's room, talking. Peggy suddenly straightened up, shrugged her shoulders bravely and said it.

"Peggy!"

"I don't care. Everybody knows it. She brought men home and I was right in the other room."

"You heard them?" Kate's immediate curiosity gave her a shiver of cold, because she really wanted to make Peggy tell what she had heard, and this made her feel cruel.

"I heard them all right. It was awful. Sometimes they'd curse each other all the time and call each other nasty names, and all the time the bed was going up and down."

"What did they say?"

"Nasty things."

"Like what?"

"Just nasty things." Peggy's face turned dark and primitive, and Kate knew she wouldn't say the words.

But Kate had kept thinking about that, thinking of the man and woman snarling like beasts and all the while joined by each other's flesh. At night she thought of it, and in the mornings before she got up she thought of it, when she lay soft and lazy in her bed. She wondered what Peggy had felt, what terrible fright and disgust. It was her own mother. But she would like to have known little Peggy's feelings. One Sunday morning instead of getting up, she'd gone back to sleep and had a curious dream, a wrong sort of dream, but it hadn't bothered her very much. In the dream she had put her arms around Peggy when Peggy was naked. Just that, the smooth skin, and Peggy didn't seem to think it strange. It was curious because she had never been the type to want to pet other girls. She'd never had that kind of a crush. The dream remained as a slightly haunting little experience—interesting, as were so many of the things happening to her senses lately. She would wander through the dim servants' quarters with their low ceilings and squat, varnished furniture, look out the small windows and want to cry because of the dingy, squalid feeling of the past. Today in such a mood she had climbed here to her tower and wiped cobwebs from the windows, opened them all and stood letting the thick summer air pass over her, holding her bare arms out as if to a lover. She was alone above the trees, in the open sky, but no one could see her, only birds and wasps. Swallows flew twisting on wings like bending little blades. Everything mounted and grew in the green heat.

But the summer was passing, moving of its own momentum toward its end, and she felt this with sadness; she longed for and yet dreaded something undefined that could only be in the fu-

ture. She had begun to notice a slight acceleration in time. Things happened too surely, as if on a barbarous schedule no one could control. The war went on, one violent, cruel battle after another. Wood, who had only just gone, it seemed, was now at Fort Benning, Georgia, being made into an officer. She could see Leah changing too, so fast she could see it. Troop trains came through Leah, full of Canadian soldiers who carried rifles with little tea-caddylike things wrapped around the trigger parts. As the train stopped, the soldiers stamped out onto the platform, formed lines and drilled, the sergeants screaming hysterically. They stamped and turned and postured like stiff wooden soldiers for five minutes, then marched back onto the train again, to go south, to go overseas to kill and to be killed. Prudence Trask's brother John was dead, and in the second-story window above the pharmacy they had changed the blue star on the service flag to gold. Mrs. Trask was now a gold-star mother, the mother of a dead boy. The new ball-bearing factory had brought in hundreds of strangers, and the dances at The Blue Moon had become drunken and dangerous. A girl in the sophomore class, Marcia Warwick, was pregnant, and wouldn't be coming back to school in the fall. There were rumors of trench mouth and even worse things. David made a dollar an hour, now—that child David, who was as much a child as she was—making a dollar an hour. Everybody had too much money to show, dollars and dollars packed into their wallets.

Her father's tenements were all full, and he was always excited or morose; his good news seemed at once to make him sad, and he sat all day in his counting house, the living room, which he sometimes called the great hall, mumbling, yelling or staring around him like a visitor in a museum. Sometimes his staring didn't mean he was unhappy. He'd say, "How do you like this bloody castle of mine, Princess? Some place, huh?" This would be most likely in the late afternoon when he had a drink of whiskey in his hand. Or he'd kid with Peggy, whom he seemed to like better than anybody else, and she'd smile and blush. But most of the time he scribbled and mumbled.

It was hard to remember that other man who'd been their father. When she was eight or nine all of them seemed to bounce around, all of the Whipples. He never sat still for very long; in fact she could hardly remember that man sitting down at all. They

had the great big open car then—a Packard—with running boards almost as high as her waist. They'd go for rides, all of them in the big red car, and people would wave and shout as the Whipples went by, all of the Whipples laughing and singing as they rode through Leah in the late summer light. They sat high above all the other cars, and they could hear the engine working inside the long red hood, slow and lazy. It was the only car like it in town, and her father was very fond of it. On Saturdays he'd wash it and simonize it, and if it wasn't raining they'd all go on the ride around town that always seemed triumphal, as though their father had just conquered the town, or become king.

That was the car he'd been driving when the people in the Ford came out of a side road and hit him. For a month after that the Packard had been more or less on display down at Hayes's garage, buckled and rusting, with the maple blossoms falling all over the seats and hood, and the glass slivers on the floor. Then it disappeared; where had that big car gone? She had never seen another one like it.

Horrible things happened, even to your own family, to change life forever. She knew that from the past. And now the war, and all the boys and men going where it was even more dangerous. She wasn't as frightened as Horace, but it was still bad. The war mixed with all of the future to make the future so ominous. "What will become of us?" she said to the summer air. How flamboyant, she thought. What a gesture! Again she opened her arms as if to a dangerous and irresistible lover. Suddenly the world changed, and she was no longer acting. Pain changed the color of the leaves to orange, and she almost fainted, was almost sick enough to vomit. It was like being nailed. Her arm above the elbow, in the tenderest soft place, writhed and burned, and the black wasp fell to the sill, its white face jerking and nodding. She jumped back and held her arm with her other hand as if in a tourniquet to stop the pain. It was so horrible, so unasked for. It was betrayal, because she had only wished them well. She would not moan or cry, but her eyes filled with bitter tears.

Harvey Watson Whipple. He signed upon the receipt the crisp signature that never seemed to change. All that remained of him and his power and hope were the legal things, things of paper.

He was making money, but he had nothing to buy. He had heard of misers who wanted nothing but the money; they couldn't bear to spend it, because it was the heavy gold or the crisp official green they wanted. If only he could find their secret. He wanted . . . *things!* But the things he wanted he could no longer want. How could he own them with the firm, manly caress of his hands when he had no hope? Each day he spent in this slug of a body, his life was shortened by more than a day. He knew what the actuaries would say about that. He dreamed of running, of sailing before the wind toward a harbor where he would find good food and drink, and love he was worthy of because of his strength. Now all that was gone, could he believe it?

I can't believe it.

Memory is worse than oblivion. Sure. Believe it. He remembered when his young wife was dark golden, her hair black as a crow's wing, and light as that day's August wind coming down the lake toward camp. How old were they that good year? He was twenty-eight and she was twenty-three. Wood was a year old, and her belly was smooth again, with only the silvery little stretch marks slanting V-like from her hipbones. In the lake was that little no-class sloop Harry Thibodeau built for him, and it rode easy beside the dock—lapstraked, white, green canvas over the foredeck. Let's take a jar of martinis and sail up the lake and come back with the spinnaker (a half-spinnaker, really; and as for the gin and vermouth, he knew a driver on the Canada run. He knew everything there was to know, then).

Aunt Mary Watson was alive then to mind the baby, who would always be a baby, just a cute little fella, always new, a new idea, just their baby.

When they grow up, you grow old.

They were skimming back down the lake under spinnaker and sail, centerboard up, cutting in the dusk, the yellow sun just gone. She leaned back against him, and felt him, and they stopped at the deep end of Pine Island, tied up on a root and slid into the cool water. They helped each other off with their knit cotton bathing suits. The lovely ache of a hard-on in cool water, scrotum hard as walnuts, and her cool cold skin, cool lips hot inside. A rubbery rub and then the always miraculous oil. God, the in-

visible unoily oil. Welcome. No. More than welcome. "You're in me," she said.

Oh, God. He watched his death so soon.

How would he go? Heart? Cancer? Flu? Anything could take him out now. A hangnail. Everybody died, didn't he know that all the time? He must have known it in his twenties, in his thirties. He must have known it and yet he joked about it. He remembered the jokes. Croak. Kick the bucket. He knew it all the time, and that what was him would turn alive in the ground another way. It was all so logical, so right, so instinctively right. By other instincts than his would he boil—try not to remember that.

But weren't there people not bothered by . . . death? He couldn't even think of that word without breathlessness, fear in his hollow. No, not him. He was all there was of him!

What about Sally? She was over seventy, for God's sake! Did she wake up at four in the morning with black nothing leaning over her, eye to eye? Maybe some lived for a purpose, died for a purpose. What purpose? All men died. If you were going to die, what was the purpose? For your children? Shit, they had to live their own lives and die their own deaths. That was their problem. Not that he was indifferent. No, he wasn't. It was all terrible.

Oh, God, he needed some medicine. He needed the drink he hated the taste of. He'd rather taste a blueberry warmed by the sun on top of Cascom Mountain. One firm blueberry pierced by his white teeth, and the acidy blue taste that meant lakes and mountains down and away, boats on the lakes, trees, gray granite, grouse, deer.

What about religion, buddy? You desperate?

He'd never had any, and that was the truth. He was an American; he wasn't haunted by anything but Nothing. Ancestors? That all washed out long ago, buddy. Some kind of a lemur, scared of snakes and cats but thought he'd live forever. Now cursed with predilection. Some of the more recent ones were human, and they had their scary solutions too. Scary because so obviously impossible to believe. Genealogies, Bibles—they were the property of certain idle aunts, all dead now, their spidery findings stored in attics or cellars.

He always said he'd never commit suicide. He wasn't the type, nope. Maybe he still wasn't. Christ, you don't cut your

throat to cure a canker sore. But what was the use of living, when you had to die? He'd heard that question before, but couldn't remember the answer. Funny he couldn't remember the answer. Very funny.

Buddy, you're choking in the clutch. But it isn't a clutch, friend. That's a myth. He'd got out of many a clutch. Them he could handle. It was dead certainty that choked him up. He was a gambler, an American; he had to have odds. Save me some sweet innocent odds, God. Shit. Cry, you poor bastard.

He sat in his wheelchair dry-eyed.

Peggy came running across the grass toward him, and he was afraid he wouldn't stop pushing the lawn mower in time; he would do something dumb. "Horace! Horace!" she cried. The maples dipped toward her, thick oily green, and once she slipped on the wet cut grass, her little ankle slipping out and her shoulders tilting to counteract it. With a little hop she righted herself and came on toward him. She had worried him with her running and crying out his name, but her dark little face wasn't panicky. He stepped between her and the teeth of the lawn mower as she came up to him. She stopped, smiling, her hands on his arms, and looked up at him. "Your father wants you," she said.

"Oh."

"It's all right. He's not mad or anything." She frowned at his worry, and squeezed his arms with her little bird hands.

He looked up the lawn toward the house. His father sat inside its bulk and darkness. It grew beyond and above the trees, and the grass ended at the black dirt under the hedges and the lilacs rooted next to the gray granite blocks of its foundations. It was the house he had always lived in, yet there were windows in odd and irregular shapes, mouth- and eye-like, whose rooms he wasn't sure of. There were windows in closets, in stairwells, windows peering out of rooms he may have never dared to discover. The four towers led up into green; David's, Wood's, Kate's and . . . his. He never went there. They told him it was his tower—David and Kate had—but he was afraid to go there. He'd seen it from David's tower, and it looked, the little square room on its high shaft,

empty of all but cobwebs. But he couldn't see down over the sills, and he couldn't see up into the ceiling. He'd lied to Kate, and said he'd gone up in it. He was afraid something else lived there.

"Go on, Horace," Peggy said, pulling his arms.

In the big room his father turned with a creak, the white face coming around slowly, its power turning.

"You're tracking grass all over the place. Can't you learn to wipe your feet?"

Horace looked back along his path through the hall and saw some blades of grass on the red carpet.

"Yes, it's grass," his father said wearily, "and it's all over the sides of your shoes, and the tops of your shoes, and in your cuffs, and hanging from your knees." His father shook his head, as if at himself for going on so. "I want you to do some errands for me." He looked up, calculating. "Do you think you can? Maybe if I write them down in block letters?"

"I'm not stupid!" Horace said, his hurt turning toward fear.

"Look, I just want the errands done. Whether you're stupid or not is another matter."

His mother's voice came from the dining-room archway. "Cruel!" she said.

"Shut up! You're the one says he ought to be trusted more!"

"You would say that in front of him, wouldn't you!"

"God damn it! Who asked you for your two cents' worth? Go on back and button your pudding irons, or whatever the fuck you were doing!"

"I ought to let you sit in that chair and rot!"

"What do you think I am doing, you stinking bitch!"

Horace felt like a tree; no one had given him the permission or the power to get away from this violence. They went on, cold words shouted, hatred in their icy faces, frowns of absolute zero.

His mother turned, her face set in that coldness, and went back to the kitchen.

For a moment his father looked down at his table, his hands over his face. They were pale, fat hands, the nails bitten down halfway, and here and there in the cracks beside what were left of the nails were traces of dried blood. His father wrung his face with those hands, then looked up.

"Now," he said. "If that's all over, I'll ask you again if you can be trusted to do a couple of errands for me. Wipe your nose."

Horace had no handkerchief.

"Take a Kleenex tissue. Here!"

Horace took one of the filmy, inconsequential things from the box his father held out to him, and wiped his nose. He felt the wet snot come through on his fingers.

"Put it in the wastebasket. Now. First I want you to go to the bank. All you have to do is give this envelope to Mr. Ward or Mrs. Wilson. Got it?"

Horace nodded. Then his father told him to go to the Water Street tenement and get the rents that had come due that week from Sam Davis. Sam Davis was supposed to get up at one o'clock in the afternoon, so he'd be awake, right?

Horace accepted the two envelopes, one to be given to the bank, one to be filled and brought home. He placed them both deep in the side pocket of his pants, and then he was allowed to go. His bike had a flat tire, so he had to walk.

Downstreet among all the eyes he hulked, looked down and into corners, avoiding the eyes as much as possible. The bank was echoey and cool, and Mrs. Wilson smiled voraciously through her teller's window as he pulled the envelopes from his pocket. One said BANK, underlined, and she seemed too pleased to accept it. She was thinking of the money he stole, she must be, and that he must be rehabilitated or something if his father trusted him. On the way out he was careful not to bump into Miss Colchester, who was just coming through the big doors. "Hello, Horace!" she said, but he noticed how careful she was of him. "My, you've grown," she said, moving out of range.

On Water Street he came to the stoop of the tenement, where grass and cindery dirt competed for the narrow strip between the steps and the crumbling sidewalk. The stoop and steps had been painted gray over the gray weathered wood, to keep down splinters. The glass in the front door had been painted gray too, for some reason. He entered the hallway, which was lighted from the far end by a grimy double-hung window, and from the front by a transom so deep in spider webs the light was brown. It smelled, the hall and its painted walls, of something that had once been hot, and had cooled. Some kind of food, or maybe even

clothes. Cellar air leaked up through the floorboards, potatoey, mixed with coal fumes.

He knocked on Sam Davis' apartment door, the first on the right, and heard quick steps coming. The door opened. It was Susie, and his heart began to skip and hammer. He stuttered something about his father. She smiled and smiled, wider and more delighted and happier to see him. Even her combed brown hair, with the comb furrows in it, seemed to spread away from her ears as she welcomed him.

"Come in, Horace! My goodness! I haven't seen you all summer! Come in and sit down!"

He sat at the kitchen table, careful to keep his arms and hands off the table and in his lap. He was so pleased and excited he was frightened of his pleasure. The table and the chairs, the jar of brown-eyed susans, the ashtray with a lipsticked butt in it—all the delicate things seemed to have been placed according to exact and precise measurements, and he must not alter any part of that plan by the millionth of an inch.

"Are you surprised to see me?" Susie said. She pulled her chair recklessly next to his, took his hands in hers and squeezed them. He wanted to run away, because she seemed to be giving him too much, too much all at once. "Horace, my good, good friend!" she said. Then her expression seemed to say: Back to the subject. "You see, we're on split shifts, or something like that. The war. Friday's my day off, now, so if you come regular for the rent money I'll be the one here. Won't that be nice, Horace? My dad's over to the other building this after . . . I think, anyway." A dark bit of worry crossed her face. "He's been . . . sad since we lost the farm. You know. And poor Mrs. Garner had to go to the County Farm."

"Oh," Horace said.

"But this is so nice! You want a Coke? I've got some cold in the icebox, and I'll have one too." She squeezed his hands and got up, so happy-looking and walking so lightly, almost dancing to the refrigerator. "We'll see each other every Friday. Won't that be nice? I'll look forward to it, won't you, Horace? I see David sweeping up the scraps and thread all the time, but I never see you! But now we can have a nice visit every week!"

She poured him his Coke and sat beside him, asking him

questions about himself only, no one else. He told her he was making twenty-five cents an hour. It was all love and pleasantness, and he began to grow calm inside, as though some sort of fusion of intent had occurred between his needs and his muscles. Calm and control; his arms did no more than his will bade them to. He drank from his glass and set it on the table lightly, easily. No fear of dribbling on his chin or on his shirt made his throat perversely contract, and he felt no need to squeeze the glass, nor to measure the distance to the table with his eye before putting it down. It descended lightly and surely to the oilcloth, with no bump at all.

Through the small clean panes of the side window were the sprung, flaking white clapboards of the next building. Past the front window's white curtains was part of Petrosky's Tavern sign— blue neon, flickering—and past the corner of that old building, once a private house, he could see down Water Street as it turned to the railroad tracks where the black and white wooden bars now slowly descended. The floor hummed from the train that was coming from Vermont, maybe all the way from Montreal, but he couldn't hear the jangling bell he knew rang from the black box. The alternate red lights blinked on and off, as though one stole the other's light, then gave it back. Susie stopped whatever she was saying and they both watched as the train became the only thing happening on the street. Two long black engines, whooshing oily black smoke in ponderous rhythm led the train. The second engine was turned around backwards, so that it looked somehow more violent than the other, as if it were being punished, and its power and pressure were that of resentment. Freight cars slid heavily past; he counted forty, then stopped counting. The building seemed tuned to the deep rumble, each room a sounding box, each doorway growling. The heavy rumble seemed to be louder in the room behind him than it was in the kitchen. Then, finally, when he'd almost got used to that deep continuing presence, another black engine, longer and lower than the others, pushed by greasily and with it the sound diminished. The black and white bars of the warning gate went up lightly, and now they seemed frail, as their counterweights fell and they pointed straight up again.

It was as though he came back into the room. Susie's smile seemed frail too, very tender and fleeting.

He didn't want to leave her, but he said he guessed he'd better because his father would suspect he'd fouled up again. She frowned, concerned. "I know you did something for me, Horace," she said, and she blushed and looked down at the table. He couldn't think what she meant. "I heard," she said. "I know you meant well, about the money, but I wouldn't have gone with them. You believe that, don't you, Horace?"

That. "It was stupid," he said, stammering. "Sus-stupid. Stupid. I threw it away and Wood had to pay it back."

"But did you think I'd go with them, really?" She was very serious.

"They seemed so strong," he said.

"I wouldn't have gone. Gordon asked me, but I wouldn't have gone, Horace. After what he did to me. I wouldn't have gone, not for anything."

"Yes," he said. He couldn't understand why she cared so much what he thought. Of course she wouldn't have gone of her own free will. Didn't she understand that?

"Do you believe me?" Tears slid back and forth at the bottoms of her eyes. Each tear was a little globe, and her eyes were so blue. His throat began to ache.

"Don't cry," he said. "That isn't it. Of course you wouldn't say you'd go. Yes! I believe you!" He sounded as if he were mad at her. His voice came out that way, like one of his accidents, and he was afraid she wouldn't understand.

"Oh, I know you believe me, Horace!" She said that and leaned over toward him, getting bigger and bigger and more lovely and powerful and she put her lips on his forehead. He sat shocked as she went to the sink and wiped her eyes, a quick dab at each eye with the damp dishcloth. He stood up, and she came back to him, a strange interest in her eyes that melted him. He couldn't move, he couldn't understand, until she took the dishcloth and cleaned the lipstick from his forehead. "See?" She showed him the red that had been on his skin, and was now on the cloth. "I got lipstick on you." She laughed, and he laughed back, a quick bark that was strange to him because he seldom laughed.

They would see each other again next Friday, whether he

271

was given the errand or not. As he walked home he saw clearly, almost too clearly, the sun on the houses, the elms shining, glints of reflected sun on windows. All the lawns seemed a brighter green. For a moment he felt his strength—a moment of daring, because his strength couldn't be trusted. But he raised his arms over his head, clasped his hands and pulled until something in his shoulder nearly broke: a warning. But a deep thing had happened, a thing almost to hurt, an alliance, a secret deep thing. They had touched deeply, where nothing was hidden. Nothing came between the feelings they had for each other, no disgrace, no freak disaster, nothing mean and cramped and murderous at all.

He saw her every Friday afternoon, and that brief half-hour became his counter for time itself. She always had the rent money ready, and never let him forget it when he left. When he arrived she hugged him briefly, and they talked, sitting at the kitchen table. Always at the back of his mind was the question "Why does she regard me with such joy?" Me. She was in love with Wood, and that seemed right. He had fantasies of a family—Wood, Susie, children. What justice and calm! And he would somehow be part of that family, almost as a child. But no, there was something else he would be, and this part he shied from, because he felt danger. As if he were a soldier. Something like a soldier, only secret, a secret force to avenge, to obliterate the murderers who crept, scaly and cold, toward the children's windows. He shivered with fear when this began to come to mind, but it was not fear for himself. He couldn't place it. He couldn't get it straight.

But in his nights a strange thing began to happen. Sometimes it was as though Leverah and Zoster and the Herpes crept out, their cellar stench falling from scale and tooth, but not for him. Toward him, but not for him. *Beyond* him, and he was the last outpost of the warmth. Arm thyself, he seemed to hear whispered. Monsters. They are monsters.

19

In Leah Town Square the sun met the summery September fog,
and the town, hot and sleepy, seemed totally deserted. It had
been a warm night—as warm as day—and now day had come back
to find the streets as empty as they had been in the darkest part
of the night. Already David's shirt stuck to his shoulder blades,
and he had fifteen miles to go. The few automobiles that had
been left parked overnight looked abandoned. The marquee of the
Strand, in this new light, revealed the necessities of its construction: bolts, iron rods, white block letters uneven on their slides,
spelling out THE MONSTER OF THE DEEP.

Goodbye! he thought exultantly. The stores and trees, that
had been too familiar, now in the humid dust of fog passed behind him newly, as if forever. "The monster of the deep," he
said out loud. "The monster of the deep." Did a monster lurk
within the Strand, living on dried chewing gum? And because
he pedaled with an unhurried rhythm, the phrase "The monster
of the deep" stayed with him all that morning, and recurred later,
miles later, coming up upon his breath.

As he rode down the slight grade of Bank Street he passed
the houses whose families he knew, the white clapboard houses
under elms and maples, then the red-brick high school he would
no longer attend. He would have little nostalgia for that building,
even though his friends would be seniors this fall. Not Ben Caswell, though, who still slept in Northlee Hospital, fed through a
tube, still powerful, still a presence, though fading sadly from the
minds of his friends. One had to get on with it, to move toward
something real. The only half-stable thing in that school now
seemed to be the anarchical rule of the students themselves, who

had all turned into something like prisoners of war, bound upon their honor to give back to their guards as little information as possible.

He had taken to turning on his radio late at night, so low no one else in the house could possibly hear it, and from some distant city heard classical music, its clean, deliberate dignity of cadence and sound. He would somehow translate himself through all that distance, through the medium of that clean, intelligent sound, into the great world where he wanted to be. And this journey might be the first step.

He had been taken to Dexter-Benham once, for an interview. Its buildings were Georgian, arranged around a mall on top of a hill under huge elms. The students wore sport coats with leather elbow patches, and white shirts with striped neckties. The headmaster, Mr. Barnes, a tall man with light blue eyes, had shaken his hand and led him into a round office with tall windows, where everything was polished and light. The furniture seemed very old, permanent, and at the same time fragile. Mr. Barnes was very formal in his manner, yet friendly. He told David to call him "Chief," and through the friendliness David seemed to see the one reservation he wanted to see—that he must do well, that he must perform, that there was no substitute for this. All would be serious, dignified. Rules would be respected and upheld. They would all be men.

As he rode out of Leah, his tin suitcase creaked and crackled as it moved within its bindings of clothesline tied with many doubtful knots. His trunk was being sent on to Dark Hill Farm, where he would live. That had been arranged by his mother, and he didn't worry about it.

He rode east on a narrow asphalt road, past well-kept houses that had once been farmhouses, although on this road the fields grew smaller as the land rose, and the stone walls that had once marked their borders were deep in the woods, submerged in the dark spruce that advanced behind hardwood brush. Dark little houses, then, that stood in clearings small as rooms, and then a few shacks covered roof and sides with tarpaper, some with no windows. These sat in clearings that seemed to have been claimed from the woods by no cutting instruments at all, but trodden out by feet. And then only the dark woods.

The road climbed, then for a short relief ran level, then climbed again, so that he had to stand upon his pedals and pump against the achy weakness that crept into his knees—a hint of mortality he knew all about. The asphalt seemed to breathe away his breath as it drew the green heat from the ferns and trees along the road. After a few miles he stopped to rest, not because he was exhausted, but to feel the pleasure of his muscles as they cleared again. He let his bike lean against the springy brush, and stood bemused—slightly dazed by the heat of the sun, looking into the thickness of the green, where blackberries hung shiny as coal upon their sticks among the heavy ferns. It was early in September, and bees hummed over the last of the wild asters. The gravel smell of the shoulder of the road was pleasant where the heat sucked it up, and where the dust had settled on the ferns the two odors mixed—the mineral one seductive as a sneeze, the furry green one rich and forbidding.

He was not in a hurry. The bees buzzed here with as much intensity as anywhere, and the sweet hot air was as much alive. Where he was, was life enough to let him know he was still in the world. And so he stood, scratching his elbow. A car passed, and shortly afterward a pickup truck, but there were few cars because of gasoline and tire rationing.

After a while he straightened up his bike and noticed that his suitcase had begun to slide off to the right. No minor adjustments of the clothesline seemed to help, so he undid all the knots and put his suitcase down in the ferns. It was an interesting problem, and while he thought about it he idly opened the snaps of the suitcase and looked inside. On top was his raincoat. He moved the raincoat and looked—pretending that it was a discovery to him—at the .32 caliber Iver Johnson revolver that pressed heavily on his one sport coat. He thought how it would have been a thrill to discover such a real and heavy thing in a suitcase among clothes. Even though he knew it was there, each time he looked at it he got a small surprise. Still thinking of discovery, he cautiously picked it up, opened it and looked at the cylinder to see if it was loaded, although he knew it was. He'd bought it from the Leah High School janitor, for the price of a pint of Schenley's and a fifth of muscatel. He hadn't fired any of the real cartridges that came with it because they couldn't be replaced; none of the hard-

ware stores had ammunition to sell any more. He had found one box of blanks in one store, and these he unloaded, reamed out and reloaded with black powder and lead balls.

He knew that the smokeless powder in the blank cartridges was too quick to use with balls, and might have caused dangerous pressures in the old gun. His attitude toward this hobby of his was mixed, especially now that he was leaving Leah for the winter. What had guns, even though guns were real, and not exactly toys, to do with the new life he wanted? He aimed the revolver at a tree, then put it carefully back on his sport coat, tied his suitcase on again and continued his long ride.

Hours later he came into Cascom above the lake, and had to climb, pushing his bike for miles, it seemed to him. The road turned as it climbed the mountain, and came out of big pines into what had once been a field, but now was grown up with small poplars and pin cherries. The road was a corridor between these low walls of thick gray and green. Here, after the deep pines, David felt exposed, trapped by the density of the saplings on either side of him. Soon the road leveled, and he could ride for a while, even though the gravel was at times mushy and difficult. But then the road climbed again, and he found it easier to get off and push. The darkest woods were just before the farm—spruce in impenetrable groves, their branches interlocked, under them only a black crawl space where the passages led, deep in needles, among the trunks and dead lower branches.

Past a hundred yards of these, with the sky darkening, he came to the farm. It was as it had been described to him; on the left, beneath tall pines and backed up against the granite outcroppings of a steep hill, the house seemed to be in hiding. It had once been a standard colonial farmhouse, but tall bay windows had been added to the front and to a newer wing, and it was painted a dark, barn red. Across the road from it the land opened up around two black, unpainted barns. On that side was a huge field, opening out pie-shaped behind the barns—a whole hill of field. Past the opening the road was immediately enclosed again by the thick spruce, as though it went straight into a black hole.

No one was in sight, but he'd been hearing a raucous, tinny sound coming from the house, and as he pushed his bike

up over the pine needles that were the lawn, he recognized the song "Chattanooga Choo Choo," the record made by Johnny Mercer.

> Can I afford to board
> Chattanooga Choo Choo?
> I've got my fare,
> And just a nickel to spare

—sang the nasal voice. The record was being played too fast, and the voice sounded somewhat like an angry squirrel.

He leaned his bike against the side porch—no track seemed to go to the front door—and went up the steps. He couldn't help seeing, through the bay window, some violent motion in the room. He looked, feeling himself to be a spy. Inside was a young girl in a blue dress, with long dark hair, who jitterbugged with no partner, and made all the expert shakes and squirms and twirls of that dance, her bobbysocks flashing as she kicked and twirled. On her rather long, pale face was the standard, expert miming of ecstasy that jitterbugging seemed to demand.

To David it would have been somewhat shameful to be caught like that, so he wasn't sure he ought to disturb her. He decided that she probably wouldn't hear his knock anyway above the noise, and decided to wait until the record ended.

When it did, and the girl had moved out of sight, he clumped his feet on the porch and knocked. He heard her stop cranking the Victrola, listen, then crank a few more times, hard, before she came to the door.

"Well, well," she said, and looked him up and down, her eyebrows raised. Her pale face was long and delicate, with a long thin nose and a wide, thin-lipped mouth scarlet with lipstick. Her eyes were gray-green. He thought she was beautiful. In spite of the jitterbugging—which he knew how to do, but had learned only because it was a way to get to put one's arms around girls—she seemed very upper-class and intellectual-looking.

"Well," she said. She pursed her lips and shrugged her shoulders, as if to say *Not bad, but nothing too special.* "Come in. Perk and Myrna are down in the barn."

That was devastating, that she called her parents by their first

names. He became desperately aware that he hadn't said anything yet.

"You're Tucker," he said.

"Me Tucker. You David," she said.

He knew he should go along at once with this Tarzan business, but he couldn't, because he didn't want her to act this way.

"Well, come on in, don't just stand there with your face hanging out," she said, and backed slowly away from him, beckoning with her hands.

Thunder sounded; it seemed to hit the hill behind the house and roll down upon them and past them as it broke into pieces. Tucker went to the Victrola and put another record on—"String of Pearls"—and came up to him to dance.

"Don't tell me you don't dance," she said, and put her left arm on his shoulder. She wore perfume that smelled a little bit like spoiled oranges. As he put his arm around her back, above her narrow waist, her dark hair brushed his cheek and he looked down into her clear, hard little eyes. Her dress had exaggerated shoulders, and it was of a blue, woven material that moved in its weave under his fingers. He had trouble beginning with the rhythm, but then began to do well, for him, and after she had twirled by herself and come back to him he brought her up against him tight, the whole line of her body against him.

"Hey! Down, boy!" she said. "You like to squeeze, huh?"

She was a little hard, a little too aggressively muscular against him, but he was ready to forgive that. He didn't like girls who were too doughy and limp, anyway.

When the record ended, loud, eccentric scratching began. He wanted to hold her, yet he wanted to get his balance. He hadn't even had time to look around the place before he had the girl in his arms, and that was too soon. He wanted it to happen, but it should happen according to his schedule, not someone else's.

The problem was solved by a dog, who appeared in the doorway with all of his teeth showing, his snarls at that pitch near strangulation that meant nothing but business. "Meet Heinz," Tucker said calmly. "Thirty-seven varieties."

Heinz was a big brownish-blackish animal, with thick, wiry hair, who looked somewhat like an oversized Airedale, yet had

softly hanging hound-dog ears. Though he still communicated the intent to kill, the wolf in him was gradually receding. David could tell that the hound in him was taking over, because the madness in his eyes was just a little put on; he was thinking too much.

Tucker had been watching, and he could feel her interest in the situation like a small piece of ice against his skin. She introduced the two of them. Heinz had to go through the motions of wariness and warning, but David could see that he was coming around. He growled too threateningly to really mean it, and allowed his hound ears to be rumpled.

It had begun to rain. Perkins and Myrna Cross came up on the porch, both dressed in yellow oilskins, and stamped and whooshed some of the water off them before they came in, their oilskins ballooning and sliding off over their arms. David's first impression of them was one of weight and substance, and it was true that neither was small. Perkins, whom he had been told was a writer, was a tall, violently freckled man, with a high, tenor voice that could turn hard as glass. Myrna was a plump, plain woman whose graying hair fell like a yoke over her shoulders. Her dress was black, with white piping, and it was somehow over-simple—one that might have been worn in the early 1800s by a girl of twelve.

Perkins affected a Western, ranchy look, with a checked cotton flannel shirt, Bull Durham tag hanging from a breast pocket, and Levis.

Myrna wiped some water from her face, using the back of her chubby hand, and with her face shining and wet came up to David.

"This must be David Whipple, then!" she said in a voice that seemed too glad. She smiled, yet her smile moved, as though something were running around underneath it, trying to get loose. Parts of it would fade, and then come back into a smile again, all this happening very fast. "We've heard what a fine young man you are!" Because of the unfocused quality of her expression he couldn't tell how she meant this.

"He can even dance," Tucker said, and at this Perkins looked stern.

"Can you handle an ax?"

"I think so," David said.

"You *think* so? Can you split wood and not your shins?"

"My mother cooks on a woodstove," David said. This, to David's surprise, seemed to impress Perkins very much—almost to overawe him, because he immediately became conciliatory, his tone of accusation gone.

"Hey!" he said. "Let's show this young man where he's going to live. You hungry? What the hell time is it? How about some grub, Myrna?"

The room they were in was called the library. On unfinished shelves all around it, even above and below the windows, were, they told him, a thousand books. The furniture consisted of several Morris chairs with marble-topped tables next to them on which stood oil mantle lamps—machines he was going to have to learn to run—the chest-high Victrola and a potbellied stove that was meticulously blacked and polished. Its brass trim shone too, and David appreciated how much work had gone into that job. When he commented upon it Tucker looked at him disgustedly, and Perkins assumed a rather complicated expression, which seemed to approve and yet be terribly bothered at the same time. Tucker, David later found, had been forced to clean and polish the stove, and so it was still a touchy subject among them. With this first error of his constraining him, he was shown the rest of the house.

The living room was long and narrow; the bay window took up the whole front end of it, and at one end was a dining area with a long harvest table dominated by a huge highboy that tilted ominously forward, suggesting that sometime it might crash over onto the table, smashing dishes and lamps and heads.

They went upstairs, where he was shown his bedroom, a small neat room with a high old-fashioned metal bed, a desk, chair and lamp. The one window looked across the yard beneath the high branches of the pines; the view stopped where the road entered the black spruce.

"Your suitcase!" Myrna suddenly shouted, so loudly she might have been calling to someone a hundred yards away. David jumped, but neither Tucker nor Perkins seemed to notice anything strange at all; they might have been deaf.

"It's all right," David said nervously. "It's tin, so it won't

leak." Again he felt he'd said something wrong. Myrna gave no sign of response, and never mentioned the suitcase again.

They went downstairs, and he was shown, by lamplight, the earth cellar, where eggs lay in crocks under water glass. Everything that could possibly be preserved in jars was preserved— meat, berries, vegetables, even a green vegetable he'd never heard of before, called lambs' quarters. There were all sorts of mushrooms, some looking like sea plants and animals, with strange, meaty tentacles that seemed to suck against the glass. The cellar smelled of earth, but also of cool, tangy things like horse radish and crushed potato skin. In another, deeper cellar room a half-carcass of a sheep hung on a mean-looking hook between damp, sawdust-leaking boards. Behind the boards, Perkins proudly told him, were thousands of pounds of ice he'd cut himself on Diddleneck Pond.

"Some of that ice is from the year before last," Perkins said. "That's how cold it is down here. The only thing we have to import is the goddam mail!" Then he added in an irritated voice, "And milk, damn it. Our goddam cow—"

"Martha," Myrna said, and Perkins scowled at her.

"Our goddam cow went dry on us. Got to get her freshened up, or whatever it is. I don't understand cows, and I don't like cows. There's always some damn thing going wrong with their plumbing."

The wood-burning furnace, Perkins told him, was in a separate cellar altogether, so the earth cellar would stay cool. "We'll be cutting wood. You sure you know how to split wood?"

"I like to split wood," David said, and then, tentatively, he tried to make a little joke. "I just don't like to carry it."

"Well, you better get over that," Perkins said seriously, and David could think of nothing at all to say; again the ensuing silence seemed to have a heavy, unspeakable meaning.

When they came up into daylight again, they went into the big kitchen with its black range and water-heating coils, heavy slate sinks and zinc-covered counters. Here Myrna took on more authority, and rather gaily, as if she knew that Perkins wouldn't interrupt her here, showed David her collection of herbs, many of them grown in her own herb garden.

"Smell!" she ordered him, holding a small jar under his nose.

It smelled like the brown ointment he'd once had to smear on his hand after a firecracker had printed blood blisters all over his palm and fingers. Another jar smelled like the inside of his father's car when it was new. "That's one I don't know the name of," Myrna said, "but doesn't it smell funny?"

He agreed. He considered telling her it smelled like the inside of a new car, but by now he'd come to feel that they either didn't hear him, or that they resented his venturing anything more than yes or no.

"I can't find it in any book! So! You know what we think?" She cocked her head like a gray-haired bird, her arch, tremulous smile flickering at him. He shook his head.

"We think it's a varietal—a sort of freak! It *looks* like partridgeberry, but the fruit is *bluish!* Isn't that interesting?"

"Very interesting," he said, playing it safe.

When the rain stopped, and his only slightly damp belongings had been arranged in his room and its small closet, Perkins took him on a tour of the barns. Heinz accompanied them this time, but he wouldn't actually go into the barns. He stood rigid in the doorways, with his tail stiffly curled down between his legs, and gave out low howls, so soft and hollow they seemed to come from somewhere inside David's own head. Tucker had come down after them, and as she came up behind Heinz she gave him a little push. He screamed, turned with his paws kicking up straw and manure, and nearly knocked her over on his way out.

"What's the matter with him?" David asked.

"He's afraid of the animals," Perkins said.

"Especially he's afraid of Lucifer. Lucifer chases him all over the place," Tucker said.

"Lucifer?"

"You'll see him," Perkins said. "Just don't let him get behind you."

"He's a black ram, but he looks more like a goat," Tucker said.

"He's a beautiful goddam animal," Perkins said. "The only thing is, he's got too damn much karakul in him."

They stood in the wide doorway of the first barn, on hard earth, scattered hay and sheep droppings—little messes of blackberries. David's eyes had adjusted to the gloom inside, and in the

light from the high door and from between the shrunken boards, he could make out a high, hay-filled loft at one end, and a platform that ran along the length of the barn. Below were pens of various sizes, with all the gates open, and in them and beside them dim, woolly things lay or moved, skittish and sullen, like prisoners, blatting now and then for no apparent reason.

Something bigger moved, back in a corner, and the ewes stamped nervously, then several of them stampeded away from whatever it was, swirled at the wooden bars and came out the pen door, hysterical blats issuing from their sober faces. The faces never changed; they might have been carved from gray-black stone. The ewes stopped in front of them and stamped their feet, and Lucifer, his black curly horns and hair shining like coal, pranced on his long legs out behind them. He paid no attention to the three people, but in the light of the doorway mounted one of the immobilized ewes. His bright red penis, bright as blood, stabbed past the dingleberries, in and out of the black folds of the ewe. Neither sheep changed expression at all, although it seemed to David that the gnarled horn and curved bone of their faces had been carved into such violent immobility they must have been aware of pain and death. He watched—there was nothing else to see—and out of the corners of his eyes saw Tucker and her father watching Lucifer's gaunt spasms over the stolid ewe. He was embarrassed, yet because there was nothing else to see, nowhere to turn that wouldn't put him face to face with another witness to the act, he had to watch until Lucifer uncurled his forelegs and let the ewe run back into the darkness.

Lucifer stood looking at them, and Perkins turned to lead them to the other barn, where the cow and two horses were kept. He turned carefully, and said, "Don't let him get behind you, or he'll bunt, and he's got a head like a rock."

Lucifer did follow them a few feet, stopped when Perkins turned toward him, then came on again, walking slowly with his head down. Perkins ran over to a shed and got a two-by-four that was leaning against it, came back and without a word bashed Lucifer across the back. This brought Lucifer's head up, and he stopped walking forward.

"Git!" Perkins yelled, bashing him over the shoulders. Lucifer turned and walked diagonally away, keeping one golden eye

on Perkins. "If you hit him on the head it just makes him feel good," Perkins said. "He's a mean son of a bitch."

David was shown the other barn, this one floored, except for the stalls, by generations of cow and horse manure. The cow and the two brown, phlegmatic workhorses paid no attention to them at all. In a small, muddy pen near the barn was a huge pig, surrounded by its bitter odor, and next to the pigpen a chicken coop—or rather a roost, for the chickens were here and there all around the barnyard. On the way back toward the house they stopped and entered the shed where Perkins did his writing. Part of its sloping roof was glass, and in the middle was a huge table covered by very realistic cardboard buildings—stores, houses and churches—representing a small New England town.

"Exactly to scale!" Perkins said accusingly. "Exact! They'll never catch *me* making the sun rise in the west. Look!" He pointed to a little street, with little automobiles in it, cementlike sidewalks, and infinitely perfect little fire hydrants and trash cans. "If a man walks down Main Street to this drugstore, by God I know just how many steps he has to take. Accurate!"

David was fascinated by the little town. The trees were made of some kind of weed that looked like elm trees. Even the cars were identifiable as to make and year. The store windows were cellophane, behind which tiny but identifiable pieces of merchandise were displayed. Perkins eagerly showed him more of its wonders—a milk bottle not much bigger than a match head, and a perfect little strew of horse manure down the center of a street, with English sparrows small as mites pecking in it. But then there came a clanging from the house, and Myrna's high, breaky voice calling, "Yoo hoo! Yoo hoo! Everybody! Yoo hoo!" They went back to the house for supper.

David washed in the bathroom, which the Crosses were proud of because it was tiled, modern, and really worked, and which they deprecated for the same reasons. The water was gravity fed from a spring in the hill behind the house, and heated in the coil and reservoir of the kitchen range. He did catch a whiff of the chocolaty odor of septic tank, but that was probably because the recent heavy rains had flooded the drainfields.

When he came back the Edison lamp on the dining table was lit, giving a white, slightly muted, pleasing light. Tucker was

setting the table with large old plates and heavy silverware, and he stood rather awkwardly, trying to think of something he ought to do rather than watch her.

"Can I help?" he finally asked.

"Probably not," she said, and clanked the silver down on the place mats too hard, a bored, somewhat sullen expression on her face, as though she were imitating some tough doll from the movies. He wanted to forgive her this crudeness, and did forgive her, because she was so trim and neat. There were her young breasts, her narrow waist in the lamplight. If only she wouldn't imitate crudeness, swinging her hind end like a bored whore. Perhaps he could teach her to be the way he wanted her to be: she would swoon in his arms, melt because of love into the simple yet passionate girl she must be underneath. How could she have that long, pale, aristocratic face, yet still act this way? He decided that she was a prisoner of this act, that the real Tucker might escape from it. It was the act of youth, which he wanted to discard in himself, and its symptoms were the code words, fads and signals of the time.

> "I dropped my eyeball
> Into my highball"

Tucker sang with a bored look. Her alphabet-soup name pin hung from the heavy sweater she'd put on over her dress—and next to it another name pin he couldn't read in this light (a hard twinge of jealousy; he'd have to look into that). Her bobbysocks and saddle shoes, the scarlet lipstick put on too thick and too high, so that all of it didn't move when she moved her lips—these things jarred him too much, and he wondered why, because a few months before they would have seemed, along with, say, fingertip reversible coats, to be the very standard marks of fashion.

> "I've got my fare
> And just a nickel to spare"

Tucker sang as she danced down the length of the table. When she came around to his side he read the alphabet-soup name pin: Joe Cilley. He would have to meet this Joe Cilley. But in any

case he would have her here, in the long winter evenings, even if what he wanted of her remained almost too vague to define. One thing was that she should grow up, and forget all that jazzy high-school stuff. She should be a lady—like, for instance, Ingrid Bergman, or Constance Bennett. And of course she should love him terribly, yet with some constraint, some shyness. They should talk seriously of important things, even of the war; of ideas and ideals. He wasn't quite sure what ideas, but of the tone of voice, the tolerance and love with which they would converse, he was certain.

"Hey, blivet-head. You can move now," she said.

He stepped back from the table to let her pass, and her strong perfume stung his nose.

Perkins had come in, and sat in a rocking chair, making little subterranean grunts and complaints. Finally he called, "Myrna! Where do you suppose Old Fornication is? He's three hours late!"

Myrna came in from the kitchen. "What?" she said, waving a long wooden spoon.

"That's Forneau he means," Tucker said. "He lives up the road."

"He's crazy," Perkins said. "He works in the tack factory in Cascom. Anyway, he brings our mail and the paper, when he doesn't forget. He's half soused on beer by the time he gets home, anyway."

"Tell him what he does with the beer cans," Tucker said.

"Oh, let me tell him!" Myrna said, turning toward David with a grinning, glowing, trembling face. "Let me tell it!"

Just then something hard poked into David's leg, and he jumped. It was Heinz, who had a short, heavy stick in his mouth. Again he poked it into David's leg.

"Heinz!" Myrna screamed. Heinz paid no attention, but growled at David and hooked him again with the end of the stick.

"Heinz! You go away and let me tell it!" Myrna seemed about to burst into tears, but when David tried to push Heinz away he growled louder and shook his head harder. In order to protect his shins, David had to grab hold of the stick, which only caused Heinz to become more aggressive. The stick was dented and wet, and no matter how hard he tried to hold it still, it moved in his hands.

"*Heinz!*" Myrna screamed again.

Perkins had been sitting very still, watching all this with a distant, pensive expression, and finally Tucker said "Hey, Poik," and motioned toward the dog. Perkins immediately jumped up. With what seemed to David to be just a little too much savagery, he grabbed the stick and wrestled the choking, snarling dog over onto his back. Heinz wouldn't let go; he still gargled and shook, and by what looked like sheer force got to his feet again. The stick was white with foam, and their wrestling didn't seem to be a game at all. The dog screamed through his white teeth, Perkins making the same kind of noises. Just when David began to think the two were in a fight to the death, when it seemed they could never stop, Perkins, with a triumphant yell, tore the stick out of Heinz's foaming mouth and tossed it on the floor behind him. Heinz didn't look for the stick, he stared at Perkins' hand, the whites gleaming all around his eyes, too much gum showing above his long teeth. Then he leapt, and Perkins gave him the hand, as if to say "Here, bite me!" In midair Heinz shut his mouth and passed right by. When he landed he cowered as if he had been whipped. With his thick tail tucked down tight he crawled into a corner, and for a long time he yelped softly, and clicked his teeth.

Myrna had gone back to the kitchen, and when she came back out, bearing a platter of lamb chops surrounded by browned potatoes, garnished with parsley, she didn't attempt again to tell him what Forneau did with his empty beer cans.

Along with the lamb chops, which tasted more strongly of mutton than any he'd ever had before, they had the vegetable called lambs' quarters, which David found good enough—something like spinach, but it left a coating on the inside of the mouth like the tallow of venison. All the food seemed dark with flavor, and rich. Perkins and Myrna had a glass of yellowish wine, and David and Tucker had raw milk which came from the Warren farm.

"We're eating Alice," Myrna said, wiping a little grease from her chin.

"Look," Perkins said, "do we have to go into it?" Tucker, too, had stopped eating, and looked disgustedly at her mother.

"I raised Alice on a bottle," Myrna said. "She used to come

and bunt me all the time because she thought I was her mother. One time she bunted me so hard I sat on the butter."

"Well, let's forget it for now, okay?" Perkins said. He looked at David. "Always we've got to have names for the animals, so I've got to butcher our goddam friends."

"Alice B. Toklas," Myrna said.

"The pig is Gertrude Stein," Tucker said.

"And the rooster is Tristan Tzara, and I've got to cut his goddam head off tomorrow or the next day."

"One horse is Ernest," Tucker said.

"The gelding!" Perkins shouted, and laughed. He didn't mind this; later David found that Ernest Hemingway had publicly insulted Perkins, before Tucker was born, when he and Myrna had lived in Paris.

"The other horse is called Other Horse," Tucker said.

"They've all got names—all of them," Perkins said, and began morosely to eat again. David wanted to ask what Forneau did with the empty beer cans, yet somehow he was almost afraid to know. And who was Alice B. Toklas, whose flesh they ate? Gertrude Stein—he had heard the name, but who was she, with her crumpled ears and bitter smell? It seemed this whole day had been too full of hints and shreds of information, so many small parts, with ominous larger parts unexplained, and that nearly everything had almost fit his preconceptions—his daydreams, even. They had so nearly fit his daydreams that this day had in it too many of the quick shifts of meaning, expected yet still too startling, of a nightmare.

When they had finished eating, and got up from the table, he was for a moment dizzy. As the lamp moved, and the walls and the tall highboy leaned in toward him, he wondered if it weren't a terrible error for him to have come away from his home, his room with all its comforting relics of his childhood, his brother and his sister, whom he understood so easily. The small wave of homesickness was physical; he tasted mutton. Then it went away. He would decide how to cope with whatever came.

But that night as he went to sleep, when the groaning old house had ceased to startle him with its deep complaints, and the pines sighing above his window had become merely pines in the wind, the houses and people and animals moved and changed

places with each other. His revolver, so powerful it lived, rested in his suitcase beneath his bed. He had left his home, and in one long day ridden strange roads, seen the ewe hump and set her hooves under Lucifer's demonic penetration—Lucifer, who now prowled the darkness below, his brainless golden eyes shining like flashlights. And somewhere close by lay the young, smooth new girl he had held in his arms, her sides white, her hair black silk, her belly tender and forbidden; yet now was she forbidden, that he could think of her lying full naked up and down his body? Under the sheet. He thought for a moment of masturbating, dreaming of his entering her. She was like the sweet pain of his tooth when he worried it out a long time ago, when he was a little boy. But there were too many other things, things that he didn't understand, that hid in the dark places. He let the sweet, gumlike pain flicker over him and through him, deep little shocks along his bones, until he went to sleep.

That was his first day away from home, from his family's great house in Leah. He had been so tired he could not stay awake long enough to think about that day, and he had to leave all his questions circling in the air, out of order. But in his dreams they seemed to be answered, and answered wrong. He woke in the morning with a deep feeling of their having been answered, that he knew much more than he did. It seemed that he had known them all long ago—Lucifer, Heinz, Perkins, even Forneau, whom he'd never seen. And Myrna too, long ago before all the crabbed emotions in the world swarmed across her face at once. And Tucker before she had lost the pure, straight dignity of a child.

20

In October, just as the leaves turned, when the last few tomatoes no one could possibly find a use for were overripe and rotting in the garden, Henrietta was pulling up cornstalks and putting them on the compost pile. She happened to see something brown moving down by the end of the driveway, past the barberry hedge. She looked again, squeezing her eyes, then pushed her glasses away from the always sensitive grooves they made in the bridge of her nose. There was a tall man, a soldier, and she wondered why he turned from the road and came walking up their driveway, a bulging canvas suitcase in his hand.

A soldier, she thought. What is that soldier coming here for? The day was bright, the light hard, and leaves blew past her eyes as she watched him. The maples were red and gold, and here came this soldier, out of place on their street. He waved. Suddenly she recognized him by his gesture as she hadn't by his face, and it was her child in the dangerous foreign clothing. Wood, her first-born, who had shed all of his need for her, piece by piece, and now came back, big as a man in clothes she hadn't chosen for him. He set down his bag and came toward her over the grass, smiling, all blurred by her tears. Gold glinted from his uniform and from his hat, from the leaves, from the odd imperfect lenses of her tears.

"Goodness!" she said. "Wood?"

He reached her and put his arms around her, and for a moment she felt as if she had walked up to the side of a house. He was so unexpectedly big. The gold buttons and bars of his uniform jacket wavered and shone. She leaned back and her eyes focused again. His face was different. It was older and smoother and harder, more muscular and handsome. His chin was hard-

ened by the even shadow of his shaven beard, and his throat was reddish and hard. She stared at the strange devices upon his chest; suddenly she recognized in gold the crossed rifles. Rifles. He wore the insignia of his new calling.

"Oh, come in," she said. "Come in and see your father." Wood had said something. What had he said? He looked down at her for a moment.

"I'll get my bag," he said. She still held him, but now she remembered to let him go, and he strode away. She wiped her hands hard on her smock.

He came back to her and they walked toward the kitchen door. "I'm sorry I had to surprise you," he said. "I tried to call but I couldn't get off the train until Boston, and then it didn't seem worth the money."

"You wrote it might be next week."

"Yeah, they . . ." His hesitation struck her with worry.

"They what?"

"They're just speeding things up a little."

"Speeding up?"

"Well, not very much," he said, and held the door for her. She didn't understand, but before she would ask him about it he must meet his father.

"Harvey!" she called as they came through the dining room. "Wood's home! Look who's here!"

As the wheelchair turned, his tortured white face came around, grimacing. "Oh," he said. "You caught me at a . . . At a bad time hello Wood." The words slurred. "Sorry," he said. A glass half full of whiskey sat next to his adding machine. "So sorry, really. Don't feel good." He tried to shake it off. "So he's a shavetail! I can see that. R.O.T.C., y'know." An agonized expression, the teeth bared; he tried to shake it off, to be sober. "Don't do this often, Wood. Lieutenant. Honest. True, Hank? True? True? Feel better later. I mean it, so glad. Happy. Proud."

He turned his face away with a jerk, as if from a blow. Wood took a step toward him and stopped. "Dad," he said.

"See you later. Don't feel good. You understand. Hanky, wheel the guts out of here, will you?"

Something made her look to Wood, and he nodded, serious and concerned. She wheeled Harvey into their bedroom and

shut the door behind them. He raised himself from his wheelchair, shaking and sweating, then awkwardly rolled over onto the bed. She loosened his shirt and pants and took the pencils, pen and matches from his shirt pocket. "Do you want something over you?" she asked him.

His eyes were open, staring at her with an intensity she first thought was rage, or vindictiveness. She braced, waiting, but nothing else happened. He stared. Whatever words moiled in his head didn't come out. He stared for a while, then blinked several times before his plump white hand gestured for hers. She let the hand take hers, conscious of her calloused hard hand, a rock in the soft white.

"Does he remember me?" Harvey asked.

"We all remember you," she said.

"I don't . . . Don't humor me. Don't mean wormy dog shit I am now. Inside 'n out. He rember? Remember. Taught him how to shoot?"

"Go to sleep and you'll be all right at suppertime," she said.

"God damn it," he said. "Pile of shit."

"Of course we all remember," she said. "Now go to sleep."

Soon he was sleeping, his red lips open slightly. In the corner of his mouth a bubble of spit trembled in each heavy breath.

She came out, shutting the door quietly. Wood wasn't there; of course he wouldn't have taken a chance of hearing what they'd said. She stood in the high room Harvey loved so much—or used to, until it had become his prison. The curving staircase, light flowing across the vast dustiness of the air, the ornate false balcony so high up she could trick her eyes into believing it was a real balcony in some great Gothic hall. The stained-glass window on the landing beamed its rich colors down through the balustrade to the parquet floor and dark wall paneling: green on brown, red on oak. The parlor, now their bedroom, had been Harvey's gun and trophy room, where antlers bristled yellow on the walls, and rifles, shotguns, nets, fishing rods—all his gear and tackle— were displayed on racks and in glassed cabinets. Now they had all been put away in an attic storeroom. Harvey had loved his gun room so much he used to stand in the doorway, just looking at it. He'd even go around on the porch and look in at it through the tall windows, an expression of surprise and wonder on his face.

The things he liked had never lost their wonder, then. His Orvis fly rods, his Packard phaeton, his sailboat, his castle, his incredibly obedient reflexes. How he had enjoyed them all.

And yet there should be something left. Were the things of his times of triumph all there were? And had she been merely another of his pretty toys—smooth, well made, obedient protoplasm?

She pitied him; she loved the man, but back inside somewhere, somewhere in her feelings for him, was that judgment: grow up. We must all grow old and brittle and useless at children's games. That is one of the rules we were born to, and we accept our pleasures, knowing that we must pay when the time comes.

But then she thought of Wood, who couldn't live his own life even at nineteen. Nineteen, and they made him wear a uniform decorated with their murderous symbols. They. They were only men, and had no right. They had no right to set the children to killing each other. All the armies were made of children. The pilots were children, and the sailors, all of them flattered into thinking they were men and then having to go out and die real deaths. Most of them had no idea of the meaning of the pain they inflicted or would have to suffer, no idea of that iron on the tongue. Stupid, stupid! Wood was coming down the stairs, and she turned away, her tears blurring and refracting the afternoon sunlight that fell so richly across the room.

Peggy had choir practice after school. They were going to sing for Thanksgiving in the school auditorium before vacation, in the Town Hall the day of Town Meeting, and at the Thanksgiving services in the Congregational Church. They didn't have to practice "God Bless America" or "Goin' Over Jordan" so much as the Bach chorales. For an encore (except in the church) they had "Oh, What a Beautiful Mornin'" and "That Old Black Magic." She wouldn't get home—back to the Whipples' house—until just before supper, so Kate would have set the table and done all the things Peggy usually helped with.

After rehearsal she came up High Street in the dusk of the clear day; the sun was gone, and darkness seemed to flow along the ground, past tree trunks, flowers, hedges, the sides of houses—like dimming fog, while the sky above was still clear daylight,

still bright blue. She had always come home this way, but now she wouldn't go on past the big house to the woods road, she would go right up to the house, let it loom with all its strength and warmth, its turrets and battlements, right over her head. Up in the woods the little sugarhouse was all alone, dark and damp. She'd gone up to see it once, in the summer, and it had grown so small and dingy she wondered how anyone could have considered it home. It had smelled of earth, and the door was stuck so firmly to its jamb she'd had to take an old leaf spring that was lying there and pry it open.

The oil stove had rusted in the places where the enamel had cracked off that time her mother had nearly burned them out. Bluish, fuzzy mold had taken over the fleece slippers her mother had left in the closet-place. The little Christmas tree was a brown skeleton, pitiful with ribbons and balls, standing in a soft bed of its own needles. Mice had been everywhere, and their little dashes lay scattered all over the sink and table, the stove top, in the coffee mugs, the soap dish, the spoons and on the blades of table knives. Her father's deer rifle was rusty, and she took it with her so David could clean it. When she left the little house she jammed the warped door back shut again. Sadness had come in waves.

As it did now, only now it seemed more the happy anticipations that came in waves above an old sadness. She came toward the Whipples' house that would be full of light and human voices. Kate and Horace, Mr. and Mrs. Whipple would be there, and almost as reassuring and important would be their lives and their problems going on, going on, surely and independently of her. Yet she was allowed, and given a place at their table.

The house rose up, lights in windows. She went in through the kitchen, into that busy place. Kate and Mrs. Whipple were getting supper; something steamed on the black warm presence of the woodstove, and dishes warmed on the reservoir.

"Peggy!" Kate said.

"I'll be right down," she said, and ran up the back stairs to take her music and her books to her room. There had been something a little more imperative and excited than usual in Kate's voice. Even in the tempo of the kitchen's bustle, somehow. Mrs. Whipple had been beating something in a bowl—beating (was

it all imagination?) faster than usual, her shoulders hunched a little more. What was it? She washed quickly and came back down.

Now Kate had changed—she was very calm and matter-of-fact. But different, still. Some kind of pressure, some excitement glowed behind her perfect calm, behind the always startling beauty of her face.

"What is it?"

"What's what?" Kate said, turning away and pretending to straighten the pile of plates.

"You're acting funny."

"Me?"

"Now, Kate," Mrs. Whipple said, smiling. She was obviously in on it.

"Oh, Peggy," Kate said. "The plates aren't on yet. Would you put them on? I've got to grease the biscuit pans."

Mystified, half trying not to believe anything was going on, Peggy picked up the pile of warm plates, took them into the dining room and began to place them around the table. Kate and Mrs. Whipple came in and seemed to be watching her, and when she got around so her back was to the living-room arch, big warm hands came from behind and covered her eyes.

"Who is it? Who is it?" Kate shouted.

Horace? David back from the farm at Cascom? Not Mr. Whipple. The hands, warm and dry, never moved, but there was a low laugh, a man's, and from farther back Horace's pleased bark.

Wood.

She put her hands over those warm hands and nodded her head because she couldn't quite say his name. Tears were coming out of her eyes, and she had to take a quick, deep breath.

"Why, Peggy," Wood said, concerned and it seemed to her pleased and amused. No, different than that. He turned her around and there he was, looking down at her, happy to see her.

"Hey, hey," he said to her tears, and picked her up, his hands like great warm slings cupping her rib cage, his fingers on her spine. "You're growing up!" he said. She came up toward his strong face, his dark hair and eyes, as though she were his equal in height. Yet her feet dangled like a child's, and she didn't dare put her hands on his shoulders, though it seemed powerfully the thing to do, for balance, for some demand of the playfulness of

the moment; perhaps it was fear of doing something too grown-up, when she was only a child. Fear, yes, of something too momentous and gigantic, an impending sacred fusion; she loved him too much, she would catch fire, she would die, she did not love him as a child. But the child judged still.

"I'm fourteen!" she said.

"Fourteen!" he said wonderingly, and put her down. "My goodness, everybody's growing up. Except me. I feel younger every day."

"Sure!" Horace said. "Oh, sure!"

"We're all growing up," Kate said. "We can't stop it."

Then they were all quiet. They had heard the glee in Kate's voice, but it had changed to something else and become sad. With one unformulated intent they looked at Mrs. Whipple.

"And I'm grown-up already, is that it?" she said, smiling sadly. "Well, it's not much of a time to grow up in."

"It's no time," Kate said. "David said that. The war and all. He said . . ." She stopped, and looked at her mother. Then they all looked at Wood, handsome and straight in his uniform.

"I wish David were here," Kate said.

They sat down to supper without Mr. Whipple, who wasn't feeling good. Wood told them that he had almost a month before he had to go back. As he said this, time began with an almost tangible lurch to move forward.

Everybody mashed his potatoes, clink, clink. The seconds passed, the minutes passed. Horace made a potato pool and poured his gravy in it—white chicken gravy. The platter of roast chicken, country-style the way Wood liked it, had no bones in it. Wood liked the white meat, with cheese and bread-and-butter pickles, olives, canned beet greens with vinegar. He'd gone downtown that afternoon and bought some beer, so he and Mrs. Whipple drank beer. Kate had a juice glass of it, but said it was bitter. Peggy couldn't stand the smell of it, close, but she liked the smell of it from farther away. She liked Wood drinking it, the man drinking beer and eating his supper.

He wore his uniform shirt with his tie off—the crossed gold rifles on one side of the collar, the gold bar on the other. Mrs. Whipple said wasn't he young to be an officer, and Wood said maybe a little, but they wanted young officers in the infantry.

Horace said why did they call it infantry—was it like infants? Wood said yes, it came from that word, because they had to be young. They needed young men because the old ones couldn't stand the marches and the running. Mrs. Whipple, looking unhappy, nodded her head.

"My captain in basic training was only twenty-four," Wood said.

"It was illegal for you to buy this beer," Mrs. Whipple said. "You're not even twenty, much less twenty-one."

"That's crazy," Kate said.

Wood shrugged. "In Phenix City you could buy anything."

Peggy watched them talk. Clear light rose from the tablecloth to shine upon their faces. A glint from a piece of silverware touched Wood's cheek. Next to Wood, Horace seemed random and unformed, not quite a complete person yet. Kate was so alive she gave off a kind of glow, almost like vibrations, that everybody had to be aware of. Her light brown hair—honey-colored, or maybe almost the color of light toast, or of the clean sand at the beach on Cascom Lake—fell lively and even about her face.

Horace grinned at Wood, big teeth with slots between them, grinning, yet his pale sunken eyes might as easily have been crying if you looked at them alone. He told Wood that he could go down cellar now.

"You've got over your fear, then," Wood said.

"No, it's just different."

"That's wonderful, anyway," Wood said.

"I sweat like a pig!"

"How did you make yourself do it?"

"It's funny. I've got to think right." Horace blushed, and looked quickly around the table.

"Think right?" Kate said.

"Yeah, I've got to think right."

"Like what?" Kate said.

"Well, I think of . . ." Horace blushed some more, and grinned so hard it must have hurt his cheeks. "I think of Susie Davis, as a matter of fact."

"And that works?" Wood said.

"That does the trick?" Kate said.

Wood gave Kate a quick look, for some reason, but then appeared satisfied with what he'd seen.

"Horace is sweet on Susie," Kate said.

"That's all right!" Horace said, nearly shouting. "Maybe I am!"

"That's all right, Horsie," Kate said. "That's all right. Susie's nice. She's awfully nice."

"Okay," Horace said.

"Horace has changed a lot," Mrs. Whipple said to Wood. Horace nodded. "He wasn't too good right after you left, for a while," she added. Horace nodded. Wood looked closely at Horace, as if he might read those changes in his face.

"I take care of the furnace now," Horace said proudly.

"That's wonderful," Wood said. "That's really wonderful, Horace." He looked at Horace curiously, and finally said, "Does Susie protect you from those things?"

"No," Horace said. His face had grown dark and secretive, as if he'd said too much. He peered out furtively, and his eyes touched each of them in turn, seeming to find no one to trust. It was odd, even for Horace, that he would admit that about Susie Davis, yet say nothing else. Peggy had always found him secretive about those things that frightened him, even when she had tried to help him. He was grateful, but he said nothing. He'd get that same dense, watchful look, even begin to sweat. His teeth would clamp and grind, as they did now. Not so she could hear them, but little bulges of muscle came and went along his jaw. It was frightening, even if it was Horace, because the tension in him was too great. His muscles grew, and quivered under his skin. It was not just fright, either, not just shivering. He fought some terrible fight inside himself, seeming to grow unhuman, almost monstrous, right before her eyes.

Then he would come out of it, piece by piece. Something broke, and something snapped, and he'd seem to get his jaw loose, and then maybe an arm, and then his neck would loosen up. She felt so sorry for him, yet there was a kind of triumph too, as he came back to them. He did come back, and then he was Horace again, who was so kind, who wouldn't hurt a fly. She thought that about the fly, then realized it was true.

No one said anything about Horace's trouble. They had all

seen it happen to him before, so they went on eating, pretending not to notice. Soon he was eating again too, bite by bite narrowing the edges of his potato pool of chicken gravy.

Wood's leave went fast for the first week, but then he began to get restless. He had nothing really to do in Leah. Lois Potter came home from college for the weekend, and they went to the last dance of the season at the Blue Moon, on the lake. She was so proud of his uniform, it made him uneasy. Everything was too smooth and perfect, too moony-spoony. She acted as if she were an actress in the sweet-furlough interlude of a movie, with just the right amount of stiff upper lip for what lay ahead. But she cried when she had to go back, and he felt some of that romance too. It was a real war, and she was a lovely girl. He just didn't love Lois. It made him feel nasty when he admitted this to himself, as if he were a cheat, an impostor (which he was). He could never tell Lois the truth. He'd never be able to. Maybe time would take care of that problem. Maybe he'd get killed; that would solve it, if in a rather drastic fashion.

David hitchhiked from Cascom to see him on the second weekend. He lived, he said, on a farm with slightly crazy people, but it was interesting. He'd never had so much homework in his life, but he guessed he was learning things. The boys who lived at Dexter-Benham had to be in their rooms during study hours at night. In fact they practically locked them in, and they didn't have much else to do. So they really piled the homework on.

David made him talk about the Army, especially about the weapons. Had he fired the .50 caliber machine gun? The bazooka? Yes, he'd fired them all, at one time or another, and taken most of them apart in the dark and put them together again. Had he fired the bazooka at a tank? Yes, at an old hulk of a medium tank that had been hit hundreds of times. They all missed the first time because they were nervous, but then on the second shot they found that a bazooka didn't kick or burn, so they took a careful sight picture and hit the tank. He had to explain to David about the "shaped charge," the rocket, the use of molten metal as the killer inside the tank. He told him how two colored kids, news vendors about ten years old, had out of curiosity poked around

on the bazooka range—this at Camp Wheeler—and found a dud round. Somehow they had tapped it, or dropped it, and it had killed them both.

What had it done to them? David wanted to know.

Wood said he hadn't seen the bodies and hadn't wanted to.

"Just curious," David said.

"Do you want to get into the war?"

"I don't want to get killed," David said. "But the war's what's going on, isn't it?"

"It's men getting killed, or being so bored they think goosing each other is high entertainment. Don't be a sucker."

David was pleased by this. "That doesn't sound like you," he said. "Well, anyway, maybe it isn't the war. What I want to do, mostly, is grow up."

"I hope you like it when you get there," Wood said, and David looked at him again, quickly, pleased and surprised that Wood should say such a thing. For a moment Wood resented this as being slightly patronizing. But then he reconsidered: he had changed a lot in a year, in this last year, and maybe David had a right to be surprised.

"I'll be seventeen in a little over a month," David said.

On Sunday afternoon when David had to start hitchhiking back to Cascom, he said goodbye. "I don't like to say goodbye," he said, with some difficulty. "When I left for Cascom last month I sort of snuck out before anybody was up."

"Let's keep in touch, though," Wood said. They shook hands.

"Um," David said. His jaw twitched as he clamped down on a word. "Take." He cleared his throat. "Take care of yourself, huh?" And then something shifted in David's head; Wood had seen this happen before. For the emotion that kept him from speaking he substituted a sort of swooping garrulity that could touch lightly upon any subject. "I mean," David said, taking a breath. "I mean it always seemed to me that I was the one that lived with reality, you know? And you lived a kind of crazy ideal life that made you have to ignore about eighty percent of what was going on. You know what I mean? Boy scout stuff, you know? DeMolay. Reverend Bledsoe's Wednesday Evening Discussion Group. Nobody's ever queer, nasty, nobody wants to play with his own crap, nobody's born cruel."

"I think you've got it a bit wrong," Wood said. "Trying and ignoring are different."

"I know. Maybe I know. I've got a lot of nerve, anyway. Christ, here you are, a second lieutenant in the infantry, you've been down South for half a year. Who the hell am I? But what made you . . . made you *able*, for instance, to go see Susie Davis last winter and face up to her father. Jesus! Sam Davis! He'd suck woodpecker eggs!"

"I felt responsible for Susie."

"Why? Did you lay her? Now, wait a minute. Don't go all stern on me, Wood. Sure, it's cruel and all that, but Susie'll go out with anybody. I've seen her in Bruce Cotter's car parked up by Scrotum Pond, for God's sake. And Bruce Cotter's no sparkling conversationalist."

"All right, David," he said.

"I mean, Bruce Cotter's about the definition of anybody."

"Don't say anything like that in front of Horace."

"See? That's what I mean!" David shook his head in disbelief, then turned serious and shy. "That's just what we mean about you, Wood."

He heard love and respect, as near as David could get to uttering those ideas, and because he understood the burden their brotherhood carried, of irony and history going back to all the indignity and self-protection of childhood, he was touched. David moved away from the porch across the lawn strewn with bright maple leaves, and jumped lightly over the barberry hedge, itself festooned with impaled leaves quivering in the dry October breeze.

"So long!" he called back. He had neglected to say goodbye to anyone else, Wood noticed.

"So long, Davy!"

David waved, turned and strode lightly away, with a hop and a skip to kick flying a pile of leaves the wind had rolled up just for him, for the lightness and energy of what was left of his childhood.

One evening the October air began to bite. The temperature fell into the twenties, and as the registers grew warm, the big house

began to creak away its summer tensions. Horace brought in a pile of split hardwood logs for the big fireplace. He wouldn't let Wood help with the furnace or with the fire, and even Harvey Whipple evidently decided not to unnerve Horace with remonstrations, or with directions about how to place the paper and kindling. Wood sat near his father's oak table, drinking a glass of his father's whiskey mixed with water. After starting the fire, Horace left them with, Wood suspected, a touch of discretion, and he wondered if his mother had anything to do with the setting of this scene of father and oldest son alone with their toddies before the baronial fire.

They were alone, sipping their drinks as they watched the fire grow into its familiar limits. The massive owl's-head andirons blinked through their reddish crystal eyes, and above the high mantle the heavy and ornate wood paneling glowed soft as old gunstocks. Lamps made circles of muted light in the high room, and they began to feel the fire's benevolent push against the chill. Wood began to feel that inner dullness, or looseness, caused by the whiskey—perhaps also a benevolent force. He rarely drank hard stuff, and the reason seemed to be a voice that suggested—not a command, but evidently a powerful suggestion—that he keep ready, keep awake, that he might have need of the edge whiskey so subtly stole from him. It was a voice he could at times resent.

His father lit a pipe, waved out his kitchen match and flicked it into the fire. "I always wondered why you didn't start college," his father said.

"The colonel who was head of the OCS Board asked me that too. I told him I knew I was going in the service within a year anyway, and my heart wouldn't have been in it. I can wait. Anyway, I'll save some money in the Army."

"I always intended to pay your tuition, you know."

"I know that," Wood said. When he looked at his father, his father turned his head back to the fire.

"Maybe it's that I hate to be a cripple. I wonder if you know. To ask people to wait on me."

"I think I understand," Wood said. He did understand all that had been skipped, how his father had come right to the point.

302

"Me!" his father said with wonder. "I just never will get over it. I don't seem to have any . . . resources. You understand? This is a confession. What have I got to lose? You've got me beat all hollow. I never got into the last war because it ended before I got my commission. It's in my mind like a worm, maybe more like a little jewel, a cyst, that I would have been damned good. I knew I was a leader—everybody did what I suggested. They followed me. I'm no good, sitting around stinking and thinking. Never been any good at that. What I've been is a man of action, and I'm not going to sit here and smile at myself with any goddam deprecation or modesty or whatever it is you're supposed to do in such a case. I've got no medals to prove anything, only a bunch of trophies and cups saying I was a captain of sports. Games. But I can't tell you how much I envy you. I envy you so much I can taste it. It's like copper on my tongue. Your mother tells me I ought to grow up, and I suppose she's right, as usual. I'm supposed to bow gracefully to rot. Shit, what I used to do was jump gracefully. I never bowed. I used to run up the trunks of trees. And then you come home on leave looking like a recruiting poster, bigger than life, and you find a drunken slob indulging himself in a messy little fit of self-pity. This is all by way of excuse, you understand. Or apology, I don't know which."

"I do understand," Wood said.

"Yeah, but it's an apology you'd never have to make. How do you think that feels stuffed in my craw?"

"How do you know that? I've never been put in your position. How do you know I could stand it at all?"

"I do know, and that's what hurts. It's why I've never been able to—Christ, since the accident—never been able to talk to my own son, nor you to me."

"We're talking now," Wood said, but his father shook his head, his white jowls moving.

"Not really. No. I'm not big enough. I'm putting on a show, can't you tell? Tough Harvey Whipple, bowed but unbent—what is it? A poem, 'Out of the Night,' is it? No, it had a Latin name to it. Bloody but unbowed. Christ! William Ernest Henley. Bunch of crap. I remember the goddam thing from college. See? I can't stop talking, acting."

But then he did stop, and he did several little things in

quick, mechanical succession, as if each were allotted a certain number of seconds. He took a drink, tapped out his pipe, lit a cigarette and adjusted himself in his chair.

"But," he said finally, "it's a two-way street, isn't it? Am I supposed to take all the blame for it?"

"No, I realize—" Wood said.

"As a matter of fact," his father said quickly, "something very peculiar began to happen to you . . . to me . . . a long time ago. I've never been a man with any *reticence*. You know what I mean? Like right now. It's go on or stop, even though I'm blabbing too much and I resent you for hearing it, and making any of your callow judgments of me. See, you can hear it. It creeps in. 'Callow.' You're only nineteen. I resent that. I'm a typical Yankee blabbermouth and you keep your mouth shut and think too much. Christ, you were born looking around and making judgments. Even when I dumped crap out of your diapers you were watching me. When I spanked you, you gave me the feeling it was only my superior strength, power, that made you cry, not right or justice or shame—no matter what you'd done to deserve it. You always seemed to be ahead of me on morals. When I taught you something you were grateful. You weren't like me at all. It was a nightmare. Here I was . . . am . . . a sinner, a hypocrite, a normal goddam puling, bragging specimen of humanity, and it looked like I had a son who was going to be everything I pretended to believe in. Every time I looked at you it knocked the shit out of my cynicism, and man, that hurt!"

His father stopped, looked at him quickly, then finished his drink. "Shit," he said in a calmer voice, "I can't make anybody answer that. How about getting us another?"

Wood took their glasses to the kitchen, thinking how he could answer his father. He should try to say something that would make the man feel better, of course. But was that right, and wouldn't his father see immediately, almost before he opened his mouth, that it was all happening again, that he was being given therapy, moral superiority? At least that was how his father would see it. What his father said was true. It was a nightmare; it was all upside down. The child was father to the man. What came first, the chicken or the egg? He couldn't find much resentment toward his father, either. All was forgiven; the nightmare was that

all was forgiven. And no attempt to recount his own sins would be anything but a kind device. He wondered how David and his father managed with hardly any words at all to be easy, to be all right with each other. Nothing seemed to hang over their heads, even when it came to shouting.

He brought the drinks back to the living room.

"Ah, thanks," his father said. They were silent for a while, listening to the smooth breath of the fire.

"I don't know what to say," Wood said finally.

"I don't blame you."

More silence, and then his father said, "It's funny how I don't seem to be able to get rid of this jealousy. It's competition, I suppose, which is overweening pride—in myself. Take Gordon Ward, for instance. I mean Gordon, Sr. Evidently Gordon, Jr., is quite a hero. Did you hear that?"

Wood nodded. He'd read about it in the *Leah Free Press*.

"Anyway, he's getting some kind of big medal and a battle-field promotion. Gordon, Sr., called me up and banged my ear about it for three quarters of an hour. Christ, he knows more military shop talk now than Sergeant York. But I suppose some of his excitement was pure surprise. I always thought the boy would end up in the guardhouse. But proud? You ought to have heard him. I sat there, listening and saying 'Ayuh,' and 'My, isn't that fine,' but all the time I was thinking: Well, I *know* a father ought to feel that way, because that's what I've always heard and seen— but it still made me wonder. Now, I admire what you've done. You're young to be an officer and so on. I admire you, and I give you the compliment of being jealous, but I could no more go and brag on you, as if I'd had anything to do with it, than I could run rabbits and bark at the moon. You understand?"

"I guess so. It seems logical, anyway," Wood said.

"Sure, but it's sick. Is that what you mean?"

"People are proud of their flesh and blood, sort of, aren't they?"

"Oh, sure, but that always seemed kind of stupid to me. It's only one half of the blood right at the start, anyway, unless you think of a woman as just a kind of incubator. And then don't start looking back, or you'll scare yourself to death. One of your great-grandfathers was a brilliant man, a college president, and his son

got senile at fifty and pissed his pants every three hours for the rest of his life. Or look at Peggy Mudd. How the hell could blood ever account for that girl? She's got her father's ugly puss, all right, but where'd she get that intelligence?"

Wood shook his head. As he'd listened to his father he could remember very clearly the quick, slim man he used to be. His voice was lean, a little high, and the clipped, slightly breathless sharp phrases were still the same.

He'd always been impatient, with his teammates and his children, but before the accident he would show it by a sudden stiff smile and a nervous turning away of his head, as though he didn't want to see such awkwardness. The smile would be gone when he turned back to whatever clumsy human he had to teach. Whatever activity it was, he'd say "Here, let me show you," and do it so perfectly, the various moves would blend into each other and disappear, and the example would be useless to the pupil. Casting a fly line, shooting, throwing a ball—whatever it was, his father seemed to flash into his stance, and then it was over; the fly floated lightly down upon the exact center of the rise, the clay bird turned to black dust, the ball appeared, stationary, in the pocket of the mitt. He was a leader, but no teacher. It was poor Horace who really suffered from this impatience. The rest were quick enough on their own, especially David, who was obviously his father's favorite, who looked most like him too. Wood thought of asking him if he were jealous of David, then shied away from that. His father had chosen the subjects for his evening of confession, and it would be a touchy thing to tamper with. Let sleeping dogs lie.

Then Wood was filled, overcome, drowned in the knowledge of his own coldness, presumption, intolerance. The words fell about him like the stern judgments of God. The child is father to the man! No, youth is selfish and intolerant. To forgive is to be indifferent, and youth wants away.

His father sat there a prisoner of his pain and the soft, fat body he must despise. He looked like a melting snowman—if a snowman could quiver so precariously. His father had offered him a great deal, but he couldn't use it. He couldn't think of anything to say. Their history was too full of stalking, still-hunting, avoidance. They had no common jokes, no common ironies.

What if he were to confess how he'd betrayed his friend

Stefan? How would he begin? What tone would he assume? If this were a night for confession, why not try?

Because his father would consider that cuckolding a triumph, and it was not a triumph. The world of smut was subtle and was everywhere. No one could be trusted with that knowledge. He'd gone back to Lenore whenever he could get a pass, and though Perrone and Quillen were suspicious, they never knew. Each time he'd curse himself and vow not to go on with it, but he knew where he was going and what he would do. She purred like a cat, and yowled softly in his ear. He couldn't stop hearing that curving, modulant warble in his ear, day and night. He was out of his mind. He would betray helplessness, the most utter helplessness. Now the outfit had gone to Europe, Stefan, God help him, included; Lenore was back in Ohio. At infantry school at Fort Benning he'd received a letter from her every day. At every mail call the blue envelope he dreaded was pressed into his helpless hand. Sheets of blue paper, her round, sincere, half-literate handwriting, the *i*'s dotted with huge circles: *Wood my darling my dearest lover I lay all night thru dreaming of you in my arms.* He read each letter in a fit of self-disgust, even breaking into sweat. *O Wood sweetheart do you think of "doing it" with me my handsome "beast." O my goodness some of the things I say you could black mail me so burn this!*

And he would groan for pity. Pity for her, pity for himself. He never answered, and finally the letters stopped. No, it was a confession he would never make. She sent her pitiful letters out into nowhere. If he could treat any person that way he would take his sin, unalloyed and unabsolved, to the final judgment.

"You don't talk much, do you?" his father said.

"No, I guess I never have."

"We never talked," his father said.

There was a hint of sadness—his father's kind, perhaps—a sort of cynical jauntiness, if that was possible. His father had given nothing up, really, and would give nothing up. Nothing would become so painful or so lost it couldn't be mentioned. Wood stretched his own healthy legs toward the fire, calves and thighs pleasurably defining themselves. His father's glass was empty, so he finished his and got up to make them another drink. "Maybe another of these will prime the pump," he said.

His father's answering smile was knowing, grateful, and Wood yearned to do something for him. He wanted to touch him, but how did one comfort his father? He couldn't figure out how to do it—he couldn't feel how to do it. Something powerful gleamed from that face sick with corpulence. Memories of pride in his father stirred, were still there from long ago. Also fear, but more a sense of residing justice that might or might not have been a child's standard delusion. He turned away, a glass in each hand, conscious of the breadth and strength of his own young body. He was his father's son; he perceived that knowledge in the other person. Though he might never hear pride expressed, they would sit late, drink, and watch the embering fire they had in common.

21

Dark Hill Farm seemed dark for more reasons than the acres of spruce that surrounded the fields like black dwarves with their arms, even their dead arms, interlocked. The reluctant winter sun was pale as it came across the hill, and the house beneath its grove of pines was dim, lantern-lit. As the winter came on, the floorboards cracked underfoot, almost fractured in the cold. David had to get up before daylight, make his breakfast of cereal and milk by oil lamp, then walk a mile down the dim frozen road to wait with the other townies for the Dexter-Benham station wagon. He waited there by the Jaspers' mailbox with Billy Warren, Harold Pittman and Howard Jasper, all of them cold, stamping, shivering as they waited. Howard Jasper was a freshman, and the other two were sophomores. Howard was small and fragile-looking; they were all scared by Al Roux, the driver, and hoped that if he were going to run the station wagon off the road he would do it before he picked them up, but Howard was often frightened into tears.

Sometimes when they got to the academy Al Roux would run the car onto the football field and slew around, laughing past his cigarette and blowing ashes into the defroster fan. Poor Howard would grab David's arm and hide his head in David's side. Billy and Harold would grit their teeth and watch whatever was coming.

After school it was again dark when they were let off, sometimes on cloudy days so dark David would have to stare above him at the faint radiance of the sky, following that in order to keep on the road. He was quite often afraid. Too many new and unsettling things were happening to him, and his life seemed to be a series of anxious waits for danger, real or not. He was ashamed because he was unable to destroy in his mind whatever evil shapes, animal or man or monster, lurked beneath the perpetual night of the spruce. He didn't dare take his revolver to school with him because he had no certain place to hide it during those bright, official hours. In the daylight his fear dimmed, but always the dark hill waited, and at the end of the hill the presence of Lucifer transformed every shade of darkness, perceived only from the corners of his eyes, into a softly moving force.

Then he would approach the house, where lamplight dimly gleamed. He walked tensely those last few hundred feet, listening carefully for breathing or the tick of hooves. And once he made the house there was still danger, but of another kind. Perkins Cross, that temperamental genius, would have decided what sort of mood he would assume in order to dominate the room, the evening, the world he had created in which his presence was to be celebrated. Though David saw through this acting, nevertheless Perkins was the master here. He was the adult. He didn't exactly frighten, but he jarred, he irritated, he demanded a reaction, whether to his anger or his humor. David watched, because he had to, and felt dishonorable when he forced himself to laugh at Perkins' little jokes. He wanted to say, "Not you, Mr. Cross, but I, I am the most important person here. I will be the future, and the main adventure will be my transformation of your beautiful daughter from a shallow nitwit into a sensitive and lovely girl."

He still believed that; it was what got him up the dark hill, got him up in the morning. It was the thought that changed his

tender skin from a child's to a man's, and let him slide into his frozen sheets at night.

But there Tucker sat, plastered with lipstick, Joe Cilley's alphabet-soup name pin grossly skewered to her sweater, reading a pulp magazine, dangling her bobbysocks and saddle shoes over the arm of the Morris chair. She liked—God help him, he was embarrassed for her—*True Romance* and *True Confession*. And yet the pure light of the Edison lamp, in cruel chiaroscuro, revealed the smoothness of her skin, her delicate wrists, her black silken hair, her narrow aristocratic nose. It hurt to look at her. She was merely enchanted, and he must somehow break that shoddy spell.

Weekends he worked with Perkins in the wood lot, sawing four-foot lengths of maple, pin cherry, beech and ash with a two-man crosscut saw—grinding, wearisome work. He kept up, and felt some approval in Perkins. Always just as David felt he couldn't pull the saw another time, Perkins would stop, set the saw aside, and roll himself a cigarette with fingers trembling from labor. Sometimes Perkins' face was so wildly red and white David found himself taking care not to look at it.

He had nowhere Perkins' brute strength, but he kept up. He couldn't sink an ax half as far into a tree to make a notch, but he could trim branches well enough, and keep going. Once when they went back to the barn to harness Ernest and Other Horse, he realized that Perkins was trying to disguise a limp, that he had worked too hard in order to impress David—or perhaps not to spoil him for hard work.

They tossed the stiff black harnesses over the horses and cinched the ancient straps and buckles onto the worn places on the horses' coats. David watched, helping only when some obvious strap had to be handed over or lifted. Then they walked the big horses out of the barn and over to the wagon, traces swaying like slow pendulums about the thick legs and broad hooves; then came the hesitation of backing, and the ponderous, nervous thud of hooves as the horses felt their way backwards onto the shaft, to the whiffletrees. Other Horse's black rectum swelled, and out came the huge orange falling biscuits.

They rode on the flat bed of the wagon around the house and up the logging road to where they had been cutting, and piled

the wood between the body stakes, all the while saying very little. Perkins said "Okay" or "That'll do" whenever some part of their morning's work was done. Occasionally he would say to Myrna "He works, all right," grudgingly.

It was only at night, with his wife and daughter as audience, that he demanded full attention from everybody. Weekdays he spent in his shed, working on his novel or on his model town. Only once did David ever find anything he had written, and he soon began to suspect that the little cardboard town was more important than anything Perkins might write about it. He found the one piece of writing in the library, in a large magazine with a thick cardboard cover. The magazine was called *Modernity*. Perkins' article was about Peter the Great, and told how the great Czar (spelled "Tsar" in the article) amused himself as a boy by throwing dogs and servants off the Kremlin walls. Strangely, all the rest of the pages were blank. It had been printed in 1925, before David was born.

Tucker's school bus came an hour later than the Dexter-Benham station wagon, and brought her back to the Jaspers' mailbox an hour earlier, while it was still daylight, so he never saw her except in the evenings. As far as he could tell, she never had any homework at all. He had met Joe Cilley early in September, an ominous meeting during which Joe beat up his brother William as a lesson to David. He'd been at Dark Hill Farm less than a week, when one hot afternoon a wagon full of kids, including Tucker, pulled by a gaunt old horse, came up the road and stopped in front of the house. David had been looking through the books in the library, and when he came out, Tucker called, "Hey, blivet! You want to go swimming?"

He could see that she wasn't too interested in having him come, but had to show him to the others. Tucker said, "That's him."

There were four boys about his age, and several smaller boys and girls, who didn't count. One of the four boys was big and fat. He wore a T-shirt over his breasts and belly, and had a mean, inquiring smile on his soft face. Another was tall and muscular, tanned all over, with a face of sharp edges, and shiny black hair. This one he knew immediately to be his rival, Joe Cilley. The other two boys were friendly and curious—farm boys with

tanned faces and hands, and pale chests and legs, gawky and lean.

Myrna had come bustling down upon them, her apron rolled up upon whatever she had been working on. "Oh, isn't this nice!" she said. "You've all come to take David swimming! This is David Whipple. David, this is Joe Cilley and his brother William, and this is Harold Pittman and Billy Warren!"

He had been right. The dangerous one was Joe Cilley. The fat one was his brother. As Myrna said "William," he thought of "Willy Cilley," and smiled a little; the fat one saw, and his smile in return was chilling. Joe Cilley's face didn't change at all, except for his lower jaw, which moved down a quarter of an inch as he said "Hi," then moved up again. Harold Pittman and Billy Warren smiled openly and said "Hi."

Tucker had either worn her bathing suit under her dungarees that morning, or had changed down at the Cilleys', or someplace. This seemed dangerous to him; as he looked at her slim legs Joe Cilley's black little eyes looked straight at him: *Watch out.* He read this easily, and was a little afraid even as the muscles in his arms, which felt hard and capable after all the woodcutting of the last few days, became taut under his shirt.

He went back to the house to change into his trunks, and as he undressed, his hands shook just a little bit. But on the way to Diddleneck Pond, Joe paid no attention to him at all, even when they stopped to admire what Romeo Forneau did with all his empty beer cans. The old horse stopped when Joe pulled the reins, stamped and swung his head in irritation, foam flying from the bit. Then David heard a soft, xylophonelike sound coming from the woods—a gentle, many-toned clanking. In silence the children got down from the wagon bed and crossed the stone wall. David followed Harold Pittman and Billy Warren, who without explanation had followed the little children. In a clearing surrounded by spruce, a small maple tree moved in the wind, and from its branches came the metallic music. An old gray ladder leaned against the trunk, and nearly every branch was full of beer cans that had been jammed down over twigs—clusters of the bronze and silver and white cans. There were almost as many cans as leaves.

"It's a wonder, ain't?" Billy Warren said in a hushed voice. The little children stared, and the tree played its music.

A sharp whistle from the road called them back. As they came across the stone wall they found Tucker and Joe Cilley in an elaborate Hollywood clinch, Tucker's slender back bent, everything bent. His crude hand lay on her ribs. With a smirk, Joe turned away from her and wiped his mouth with a red bandanna. He didn't look at David then, but later as they swam in the cold water above the mucky bottom of Diddleneck Pond he suddenly turned on his brother and hit him in the arm, on the back of the head, on the chest, in the kidneys, on the back—vicious short blows that actually echoed from the woods across the pond. Willy didn't begin to bawl until he had been hit five or six times, the blows had come so suddenly. After Willy had floundered out of the water, black muck on his fat thighs, David looked to find Joe's eyes hard upon his own. It was a warning. That was the first time they met, and David thought: Okay, but I'll have her to myself in the long evenings.

He did, on many of those evenings. They danced to the phonograph, and she let him hold her close, his hand on her waist above the delicate surges of her muscles, her breath on his neck. He'd see stars. But her pose was bored sophistication; he couldn't get hold of her mind, which seemed as smoothly inaccessible in its perfection of attitude as a jewel, a pearl.

She was afraid of the dark, and for this he was grateful. His own marginal fear of the dark of course disappeared when he was with her—darkness became so easily then the soft setting of his daydreams, in which he could have taken on a werewolf, a bear, any monster large enough to warrant his dreamed-of reward. It was because of her fear of the dark that she let him walk her down the hill sometimes after supper. She hated to be home. In love with lights and dancing, as she was, she hated the farm, the sheep, the reasons for having to live there. She had vicious fights with her father when he wanted her to help with the chores. Her voice would turn flat and mean, and David would try to protect the vision of Tucker he thought to be possible.

They would walk together down the hill to the crossroads, where, in December, they skated with the other kids around a bonfire on the millpond. From Joe Cilley he expected violence at any moment, and again one night on the ice Joe beat Willy up; another lesson. David had never seen anyone hit so hard. Joe's

fists would have broken boards. He leaped straight upon Willy, skates flashing in the firelight, and knocked him down flat upon the ice with one blow to the shoulder. Using his fists and arms like hammers, he beat upon his screaming brother's head, arms, back, until the screams turned really desperate. Then he stopped, and Willy, who at fifteen was as big as a man, ran crying home upon his skates, right across the road, his weak ankles bending nearly flat.

Joe didn't bother to watch his brother run home, and David saw his face, then, above the fire. His black hair shone. Set into the smooth plane of his face were four black holes, all about the same size—his eyes and the holes of his nostrils. His nose was very small and sharp. Sometimes he seemed unreal, a character from a movie in which a man could be as brilliantly cold and cruel as he wanted to be. When Joe hit there was no hesitation at all, no caution, none of the involuntary mercy that kept most people from hurting each other. Except toward his brother, he wasn't really mean. He bullied no one else, but when he hit, even in play, he hit too hard, and no one ever dared to challenge him.

And Tucker was so frail. David was afraid he would hurt her, brutalize her in some dark and violent way he hardly dared to think about.

As for Willy, he tried his revenge several times, jumping David from behind and trying to crush him. Joe watched these episodes coolly. David always managed to get out from under and pin Willy, and finally he said, "Look, you tub of lard, it appears that I'm stronger than you, so why don't you lay off?" He never hit Willy, and he often wondered why, thinking that perhaps it was fear of Joe. He wasn't really certain of this at all, and this possibly dishonorable indecision was added to all the others, brutal or merely irritating, that surrounded his days and nights.

Sometimes after skating, Joe would consent to walk Tucker home, and David would walk ahead of them.

"You keep on the road, now, David," Joe would call, "and make some noise, because I ain't looking where I'm going." And Tucker would laugh for him, a delicate, ladylike chime so beautifully cruel that even in his pain David had to admire its skill. If Joe decided not to walk her home she would have David walk

next to her, and he was not too proud to put his arm around her. Once, just before they reached the house, he turned and tried to kiss her. She punched him painfully in the stomach and said, "Down, Rover, down, boy."

Perhaps that was the first time a certain small question flicked past his consciousness: what was he doing here? In his cold bed that night as he shivered and waited for the sheets to warm he looked carefully at his idea of himself. Just how had he come to accept this degradation?

At Dexter-Benham, once the wild ride in the station wagon was over, and the sensation of sliding rear wheels had faded into only a small trace of anxiety, the days were sober and neat. He was good at what he was good at—sports and subjects other than math. In grammar school he had developed, out of the void, a system based upon three rather than ten, and although he understood the decimal system in principle, in any sort of stress he reverted to what he called his "tricimal" system, in which, for example, seventy-three became for purposes of common interchange twenty threes plus three threes plus one plus three, or, twenty-four threes plus one. He was aware of the cumbersomeness of his system, but it was the one native to his blood.

The regular Dexter-Benham boys perhaps changed their striped neckties and real Argyle socks a little too often for his taste—sometimes before lunch—and tended to brag rather blatantly of what they had done over vacation late at night in their families' rumpus rooms or in their fathers' Lincoln Continentals. Many of them seemed to be obsessed by Jews; a tall, red-headed boy named McLeod, from Des Moines, whose pride in basketball was to pass the ball so hard at close range no one on his own team could catch it, asked David if Whipple was a Jewish name. David's blank astonishment at the relevance of this question was assumed by several others to be a fine Yankee putdown of McLeod. In any case he began to have certain friends.

After the chaos of Leah High School, his instructors did, at least at first, personify the world of intelligence and logic he desired. His homework had to be done, and it had to be neat and precise. If he began to find in his instructors areas of prejudice or of political rigidity, he only wondered where he'd got his own beliefs. He came to the conclusion that the few and muted dia-

logues on these subjects between his mother and father had given him opinions, mostly his mother's because she tended to speak from knowledge. He found to his surprise that his occasional reading of the books she brought home was, in the aggregate, an accomplishment that was astounding to his instructors and his new friends. He was not always sure that his questions wouldn't embarrass his instructors, and he grew careful. Little by little he began to feel that no one on that bright and civilized hill knew or cared what the war was all about. Perhaps they were right, and his baggage of terms such as fascist, democrat, communist, liberal, reactionary, anti-Semite had very little to do with why his country fought the war.

But these qualifications were slow in coming, and the school charmed him and flattered him in many little ways. His friends —Lance Vandenbree, Judson Gay, Hoppy Hopright, Swivelhead Downing and others—with their screwy and even sometimes witty jargon, were set in his mind against the dangerous journey back to Cascom and the nervous weary load of fear and frustration he would carry up the hill into that perpetual night.

On weekends sometimes, at dusk and with the Crosses' blessings, he shot brown rats off the ridgepole of the sheep barn. The Crosses had a whole case of prewar .22 Longs, an inferior cartridge though adequate for rats, and a single-shot Remington .22 rifle. The rats seemed to have an evening trek that took them along the ridgepole, and against the sky they made interesting if gruesome running targets. The rifle cracked and he heard the thunk as the bullets wiped the rats away. At dark he took a paper bag and a flashlight and gathered the dead rats that had tumbled down the roof to the back of the barn. Once, passing the pigpen, he gingerly picked a rat out of the bag by the tail and tossed it into the trough. Gertrude Stein, snorting in the near darkness, swayed obesely up to the trough, and the rat's bones crunched. He buried the others.

Lucifer was part karakul, part Dorset Horn, part some odd mutant spirit that appealed in the darkest way to Perkins Cross. They seemed violent enemies and yet there was an intimacy between them that David couldn't help observing—a kind of equality, as though Lucifer were not quite unhuman. When the proper ewes came in heat and Lucifer was allowed among them, Perkins

stood at the door of his writing shed and watched as Lucifer, his scrotum on its narrow strap swinging as wildly as a punching bag, took them one by one whenever they crossed his skewed stare. The ewes dutifully stood for him, and dutifully grew deep-bellied with lambs. These lambs would be born in February, for a special restaurant market—early lambs, hard to keep alive in the coldest part of the year.

When not allowed to rut, Lucifer seemed to take perverse pleasure in bunting and pushing against the side of Perkins' shed, and if Perkins was inside it, he'd grab his lantern and the two-by-four he kept for the purpose, come out cursing, carefully put the lantern down and bash Lucifer across the shoulders. Lucifer ran just out of the light, then turned a dull gold eye on Perkins before moving back into the dark.

David went home for Christmas still puzzled by his new life, aware that he gave vague answers to his family about Cascom and Dexter-Benham. Christmas was strange without Wood, who was in Texas and couldn't get leave to come home. He and Horace put up the tree, and he drove Sally De Oestris on her Christmas rounds. He felt a little like an impostor—that because it was not Wood who chose and set the tree, the tree was not quite real. Christmas seemed an imitation of itself. He came back to Cascom by way of Dexter-Benham, slept overnight in Hoppy Hopright's room, and the next day resumed, by way of Al Roux's careening station wagon, his oddly split existence.

In February, that gray, frozen month, the lambs came due. Snow lay three feet deep, and the banks along the road, plowed for the town by Romeo Forneau, were as high as David's head. A path one shovel wide came down from the house, cut through the banks and deltaed out among the sheds and barns, a diagram of chores.

On alternate nights he found himself sleeping, by what reasoning or tacit agreement on his part he could not quite follow or remember, on a cot in the barn loft just above what Myrna Cross called "The Maternity Ward." His revolver under his pillow, his head beneath the covers against the barn's vast darkness of rafter and purlin, cobweb and rat run, the rich heat of the ewes rose up around him and made him sweat. Every two hours an alarm clock woke him, and he lit an oil lantern and

climbed down to the ewes, where they skittishly bumped their horns and rumps against the bars.

If one of the ewes did not move away, but stood stiffly, neck extended, hooves spread, then he would take down the bottle of linseed oil, the sharp hunting knife, and attend a birth. Maybe it was Lucifer's long legs that had got onto those lambs; a lamb's forefeet had to come out neatly beneath its nose, and too often these did not. He had to arrange things, even push back, sometimes, against the force of birth. Sometimes it was necessary to cut the ewe's taut perineum, sometimes to kill a lamb, cut it off piecemeal in order to save its twin or its mother. For these major disasters he called for help by ringing an iron triangle that hung outside the barn door. No matter what occurred, the ewe would never make a sound, except for long breaths, her hind feet set in the brown dirt floor.

Not all of the ewes had names—there were too many of them —but two of them were always spoken of by name because their mothers had died when they were born, and they had been raised, until weaned, in the house on baby bottles. One was Grace, who died of the same mysterious complaint her mother died of— a kind of weakness in the attachment of the womb, which caused her to bleed to death. Her lamb was called "Harold." Myrna called him—"Here, Harold"—and he would see the bottle and come at her, his soft, stupid eyes gleaming, and butt her with accurate, primal force, all greedy appetite.

Grace had died late in the morning, while he was at Dexter-Benham. It had been a typical day—chapel in the morning, the boys' proud, polite and breaking voices singing of the Holy Trinity, their button-down shirts white, their ties conservatively striped, their faces clean in the morning light. David looked like one of them. In English class they politely discussed, with Mr. Barkham, who looked like one of them a few years older, Gray's "Elegy." In science class they watched a radiometer turn in the sunlight. David studied in one of his friends' rooms, not with the other townies, who studied in the library. It always seemed unnatural to his friends that he didn't live at school. Sometimes at night, they told him, they put a penny in the floor master's light socket, and every time he changed the fuse, he blew it out again himself.

Then David came back to the farm, up the long hill in the heavy darkness among the trees. He felt like an explorer in his thin foreign clothes, and when he reached the house he reluctantly took off his white shirt, Ivy League jacket and regimental-striped tie and carefully hung them in his closet.

The Crosses had nearly finished butchering Grace. By the time he'd changed into dungarees, rubber boots and his canvas mackinaw, all that could be used of her, including the intestines which would be used for sutures, was packaged and ready to be picked up and taken to the freezer in the village.

The other orphan was Amantha, who waited until it was David's shift to try to have her twins.

He awoke in his damp blankets before the alarm clock rang, thinking he'd heard voices. It was, by the clock's dim green face, nearly one in the morning. With an arm aching from sleep he pushed down the alarm button before it rang, and fumbled for the lantern.

A giggle, not made by any sheep, came from below, and he knew it was Tucker. Wild thoughts: had she come sneaking down to see him? Would she think it a great joke to come creeping upon him, then, after startling him, to slide softly under the covers with him? He didn't move, but the ewes stamped and bumped below. There seemed to be a nervous increase in their rising warmth, in the oily smell of wool. Tucker would climb the ladder and slide her thin hands coolly down his chest, and her hair would cover his face as she slipped lightly into his bed. She giggled again, and this time reality, another sound, pierced him; cold damp shame at his wishfulness. Joe Cilley's chuckle climbed over hers, a dry, unbroken sound calculated not to show too much amusement, the standard noise he made whenever something of the sort was called for. Now David knew where these cruel noises came from—the bay next to the ewes' pen, where hay was kept.

"Shhhh!" Tucker whispered. Then came a soft breath of hay, a slight sound like sweeping, and they were quiet. They were waiting for the alarm to go off, no doubt, and they would lie still in each other's arms until he'd looked at the sheep and gone back to sleep. Joe Cilley was eighteen, Tucker seventeen; they were a man and a woman there in the hay, the warmest place they could find on the farm. In the hay. Could Joe Cilley? Would

she let him? Did he have her pajama pants down, now, and the soft parts of her open? David shriveled at this danger to her. He seemed to hear huge, raucous laughter bounding about in the silent barn. Scorned, betrayed, cuckolded, he lay breathing hard, seeing that brutish engorgement, and the delicate petals of Tucker's enthralled body.

No sound from below. He had to make his inspection even though self-pity, the terrible weakness of betrayal, dragged at him as though a chain were wrapped around each leg. What was he doing here? He pulled the alarm button, let it ring for a second, then shut it off. He lit the lantern, dragged on his pants and mackinaw, stepped into his icy boots and climbed down to the ewes, who began their half-serious dance of fear.

All but one—Amantha. Her breaths were harsh sighs, and her neck arched and shuddered. He knew immediately that it was Amantha because she was longer and thinner in the body than any of the others, and her gray wool, especially around her neck, formed precise, circular ruffs where the wool split into cracks as well defined as cracks along the grain of wood. She looked much like a picture of Queen Elizabeth in her ruffs, as though someone had superimposed upon that picture in his history book a sheep's dignified, dull face—the convex forehead-nose, the scalloped horns like thickly curled hair.

He brought the lantern around to find the beginnings of a breech birth. One hind leg had emerged from the hugely distended black vagina, and he had to pour linseed oil on his hands and place them on the lamb. Part of its rump was visible, glossy as a candied apple; the contractions of Amantha's sheep flesh pushed against an impossible counterforce. He couldn't move the lamb. As he probed into Amantha's warm membranes he found that the visible leg did not belong to the rump he tried to move. There were two lambs in there—a deep-sea vision of two entangled lives. He tried to pull, digging in his heels, but could only bend the lamb's leg. Amantha's breaths grew harsh, and her hind hooves made grooves in the dirt. A dark red jelly stained her woolly loins.

Joe Cilley and Tucker: did they watch and listen from their hot bed in the hay? He jumped up and ran, cartwheeling over the pen bars, to the barn door, grabbed the short piece of reinforc-

ing rod that hung there and beat upon the triangle as hard as he could. Its clangs swarmed in the frosty night. A sheep *baa*ed, an explosive sound that seemed full of panic. Joe Cilley ran past him without a word. Tucker followed, her bathrobe flying. "Oh dear, oh *dear!*" she said, as though this real emergency had caused in her a more civilized response than usual. David clanged the triangle remorselessly. "Terror, panic, disaster!" he felt his arm proclaim. The steel stung his hand.

Tucker would have to hope that her parents wouldn't look into her room. She would have to hide until they came to the barn, then sneak back into bed. It wouldn't work, David knew. He had seen Perkins and Myrna consider Joe Cilley too many times, and seen Tucker and Perkins fight too many times. Her parents watched her more closely than she knew.

In a few minutes Myrna's voice came clearly from the porch, high, strangely cultured in its fragmented breaks into alto. "Tucker? Tucker?" At first as though she were gently chiding, reminding her daughter of something, then a descent into anger. "Tucker! Tucker!" Then a grating cry with sobs interspersed: "*Tuck*er! *Tuck*er!"

With great huffs and groans, bathrobe billowing and snow flying, Perkins came charging down the narrow path between the snow. His overshoes were open, full of snow from his having stepped off the path. His high, whiney voice complained and despaired. He, too, yelled "*Tucker!*" whenever he got his breath.

David had ceased beating the alarm. He stood like a spectator now, listening to all this family panic. And then, as Tucker's voice came down from her window, she finally managed to prove that she was hopeless to his fantasies, that within her lovely body his gentle girl did not exist. Perhaps it was her lack of talent. "Whaaat?" she yelled, trying to sound sleepy, interrupted, irritated, bored. "Whaaat?" It was all so patently a lie, such crudely bad acting. In David's secret mind almost audibly something clicked, and no more strength came to him from any ideal conception of that girl. He began to shiver, and couldn't stop. Inside the barn Amantha slowly tore herself apart.

Perkins took one look at Amantha and stamped his foot. Soon Myrna pushed Tucker, sullen and dark around the eyes, into the light. Perkins looked at her, vibrating. "Where's Joe Cilley?" he

said. "I saw something run down the road, Miss. Is that who it was?"

Tucker didn't answer.

"She was covered with hay," Myrna said.

"Ah," Perkins said. "Did you have a roll in the hay, Miss?"

David didn't want to witness this.

Myrna said, with astounding vindictiveness, "Did he get your cherry? Did you give it away?" Her smile seemed at one moment to express pleasure and goodwill, at the next the most vicious hatred.

"Give what away?" Tucker said.

"Why, your little maidenhead, dear," Myrna said. "Don't you even know the name of the merchandise?"

"We didn't go all the way, if that's what you mean," Tucker said. Her father took one step and slapped her so hard she fell down. Hoarse blats came from her little mouth.

The observer asked himself what he was doing here.

When Tucker stopped bawling they heard Amantha's breaths. There was nothing to be done for her alive. David waited with her while the Crosses went to change into their clothes, to get the saw, the knives and stones. When they returned, Tucker sullen, the side of her face swelling, they put their hands deep into Amantha's wool and rolled her onto an old Flexible Flyer. With Myrna holding her on, Perkins and David pulled her over to the shed. Tucker was sent to get more lamps while David helped Perkins remove the cardboard town from the trestle table. "Careful, by God! Now be careful!" Perkins muttered. They lifted the plywood sheet, streets, buildings, cars, trees, horse manure and mosquito-sized sparrows turning vertical, a dizzy great upheaval of that part of the world, and finally set the plywood against the rear wall of the shed. Myrna covered the table with newspapers. Perkins lit the oil space heater, and the metal creaked as it warmed. The block and tackle was arranged, roped to a beam so that it hung next to the table.

Amantha still took long breaths. The shed leaked air in places, and the amber light moved in the lamp chimneys. When Tucker asked if she could go to bed, her mother said, "You'll get your little hands in it." Tucker held out her pale hands, manicured nails enameled bright red.

David waited, shivering still, for the necessary violence. Amantha's throat must be cut, she must be hung above the floor, above a tub, and they must take her all apart. This was done. He remembered certain moments, flashes of silence, the pale odor and the reluctant spasm of death. With a sigh, life became meat. Weariness, too, in his own fingers as they pried loose the adamant skin.

The hide lay on the table like a heavy overcoat someone had taken off and dropped in folds. But the skin had come off with it, and it seemed there must be a living creature, not that pile of meat, who somewhere gibbered in agony. The intestines lay in round piles like casual pillows, the little waves of peristalsis continuing to flow down the silk. Tucker was made to clean the gut, and she cried bitterly as she squeezed an iridescent blue tube as big around as her arm. Blood spotted her gabardine ski pants. On the table lay bundles and clubs of bright red meat and pink fat; in a corner the two dead lambs were stacked like dirty rags. Buckets and washtubs filled with blood, hunks of bone and fat. Tallow climbed David's arms and made his knife slippery in his hand.

Heinz pushed through the door, looking as guilty as if he had caused all the mayhem he saw, and before he was chased out he quickly licked at a run of blood. He cringed and bristled almost hysterically, as though the wolf's hunger and the jackal's taboos fought each other over all that gore. The jackal won, and he ran whining off into the dark.

The block and tackle slipped, and Perkins had to catch, in his bare arms, against his shirt, half the bright carcass. He staggered back against his town and crushed whole streets of houses. "What's the use?" he cried. "What's the use?" His freckles were like spots of paint, the orange-red of his face clashing with the red of the meat. Just then the shed moved; Lucifer was pushing against it.

Later, recollected in whatever tranquillity David recognized as it fleeted through his life that spring, his actions at that moment would haunt him, and seem to resound with all sorts of meanings, some more obvious than others, some obscured by shame, perhaps forever.

Perkins heaved the carcass on the table, then merely sat down, sighing wearily. David took the two-by-four and lantern and

went outside. Lucifer took several dainty steps and bumped the shed again. The boards rattled. He backed up and cocked his head, and David hit him across the shoulders. Lucifer seemed surprised; he lowered his head at David. It was that slight challenge, that moment of suggested aggression that turned David loose, that lost him to rage. He brought the two-by-four down in a precise arc, feeling its cold efficiency in his arms, and hurt Lucifer badly. Lucifer turned to run away, but David hit him again, directly across the nose. His head went down and he stumbled as he tried to turn; his face turned, brutal and bland, and the two-by-four caught him straight across his exposed ribs. He managed to get to his feet before the next inevitable descent of the wood, but it got him and he ran away, humping and jerking on three legs. He didn't stop to show his golden eye.

David never found out how badly he hurt Lucifer, and it would be some time before he felt shame or responsibility for that fit of rage. The black ram would have been killed if he hadn't run; that was the bare knowledge David finally possessed.

That night he packed his trunk and his suitcase. His trunk and bicycle could be picked up later—or not, as far as he was concerned. He had finally answered the question about what he was doing at Dark Hill Farm. In the morning he was ready long before light, and flagged down Romeo Forneau's Ford.

"You leavin' them people?" Forneau asked him as they swayed and slid down the long hill. "Crazy bastards, ain't they? I hear tell she's rich as Rockefeller. You know that?"

"No, I didn't," David said.

Forneau took him as far as Cascom, and he hitchhiked home from there.

From his room at Dexter-Benham he could see the little square with the white wooden chapel on one side and the tennis courts on the other. The high elms, evenly spaced, seemed the guardians of the square's neat formality. His room was small and bright, with a fluorescent lamp at his desk. He didn't think of the Cross farm very much that spring, and at Dexter-Benham he lost his ideal of learning and of logic slowly and without apparent pain. There were certain rules one broke at one's peril—smoking was

probably the worst crime of all. Infractions of lesser rules were punished too, and the greatest of these was to be late for a meal.

One March day, a half-hour before lunch, Hoppy Hopright came into David's room. He was a tall, lumpy-faced boy with woolly blond hair, and his usually humorous face was now full of anxiety. Something was bothering him very much, and he held a towel over his fly.

"Oh, Jesus, Dave," he said, "I did a goddam dumb-ass thing."

"What?" David said.

"If you've got a cruel streak in you, you'll laugh your ass off."

"Not me," David said. "Of course, it depends. What's the matter?"

"I don't want to see hilarity in any form," Hoppy said. He blushed red, and his forehead was wet. "Oh, I'm a prize idiot!"

"Well, what is it?" David said. He looked at the towel Hoppy held in front of him.

"You see, I got this new idea how to jerk off. I no longer recommend it, you understand."

"Yeah?"

"I had this half-pint milk bottle, see, and I was thinking about how the hole was just about the right size?" Hoppy blushed and shook his head. "Jesus, what a brain! Well, to make a long story short, I was wrong." He removed the towel, and what he revealed didn't look so much like a half-pint milk bottle as a piece of meat in the form of a half-pint milk bottle. "It's stuck!" Hoppy said desperately. "I can't get it off. I've been trying to pull the bastard off over an hour! I'm going out of my mind!"

"What about soap and water?" David said.

"Christ, I tried that first off. No dice."

"Maybe if you used cold water you could shrink it."

"I tried that, but it doesn't want to shrink." Hoppy groaned. "Christ! Hung up on a milk bottle!"

Hoppy held the bottle gingerly, and David could see veins, skin, all the parts, but bloated, magnified by the thick glass.

"You've evidently got a half-pint size," he said.

"Don't laugh! God damn it, lunch is in twenty minutes!"

"How about sticking the whole works in your pants?"

"It shows. I tried. I can't even walk without holding on to it."

The door suddenly opened. Hoppy grabbed for the towel, and Judson Gay appeared. He stood looking at them, and Hoppy stared up into his head in resignation.

"Did I interrupt something?" Judson asked. His characteristic expression was of an irony so distinct that sometimes his nose appeared to be on a different side of his face than his mouth.

"Tell him," Hoppy said. "Tell them all."

"What?" Judson asked.

"Hoppy got his pecker stuck in a milk bottle."

"What?" Judson said.

"You didn't have to be so crudely precise," Hoppy said.

"What?" Judson said.

"Tell him again," Hoppy said. "Tell everybody."

"Let's see it," Judson said. He whistled. "My God! It looks like a bottle of pickled pigs' feet!"

"That's helpful as all hell," Hoppy said. "Look, I've got to get it *off!* Think! Think!"

They explained to Judson what had been tried already.

"The radiator," Judson said after much thought. "We'll just tap it on the radiator."

"Agh!" Hoppy said. "The radiator! Good God!"

"We'll just tap it gently, until it cracks—"

"No cracks! Forget it!"

"Maybe Swivelhead could think of something," David suggested.

"I'd just as soon keep the number of witnesses down," Hoppy said. "Sort of at a minimum."

Swivelhead was summoned.

"Jesus!" he said. "What in hell did you go stick your dink in a h-p for?"

"For the thrill of it," Hoppy said.

"You ever try slamming a window on it?"

"A lot of help he's going to be," Hoppy said miserably.

Nothing was any help, and at the last minute, out of real desperation, they went to the floor master, Mr. Cheevy, whom they'd tormented with pennies in his light socket. This was slightly degrading in many ways, and worst of all it proved that, seventeen or not, they were not as wise as the little man they had professed to despise. After one look he went to his bathroom

and came back with a soaped tongue depressor. This he slid down into the bottle, letting in air, and the bottle slid off fairly easily.

"You had created a vacuum," he said, insultingly unsurprised by the whole business. He told no one, either, and of course they could never torment him again.

In May, David took some tests given at the school by the Army, and was admitted to something called the Army Specialized Training Reserve Program. After graduation in June he would be in uniform. When he became eighteen he would go into the Army proper, but until then the Army would feed and clothe him and send him to college.

One day during spring vacation he sat at home, at his desk below the head of the dusty De Oestris moose. His room seemed smaller after his absences, cluttered, half his possessions childish. The maple roll-top desk was full of toys such as bullet molds, knives; plans, half conceived, of odd gadgets, boats, airplanes. There were manuscripts, pretentious in their titles ("A History of the Underhammer Pistol"), that tapered off after a few pages from lack of research and real interest. Behind the desk were some embarrassingly bad paintings that ought to be destroyed.

From a small drawer he took his revolver and spun the magazine, opened it upon the round, still-powerful faces of the primers, clicked it shut and put it back in its drawer. It was silver-plated—real, but decorated like a toy. The real guns were blued nearly black, or painted olive drab, and they fired in the real wars in Europe and in Asia. In A *Farewell to Arms*, Lieutenant Rinaldi kept toilet paper in his pistol holster. At first David had thought it was because he hated guns, but then it occurred to him—and this seemed a powerful insight still—that he kept the toilet paper to use as toilet paper, and the implied comment was so much more powerful than the direct one he'd first supposed. And beautiful Catherine Barkley. Would the war reveal to him a girl like that somewhere, somehow? Or was she real at all, that brave nurse? Were all girls somehow half there— pretty but rather stupid like Carol Oakes, in love with you but bland and plain like Mary Denney, beautiful and striking like Tucker Cross, but a slut at heart? No, how about Katie, who was so pretty and so alive? He was surprised by a surge of brotherly

327

love for that lively sister. But surely there must be a girl out there for him, for him to be worthy of.

In a month or so the uniform of his country's Army would declare him a man, and he would leave boyhood, its humiliations, its accidents, his friends (like Ben, he thought; poor Ben, who still breathed and was fed by tube, forever a child). *Are you out there?* he whispered, meaning the girl, the world, something like a life, serious and meaningful unto death.

22

In the year 1944 a strange thing began to happen to Harvey Watson Whipple—an amelioration so gradual, so slow it was there working in his diseased bones without his knowledge. If he took a few less aspirin a week, how could he notice that? Or if he found it necessary to drink, later on, only one two-ounce ration of whiskey before he went to bed, had he ever measured his need in ounces? His healing was a forgetting, a slow fading of what once had been so positive a force. There were new drugs that may have had something to do with it, drugs developed because of the war, and the doctors at the clinic in Northlee had begun to use these in his prescriptions. Once, standing in the bathroom, he found that he had stood his left crutch against the wall by the medicine cabinet. Yes, there it was, and for a moment he felt a thrill almost of amputation, reached quickly for the crutch as though he might be falling, then realized that he had been standing not just upon his left leg. Ounces of weight—a delicate touch of the ball of the foot for balance—had been placed upon the right leg, yet there was no pain, only a certain achelike stiffness, or pressure, in the socket of his hip. Now, all at once, he took careful notice. In the massive leanings of his pain, which were

still there, certain strengths that before had been ominous in their reserves and predictions, now waned. His pulse beat lighter in their surges, as though his heart were his own again, not part traitor.

Careful, careful, he thought, afraid of the despair he had lived with so long; he wanted no redefinement of it. All this could be a nasty trick, a plot to renew his anguish. He told no one, which was a measure of his fear.

He didn't tell his wife, but of course she noticed. Long before he made his first experiments with his disused nerves and muscles, she noticed. Once she woke to find him sleeping on his stomach. Once he forgot to take his aspirin in the morning. One night they made love, the real way, not just her helping him, or having to be so careful.

Finally he was ready to tell her, but of course she had seen changes, by then, not only in his mind but in the shape, the roundness and length, of the muscles in his atrophied leg. His thigh began to turn round again. No longer a shank of bone in a loose bag of fat, its surfaces returned, and the scars and tears and stitch marks arched, now, around the growing muscles they defined.

One morning in late summer, a humid morning when all was finely misted as in an old painting, she woke to find him standing in front of the high window of their bedroom. He held one crutch by its handhold, using it as a cane. He took a step, and her hip tingled and stung in sympathy. He grimaced, but it was partly triumph. When he saw her watching him his face fell and he looked trapped, guilty. "Hanky," he said. "Did you see me?"

"I saw."

He sobbed, and took another step. "Nobody'll ever understand," he said. "I don't care if they don't. I don't give a shit if you see me bawl. I do, Hanky, I do. But if this leg is going to even half-ass work again, I . . ." He turned to the window, and looked for a long time across the lawn and into the woods.

Horace sat at David's desk, staring into the small drawer that held David's revolver. Could he pick it up? That instrument was made for a hand, a hand like his own. Once wed to a hand, power

in lines of force enlarged one man, made him master of all within range of that small glittering instrument. Miraculous, and dangerous too. It was necessary to have complete dominance over its parts, its springs, its cams and pressures. Now. Coolly, rationally, one's brain runs one's body. Reach down and pick it up.

He jumped back, crying softly. Had it coiled and lashed at his hand? Hadn't it waited coldly until he was too close, then jumped? Something had. No, now wait. Something can be nothing. Something can happen inside that seems to have happened outside.

His new power waxed and waned, but he felt progress. When he went down cellar to take out clinkers, to get the furnace ready for fall, his magic was to die. All right, he said each time, I will die. But I will take certain ones with me. He had challenged them. Zoster was too wise, but Leverah was dead—or at least badly injured. The Herpes were little yappers he would someday catch, one by one in his hands of steel and wrench them apart, their little yapping mouths still talking as he flung their dismembered bodies through that space, heads rolling, arms tumbling, joints flying. But how he had tricked Leverah, in his room! He knew she was there, blue coals of eyes, hair like clamworms, brown rotten banana fingers. All right, he said, now! He'd jumped up and rushed to the window, his eyes bugged out. A flash of blood smeared the glass on the outside and then came the long dying echo of a witch's scream as she fell, bleeding and burning. He felt no pity whatsoever, and his strength grew.

For they were the souls of the enemies. He would be a victim no longer. A victim is worthless, hardly even pitiful. He knew that from plenty of experience. He'd pleaded with them, he'd pleaded with *them*, and pleading did no good. Even in Wood such despised helplessness had caused disgust. Wood had to get away from that person he had been. He understood. It was not Wood's fault. Wood had taught him a lesson.

Susie had recognized right off that he was no longer a victim, because she loved to have him near her. He was strong, now, and she knew he would protect her with his life.

But the revolver lay crouched in its drawer, and he watched it. It was so quiet. Don't be a sap! Guns aren't alive, you jerk! They aren't alive at all until you pull the trigger. Then they jump.

But then they jump in your hand. That's wrong. The revolver becomes you, part of *you*, and it sends its authority, which is yours, out in that line you choose, which is yours, and kills what you have directed it to kill.

Several days later he got his hand on it, and nothing happened, so he picked it up. It seemed to give a satisfied little twitch as it snuggled into his hand. Later he found how to open it up. The shells came up out of their holes all at once, sort of as if the revolver vomited as he bent it. No hard feelings, though. Soon he kept it in his room, in the drawer of the table by his bed. When David came home on furlough from the Army he put it back, of course, then kept it near his bed again. He had made peace with Wood's shotgun too; its black tubes and dark wood stood in the corner by his door.

That was the Christmas neither Wood nor David came home, and Horace cut and dragged in and set up the tree. Horace! Peggy watched him proudly, and from the balcony handed him the angel. Kate steadied the stepladder. They were all proud of Horace. Sally De Oestris had to hire a man to drive her on her rounds that year, an old man who used to drive a taxi. Fortunately there was little snow, and she could get around well enough on her canes. Peggy went with her. Sally had taken a great notion to Peggy, and she worked at Sally's house two or three days a week.

Peggy hadn't heard from her mother in six months, and there was no word from her at all that Christmas.

Sally came hobbling out to the kitchen, where she found Henrietta alone. She tried to whisper, but her whispers were still somehow voiced and penetrating.

"That woman's abandoned her child," Sally said, her little blue eyes flashing above her diamonds and silver, out of her wrinkles. Her hair was white-silver as the artificial snow beneath the tree, but in her seriousness she seemed to turn before Henrietta's eyes from a decorative object into a stern, real person.

"I know."

"Cheap bitch," Sally said. "The girl's well rid of her."

"She'll be all right here with us," Henrietta said.

"She seems smart's a whip. How smart is she?"

"She gets good grades in school. Is that what you mean?"

"How good?"

"A's and B's. Like Kate."

"Tell me, now, Henrietta. I know her mother's a stupid woman. I had her in to help once and I swear to God! And her father's no genius either. Is she college material?"

"Why ask me?"

"Oh, come on! I'm too old for that bloody sensitivity. God damn it, I know you didn't go to college, so *can it!* We got over that years ago, didn't we?"

"I'm sorry," Henrietta said, and she meant it. Her sudden defensiveness had surprised her. "I'm sorry, Sally," she said.

"*Okay!*"

"Peggy's smart, all right. She's very smart."

"I'm going to put her through college, when the time comes. I saw Fred Pike about it a week ago Friday, and he's setting it up. Now I don't want the girl to know this just yet, but I do think she ought to know. It's a dilemma. Don't want gratitude, but if she can go to college I want her to take the college prep and not settle for some fiddle-faddle like secretarial studies or home ec. See what I mean?"

"Yes, but I think you'll have to suffer the gratitude. Mine too."

"Ah, yes," Sally said. She sighed. "Yours I'll suffer gladly. It's just that I don't want the girl beholden to me. It's two years before she'd be going off, and I like to have her around, but not as any sort of *ward*, you know? Now maybe this is too much to ask, but I wonder if you could just give her the impression somehow that if she wants to go on with her education, she can?"

"Great Expectations," Henrietta said.

"What? Oh yes. Well, how about it? Talk it over with Harvey. 'Course if you don't want to go along with my little white lie, or whatever it is, that's all right. I'm an old woman, is all, probably ready to kick the bucket, and that's the reason I give for asking."

"We'll see, then," Henrietta said, and Sally tapped her affectionately on the hip with one of her canes.

Peggy had been helping decorate the tree, but just before this conversation had begun, she'd gone to her room to get her presents for the Whipples out from under her bed. She'd just knelt by the floor register and reached for the tissue-wrapped boxes, and she heard every word as clearly as if she'd been standing beside them.

It was the goodwill, that wave of warmth come up with the kitchen smells and warm dry air from the range. First that about her mother—hard but true; they had a right to say what they'd said, and she shouldn't resent it. Then their concern for her, bringing tears. She put her face on the bed. How had the Whipples happened to be here, and Sally De Oestris? Why should they take her in? So many kids lived in shacks in the woods, and came to school hungry too, with that beat-up look about the eyes, and constant toothaches. She used to recognize them, and they her, and feel that none of them really belonged in school or would be there very long. Sixteen was when you quit school—it was a fact nobody thought much about.

She felt gawky and rawboned, and she knew her eyes were red. She'd grown taller, into an awkward bony thing. She'd begun to have arguments with people when she disagreed with them. She'd begun to have opinions, even to look things up in the encyclopedia, and to read the newspapers and magazines. She'd begun to feel that she wasn't really a nice person—as if this research were a form of cheating. She'd had an argument with Mr. Whipple about Roosevelt and Dewey and he'd got so mad he whacked his cane down across his table and roared at her how the President was a dictator worse than Hitler. That was because he'd got Donald Nelson and Harold Ickes mixed up, and she'd corrected him.

And now to hear Sally and Mrs. Whipple talk of her with no reference to this hardness that had come over her, this snottiness she couldn't seem to control sometimes. She had to *deserve* whatever concern anyone had for her. What other right could she possibly have for being here, for living in this house? She could

not deserve their kindness, yet they gave it anyway. And even after her argument with Mr. Whipple—right afterwards, with the echoes still flying—he'd asked her in the nicest way to get him another cup of coffee, as though nothing had happened.

Then, beyond what warmth of gratitude she'd felt as she listened to their power and concern, she thought of the gift itself. She had never thought of going to college. People like her didn't go to college, period. It was odd if they finished high school. She *had* been planning to major in the secretarial course. But now the possibilities scarily opened out. Now she could be anything. She could be *anything*. She knew she would never get married, and now she could learn things beyond the mere information and mechanical skills of high school. In college you learned how to make a profession out of your knowledge. She could be a teacher, a scientist, she could take Latin two more years if she wanted, and it would help her, not just be something she liked. Her whole future now opened out in warm colors, something to anticipate with fear and joy.

Then shut, with a chill shiver. She had forgotten the war, forgotten that Wood was in constant danger. Her father too. Even David was now in the real Army, training down in the South. She could not look ahead at all, not beyond Wood's safe return. They were all trapped to right here and right now. Again her essential selfishness had appeared, a little cold selfish thing like a snake, that made her say *me, me,* that slithered its cold head in and out of her mind, not under her control.

That Christmas, after the presents were opened, they were all silent, all at once, thinking of Wood. So many men and boys were overseas, or gone from Leah. Bertram Mudd was somewhere in the Pacific, and so was Wood. David was in the Army in the South, and so was John Cotter. Keith Joubert was in Europe. Donald Ramsey was in the Marines. Michael Spinelli was in a submarine. Gordon Ward had been wounded again in Italy. Eddie Kusacs was dead, still sitting inside his Marine fighter plane, deep in the Pacific Ocean; he'd crashed trying to land on his carrier and slid off over the side, leaving his wings, so he sank like

a stone. Sylvia Beaudette's husband, Phil, was dead, missing over Germany but seen to explode, his "Flying Fortress" blowing up like one bomb, and she'd gone home to Maine to live with her parents. Others were dead, or missing, or wounded so badly they couldn't come home. The war was being won, but what consolation was that when all the hostages, the boys who ought not to have to die, were off in deadly foreign places? It was the winter for death.

Henrietta sat by the fire, seeing empty places in the room. It was the winter for death. Let them crow of the victories happening or to come. Victories over what, over whom? Some kind of monster out of space, was it? Was it a victory over fascism, now, fought by boys and men who didn't know fascism from German measles?

In the smiles of victory she saw the same vicious triumph she'd seen on Hitler's face at the fall of France. She saw the same primitive joy in giving death. Patton, for instance, wearing his six-shooters. She saw it in Harvey. She saw it all over town. She read it in the papers and heard it on the radio. They were fighting the war for a new car and a new refrigerator, according to the ads, and that was a good way to put it, because they didn't give a hoot in hell for anybody else; they killed vermin, everybody was killing vermin, to get them out of the way so they could get theirs, the things they wanted, and it was a nice nasty way to put it, to hide it, that they fought for a new car and a new refrigerator.

But then she thought of Wood, and her bitterness melted. He looked like them all, so broad and manly and upright, but she could not see death in his squarish, unhumorous face. She never had. But then he'd rarely let his face be read, even as a child. She tried to pray for him, but even as she considered it she saw how silly and stupid it would be, because she'd never prayed out of real belief in her life. There'd have to be too many ifs, ands and buts in any prayer she'd make.

But she loved and honored her son. What else could she do for him?

Nothing.

Suddenly a big hand was on her shoulder. It was Horace, who stood leaning massively over her, his coarse face staring fiercely, meaning to comfort her.

335

That winter and spring Horace continued to do errands for his father concerning the tenements. He had changed a great deal, and everybody noticed it. When he moved his body now, it was with purpose, almost aggressive purpose, and this new tension in his muscles caused him to have control he'd never had before. When he reached for his glass at the table, he believed, now, that the glass would stay there until his hand got ready to grasp it. Inanimate things were no longer quite as aggressive toward him. In a dream he had even killed a Herpes with his hands. The others got away. He knew they were only in his mind, but somehow this thought was frightening, so he tried not to know, knowing all the time that Zoster and the Herpes were in his mind.

Zoster skulked in the cellar, and when Horace went to the cellar he thought of Susie's warmth and frailty. He carried David's loaded revolver in his back pocket under his handkerchief, but he would not shoot Zoster, he would kill him with his bare hands if he appeared in conjunction with Susie's goodness. Then why the gun? he sometimes asked himself. If he actually shot it in the house someone would hear it and all hell would break loose. But in spite of these disturbing questions, his power grew. No longer did he have to make a pact with his own death each time he descended into the cellar's stench of earth, potatoes, vegetable rot and the wisps from the coal fire. His shoulders squared; hard as iron, he challenged Zoster. If he turned, he turned slowly in his strength, his rage contained, his fear contained, deliberately wanting to look upon the scaled head that had never yet dared to face him. He held out an arm, an offering to that mouth, but kept the other ready. He had never seen Zoster but he knew what he looked like, how the scales overlapped, the long teeth clashed, the eyes shone with triumphant, smutty mirth. He knew where the joint was in that neck, the main joint where reptilian horn glided in cold oil to protect the black nerves and blood.

But then, the fire shaken down—not too far, as David had shown him, the drafts right, the cleanout door shut—he left the furnace creaking contentedly like a huge, fairly friendly domesticated animal in its stall and climbed the stairs into the real world again. Sweat always beaded his spine at his escape from the confrontation with Zoster, and it turned cool as he shut the door

and strode, not too fast, through the shelf pantry into the kitchen.

"You're not afraid of the cellar any more?" his mother asked.

"Not exactly," he said. "I mean, I can go down there now."

But he was not sure that he could go down there, just himself, just Horace Whipple. He became something else, a sort of warrior, not that little boy who cringed in terror under his damp bedclothes. It was like dying and being born again into that stern duty. It took a great carefulness of thought, and thought was a dangerous thing to weave into spells, because it might trick you.

On Friday afternoons he trembled as he tapped on Susie's door. She always smiled and kissed him on the forehead, sometimes putting her arms around him for a second. But sometimes she seemed tired, and he grew worried. Sometimes she would seem listless and distracted, though always friendly. But then he'd come the next Friday and she'd greet him all lively and full of excitement again, and they'd sit at the table and talk. Her eyes were dark blue, blue as plums, and her wide cheeks bowed when she smiled, she smiled so wide. He liked it best when she wore no lipstick, because without the lipstick's hard red proclamation to be seen, her face was softer, and she seemed more intimate with him.

What he didn't like at all was to find Mrs. Palmer sitting at Susie's table, sometimes with a bottle of beer. Susie called her "Candy," and they made references to things Horace wasn't sure about. Candy was Beady Palmer's wife, and she had four little kids to take care of—three of them the children of her first husband. She lived in the apartment across the hall, in the only three-bedroom apartment in the building, and she left the doors open so she could hear if the little kids started screaming. She was four or five years older than Beady, with that smooth hard look about her, her blond hair too much fussed with, that Horace understood was supposed to be attractive to men. When he'd first seen her there he stood silent and embarrassed, he was so surprised. A slithery green dressing gown fell loosely from her shoulders, and underneath were only pink bands and smooth, cuplike structures of pink silk. As Susie introduced him to her she drew the green material across her breasts and over her thighs.

"Jesus," she said. "You said he was a kid. He's as big as a man!"

Susie laughed and put her arm around him. "He's my Horace," she said gaily.

Candy winked and mashed a pink cigarette butt into the ashtray. "Well, I say he's as big as a man," she said. The way she said it Horace wasn't sure she meant just his size. There had to be some other meaning, the way she said it, as though at least one of the words she'd used didn't mean what it usually meant.

Susie would start using this strange language too, only not so much. It seemed she used it only to be polite to Candy, although she laughed when Horace couldn't laugh, and then she seemed to have gone away from him.

Once when Candy was there Beady Palmer came home from work.

"Hey, Candy!" he began shouting in the other apartment. Candy yelled, "In here, lover boy!" Then in a lower voice she said, "If he can find his way." She and Susie laughed.

Beady came in, moving his dented cheeks from side to side so his eyes could see everything. "Well," he said, recognizing Horace, "our illustrious landlord's son and heir!" He saw the beer on the table. "Hey, Suze, let me trade you a hot one for a cold one," he said. They all laughed, and Beady went to his apartment and brought back a quart bottle of Beverwyck Ale, which he put in Susie's refrigerator. Susie poured him a glass from another quart that was evidently colder. But why the laughter?

"I don't want you to do no trading unless I'm present and accounted for," Candy said. They laughed.

"How about a beer for the kid?" Candy said. Horace said no, thank you, and they laughed. Susie patted his hand and smiled at him.

But what caused the greatest laughter of all was later, when Beady put his hand on Candy's leg and said, "Hey, kid, I'm tired. Let's go to bed."

After the laughter Beady said, "No kidding, we got to eat and git ready if we're going out on the town."

"Some town," Candy said. "You mean the hog wrastle."

" 'Blue Moooon, da da di yadda di da,' " Beady sang.

When they got up to go, Candy thanked Susie, who was

going to leave the doors open so she could keep an ear out for the kids. "Rain or shine, we'll be back at twelve, Suze, and thanks a million, huh?"

"You're a sweetheart, Suze," Beady said. "I wish I could thank you in a more personal way." They all laughed, and Candy punched him on the arm.

When they were gone, Susie looked a little sad, and Horace asked her what was the matter.

"Oh, it's just life, I guess," she said, sighing. "A girl gets lonely, Horace. You know what I mean?"

"I'll keep you company," he said.

"You're a darling," she said, squeezing his arm. But she still looked so sad he moved his chair over next to hers and put his arm around her. For a minute she put her head on his chest. His heart beat in his throat. He smelled her rich brown hair, oily and soapy. Her body was warm and soft, all encircled by his strong arm. His hand, wide and living on her side, felt her breathe.

Finally, in a businesslike way, she straightened up and shook her head, then with an affectionate pat on his ribs she got up and began to clear the table.

"You're a love, Horace. You're so nice. You really are."

"I love you," he said.

"Oh, Horace!" she said, smiling. "And I love you too. Very much!"

But the next Friday when he came she looked awful. She looked older, with puffy places below her eyes and even at the sides of her mouth.

"What's the matter?" he asked. She sat hunched over, drinking black coffee. Her white blouse was dirty.

"Oh me," she said, trying to smile. "It's a combination of a hangover and the wrong time of the month, I guess."

"Oh," he said.

"Maybe I'll have a little hair of the dog," she said. "Ooo, my achin' head!"

Black visions swam through his mind. Monthly, hangover, hair of the dog. He knew vaguely that women had a bad thing at certain phases of the moon. It was a curse they bore for being women, for being able to give birth. They bled. The hair of a

dog he didn't understand, but it was monstrous, bestial enough to go with the other.

"A little hair of the dog that bit me," she said, and got a bottle of beer from the refrigerator. "It's a saying, Horace, when the dog is alcohol. Oh, here, before my mind goes blank."

She had the due rents ready, and a list of materials her father had bought for repairs to the two buildings—toilet floats, faucet washers, lumber, nails, paint, glazing compound, and three 7" x 9" lights. Horace was learning about these things, and now knew that lights meant panes of glass and not light bulbs.

"Are you going to be all right?" he asked. She stood at the table, leaning on the knuckles of one hand while she drank out of the bottle.

"Oh, Horace, I'm sorry to be such a slob. I meant to take a bath and change before you came, but I crapped out on the davenport."

"That's okay," he said.

She sat down and leaned back in the kitchen chair, her eyes shut. "I know it's awful, but a girl gets lonely, Horace. You know what I mean?" She opened her dark blue eyes and stared seriously at him while she thought.

"I don't know exactly," he said.

"To sit alone, nobody around, and hear music from somewhere? People laughing?"

"I don't have any friends except at home," he said. "And you."

"Neither do I, really," she said. "I mean Candy and Beady are sort of fun, but they have their own lives. Not that Beady wouldn't try plenty if I didn't slap him down once in a while." She chuckled wearily.

"Slap him down?"

"Oh, he's a good guy, Horace. Don't get excited. My goodness, you *are* all het up!"

"I wouldn't let anybody hurt you!"

"Well, he wouldn't *hurt* me, Horace," she said, and laughed, then grimaced and held her head. "Ow! It only hurts when I laugh."

"Don't talk like that," he said.

She opened her eyes wide. "What?"

"When you joke about whatever it is. You aren't you."

"Oh, dear. I'm afraid I am me, Horace. I'm afraid I am me, and it's not so nice."

"What's hurting you?" he asked her. He knew that his own experiences might really qualify him to help. "Please tell me, Susie. Maybe I can help you. Really."

"Life," she said. "It hurts."

"Why?"

"Oh, Horace," she said sadly. "You don't want to know."

"I want to know."

She shook her head loosely. Dusk was coming into the room, and with it the cold ghostly blue of Futzie Petrosky's tavern sign. He wondered if he ought to reach up above the table and turn on the light.

"Horace, would you go into my room and get me the pack of Chesterfields on the bed table? The room on the left in there?"

He went through the small living room, where the dark, bulky stuffed furniture was, dim rolled shapes that shouldered up into the windows. He felt his way, not knowing where any light switches were, past the toothpaste-watery smell of the bathroom. Her room smelled of her, and beside the bed the white pack of cigarettes gleamed on the table. Her bed was mussed, unmade, and he went quickly to his knees and put his head down underneath the covers in the wrinkled sheets, deep in her powerful smells where her body had lain. It was sweet, and he breathed deeply that heavy sweetness edged with sour.

Back in the kitchen she took the cigarettes and lit one, her face edged black in the matchlight. She sipped her beer and then took a deep red drag on the cigarette. "Don't turn on the light," she said. "Futzie's sign is bad enough when you look like a zombie."

"I want to help you," he said. In the dusk his voice seemed grown-up and strange to him.

"There's nothing to do to help."

"You can tell me what's making you so sad," his grown-up voice said.

"I was in high school once," she began, as though she were telling a bedtime story. "I was in high school and I was a good

341

girl and got good grades. I was maybe a little plump, but everybody said how pretty I was anyway. What was wrong with me was I was too friendly and I believed everything another person said. I just couldn't believe anybody would lie. Now, that's pretty stupid."

"And then?"

"And I was in love with Wood. A lot of girls were in love with Wood Spencer Whipple. I guess I showed it more than anybody."

"Do you still love Wood?"

"I threw that chance away a long time ago, Horace."

"Chance?"

"Yes. Anyway . . ." She took a drink of beer; he heard the liquid gurgle in the bottle. "Anyway, one day at school I found a note in my desk, and I'll tell you word for word what it said. It said, 'Dear Susie, I think you are swell. I like you a lot. Would you meet me at 9:30 after DeMolay by the big pine next to the Congregational Church? Love, Wood W.'

"That's what the note said. Naturally I thought it was from Wood. But it wasn't, because he told me about six months later, as nice as he could, that it wasn't from him. So I'm waiting in the shadow of that big pine and my heart's beating a thousand times a minute. I'm all dressed up, all fixed up as good as I can, and I see a tall boy—I can see his outline against the lights of the square . . . Well, it was Gordon Ward, saying that because of something or other at DeMolay, Wood couldn't come, but he'd asked Gordon to take me home. Boy, was he smart! He figured everything. I couldn't stand him, you see. He used to goose me in school. And now he had a chance to be so nice, and Wood never sent me another note or anything, so I kind of rebounded. I was lonely anyway, living three miles out on the farm and not getting into town for things. It was a long ride on a bicycle, and scary after dark. And Gordon had his Plymouth convertible coupé, so he could stick my bike in the rumble seat."

"Gordon Ward," Horace said.

"Oh, that's all history," Susie said. "Water under the dam. Now everybody's in the service. Gordon's a hero. Poor Wood's overseas too. Wood was so kind to me, Horace. He came to the farm, and my father pointed his shotgun at him. Now people are really shooting at him. I pray he won't get hurt!"

"I pray Gordon Ward gets killed," Horace said.

"Don't say that! Oh, my God, Horace! Don't say such a thing! It's wrong!"

"There's others too," Horace said, "I wouldn't mind seeing dead."

"Horace!" she said. A chair scraped, and she stood up. "Please, Horace, never say things like that!"

He got up slowly and went to her, so strong he could hardly move. She smelled of beer, that bread smell, and sharp sweat, and the deep, hurt sweetness that was part of her skin and glands or whatever. He brought her against his chest.

"Horace?" she asked, her arms against her sides.

"I'm not going to let anybody hurt you," he said slowly, hearing that new odd timbre in his voice. He wanted to convince her that he had seen death as close as anyone, that he was deadly serious and did not wish upon death lightly.

"Oh, I feel awful," she said, tapping his sides as a signal that he should let her go. "And I've got to work tonight. I'm taking Bessie Higgins' shift for her, and it's going to be sheer purgatory."

"How can I take care of you if you won't tell me what's wrong?" he asked.

"You can't take care of me, Horace." He hadn't let her go, so she stood on her toes, kissed him on the mouth and pushed him away. "You can't. Nobody can. I don't even trust myself with you. It's too late for me."

"No."

"You're so good, Horace. I don't blame you for feeling that way about Gordon and those others that . . . you know. But you're not like that, really. You're so good, so sweet. You're the nicest thing in my whole life, and I mean that."

"I love you," he said.

"And I love you, an awful lot."

She had to take a bath and change for work, so he left, and walked home in the night. He went carefully up Water Street, then through the square that was now busy before the first show at the Strand, past all the frail people of the town. She was wrong, but of course she didn't know. She had no idea of his power.

23

Kate sat in *The Quill* office in the teachers' lounge, where no teacher ever lounged. She was the editor, and felt a great responsibility to maintain the standards of originality Wayne had set last year and the year before. He was at the university now, but she sent him copies of *The Quill* for criticism. One hard thing was to think up cover pictures that would do justice to Wayne's idea of "beauty with a sting in it." Without being positively morbid—like an arrow stuck into somebody—it was hard to continue the play on the word "quill." One idea she liked, and so did Wayne, was the cover with a quill pen stuck into a large black beetle. That is, the beetle was really an inkwell made in the shape of a very realistic beetle. Wayne was enthusiastic about that one, and praised her originality. She had copied the beetle from a book of Japanese woodcuts that belonged to Sally De Oestris.

She had his letter, written in brown ink on beige paper, beside the typewriter.

106 South Hall
April 5, 1945

My dear Kate,

Your beautiful bug impaled by the pen is superb! Nice drawing too; not only are you original, you have a sensitive Pre-Raphaelite line—whether copied or not. Like poetry, line is hardest to translate.

Some of the contributions in this issue are of doubtful quality, but that is life. We both know that few flowers grow in a cultural desert (certain ones do, however, *viz.*:

you and I). Your poem has some nice lines in it, and at least one fascinating conceit. The pottery fragments ". . . which man made alien to clay . . ." is utterly superb. Perhaps someday one will have to admit that your talent equals your beauty.

Kate blushed each time she read that part. Although she could sense Wayne's admiration of his own prose style, she still flushed with pleasure—flattery or not—whenever anybody said she had something to her besides "beauty."

His letter continued:

As far as this university is concerned, I have had few triumphs since last fall, when I convinced the powers that be that I had no need of "freshman rhetoric." One sits in enough classes as it is full of dull clods whose primal desire is only to graduate out of boredom into a secure job (after the war) in which they will manifest all the human alternatives and glories of a screwdriver. And full of dull female clods that (pardon me) want only to be the recipients of what that tool drives. The College of Matrimonial Arts, perhaps it should be called. There are so few males here that the dishonor of civilian clothes hardly makes a difference, and even I find myself considered possibly eligible in the eyes of these desperately man-hungry, beef-headed, bladder-prowed matrons of the future. And when they aren't rather aggressive they are excruciatingly shy, as though heartily ashamed of their female parts. They walk about hunched, avoiding eyes, squinched in as though afraid some sweating wild man will emerge, roaring, from the lilacs, overwhelm and ravish them, Kleenex, pens and textbooks flying, upon the sacred walks of the Administration Building.

Among all of them, dear Kate, you would move as a goddess among kine.

Thank you for saying "hello" to my mother. I must admit I don't write her as often as I probably should. Unfortunately we don't speak the same language, although the dear old thing tries.

Ciao, K,
Wayne

345

She read the letter through again, again blushing at his flattery. As for his horrible picture of the university, this depressed her a little even though, knowing Wayne's exaggerated opinions, she knew it couldn't be anywhere near that bad.

She would go to the university too, and Wayne would still be there, an upperclassman, when she was a freshman. It would be an exciting time, full of new experiences. And triumphs? Let's face it, she thought, that too.

But now with the war being won, Leah did seem an awful backwater. All the people working on *The Quill* seemed about half there. Her thoughts always went out to the soldiers and sailors. Wood was in combat again, that much he let them know. You could see in his short V-mail letters how he tried not to worry his mother, and how she knew he didn't say much so as not to worry anybody.

Davy's letters were different, but of course he wasn't overseas. He positively bragged about shooting "expert" with the rifle, and about all the big explosive things he was shooting off. You'd think David was the one in combat, from his letters. But she knew him; he was probably having a fine time strutting around, playing soldier. But then she thought: Yes, but when would the war really end? Would it ever really end altogether? Wouldn't they have to fight all the way up through China? Maybe David would really have to go and be really *shot* at. She shivered—almost a paroxysm, really, and it was fear, real fear for David. He shouldn't have to do that. He shouldn't be made to take such real risks.

But what about Wood? Sometimes she found herself getting almost used to the idea that Wood was fighting. It was terrible, because she would die if Wood were hurt. They all would. Sometimes she would find her mother staring, white with fear. And Peggy would go into long silences, suffering for Wood. No, it couldn't happen. Certain things simply could not happen, not to her family. There had been her father's accident, yes—that was a real thing and it had happened to them, but now he was getting better all the time. Sometimes he walked down the driveway, using canes. And Horace had changed so much. He was so dependable now, and you didn't have to watch out for him all the time. Out of the shadow that was over them all, things seemed

little by little to be getting better for them. Cross fingers, knock on wood, pray Dear God Wood and Davy come home all right.

On the afternoon of Thursday, April 12, Harvey and Henrietta were waiting for the news. Gene Krupa or somebody was doing something called a "triple paradiddle," on drums, and they had toned this down while they waited. Suddenly the band music was cut off, and Henrietta began to get up to see if it was something wrong with the radio.

Then came a strange sound to hear over the air, a long, ragged breath. Without introduction the announcer's voice, phlegmy and broken, said, "President Roosevelt is dead." There were odd peeps and breaks in the voice. "In Warm Springs, Georgia. The President, according to his doctors, suffered . . ." From the radio came part of a sob, then the total quiet of cutoff, then the voice again, stronger after that blank moment of imposed control, "The President suffered a massive cerebral hemorrhage and . . . died . . . at approximately 3:35 P.M."

It was as though the announcer's sorrowing voice had fallen through her own mouth, and for a moment Henrietta couldn't take a breath. She did not think of herself as the kind who could love a public man, but this sudden emptiness was love torn from her. Suddenly it was that void.

The day was warm, an early rush of spring, and windows in the big room were open. The long curtains folded and unfolded in the breeze that brought in earth smells. She seemed to hear above the spring day the distant boom and crack of the war, and suddenly it was all without direction, pure madness, and all the violence was being done by doubtful little men. Words continued to come from the radio, but nothing much more was known. When the music continued it was muted and funereal.

"Well, goddam!" Harvey said. She looked at him, at that blankness of care.

After a minute or two the telephone rang, and automatically she picked it up. Gordon Ward, Sr.'s, elated voice said, "Harvey! Have you heard? The son of a bitch is dead! Harvey?"

She handed him the phone.

347

"Yeah, I just heard." He looked at her somewhat furtively, and said, "Yeah, Gordon. Yeah. Yeah, old Rosenfeld."

"Go ahead and chortle," she said. "It's no dirtier now than it's been for all these years." Tears were running down her face, and as she looked at his furtive grin of collusion with Gordon Ward, she despaired of him, of them all. This was the void left, that people like these waited for.

Horace came into the hall at that moment, and immediately felt the badness. He stopped and stood quietly against the wall, just out of their sight. His father hung up the telephone and began to shout at his mother. "What the hell do you know about it, anyway?"

"Not the vicious slander you get from the likes of Gordon Ward."

"That man was trying to destroy the country! He was a dictator! He got us in the war to save the Bolshies, and don't forget it! He was a maniac, and how the hell do you know he's even dead? Gordon says they probably carted him off to the funny farm!"

"Shut up," she said coldly. "You don't know anything now and you never have. You've always preferred plots and rumors to learning."

"Why, you dumb bitch! Try earning a living in this country!"

"A great man has died. Of course all you can think about is your money. You're a Republican. But he saved this country. Yes, literally saved it, what was good in it, and you small cold people hate him still. You always will, because it's your nature. Go on making things up about him. What was it a while ago? Eleanor gave him syphilis, and she got it from Paul Robeson? All you believe in is selfishness, that's the whole thing, and I figured that out a long, long time ago. You'll never understand *anybody* who wants to help other people. You're rotten, you and all the other Gordon Wards. Your pleasure is to kill goodness. Your faces were made to smirk, and that's all! Oh, I see you all the time, everywhere! Did you ever look at Hitler? You might as well look into the mirror!"

Horace heard all this as he stood in the shadow. His father began screaming again, almost desperately, his words tumbling

among curses. "Packing Supreme Court! Double cross! How about that? Do you deny, you asshole? How about the NRA? How about AAA? Unconstitutional! How about those half-baked Reds and all their fucking alphabet soup? Christ Almighty, what the hell did that bunch of Jews and Communists save? Stalin's ass, that's what they saved, and we're paying for it!"

Carefully, Horace eased back. His mother was crying, trying to speak but having to sob. "God help us," she finally said. "Oh, God help us now!"

He stood in hiding against the wall, waiting, cool and ready. His mother rushed past without seeing him and ran up the stairs, still crying. He stayed where he was, calm and steady and unseen, one center of the world upon which they could not descend. He was here, broadcasting that information on the wavelength of his mind so that they should all know, all of them in their holes and foul cellar cracks, that he was neither dead nor incapacitated. And somewhere Wood steadfastly kept that vigil too.

First, he is exhausted. He has run too far, too fast, too many times today, uphill, carrying too much—carbine, four grenades, canteen and mess kit, clips of ammo besides those in stock pouches, steel helmet, bayonet knife, entrenching tool, binoculars, map case, first-aid packet, webbed belt, boots, clothing, sweat, crud. As always, he is afraid. Certain secretions have been shot by glands too often for too long into his gaunt body, compounding exhaustion. He runs on nerve, burning. He is twenty years old, a first lieutenant; he has been acting company commander for five days, on the point for more than a month. He is in sorrow, crying the way he has come to cry, with no tears but a piece of clay in the throat he cannot swallow. He has just lost five men, two of them killed outright. Wilcox and Malins, whose dog tags jingle in his pocket, Wilcox's and Malins' jingling together. He knew them well.

What action, what elaboration can help? This is the only activity of men. The dust, the death-gray of battle covering what had been the washed green of this little valley. Cordite, fulminate of mercury, raw flamethrower oil, the flutter of shells, the blind-

ness of war. You can't see anything. You can't see enough. Where is? What coordinates? Where? By sound he has identified what it was, a nine-millimeter Nambu machine gun. One could have looked more closely at the hole in Malins' helmet, but what does it matter? Able Baker Charlie Dog. He is Charlie One. Where does Charlie One think that Nambu is now?

Then he has made a mistake, because a sudden hand comes down as if from the vast sky, from all sides at once, and swats him down out of erectness into the ground as a fly is swatted into a table. He is conscious but with the knowledge that time, that vacuum, has passed unneedful of him. He stares at blue that is wavering now—how can it when it has no reference points? It moves, and in shock he knows that it is part of shock, the reverie of shock. It has happened to him. Shock is the presence of all the nausea of one's life come back at once in an aura, now, of white birds broken and falling. The cold oil of nausea. Ice in the extremities. Pain comes, and is not negotiable. Formal notice of power. Oh, my God.

Third Platoon, his old platoon, has seen him hit. Now good men in their sorrow risk themselves to kill. He does not want them to come across there, and waves them back with his right arm. They see his weakness and do not obey. The Nambu fires short professional bursts, and he is terrified for them, but soon their warm sweat and friendly stench surround him, and he hears from above the execution of the Japanese gunners: "*O-isogi de!* *Hayaku, hayaku!*" a Japanese says. This means hurry up, and the irony is lost on Corporal Wilson, who is quick enough as it is.

"*Medic! Medic! Medic!*" Wood hears that old sobbing cry. "*Oh, Christ!*" he hears. "*He's hurtin'! Give him a shot!*" He hears this, hears it even though he is drowning. Then someone cuts at his throat and the suffocation is suddenly gone. He feels the manipulation, feels the leathery resistance of his own skin, and also the pain of the cut. Separate, yet the same. He believes that he is dying, which is not a strange idea at all. He believes in the magnitude of the force that hit him; surely it was great enough to kill a hundred times, a thousand times.

Then nothing. Then he wakes, and time has passed without his attention to any of its details. It is now independent of him,

and he is not necessary after all. Morphine-borne, he drifts off into the days.

—th Regiment
96th Infantry Division
Naha, Okinawa
7 July, 1945

Mr. and Mrs. Harvey W. Whipple
10 High St.
Leah, New Hampshire

Dear Mr. and Mrs. Whipple:

Wood has asked me to write to you and to tell you that he is fine. I have decided that without his consent I will tell you more.

At present he is aboard the hospital ship Alaria, where I visited him this morning. After a long talk with his doctors, they assure me that he will be all right, able to live a normal life. But it will take some time, and at least three, maybe more, operations will be necessary to restore his larynx, his left wrist, and to form a cushion on his left thigh to enable him to bear weight on the necessary prosthesis, or artificial limb, that he will have to wear. His left eye is gone, but all indications are that the right one will have few sympathetic reactions and will be all right. I'm sorry to have to list all these things at once, but in my judgment it is always better that you know.

It might also help to know that Lieutenant Whipple has been awarded the Bronze Star Medal and has been recommended twice for the Silver Star. I am informed that this medal will most certainly be awarded.

On 5 June, while acting company commander, "C" Company, 4th Battalion, he was hit by four machine-gun bullets. It is on record that were it not for the devotion of his men, who took several casualties in order to silence the machine gun and to reach him immediately, he would not have lived. S/Sgt. Daniel P. Furlin performed an emergency tracheotomy that enabled him to breathe. This action most definitely saved his life. S/Sgt. Furlin's home address is 141 Belmont St., Clareville, Ky.

I would like also to say something of our extreme pride in your son, one of our finest young officers. His devotion to the welfare of his men, and their devotion to him, was always manifest. With the strength of character Lieutenant Whipple possesses, I am most certain he will overcome his disabilities and lead a meaningful and productive life.

Sincerely yours,

William H. Halberstadt
Lt. Col., Infantry
A.U.S.

PART III

And from there those that lifted eyes could count
Five mountain ranges one behind the other
Under the sunset far into Vermont.

Robert Frost: "Out, Out—"

24

The war had receded, leaving its scum of unusable knowledge. It was the second week of June, 1948.

Wood sat out at the end of the porch, quietly reading. He hardly ever moved, except to turn pages or to brush away a mosquito, and his calmness seemed unnatural to Henrietta. His quietness was unnerving because it was constant, and although he read all the time, he hardly seemed interested. He just read steadily, carefully, as though studying.

In the fall he had had the last—hopefully the last—operation on his throat, and although his voice was still windy, there was something of voice in it. It was no longer the harsh, painful whisper it had been. But he'd got used to saying very little. When she asked him why he did nothing but read—why he didn't see about going to college, getting on with life—he said "I want to see where I've been," smiling, but saying nothing more.

He wore a patch over his left eye, where his left eye had been. When she had asked to see his eye, he removed the patch and it was shocking because nothing but skin wrapped his face between his nose and ear, as though the eye itself had been a wound that had healed over with hardly a scar. He had told her in technical language as calmly as a doctor the information relative to his wounds: a nine-millimeter machine-gun bullet at maximum velocity hit his knee squarely. The bullet may have been defective, for it shattered, doing more damage. Parts of that bullet probably struck his left wrist. He was running at the time, stooped

over. Another bullet hit his left leg just below the knee. Another bullet grazed his left eye and took away part of the temple; another bullet pierced his larynx.

"I was lucky," he'd whispered. "I'd done a stupid thing and they had me dead to rights."

"What was so stupid?"

"It was strange," he said.

"What was strange?"

"I almost think I knew where that machine gun was." He looked at her and evidently saw her expression of concern. "Of course I didn't really know where it was. But you get so tired," he'd said, this in his former scratchy whisper. "You get so tired."

She stood now, watching him from the bay window of a parlorlike room they hardly ever used, feeling guilty of peeping because she had no real business in that dusty room. He was reading another book about the war, this one by a moderately liberal war correspondent. She had noticed that he carried around with him certain old magazines, which always seemed to be rather casually lying near him. She had picked them up and looked through them, finding immediately those pages he studied. Some were pictures of Hiroshima—a little girl whose back and arm grew bubbly and white. Another had a series of pictures of concentration camps. At Dachau or Belsen husky German girls threw sticklike corpses into a trench. He studied the charnel houses— now cities, even countries, it seemed, of the world. She had looked up from the pictures of Hiroshima and caught his eye. He looked away.

"But we weren't . . ." she began to say that time; his dark eye had turned toward her again and she had stopped.

Someone had sent him the papers found on the body of the Japanese soldier who had shot him, and he kept these near him too, in that informal pile of magazines and pictures. Last fall he had sent the papers to David, who was at the University of Chicago, and David had gone to the Oriental Institute and got somebody to translate them. The soldier was Jōtōhei, or Superior Private, Ichiro Watanabe, twenty-two years old when he died. A letter among the papers was from his parents. They lived in Asakusa, a ward of Tokyo, and Wood had sent them the papers, with a note, but had heard nothing. In the spring the envelope

came back. Written on it in English was a note saying that street hadn't existed since the B-29 fire raid of March 10, 1945. Then Wood learned that eighty-three thousand people had died in that fire raid.

"My little gesture," he'd said to Henrietta.

Now he sat there by the grapevine, in the high-backed old rocking chair, his artificial leg unlocked so the knee of it bent. He stopped reading to light his pipe. He was twenty-three years old, which seemed to her so young, a happy age to be. Twenty-three. When she was that age Wood was a year old, and she remembered those times. She was having babies, and it was so much fun. That was about it. They wanted the babies and they had the money and they loved to do what caused the babies. The world seemed such a wonderful place to make love and have babies in.

And now, cursed every day by the news she could no longer ignore, the world was all pain and hatred and murder. It was stupid. The world was stupid. But people hurt just as much as they ever did. Wood had hurt just as much as she would have if they'd cut off her leg and poked out her eye and shot her in the throat.

For a while after the war, in spite of everything, there had been hope, but now hatred had settled in all over the world again like a disease spawned in the war. If a good man tried to do something they assassinated him, like Gandhi, or somehow he died or was slandered, sacrificed to the universal stupidity.

She was weeping, clenching her fists and weeping.

Wood had spent quite a few months of those three years in Army and VA hospitals in Seattle, Chicago, and finally in Vermont. His mother had flown for the first time in her life to visit him in Seattle, a few months after his return on the *Alaria* to the States.

In late 1946, when his prosthesis began to work for him and he could walk without crutches, and when most of the strength in his left hand had returned, he obtained a car through the VA—a 1946 Hudson with a hand clutch—and drove east

from Chicago. That trip had taken months, because it led to many places, east, west and south. He spent three months, including Christmas of 1946, in Columbus, Ohio, with George Murchison, who had been a buck sergeant, then second lieutenant and platoon leader, then was badly wounded in the fourth week on Okinawa. Wood had intended to stop for a day or two, to keep a promise, but George, his wife and her parents, who lived in a big old stucco house, had all conspired to keep him there forever. George had been hit by shell fragments in both legs and in the head, and wore a titanium plate in his skull. He was a dark, short man who looked fierce. His sense of humor was gentle and generous, and he liked without apology to talk of what he called "big" things. The two of them spent most of their time limping about among the falling leaves, throwing rocks in the frog pond or sitting on the rail fence, watching the horses in the fields of the working farm next door.

When it grew cold they sat in the second living room, George, his wife Bev, and Wood, in front of a ragged stone fireplace. Sometimes Bev's mother and father would come in, although they had their own part of the big house. Bev's father was a doctor who had a somehow engaging, ironic fondness for military titles. He called George "Lieutenant," and Wood "Captain." Bev was a warm, big girl with a very pretty face and trim, birdlike little legs. She brought them beer, apples, cheese and whatever else they wanted. She watched them play chess, and played darts better than either of them. In a strange and relaxing way that caused Wood to feel peaceful, he fell in love with Bev, or maybe it was with both of them, with the sight of Bev sitting on the arm of George's chair, both of them seriously trying to make the same point, yet disagreeing vehemently about how to make it.

George wanted Wood to go into business with him.

"What kind of business?" Wood asked in his tremulous whisper.

"Any kind. We've got to look around. In the spring we'll case the whole area."

"I ought to go to college, I suppose," Wood said.

"What about Ohio State?" Bev said eagerly.

"There's a lot worse places than O.S.U.," George said.

Wood swallowed, trying to arrange his vocal cords, and whispered, "But I shouldn't stay here. I've got errands to do."

George nodded, then shook his head. Wood had admitted to them that he intended to visit the families of Wilcox, Malins, Strecher, Forman, Hawkes, Dreher and Smith.

"Why do you feel you have to do that?" George asked again.

"I'm not sure," Wood said.

Bev's eyes glistened. "My God, what a terrible thing to have to do. But it's beautiful. I know how much it means to those people. It makes it all for something."

"Yes, that's it. I feel responsible," Wood said.

"For what?" George said. "Christ, if any platoon leader did all he could to keep his men alive, it was you."

"I don't mean personally responsible," Wood said. "Maybe I don't know what I mean. Maybe it's my country that blotted them out. No, not really that, either."

George frowned at him. "That's dangerous, Wood. That's dangerous. I think you ought to gab more, like me, and get it out of your system. I don't like you to think along those lines, buddy."

He left the Murchisons after Christmas. Each of his duty visits was a blow that shook him as badly as the last. He dreaded seeing the town signs come up, then the street signs that led him to those houses empty of their sons. Parents, sometimes wives and children, found him on their doorstep. He was aware of the authority of his scars, his eye patch and obvious false leg—his credentials—how they all helped to raise up memory and regard. He did make those deaths seem more than a blotting out, and he was given gratitude.

He grew sad and morose. He couldn't eat. It was all fake and useless, even their emotion. What was he giving them? Why had he given himself this duty?

Then to enter a town, its looming water tower printed with the fateful name, search out the street and house, and at the door the mother's face as he tells her in his cracked, half-voiced whisper that he knew her son. "Herman? You knew Herman?" she says. The father gets up, folding his glasses, and reaches out the always bent, tentative hand, as though he might be touching the dead son.

Once, while doing sixty-five miles an hour on a narrow Iowa highway, he considered driving into an approaching concrete bridge abutment. The smooth cement was like an empty page, and with the slightest easy movement of his arm he could make an end. Nothing. His whole body was suddenly at war with and against this idea. The engagement was in fact so inconclusive that he stopped on down the road and sat shaking and sweating for a long time.

After he came home he'd sought out no one, but they had all come to do their duty by him. Lois Potter cried and was brave over his disfigurements, and he could see and understand how terribly upset she was over these new considerations. Al Coutermarsh had stopped by soon after he first came home, and although they were at ease with each other they had little to say. Foster Greenwood came too. He and Jean had finally married, and Foster told him how he was learning to be a Catholic. "I don't know whether I ought to fake it or believe it," Foster said.

A rather subdued Gordon Ward came to see him too. Gordon had always had a presence that demanded attention, and he still had this. But he was more serious now, as though certain doubts hovered behind his eyes somewhere. He told Wood that the two wounds he'd got in Italy were "Beautiful. Timed just right. Beautiful blighties. I really had it lucky." The new Gordon had something on his mind. "I know a lot of things happened a long time ago, Wood. We never got along and there were damn good reasons for it."

Wood nodded. Gordon sat on the porch rail, wearing Army suntan pants and a Dartmouth T-shirt. On one of his long, freckled arms a shiny burn scar smeared his freckles from elbow to wrist. His red hair stood like springs, coiled and flaming above the green eyes. He was such a flamboyant creature, Wood wondered if his unconventional behavior hadn't been forced upon him, the way one felt a hush of expectation in the presence of a brightly colored snake. He had always caused nervousness, trepidation, just by his looks. Now, trying to look sincere and mature, he did project those qualities, but at this range it all began to seem synthetic.

"I know, I know," Gordon said. "Some lousy juvenile things

happened back there. But I think we've all grown up, now. We're older, and we've been through hell."

Wood thought of asking Gordon what changes occurred in that process, but didn't ask. Gordon was not asking for forgiveness; his allusion to their old dislike of each other was merely something to say, perhaps the only thing Gordon could think of at that moment.

"I guess you're right," Wood said.

"Well, I've got to get going, I guess," Gordon said. "Take care of yourself, now."

"Okay, Gordon."

Gordon jogged down the lawn and swung into the seat of his car, a sporty black 1939 Mercury convertible. He waved as he took off, and Wood could see relief on his big pale face.

Everyone was coming home from college that summer. The summer before, David had worked in Pasadena, digging up streets, laying cable for the Pasadena Light and Power Company. Peggy and Sally De Oestris had taken the *Mauretania* to England, its first voyage after having been a troopship. In Southampton they hired a chauffeur-driven car and traveled, visiting those few old friends of Sally's who were still alive. Sally still loved to travel, and she sat brightly on the jump seat of the Daimler, pointing out to Peggy the landmarks of her history as well as England's.

But this summer David was going to look for a job in Leah, and Sally had decided that she was too old to cope with "English food and French bacteria. In the old days," she said, "when it came to food, I much preferred the French bacteria."

Peggy was a sophomore at Bennington, a school Sally had something vaguely official to do with. She had either been one of its founders or was a friend of one of them, Peggy wasn't certain.

Peggy's mother hadn't been heard from for more than three years. Her father had come home in 1946, looked at the rotting sugarhouse and gone away. She got a card from him a month later from Tucson, Arizona, where an Army buddy had given him a job. She hadn't heard from him now for over a year, and though she felt slightly guilty about him—about both of them, because they were her family—they seemed more and more like

distant relations, or maybe more like children she had once known who had moved away. Soon she would be nineteen, as old as her mother had been when she was born. She had changed so much even she could see the changes. That other Peggy Mudd who once lived in the sugarhouse seemed as distant as her parents. Sally De Oestris had more or less adopted her, and she lived at Sally's house, helping in the summers. Sally paid her a salary, but it was really more like an allowance to a member of the family. Sylvia Beaudette, who had come back from Maine, was the real maid and cook for Sally.

But the changes she saw in herself, physical and otherwise, were always contrasted with those shadowy yesterdays. Most of the girls she knew at college were what they'd always been, and even their wonderment and involvement with all the new ideas were more an evolution than not. She saw that she would never be quite like them, that the Peggy Mudd who now argued so vehemently about T. S. Eliot's anti-Semitism, or Henry Wallace's enlightened capitalism, or *The Prophet*, or "This Is My Beloved" had once as a child, listening in the smelly dark, wondered if her mother knew anything about birth control or venereal disease. That other girl had learned at twelve to gauge with mortal precision, against fire and disaster, the subtle degrees of drunkenness and irresponsibility.

And always was the knowledge that she might have gone the way of those other children, those waifs of the woods slums.

Horace had commuted to Northlee College for a year and then stopped. He said he wasn't interested. He had taken over from Sam Davis the janitorship of his father's two tenements, and even his father had to admit that he did a good job. There had been a third tenement too, but his father had sold it at a profit and was more interested in the stock market now than in owning real estate. He'd gone back to selling insurance too and had reopened his agency office in the Tuttle Block on the square.

Sam Davis had lost one job after another. Now, Horace knew, Susie gave him enough money so he could spend his days in Futzie Petrosky's Tavern. All he really wanted to be, he said, was a farmer, but he couldn't work for another man. Sometimes

he'd come home when Horace was there, and go on for hours, friendly, drunken, dangerous, about what a good man Horace's father was, and how someday he was going to get Gordon Ward —Sr. and Jr. both—and wouldn't he let all kinds of cats out of the bag, and how good a farmer he'd been but the dirty bastards cheated him out of everything. He'd sometimes stop, bang his beer bottle on the table, cant his bristly gray head and smile broadly at Horace, teeth yellow, brown, missing. Horace thought him mad. He'd tell one story twice in a row. Of course, he was always drunk. He had beer for breakfast and beer for lunch. He couldn't do anything without having a beer first. If Susie had any harder stuff she had to leave it in Candy Palmer's apartment, because she said her father went off his rocker altogether on the hard stuff. He got violent, she said. He was too violent as it was, with his stories of dark plots, of vicious men out to get him, and how he would get his revenge. Horace was constantly worried about Susie, even though she had been doing very well for nearly a year. Seldom did he find her drunk or sick. Very seldom.

Kate was a sophomore at the University of New Hampshire, where Wayne Facieux would be a senior next year. He'd left school for what would ordinarily have been his senior year to work in New York for what he called a "vanity press." Interesting, illuminating and disgusting, he'd written. He was going to be in Leah this summer too because his mother had to have an operation at Northlee Hospital. He already had a job—one he hated, of course—selling shoes at Thom McAn. In spite of these things he was not at all discouraged, really. As a junior he'd won the *Atlantic Monthly* poetry contest for undergraduates, and he was working on a book of poems for submission to the Yale Younger Poets series.

He did not approve of Kate's joining Chi O, and in some ways she didn't either. They had charmed her practically to death, however, so she had joined, and sometimes now she felt rather as if she'd been had. There were two parts of college, the idea part and the social part, and she still wanted to believe they could be reconciled. Wayne said they couldn't. Maybe he was right, but

she didn't want to give up some of the Greek things. In any case, this would be a summer to think hard about that.

This last year she had been on too many dates, and gone to too many parties. Her marks hadn't gone down, and that was depressing because she knew she wasn't doing what she should. She felt like a butterfly, something pretty to have around. She was very low on herself. In one of her courses she was supposed to have read *Anna Karenina*, but she'd read about a quarter of it, got the rest out of *Master Plots* and got an A on the exam. Such things ate into her ideal of college; it was the sophomore syndrome—that it was a racket. She saw the cheating going on around her, and she even whispered answers to a sister or two. The war veterans, most of them, were just as unserious as the nonveterans, just as fraternity gung ho too, it seemed. Many of them wore parts of their uniforms with insignia still attached just to brag about what heroes they were.

But she couldn't blame anybody for her frivolous sophomore year, so she came home that summer depressed, even noticeably quiet. Mainly she wanted to see Wayne, to see if his wonderful enthusiasm could bring her back. She still shivered at the thought of him, his intelligent face, his long wrists. She had missed him. And Davy would be back too. She wanted to have a long, long talk with Davy.

This was the first summer of what Harvey Whipple called "the Truman Depression," and David had trouble finding a job that in any way pleased him. The Whipple cabin on Lake Cascom, however, was in bad repair, so David contracted with his father to repair it. It had been seldom used during the war and various sorts of disintegration had set in. The boathouse had been uprooted by ice and had fallen in, the dock had disappeared altogether, the roof leaked in several places, the gutters had filled with pine needles and rotted out, and the steps down to the lake were punky and dangerous.

David's greatest coup was to talk his father into advancing him $125 to buy a 1935 Ford pickup truck. All it needed was a clutch, and it only burned oil going downhill. For another $25 he had the clutch installed, and he had a going rig. He pounded out

most of the dents, painted it with gray primer, and suddenly it was the jauntiest, most toylike little truck he'd ever seen. He envied no one, not even Gordon Ward with his milled-head, dual-carburetor Mercury.

The Ford was nice, and gave him a kind of freedom, but that was not his ideal vision of this summer. It was to be his Thoreauesque, or philosophical, or decisional summer. He would live at the cabin by himself, take a dip in the cold lake each morning, work himself hard at the clean carpentering, nailing and brush clearing. In Chicago he lived with a girl to whom he had lied about his age, saying that he was twenty-four, when he wouldn't even be twenty-two until December 5. She was twenty-four, and he was almost certain he was in love with her. Yet there was the lie, and his awful youth, which seemed so absurd after two and a half years in the Army. He felt that he was a fake, that Letty gave her sweet gifts of passion and comradeship to a child who used her in a masquerade.

They lived on South Greenwood, in Mrs. Salamonsky's Rooming House, where anything went—political, psychological, chemical. They had the old second-floor dining room, and shared the kitchen with the two Trotskyites, with the two homosexual communists, with the prim and quiet couple, she white, he Negro, who never went outside the building in each other's company, and with the peculiar little Cuban who lived in what had been the pantry, who declared that if his grandmother became a communist he would cut her throat on the spot and pulled out a great switchblade knife to prove it. One girl was a periodical nymphomaniac, and sometimes in the night raunchy characters, even old bums, could be heard crooning her name in the alley, staring hopefully up at her window. The male Trotskyite was a recidivist Roman Catholic named Halloran, and the female Trotskyite was a beautifully statuesque Jewish kleptomaniac undergoing perpetual analysis by a Trotskyite analyst. They all lived together, somehow, in a kind of joyful clamor, the smell of marijuana mixing with liver and onions, garlic and toothpaste.

But David wanted this summer out of Chicago, out of that city all gray and darker gray. Letty was going back to her family for the summer too, to conduct her annual campaign for funds. They were Scandinavian farmers in North Dakota, who couldn't

understand why she wanted to be a perpetual student. She already had a degree, the Ph.B. given at Chicago, and now she wanted a master's in anthropology. She had to treat them carefully, but such was their respect for education they would most likely stake her for another year.

David was more or less wandering around in the humanities division, taking courses here and there. He was vaguely depressed by college. He had odd urges to transfer to the University of Hawaii or the University of Paris, or to try to get on a whaling ship, or to marry Letty, learn some sort of a profession and live in San Francisco. When he was away from her he felt sadness and relief. At other times he yearned for her, the way she came back down the hall in his bathrobe, smelling of soap, to kneel on their bed—a box spring supported by textbooks—and make a tent over his face with her dark blond hair. Their two faces were so serious under that soft canopy.

She thought him funny, and they would lie in bed all morning, chuckling and laughing at each other's remarks, none of which they could ever remember afterwards. The two homosexual communists would sometimes make coffee and knock on their door to bring them some. They treated him and Letty as if they were delightful pets, even though David was sometimes exasperated by their evasions of Lysenkoist doctrine, and would confuse them by making up false history complete with Russian-sounding names, ships bringing phosphates to Ciano's legions, dates in the late thirties of deals, purges, treacheries. They could not cope, it seemed, with spurious facts. Letty would pinch him under the covers, and he would lose his exasperation and actually feel contrite.

He wrote to Letty, feeling even more fake as he tried to be amusing, and her letter crossed his in the mails, saying North Dakota was sheer hell, and she loved him, loved him. He was frightened, and went back to the clean pine planks he was fashioning into stairs.

25

It was a blue and gold Sunday in June, and they were all spending it at the cabin. David had repaired the steps and rebuilt the dock, but nobody else would be staying overnight because he had ripped up half the floor of the living room.

A cool breeze from the lake blew the bugs back toward the woods. Small waves splashed among the dark rocks. This was the piney, deep side of the lake, where the bottom fell quickly into cold springs among boulders, so the dock had to run parallel to the shore. Perch and bass cruised among the pilings, and deeper in the lake were salmon and lake trout. Across the blue water was the more populated shore, two miles away, and behind the shore fringe the round hills of the Cascom range rose up beyond pastures into darker spruce.

The boards of the dock were still yellow and new, as were the stairs. Wood and Harvey sat on the bottom step, and Sally De Oestris was installed on a straight chair on the dock beside them. David, Kate, Horace and Peggy dove and splashed, in and out of the water, shivering and basking. Horace deliberately belly-flopped—a great spank and a sheet of water peeled out from under him, then huge waves. David could do a front somersault; they were both showing off. Henrietta was up on the bank, getting the food ready. She had split all the hot-dog buns, lit the fire David had set up in the outdoor fireplace and set the trestle table with the old, cracked, chipped and mismatched dishes, the worn and bent pot-metal silverware of the cabin.

"Hey, Hank!" Harvey yelled. "You gonna swim?"

She looked down at them, feeling old and soft. The youngsters were thrashing and laughing, all muscle and tendon—dyna-

mos. She could barely remember the joy of mere movement. Compared to them she would look like an old mother seal. Her swimsuit was out of date too. She shook her head.

"How about you?" she said. "You want to display your age?"

"Well, maybe I will!" But he didn't move. Wood looked on, smiling when a smile was called for. No one had dared ask him if he was going to swim or not, and she wondered what he felt about showing his leg and eye. They could get used to it; she wondered if he knew how easy it would be. He sat quietly, smoking a cigarette and looking on. David flexed his shoulder muscles and did his front somersault.

But the two girls, who now stood together, laughing at something Sally had said—they gave her an ache in the heart. Kate was so beautiful it took her breath, and Peggy had . . . bloomed. She wasn't the old Peggy at all. She had grown as tall as Kate. In repose, her face might suggest the kinship between this Peggy and the old funny little Peggy with the uncertain eyes and the thin mouth that didn't know which way to quiver. Now all the little things had changed—her glance, the glint of humor. She acted as though she deserved to occupy the space she occupied. Maybe that was it. She was so dark, and the wide mouth could now afford to laugh and be generous. Dark, in a black swimsuit, a night to Kate's day, but equal. She was no longer a satellite to Kate's beauty. Water flowed over her almost olive skin, clean and flashing. Henrietta had seen both Horace and David look at Peggy with surprise and even consternation, as if she were a girl they hadn't yet been introduced to.

Sally watched too, grinning and crinkling and tapping her canes on the dock as if she were applauding all this energy and smoothness of skin. Horace roared, made a cross-eyed, tongue-out idiot face and slowly, stiffly fell over backward, to hit the water like a flat board. That must have hurt. He came up lunging and grinning, and both Kate and Peggy, in yellow and black, slim as birds, dove in neat arcs on either side of him. He grabbed them, one in each arm, and his grin of pleasure made Henrietta's cheeks hurt. They ducked him, and as he came up blowing and sputtering, his bellow of mock outrage was so loud, so almost brutal it caused in her the surge of emergency. But of course it was all play. Horace was having the time of his life.

David came running up the stairs, dancing on tender feet. "Hey! HEY!" he said from sheer exuberance. "Hubba, hubba!" He went onto the screened porch of the cabin and came back with an inflated inner tube. "Forgot all about this," he said. Suddenly calm, he stopped next to her and looked down at the stairs and dock.

"Well," he said.

"Well, what?" she asked him.

"Here we are."

"We?" she said.

"Why, we the Whipples," he said, turning his bland, smooth face to her. He reminded her so much of Harvey—just to look at. A sort of smaller antelope, ready to nuzzle or to jump.

"Yes, we're all together again," she said.

"With certain changes," he said.

"Oh yes."

"The Whip looks great."

"He feels better, that's for certain," she said. They both looked down at him. He even had some color. He had his cane hooked in the right pocket of his print sport shirt (his Harry Truman shirt, she called it to aggravate him) and he was telling a story to Sally, who rumbled in preparation for the eruption at the end. Wood half smiled as he listened.

"I'm going to put a rail down these stairs," David said. That would be for their cripples. She looked at him and saw that he knew he had brought up the subject. Harvey had said once, "We ought to have an act, Wood and me—sort of soft shoe. 'The Whipple Gimp,' we could call it." Wood had smiled.

"For Sally too," David said.

"And me," she said. "I'm not getting any younger."

David laughed and patted her on the shoulder. "You're in great shape," he said. They watched Kate and Peggy climb out of the water, legs flashing in the sun.

"Peggy's changed," David said. "She's got muscles now."

"She's a lovely girl," Henrietta said.

David looked startled, then he said, "Yes. That's right. That's a good word for it." He thought awhile. "She's still got a kind of funny face, but it's not homely any more."

The girls stood together, looking up, aware that they were being examined. David pointed at them, and they both giggled.

369

"Come on, Davy!" Kate said. "Bring the inner tube!"

"You know," David said, "when Peggy tans up she'll look like a Masai princess."

"Come *on!*" Kate yelled.

"All of a sudden she's built," David said.

"What?"

"She's built. Peggy. Meaning she had good bones all the time."

Henrietta looked at him closely. Something about his new regard of Peggy struck her as dangerous. "Don't you hurt her, Davy," she said.

"What?" He laughed, surprised and even flattered. "Me? But why should I hurt her?"

"Because you could," she said.

He laughed, partly embarrassed, still pleased. At least she had startled him out of his sophistication for a moment.

"Maybe I could," he said. There was some little-boy bragging in this; maybe that was what struck her as dangerous in him. He looked closely at the two girls, a speculative look. "But you know, I've got a girl, at Chicago. She's in North Dakota right now." This made him thoughtful, even a little sad. He sailed the inner tube down across the dock into the water, and Horace lunged after it, followed by the two girls. "Maybe you shouldn't trust me," he said. "I don't know. But Peggy? That would be almost like incest, wouldn't it? Peggy's a member of the family."

"You are dangerous, Davy. I don't mean to flatter you, either," she said. "Please don't get involved with Peggy. She's changing a lot right now, and I think she's still confused. We all mean too much to her still. It wouldn't be fair if you used that."

He laughed again and patted her on the back. "You know, you're not so dumb," he said. "For a mother, I mean! Sorry! But I promise. Besides, Peggy's been crazy about Wood since she was knee high to a mouse."

"But not in that way."

"Ah, but she wasn't this way then." They watched Peggy climb out of the water and pull down her black suit. Her waist was narrow. She was shy of her hips, and reached for her towel with a turning, feminine bend of the knees. She looked at Wood; they both saw that.

After the hot dogs and potato salad they all sat around, Wood and Harvey drinking beer out of cans, Sally and Henrietta out of jelly glasses. David and Kate sat on the dock in the afternoon sun, dangling their feet in the water, and Horace lay stretched out on his stomach, peering down through the interstices of the boards at the perch that hung among the boulders. Every once in a while he would creep like a big reddish lizard to a better crack, his glasses almost touching the boards.

David lay back, his hands protecting his eyes from the sun, and Kate lifted his head to put a towel underneath it.

"There," she said.

"You take good care of me, Sis," he said. He liked that caring touch of her hands, and raised his fingers to look at her. Sunlight haloed her head, and a flash of sun blinded him.

"What's Chicago like, Davy?"

"It's crazy," he said. "It's a nuthouse."

"Don't you like it?"

"I don't know. Sometimes."

"I mean, is it serious? Are you learning a lot?"

"I guess so."

"Is it hard?"

"No."

"Neither is U.N.H.," she said. He heard the sadness in her voice, and risked a glance at her, but the sun blinded him again. In his shut eyes he saw the outline of her head and neck, graceful in light blue against black, flashing blue and green, yellow and black and blue in the middle of his head.

"You can't look at the sun," she said.

"But I'm your brother," he said, and she laughed and hit him on the shoulder. It hurt.

"Ow!" he said. "If I wasn't blind I'd tickle you to death."

"Come on, Davy! I want to be serious!"

"All right."

"Tell me about that place where you live."

"Mrs. Salamonsky's Madhouse?"

"And you have a mistress."

"That's a funny word. I never thought of it that way." He liked the word in a way, and was then repelled by it.

"But you do," Kate said. "You actually live with this girl.

That's what you said. What I want to know is do you love her very much? Is it good?"

"It's good, I guess." He was a little ashamed of his romantic sadness.

"But is she nice? What does she look like?"

"She's pretty. I think so, anyway. She's handsome—a little blonder than you, and maybe an inch shorter. Is that the kind of details you want?"

"Does she love you very much?"

"I . . ." He began to say that he thought so. Did she love him very much? Yes, she did. Yes. "I think . . . I'm afraid she really does."

"You're afraid because you don't love her?"

"No, I think I do."

"You can't even mention the word 'love.' You can't even say it!"

"I love you, kiddo," he said.

"Oh, shut up." She was silent for a while. The water licked the bottoms of his feet, cool little kisses from the lake.

Finally Kate said, "Can't you be serious, Davy? I really need to find out some things. Honest, I'm not just prying, I mean it. About boys and girls. I don't mean birds and bees stuff, either. I know all that. But I'm having problems, Davy."

"What kind?" he said quickly. A hard pang of concern, maybe even jealousy, startled and confused him. He rose up on his elbow and looked at her. He didn't even care if she saw his concern. Her valuable self, his Katie out among the predators. There were her delicate lashes, her grave, gray-blue eyes. None of the wolves and foxes was a millionth-part worthy of her. "What kind of problems?" he asked. She was very serious, and her eyes stared soberly into his.

"It's mostly about Wayne," she said.

"What about him?"

"Well, I don't think I understand him. I mean what he wants from me. What he wants me *for.*"

"What do you mean?" Through his mind passed that gangling, unmanly creature named Wayne Facieux, skunkheaded, supercilious and dangerous, probably queer, and a vision of Kate being used by Wayne and his flitty friends, if he had any, in

strange, vile communal rites of sodomy and degradation. He grew cool with anger.

"No, David. Take it easy," she said. "You don't have to get all upset! But you are, aren't you?"

"Yes, all right, I'm upset."

"Well, you don't have to be. It's nothing like you think."

"How do you know what I think?" He couldn't keep a self-belittling anger out of his voice.

"You know," she said.

"No, I don't."

"Yes you do. He's never . . . made love to me. That's a euphemism."

"Is that what you want him to do?"

"No! That's what you *thought*. Now, come on! That's what's so confusing. Shouldn't I at least want him to want to?"

"Well, you startled me," he said.

"Well, don't treat me like a child, Davy. I'm a big girl now."

He wanted to ask her questions he wasn't sure he wanted the answers to. He said, finally, "I just don't want you to get in any trouble, Katie. I want you to be happy."

"Thank you, Davy," she said in a low voice. Her eyes grew dark and concerned; she touched him on the cheek. Her emotion seemed a flaw in her beauty, and he knew how much he loved her —how much he really did, far and beyond all the kidding around and the ego points, that game they used to play.

A breeze had come up again, and Kate's light brown hair blew in long strands across her nose. She pushed them away. From above came Sally's raucous, rumbling laughter.

"Anything you want to know," he said.

"Okay. Well, tell me . . ." She blushed. "Tell me what you do when you make love to her. To Letty. I don't mean all the way to the final sexual part. I presume that's pretty mechanical once it gets down to that, although maybe I'm wrong. But how do you begin? What do you say? Like that. I mean, how does it start, from not feeling like making love to starting to?"

He thought. "It's a look," he said. "It's a funny little look, sort of steady and serious. It lasts about a second."

"You both have it?"

"Yes. It sort of says 'I'm a man,' and hers says 'I'm a woman.'

I never thought about it before. But it can happen any time. Sometimes it happens when we just happen to pass each other going back and forth to classes, and then we know all day long that we'll make love that night."

"Do you both always feel the same? At the same instant?"

"No, but it's always better when we do."

"You mean you make love without that look?"

"One can more or less persuade the other to, anyway," he said.

"But that's not so nice?"

"Not quite."

"Then what do you do? After the look."

"We touch each other."

"Do you kiss?"

"Yes. Not always on the mouth, though. At least not at first."

"Where?"

"On the neck, maybe. And other places. She has favorite places."

"It sounds lovely, Davy." Kate sighed. "I'm sure it's lovely for both of you." She seemed thoughtful and rather unhappy. They sat up and kicked their feet in the water. Then she said, "Do you ever comb her hair?"

"No, I never have. She never asked me to."

"Hmm," Kate said. "Wayne likes to comb mine."

"What is he, a hair stylist or something? It sounds awfully queer to me."

"You mean strange?" she asked.

"No, queer."

"You mean homosexual? I don't think so. I'm kind of vague on the subject. But Davy, Wayne's the only boy that ever treated me like a human being. I thought in college it would be different, but it isn't. He's the only one that talks to me—I mean straight to me, like what he wants to say he wants me to understand, because what he's saying is important for itself. The others all treat me like a *thing*. I mean it. I'm not being paranoid, either."

"I know," he said. "I guess I know how they feel."

"Sometimes I get so blue, and even angry, Davy. I feel I ought to do something drastic, or even shameful. You know? It's being a *thing*, and I can't stand it! Sometimes I think I ought

374

to paint my teeth black, or never wash my hair, but I'm scared to do that!"

"Katie."

"Well, *damn* it all!"

"Hey, Kate," he said. She was crying, actually crying, and he almost felt like crying too, just looking at her. This was impossible, especially here on the breezy lake, with the gabbing and laughter coming down from above. Horace had gone up there with the others.

Kate rubbed her eyes and gave him a quick, contrite look.

"Davy, I'm sorry! But I've been throwing college away. It's only as easy as you make it, and I've been partying and cramming instead of getting involved. It's all so silly. The whole thing. Sometimes I want to stand up and yell the worst thing I can think of. My *profs* can't even look me in the eye. I want to stand up in class sometime and yell '*Fuck*' or something. There!"

A sailboat had been coming across the lake on a tack directly toward them. Now it came about with the white flash of sail and jib. David could barely make out that its sides were red, and he could just see a trace of white foam at its bow as it cut back on a better angle to the wind.

"I don't want to *smile* any more," Kate said.

The sailboat went behind Pine Island, moving fast. It would come out the other side soon, then probably take the slower tack back toward them.

"I wish I could help you be happier, Katie," he said.

"I don't even talk like this with Wayne," she said bitterly. "He does all the talking, anyway. That's all he does is talk. Talk, talk, talk. He hardly ever listens."

"That sounds like him, all right," David said.

"Well, he's brilliant!"

"All right already!"

"He is, Davy. But dammit all." She stared morosely toward Pine Island, waiting, as he was, for the sailboat to reappear.

He thought of going to see Wayne: *Suh, I have come in order to determine the quality of yo' intentions, suh, in ree-gard to a certain lady.* But was Wayne a faggot? He didn't resemble, in his small gestures, either of the two tame communists at Mrs. Salamonsky's, but homosexual communists were rare birds any-

way. Wayne had sold him a pair of sneakers last week, and he seemed odd enough, but not in that way. He had wanted to know all about the University of Chicago, and did they have any poets besides J. V. Cunningham (which Wayne pronounced J. V. Cunningum).

But suppose he did go to see Wayne? The whole thing was ridiculous. He might tell Wayne to turn into a nice, square, honorable, straightforward type, undangerous and predictable, who would then drop his jaw and gaze upon Kate with that typical stunned awe that she despised. Or he could deal with this complex problem, using the methods of the Black Hand; how would Wayne look with his feet encased in a washtub of cement, his striped hair flowing, deep in the Cascom River? A strange weed down among the cans and bottles and the passing condoms. The idea seemed a little more feasible than it should have.

The sailboat came into sight, nearer now. It came about onto an approaching tack, its bow waves curling like a little white mustache. It was a pretty little boat, leaning jauntily as it splashed across the waves. Its helmsman leaned the other way. *Ensconced*, David thought. No, what was the word for that rakish, somewhat regal pose there in the stern? He envied that sailor.

Because it came straight toward them, the boat caught their attention; it seemed to have them in mind, the way anything that points, like an arrow or a gun, suggests a dreamlike intention to the eye. It came on until that vague idea of collision changed into the possible. It was like waking up, and there was the little sloop, red with a white deck forward, its stays and braces trim and neat. The sailor was Gordon Ward, Jr., all muscles and freckles and clashing red hair. The gusty wind had brought up whitecaps, and he worked his sheet constantly to keep on course. He came within ten yards of the dock and suddenly hove to, his sail fluttering. "Ahoy!" he called.

"Avast!" David called back.

"That's a honey of a boat!" Harvey called from above.

"You used to own it!" Gordon yelled.

"Son of a bitch! Goddam!" Harvey yelled. "I didn't recognize it! Used to be green and white. Well, it *is* a damn pretty boat!"

Gordon was gathering sternway in the stiff wind. During this exchange he kept looking (who wouldn't? David thought) at Kate.

The damn pretty boat was in danger of bumping into the rocks, and though Gordon's mouth didn't hang open, David was quite sure of what was going on in his head. People always looked at Kate twice, then had to drag their eyes away. It was as if they searched hungrily for an imperfection—just one, something, anything. She seemed to glow, her skin lighted from an inner source.

Gordon had a little paddle out now, and was barely holding against the wind. "Anybody want a ride?" he called. "It's great!"

David got up and looked up the stairs. Peggy was sitting near Wood, talking to him and not paying any attention to Gordon and his boat. Horace was nowhere in sight. Then, behind him, he heard a splash. He was held for that second, having that choice, then turned swiftly and dove straight at the horizon.

Gordon reached down, pulled Kate up and sat her lightly on the side of the cockpit. David clambered aboard the foredeck. They were dangerously close to the rocks, but with one swing of the tiller, the little boat turned, mainsail and jib snapped taut, and they were tearing out into open water.

The dock receded, the cabin began to fade into its trees. Then he saw where Horace had been all this time. He must have been hiding, because he appeared beside the one boathouse wall that was still more or less vertical. He squatted there now, on a rock, gazing after them.

26

David had reason to remember Horace hiding there, because a week or so later he thought he saw Horace doing something like that again. He was at Futzie's Tavern with Gordon one night, and he turned toward the front window to see what he thought was Horace's wide, cragged face lit by the ghastly blue neon,

staring in through the grime of the front window. Then the face was gone, but he was quite sure he'd seen it.

Gordon had decided to take David up. He stopped by the cabin several times, twice in the sailboat, this night in his Mercury convertible. They had been in the murky brown barroom for an hour or more, beer sticky on the booth table, smoke flowing slowly toward the exhaust fan above the door. Gordon was telling a story about leave in Naples, while David tried and gave up trying to find anything comparably exotic in his own stateside service. He could feel the beer, and felt like bragging about something or other, but decided that being seen with Gordon, that legitimate hero, was enough to confer upon him an aura, at least, of veteran service and heroics. He wore his Ike jacket, minus insignia. He also felt vaguely traitorous to aspirations of his that were not public and did not concern bragging or posing at all. Letty was real, perhaps even more so at this distance, and his future was real. Whatever talent and passion he had for this life waited, he knew, while Gordon tried to charm him. One of Gordon's methods was an undefined assumption that David, too, had seen and been through much. Never would he allude to David's merely stateside service. It was a strange, collusive situation, in which he was not always sure why he was being charmed. It had much to do with Kate, of course; whenever Gordon thought of her or tried to speak of her his green eyes flickered, as if a sneaky little wind had nearly blown them out.

At the bar several old men, the regulars, sat on the stools and leaned into their beers. One woman at the end of the bar sat alone, wearing a pre-new-look dress that showed her baggy milk-white legs. Donald Ramsey and his girl had been in for a quick rye and ginger before the movie, and in the booths a few of the old Trask's Pharmacy crowd, now graduated to beer, fed the jukebox here as they had the Wurlitzer at Trask's. "Peg O' My Heart" was playing, and it gave David a sad, chill memory of Letty, if only for the reason that they had heard it so often at the University Tavern on Fifty-fifth Street.

Sam Davis pushed the door open, stepped halfway into the doorway, and the door came back to hit him a light but nearly staggering blow on the shoulder. He was very drunk. When he regained his balance he came carefully down the aisle of booths

toward Gordon's outstretched legs. Something like vomit, or at least something distributed like vomit, discolored his green work clothes. His eyes were all one shade of dull pink, his face and neck covered with gray bristles. Futzie had been serving a booth toward the front, but he cut around to head Sam Davis off.

Sam managed to see Gordon's legs sprawled across the aisle, and he stopped tipsily and glared down at them. "Git your goddam legs out of the way!" he said. Then he saw whose legs they were. Gordon looked up at him with fierce but not unfriendly interest. "Now, Sam," he said.

Futzie arrived, and took Sam by the shoulder. "Sam, you're too drunk to be in here you! You wanna lose my license?"

Sam stared at Gordon. "Son of a bitch," he said.

"Sam?" Gordon said, smiling at him. "Sit down and I'll buy you a drink."

"Son of a *bitch*," Sam said. His shoulders straightened with a proud jerk, but this only seemed to stun him.

"Sam, you go home," Futzie said, wiping his hands nervously on his apron. "You been sick too. I can smell it."

"Snakes, pigs, buzzards, pig fuckers," Sam said.

"Sam!" Futzie said, shocked.

"Now wait. Wait," Gordon said. "He needs a drink, Futz, and I'm buying. Don't worry, I'll take care of old Sam Davis. Go on, now, Futz." While saying this he'd got up and actually forced Sam down into the booth—manhandled him. "What's your pleasure, Sam?" he asked.

Sam growled like a dog. He couldn't see straight, and he fumbled for the table edge with both hands. His head nodded and nodded. He looked sick to death.

"All right," Futzie said. "One beer, you get him the hell out."

"We'll take him home and tuck him in bed. Right, David?" Gordon winked.

It was then David thought he saw Horace's pale blue face at the window.

Sam poured half his beer on his chest and passed out, so they took him by the armpits and carried him, his feet dragging, across the street and into the tenement. Gordon knocked on the apartment door. "Papa, dear Papa, come home with me now," he said.

The door opened upon Beady Palmer's friendly, ridged and jerky face. His eyes plotted them out. "One, two, three!" he said. He turned toward the room behind him and said, "Special delivery, C.O.D."

They carried Sam into the kitchen, where Candy Palmer sat at the table with Susie Davis.

"Is he just drunk?" Susie said. She tossed her thick brown hair back and got up. "God, he's a mess!" she said. "Bring him into the bathroom." She led the way through a dark room, into a little hallway and switched on the bathroom light. "Somebody must have got him some hard stuff again. Where'd you find him?"

"He wandered into Futzie's, where he met a couple of good Samaritans," Gordon said.

"Oh, sure," Susie said. "Hello, David."

"Hi," David said.

"He needs some sleep and I need a drink," Susie said. "Leave him in the bathtub and I'll take care of him later."

"Hell, Suze, leave us do it. We'll hose him off and tuck him in," Gordon said.

"Well, make sure he's through puking before you put him in bed."

"Okey-doke."

They looked down at the wreck in the bathtub. His red neck was lined and crosshatched; tendons and veins laced it like half-unraveled knots. All but the shreds of the vomit had soaked into his shirt and pants. Water from the faucets was dripping on one of his run-over work shoes, and David, his shoulder against the moist commode reservoir, untied his laces and pulled the shoes from strangely clean white socks. Gordon went after the shirt buttons.

"Glah," Gordon said, averting his face for a moment. "In combat we'd cut his clothes off."

David was startled by Sam's baby-smooth, ivory feet. As they removed his shirt and pants, this strange metamorphosis continued. They peeled away his long underwear, and his smooth white skin was as pure and unblemished as a peeled egg. A delicate blue vein shone through the translucent white of his chest, where a few limp blond hairs grew. This could hardly be the body that had grown that ravaged head and those scarred and filthy

wrists and hands. His genitals looked young and unmarked; relaxed, familiar between the alabaster thighs, they looked like David's own. Sam's bellybutton hid in its little dent and crease. They looked for something to pour water from. Gordon found Susie's douche bag hanging under her housecoat on the back of the door, so they filled it with warm water and squirted Sam with its little hose. Gordon thought this was funny.

"The old coot," he said, chuckling as he hosed him down from chin to crotch. "If he only knew!"

There was the grizzled head, mouth hanging open to show an ancient brown tooth, then a pallor of chest that was deathlike, yet new. The man was such a total drunk he must be close to the idea of his own death. He would take with him to the embalmer's whatever fair skin and working organs he had left. It seemed unfair to the good parts of him that they should have to die.

They toweled him off, at least the top of him, and hauled him into his room down the hallway, David taking the smooth white feet. Gordon seemed to know his way around the place. They hoisted Sam into the deepest depression of the hammocky bed and pulled a sheet over him.

"Man, is he *out* of it," Gordon said. "He doesn't even know what a nice douche we gave him. You know *douche* means a regular shower in French? Did you know that?"

They went back to the kitchen. "We put him beddie-bye," Gordon said. "He's dreaming of great brown bottles and elephant cunts."

"Don't be such a foul mouth," Susie said, glancing at David.

Candy Palmer had reared back to laugh, her breasts heaving under her silky blouse. David could smell her perfume all around her in the air, and he wondered if she could smell it. She wore a pair of shorts so short they were practically panties, and she moved on her chair so that he and Gordon could see more of her. Before she stopped giggling she adjusted a breast and touched her white-blond hair. She was so made-up, so somehow meant only to be looked at, he thought how strange it would seem if she had to do anything—like get a meal or clean up the sink. She didn't seem made for anything like that. She was a bit old for this glamour act, however; tiny red lines appeared here and there on

her thighs, and there was a slight downiness to her chin. He had heard she was older than Beady, who now reached over and put his hand on her knee as if to prove his ownership of this showboat.

"I call my sugar 'Candy,'" he said, "'cause she makes my peanut brittle! Haw! Haw! Hee! Hee!"

"Oh, Jesus, here we go," Susie said. "I need another drink. Gordon, get us and you and David a drink."

Susie had little brown shadings under her eyes now, so she looked softer than the last time he'd seen her, and a little tired. Her dark blue eyes were bigger and more vulnerable. She'd lost all traces of baby fat too, and she didn't seem anywhere near as big a girl as she once had—but he supposed his own attitudes had changed a great deal. Perhaps a woman would just not seem as big to him now.

The fifth on the refrigerator was dead, but Susie and the Palmers had a new fifth of blended whiskey they'd chipped in on —Beady and Candy had to keep it in their apartment, Susie said, or else her father would soak it up like a blotter. Gordon had a fifth of bourbon in the trunk of his car, so he went to get that while Beady went for his fifth.

"We'll make a party!" Candy said. "We need a girl for little David, though. My Jesus, ain't he cute? I could go for him myself!"

"How's Wood, David? How's he doing now?" Susie asked seriously, ignoring Candy.

"He's kind of quiet. He reads all the time," he said.

"I cried and cried when I heard," Susie said. Tears jumped into her eyes. "He's the nicest person I ever knew."

"Hey!" Candy said. "Cut that gloom stuff! Turn on the radio! We're going to make a party! How about that little girl upstairs. What's her name? How about it, Suze?"

"Phyllis?" Susie said. David felt that in his presence Susie was being polite, or at least acting in a way that surprised Candy Palmer.

"Yeah. Phyllis. Why not? She's got a cute little set of boobs even if she is a little homely."

"Well, you could ask her," Susie said doubtfully. "She's awful young—I mean with drinking and all."

"Coming from that family? Come on, honey."

"Her mother and father's home tonight. I saw them come in."

"They could give a shit and you know it." Candy got up and went to the telephone. "Hon, I forgot my glasses. What's their number?"

"Maybe David—"

"What? She's not going to scare li'l David." Candy winked at him. The heel of one of her red pumps tapped the floor. She had a nice figure, even if she was pretty old, and suddenly David did want another woman around to make it even.

"Call her," he said. "What the hell?"

So Susie looked up the number and Candy spoke to the girl.

"Hi, hon. This is Candy Palmer, and we've got a swell party going down to Susie's place. Only thing is, we've got an extra boy, so we thought maybe you'd like to stop by and meet him? Well, tell them you're baby-sitting for us. Aw, come on! He's a good-looker, hon, no kidding. Come on, now! What?" Candy laughed. "Don't you worry none about that at *all!* For one thing, I don't think so, and for another thing I know it's not true! You're one of the most attractive persons I know. What, honey? Speak up! No, he's not listening."

She winked at them and drew her mouth down humorously. The listening and convincing went on for a while. Beady and Gordon came back, and were shushed while Candy listened and cajoled. Finally Candy looked at them and nodded her head in triumph. "Oh, fine, honey. Goooood. Ten minutes? See you then!" She hung up. "Poor little thing don't think she's much, you know? But she's awfully sweet. A sweet kid if I ever saw one. You'll love her, Davy."

"Does she?" Gordon said.

"Oh, shut *up*, Gordon!" Susie said.

"She's got a great personality!" Beady said. "Haw, haw!"

"You cut that out!" Candy said, and turned to David. "I wouldn't sic no ugly on you Davy, now I mean it. You'll see. Phyllis is a peach of a little thing."

"Now you've got me all nerved up and interested," Gordon said.

"Okay," David said. "You take Phyllis and I'll take Susie." Susie looked at him quickly, and he saw that they were all pleased by this first positive thing he'd said.

"All right," Susie said, half jokingly. She came up close to him. "My goodness, Davy. You're a lot taller than me now. I think you grew in the Army!"

Gordon laughed hard at that.

Candy was tuning the radio, trying to find the kind of dance music she wanted, while Beady and Gordon made drinks. Beady went to their place to get the ginger ale Susie and Candy liked with their whiskey.

It was a warm night and getting warmer in the room. When Candy found the right music, fast but not too fast, she said, she came up behind David and pulled off his Ike jacket. The T-shirt under it was paint-splattered but clean, and this informality— especially the rakish splotches of green paint—made David feel at ease and a little reckless. He danced with Candy, her perfume so heady and thick it was like putting his head in a box. She was slippery silk, and light on her feet. When he pulled her hard against him she giggled and rubbed back. The next song was "Nature Boy," so they stopped and picked up their drinks.

"You know what 'Nature Boy' is backwards?" Beady said. " 'Serutan Yob.' "

"That'd be 'Natures Boy,' " Candy said. "Did you see the picture of the fellow that wrote it? He's sitting there naked! I mean bare-assed, and his little skinny legs are crossed, and he hasn't got any tummy! I swear, you can see his little backbone sticking right through, he's got himself so sucked in. And the prettiest blond hair you ever saw."

. . . a very strange enchanted boy . . .

the sugary voice sang from the radio.

"A queer," Gordon said.

"I bet he's not," Candy said. "He's too queer to be a queer."

David's drink was bourbon and water; Gordon had made it, and it was strong. He put it on the refrigerator and danced with Susie, prim and proper at first. Although he'd known Susie all his life, he'd never put his hands on her. It was strange to feel her muscles and soft places against him, her breath whiskey-sweet against his neck. They moved around the table and she let her head rest on his shoulder like a little girl. His lips touched her

384

ear and he began to get an erection, which seemed strange because he had really never before in his life thought of Susie that way. The gang-bang incident in high school hadn't made him think of her as a sexual object, but as a legal, social sort of object—a victim. But now she was, suddenly, singular and real. Her light cotton dress became unsubstantial under his hands, as though some chemical process were disintegrating its fibers, and all he had in his arms was the smooth naked girl.

Gordon and Candy were dancing and laughing, while Beady drummed on Susie's canister set. David didn't know the name of the song, but it had a simple rhythm he could follow easily. When it was over, Susie gave him a long, serious look. It was a dark look, and he could read it, or part of it. Her plum-dark eyes looked right into his mind, and what he thought he saw her considering was him in bed with her. He had occurred to her just as she had occurred to him. This thrilled him and made him jumpy. But why not? Why not?

A hesitant little knock on the door. Beady opened it. "Open the door, Richard," Beady sang, "or don't shut the door on me dick!" In stepped a little girl in a plain, light brown dress. She looked about twelve years old, but David looked again and the little twelve-year-old had hips and a waist. She was very shy, and stood aside with her hands clasped together in her skirt. Her face was dim, but upon close examination it looked like a monkey's face, with tiny little nail-hole eyes and a pug nose like a peanut stuck on sideways. She smiled widely and shyly, revealing thousands of sharp little teeth. It was a barely human face, dark and twisted by self-shame. It quivered, and he saw that she was being very brave. Susie introduced her, but David immediately forgot her last name. He got her a drink of whiskey and ginger and they stood, a rather formal maneuver into position, by the telephone stand, in order to introduce themselves and talk.

David was becoming glib on the whiskey, and felt himself to be extremely sophisticated and cosmopolitan. Phyllis lisped. She took a sip and said in a voice he could hardly hear, "Thank you. Thith ith nythe." She was nineteen, and she worked at the Leah Laundry. He could smell the Clorox on her—just a whiff. It was awkward talking to her because he looked down upon the top of her head at her black hair salted with dandruff, and her upper

lip stuck out farther than her nose. He suggested they sit down, so they sat down at the table while the others danced. He had the weird feeling that he was not engaged in a really human pursuit, and he'd glance at Susie as if over there where she was, dancing wildly now with Gordon, the really human world was going on.

They drank. He danced with Phyllis, but the top of her head came to his sternum. Beady grew red, flaming red in the face, and danced with everybody and then with himself. The room developed a rotatory tendency. Later, when Susie and Gordon disappeared, Candy danced with herself. Beady would jerk himself into a kind of sobriety and drum on the canisters. "Sweet Eloise has a social disease," he sang, "crabs in her hair and a crotch full of cheese!" Candy cursed him for a drunken slob and said she didn't want to go home, so he'd better sober up and dance. David felt himself to be drunk. He was no longer listening to Phyllis' answers, or even to his own questions. And she would not talk except to answer his stupid questions. Her eyes were like tiny black spiders crouched back in their holes, and he'd peer around and up into the holes to see if he could make out a small glimmer of intent.

He wondered what Gordon and Susie were doing. Had they taken the couch in the next room or gone to Susie's room, or what? Finally he took Phyllis by the hand and led her into the next room. First they sat on the couch and then they lay on the couch. He couldn't bear to kiss the poor girl. All those tiny teeth intimidated him. He felt like a shit, an utter shit; he remembered saying this out loud. Then he did kiss her, and her mouth was human and sweet. She moaned, and said nothing at all about his hands. She did have hard little breasts, hard as apples. Once he kissed her where Letty loved to be kissed; this shocked him—the shock of faithlessness, of adultery. He couldn't understand this little girl, didn't know her. Why should he get her all messed up? If he did, if he went ahead, in the morning he would feel bad, sick, lousy. It was as though she'd never heard of resistance, that a girl might say *no* to a boy. He had her pants down around one ankle and was poised, about to enter her, when he stopped. "Are you a virgin?" he asked. "Yeth," she said. "Do you want me to?" he asked her. No answer. "Do you want me to go ahead with

it?" She wouldn't answer, but she moaned. She was all liquid and passive, and he ached. But then a lawyerlike stricture seemed to take over his brain. What did he want the girl to do, sign a statement to the effect that David Abbott Whipple, hereinafter referred to the party of the first part, is given permission to have sexual intercourse with Phyllis Simian, hereinafter et cetera? What if she really was a virgin? He had no rubbers and he might get her pregnant. David, do you take this woman? Ow! And why had she not resisted at all, in any way?

"I'll get us a drink," he said, and gracelessly removed himself from her. He pulled up his pants and hid his erection as best he could, pulling his T-shirt down over it.

In the kitchen Candy sat morosely across from a snoring, crapped-out Beady Palmer. "Cheers," she said. "Some party. Everybody goes off to neck and leaves the old married slobs looking at each other."

He felt steadier in the light, and he made the drinks with the last of the ice cubes. Candy came over to him, her drink in her hand, and slipped in between his arms. "One more waltz for the old dame, huh, Davy?" He put the glasses down. What the hell? The radio had faded down and they could hardly hear the music, but they danced slowly around the table. She felt his erection immediately, rubbed against it and smiled, then really pushed and did a slow bump and grind on it. Beady slept on. She did the most exaggerated bumps and grinds, bending her knees and coming up against him. When they came around behind Beady she poured part of her drink on his head, but he snored on. Her left hand was under David's belt in back, pulling him up against her. "Mmmmm," she hummed in his ear.

Out of the corner of his eye he saw a slight, quick, brownish thing pass by. He was only vaguely curious, but then the door to the hall opened and closed and he knew it was little Phyllis.

He danced Candy through the door to the next room, and they stood kissing and grabbing at each other. She hummed even when their mouths were locked and her tongue was all over his teeth and in between his jaws. He pulled her toward the couch and started to pull her down on it.

But she didn't want to lie down on the couch.

"Unh, unh, unh," she said. She wanted to stand up. He

unzipped her shorts and she zipped them up again, and all the time their tongues were touching. He became a little firmer, and she resisted a little more firmly. Suddenly all the kissing and hugging was ridiculous, flimsy, frustrating. He picked her up and put her down on her back on the couch. She fought silently, but he pinned both arms beneath her and leaned on her chest, his arm free to work at her shorts.

"Jesus Christ!" she whispered furiously. "For Christ's sake, can't you take a joke? Get *off!*"

"Unh, unh," he said.

"Look, David, get your hand out of there!" She was really angry. "I was just kidding around, now cut it out! Let me up!"

He had his thumb in her, to see if the way was clear. She was wet and ready, but dammit, he had to get the shorts off.

"You want him to hear?" she whispered, hissing at him. "Jesus Christ, he's just sitting there, you bastard! I mean it! I'm absolutely serious, now! Let me up! I do not want you to *screw* me. Is that *clear?*"

He had the shorts unzipped and down to her knees, but she held her legs tightly together and he couldn't get them any farther down.

"Let me *up!* Get off me! You want me to yell for help? You want me to scream?" When he didn't answer, but just kept working, she began to grind her teeth, to try to bite him or butt him with her head. Both her wrists were in his left hand, and he could feel the hands writhing, trying to scratch and gouge. She made the mistake of trying to use a leg for leverage and he whipped the shorts past this break in her defenses. Her silk pants came apart easily, as if they had been made of tissue paper.

"David," she whispered, trying a new, calmer method. "Listen to me. You are *raping* me. Do you understand that? And also I detest being manhandled by men. I cannot *stand* it! Do you know what the penalty is for rape?"

He had his pants and shorts off by this time. He'd considered just pulling them down partway, but he'd need his legs completely free.

"If you go on with this," she said in a really vicious, pressured whisper. "If you continue to go on with this terrible thing, I am going to call the *police*. Do you understand that? I will call the

police and a doctor, who will examine me and prove that I have been forcibly raped and misused. This, I promise you!"

He got a knee between her legs and began to pry them apart with superior leverage.

"*I can't stand this! I can't stand it!*" she hissed.

With a quick shift and jump both his knees slid between her legs. He let one of her wrists go and her hand came up to rake his face, but he ducked it and pulled the cushion out from under her shoulders so he had her bent back and down, then caught that flicking hand and had her pinned like a wrestler. She tried to kick loose, tried to avoid him with her pelvis, desperately moving it up and down and sideways, but she was open to him now and he went deep into her, to her moist center.

She gurgled and hissed, cursed him, whined and cursed him, still trying to get away. He began to move soft and easy now, hard and slow and soft and easy, and soon her attempts to move her pelvis away from him chimed with his movements, and she stopped cursing him and let him ride her, pushing with greed against him. In the dim light from the doorway her frizzled hair glowed; she arched her neck, and her mouth was open as though she were screaming. He let her arms loose and she pulled her blouse and bra up away from her breasts, then pulled up his T-shirt so their chests could come together. Her hands hooked his buttocks. Her breaths came shorter and shorter until they were hardly breaths at all and finally he thought: All right, you bitch, sue me now. And the back of his head melted, his lower back congealed with an ooze of sweetness and he became a great hose that semen rushed gushing and tumbling through, boiling oil and chunks of ice, hot and deep into the woman.

She mumbled words that meant nothing. Clicks and random vowels. She couldn't seem to get her breath, and he pulled out the hose and put his feet on the floor. Then he was stunned by a blow on the side of his face. She had one of her red pumps, and she got him again, so hard he thought it must have drawn blood. He disarmed her and she went after his eyes with the other hand. Finally he had both of her hands. Because of her earlier capitulation, he was astounded. "What the hell's wrong with you?" he asked.

"You *brute!*" she said, low and vicious.

"What?"

"You *raped* me! You forced me! I'll tear your eyes out!"

"Now, wait a minute," he said.

She struggled and hissed. "Dumped your load in *me!*"

He was uncomfortably aware that, naked himself, he held this naked wildcat, both of them disarrayed indeed, within twenty feet of her sleeping husband.

"Brute! Brute! *Brute!*"

He wondered just how the situation could have been worse. My God, he thought. It couldn't have been planned better. With a sudden impulse that was perhaps suicidal he pulled her over on his lap and said into her captive ear, "In a minute I'm going to give it to you again, you prick-teasing bitch!"

She tried to bite his arm. One thing he knew, and had known from the beginning, was that she didn't want Beady to know anything about this. The most violent of her outbursts had been muted so as not to arouse her husband from his stupor. Now, given that fact, the object was to get the hell away from this woman with the loss of as little skin and blood as possible. "We'll wake Beady up," he said. He had an urge to whack her backside with the flat of his hand; maybe that would bring her sanity back. She still tried to bite him. "If I let you go, will you calm down?" he said reasonably.

She went limp, and though he didn't trust her he let her up, carefully. She sat there breathing hard, then pulled her clothes around and down over her breasts, obliterating those two black eyes. Even in this light she was a mess of lipstick and frazzled platinum hair. Between them their heat rose tiredly. He found her shorts and the remains of her underpants and handed them to her. She slid into the shorts, searched for her pumps and put them on, then stood and stretched as though she'd just got up in the morning. A little wobbly on her heels, but with no further words, she walked out into the kitchen. He heard the outer door slam.

He went to the bathroom and washed himself, trying to get her oil, her stink of perfume and his sweat off him, got dressed and went back to the kitchen, where Beady still snored. Obviously if she didn't want Beady to know she wouldn't pull any of that crap about the police. The two drinks he'd fixed were there, the

ice all melted, and he drank part of one of them. It was three in the morning and he had no way to get back to the lake. Dammit, he should have taken his truck tonight. He wished he were back in his bunk at the cabin, dreaming of Letty, of pure sweet Letty, who was a thousand miles away.

One cigarette was left in a pack on the table—Candy's pack—and he lit that. He felt sordid, tawdry, stupid. His cheekbone was numb where she'd pasted him with her shoe. All around him were the shoddy remains of gaiety—cigarette butts, ashes, greasy glasses smeared with lipstick—he couldn't even get all the lipstick off his jowls. No one in this dingy building was anyone he wanted to see. That poor little monkey girl, what had he done to her, and what must she be thinking about herself?

Candy Palmer's perfume hung in his nose like ancient fruit. He'd go home to High Street, a long walk he didn't want to make, and sleep in his room tonight. Where the hell was his Ike jacket? There it was, where Candy Palmer, back when she'd been made up like a confectioner's masterpiece, had put it solicitously over the back of a chair. When she took it off him she had no idea what else would come off, that seemed quite certain now. He was empty, cruel, weary from the alcohol and that brutal, demeaning wrestle. He had never considered himself a rapist; none of his dreams of sex had ever been without mutual and tender consent. He let himself out into the fumy hall and then to the grimy, narrow old street damp with dew. Across the street Futzie's was closed and empty. The night light behind the bar, a raw bulb, shone harsh yet dim, like the gleam in a drunken eye.

27

"Okay," Harvey Whipple said, "so the Jews have a country of their own now. Good! I hope they all go there!"

When his wife's expression showed contempt, he added, "I mean you've got to give them credit, because they fought for it. That, I've got to admit. Nobody would have thought it, but they stood up and fought like men."

Wood listened. He always listened, and the words came belling like retribution, remorseless but just. He had argued the case time and time again, in chambers, in the horror gallery of his mind, but he always lost. Always the punishment was apt and the administering force implacable but just.

His father's smooth, self-satisfied ignorance was no real defect, it was only a symptom of the one grave one. He was a man. But Wood had known this, all of this, since he was a child, and why should that knowledge now have turned into constant anxiety? It was anxiety, a needle forever poised against the heart, the feeling that makes all feelings meaningless. He'd felt it a thousand times in combat, but then it lasted only hours or minutes, even seconds. Now, though everyone thought him calm, inside he was desperate; he fluttered and gasped for fear of something, but he couldn't quite find that something. Perhaps he was afraid to find it, to define it. He could only concentrate upon those things that gave him horror, pure and powerful beyond the constant breathless flutter below his heart.

"The only Jew you've done business with you cheated, because you didn't pay him what his tenement was worth," Henrietta said.

"Dot's beesniss," Harvey Whipple said, shrugging and raising

his palms. Then, seriously: "I've done business with *plenty* of them."

The flutter below Wood's heart increased, and he took a breath. What was the knowledge he feared to have? He'd had a dream in which he came sailing across a blue sea on a day of high cumulus clouds that were at first only interestingly dangerous. They grew from within, massive explosions of clouds that moved ponderously along the horizon, over the curve of the world. Far off, beneath their blackness, lightning forked into a sea grown dark green. But he sailed under blue sky in a light but energetic wind, going before that friendly wind with jib opposite mainsail, to catch it all. He was coming up on an island, or perhaps a mainland, but whatever land it was he didn't want to go there. Suddenly the wind stiffened and he was afraid he'd jibe. If he came about he was sure he'd swamp, and so he sailed on toward that dark land, searching the breakers for a harbor or a cove. Behind the beach, tall trees, elmlike yet more lissome and ominously flexible, waved and flashed the silver undersides of leaves. On one beach lay a boat, a catamaran broken and bleached out, with the sand smooth around it. A rag of sail no bigger than a handkerchief fluttered from its curved mast.

In the dream the sea hissed around his prow and in his wake. At that moment he must decide whether to tack or to sail on into the breakers. Right now he must make the decision. Right now!

And just as he became vividly afraid, full of the sharp, clean fear of breaker and wind and the power of the sea, the thunder finally released itself—the voices of those massive clouds far off on the horizon, and it came in the form of a deep and resonant voice saying: *It doesn't matter.*

But he woke from that dream remembering almost with nostalgia the clean decision he had to make, and the wild trees flashing along the shore.

Harvey Whipple leaned half on his cane and half against the wood paneling next to the fireplace. Outdoors it was a raw day of rain and drizzle, but in the big room a fire burned bright orange. Wood got up and locked his leg before he limped to the hall closet.

"Going someplace?" Harvey asked.

Wood came back with his green Army raincoat and an old duck hunter's cap. "I guess I'll take a stack of books back to North-lee Library," he said.

"You sure do a lot of reading," Harvey said, meaning *When are you going to do something?*

"Yeah, I guess I do," Wood said. He saw his father fail to meet his eye—or rather his eye patch.

When Wood had gone, Henrietta put down her book—a silly little story she didn't think she'd finish anyway—and stared into the fire.

"What's the matter?" Harvey said.

"Wood," she said.

"He's all right, Hanky. It takes time to get used to some things." They usually reassured each other; when he worried about Wood, she told him to be patient.

"Did you ever get used to your arthritis?" she said.

"No," he had to admit. "But Wood's thing is different. You know, the eye too. God!"

"I hope that's all that's bothering him," she said.

"What do you mean?"

"I don't like a lot of the things he studies all the time. Torture, death. The awful things people do to each other. He clips things out of the paper. Did you see where that Negro soldier had his eyes gouged out by a policeman? In a railroad station? He clipped that one out. I saw where it was missing when I put the old papers out."

"What's he do that for?"

"I don't know. I can see where a lot of people would find that sort of thing fascinating. But not Wood. I don't understand it!"

"Hey, don't get all upset, Hanky. Come on, now."

"He collects pictures. God-awful pictures. There's one where the S.S. locked all these prisoners in a sort of a shed and set fire to it. This one man tried to dig and push his way out underneath the boards, but he just got his head and part of his shoulder out. He's so *trapped,* and you can feel how he tried to push, but it's just *impossible.* There's blood that's come out of his nose. It

makes you want to jump up and shake yourself. It's a terrible picture! And Wood studies it. He sits and studies that picture."

"Did you ask him about it?"

"No."

"Why not?"

She jumped up. "Oh, you make me sick!" she said, and went toward the dining room. He came hobbling over and caught her by the arm.

"Hanky," he said.

"You know what I mean! You and your Jews and your communists and all those other words! Your goddam chamber-of-commerce language!" She felt so mean and guilty she couldn't stop. "What do you think you can do for the rest of your life, parrot everything you hear? You think that will do for a . . . a *philosophy?*"

His mouth hung open; astounded and hurt, he let go of her arm and turned away. His old golf sweater had holes all over it, and one armpit was unraveled, but he wouldn't let her throw it away.

"You think I'm so goddam happy?" he said.

She began to cry, and went through the dining room into the kitchen, where she sat in a wooden chair and rubbed her eyes. Her glasses were all dirty, probably, so she wiped them with her skirt. She couldn't see them clearly without wearing her other pair. She was hot; she knew that if she looked into the mirror over the sink she'd have a red blotch on her forehead, and her ears would be flaming. And soon she'd have a chill—just the opposite. She was forty-five years old, and she knew what it was—it was glands and all that wearisome business.

But no matter what the excuse she shouldn't be mean to Harvey. He was what he was, and he wasn't really a mean man. He couldn't help whatever was wrong with Wood, and she couldn't expect him to. And another reason she'd been mean to him was she'd seen him smirking over his accounts and his "portfolio." He'd made some money and he was savoring it before he announced it to her. This irritated her so much, for no reason, that she'd been on edge for days.

She was trembling. She felt like that man trying to mole himself out of the fire and could never make it.

On the way down Bank Street toward the square, Wood began to have trouble controlling his car. The hand clutch seemed at first unfamiliar to him, and his leg jerked toward the pedal that wasn't there. He kept thinking of the rear wheels going around, then the transmission with all its gnashing little teeth swimming in black oil. It was a various and violent machine altogether, and he doubted his authority to make it go where he wanted it to. When he came to the square he pulled over next to the corroded green Civil War veteran who leaned on his gun, his bronze hands dangerously capped over the muzzle. He turned off the engine and sat there, letting his wits settle. One of the results of whatever was bothering him was a recurring physical weakness. He would find himself struggling silently but frantically to get his keys out of his pocket, as though little wires bound his fingers together. While driving he would wonder if, when he turned the wheel, the front wheels would obey.

The elms leaned over the wet grass, cars passed and confidently turned around the square. Rain bleared and streaked his windshield. In spite of the rain, the town went hurrying along on its business. People walked jerkily along the sidewalks, ducking the rain as if it were chunks and fragments they could see to duck, hurrying for awnings and overhangs. Store windows were lighted against the gray rain, and the matinee at the Strand let out humped, two-legged creatures who ran for Trask's or their cars or stood forlornly and impatiently beneath the marquee, looking at the shiny wet all around them.

According to his records, this was his town. Leah—a strange name. A woman in the Bible. Beautiful Rachel and fruitful Leah. Ugly Leah. It depended upon the view you took of it. In a place back in his mind that seemed as isolated as a prison cell, yet brightly lit, clear, cool, he knew that Leah was not an ugly town, as towns went. You could stand in many places and see the great elms, the neat old houses, the ancient maples rooted in green. A matter of some civic pride. He wanted to vomit.

Wait a minute. He shut his eyes (eye) and let his head fall back. There was nothing he wanted to do, and nothing, no miracle, could give him joy. It was worse to follow any thought at all, because he forgot for a moment the flutter of anxiety, and it came back new again to take his breath before it settled into the

almost tolerable, the low-grade fear, fever fear. Death was preferable to the fear of death, but what was this fear that was not really the fear of death? Perhaps he would like to kill someone.

Now the dream came toward him as he pondered helplessly upon its variations. The vision grew behind his eyes, where he couldn't shut it out: a room, an institutional yet temporary room, mustard-walled. The construction of the room is hasty, crude. The windows have multiframed lights, and one doesn't quite match the other because they have been taken from other buildings, even perhaps from houses. The glass is covered by heavy-gauge hardware cloth. Beyond the windows is a high wire fence—electrified, from the evidence of white ceramic insulators. Six strands of barbed wire form an inner fence to keep the electrified one from being touched accidentally—a bit of prevention related almost to benevolence. Or perhaps the barbed wire is to keep back those who would prefer to embrace the current.

On the far side of the fences can be seen the legs of a wooden tower, wet snow blown against the creosoted poles like frosting, dingy and gray. Stairs angle toward the apex of the tower, an ominous black slitted box.

Inside the room it is miserably cold. Chill moisture with the look of grease covers the linoleum floor, upon which stand three strange living creatures resembling praying mantises. Each is as large as a human adult. Vividly green, they move and nod, raising their tubular forearms in an awkward fashion that suggests great, if unlimber, strength. Certain relationships can be discerned; the very largest mantis is of lesser authority than the other two. His (or her) black compound eyes glitter, but with a lesser sheen, and he (or she) stands still near the door while the other two jabber in a strange, glottal language, and gesture over what seems to interest them—a large bathtub which they are filling by means of a red rubber hose connected to a faucet. The mantises don't seem to feel the cold, but they are interested in temperature, for they have several kinds of thermometers, sensory devices connected to wires, tubes, dials, some even suggesting cooking thermometers. One dial records the water in the tub to be 33 degrees Fahrenheit. Room temperature, indicated, is 41 degrees Fahrenheit. Though the damp floor is even puddled in

places, the feet of the mantises, encased in the green exoskeletal chitin, do not seem to be wet.

The mantises speak in voices one does not expect to have the lilt of human speech. One gives what is, however, an obvious order, and the second repeats this order to the third. This one's voice is deeper. Perhaps this one is a male, although in these creatures a deep voice might indicate femaleness, one can't tell. Perhaps they have no separate sexes, and procreate by some other process.

The deep-voiced one nods to the large one by the door, who nods back, turns and goes out.

Immediately comes the terrified scream of a human, and in a moment the largest mantis comes back pulling a small human dressed in a ragged uniform that was once striped gray and blue. Without further ado the mantis forcibly removes the shirt and pants of the uniform. The subject, or Test Person, is revealed to be a human girl child of nine or ten years, the hypogastric region naked of hair, the mammary glands undeveloped. She is weeping, a sound rather like the mewing of kittens, and shivering violently. The papillae of her pale skin are erect, as are the immature teats, and wide areas of a bluish cast attest to her discomfort. Her trembling interests the mantises, and they push her to the center of the room, next to the filled bathtub, in order to examine her more closely. When they touch her she screams frantically, but they are intent upon their observations and take many notes, writing with fountain pens upon paper held in clipboards.

Sometimes words form in her weeping and screaming: "*Ooo-hoo eeeuw mama anh anh oh oh anh eeow hawn ee mama maahmaanh!*" Her arms are crossed upon the ridges of her ribs, and her head, covered with short, dirty brown hair, seems to be trying to hide against her thin chest. She is dirtiest around the feet and ankles, and her thighs and trunk are splotched by infected insect bites.

The mantises observe, remark upon her characteristics, then write the data into their records.

"*Oh oh oh aaaee hawn no no anh hah!*" the child cries in panic weakness. The cries, in this room, seem the long echo of all hopelessness, as though the very plaster of the walls has absorbed all the misery it can and is now impervious. At a nod from one

mantis, the other takes a metal tube three centimeters in diameter and ten centimeters long, attaches a wire and dial to this tube and swiftly inserts it in the child's anus. The volume and rising tonality of her cries indicate pain. The largest mantis comes forward to prevent her from removing the tube and wire; because she is not cooperative he binds her wrists together in front with strong wire.

The mantises talk and observe. The child cries again and again for her mother.

The largest mantis takes the shivering and struggling child in his sticklike arms and forces her into the bathtub. At the touch of the cold water she screams and kicks her legs, which then have to be bound, knees and ankles, with strong wire. She still cries and struggles, slopping some water on the linoleum floor. The iron-cold room seems to have heard, again and again, every variation of the blat of terror. There is a heavy sense of familiarity.

The high-voiced mantis moves to the edge of the bathtub, not seeming to mind the child's high, fragmented screams, and inserts a metal needle, again with wire attached, several centimeters into the starved flesh of her thigh. Notes are made, and much attention is paid to the clock. The child's screams grow weaker as the long minutes pass. One mantis holds the child's upper arm in his "hand," seeming to count her pulse. Soon she screams no more. Later her teeth stop chattering. Labial tissue turns grayish-blue, and examination of the eyes reveals the pupils turned up into the head.

One mantis holds a metal spike with a round dial at the end similar to a roast thermometer. At a nod from the pulse watcher he reaches down and with even strength presses the spike through the tough chest skin, between two ribs, into the child's heart. The mantises converse, taking a few more notes before nodding to the largest mantis, who comes forward seeming to be quite familiar with his duties.

The scene shifts, and we are in the deep woods, a mile from the electrified fence and its towers. Colors sharpen; as if the clear call of a bugle had dispelled the weight of despair, the world is clean again. Tall fir trees drip with the melting snow, and several armed men are standing by a cheerful fire, talking in steady, low voices. Resolute, clear-eyed, good-looking men, it is a relief to see

them, and to note that in every gesture of these avengers is the strength of right and justice, et cetera, et cetera.

Back in the car on the rainy street, the smile Wood felt upon his own face was as bitter as a snarl. He could not help going back to the little girl, whom they hadn't yet forced into the icy water. She is going to die, and she knows it. A child's terror is close to the skin. All phenomena are brighter, colder, hotter, more lovely or terrifying. She pleads for life. It is to men she pleads. She pleads not to be hurt. But they do it anyway. It is inevitable. It is *inevitable.*

Peggy found him sitting in his car. She had seen it parked there on her way downtown, and on the way back—she was driving Sally's car—noticed that Wood was still sitting there. She turned around the information booth's little island, parked behind him and went up and tapped on the window. He didn't hear or see her, yet he sat there with his eye wide open. It gave her a bad scare. Finally she opened the door and got in beside him. He seemed to nod.

"Wood?"

He nodded.

"Wood, are you all right?"

"Peggy," he said in his windy voice.

"Yes, it's me, Wood." She picked his hand from the seat and put it between her hands. It was cold, cold as meat from the refrigerator.

"Strictly speaking," he said, "I'm not all right." He kept his face in profile to her, so she could see only the black cord going across his hair, and not his eye patch. He looked so strong and confident in profile, with his straight nose and square chin. But this was Wood; he *was* strong. She turned in sudden fright and pulled his hand against her, squeezing it, trying to warm it up. "Your hand's so cold! Like ice!"

"I'm not sure what it is," he said.

"But you're cold, *cold.* We've got to warm you up. You're shivering!"

400

"I can't seem to drive the car, Peggy."

"Oh, my God!" she said, thinking of his wounds, of some possible latent damage to his nerves. "I'll get you home. Come on. I've got Sally's car. Can you walk? I'm parked right behind."

"I just came from home," he said.

"To Sally's, then. There's a nice fire."

"I really ought to get this car somewhere."

"Leave it!" she said. "Leave it!"

"It isn't that I can't drive it, Peggy. I just didn't want to there for a while."

"I want to get you warm," she said. If he only knew. She wanted to wait on him. Already she saw him with his shoes off in front of the fire, warm and glowing. She'd make him a hot drink, and she'd sit on the rug at his feet and look up at him. They would talk of things. Forever.

But now she'd have to be a little more practical. She got out of the car, went around to his side and opened the door. "Come on," she said.

"I've got all those books in the back seat," he said.

"Give me your keys and I'll put them all in the trunk."

He handed her the keys, turning his head around to her, since she was now on his blind side.

"You're strong," he said. "Did you know that, Peggy?"

"Come on, get out," she said.

The rain had let up a little. He picked up his left leg and put it outside the car, then moved over to stiffen it and lock it. He stood up and looked down at her. His officer's raincoat, with its shoulder straps, and his eye patch made him look rather rakish, like a pirate.

"I'll take care of the books," she said. "You go get in Sally's car."

"Yes, ma'am," he said, but he took a step to get out of her way and leaned against the car, his hands spread against the wet metal. She quickly put the two armloads of books in his car trunk and locked it. He still leaned against the car.

"I am," he said slowly, "what you might call 'inexplicably weak.'"

"Let me help you." She took his left arm, and they moved toward Sally's car. All he seemed to need was balance.

"You are strong," he said. "Little Peggy."

"How do you feel?" she asked. She opened the door for him.

"Now, that's funny." He sighed as he leaned back against the seat to unlock his leg. "I don't feel weak, exactly. Very peculiar." As they drove up Bank Street he said, "Very peculiar. I said to myself, 'Go over and get in Sally's car.' But it was like my muscles didn't speak the same language. They kept asking what the hell *that* meant."

"But Wood, what could it be? Is it some sort of nerve thing?" She turned into Sally's driveway and stopped next to the veranda steps.

He was looking at the dashboard. "How many times I used to drive Sally around in this antique!"

He was still shivering, and she got him into the house. Sylvia Beaudette took his coat. "Sylvia, how are you?" he said.

"I'm fine, Wood," Sylvia said with a sad smile. She looked older than she was, with red lines close around her eyes—the look of a person who weeps in private. She seemed to have shriveled since the war, and Peggy had often wondered, knowing the callow oversimpleness of the thought, how Sylvia could get herself another husband if she let herself get all red and wrinkled like that.

Sylvia took their raincoats, and Peggy and Wood went into the "comfortable" parlor, where Sally kept the old De Oestris furniture of leather and masculine bulk—furniture from the hunting branch of the family. Sally was here herself, sitting on a straight, armed chair of black wood, with brass lion-claw feet. She was utterly delighted to see Wood, and said so, her twinkly, glaring little blue eyes flashing back and forth between Wood and Peggy.

Then all Sally's vibrations stopped at once, as though she were a clockwork bird suddenly run down, only its jewels glinting. "What's the matter?" she demanded in a resonant alto. Her eyes moved back and forth to see who would give the answer. Wood sat down into the leather sofa and leaned back with a sigh.

"Wood didn't feel good," Peggy said.

"I've known that for a long time," Sally said, "and so have you. I mean why are you so upset right now, Peggy Mudd?"

"He was . . ." Peggy began. But what was he? Immobilized, somehow. "He was sitting in his car, shivering."

"I was merely sitting downstreet in my car," Wood said, obviously trying to be funny. "There I was, minding my own business, when this crazy young girl kidnaps me." His hollow, breathy voice sounded cold and shivery-still. Sally was not amused, and Peggy turned away from their tense regard of each other, which seemed all at once familial, as though she were excluded. She put another small stick on the fire.

Wood said, contritely, "I should never try to be funny. It's never worked. I was having a chill of some sort."

"Hmmm," Sally said. "You mean you're coming down with a cold?"

"I doubt it. If I was I wouldn't bring it to your house."

"Then what is your trouble? Is it mechanical or psychic? Physical or mental?"

"I'm not sure what it is," Wood said. "All I know is it's not a cold."

"I'll get you something hot to drink," Peggy said.

"Get him a cup of green tea—a mug of it—with white rum in it. Plenty of rum," Sally said.

"In other words, you've made your diagnosis already," Wood said.

"I think you're more badly hurt than you try to make out," Sally said. Peggy was standing in the doorway, about to go out, and they both looked at her, calmly, not with any real surprise that she stood there still. She turned to go. They seemed to hesitate to speak until she left, so she went on to the kitchen and made the tea.

When she came back with the tray they hesitated again, and she had the feeling they had been talking about her. Wood sat back with his legs stretched out toward the fire. His shirt was open at the neck, a blue shirt she remembered from the time before he went into the Army. His chin was down, and he stared into the fire; the eye patch was so immediately noticeable it seemed to hide both eyes. She wanted to take it off. She wouldn't mind what was underneath. There could be nothing about Wood that had to be kept from her sight or touch. That false leg, even inside the pants leg, looked too round, and the shoe didn't cover

a real, tender foot. That was part of a statue, not part of Wood.

She poured him a mug of tea, and let him add rum from the bottle according to Sally's prescription. Then she did sit on the rug near him, as she had imagined herself sitting, looking up at Wood, the presence of him. She was not unhappy that Sally was there, because she would not have to think of things to say. He needed an ashtray, so she rose quickly, conscious of the added strength his presence somehow gave to her legs.

"Look," Sally said, "I'm about to step out any day now. When I wake up in the morning I'm always just a little surprised."

"So that makes you an expert on chills?" Wood said.

Sally grinned and shook her head. "Well, as chills go, that one's pretty cold, wouldn't you say? You're so young I doubt if you've really felt that one. I don't like to pull rank on you, Captain, but I've been through a long campaign myself."

"Don't talk about dying," Peggy said.

"All right, dear," Sally said. "That suits me fine. How about getting us some sherry? For you and me, and we won't think about that subject. Sometimes I wish my brain had gone soft along with my skin and bones. Most of my generation's gone, and the only ones left spend most of their time in kiddyland. Through the looking glass." As Peggy went to the sideboard for the sherry, Sally went on, intensely now, trying to convince Wood. "Don't think about such things—whatever they are! You've got most of your body left, and it's young! Think with your blood. You're a young man. Let your skin think for you!"

"I'm afraid of my skin's conclusions," Wood said.

"Don't be facetious. Have you got some wounds you haven't told us about?"

"What sort of wounds?" Wood said, smiling.

"You're still being facetious, young man. I mean is there any physical reason why you can't act like a young man? Is there any physical reason for your *Weltschmerz?*"

Peggy saw Wood's surprise at the word. "That sounds German," he said. "What's it mean?"

"World sadness," Peggy said quickly.

"World sadness," Wood said, looking straight at her, his dark eye bright. He turned to Sally. "See how ignorant I am? You mean I'm sad about the world? No, wait, Sally. I hasten to assure you that you know about all the wounds I've got. Okay?"

"There's nothing progressive about any of them? Nothing with a bad prognosis?"

"Scout's honor and all that."

"You don't know how much we've all been worrying. Peggy's talked with me about it before. And you don't know how much your mother worries. Whenever she looks at you something gruesome happens to her face—it looks like she's pressed up against a screen. Not pleasant to see." She was still, waiting for his answer with her sherry glass poised at her lips as though she could not sip until he answered.

"I'm sorry," Wood said.

"Because you remind me of someone, an old friend who had inoperable cancer and never told anyone about it. He seemed to find all our enthusiasms mildly amusing."

Peggy had blushed when Sally mentioned her worrying about Wood, but neither of them had noticed. Now, with this casual mention of cancer and death, her heart fluttered, fearing for him.

"Weltschmerz, was it?" Wood said, musing. "Weltschmerz, huh? But I don't want to cause any worry. Maybe I ought to go away from Leah again."

"No!" Peggy said. Her outburst embarrassed her. They both looked at her seriously. "I don't think that would do at all!" she said. She saw Wood immobilized in a strange city, in a room among thousands of anonymous rooms, sitting with his eye glazed, as she had found him in his car. They waited for her to continue. "I think you should stay with us. With the ones that love you."

"Do you love him, Peggy?" Sally said.

"Of course! We all do!" Then she thought, how was this a lie? She did not love Wood "of course" and with them all in any collective way. She loved him more than anything, more than the whole world, and she had loved him since her memory began. "I want to stay with you and try to help you," she said, forgetting to be embarrassed. No, it was as a doctor or a nurse that she could say these things. "You said you weren't all right and I know it. I saw you there in your car, and I've seen you when you were so unhappy!"

"Yes," he said, staring at her in a way that was completely unself-conscious, the one eye bright, the other that patch of darkness, blankness, like night and day. "I said you were strong,"

Wood said. He still stared at her. "You've been good for us all your life."

Sally nodded. "That's true."

But what did that mean? If they hadn't been talking about her, she felt she might have understood. She was silent, confused. She took a sip of her wine and could not look back up at them. She could feel Wood's attention, as strong as a touch. There were his shoes, one for a real foot, one not, and his cuffless Army trousers. She felt as though she bowed before him, perhaps gracefully, showing the part in her hair and her meek shoulders. I am thine to do with as you wish. As thee wish? But he must do something, or she would have to do it. She would follow him, hide in the back seat of his car, peer at him through windows and the cracks of doors. When he wasn't looking she would slip under his skin. Just sitting here at his feet she was so happy.

Wood's night dreams were worse than his daydreams; the horror was more intense and less justified by where he was and what he saw. He merely felt. He dreamed of himself with two legs and two eyes, never mutilated; but in his night dreams the horror was like air or water, and covered every neutral object. When he dreamed of sailing, horror slid from the white sails. The green sea hissed, the clouds grew into anvils.

Awake, the names of raids and massacres tolled in his mind. Every day this glut of murder presented itself to him, gaunt faces staring at him or at the sky. Their pain rose like a column of heat higher than the sun, and it was his flesh swooning, exulting in that force. Clearer visions inserted themselves as counterpoint: the kamikaze comes in low, comes on forever though hit again and again. Lines, loops, banks of steel flee out, hose out to bracket, strafe, miss, return. It is an ancient biplane as primitive to this time of war as a Model T, a construction of fabric and strut with a bomb strapped to its fuselage. The fire meets and holes it time and again, but slowly and intently it comes on. It is a bomb, the pilot a boy who has become his bomb. Even the great warships seem evanescent before this will. The lover of death comes to his love forever.

Or he dreamed, awake, of his own eye discarded like a

damaged grape. They must have had places to put things like that—parts, bones, meat. Did they take them to the fantail of the *Alaria* and send them to the sharks and crabs? He saw through that warped, discarded lens dimly, as through a pinhole, a glimmer revolving slowly as it descended through the fathoms. Fish drifted by, silver and black. When would the sudden pluck turn out that tiny light? On the bottom awaited the crab's slower embrace. And the leg, the foot; when the shark's jaws crushed the ankle, rolling the bones together, he felt that ghost pain and the relief, the dissolving into union with the cold jaws.

But his night dreams, real dreams, began in peace and beauty, the fields waving amber, and a brave row of poplars, skies warm with fleece upon the blue. Then a word, a glance from some sourceless eye, and all turned to writhing. The clouds coiled in spasms, and the slimness of the poplars was that their arms were cruelly tied. Or the clear blue water of a lake turned briny and green before his eyes, and the smeared surface hid the secret of his horror yet gave it all away. Horror was the meaning of that world and yet whatever forces moved there were so stupid and obvious that he had to feel contempt. Contempt and horror—were these parts of an equation? Perhaps he hadn't the will to try to solve it. Perhaps he knew the solution already, and it was not cure but destruction.

28

Wayne looked different after his year in New York. He seemed taller, older, sallower, and the dots of his shaved whiskers formed darker islands along his jaws. He seemed less pure, and the white streak in his hair, though she knew it was a thing he was born

with, looked cosmetic, even garish—that word that had once been his favorite deprecation.

He listened even less than before. When Kate spoke, even in response to a question, a nervous, almost impatient look came over his face. Yet he wanted her company, and he liked to have her stop by at the end of the day when the clerks were totaling up the cash register. Then, usually, they would go to Trask's for coffee. She began to feel slightly official, Wayne's designated audience, object, and thus replaceable, or somehow interchangeable. But maybe that haunted most women.

One warm Sunday they sat on the grass of the square. Wayne was wearing a horrible light blue suit, white socks with a blue clock, and a gun-metal necktie with an orange ship's wheel embroidered on it. He didn't care at all about clothes, but the effect he gave was of a hick who did care. She experienced her usual guilt for making this judgment, but of course a little guilt couldn't alter it. In a way it was his arrogance that caused him to look so awkwardly formal on a warm summer day.

"Kate?" he said.

"Mmm," she answered.

"What do you want to be when you grow up?"

"I am grown-up."

"What are your aspirations?"

She felt like saying something flippant, but then she thought: How cold we all are! "Let me think," she said. What did she want? She wanted to deserve to be loved, for a start. But everyone who passed by them, on the walks and even in cars, gave a sneaky lie to this aspiration. They all looked at her too quickly, as though she hurt their eyes. Maybe she should give up. Suddenly she wanted to be talking to David. She wanted all this half-known business and its tensions gone, and to be with David, whose square hands and rugged muscles were so much the male counterparts of her own. She wished they were both in white shirts and faded dungarees, barefooted, walking along a sunlit beach. She could feel the warm clean sand between their toes.

"How to foresee a life," Wayne said. "I want to be a poet, and I've never, as far as I can remember, wanted to be anything else. There was a nasty rumor, projected by my mother, that

I wanted to be an osteopath. Where that idea came from I'll never know."

He was settling in for a long discussion of his aspirations, and suddenly Kate jumped up. "Let's go out to the lake and see David," she said. "Come on!"

"What?" he said, making a face. In one lens of his glasses she discovered a fingerprint. How could he look through that fingerprint and not be bothered by it?

Oh, she knew she was a flibbertigibbet; she'd never really amount to anything, and all she'd ever notice would be superficial things. Wayne's white socks with that awful clock made of blue triangles—it was such a pretentious piece of artwork creeping up over his bony ankle. How could he not see that? And why did he want a ship's steering wheel on his necktie? Why? He cared nothing about boats. He couldn't even swim. Maybe his mother or an aunt had given him that tie. "Where did you get that tie?" she said.

"What?" He was in the process of untangling his gangly legs, and he stopped, still sitting, to look up at her.

"Did your mother give it to you?"

"This tie?" He looked down at it. "No, I bought it last week."

"Why? Why that one?"

"Because I needed a tie to wear to work."

"But why a ship's wheel?"

"Ship's wheel?" He picked up his tie and looked at it. "Well, so that's what it is," he said, mildly interested. "I thought of symmetry, the wheel of existence, Yin and Yang—you know. But it's a nautical thing, is it? Very interesting."

"It's horrible!" she said.

"Really? Why?"

But if she told him why, she would have to tell him about all of his clothes—his suit, his socks, his shirt with the four-inch collar points—and he couldn't afford to get new clothes. "I can't understand how somebody with your sensitivity about other things—like *The Quill*, for instance—can be so blind about how you look."

"I never considered myself an esthetic object," he said.

"But don't you care how you look?"

"I put in a certain amount of time on it. Like shaving, or brushing my teeth. It's a total bore, but I don't want to get so ragged I attract attention. That's an even bigger waste of time."

She supposed he was right. He dressed the way shoe clerks in Leah dressed. Her superficiality was clear. But why shouldn't he have *some* pride in how he looked? Didn't he think he was a good animal? Maybe he thought of himself as being all mind, and the rest didn't matter. In that case part of what she wanted to be to him didn't matter, either. That sounded stupid, silly; it was confusing, nervous-making. What she knew was that she couldn't talk to Wayne about it.

"Come on!" she said, helping him to his feet. His hand was limp and warm. She had the car for the afternoon, and she pulled him across the grass toward the street. Before they could cross they heard the rattle of drums, and everybody stopped to locate that strange holiday sound. At the intersection by the Masonic block a town policeman had stopped cross traffic. Beyond him, bobbing in lines, were what looked like a company of white mushrooms. It was the helmets of the Legion Drum and Bugle Corps. Though Kate had seen them march before, and knew how precise they were in their maneuvers, seen down the files this way each man's helmet bobbed according to his own way of walking.

The high voice of command came wavering down the street: "*Column leeeft, harch!*" The voice was shrill, like a woman's, and she couldn't recognize whose it was. They always sang their commands in that strange falsetto. When the column turned to go down River Street toward the Legion Hall, their blue and gold satin uniforms caught the sunlight, and their brass instruments and insignia flashed. Even the sheen of leather gleamed, a block away. To the steady tattoo of the drums the column turned, and with a kind of ominous gaiety swung down River Street out of sight.

"Hmm," Wayne said. They crossed the street and got into the Whipples' Chevrolet. "A perfect example of culture lag. Utterly perfect."

Kate drove around the square and took the road to the lake. The familiar hills and turns made her think of all her childhood trips to the cabin. She remembered her anticipation then, how she and David and Horace counted the miles by farms and trees

and houses they had plotted by the car's mileage meter. There was the gray, leaning barn that meant five miles to go. They called it the red barn because once, long before they were born, it had been red; now only a pale reddish tinge could be seen up under the eaves, and the rest was silvery wood. Its silo had twisted down and around upon itself like pickup sticks. Then it was gone past, and she guided the car on over the hills, all the miles known and remembered, until she came down the long hill to Lake Cascom.

She drove through the tall pines along the gravel road down to the cabin. As she parked near David's little truck by the shed, they heard the hollow rap of a mallet, and voices from the shore. They got out of the car, Kate leading, and went down to the dock.

It was David and Gordon Ward, both of them rugged and dark of skin, Gordon's red hair now brighter and more metallic than the bronze freckles on his shoulders. Gordon stood waist deep in the water to steady an upright pole, while David rode a higher, horizontal beam and pegged in the pole with a huge wooden mallet. Gordon's sailboat rode at a mooring in the lake, its sail down and loosely draped over the boom. The air was fresh and glittery, and the clean blond wood fit its notch with precision.

When David saw her he smiled, surprised to see her, then swung down off his beam on a curved arm, sure and light as a gibbon. "Katie!" He came toward her on the dock. His toes were evenly tanned, and the tops of his feet were dry, the even color of toast. He held out his hands to her. "So you came to see me," he said, and tapped her shoulders lightly.

Gordon swung up onto the dock, the bright water sliding from his legs. Both he and David were so vivid; each seemed to have his color scheme—Gordon bronze-red and David golden—as though each stood in a different light.

She turned to Wayne, whose skin seemed in shadow. He leaned against the stair rail, prepared to be bored. The soles of his cheap black shoes were too thin at the edges where the stitching was; she felt embarrassed to be his sponsor here, and the guilt that sneaked in after that.

David said hello to Wayne in a friendly enough fashion, then

knelt at the edge of the dock and began to pull in a clothesline rope. His broad back seemed an acre of smooth muscle. He hauled in a net bag full of bottles of beer and straightened them out so they'd all stand upright on the dock. They would be much colder than the lake water because of the cold spring down there in the boulders. On hot days they used to swim down through the warm water to feel the caress of that chill stream. Sometimes big fish hovered as if at moorings deep between the rocks, breathing the cold water, their gills pale winking half-moons against their black sides.

David opened four bottles with the bottle opener that was tied to the beer bag, and lowered the rest of the bottles back to their cold hollow. Wayne accepted a bottle, though he didn't like beer and would hold it until it warmed in his hand. They sat on the stairs and on the dock, she and Wayne on the stairs, David and Gordon Indian-fashion on the dock. Gordon smiled at her, and his intense delight seemed at first too fierce, like the smile of a tiger about to eat her up. But nothing he said corresponded to his gaudy looks, and he was polite to Wayne. This without words, because they would have little to say to each other except hello. When their glances crossed, Gordon recognized the other's presence, and she wondered if it had been the war that had changed Gordon and subdued him. Not so much subdued him as made him sensitive. Even his past scandals could now seem more romantic than merely sordid, and his dangerousness perhaps a little challenging. He was a friend of David's, now. At that moment she decided to go out with him when he asked her to.

Let Wayne stay in his shadow; his desires seemed old, and he no longer had that careless style he once had. He was turning into a shoe clerk who wrote poetry, that was it. She thought suddenly of one of the clerks in Trotevale's—a dark, handsome man with a touch of gray at his temples, who sang a popular song or two at any community occasion. He had a good tenor voice, and sang very well, with just the amount of skill that, in a movie, signified the winning of the amateur contest. All the rest of his life he was a clerk in Trotevale's, a quiet and rather sweet man, having no force. No, surely Wayne was not like that. Perhaps he was just the opposite. But there was a mustiness

about Wayne. He smelled somehow of old age, of toothbrush glasses and fussy pill bottles, and special preparations for the relief of gas or something. He might have worn a truss, a canvas and leather affair of straps and buckles, bitter with use. He was old at twenty; he couldn't swim, couldn't dance, couldn't even drive a car. She had never seen him run. If he did, things would joggle and flap and his gold fountain pen would bounce out of his pocket, followed by the comb he kept in the breast pocket of his suit coat, followed by the other comb that was clipped like his pen to his shirt pocket, followed by God knew what other crap. She saw him full of tinny little things like the prizes from Cracker Jack boxes. He wasn't, of course—but he was full of his little metaphors and judgments, as though life were a course in criticism, a lecture at which he took constant notes. Here he sat now, listening and judging, when it didn't matter at all what anyone said. They were smooth and lively and young, beautiful as birds, and they basked here in the bright sunlight, next to the glittering clean water, having themselves, enjoying each other, tense with all their energy and possibilities. What did it matter what anyone said? David was speaking, his face shining with pleasure and goodwill. He could be speaking Portuguese, or Bantu, what did it matter?

At four o'clock, when Kate and Wayne had left for Leah, Gordon and David went for a sail around Pine Island. After starting to drink beer, David couldn't make himself go back to work on the boathouse, so they took a few bottles with them on Gordon's boat. The wind was brisk, changing around from west to south to southeast, and they heeled and jibed and got wet. When they came into the lee of Pine Island they dropped sail and let the boat drift out toward the whitecaps as they opened the beer. The sun grew warm again and dried them, and the canvas deck grew warm to David's skin. He leaned back against the mast and watched Gordon try to say something he evidently found a little difficult.

"Davy? I've been wondering," he said, looking at the hole in his bottle. He held the bottle up and sighted down into it with one green eye. "I know my history and all that around this town,

but I wonder if you'd have any objection if I asked Kate to go out with me."

David had known this was coming. Gordon's strange deference toward him had indicated it clearly enough. But still he had a chill. "I presume you wouldn't arrange a gang bang," he said.

Gordon looked up with slit eyes, then decided to laugh. "Well, I guess I did bring it up," he said ruefully. But the green eyes watched without rue. "You know better than that. That was high-school stuff, Dave."

David wondered what he did know better than. One thing was that he could not be the keeper of his sister's virtue. She would have to know crueler shits than Gordon Ward in her lifetime.

Yet he couldn't help liking Gordon—or at least he never found him boring. That electric, somehow dangerous tension in Gordon, his rakehell straight look at anything, was a little like David's own. If life presented itself to you, you looked at it. If, for instance, Candy Palmer shoved it in front of you, thinking you weren't real, or dangerous, you didn't hesitate. He thought suddenly of Lucifer the karakul, and his golden eye, and then of Ben Caswell, whom they still kept alive in Northlee Hospital. There was that skinny force in Ben that seemed more mind than muscle. Ben had looked squarely at hard things and never hesitated.

The sun pressed against his skin and the boat rolled lightly on the water. Its buoyancy seemed slightly miraculous, although the beer was partly responsible for that. He wished he hadn't begun to drink this afternoon; there should be a clarity of mind on a brisk day like this, and he shouldn't brag to himself of a strength he knew to be strictly occasional.

Gordon said, "I'm not screwing around with Susie Davis anymore, Dave. I haven't seen her since the time we hosed off old Sam."

David shrugged. He'd told Gordon about what had happened that night with Candy Palmer, and right in the middle of the telling began to wish he hadn't. But he had to tell somebody, for some powerful reason, and Gordon had been highly pleased by the story. Pleased too, David suspected, to have something sordid

on him—that was why he wished he hadn't told Gordon. Even his words and phrases came back shamefully. How he had the little monkey girl's briefs off too, and the words he used to describe Candy's parts. In retrospect the telling of that tale seemed a fit of degradation. He should have made love to the little monkey girl, as tenderly and thoroughly as he could, taken her funny little maidenhead, soothed her until she saw stars, and told no one. Half violent, half chickenshit might be a more accurate summation of his character.

One thing he was not going to tell Gordon was that he was taking Susie to the hog wrastle at the Grange Hall in Summerslee Saturday night. His plan was to bring her back by way of the cabin. Now he wished he hadn't made that date, because in his mind Susie began to grow large, powerfully female. With deep uterine authority she seemed to envelop him and his life in warm folds of silk. At other times—this morning in the shower when he washed his hard body and its tight rubbery male parts—he knew that when he first touched her with naked intent she would shrink back softly into a mere girl, and he would have the power. But she waxed and waned, dangerous and then desirable. Right now in this clear light his plan seemed foolhardy.

"What do you say, Dave? Would it make you too nervous? I . . ." Gordon hesitated, and looked at him warily. "I mean I know how you feel about Kate. Little sister and all that. But my intentions are strictly honorable—in this case." He grinned, tentatively.

"That's her business, isn't it?" David said.

"I was considering your point of view, friend."

"I haven't figured that out." No, he hadn't figured that out. "Look," he said, "it doesn't matter what I think about it. You're no worse than most people—if that's what you want me to say. You're a bit of a shit and so am I. Why the hell should you ask my permission?"

Gordon smiled. "What if I asked her to marry me?"

"You?"

"See what I mean?" Gordon laughed, this time. "You're not prejudiced—you just wouldn't want your sister to marry one!"

David felt himself blush.

415

Gordon called her that night, as she suspected he would. When her mother called her to the telephone she knew whose voice it would be but not what tone or method the gaudy, reddish boy would adopt for her benefit. She knew it would be highly planned, whatever method it was. She was curious and a little excited as she took the telephone from her mother's hand.

"It's Gordon Ward and he wants you," her mother said, surprised. Although Kate took the telephone smoothly, with no real instant of hesitation in order to discover her mother's attitude beyond surprise, she felt the darkness of her mother's thoughts.

"Hi, Kate," Gordon said. "Hey, would you like to go to the Blue Moon Saturday night?"

"Oh. Well," she said, stalling; she blushed because of that little lie. "Let's see." Another lie. "All right, Gordon."

"Good! Great! I'll pick you up around seven-thirty, okay?"

"All right," she said.

"Now, how about going sailing tomorrow? Supposed to be bright and windy. I could pick you up around eleven, we could have lunch at our cabin and sail across the lake and back. Stop in and see Davy at work on his beloved boathouse."

"Well," she said. She felt his force. Already he seemed a little too strong, a little out of control. Out of her control. She felt the tiniest bite of fear. She had answered in such a hesitant way. "Well," she'd said, and that meant she had no clear right to say no.

"All right," she said again, and again he was inordinately pleased. Did he think he had soothed her with the promise of visiting David? Or even bribed her, somehow? How calculated had been that suggestion?

"See you tomorrow then, Katie. Eleven sharp." He paused. "Hey, good night," he said.

Ah. She heard that unusual diminuendo in his voice. Awe, and even a Gordonish sort of tenderness. Yes, she heard it plain.

"Good night, Gordon," she said.

After she put the telephone down she turned in the shadowy

416

hallway. Slowly she felt her arms, hugging herself. She felt very deep, a strange deepness full of power that was not hers alone, but hers in common. She thought of her mother, and Peggy, and Letty who had that power over David. And Susie Davis—the power a woman had, though all women were inside out, to make a man turn. Men needed them. What a miracle it was that those bright, agile creatures needed the waiting emptiness. It was the power of warmth, of liquid, of gas, a lake in which the shouldery fish cruised and glittered, or it was moist air carved by the wings of flamingos.

29

Late in the summer the Whipples gathered in the great hall. There was Wood, tall and pale, his dark hair grown too long, leaning against the mantel with a slight angle to his hips that gave away his false leg. He wore a brown tweed suit for this semi-formal occasion, the celebration of his twenty-fourth birthday. The black eye patch was a shadow they had all grown used to, and his eye moved deep in the other socket, calmly surveying them all, or so they thought.

Peggy Mudd crossed the room in their sight, her faille dress rustling against her legs, hiding from them the trembling her decision had caused her, and kissed Wood upon the mouth. His hands came slowly to her waist, and he smiled. To her he seemed sadly pleased, an emotion that barred her from him as with iron. "Happy birthday," she said. When he perceived her disappointment his face grew thoughtful and remote.

From across the room, a distance great enough to place him in a different and cooler light, David began to speak in mock-stentorian tones: "Ladies, gentlemen, squires, blood cousins,

dames of quality . . ." He bowed toward Sally De Oestris who perched, blue and silver, upon her straight throne. "We have been summoned to celebrate the birthday of our brother Wood, an occasion of high rejoicing in this kingdom."

"Oyez oyez!" cried Kate from above.

David read from a paper held before him in both hands: "'Brother, son, cousin, in all ways dutiful, valorous and fair, hero wounded in the wars against the Black Evils, Cruelty and Pride, all hail!'" David nodded to Kate, who stood upon the landing in the solemn ecclesiastical glow of the stained glass. She began to recite:

> "First in his five wits he faultless was found;
> In his five fingers the man never failed . . .
> The fifth five the hero made use of, I find,
> More than all were his liberalness, love of his fellows,
> His courtesy, chasteness, unchangeable ever,
> And pity, all further traits passing. These five
> In this hero more surely were set . . ."

Her voice broke, and she turned, suddenly awkward, toward David. "I'm sorry, Davy! I can't finish!"

Everyone looked away from Kate, and then toward Wood, who frowned unhappily. The most powerful reasons they could think of for his unhappiness were not powerful enough.

"All right," David said, "we'll shorten the ceremony somewhat." He nodded to Peggy, who went to the old harmonium and took her seat upon its oak bench. The little chapel's round stained-glass window glowed dark blue and amber, and suddenly the hall's antique details—the false balcony, the various panels, sills and ornately carved and cabineted wood—all seemed to grow into deeper relief. As Peggy worked the wheezy pedals and began to play a thin and unfamiliar melody, all the pretentious ornamentations of the great hall gained authority. The song she played was ancient, bitter-sweet, as though composed for instruments with names like psaltery or dulcimer.

> "On earth, or far or near,
> It seemed as if he ought
> To be a prince sans peer
> In fields where fierce men fought.

> *"Of us this hero now*
> *Will noble manners teach;*
> *Who hear him will learn how*
> *To utter loving speech."*

Wood didn't hear the words, but the sweet voice pierced him. It did not mean what his dreams meant, yet its clarity changed the world as forcefully as the dark shutter of his dreams. The soft wind of her throat, her slender hollow throat shaped by the delicate cords and muscles she so gracefully commanded. When she glanced at him he lost his breath. She was only human, yet she carved that music out of the air—no, took the ordinary air and made this lovely order. In its returns and predictions the melody bound him, but it was not his hands tied, no one's body cruelly tied. As in a dream he felt the presence of a force he could not understand or even attempt to define. It was not to murder; of course not, on the face of it. Peggy—Margaret. Margaret. She glanced at him again and smiled. It was not like a little while ago when she kissed him and waited for the response he knew ought to be given, that he could not then give.

A *Wandervogel*, Sally had called her long ago, the Christmas she had come to live with them. That little bird had grown and changed. A German word again, from the language that meant to him cool rational insanity, or cool sane irrationality, whose harsh clean sounds stretched across his mind like steel cords. The language of the intellect.

> *"Of us this hero now*
> *Will noble manners teach;*
> *Who hear him will learn how*
> *To utter loving speech."*

As Peggy sang the verse again he understood the words, and they all took note of his wry smile. They sang him happy birthday, and Henrietta brought in a chocolate cake with twenty-four candles burning and smoking like a small bonfire in her hands. Her face was a warm moon above the fires, and her thick lenses cast brighter ovals upon her eyelids. They noticed how her hair was turning gray. The children were grown up, now. Would this be the last summer all of them would spend in Leah?

Horace felt them all going away, all but him. Wood was somehow gone already. Wood was frightened; he felt it. He knew all the symptoms. Wood took no joy in this birthday party. Kate had gone to the Blue Moon and other places with Gordon Ward, and David instead of Wood saw Susie Davis. Were they all mad? David! All this mouthing of smooth words. David had tried to teach him how to drive, but everything he said was cruel and apprehensive. *The clutch, the clutch!* he said, nervous and cold, and the truck bucked and stalled, bucked and stalled as though each wheel were as independent as the leg of a wild horse. He hated the truck. He didn't want to become its brain, its intelligence. David was so smooth and skillful with it.

Peggy kissed Wood; she was grown-up and had left herself behind—how was that? She wanted Wood to be grown-up with her. She was after something, out of herself, too old to be Peggy any more. Susie said she loved him, but she went out with— David! Look at him, so smooth and sure of himself. He hadn't died of fear a thousand times; he did not deserve! He would never marry her and make her happy. All he wanted was that part of her down there. The brown room darkened. She liked it or she wouldn't let him do it to her. But how could she give herself away to such cheap lust? He had followed them. He knew. Hiding in the pines, waiting for them to return to the cabin, his bike behind the woodpile at midnight. Through the screen he heard them thrashing, and cried inside himself, cold and silent. So cheap and so dangerous! David caused her loose laughter, said things that made her laugh. That clever brother. They were all gone away now, all of them, driven by their new desires, joining or being pursued by evil. Kate trying to be all smooth and confident with Gordon Ward, laughing with him, not caring who he was or what he had done. What had made them turn? He looked at their faces that were firmed by these alien certainties. They knew what they wanted, now, and that knowing must be a terrible forgetfulness.

Wood blew out all the candles in one breath, and they gave a cheer.

Harvey didn't want to look at Wood, at his son. Dammit, things began to go fairly well for a change and it was always somebody else's troubles that weighed you down like a wet blanket.

He thought of his money. He tried to think of his money—more money than any of them suspected, by God! Even Hanky had no idea. Those lovely zeroes. Zero, zero, zero, zero! In fact, one, five, zero, zero, zero, zero—and that didn't count real property. Had he taken chances!

He must try again to get Wood interested in the stock market. Wood had the disability check each month, for a good, even sort of ballast, and he had quite a bit in War Bonds. War Bonds, for Christ's sake! What a terrible waste of capital! Somehow he had to get to Wood and convince him. What a time they'd have together, the New York *Times* between them. Right here at this table, Wood's intelligence and his, father and son, saying to each other with calm equality those words they would both instantly understand.

He looked at his son's face—part face. *Gueules cassées*—what was that memory? No, what would an eye missing be called? No more binocular vision there, although what about Wiley Post? Famous flyer, but then he did crash. When was that? Will Rogers was with him. Stop procrastinating and look at your son. He looked.

Screw that noble sadness. Hadn't it been going on for too long a time?

He accepted a piece of cake. "Thank you!" he said, and turned toward Wood. "Many happy returns, as they say!"

"Thanks," Wood said.

Oh, Jesus, how was he going to break through? All he could do was talk, talk, talk against that impeccable, infuriating calm.

Henrietta, having cut the cake, sat back in the straight chair she rather resentfully knew to be hers, or to be generally considered hers. She had seen the others avoid it. She was not ready to consider herself an institution, like Sally, who always sat in a particular chair, just so, so she could see everybody without moving her stiffened and compressed little spine. No, she was not ready to exist as some sort of predictable adjunct to this family. She loved them—why else would she wait on them, and cry bitter tears over their wounds—but she was herself; she was hard. The whole town didn't like her sudden opinions. She was never a part of its social structure at all, and because she didn't care, they didn't like her one bit. It had been a long, long time since Harvey,

for business reasons, had hinted that she might give the ladies of the town, their charities, their study groups, their asinine fashion shows, a little of her time. She could never smile at stupidity, she could never flatter. She was considered a dangerous radical.

This made her smile, as she did not when their wit descended (or ascended?) to imitations of Eleanor Roosevelt (Rosenfeld). "Maay Daay," they would half snarl, and seeing her, stop, frozen by an audience that ruined their joke unforgivably. "Did you hear? Harry Truman died on the way to Eleanor's funeral!" Somehow she heard them all—across aisles, through walls, over hedges.

And they all knew her story, from whence she came to this castle. She thought of the time she'd flown all the way across the country to see Wood, shortly after the war, when she sat enclosed in the airplane among all those people who had been made by their adventure important and dramatic. She'd looked down to see the lights of whole cities glimmering on the earth below. What was Henrietta Sleeper doing in that Olympian company? After all these years away from Switches Corners, that ghost place in the woods that was even then doomed, gray birch in the cellar holes, she asked herself that self-acknowledging question. Yes, she was herself still, a visitor to these half-strangers. When I die, she thought, hearing the words, I will die like a cat; I will go off by myself to a private place. She spoke to herself, for no one else's ear: I will die as I once lived—alone—not because I have to but because I want to. Because I want to.

But in the kitchen Tom the cat, as if to refute her simile, lay emaciated in his washtub, on the soiled burlap, obviously dying. David was going to take him to the vet's and have him put to sleep. He was an old cat, and the magic had gone out of him. He had cancer in several places—in his belly, in his bowels—and he suffered, not always in silence. Last night they had heard his miniature roar, as though agony were another tomcat he warned away.

She listened above the murmur of their talk. A shout of Sally's laughter made Wood smile. Tom was quiet, as far as she could tell. He often slept these days with his head up; he couldn't find a way to the flexible and languorous cat ease that once let him dream, even while draped over the splintery stove wood. Now there was no more stove wood, and the kitchen had grown cold

and white. In the cellar the oil burner rumbled at its own urgings. No one went down there for weeks at a time.

Wood tried on his new sweater, and smoked his new pipe. Sally had given him a Japanese print, of carpenters ripsawing a huge beam, with Fuji in the distance.

"It's work," he said. "It's beautiful work. The sawing." He seemed to dream himself into the landscape. They were all quiet while he looked at it. He turned to them with an almost embarrassed smile. "It's beautiful, Sally."

"Glad you like it," Sally said.

"My God!" Kate said to David. "How can you drink beer and eat chocolate cake at the same time?"

"Actually, I do them separately," David said. Kate punched him affectionately on the arm as she went by him, taking her fork and plate to the kitchen.

Horace wasn't having any cake. He wasn't hungry, he said. Henrietta looked at him more closely than she had for some time. She had been so preoccupied with Wood's melancholy she hadn't had much time to worry about Horace. He was still Horace, always that tangle in the back of her mind. Poor Horace, all in snarls, pulling against himself like a jammed knot. He wouldn't even consider going to college. She had talked Harvey into keeping the one tenement, against what he called his better judgment, so Horace would have that job, at least. As long as Susie Davis lived there, Horace would take care of it. She wondered about that relationship, always skirting the idea, somehow.

Horace's crude face contained much force. He ground his teeth, and the bristles glinted along his jaw. He was a man now, wasn't he? And suddenly she let the idea come plain in her mind. Did that woman take her child in . . . what? There must be a word that contained the drama and fear she either felt, or felt that she must feel. All right, did she, Susie Davis, copulate with Horace? Had she taught the boy what to do and taken him . . . again, where? What? What about it? Susie was considered by the town to be a loose woman. There was the possibility of disease, or of her becoming pregnant. What a mess! But then, hadn't she been good for Horace? She had helped him over certain childish fears. Miraculously, he no longer seemed afraid of the dark. That woman. But weren't they both women, Susie and

423

herself? Was it jealousy? Whose job was it to help the child? Why hadn't she ever considered going to see Susie, even perhaps to thank her for what she'd done? Yes, she should do that. Of course she should. She shuddered. She could see two women facing each other; from one had come this child, labor and blood and kaput, the flesh distended, the shaved pubes, the cord, the wet placenta —all the gross intimacy of the begun life. That could not be forgotten, ever, no matter how big and old the child became. The other knowledge was how that child groaned upon the other woman, flesh of her flesh ascending toward the darkness of that other womb.

Oh, she was hard and cold; she avoided emotion like a cat. But she was not!

Quickly she got up and went to the kitchen. Kate was coming back and they collided. No, they didn't collide, Kate had seen her face and put her arms around her.

"Hey, Hanky," Kate said.

Someone had come up behind her, and some more arms came around her. "The trouble with you," David said in her ear, "is that you're an intellectual."

"What?" Kate said.

"She was wondering again. Very bad for the complexion."

"What were you wondering about, Mother?" Kate asked.

"The meaning of it all," David said. "Should never wonder about that. Bad for the pistons. Fouls the intake ports. Shrivels the baffles. Awful."

"Oh, you two," Henrietta said. "You're so pretty."

"Isn't it pretty of you to think so," David said.

"David, stop it!" Kate said.

"I should be serious."

"Yes, you should."

"Like everybody else?"

"If you're going to have an argument," Henrietta said, "do you need me in the middle?" That made them laugh, and they let her go, although both of them watched her carefully.

Kate found David looking at her. "Speaking of cake and beer," he said, "how are you and Gordon making out?"

"Nobody's making out," she said.

"That wasn't my question," he said quickly.

"Wasn't it, Davy?"

He blushed a little. She wished they hadn't begun to speak so flippantly, because she would like some serious information from David on this subject.

"You must find him interesting," David said.

"Well, he's . . ." What was it? "He's lively," she said. That was part of it. There were subjects Gordon never thought about at all, that he wouldn't ever stop to consider, but he had a charming impatience with life that kept them jumping and laughing. He was funny without wit, or at least any sort of wit she could remember afterwards. With Gordon everything had to be there at once, in context. And he handled *things* so well—material things like his sailboat and his car, and his phonograph. Things like cigarettes, lighters, cocktail shakers—they were all made for his hands. He danced lightly and knowledgeably. The people who served him seemed glad. She had little time to find him shallow, because everything they did seemed an occasion, and they were always at the center.

"Yes, he's lively," David said. "I'll grant you that."

"Why do you have to grant anything to me? He's your friend, isn't he?"

"I don't think so," David said seriously. "Maybe, but I'm not so sure."

"Well, what's a friend, Davy? You see him a lot. What do you mean by 'friend'?"

"Like you and me," David said, and it struck her. He said it so plainly. Her skin seemed to melt, and suddenly she grew shy of him. It mattered terribly that he not see her confusion. She turned away, as though casually, and rubbed a small stain from the table, a drop of juice from the beets they had at dinner.

"What's the matter?" David asked.

"Nothing."

"Where's he taking you tonight? To that thing at the Country Club?"

"Yes."

"Maybe I'll stop by later and case the joint."

"Okay, Davy," she said.

They went back into the living room to join the others. David watched Kate talk to Wood, her loved face printing upon

its surface her kindness and lightness, how she couldn't ever lie, not even to Wood about her concern. It occurred to him that none of the Whipples were liars, with the possible exception of himself. With the perfect, exact, absolute exception of himself. For one thing, Letty thought him more real, more possible, than he was. He was struck again by Letty's likeness to Kate, and as he watched Kate it was as though he had lied to her, been in some way dishonorable to her. She was so open and delicate. He thought of a flower, perhaps a daisy; only an organism as pure and mute as a flower could have Kate's symmetry and perfection. She was dressed up to go to the dance, and even in the nylons and heels, the make-up, the dress fashioned to fit over a grown woman's breasts and hips, Kate carried herself so lightly she managed to look as fit as a lovely child.

That evening when Wood took his new print to his room he found an unmarked envelope under his door. In the envelope were two ten-dollar bills and a five-dollar bill. He took the money and the envelope and put them on his desk. A present? But who would give him money like that? Twenty-five dollars. Then he knew; it was the twenty-five dollars Horace had confiscated from the school lockers long ago; now Horace marked that fund paid. Paid in full. Maybe a declaration of independence. He and Horace hadn't been very close these last years. Horace stayed by himself, and though he was as haunted-looking as ever, he always seemed busy.

Wood was trembling; he wanted peace. Even while the rational part of him considered that old debt, and Horace, and after Horace the rest of the family and their worries, there was a call from his darkness, a scream of helplessness. He took two translucent capsules from an olive-colored box, a bottle from his desk drawer, and washed the capsules down with raw whiskey. Once that would have made him gag, once upon a more innocent time. Now there seemed to be so little power in whiskey or drugs. But there was some power, thank God. He would have no more than an hour to kill before he could sleep.

Duty said he should go knock on Horace's door and find out in what spirit Horace had paid back the money. Why was there no message with it?

On his desk beside the money was a paragraph he had recently copied into his notebook:

> The entire population of Japan is a proper military target
> . . . THERE ARE NO CIVILIANS IN JAPAN. We are
> making War and making it in the all-out fashion which
> saves American lives, shortens the agony which War is
> and seeks to bring about an enduring Peace. We intend to
> seek out and destroy the enemy wherever he or she is,
> in the greatest possible numbers, in the shortest possible
> time.
>
> —Col. Harry F. Cunningham, A-2,
> Fifth Air Force. *Fifth Air Force*
> *Intelligence Review*, No. 86,
> 15–21 July, 1945

These little jewels he saved. They seemed to help his case, as though each document proved him just a little innocent. But wasn't he the prosecutor? Was it not someone else's trial, and he only the lawyer's clerk?

Fifty-five minutes, approximately.

He forced himself to go to Horace's room. Horace wasn't there. That took four minutes, what with knocking, waiting and finally opening the door, turning on the light and finding the room empty. Slowly and methodically he went to the bathroom and washed, brushed his teeth and got ready for bed. He took one more drink from the bottle of whiskey, and this time the acid shock of whiskey and toothpaste did almost make him gag. Good. He got into bed and looked at the one foot pushing up the blankets. Good. He felt the smooth depression where he once had an eye. When he tapped it, it made a hollow sound, like a loose drum. The whiskey, he had been warned, increased the effect of the barbituate, and he had found that approximately two ounces, or two swallows, was the right amount if he hadn't eaten much for supper. Beyond these dosages lay another world where he tossed without control, in the power of the drugs. Once in desperation he had taken himself by the throat and tried to kill the mind that had entertained the fantasies of that world. Now he was more careful.

427

Perhaps he shouldn't have got into bed quite so soon. He turned out the light, then quickly turned it on again, because its absence revealed the room with the mustard walls, the wooden guard tower beyond those cold, borrowed windows. This time an operating table stood in the center of the room. He had seen too much. A slender woman lay strapped to the table, her knees spread and her feet tied into stirrups. She was naked, and now his face dollied in, his face and his eyes, looking, seeing everything. Her external genitalia had been closely shaved, and were covered with the reddish scrapes of the razor. The pores stood out upon the scraped pudenda, and the flesh looked tough, like something much handled, although it hadn't been. He tried to avoid looking at her face because he knew who she was.

The clipboard said: *Zeugungs versuchsstelle: 1–004–065 (m)*. There was no question as to the inevitability of the operation, which would be performed without anesthesia, an interesting problem (it was written) in the traumatic effects of such pain; the next experiment (*Versuch*), scheduled for 1400 hours, would be upon a patient of the same approximate age and in the same approximate health. In this case spinal anesthesia would be used. What the clipboard promised would be done.

"Wood?" she said. It was Lois, as he had known. "Wood?" Her face was sick and pale. Her black hair, so dirty it was the color of slate, fell thinly to the gray paper. Canvas straps cut across her chest.

"Wood, I've changed my mind. I think I'd rather die."

"It's too late now."

"What are they going to do to me?"

Of course he knew. "Just a little operation," he said.

"Wood, I'm cold. My nose itches."

"My arms are tied," he said. "What can I do?"

"Remember when I played the duke? Remember my costume? You were the king. You were always my king."

"I'm only a prisoner!" he shouted. "Don't ask me to do anything! You should have died! You made the wrong choice and I can't help it!"

"Oh, Wood," she said softly, "don't cry, my dear. I'm so happy to be a woman." She listened, and seemed to be remembering.

428

Soon the experiment would begin, and he would hear her first long unbelieving call. His eyes were forced to the schedule on the clipboard. *Heben:* ovaries, fallopian tubes, uterus, vagina, labia majora, labia minora, clitoris, fourchette, fossa navicularis, vestibule, vestibular bulb, Skene's tubules, glands of Bartholin, hymen, vaginal introitus. Extend meatus urinarius beyond perineum. *Why had he studied their work?*

"Can't you kill me, Wood, before they come?"

He fell from the bed and crawled to the corner where his shotgun stood, but it wasn't there. He propped himself upon his stump, and his arms scythed that corner, but never found the cold gun. His box of shells was gone from the shelf. All right, he coldly thought, you have tried to disarm me. My visions are precise and even scientific; agony is considered an incidental phenomenon, below all but perhaps the mildest curiosity of the state. He stumbled and hopped to his desk and gobbled all the rest of the translucent capsules. If he drank too much whiskey with them he might vomit them up (*auswerfen*), so he did not.

At ten o'clock that evening Horace walked down Bank Street, past the windowlights of houses, past the dark high school. Today had been the first Friday that Susie hadn't been up to greet him when he came for the rents. Sam Davis had let him in, Sam Davis so drunk he drooled as he grinned, and when Sam stepped back he shoved the kitchen table so far, the electric toaster came to the end of its cord and fell to the floor. An old piece of dried toast was still in the toaster, and this struck Horace with ominous meaning, as though life had somehow ended with that small forgetting. He must get Susie out of there and away, and now, this evening, he had begun. He had six hundred dollars in traveler's checks in a neat little folder with a snap on it, and a hundred dollars in cash. They would take Grimes' taxi to Wentworth Junction and take the midnight train south. If he couldn't get her to leave tonight they would leave tomorrow; he was ready now. There were no more Herpes, and Zoster had faded, disappeared, gone away without leaving a memory of cellar stench. Below his window he'd found, long ago, a ball of mouse fur, the last sign of Leverah. He was a man now. He knew the ball of mouse fur had

been passed by a cat, probably Tom. He knew what had been in his imagination and what had not, and in his singular clarity of mind he made this new decision with no trepidation whatsoever. He had saved the seven hundred dollars out of his salary—it had taken less than a year. He would get a job, and maybe Susie would get a job when she felt better, and there would be no cheap laughter any more. She was only four years older than he was. If she couldn't do without sex, she could show him what she liked and he could do it to her. They would be married. But first he must get her away from Leah, from this terrible place. How many times had he heard them joke about her. They said she "ate the bird," and he didn't know what that meant. The lowest, filthiest men in town had the right to print her with the word "Fuck," then laugh with expressions like they had to go to the bathroom. It was Leah, this terrible place that wouldn't let you go, that remembered everything bad. They would change their names; they would never think of Leah again. They would start new, with no memories, just their own kindness.

In the square the grown people seemed furtive. Some high-school-age kids hollered and lounged on the steps of the Town Hall, flicking cigarettes ten feet across the sidewalk to the gutter, watching for girls and women so they could act their smut out upon their faces. Cruelty was everywhere. In Trask's the bright lights proclaimed those thoughts official, as though the people were on the stage. In the Strand they all sat close as a pinch or a goose in the dark, watching the murder they had paid to see. The mills and factories were closed for the night, the pale steel gears waiting to mesh.

Water Street smelled of cinders and coal and the ancient fumes of locomotives. Futzie's Tavern door opened like a mouth to let a shadow in as a bad breath of smoke and beer seeped out into the street. The mouth of hell with blue neon lips. He would take her out of Leah. The stars closed down upon the town, so close they might have been pinned to a blanket stretched across the tops of the houses. Someone came out of the tenement and quickly walked toward the railroad tracks, keeping in the shadow.

Susie's door was ajar, so he went straight on in through the empty kitchen. The toaster was still on the floor with the piece of toast sticking half out of it like a dead tongue. He heard a gag,

that despairing sound, and ran to Susie's bedroom. Her light was on, and she lay across her bed. The white balloons of her buttocks gleamed pure and cool; her bathrobe was all up around her waist, and her head hung down on the dark side of her bed.

"Again?" she said, and retched. "Didn't you get your rocks off? Can't you see I'm *sick?* Get out of here! Ugg, ugg!" Liquid splashed, with a metal-bowl sound. "Glaag! Oh, oh!" she said. "Get out!" she sighed in despair. "Oh, oh, oh!" She lost her breath, and heaved. Her hand clutched the spread, and the great pure virginal moons of her shivered and clenched.

She raised her head and looked. "Horace! Oh, my God!" She pulled her bathrobe down, turning as she tried to pull it out from under her. He saw the dark cloud between her legs, dark as a piece of twilight, furred brown as a rabbit pelt.

"I'm sorry, Horace. I'm sick," she said quickly. "Go out to the kitchen and I'll be out in a mintue."

"You're sick," he said. "Lie down." He pressed her back, his hand on her chest. He took the vomit to the bathroom and flushed the thin brownish stuff down the toilet. He found a sponge under the kitchen sink and cleaned up the splashes, then cleaned the basin. With a washcloth damp with cool water he came back and washed the sweat from her face and neck.

"Oh, Christ." She sighed. "I'm so drunk. I'm stinking drunk. Give me a cigarette." Her hand waved weakly toward the table. He got her a cigarette and lighted it for her. She took a long drag and immediately heaved, and he caught the cigarette and a string of drool in the washcloth. Her hair was all brown strings pasted to her head.

"Go away, Horace. Go away. Go home."

"No," he said. "I'm going to take care of you."

He went to the bathroom, rinsed out the washcloth with soap and came back to wash the old make-up off the bottom half of her face.

"You're washing me," she said. "You're *washing* me."

"Do you feel better?"

"Oh, God, no. I stink."

"You ought to take a bath, then."

"I stink all over."

431

He went to the bathroom, turned on the tub faucets and waited for the water to warm, then went back to her.

"The tub's filling," he said. "Come on."

When she closed her eyes, the brown hollows under them made him melt with tenderness. He touched those soft places. She opened her eyes and looked at him almost with horror. "What are you doing?"

"I just touched your eyes."

"Horace, what are you doing here?"

"From now on I'm going to be taking care of you."

"I don't understand you. I've never made you happy."

Something odd happened to her mouth, as though it weren't her moving it. "You've always made me happy," he said.

"I've made everybody else happy. I've made everybody happy but you."

"Come on. The tub's filling. It'll run over."

"I've got this thing makes them happy." She laughed, and retched, but not so badly as before.

"Come on." He took her by the arms and stood her up. She began to fall back, so he put his arm around her and began to walk her down the hall.

A door banged open behind them and Sam Davis came staggering out in his long underwear. The wrists, neck and fly of the underwear were all worn brown. He stopped, his pinkish eyes bugging out.

"Jesus Baldheaded Christ!" he yelled. "What the shit are you doing?"

Susie's head lay on Horace's shoulder, her bare feet dragging on the floor.

"Never mind," Horace said. The bathtub would run over if he didn't get there soon, but now Sam Davis ran around in front of them and blocked the way, his brown crotch sagging like a diaper and his scrawny arms braced against the wallpaper.

"I've got a right to know!" he yelled. One hand slid down the wall and he nearly followed it to the floor.

"Get out of our way," Horace said. When Sam didn't, he walked over him, and Sam fell down like several sticks.

"Christ, you didn't have to do that," Sam whined from the bathroom door. "You hurt me. I ought to call the cops."

"Oh, God," Susie said, and retched.

"Well, Jesus," Sam said plaintively, "I'm your father and you ain't got a blessed stitch on under that bathrobe. Jesus, I got a right to think I ought to be told something. Besides, I got to take a leak so bad I can taste it."

Still holding Susie, Horace bent down and turned off the faucets. "All right," he said, and walked Susie out to the hall. Sam shut the door, and they heard the splashing. Susie breathed on his neck, the sour smell of her hair and her vomit breath surrounding him. She leaned against him and she seemed to be getting drunker.

"Poor Horace," she said. "Oh, my, I'm so drunk. I'm such a drunk. I'm a filthy drunk. I'm a filthy old bag, Horace. Horse. I'm a slut. I'm a great piece of ass as the whole town knows I can't say no to anything that wears pants."

"Be quiet."

"I just want everybody to be happy, Horsie-Horse. I never played with your pickle, though, did I? I never played your piccolo?"

He would wash away all that, and they would begin again. He would tear down all that—this house—with his bare hands, and all it meant. The wallpaper exuded that rotten slime. It smelled of sweat.

"'Susie Davis, in a dream, took on the Leah football team.' Haven't you ever sang . . . sung that at a picnic?"

"Be quiet now," he said.

Sam came out of the bathroom. "I'd still like to know what you got in mind," he said.

"I'm going to give Susie a bath," Horace said.

"What? You're what?"

Horace moved Susie into the bathroom and removed her bathrobe, revealing great, achingly pure expanses of her delicate flesh. He rolled up his sleeves and lowered her into the tub. Sam stood in the door with his face averted, arguing.

"What gives you the right to look at all of her like that? Jesus Christ!"

"I'm going to make her clean again."

"Jesus, you sure do give funny answers. You're gitting me all confused."

Horace soaped her hair, and wrung the suds through it. His rough hands squeezed and rinsed the long brown hair. "Ah," Susie sighed.

"I'm gonna git me a beer," Sam said.

Horace soaped her neck and shoulders, then her sandpapery armpits. She leaned forward obligingly, as if in a dream, as he washed her back. He washed her all over, his hands at times seeming to sink deep into forbidden places, quicksand places. Her hard breasts, the pink nipples, her thighs and calves and feet; he washed the deep complications of her sexual place, amazed at his right. Under his ministering fingers passed the button of her anus. He left no part of her unclean.

Sam came back to argue, keeping his face turned so he would catch no glimpse of his daughter.

"You sure got a lot of gall," Sam ventured.

"I'm taking Susie away," Horace said. He lifted her out, and she stood leaning against him as he dried her. His shirt and pants were all wet in front.

"Taking Susie away?" Sam looked, this time, and quickly, guiltily looked away. "What d'you mean, take her away?"

"Away," Horace said. He put her bathrobe around her and led her back to her room.

"Oh, Horace," she said. "What in the world are you doing?"

"You may be the goddam janitor," Sam said, "but it don't follow you got a right to come in here and wash my girl!" A gust of drunkenness hit him and he rolled along the wall. Without spilling his beer he fell to one knee. "I ought to call the cops," he said.

"It's too late for you," Horace said.

"What? What?"

"All you are is a drunk."

"I'm a *farmer!*"

"You're a drunk."

"I'm a farmer! Susie, ain't I a farmer? Tell him!" Sam began to blubber. "If he takes you away, what happens to me? Answer me that! What happens to me?"

"If I don't take her away, what happens to her?"

"It ain't fair!" Sam cried.

434

Horace let her down on the bed and pulled the spread over her. From her bureau he began to gather her clothes.

"Horace, what are you doing?" She tried to get up on her elbow, but fell back with a groan. "I'm so drunk. It's got me."

"I'm getting your clothes together."

"What happens to me?" Sam cried.

"You've taken money from Gordon Ward," Horace said.

"Who says so?" Sam was terribly indignant.

"I've seen. Do you think I'm blind? I know everything. He buys your liquor for you."

"It ain't true!" Sam was truly indignant; no one could be accused of such a thing. Horace saw his true indignation. Sam could not believe how things could be summed up.

"Daddy," Susie called in a sick voice. "Let me talk to Horace. Go away and leave us."

"Well, I don't know, now," Sam said. "It don't seem right, somehow, to leave him in here when you got no clothes on."

"Shut up, Daddy. Go get yourself another beer."

"It don't seem proper."

"Oh, God!" Susie groaned.

Muttering and complaining, Sam went out of the room.

"Haven't you got a suitcase?" Horace said.

Susie sat up and tried to look at him. She held the spread across her chest, and her damp hair fell over her shoulder and back. "What?" she said.

"A suitcase," Horace said.

"What you doing?"

"I'm going to pack your things. You've got to tell me what you want to wear."

She had fallen back. "Sick, Horsie. Can't you see 'm sick."

He leaned over her and grabbed her face. "Listen!" he said, shaking her face back and forth. Her lips slid over her teeth; he had made that grimace with his hands, and he was afraid he hurt her. She opened her eyes.

"Can I make you happy, Horsie? I think I'm going to sleep, so hurry up."

"No!" he shouted. "Wake up! You're acting crazy!"

She tried to wake up, he could see. She shook her head. "I don't get it," she said in a rational voice. "What is it, Horace?

435

If you want to, go ahead. Go ahead if you want to." She began to pull the spread from her body, and he pulled it back and held it to her shoulders.

"I want you to go away with me," he said clearly. "Do you understand? I've saved up a lot of money, and I want to take you away from Leah. We can go right now. I've got it all planned."

"Give me a cigarette."

"Don't you understand, Susie?"

"I'm not thinking too good, Horace."

He held the match to her cigarette and she took a long drag. The blue cone of smoke sighed from her throat, and her eyes flickered.

"Susie, please listen to me!"

"Get me a beer. Maybe that'll wake me up."

"You don't want a beer!"

"I want to make you happy, Horace. It makes me happy to make you happy."

"Will you go with me?"

"Oh yes, yes. Anything you say, Horace." She dropped the cigarette and he picked it up and put it in the ashtray.

"Do you understand what I want? Susie! Do you really understand?"

"Yes, Horace."

If only he could pick her up right now and take her out of this house. But he couldn't think of a place. If only he had learned to drive when David tried to teach him, instead of freezing up tight. He groaned. If he could get her dressed he could call Grimes' taxi. But he couldn't lug her out like a sack of meal. Grimes would take one look and tell him to put her to bed, enjoying it all immensely too.

"Listen, Susie!"

"Cigarette."

He handed her the cigarette.

"Listen, Susie. I'm taking you away. We're going to start all over again, like when you were a little girl. Remember? You and me." His words seemed all at once hopeless, a weird echo of something hopeless he had heard before.

"Okay."

She didn't understand at all.

"You're so sweet, Horsie. Oh my, I feel so clean and so sleepy."

Suddenly he was discouraged. He couldn't fight her lethargy, her absent mind. Even if he managed to take her away now, it wouldn't be Susie, it would only be that bright flesh and hair he had washed and dried. He would have to leave and continue his own preparations. He hadn't even thought to pack a suitcase for himself, and he didn't want to spend their money on clothes. Evidently she didn't have a suitcase. Her drawers were full of silky female things, and strange boxes and ointments she'd probably need. These petty considerations had him caught, like a haunting blow from the past when elbows and angles always reached for him and stung him. For a second his vision turned red and he considered tearing the doorframe out of the wall. This grimy, sill-rotten building, bought with a cheat and a lie, with its stinking drains and sweating pipes.

He shouldn't leave her here even for a moment.

Susie moaned and rolled toward him. "Gimme cigarette."

He pushed her back. "Go to sleep."

"Mmm."

He put his hand on her breast; beneath the rubbery flesh was the even beat of her heart. She half woke. "Did you come, Horace? Did you like it? Did you do like to give me a baby?" With a sigh, she slept.

He melted, and wrung his face with his hands. He couldn't leave her unprotected. He considered the possibility of the eight o'clock bus to Wentworth Junction; could he get her organized by morning? He would have to leave her here for a while with no defenses, not even her wits, with that broken fool her father. Gordon Ward might come, or Keith Joubert, Donald Ramsey, Bruce Cotter, Junior Stevens, even David. No, he would keep his plan for a while longer, reorganize it and perfect it. He would consider things like suitcases this time, and train reservations. He would know their destination. It would be Springfield, Lawrence or Providence, not just some vague city to the south. He would present the plan to her not in breathless desperation but with calm strength.

She breathed evenly now, with a little repeating tick of mucus in her nose—a little-child noise he found so moving tears

came to his eyes. Her hair was drying glossy and soft, and he re-arranged it on the pillow. Beneath her lids her gentle eyes moved in a dream. He would sit beside her and be her sentinel until dawn.

They parked by the first tee and crossed the lawn in the balmy summer air, Gordon's hand lightly on her elbow. The Country Club was gay with Japanese lanterns hung all around the wide porches. As they approached, band music, laughter and light came from the windows and verandas, proclaiming a kind of disorganized joy. Tall elms stood over the Country Club like fond giants —parents, even—guarding it into the dusk. The young deserved their gaiety, did they not? They walked so firmly, breathed so easily. The air they drank was friendly to their energies.

Inside, she and Gordon danced among the others, everyone gracefully passing and turning. Gordon moved lightly on his feet, and she couldn't combine this Gordon with the Gordon Ward of high school who had seemed so big and crude. The two boys simply would not come together in her mind. It reminded her of the depth finder in her camera with its two images, one gold and the other plain. They were supposed to slide together to make one image, but her memory would not do that to the bright boy who held her. This Gordon, who was slenderer than the other one, hadn't the cruel laugh and swagger she remembered.

The song was "Sweet Eloise," the last of a set of old fox trots, so when it was over they found a table near the band and sat down. The players knew Gordon, or remembered him, and they smiled and nodded as they put their instruments down by their chairs.

She knew David was worried about her going out with Gordon, but she found herself smiling with pleasure at this thought. David had even been worried about Wayne, who had never seriously kissed her. Wayne would always have to be acting. He would bow, saying some ironic thing, and kiss her hand or her forehead. When Gordon first kissed her he knew enough to just plain take her in his arms and do it, without any joking or asking for permission or any words at all. He was very hard and strong, but very gentle in his strength. She had the sense of that restraint, of

the strong man being so gentle with her. When he held her with that powerful but gentle intent she thought she must be in love with him.

But then she would look, as she did now, at his large freckled hand sporting his class ring, the biggest model obtainable, and a sort of dull, unwelcome warning sounded. Something was wrong. And something was wrong with his watchband—a series of gold S-shaped bars that flexed and glittered. Why did these little things strike her that way? She remembered feeling the same guilt about her evidence when she looked at Wayne's hickish clothes. Gordon wasn't hickish, he was deliberately Ivy League, but was that watchband some kind of miscalculation, or what? Was it too right, or just a little wrong? In any case, Gordon looked like money and he knew he looked like money. He'd told her once that a headwaiter always looked at your shoes, and could always tell. One time they'd decided to eat at the Inn in Northlee, a rather formal place, when they'd been driving back from Vermont and were wearing sports clothes. When Gordon had asked the hostess if they were dressed too informally, a man at the reception desk had turned to another and said in their hearing, "A forty-dollar sweater and he's worried?" This pleased Gordon; he seemed pleased that people could look at your clothes and know exactly what they cost.

Were the people here appraising them in this fashion? As she looked around to see who was here, the always slightly embarrassing thing occurred; faces caught looking at her and Gordon turned slightly, eyes changed their focus slightly. There was Lois Potter, pretty dark hair and alabaster skin, and that also Ivy League boy must be her fiancé from Brown. With them were Foster and Jean Greenwood, who looked strange whenever they danced because he was so tall and she was so short. It looked just a little possible that Jean was pregnant again. John Cotter was there with, of all people, Minetta Randolf. He was a quiet, silent boy and she was as sexy-looking as Carol Oakes, only sultrier. There were a lot of couples in their early thirties, and they were the ones who were a little drunk and noisy. Some of the men had red faces and ears. She knew very few of the names of the couples in that group.

Their drinks came—a gin rickey for Gordon and a Coke for her. The waiter, probably a college boy, seemed to be a great

admirer of Gordon's. She didn't know who he was, but Gordon called him "Skink," and Skink seemed joyful at that recognition.

Mr. and Mrs. Ward came over to say hello, Gordon rising with a mock-gallant flourish to ease his mother's chair. The tall old couple were all decked out and glittering. They were both more vivid than life, with whiter hair, bigger jewels and sparklier teeth than anyone their age ought to have.

"We won't bother you youngsters for more than a minute!" Mr. Ward said. Another waiter brought their drinks from their table.

"How are you, my dear?" Mrs. Ward said. "My, you make such a striking couple. Everybody looked up when you came in!" She'd had a few drinks, evidently, because her voice was a little slurry and a little more honest in its intonations than it was when she was totally sober. She affected what David called "the East Coast upper-class accent," but all her affectations were harmless because she was a character, not a real force. Kate liked her.

She leaned toward Kate conspiratorially, her veined waxy hand glowing beneath its jewels, and said, "Like father, like son. Aren't my men *dashing?*" Gordon and his father were laughing at something, and Mrs. Ward looked at them proudly.

There was a sort of charm to that life. Kate could feel it, expensive and dashing, possessed of the richest and best of things. How gray and fussy Wayne's round of life seemed compared to the Wards'. She thought of them as walking upon their green manicured lawns, or riding in great silent cars, always having a kind of holiday.

She and Gordon danced, and the Wards went back to their friends. At the next intermission they went out to the car, where she had a real drink, a gin and collins Gordon skillfully prepared from his leather-covered portable bar. The night was warm and starry, so Gordon put down the top of the car. The sweet smell of mown grass, damp from the night sprinklers they heard busily hissing, wafted across the golf course.

After that drink of gin she seemed to dance more lightly, perhaps a little abandonedly. Gordon was always there, turning and coming back to her, pleased by her lightness. Later they went out to the car again, a tune following them across the lawn. "Falling in love with love" came smoothly from among the happy

noises inside the Country Club. The Japanese lanterns along the verandas glowed inside themselves, not casting any light at all.

"You happy, Kate?" Gordon asked. She had been humming the song.

"Yes, I guess I am," she said.

"I'm serious about you," he said.

The moon had come up, lighting the strong angles of his face, so that he seemed very noble and important. He turned and kissed her, steadily but uninsistently. When he drew his lips away she wasn't ready for that departure—it was almost like loss.

"Let's go for a drive," Gordon said. "It's such a warm night. Top down. How about it?"

As they drove she leaned her head back and watched the trees swing by overhead, dipping their great dignified branches as if in salute, as if the smoothly running car were a sort of throne, or sedan, passing down wide dark aisles. She hadn't noticed where they were going, or even that they had climbed a hill, when they stopped in front of her house.

"What?" she said, recognizing the towering house with surprise.

"I've got an idea," Gordon said. "Go get your bathing suit and we'll go for a swim. What do you say?"

"Where?"

"At our cabin, where else?"

"My goodness. What time is it?"

"Ten-thirty. It's early. Come on, Katie, it'll cool us off. Then I'll light a fire in the fireplace and warm us up again."

"I don't know." She wondered how she could tell him what her worry was. She wanted to be with him, but she was a little— just too tantalizingly little—afraid of him.

"You can trust me," he said, laughing. "Anyway, Mother and Dad'll be there at midnight, and I'll bring you home. Safe as hell! Even I can be trusted for an hour and a half!"

"All right," she said, thinking that it was peculiar but that she wanted to run her fingers over his wound, over the livid burn that smeared his freckled arm.

The Wards' cabin was on the sandy side of the lake. The cabin itself was less like a camp than a year-round house, with finished and polished furniture, a large brick fireplace and a

441

chromed and enameled modern kitchen. She changed, into her yellow one-piece suit, in Gordon's parents' bedroom, leaving her clothes on one of the twin beds.

When she came out, Gordon had already changed and was lighting the fire. When the papers flamed, his wiry hair turned red as the fire, and his chest glowed warmly. He was all live skin and curls.

He rose and turned toward her. "We'll have one for courage. Then, sploosh! Last one in's a rotten egg!" He opened a knotty-pine cabinet, revealing all kinds of bottles—short, tall, amber, green, even red and yellow ones. "I'm going to make you a special potion," he said, rubbing his hands like a movie villain. "It's small, and green, ha! ha! It will make you my slave, Kate Whipple!"

His green eyes did glitter with almost evil intent, and she shivered as she laughed.

"You may laugh, me proud beauty," he said. Then his voice changed and he came to her and took hold of her arms. "Katie, I'm absolutely serious now. I want to marry you. I love you, God damn it, and I want to marry you."

The man offered himself to her, totally, for all time, altogether. The generosity of this offer stunned her. She couldn't speak, but she found her hand sliding up the marble-smooth scar tissue on his arm. God! What had she been thinking? She knew too much, she saw too much. That contract had to be perfect, without any reservations at all. The world, something else, must still be out there for her. "Gordon," she said.

"Now, now, Katie, I know. Bad taste to spring such a proposition on you without warning, right?"

She nodded, and he said, "However, the offer stands, pending notification by the party of the first part of intent to cancel. You understand? Serious. Thought out. Even discussed with parents. I've got it so bad I look at building lots."

She couldn't think of anything to say, so she squeezed his hand. They went down to the beach, subdued and silent. The sand was cooler than the water. They eased into the black water, and she felt the motion and the pressure of the man swimming beside her, easily pushing through the warmth. They swam slowly out into the lake, where it was all water and chilly moon-

442

light. He rolled slowly, like a seal, and they swam back toward the lights of the cabin. When she could touch bottom he touched her, and she came against his cool slippery skin.

"I forgot all about the potion," he said. "I should have given you the potion first. But when you fall in love your timing gets all screwed up."

They stood in front of the fire in their bathing suits while they drank the potion, which was something with green crème de menthe in it, and then changed back into their clothes. When she came back, Gordon had moved the leather sofa up in front of the fire. His white shirt gleamed. "Here's your second portion of potion," he said, handing her the tall glass.

They sat in front of the fire. She asked him what time it was and he told her eleven-thirty. She knew he wanted to put his arms around her, and she wanted him to, but there was that sobering question. It was all too serious now, too meaningful. She had to trust him because he had declared himself. For seconds at a time she eased slowly into considering it, really considering marrying Gordon and having it all over with. All the messing around and the dating and the embarrassed glances would end, because she would be an entity not herself. She would be Mrs. Gordon Ward, who would know who she was and what she was for. She would be for this man to love, to make real love to and to have his babies. How soft and simple that would be.

No.

After a while he took her glass and put it on the floor. Such a firm, authoritative thing it was, his strong arm coming around her. She let go, wondering, melting with pleasure, yet still wondering. Soon his parents would be home, wouldn't they? Her lips made a noise like silk against the sand of his face. She was conscious of their receiving softness. They were lying next to each other; she had moved lightly as though obeying thoughts, without thinking, and let him use her own body to place them here. How had he done that so beautifully? A warning, a tick of warning. He was too good, but how could a man be too good? His hand held itself firm upon her ribs, and she didn't want him to and wanted him to move his hand up over her breasts so badly it seemed unfair that he didn't right now gently caress her breasts. The hand wouldn't move. Warning, warning, she heard.

443

Look out. She was all slow honey. One step more and she would dissolve into rapture, be impaled by rapture.

How could it remain and grow, the fresh desire for more and more of him, for more and more of his weight? Now she would let him touch her breasts; the moment she decided that, his hand moved over her breasts toward the very edge of reason. Beware, a small voice—her own from far away, a long time ago— spoke thinly. You don't know what he can do, what he will do. His lips and hands half covered her. Again and again she received his touch without satiation. How strangely slow it was, how the great movements of heat gathered and washed her, and the clean cold Kate let herself be gathered again into heat.

Hadn't hours passed? How many thousand times had they kissed? Their teeth touched—then, familiar yet always burning, their tongues. He loved her, and his moan broke her—that she caused that pain. Who was this force that grew, that before had only been a boy? His hands were everywhere—border violations, childish business, hot on the forbidden skin of her breasts, the soft brittle nipples. In a wave's trough she was afloat in a sultry tropical night. She had been prepared, made royal, and awaited the young god who had chosen her from all the virgins of the world. Bathed and delicately scented, she had been placed among ferns on the golden shore. The galleys had sailed away, heaving in the green sea, and she trembled and yearned for his power. Then he appeared, golden and gloriously naked before her, trim of body and shining with his dangerous power. He smiled, and his eyes were kind yet full of dark intent. Pain like a blue spark, a flash, and the saddle of the man was all against her. She was impaled. He was the beloved lovely rack that softly broke her, over and over.

30

David spent the night in Leah, in his old room with the cobwebby De Oestris moose sternly watching over him. He woke at dawn, feeling a strange mixture of pleasure and dread, and it was a few moments before he remembered that he had to take Tom to the vet's. It was a thing he had to do, and the pleasure came from that clear task; it would end in the most certain and final way. Tom would be out of his misery, an era would be ended, Tom would be no more. The dread came from that finality too.

He came downstairs before anyone else was up, and knelt by Tom's washtub. The old gray tiger stirred, looked up with his slit yellow eyes and gave a short rasp of a purr. If a cat could be said to have favorites, David had been that one. When Tom was younger he used to run in front of David and throw himself down with a thud upon his back, wanting his chin and belly scratched. He loved to box then too, and though in his play he sometimes bit hard enough to pinch and hurt, he never unsheathed a single one of his bodkins.

"Thomas," David said uncertainly. "Old friend, old fellow murderer, I bring sad tidings."

An evil stench came from the box of sand they had, since his sickness, kept in a corner of the kitchen. Though it caused Tom considerable pain to climb out of his bed and go to the box—pain signified by a muted, furry snarl that had given David a dull pain in his own lower regions—Tom wouldn't foul his bed. David went to shovel out the half-buried bloody stool and then remembered that they would need the box no more—the washtub could soon go to the cellar or the shed. He felt that loss. Tom had

445

been with them on and off for nearly ten years—nearly half of David's life.

Outside it was a gray day with mist on the leaves and grass, although the trunks of the maples were dry. He thought of breakfast and decided he wouldn't make himself any. He didn't like the vet or the vet's snitty wife, who had a gushing, patronizing manner toward animals that immediately sent their temperatures up. When they'd first noticed, in June, that Tom had something wrong, they took him to the vet's and Tom had become absolutely hysterical. He had screamed, arched and turned all into prongs like an animated gray cactus. David had several observable scars left from that visit. Now he had to pay that vet to kill Tom.

Another possibility occurred to him, and for a moment took his breath. He had dealt death competently enough; he had the proper tools. Should he hire out this murder? Tom was his old friend, not the vet's or the vet's wife's with all her flashing dim bicuspids. Shouldn't this quietus have some dignity about it, he and Tom alone in the woods, Tom trusting and calm even past the final clap of darkness? Suddenly he knew the place, a cathedral-like room of tall pines just above the old sugarhouse. Light filtered down green upon the soft pine needles. There was an old spade at the sugarhouse, and he would dig Tom's grave deep beneath the needles, just north of the largest white pine. The old cat could sleep there in peace.

This way (he still only considered it) Tom wouldn't have to ride in the truck—another thing that always brought out his cat apprehension. In a car he lay his ears back and watched for the first possible escape hatch.

There were all sorts of good reasons leading toward that last aim and squeeze. The barrel at the back of the head. Half a breath, and the slow squeeze.

Tom's neck trembled, and his neat little cat smile disappeared into a great yawn full of teeth, pink pallet and the curled tongue. Dry clicks came from his stretched jaws, then his head closed back down into the demure smile. "Urr," he said, and neatly licked the roots of his white whiskers. He didn't stretch because stretching gave him too much pain. The fur at the base of his tail was matted and stringy, like wet feathers. He began to

get up, then froze and gave a sudden stare and a low, warning yowl toward his hindquarters.

"All right," David said. "All right." He would no longer patronize the cat by speaking to him. He went up to his room by the back way and got his duck-hunting jacket and his Iver Johnson revolver. Six commercially loaded .32 S & W Longs were in the cylinder, but he would need to use only one.

Now wait, he thought. What was he doing? Why had he chosen the revolver rather than the shotgun, which was surer medicine? Did he want to use the revolver because he wanted to feel in his hand that quick push of death? No, he chose the revolver because he could hide it in his jacket pocket and no one would know what he was going to do. Anyway, the S & W .32 Long cartridge, with its 98-grain bullet, was more than adequate to smash the skull of a cat. Who was he arguing with? Wasn't it better to bloody your own hands and take your medicine than to hire it done?

He went back to the kitchen and watched Tom's stiff progress toward his food dish. Tom smelled the canned cat food once and then stood over it, looking at it as though wondering why he didn't want to eat it. The grainy food smelled like sardines and it had always been Tom's favorite. He turned toward David, who could have sworn the look was a question. Tom came back to his washtub; David gingerly lifted him into it and pulled a flap of burlap over him like a blanket.

"All right," David said out loud. With a feeling of at least some relief he took the washtub in his arms and left by the kitchen door, carefully opening and closing the door and screen door with hands he couldn't see. On the way up the shortcut through the woods, Tom's face swayed close to his, Tom's yellow eyes half closed. He seemed unworried by this strange journey. Didn't he know what was going to happen? He must think it strange to be carried through the woods. But animals had those they trusted as well as those they didn't trust.

The path had grown up in the last few years, in brush and poplar and gray birch saplings. Occasionally a long red blackberry stalk leaned toward him and scratched its thorns along the washtub. One caught his hand and drew across his fingers. He knew that it made him bleed, but he didn't stop to look; he didn't

want to tamper with Tom's strange calmness. A big maple branch, split from its trunk and full of dirt, had fallen across the path, and a small balsam grew from its rich center.

He decided that he would not hesitate, just put Tom down, aim and shoot. There should be no ceremony, no words, nothing but the quick and efficient deed. He might even admit to the family, if they asked, that he had done it himself. He could hear himself explaining: "Tom was my friend—it seemed the honorable thing to do. And you know how he hated the vet's."

The sugarhouse still stood, but it seemed much lower, as though the ground were rising up around it—which the ground was, he supposed. Green moss grew on its doorstep, and the rusted spade leaned against the door as if to hold it shut. With some difficulty he took the spade along with him. The tub grew heavier as he climbed into the deep woods. When he came to the place he remembered, he put the washtub on the silent needles. One side of the chamber formed by the pines was a cragged wall of ledge. The light here had a dim, interior look, as though it were allowed to enter only by design, by spaced windows high above.

Moist air, even a wafting of mist, slowly crossed. His legs were wet from the droplets on the brush he had come through. Tom turned his head, then nodded again, and David decided not to remove him from the tub. He would bury him in it. The last thing he did right was to hold the silver revolver behind him to cock it. Three cold clicks as the hammer rose and the cylinder turned and locked. He brought the gun forward and down. He aimed at the gray skull, between the delicately cocked ears, his heart thudded and he fired.

Instantly Tom was out of the tub, all wire and springs, cocked on his spread legs. He stared at David with total knowledge. His scalp was ripped like a tear in a carpet, and one ear hung on that flap. His eyes shone, wide and bright. He looked once, then was gone out of there.

David was in shock. Tom's monstrous act of escape, that judgment so accurate and instantaneous—was all the truth at once. He almost cried to Tom to stop, to be dead. His knees gave way and he went down into the needles. The bullet had keyholed the side of the washtub; that jagged hole seemed to grow. He

crawled for a moment, then got his weak legs under him and staggered across the opening toward the thicket of basswood and witch hobble where the cat had disappeared. His eyes hurt him, as though they burned like searchlights. That gray opinion, that half-life, was somewhere, betrayer and betrayed. He crashed into the thicket, his revolver cocked. He had five shots left.

When Wood hadn't come downstairs by ten o'clock, Peggy began to feel dread. She had walked up High Street at eight, in the misty light, wanting to see the turrets of the old castle at that hour. Henrietta, Harvey, Kate and Horace were just finishing breakfast, so she had a cup of coffee with them. Horace, who looked exhausted, went upstairs as soon as he finished. She and Kate sat talking at the round table in the gray light that was barely bright enough to do without the electric ones. Kate drank coffee like mad, but after three cups Peggy's hands were trembling. They talked about school, and she hadn't realized how unhappy Kate was about going back.

"But I don't necessarily want to be in Leah, either," Kate said, shrugging her shoulders. Unhappy or not, Kate glowed in the cool light. She was still the most beautiful girl Peggy had ever seen, anywhere, even in pictures.

"Doesn't Wood eat breakfast?" she said.

"Usually he does," Kate said. "He's usually up by now, anyway." Kate watched her, and suddenly said, "Why are you looking at me like that?"

"I'm sorry. Was I staring or something?"

"It reminded me of high school," Kate said. "I'm sorry I startled you, Peggy."

"I know you're not happy," Peggy said. She reached out and touched Kate's slim hand; Kate's other hand came over hers, and Kate smiled gratefully, her smile so much like the sun. When they were younger Kate had been her teacher. She'd told Peggy what to read, how to dress, how to straighten a hemline, how to fix a bra strap in an emergency. They had seldom talked of secret things, and always Peggy felt that beautiful Kate was touched by some kind of doom. It shone upon her like a sad summer light. Peggy was the one with the hard common sense.

449

"I'll tell you how screwed up I am," Kate said. "Gordon wants me to marry him and I almost said yes. It seemed like such a *relief*. I mean to get married and get it all over with."

"Oh, Kate!"

"Well, you can talk about marrying for love and all that!" Kate said angrily. "Sometimes I wish I could just drop dead and make a 'beautiful' corpse."

"No you don't!" Peggy said. She held up her hands, they were trembling so much. It was the coffee, and Kate's unhappiness, and Wood—where was he?

Kate startled her in the middle of that thought. "I know how you feel about Wood. You love him! You shine all over with it!"

Peggy's skin grew warm.

"You turned all dark," Kate said.

"I'm going up and see if he's there."

"Why, he's there, Peggy." Kate looked worried now, and with this recognition of her own dread Peggy jumped up.

"Oh!" she said, trying to get a breath. "Oh! Why am I so worried? What's the matter?"

"Go up and see. Go on, Peggy. Don't keep worrying about it."

"All right. It's silly, but all of a sudden I'm so scared. Come with me."

"All right," Kate said. They took the back stairs, up the narrow stairs past Peggy's old room in the servants' quarters. She went first and Kate followed. Peggy was almost running. They hurried down the hall, out of the servants' quarters into the bigger hall, and came to Wood's door. She stopped, feeling silly. But her dread was there still. She knocked, and they waited, both trembling. The tall heavy door was Wood's, the big brass knob should turn only at his will. There was no answer. Peggy knocked again, harder.

"Wood?" she said in a tiny, constricted voice. Then, "Wood?" They listened. A clogged, grunting sound came from inside, but that was all. "Wood!" Peggy called. They listened, unbelieving, to that strange sound, and finally Peggy took the cool knob and opened the door. She looked into the room, which all at once was a huge dark box. There was the bed, the desk, the shades pulled

over the windows. The bed—she searched the room as though feeling with her hands in a closet. In the middle of the room the grunting came again, from Wood where he lay on his bed. He seemed incomplete, out of focus. Kate ran past her and opened the shades. Wood had no eye on one side, and his face and hands were a dull rose color, as even and smooth as if he had been painted.

"What's the matter with him?" Kate cried. He breathed too slowly, with that wet sound. Kate ran out, calling for David and her mother.

Wood seemed to be strangling on his own breath, so Peggy got her arm under his broad back and hauled him up into a sitting position. His head fell over her shoulder. She knew what was wrong with him; she saw the empty pillbox, the whiskey bottle. Last semester a girl in her dorm had been found like this. The girl had taken twenty-five sleeping pills and later called the dean so they could discover her and pump out her stomach before it was too late.

"Kate!" she yelled. She shook Wood, trying to wake him up, and miraculously he did partly wake up. His eye opened, nearly all black pupil, and he coughed before going limp again. "Kate!" she yelled again, and both Kate and Henrietta came running in.

"It's pills!" she said to them. "Tell Dr. Winston what it is!" She gave them the box. "Read him what it says!" Henrietta came to Wood, and though Kate was crying she took the box. At the door she stopped and cried, "I can't! I can't!"

"Here! Hold him up and shake him! Slap him!" Peggy made them both hold Wood up, and went down to the telephone herself.

She was surprised that she remembered Dr. Winston's number, and surprised at the calmness of her voice. Thank God, he was there. "It's Wood Whipple. He's taken sleeping pills. Veronal, it says on the box—from the Veterans' Hospital."

"He's home?"

"Yes."

"How's his breathing?"

"Slow, and noisy."

"Will he wake up at all?"

"Yes, a little."

451

"All right." Dr. Winston's steady voice seemed to reflect her coolness. "Make him sit up. Keep him moving and try to keep him awake. I'll be right there."

Harvey had come out on his canes. "What in God's name?" he said. "Wood what?"

She left him with his mouth open and ran back upstairs to find Horace standing in the hall in pajamas. "What? What?" Horace said in a voice ragged from sleep.

"It's Wood," she said. "Come and help."

Harvey began to yell from the hall. "Somebody tell me what's going on! What's with Wood?"

Wood's head lolled from side to side as Kate and Henrietta pushed and pulled on him, that strange dearth place of an eye gleaming pink. Kate tried to slap his cheek, but couldn't. "Peggy!" she said desperately.

"Go get a basin of cold water and a washcloth," Peggy ordered. "Put ice cubes in it." Kate went to do this and she took Kate's place. "Horace," she said, "come help us get him up." She slapped Wood's face hard, and his eye opened. His whiskers had stung her hand.

"Yeah-yeah," he said, sighing sleepily as his eye slowly closed again.

"Is he going to be all right?" Henrietta asked. "Peggy? Peggy?"

"I think so," she said. "Here, Horace, get under his arm. Get his arm over your neck. Now lift him up."

Between them they pulled Wood from the bed, one pajama leg waving empty from above the knee. As they moved him to his desk chair the stump of his left leg banged the desk, giving Peggy such a massive twinge of sympathy pain she stumbled. Horace held them both up for a moment before they got Wood into the chair.

"Mmm-yeah," Wood mumbled.

"What the hell's going on?" Harvey demanded from the door. He was sweating and shaking from his climb up the stairs.

"He'll be all right," Peggy said, shaking Wood's head back and forth. She could feel the muscles of his neck tense to fight this motion.

"Hey," Wood said.

"That's better," she said. "Stay awake, Wood! You must stay awake!"

Harvey came into the room. The olive-colored box was crushed in his hand against his cane handle. He balanced himself and tossed the box on the desk. "So that's it," he said. "My God."

Henrietta was sitting on the bed, her head in her hands. "Why?" she asked. "I can't understand anything."

Wood began to slip out of the chair, but Horace, with a hoarse grunt, leapt back to him and pulled him up straight. "*Sit up!*" he yelled into Wood's ear. "*Sit up!*" His voice was so loud they all looked at him in surprise.

Kate came in, sloshing the ice water. "Here it is, Peggy! There was only one tray of ice cubes!"

Peggy took a handful of Wood's hair, held his head up and placed the icy cloth against his face. "What're you doing?" Wood said slowly, exhaustedly.

"See? See? He said something!" Kate said.

Peggy could feel the stronger and more deliberate force of Wood's neck muscles now, fighting against her constant manipulation of his head. She knew he would wake up. His breathing was quieter and a little faster. "Someone let Dr. Winston in, when he comes," she said. She held Wood's head in her hands, her fingers on his ears and in his hair, now on his strong jaws, feeling the smooth muscles underneath the bristly skin. She wanted to stop jerking him back and forth, to put his face against her breast. His hair was glossy and wet, all mussed and young-looking. While the washcloth soaked in the basin she risked one moment of tenderness and moved her fingers over the shiny skin where his eye had been.

When she had first entered the room and heard that sick rattle of breath it seemed as though her whole life with the Whipples had been a kind of dull green cone, a corridor of time she'd traveled slowly through to reach this dreadful apex, everything leading down smaller and more vivid to this rendezvous. The Whipples sat and stood around her now, watching her authority with some awe in spite of their apprehension. Death had touched all their faces and made them gray.

No one had to let Dr. Winston in. He was already there, a tall, stooped man in his fifties who always spoke calmly and

always seemed in memory to be moving forward; they had all seen his gaunt face loom toward their beds as he raised his black gladstone bag toward a table or a chair. "Ah," he said, looking at the crushed green box. Peggy saw him notice the whiskey bottle beneath the bed, next to the straps and hinges of the artificial leg. He looked then at Wood, tapped Wood's jaw sharply and nodded at the flash of consciousness it caused.

"Who was it called me?" he asked.

"I did," Peggy said.

He nodded, seeming pleased with her. He looked carefully at the others. "Horace, help me get him to the bathroom. Margaret Mudd, take my bag. The rest of you might as well stay out. We've got to wash him out inside and that won't be pleasant. Henrietta, you make some strong coffee."

"Is he going to be all right?" Henrietta asked.

"Why, yes, I think so, Henrietta. There might be a chance of pneumonia, but we can take care of that if the time comes. My guess is he took the Veronal quite a few hours back, you see. If it had a mind to kill him, it would have by now."

Henrietta shuddered as she drew a breath.

"Now, now, Henrietta," he said, "and Harvey. It very well could have been an accident. 'An accidental overdose,' we'll call it for the time being. You understand?"

Henrietta nodded, shaking her head at the same time. A small squeak of fear escaped her, and she cleared her throat to try to hide it.

At the foot of Wood's rumpled bed, Harvey leaned on his canes and stared at the doctor's face.

He was wet all through, and bled from a lacework of pricks and scratches across his hands and face. The water, coming from leaves and stalks, stung like acid. Now he crept over the top of a granite outcropping, just above the prickly brush that surrounded it. He had seen Tom twice in the last hour or so—a quick sliding of gray once; the other time what he'd taken for a piece of stone had been carefully watching him until it slid away. In desperation he'd even tried calling to Tom, as though the cat were so stupid he would come toward his betrayer and ask for death. In near-

hysteria he'd plunged after the cat, and a maple sapling just too big to swing out of the way had caught him like a club on the forehead, unhinging his knees. Soon after he slipped on a mossy ledge and fell on his knee. A hollow throb worked there, predicting later pain.

He could see down into the blackberries here. Their leaves were old and slightly shriveled, and the shiny berries were almost ripe. His eyes moved so quickly, in such a frenzy of search he felt their tired muscles pull. Where was the cat? Tom, his old friend—he must shut off that judging brain. Wasn't it a favor he was doing? Tom had made a terrible misinterpretation.

If he didn't calm himself he wouldn't be able to hit anything with the pistol. When he held it out in front of him, the narrow sights wavered so badly he could hardly find the front blade in the grooves. Deep breaths, he told himself. Now wait awhile and try to listen. The old pistol was inaccurate under the best conditions. There was a tick, and another down in the fuzz of stalks, beneath the gray-green leaves somewhere. He held his breath, feeling movement down there. Something crept, about ten feet away, just barely out of sight. He found a piece of gray next to what must have been an old stump with a white mushroom tray on its side, and tried to find an open corridor in the interstices of stalks and branches. He knew better than to shoot at hair; he should see the whole animal and know what he aimed at, what part he aimed at, but this was the first time he had a chance to shoot at all, so he held the pistol in both hands, steady against the moss, found the blade against that wisp of gray and fired.

A high yowl of pain and anger proved the gray to be alive. Screaming, Tom rolled out into clear sight. He fought his rear legs, clawing and biting so fiercely he seemed to be two cats at once. Then, as though he'd met a stronger cat and knew it, he tried to escape the force that hurt him. One haunch, pierced and broken, dragged at a splayed, impossible angle. Blood appeared upon the old leaves. When Tom stopped and tried again to fight whatever had him in its jaws, David fired into that gray tangle, knowing all the time he should have waited. He hurt Tom again; the yowl wavered and became lower, more intense, closer, as though it came from David's own head. The gray bundle con-

vulsed, appeared catlike and then became a ball of ragged blood and hair. David fired again, knowing immediately he'd missed, and again, knowing he'd missed by more than a foot. Did he have another unspent cartridge in the cylinder? It occurred to him that he might have shot Tom through his sick place, through the cancer, and with this horror he jumped and slid down the jagged ledge into the brush. A branch whipped his face and blinded him, then his eyes opened onto glittery tears and prisms. He hadn't stopped running and was afraid he'd gone past Tom, but there Tom was, trying to get enough of his legs under him to run away, to drag himself away from David. He cast a yellow glance over his shoulder, knowing from whom he tried to escape. David reached as close as he could, as he dared, and fired into Tom's body, hurting him badly. A loop of putty-colored intestine picked up dirt and shreds of matter from the ground. The next shot was a heartless empty click, and David fought through the branches, fell to one knee and was forced back by their combined resilient push before he got through to stamp Tom's head into the punky dirt. He stamped and heel-pounded the head until it was dirty and shapeless. The torn skin slipped off the eyes and jaws. Some time later the cat was dead.

Dull-witted and sick, he staggered back down through the woods toward the house. His face and hands stung, laced as they were with thorn scratches and punctures. Pale reddish water and seeds were on his palms. His wet pants clung heavily, and he fell over a branch he could easily have avoided. He lay with his face in the rotten leaves, feeling the sticky, sickish water on his thighs. He might as well stay here for a while, one foot hung over the branch that tripped him, shin in pain—the disorganized posture of a corpse. Tom's body had been splayed thus, horribly out of character for a cat, filthy, ragged and unnatural.

Let the grubs and newts crawl up his nose and out his ears. The hell with it. The cellar odor of rotting leaves was deep, buried, but contained the peppery bite of toadstool. Fragrant rot. For one thing, he would make a vow: never again consider David Abbott Whipple of adequate talent in the matter of death. Certain decisions simply are not David Abbott Whipple's to make. Let him flit charmingly among the women, saying clever things and dipping his little wick in the honey, but let him eschew death.

Eschew it. *Gesundheit. Ave atque vale.* He would never consider that subject again.

He lay there until he grew cold, past shivering. Something walked six- or eight-legged over the back of his neck, and when he moved to brush it off he became aware that he was hungry. He got up, the oil in his joints gummy with cold. His knee throbbed as he trudged out of the woods.

No one was in the kitchen, so he sneaked up the back stairs and made it to his room without being seen. He put his revolver on his desk; why hadn't he considered burying it with the cat? Was his oath a lie, then? The fact was, he wanted the revolver. He still wanted that instrument of murder. He would let it lie there in its own darkness, to be considered later.

He toweled himself off with a dirty shirt and had just changed into dry pants when Kate opened his door without knocking and came running in. "Davy!" she said. "Where have you been all this time?"

Murdering, he thought, then saw that she had been crying. She came up as if to touch him, then shied back. He put on a clean shirt, and she began to cry. "Wood," she said in a weak, hilly voice. She was all shiny and disorganized; something odd had happened to the symmetry of her face.

"What? Wood what?" he said, badly frightened now.

"He tried . . . tried to commit suicide."

"Tried to?"

"With pills but they didn't work, and Peggy got worried so we went up and found him. Dr. Winston came, and oh, goodness, Davy! Everything's gone wrong!"

"Is Wood all right now?"

"He's all jittery because of the hypodermic and black coffee and all that." She cried and hiccuped into her hands. She seemed to be blind with her tears, so he led her to his easy chair and pushed her down into it. Finally she got hold of herself and could speak. "Give me a Kleenex or something."

He gave her a clean handkerchief and she wiped her face. "I knew you were here because your truck was here, Davy."

"How is he now? Is he home?"

"He's in his room. He has to sit up, because of his lungs or

something. Peggy's taking care of him. Davy, when we found him he was all pink! My God!"

"Should I go see him?" David said.

"What good is anything if he wants to die?"

"I guess I'd better go see him."

"You don't have to now, Davy. You can wait until he's better. He's really shaking now. It hurts to look at him."

"Okay, I'll wait awhile," he said with shame and relief. He tried to imagine Wood wanting to die, choosing to die. Wood! They all knew he was unhappy. There were the conventional explanations about returning combat veterans and all that, but they didn't seem to apply. His disfigurements? No, that couldn't be it, not with Wood. But you never knew what got to people. He wished, suddenly, with a real force that surprised him, that he and Wood could divide those wounds. He'd take either the leg or the eye, whichever bothered Wood the most. Yes, he would, right now. His eyes grew moist, but at what part of that thought? His love and sorrow for his brother, or his own nobility? Both? Every emotion he ever had was just slightly infected.

"How's mother taking it?" he said.

"Quietly. She sort of chirped and then she was quiet."

"Dad?"

"I don't know. He came upstairs on his canes and now he's back downstairs. Horace helped carry Wood around, but Peggy really took charge of the whole thing until Dr. Winston got here."

"She would," he said. "I can see that."

"I don't think he even sees her," Kate said.

"Sees her?"

"I mean she loves him so much."

"What's bothering him, anyway? Have you got any idea, Katie? Is it his leg and eye? I can't understand it if it's that."

"I don't know. He's so unhappy. Nobody knows. Even Dad asked me if I knew." She looked at him as though her eyes had focused for the first time since she'd entered the room. "Davy? What are all those scratches all over your face?"

He thought, perhaps too long. "I was hunting and I got caught in a blackberry patch."

"Oh," she said. "Hunting."

"I better go see him, Katie. You know I have to."

"Yes." She lay back in the chair, looking exhausted and small. She wore her faded dungarees and an old blue dress shirt he'd given her at the beginning of the summer. Her pretty arms, coming out of the rolled sleeves of his old shirt, showed how slender she really was, compared to him.

"Hey, kid," he said. "I bet we'll get all this straightened out."

She stared up toward the moose, but not as though she saw it. "Davy, I thought you were going to show up at the dance last night."

"I couldn't find a clean shirt. They're all out at the cabin."

"Oh."

"Did you have a good time?"

She looked at him, frowning unhappily. "I don't know. Davy, come back and talk to me, will you? After you see Wood? Can I stay here and wait for you?"

"Of course you can," he said, but he thought: Oh, God, what did that shit do to her? He felt sick and responsible. In a way, he didn't want to hear, just as in one way he didn't want to have to see Wood.

He left her in his room and went to the bathroom to see how scratched up he really was. He washed off a few crusty lines of dried blood, but he'd still have explanations (lies) to make if anyone looked at him closely. Then he remembered that he hadn't taken Tom's sandbox out. He must get rid of any evidence that there had ever been a cat. Yes, quickly. He went down the back stairs to the kitchen, took the stinking box in his arms, lugged it out across the driveway and dumped the sand in the underbrush. The box he stamped flat and jammed into one of the trash cans. There.

But his mother was waiting for him in the kitchen, looking as though she knew something. "David, you've got to help us," she said.

He was relieved, first, then a little frightened and wary. He thought of saying, "*I don't live here, you know. Just visiting, sort of.*"

"It's about Wood. Your father and I can't . . ."

She was so upset. Her magnified eyes swiveled back and forth in her lenses.

"I know," he said. "I'm going to see him now."

"See your father too, Davy. Oh!"

"Don't cry, now, Hank," he said. "You just wait and see if we don't get this all straightened out." Liar, coward. He patted her shoulder, an easy gesture, and went through the dining room. Strange, knowing what he knew, that he yearned to have his father tell him what to do about Wood.

His father sat at his oak table, pale and overweight, a glaze of sweat on his forehead. He seemed at first to be reading the newspaper that lay on the table before him, but David saw that his eyes were distant and still.

"Dave," he said. His eyes had flicked over and gone back. "God knows you must be closer to him than I ever was. What's eating him?" When he turned his head he looked old. His hair was sparse, darker and thinner than David had ever noticed before. His eyes were gummy in the whites, with brownish striations radiating out of the irises, as though the irises were slowly melting with age. When David looked away he saw in his mind a different picture of his father—in fact two different pictures, one fatter but more fierce and powerful, one a younger man startlingly like himself. It was the first time he'd ever considered himself to be what his father once was, and the cold hand of age and death brushed over them both.

"I don't know, unless it's his leg and all that."

"But Christ, don't you think I know what it's like to be a cripple? Whipple the Cripple. For God knows how many years I was in pain all the time and I never tried to scrag myself!"

"Maybe it's something else," David said.

"Jesus. Don't you kids think we ever loved you?"

"Yes, I guess so," David said. His father seemed a little gross in his looseness of skin and emotion. Long curly hairs grew out of his nose.

"Of course we did!" his father said. "There was always a lot of yelling and screaming around our house, but when the chips were down, you goddam well knew your mother and I loved you!"

Was his father talking to Wood? "Maybe that isn't it either," David said.

"What? Well, what is it? Why? Was it Lois Potter giving him the old heave-ho?"

"I think he more or less gave her the old heave-ho," David said, regretting his repetition of those words.

"What? He did?" His father looked at him with real curiosity. "Lois Potter? Why, she's so pretty she'd give asthma to a brass monkey. You mean to say he broke it off?"

"That's what I think. She cried on my shoulder about it, anyway. Once she got over the shock of the leg and eye, she wanted him back. I think she was telling the truth about it. Maybe she just felt guilty, I don't know." That had been a strange session, because at the same time he had been feeling genuinely sorry for Lois and patting her on the back, a sweet push of desire had come over him and he sneezed on her neck.

"I can't figure anything," his father said.

"Me either."

"Try to find out, Dave, will you? Christ, sometimes I don't think I have the right to feel so bad about it, I'm such a selfish son of a bitch. But I love that boy!" His father's voice broke and he turned his head directly away from David—an awkward, strained position. It was all wrong. There must still be power in this thronelike center of the great hall. When he thought of home, no matter where he was, it was first the man sitting tensely here, powerful and exciting, and then the other rooms and towers, all held together by the father at his broad oak table. He could laugh at him, and sometimes even half despise him, but the power had always been there.

"All right," he said. Not wanting to look at his father any longer, he turned to go.

"Oh, Dave," his father said.

"Yes?" His father's tone meant a change of subject.

"I meant to tell you about Ben Caswell."

"What?"

His father turned the *Free Press* around on the table so he could see the short notice. After five years in a coma, Benjamin R. Caswell, twenty-one, had died of pneumonia.

"I guess it was a good thing," his father said. "Their medical expenses must have been out of sight."

"Good thing?" David said. He felt numb, really. He hadn't thought—not a trace of a thought—of Ben for a long time. It was as if the dead friend had risen from the grave for a last look into

461

his concern before passing away. It had happened, Ben's accident, so long ago. So many things had happened since, things that Ben had never heard about.

"About Wood, Dave. We'll get this straightened out," his father said.

Those words haunted David up the stairs.

31

Kate sat in David's big chair, waiting for him to come back. She smoked two of his cigarettes, trembling and then not trembling. For minutes at a time she thought neither of Wood nor of Gordon, but then she would have to come back to right now. She squirmed in sudden ghost pain, feeling things swimming inside her, where she was unprotected.

Last night when she'd come to her senses it was like coming up out of deep water, like a diver coming slowly back to the pressures and rules of another atmosphere. She was appalled at what she'd let him do. She hadn't remembered opening her legs. She'd cried for shame. But even now, horrified as she was, she remembered that delicious melting. She moved, half in shame and half in luxury. Then shame bleared the room.

All Gordon had seemed to feel afterwards was a good-humored sort of pleasure. He even tried to kid her about it, saying how she'd have to marry him. "You're used goods now, Kate," he'd said. Then, quickly, he was tender. "Did I hurt you? I felt that little ring."

"No," she'd said coldly. She'd contemplated her new situation. She had been sexually used. Virginity did not seem a funny idea at all. How callous were the jokes she had once laughed at! While she lay there, confronting the enormity of what had hap-

pened to her, he took off the rest of his clothes. Of course it was a lie about his parents coming. In the firelight she saw his enormous penis shining. Then she was angry, nearly hysterical, and made him take her home.

He didn't speak until they stopped in the Whipples' driveway, then formally said again that he wanted to marry her, that he damned well would marry her, that he deliberately hadn't "used" anything because he wouldn't mind at all if he made her pregnant. He seemed so pleased at how he'd managed everything. She left him without answering and ran to the house.

And now, as if to show her how one didn't lightly play with life, Wood had tried to kill himself. Everything was too serious and deadly. She could hardly get a breath. When David came back she ran to him and held onto him. "David, I'm so unhappy! I don't know what to do!"

"Hey, Katie," he said. His arms surrounded her, holding her steady, her nose pressed against his musty old shirt. "Hey, hey, Kate, now. What's the matter?"

She bawled against his chest, the noises coming out of her chest with pain, as though they were chunks of things. He patted her and patted her, crooning comforting sounds into her ear. Finally she could stop crying. She didn't want to let him go, but she had to blow her drippy nose. She didn't know how to tell him what she had to tell him.

"Is it Wood?" he said.

"Yes, but other things too, Davy. I feel so selfish! I should shut up." She saw how worried he was. "How's Wood?" she managed to ask.

"Well, Peggy's taken over, I guess. But Katie—"

"How does he look, Davy?"

"He looks at Peggy—like he's looking at a ghost." David took hold of her at arm's length and stared at her. "What else is it, Katie?"

"I don't know if I can tell you!" She was trembling so much he shook her a little as if to jar her out of it. "Davy, everything's mixed up. I feel like I'm being electrocuted or something."

"Gordon Ward," he said. His face grew cold, lumpy along his jaws.

"Yes, Davy, but—"

"What did the son of a bitch do to you?"

"I've got to tell somebody, Davy, and there isn't anybody but you."

"Okay," he said, obviously trying to be calm. "Sit down and I'll try not to act like your big brother." Gently he sat her down in his easy chair again. He sat at his desk and gave her a cigarette. "I'm sorry, Katie. I've had a bad day too. Like a goddam nightmare. But we can talk, can't we?"

"Yes, Davy," she said gratefully.

"We could always talk, couldn't we?" he said.

They were silent for a while.

"He asked me to marry him, for one thing," she said finally.

"Katie, he's charming and all that, when he wants to be."

"Don't I know it."

"But he's a shit."

"I guess so."

"Did he . . . ?"

"Yes." It seemed too important a thing to answer yes or no to, but there it was. You did it or you didn't do it, and she had let Gordon do it. "But it was a combination of things, Davy!" She had to explain to him why it was so much an accident, because of everything that led up to it.

"Okay, tell me if you want to, Katie," he said, and she knew she loved David and could trust him. She told him most of what had happened—the parts she could make words go around, with the words that were utterable in his presence.

"Are you sure he didn't use anything?" David said sternly. She felt that he was trying to salvage that part of the damaged goods that was salvageable.

"I'm not sure of anything, Davy. I mean it. I was out of my mind. I couldn't stop, you know? It felt so . . . like I was having a dream or something."

"Did he pull out? Did he withdraw?"

"God, Davy. I wouldn't know. I'm not even sure what that means. I'm sorry."

"He sure likes to get what he wants, doesn't he? The son of a bitch is thinking all the time. If it would do any good I'd maim him a little."

"I think I loved him, Davy. I thought about marrying him."

He got all excited. "For God's sake, don't even think about that! Don't even consider it! You could come to Chicago and we could take care of it. I mean it! By a real doctor too, no fly-by-night outfit."

"God," she said. She felt sick.

"You're too valuable to give to Gordon Ward. He doesn't even think the way you do, Katie. Listen to me! He's not like us—not like you, I mean. He's a different *species* or something from us. Just think of Wood and then think of him. Do you see what I mean? He's cold. He's like a fucking crocodile, Katie!"

Why, she thought, David has tears in his eyes. He has tears in his eyes, he means that so much.

"Oh, Davy, I love you," she said. "There isn't anybody in the world I love as much as you."

He took her hand. "Katie, this isn't the end of the world, you know. It was just the first time for you, and girls always have to be in love, or think they are. The only complication is if you get . . ." He had trouble with a word. "Pregnant. I can raise the money, though, easy. It's three hundred bucks. Nobody'd ever know about it. You could fly out and back, from school, and nobody'd ever know you were gone."

"I could meet Letty," she said.

"That's right!" He laughed. "You're fine, Katie. Always look on the bright side. We'd have a great time."

How she would love to live near David in Chicago. He and Letty would be there, secure in their love for each other, and she would go out to dinner with them sometimes, she and Letty like loving sisters. She would tell Letty about David as a little boy, about some of his foibles, about the secret paintings hidden behind his desk.

David had got up and gone to the window. "What's that?" he said, listening intently, frozen for a moment into silence. He didn't seem to breathe, yet he wasn't all that excited.

"What's what?" she said.

"Listen," he said.

On the wind over Leah came a sound that was rare though familiar. It was the breathy moo that always dipped strangely into focus. Not the noon whistle—that had to be rejected first. It was now deep in the afternoon, and that windy, hoarse cow's

roar meant a fire somewhere. It rose and fell as the wind took it
—the warm wind of this August afternoon. Then she began to try
to count the number of short moos and long moos.

"It's the fire whistle," David said calmly, now that he had
identified it. "I wonder where the fire is." He came back to her and
leaned his threadbare knee on the arm of the easy chair. "Anyway,
Sis, take it easy. All this 'pregnant' talk is probably hysterical. It
depends on whether you're in a fertile period and all that, and
who knows when that is? It only lasts for a day or two—I think,
anyway—out of the whole month." He picked something off her
shoulder and held it up to the light. "You know we've got the
same hair?"

"But it means so much to a girl, Davy. I didn't think it
would hit me like that. And then Wood did what he did."

"I know," he said, suddenly growing nervous. "And you know
what I did this morning? I took Tom out in the woods and
murdered the poor old bastard."

"Oh, Davy!"

"I couldn't even do that right," he said. "Christ, he ran off
with one ear hanging. The thing was, I thought I was doing him
a favor, but then he found out I was trying to kill him. He
looked right at me. I had to hunt him all morning, and he knew
all the time who was coming after him. Uh!" He shuddered.

"And you think you did something bad?"

"But you didn't *mean* to . . ." She had no idea how to finish
that sentence.

"I'm scared about what I meant to do," he said. "Certain
parts of it I remember with a creepy sort of pleasure."

"But he had to be put away, Davy!"

"Sure. And I elected myself executioner. I won't go into all
the fraudulent reasons." He shook himself. "Anyway, Katie, I
think it's fading out. Everything fades out, you know? Don't you
feel a little better now about last night?"

"Yes, I do." She got up and tucked in her shirt, thinking how
that must represent a kind of symbolic return to order—Wayne
would say that. Like tucking in the mind.

The fire whistle continued its vaguely hysterical mooing.
They both listened, trying to count the longs and shorts, but
the wind blew some of the moos away off toward Vermont. She

466

hoped no one was afraid because of that fire, wherever it was.

"Just talking to you about it helped an awful lot," she said.

"I mean that about getting it taken care of, Katie, if anything happens. If you miss your period and all."

She was so grateful that he should know how simple and human it was—she was—to have periods. It was natural, wasn't it? Everything was only natural. It was really no terrible thing she'd done with Gordon. She felt she must tell this to David.

"Nobody was hurt. I mean, he didn't hurt me. Maybe I made too much of the virgin bit."

"That's right, Katie."

"And I loved it, Davy. I was out of my mind, I loved it so much." She had to tell him how marvelous it was. "There was just this little tick of pain, that's all, and then it was like I was all hollow and empty and he *filled* me."

"Katie," he said. He was upset, she could tell, and this gave her a funny feeling of power and pleasure. He stood there so trim and young in his raggedy old clothes. He had that authority she had always admired—a sort of authority over his limbs and all the parts of him. The scratches on his face and hands seemed very uncharacteristic, but these were peculiar times.

"It's Wood we have to worry about now," he said. "Maybe it's too deep for us."

"Yes. But thank you, Davy," she said, and lost her breath. She kissed him on the cheek, turned and left him there in his room.

The wind belled Wood's curtains and let them fall back to the sides of the windows like the skirts of dancers. But they hadn't the reassuring rhythm of dancers, so they were always just a little startling, those flamboyant flourishes. The day had cleared and grown harshly bright in that dry wind. The checked pattern of the curtains had a slightly unpleasant, hallucinatory effect on Peggy; were those little checks upside down or not?

She would not ask Wood why he had done what he had done. She would be his nurse—efficient, observant, always present. Perhaps it really had been an accidental overdose, although Dr. Winston obviously didn't think so. She looked up and found

Wood staring at her. He sat in his desk chair, keeping himself upright. At first he'd been tied upright with a bathrobe sash around his chest under his arms. The injection of picrotoxin was wearing off, and he seemed a little less jittery. He stared, and she looked straight back at that dark eye, looking for recognition. She found that he was looking at her and thinking about her, but he wasn't aware that her look asked for recognition. She was being studied by that consciousness that had tried to end itself, to end all its processes. Earlier, when he was still extremely groggy, Wood had mumbled, "Oh, God, I'm awake."

It must have been a disappointment to him to wake into a world he never wanted to see again. He hadn't wanted to see daylight again. How could he want to leave, when all she wanted in the world was to be near him? There was no balance, no fairness in it. That he could want to end himself! Somehow she must get inside him and find out what was wrong. She must ask, and if that failed she would have to do something else. But she was still shy. She could not, even for the most urgent of reasons, get over that shyness. It was still like iron. When she made up declarations of love they appeared in her mind already mute and doomed. She could not even muster up a chiding anger; she had become his nurse, just his nurse.

His robe had fallen open across his chest, where the shining hairs were springy and alive against his skin. His bathrobe was maroon, warm as blood; his skin was too vivid against it, suggesting the parts of a wound. She began to shake, as if it had been she who had taken the injection of stimulant. He seemed to notice her trembling; a slight frown made lines on one side of his forehead. The string of his eye patch cut those lines off short, so the eyeless side remained clear as unmarked paper.

Though she was frightened and unhappy about him now, memory told her, as it always seemed to do no matter what troubles she had at the moment, that she had come a long way toward Wood. When she was ten, he was fifteen; they had been separated by those five years from any sort of equality. She had been the little girl he was kind and friendly toward. He had always been the leader, not really named as such, but the power behind a zone of protection that had surrounded her all of her life. Ever since she could remember, she had lived in a world where there

was an ultimate authority who could be trusted. Yes, and how peculiar it was for her to claim poverty and stupid drunkenness as her childhood environment when Wood had always been nearby. He was her environment too, wasn't he? The Whipples were her environment long before she came to live with them, and always that dark, quiet boy was there, the one person in the world she knew would never betray her. She had lain in her damp bed up in the sugarhouse, listening to the dangerous, stupid conversation between her mother and father or between her mother and other men, frightened half out of her wits by their crashing and thrashing because she didn't know what kept them at it. If they could say such crude things to each other and seem to hate each other, why didn't they keep away from each other? She really hadn't known until Wood explained it to her. Well, not really explained everything, she supposed, but at least he told her there was a reason, that it wasn't all pure madness. That was when she was nine or ten. What had been Wood's explanation? He had wiped off her tears with a rather dirty handkerchief—she remembered that. They were sitting on one of the porches of the Whipple house—he had been sitting there, that is. It was raining but warm. All that day in school she had been nervous, on the edge of whimpering, because of what had happened the night before. On the way home she'd seen him sitting there reading and come running across the lawn. His kindness made her cry. She asked him what made her mother have to do what she hated so much. "Don't you know, Peggy?" he said. He was fourteen or fifteen, yet even so she trusted him not to giggle or to evade any question. This seemed more of a miracle every year. She had known then, of course, that what she spoke of was wrong, dirty, sinful, giggle-making. She knew that much, maybe more, because now she couldn't remember the exact words of his explanation. He had made it something she could live with, though. What had he said? That there was a strong attraction between male and female. "Strong attraction"—she remembered that clearly. She'd already known that. But then he went on to say that even though her mother sounded as though she didn't like it, she did like it, very much; that it was only a kind of game to say the words that meant the opposite of what you felt. Good God! she thought now, the boy had actually said that to her!

It had to do with her shyness now—not just that incident, but all the times he had kept the world meaningful. He still did. If only she could get angry with him, or even make fun of him! Then she might get her tongue back. But he was invulnerable. He was too important.

She was getting so jittery herself she couldn't even think straight. There he sat. There he was, yet right in this room last night he had almost gone out of himself. She must keep him here—a crazy vision of herself holding him down, like a wrestler. She could get her arms around his waist and hold him down on the bed so he couldn't do anything. She could wrap her legs around him so he couldn't even move; she would hold him quiet and soft until her warmth melted into him and he was calm.

A knock on the door startled her so much the wind went out of her chest. It was Dr. Winston back again. As he came in he gave her a quizzical, smiling little look, half secretive. "How's your patient?" he said, putting his bag on the chair she'd been sitting in.

"I think he's better."

"You'd know if he was better or not," Dr. Winston said. "In any case, it's not the physical part I'm interested in now. The danger of the hypostatic pneumonia is over, to my thinking. He's young. Even if he is a little flabby from sitting on his butt all the time, he's pretty strong." While he spoke he handled Wood—peered with the help of a little flashlight into his eye, then reached down into his bathrobe to thump his chest and squeeze his stomach. He didn't speak directly to Wood, or even ask him to do anything. "Will he talk to you?" he asked.

"I haven't asked him to," Peggy said.

"Well, I'll do some straight talking. Are you listening, Wood?" Wood nodded.

"Are you going to try this again? Because if you do it's going to be a little messy for me. Ordinarily I'd have to refer you to the psychiatrist at the clinic, and this business would be on your record. But there's something peculiar about you and all the other people around here. I've been around a long time, and I can smell it. This young lady here, for instance. She doesn't want you to go off and leave us, so I don't expect you will. I don't think you'd want to do that to your mother and father. There's too

strong a current running around in this house. And I think I know you. I've known you for a long time, off and on all your life, and I know your war record. I don't know the details of whatever sort of hell you found yourself in last night. It must have been god-awful. But you're not the type to hurt other people that much, now that you can think about it. You're going to have to live with whatever it is. What I mean to say is you've got a duty toward the people who love you and want you alive. You're not free to commit suicide."

Dr. Winston shut his thin lips and nodded once, as if to say "There."

Wood glanced at him and then away. "All right," he said wearily.

"All right," Dr. Winston said. He packed his bag and strode out on his long legs. As he went through the door he instinctively ducked his head, though the door was much taller than he was. Before he shut the door he turned around with a look of exasperation, as though Wood's short answer had cut him off.

"Look!" he said. "As far as I'm concerned there's nothing morally wrong with suicide. You understand that? In the proper circumstances, who can say? And you know as well as I do that 'duty' is a highly abused term, to say the least. I just want you to know I'm aware of that."

"Yes," Wood said, nodding his head.

"All right." Dr. Winston shut the door.

Peggy turned back to Wood, to find him staring at her again. What was he seeing? She looked away. She wanted him to understand how much she loved him; he must see that. But maybe he didn't want that love all over him, piled on like chocolate sauce over a sundae. Maybe he wanted Lois Potter. Jealousy pierced her so sharply she almost said "Ow."

"What are you looking at?" she said. Her words slowly went into his head; she could almost see them disappearing into his mind, and she waited, shivering, to see what happened.

He turned shy, and looked away. "I was thinking how you've grown up," he said.

"I've caught up to you."

"Peggy, you've passed me. I haven't even been to college."

471

"No, I haven't!" She didn't know if her outburst was from anger or from fear of crying.

"Peggy," he said. She heard his concern, then watched it change. Slowly it submerged into his usual immobility. She wondered if she considered herself worthy of him because he had been crippled. If he hadn't been so maimed he would of course belong to someone like Lois Potter. Did she think she could sneak into his life because of what a machine gun had done to him?

"I'm sorry," she said.

"You're sorry?" He seemed genuinely surprised. "What have you ever done to be sorry about?"

"I wish I could get mad," she said. Maybe she was getting angry. He kept making her breathless, knocking the wind out of her. Maybe he was the one who ought to wake up and see what was going on. "You sit there," she said. "You *sit* there." Now, that didn't make sense. She had too much pride to tell him the truth right out straight, no matter what had happened. But what kind of pride was that? It was the pride that didn't want him to treat her with kindness—not that goddam *kindness!*

"You're angry," he said.

"Well, don't say you don't blame me or something!"

"Peggy, I don't think I can explain what happened to me last night."

She saw the pain, but that wasn't exactly what she had been talking about. He'd knocked the wind out of her again. Maybe he would always be able to do that. How could she explain that she wanted to be a woman to him?

"You tried to kill yourself!" she said. She almost added, "I *can't use you dead!*" She was selfish, why not? He couldn't use her, either, if he were dead. She had to get to him, right next to him. They had to burn up together so she could cure that death thing. "I'm not a little girl any more!" she said.

"I can see that," he said, smiling a little. Icicles touched her waist, and then her breasts. For a moment she was burning up, confused. She'd put her hands on her stomach, and it embarrassed her terribly that he might know why. He just looked at her and she had gone all to pieces.

Outside, the leaves streamed and glittered in the wind. The curtains made their graceful but frantic swirls against the dark

carved window frames. The fire whistle had been windily calling, hoarse and urgent, but it was so distant in this wind it might have been calling from another town, or even another country. It was such a distant urgency, so far away it might have even come from another time. Another brush fire, she supposed, in this dry year. Although this morning's dew had been deceptively heavy, the wind had blown it all away. She listened, but it was impossible to count the number of whistles.

Wood looked at her as she turned away toward the window. She gave him a strangely sinful feeling, like the memory of stolen looks at girls in childhood. Maybe it had something to do with a time long ago when for one shocking second he'd seen Peggy Mudd naked. He'd nearly forgotten about it. She was only a child. He'd been hunting partridge up by the reservoir, and coming suddenly upon the sugarhouse he'd stepped to a window and looked in. She stood in a washtub next to the sink, shining wet and naked, so smoothly pure, unmarked by body hair. He'd fled at once.

The two images slid into place: little Peggy and the little girl murdered by freezing, a ghost function of his missing eye, impossible diplopia. He put his hand to his eye, and as if he'd touched her, she spoke. "What is it? What is it?" She leaned over him, her warmth on his face and on the back of his hand. "Do you hurt or something, Wood?" Firmly she took his hand down from his eye, and looked into his head. He shut his eye tight, trying to keep her from that scene. "What's the matter? What's the matter?" she cried. "Stop it, Wood!" She pulled his face against her—muscle and softness, the presence of bone and the flutter of her heart. In that mustard-colored room her warmth could only bleed before the cold noneye, the flame-green intent that should not ever touch her.

It was so dangerous he couldn't move.

"Wood!" he heard her call from outside. "Wood!" She seemed to have more than a small power of warmth. Her heart beat against him like the heart of a bird whose warm wings enfolded him. As long as they could not subdue that strong idea, all would be precariously safe. But it was Peggy, and he knew she was not a

473

prisoner; she was here in his room, holding his head in her arms as fiercely as one holds a contested basketball. A peculiar sight, signifying that perhaps this was not Auschwitz, Maidanek, Sibibor, Chelmno, Wolzek, Treblinka. Leah; so it was Leah. The cold ones waited everywhere for their chance at power. *Vernichtungslager* in Russian or in English would smell as sweet. Or in Chinese or Japanese. The nasty little two-legged things, indifferent or deadly, had come down into him by that ageless diffusion of characteristics. He opened his eye to a crack of sun, a flash like a strobe light illuminating the familiar cold room, the tower legs and barbed wire outside that strangely borrowed window.

She still called to him, caring for him. There was that power, and he came back to her, his face pressed against her body. He heard the little gurglings inside her, and the light thud of her heart. Her smooth arms slid around his head and neck, searching for better ways to hold onto him. So he came back into the August afternoon.

It was the first time they hadn't meticulously continued. Always before they went all the way until the screaming stopped and the Test Person was comatose or dead.

Peggy was scared, and he tried to comfort her.

"Where did you go?" she kept asking him. "Where did you go, Wood?"

"Nowhere," he said. "I've been right here with you all the time." She held his face in her hands, making him look at her.

"Wood! I'm sorry, but I love you so much you can't do that. You had a sort of fit, and you mustn't do that!"

"No, I really didn't have the fit that time. You kept me from having it, Peggy." That was true, perhaps.

"You've got to tell me what's the matter," she said in that nervous, serious voice that comes straight down to a hard question. He was fascinated by the montage of Peggy's child face upon this woman's. The wide mouth, the high, Indian cheekbones, the even darkness of skin. The other girl had looked almost sickly around the eyes, but this woman's were clear and demanding. This woman was, however, Margaret Marcia Mudd. The lovely flesh, though it cradled old memories and fears, had changed so much. He touched her hipbones, now subtly sheathed where

474

once they had been starved, canted, it had seemed, like the edges of a dish.

They were poised there, looking straight at each other, Peggy's hands on his shoulders, when a clatter and unintelligible voices approached the door. Peggy went to open it, and in the door appeared Sally De Oestris, supported gingerly by David and Henrietta. She got her canes straightened out and came on in, seeming to look up and out from her bent spine. "What's all this they tell me?" she demanded.

"Now, Sally," Henrietta said, cautioning her.

"He looks all right," Sally said. "Peggy, how is he?"

"I think he's much better. Physically."

"Oh yeah? Physically. Well now, as I'm the nearest to going where he had a mind to go last night, I'd like to talk to him alone. You can go wash your face or something, Peggy, while I talk to him." She shooed them all out. "I'll have to ask you for that chair, Wood."

He gave her the chair and sat on the edge of his bed. His stump tingled. All his joints felt slow and old, as if filled with heavy grease.

"So you tried to step out," she said. "Is the reason a secret? They tell me you didn't bother to leave a note."

"Maybe it was an accident," he said.

"Puh!"

"All right, Sally."

"I'm not what you'd call a curious old woman. I used to be a curious young woman, but my curiosity rewarded me with too much knowledge. I thought, presumptuous as it might sound, that I could help." She gleamed brightly, and though she sat erect—she had to sit erect—her knees were spread awkwardly for balance. She held her canes in one hand, her blotched, arthritic fingers flattened against the crooks. Her fingers seemed to articulate only at their first joints. It was hard to think of that wizened, softly wrinkled face as having been young. It seemed to him that Sally had been just as old as this for as long as he had been alive. Just old, a state that everyone a decade or so older than yourself had entered. But Sally had been nearly fifty years old when he was born. From all the myths and rumors about her, she had lived quite a life by then.

"Well?" she said.

"I don't think I'd know how to talk about it."

"What I don't see is why you're in such a bloody hurry. You'll be dead soon enough as it is. Even if you live as long as this old bag of bones, you'll look back and your life will seem short. Too short."

"Yes, I suppose so," he said. He was afraid for Sally, and guilty because he had made death the subject of this day. She would have to get back down the stairs without his help, and he trusted no one else to keep her from falling. His hip joints tingled for her fragile old bones—another form of the anxiety, familiar as a scream laid lightly on the nerves.

"Do you mind if I rattle on?" Sally asked—really asking it as a question. He shook his head, and she took a breath. "All right. All right," she said. "I don't think you're afraid of much. Tell me if I'm getting warm. No. Let me tell you about the De Oestrises—a crazy tribe but the world hasn't been exactly destroyed by their presence on it. One branch of the family made its money in mines. Gold mines. I suppose you know something about that. And silver mines and iron mines. That's what I call the Rough Rider branch, the hunters, the Wild and Woolies. The other branch settled down around here and played with stores and mills. That branch wore spectacles and sleeve garters— you know what I mean? They owned land too, but hired somebody else to lumber it. This goes way back, before the log drives on the Connecticut River. Back to the time of Governor Wentworth, and before that.

"The name sounds sort of Dutch, don't it? Sounds like something to do with eggs. In Greek ôistros means gadfly, and in Latin oestrus means frenzy, passion. Oestrus in English has to do with the whole cycle of fertility in female mammals. Hell of a name, ain't it? You call yourself a Whipple, but you're really a De Oestris, because the line's dominant over Whipples and Sleepers. Anyway, I know because you're crazy like a De Oestris. I meant to say the line went batty in my generation. Crazy as hoot owls. Now, pardon an old woman—you'll find old women are dippy about blood lines and all that. It's all they've got left to talk about or be proud of. But you had the De Oestris mark on you when you came home from the hospital. The eyes—it's in the

eyes. I took one look and there it was. Your mother was such a strong, healthy girl—peaches and cream and raven black hair. She was a country beauty, full of good rich milk and strong as an ox. She was okay. But the De Oestris mark was on every one of her children, the poor girl." Sally shook her head and sighed.

"Oh, come on, Sally," he said.

She laughed—a great bellow of laughter that shook her. "Now they'll wonder what in the world we're laughing about," she said. "Oh, my! Oh, dear! Now tell me why you took all those sleeping pills."

"Because I can't stand . . . I couldn't . . ." He heard his words. They hung in the air while he read them and saw that they hadn't said anything yet. "I couldn't stand being a witness."

"A witness to what?" She squinted carefully, like a sharpshooter.

"To torture. Murder." The words were dangerous to say. He looked around for Peggy. Even in his anxiety he found it interesting that he'd looked for Peggy. Where was she? He wondered if she were in any danger; the thought caused a sharp pain in his throat.

"I see. Yes," Sally said. "Are you going to do it again?"

"I don't know. Maybe not."

"What about Margaret Mudd?"

"What?" he said, startled. Sally's words had superimposed themselves upon those identical words in his own mind. Maybe Sally was a little magic—like all old people who could still think. That was it, he supposed. You got used to old people being so dim; when one wasn't, it was as strange as hearing a talking dog.

"I said, 'What about Margaret Mudd?' "

"What about her?" he said defensively.

"Have you discovered she's a woman yet?"

"Well, yes. I know she's growing up."

"Growing up!" Sally said disgustedly.

He shied away from this talk; it was like glancing away from direct sunlight, turning away from heat. He knew what he was doing. There was a memory that had been flitting around just outside of memory, that he couldn't quite get hold of. Ah. The barn. One of the De Oestrises—his great-uncle Walter—had a farm on the Cascom road where he kept horses. A long time ago Wood had spent a whole afternoon climbing a ladder made of

477

boards nailed to an upright, climbing up through the hay-dusty air toward the great hollow peak, to a tie beam that crossed twenty or thirty feet above the loose hay. Then to fall through all that air and space. Each time was like the first time. No amount of repetition dimmed that lovely giving-way. In the absolute of gravity, falling, falling, his bowels shivery with delicious apprehension at that freedom. While he fell he was in thrall. Then to climb again. Though he visited the farm often when he was a boy, that one afternoon was the only time the level of hay had been just right. When his father was ready to go he had called and called, but Wood took one more fall, then one more, and his father had to come and get him. It wasn't like him to pretend not to hear; maybe that had helped to fix the memory.

The barn burned one August because of damp hay—"spontaneous combustion" they called it—and the house was later sold to summer people.

The falling haunted him. The memory had come back at odd times ever since, full of complicated nostalgia. When he couldn't stay away from Lenore Stefan it had returned often—then painful and full of yearning. He had to go to her, to let go, but he could never really let go. He had no right to use her.

"Where did you go off to?" Sally said. She looked at him with curiosity and suspicion.

"I had a memory," he said.

"I hope you're not such a damned fool you prefer memories to real kisses."

"What?"

"I said the girl's out of her mind for you, and you just sit there."

"Who?"

"You nitwit!"

"What do you want me to do?" he said, suddenly exasperated. "I don't know! Maybe I don't feel that way. Who am I to even . . . Maybe I don't feel that way!"

"Who said you have to be full of moonbeams? I'm thinking of Peggy, not you. I'm a woman, after all. At least I used to be one before I turned into a bloody ancient gnome. She's a young, attractive woman. Why don't you make love to her? You can any time you want to! If there's anything that drives me insane with

anger it's when a man won't do what he can do! There's nothing in the world hurts a woman more, that's meaner, that shows her how helpless she is, than a . . . *limp* man."

"Maybe she doesn't feel that way," he said.

"If she don't, things have changed since I was a girl. Maybe they have. God knows I was always a strange critter anyway." Sally sighed. She looked a little defeated, perhaps even embarrassed.

"Listen," she said. "I've been doing a good deal of thinking on this subject. And of course I'm thinking of you too. I'm thinking of both of you, because I care more for you two people than anything in the world. That don't come halfway to saying it. Maybe I'm a nut. I'm an old 'maiden' lady voyeur, maybe, who wants to breed Whipples instead of cocker spaniels!" She laughed. "Anyway, you remember what I told you once? Think with your skin—while you've got one. Examine your life with the glands. Instead of all this internal bleeding. You were always so damned sensitive, afraid somebody was going to get hurt. God knows they did get hurt. But you're not being good to Peggy, you know. I think you'll find that a certain kind of violent use of her will please her as much as it will you."

Sally shut her eyes and moved her head from side to side as though she were very tired, tired to death. "It's taken a good deal of energy to say this, to care enough to say it. I'd like to find out what my own reasons are for saying it. I think I've been cursed by a strange enthusiasm. Cursed by it all my life. I had a child, a girl. She died of cholera infantum when she was four. I was three thousand miles away at the time. You know how long ago that was? She died April 14, 1899, in Essex, Massachusetts. I was in Paris. I was twenty-five years old—about your age. I felt pretty bad. She was Aranpo's child, and he was dead too. I was twenty-five. I wasn't dead."

Sally stared intently at the print of the carpenters sawing the big beam. "A long time ago. What I mean to say is I was still very much alive."

Wood looked at her ancient skin, at her cramped, misshapen body. Her trunk was rigid, almost exoskeletal, but the soft, powdery parts of her—her face and forearms—hung limply on the inner bones. Her legs were encased in strong lisle, a weave so hard it shone. She seemed very tired now.

479

She was looking at him. "Now I'm so old it hardly matters. Why don't I keep my mouth shut? Even my jaw muscles get tired. It's that I ain't dead, I guess. I'd better get on home." It took her several heaves to get up from the chair. Three or four of them were practice, or aiming heaves, before the real one that brought her to her feet and canes. Again he had those quick shocks of sympathy.

"Be careful," he said.

She grinned at him. "Be careful," she said, imitating him. "Be careful. Be careful."

She met her escort in the hall. Wood almost called out to them to be careful. They got her downstairs all right, and soon Peggy came back, with David following her.

"Okay, boss," David said to her, and she smiled. "How's it going?" David asked.

"Better," Wood said.

"Good!" David seemed shy. Then he said, "Where was the fire, anyway? Did you hear it?"

"We couldn't count the whistles," Peggy said.

"I just wondered. Hank said Horace took off right out straight, and now she doesn't know whether she ought to be worried or not. She won't call up to find out for sure where it is."

"She wouldn't do that," Peggy said.

David turned to go. Before he reached the door they heard, distinctly this time, the two short whistles that meant the fire was out. Downstairs the telephone began to ring.

"I've got to take Sally back home," David said. "You take good care of Wood, Peggy. Make him happy."

"I'll try," Peggy said.

The ringing of the telephone quieted as David shut the door. Wood had been noticing that everyone rather carefully shut the door upon the two of them. Peggy was blushing, rose and dark gold, at what, he didn't know.

"Well," he said.

"Yes?" She turned to him, still smiling and blushing, glowing with some interior idea. Confused, he hopped back to his chair and arranged himself on it, pulling his robe together and

draping it over his stump. She came and sat near him on the arm of his easy chair.

"Do you think I'd mind seeing that?" she said, pointing at his leg.

"It's not pretty."

"I've seen it already, and I saw where your eye used to be. I touched that place. It didn't bother me at all."

He heard that confession of love; but would the court accept it?

There was Sally's advice, the "violent use" he might make of Peggy. Peggy Mudd! Suddenly he was so shy and nervous he couldn't speak. He turned toward the windows, the main arched window with the narrow arched lights on each side. The curtains swirled before the dry windy day, bright as the light beyond them. In each gust the maple leaves glittered and hissed furiously. She was watching him, and he held back the visions of that violent use. She was still that skinny little girl-child, almost a baby, who had the sniffles every winter. It had been her mother he had often thought about in his early fantasies, never the child. When he had stepped to the window of the sugarhouse it was the mother that had made his throat thick and dry, the older woman who had in fact once looked at him in an appraising way. Just a glance, but it had been enough to set him vibrating for days when he was sixteen.

"Are you all right, Wood?" Peggy said close to his ear.

He had told Sally he couldn't stand being a witness to what he saw, but of course he had always been more than a witness. Peggy's cool hands slid along his jaws, to his throat, pulled his collar open and began to massage the tense muscles at the base of his neck. "Do you like that?" she asked in a low, hollow voice. Her hands moved. "Do you like it, Wood? If you don't I'll stop, but you looked like a knot."

"Yes," he said.

"See? You're getting softer. You're untangling."

"Oh, sure," he said.

"Don't scoff. I'll untangle you. You let me stay with you and I'll untangle you. I feel sort of powerful all of a sudden. You know what my zoology instructor said once? He said mammals like to touch each other. Did you ever think of that? I mean it's one

common characteristic of mammals—they enjoy touching each other."

"Yes, I can see that," he said. Then knives flashed in his mind. Meat thermometers, dull greasy metal. No, not greasy, but dulled by constant autoclaving, racking; the anonymous handiness of things kept in use.

"Relax, now," she whispered, her lips at his ear. Her hair touched his cheek. "You're tangled up again. Don't go away from me like that." Her hands came back to his skin, and the knives were gone. "There. See? I can tell," she said.

It was true. He could have groaned with relief. She would stay with him, do anything to help him. Perhaps someday he could let go in her presence, but that would be some other time. In the meanwhile his gratitude welled up and was held. That control had been too long in the making. He was singular in this world; they needed him calm, with all his wits about him. She needed him. Who would protect them? Who would protect her? His men were dying! He must protect them against themselves, the killers of children.

"Wood! Wood!" she called.

Slowly he came back to the brown room. The curtains belled out, spilling wind, revealing all the wild energy in the maple leaves. At least not human. But her arms were. She had pulled him back again. When would he be safe enough to reveal his gratitude? He must let go and fall. But he was all cockeyed, asymmetrical, awkward. He would land on his head and break his neck, or somebody's neck. He would kick out a foot that wasn't there any more, get clubbed by a beam on his blind side.

She was crying because of him. With much effort he unclenched his dangerous fists and smoothed her hair away from her forehead. How round her forehead was! He had never noticed that roundness before, and the wonder of it calmed him, he had no idea how. It was a marvel. All right, it was a marvel. She liked his touch; like a cat she moved into his touch.

"Peggy," he said, being careful of this calmness.

"What?" she said.

"I think I want you to stay with me. I mean I appreciate it very much."

"It's all I want to do," she said.

32

Horace read the whistles at the first signal. Seven long, four short: Main Street to railroad tracks, from Cascom River Bridge to Bank Street intersection. First he tried to find a bicycle, but all the tires were flat. No one seemed to ride any of the bicycles any more. They were all dusty and out of order, so he left them in a pile and ran all the way downstreet, to arrive exhausted and gagging at the busy scene of the fire.

Because he had run in fear, he was sick almost to death. The old Leah pumper blocked Water Street, its engine coughing at idle. Brass valves moved, shiny rods humped like leisurely elbows. Water dripped everywhere down its red enameled sides. Smoke, dark gray and not much of it, flew in long wisps down the street above the heads of the people he pushed through. They let him by, gazing as they were, calmly talking to each other. Down the other way the street was blue and white, shiny with the parade uniforms of the legionnaires. "Hey!" someone yelled at him. The canvas hose bulged, wanting to straighten itself but having to crimp where it twisted through the front doorway. The kitchen windows were broken, and thick smoke tumbled out to be whipped into streamers and rags. He followed the hose. "Hey! You!" they yelled imperiously. Chief Tuttle cut him off and tried to take his arm, but the old man's hands slid off and away. He took a last breath before entering the smoke. The stink of burning cloth, of string, struck his nose even though he wouldn't breathe. His eyes had to shut tight; immediately he collided with wet oilskins and fell into the rush of water. He fell through the parlor toward her room. Glass tinkled at all the windows. With his nose at the baseboard he got part of a breath, and as he got to his feet a fireman

brushed past him, oilskins flapping. Then another. He was weaker than he thought; he had forgotten not to breathe. Susie, where was she? He fell, not aware that he was falling until his head hit the floor and the world turned flat again. Someone had his feet. His head rattled across doorsills, slid on linoleum. The legs of a table became involved with him, then tumbled away. He swung, loose as a rope, into the light. Someone had his arm. He was on his knees, but they smothered him like wrestlers, turned him over too easily against his will and stared down at him from a great height. Their faces circled him, tilting down.

"It's Horace Whipple," Chief Tuttle said. Someone else knelt down and felt him over. "He's not in bad shape," that voice said. They all straightened up. "How's the woman?"

"Forget it."

"Get him across the street."

They let him stand, but led him firmly across. He stumbled at the curb in front of Futzie's Tavern, where on the sidewalk a mound of gray blankets lay. Near the straps and canvas, beside the kneeling uniformed men, a metal box with a red light on it pumped and wheezed. From the pile of blankets a black hand protruded, shiny and cracked as coal.

That evening the Whipples, all except Horace, had gathered in the great hall, around Harvey's broad oak table. Their faces were constrained against the thrill of it all. Each was conscious of his own expression—noncommittal, stopped. Words seemed too clear, too calmly said.

"This will *kill* Horace," Kate said.

They were silent at the wonder of it. When Wood lit his pipe they were startled by the match. He was still sick, but he wouldn't stay upstairs.

"Poor Susie Davis," Henrietta said.

"Poor old Sam too," David said. "What's he going to do now?" All their words were careful; none of them could understand why they were so excitedly pretending to be calm.

"That damned building was insured to the hilt, anyway," Harvey said.

"How's Horace taking it?" Peggy asked David, who had just come downstairs.

"I don't know."

"What do you mean?" Henrietta said, getting up.

"He wouldn't let me in, either."

"I'm going up again!" Henrietta said. They watched her climb the stairs. With a hand on the rail she pulled herself up, limping with tiredness.

At that moment Wood recalled that his shotgun was missing. But it had been missing last night, before this happened. He was confused. It might possibly have been a deliberate act of Horace's toward him; perhaps it had saved his life. Because of course Horace must have the gun. Horace had been fascinated and slightly afraid of it for a long time, had even borrowed it once to try it out up behind the house. Was there anything to worry about right now—that was the question he must examine very carefully. He didn't seem to have enough information, enough data, to make a decision about Horace and the gun. It was as if his long sleep had cut him out of time, away from all of them and their problems, and suddenly all he could think of wanting was peace. Poor Susie—it seemed that she had been lost long ago, in his or in someone else's childhood, an old, old story. It was too late for her. Nothing could be done there. She was dead, she was in peace.

Now Peggy must stay with him and do whatever mysterious thing she did to keep him from the visions. If he touched her the visions could not happen, so he reached for her hand. She had been watching him, sensed the slight desperation in his movement toward her, and took his hand in both of hers. Her touch did more to him than he expected. He had known perfectly that she would respond; that he had known this was astounding. There had been no doubt at all. He was filled with so much knowledge of what she would do in response to him, how she would turn her head, close her eyes, move her lips. He saw it all ahead. She was smiling: the little teeth—needles in her softness. He blinked and squinted at her. How could he not believe all he knew? Those eyes were looking at him and thinking. That other intelligence! Slowly he became aware, admitted that he owned her, this other force. Need was another matter. Her taut dark

485

skin was his, her hair, the joints of her bones. He sat dazed and still frightened, knowing that he always would be frightened, as this strange adjustment occurred before his eyes. It seemed now that he must have known this all the time, ever since she was a child.

She stood up and pulled his hands, asking him to stand. "Let's go outside," she said. He stood and locked his leg. The suggestion didn't seem an unnatural one for her to make. She didn't seem to be aware of the possibility of refusal. They had arrived, he saw at once, at their next relationship. Perhaps she had read his mind at the moment she had changed. He couldn't define his nervousness as fear, exactly, but it was a remembered feeling—the half-joyous apprehension of too much awareness, of any heightening.

They stood in the dark on the front steps, with the wind whispering near-words through the hedges and along the grass. She put her arm around his waist, easily, naturally. That easiness shocked him into another realization: she had always been the wanton girl of his imaginings. All the time. It was strange that his protectiveness should have hidden that deeper feeling, or prediction, or perversion—whatever it was. She was the open, friendly, wanton girl that so easily broke him in his dream. No stranger at all, but his ward, part sister, part daughter. It was all uncontrollably sweet, misty, miasmic.

She turned toward him, her other arm coming around his ribs, her face against his shirt. "Everything looks different," she said. "The lights down there. Everything. Too many things are happening."

Harvey said, "So they were all crocked before noon."

David and Kate nodded. They knew all those interesting, first-told details. Susie had passed out sometime toward the end of the afternoon, and the boys had left. Those names were not being given out officially—Donald Ramsey, for instance, being married. But nearly everyone knew who they were, especially since those who were legionnaires arrived fairly drunk at the Legion Drum and Bugle Corps practice. Keith Joubert, Junior Stevens and the rest. Bruce Cotter had been there too, and Herb Den-

ney. Beady and Candy Palmer both said that it wasn't their kind of party, that Susie had been getting crazier and crazier lately. Sam Davis was across the street in Futzie's all day. Evidently Susie woke up long enough to light a cigarette. The damage to the apartment was mostly from smoke and water.

"So they had a little gang bang," Harvey said. "That's the way it all began, a long time back."

"With Gordon Ward," David said. "It began in high school with Gordon." He glanced at Kate, who looked away.

Henrietta's voice came down to them from the landing, where she stood grasping the banister rail. Her voice was weak, calmly matter-of-fact but weak, as if from age. "He doesn't seem to be here at all," she said. "I've looked everywhere for him."

David felt danger. Kate jumped up. "Davy!" she whispered.

"Take it easy," he said. He could think of nothing to do about it. Even if he could think of something, he wasn't the one to do it. Asshole, fuckup. Whatever he touched got out of hand. Susie was a corpse—cold, burned. He hadn't been in on the cause of her ruin, but he had taken advantage of it. He shriveled, shivered at the memory of her companionable willingness. She had been a lot of fun because she knew every time was the last. She had the gaiety of despair, the sense of humor of a whore. No love possible there; it was a joke she laughed at, and the joke was always on her.

"David," his mother called down to him. "You've got to find him." Her wavery voice was on the edge. Kate ran up the stairs to her. "You've got to find him, David. You know, you're the only one left who can walk. I'm so afraid of what he'll do. He might hurt himself!"

He looked at his father, who seemed to have retired from such decisions. He stared dimly, his dark eyes like rust spots on the sickish pale skin of his head. In spite of his own fear, or because of it, David distinctly thought that he would not like to be in his father's position right now. They were too much alike; he felt the weight of his father's relationship with Horace all too well. He himself was not without dishonor in that respect. Also, he had a pretty good idea that Horace knew of the times he'd taken Susie to the cabin. There was that stern, broad face again,

487

blue with cold neon, staring at him through Futzie's window. He did not like the memory of that judgment.

His mother still looked at him, asking him to take charge of Horace. What could he say?

"All right," he said. Already he saw himself merely cruising around, goldbricking, safe in the cab of his truck, looking around with no real idea of finding Horace.

His father was silent.

The wind was a constant hiss in the trees. Against the moon or windowlights the leaves streamed and fluttered frantic signals, as if to warn against him. But none of Them would listen. Long ago he had found that the cruel were stupid. They were indifferent, and wouldn't understand. Not that he hadn't taken precautions. It was a warm night to be wearing a mackinaw, but it hid the two sections of Wood's shotgun he had cleverly tied together so they hung on clothesline around his neck. Without untying the line he could lift it over his head, fit the barrel to the action with a quick twist, then feed the shells from his pocket into the magazine. Now he walked, without visible agitation, down High Street to the left, the back way to the Town Square. They would soon discover his absence and might try pursuit. David in his truck, of course, but David would go down Bank Street. They were all so stupid. If they were not stupid they would see him burning bright as a torch along the dark streets.

The warm houselights were the deceptions they put on like smiles. If you looked closely, past the thin lace veils of those windows, just as you might look into a smile to see the cruelty, you saw the cold people. They were all enemies, laughing among themselves at Susie, at himself. They thought it thrilling to see her destruction. At his own dinner table he had once heard them snicker and call her names. The names were true, of course, according to their judgments, and could not be answered in their language. He could not call them wrong.

Up the street a car began to turn toward him, but before its lights came around he stepped smoothly into a lilac bush to watch it come blazing arrogantly toward him and pass with its swish of engine and tires. Hung around his neck he had the power

488

to stop anything. He had seen what Wood's shotgun could do. One shot had cut down a poplar sapling three inches in diameter, blown its white pulpy wood into gruel.

He would make her death a little more important. There was a kind of justice they didn't understand, not having gone to hell and seen the resemblance between their indifference and hell's indifference. He was scourged, free, shining. He had outfaced Leverah and the Herpes, wept for their victims but not become one. Nothing left on earth could frighten him as badly as the Herpes had frightened him. Now he had no one to protect, so he was free. They had no hostages now. Wood no longer cared, Kate had been taken and turned, Peggy was lost in poor broken Wood, Susie was dead.

He fell to the ground beside a white garage—the Martins' garage. Giant rhubarb leaves, the furry smell of rhubarb, covered him. With his face on the cool earth, he was a part of that forest. He could mourn quietly because he was free. A car passed with a familiar clank of metal—David's truck. This would hurt his mother, and he was sorry for that, but no one else would do what had to be done. She would get over it soon because after tonight she would never have to worry about him again. He would never have to see her face break into fragments again, nor see her big eyes glaze and shake behind her glasses. He wanted no pity and had never asked it of them. Only in the coldest fear had he ever asked for it, and then, to his shame, it had been from Zoster and the Herpes. They had made him whimper as his father had once made him whimper, asking for fairness, that child's cry. Let them ask him for fairness now. Let them complain that it wasn't fair.

He took the cinder alley to Union Street, crossed Maple Street to avoid a woman who walked a small, brittle-legged dog, and turned east on Locust Street. Lights were on in the basement of the Methodist Church, where women washed pots and dishes down there in the brightness. He would have to cross Summerslee Street to get into the darkness behind the grammar school. Then he would be among the gravestones and the arbor vitae, whose formal lanes would take him up behind the Congregational Church and the Wards' house. He was sweating now—a hazard because his glasses fogged and became slippery over his ears and

nose. He stopped in a shadow and hastily wiped them with his handkerchief.

As he crossed Summerslee Street a car caught him unexpectedly in its headlights. It must have turned out from a side street. He kept himself from running, and it passed, not seeming to care, its taillights narrowing steadily south. The worn playground brought memories of degradation. The great tube of the fire-escape slide came like an arm akimbo from the second story of the dark school. Once in fire drill he had slid into its hollow and been deposited on the ground, still among strangers. In this building he had broken Mabel Andrews' tooth and nearly died of shame and horror that his touch could hurt her. His life had ripped apart like cloth when she screamed, and after that she had to wear a false tooth forever. All the rest of her life that artificial part of her would be in view because of him.

He climbed the wooden fence and dropped onto the smooth grass of the cemetery. This time his touch would be for justice, not for love. Following the odd lines of shadows, he crouched and moved quietly over the tended lawn between the stones. He was not a person, not even an animal, but the force of justice moving with perfect authority toward its culmination.

Voices murmured from his left, and he crouched behind a block of polished granite smooth as glass. Along the ground, not too far away, came the harsh purr of a man, then the higher one of a girl, a hummed assent, over and over: "Yum yum yum yum." Absorbed in their noises, they wouldn't hear him pass. Further on he had to cross a graveled path, the crunch of his shoes half taken by the wind, then onto dark lawn again. The white steeple of the Congregational Church was outlined in pink by the store lights across the square. To its right the gables of the Wards' house crouched among the elms, black from this side. He stopped to listen; a cricket ticked next to his hand. It was here somewhere, among these graves, Gordon had offered Susie to his teammates. He saw their hard, handsome faces, their thick necks. Gordon's orange freckles glowed. He could hear their exuberant, stifled voices as they watched each other mount the girl.

It was that betrayal he'd lived over and over. She had come to Gordon's house, thinking she would meet his parents, that she was serious to Gordon. "Mother, Father, this is Susan Davis."

"How do you do, my dear?" She had told him what Gordon promised. Her aspirations—what a joke. He groaned for pity of her trust. No parents were home, but the football players giggled manfully in the barn or somewhere. She said she wore a pretty dress.

No more. Beneath a tall blue spruce he assembled Wood's shotgun and loaded five of the number-six shells into the magazine, pumped one into the chamber and slid one more into the magazine. No one heard the clash of the metal. As he moved toward the barn-garage he held the gun, barrel-down, alongside his leg. From shadow to shadow he slid, a shadow himself, to the dark along the wooden wall. Sweet peas on their strings swayed like marionettes, and somewhere a door bumped and creaked in the wind. A glassless window passed like a mouth, revealing a darkness inside so palpable it seemed to bulge softly, like velvet. He waited for a cloud to cross the moon before going around the corner. The first cloud turned silver and rushed by, missing the moon, so he waited. On such a warm night people might be sitting in the dark on the porch next door. He had no fear of them because he was the power here. He had no need of fear or rage; he merely regretted their coldness. They felt pain—their own pain, that is—and he had no desire to give pain or to make anyone fear him. So he was careful not to involve the neighbors in Gordon's execution. They would know about it soon enough.

When the clouds came over the moon he slipped into the garage. If Gordon's car was not here, he would wait. In the darkness he felt around for the cars. He could smell them, almost feel them in his head. An emptiness there ahead of him—he could feel it, or hear it. But there, to the right, something took up space. He touched its smooth enamel and ran his hand up its side. The grainy texture of canvas made it Gordon's convertible.

He had been in the Wards' house several times, and knew the downstairs part of it well. The back hall led past several pantries into the kitchen. All right. He crossed the driveway and entered the house. It had seemed that he was totally committed to what he must do, but now, in the house itself, among its own odors and vibrations, there was a new intensity of purpose. The kitchen overhead light was on, but he walked casually through that busy room. Stove, refrigerator, sink—they seemed needless

now, and unsubstantial. He stepped into the unlighted dining room, hearing a voice. Two steps down from the dining room, at the hall telephone, Gordon leaned against the wall. He was relaxed, even happy in his posture, making a comma against the wall. His white shirt was too clean, his chinos and loafers too new and crisp. His hair flamed into thousands of tight curls and angles.

"Okay, what time you want to start?" said Gordon's easy voice. "Yeah, yeah," he said with a wry grin, "we'll make it a sort of wake. Hmm? I'll bring a couple new decks of Bicycles and take out of the pot. You get the beer. Okay, Don? Nine o'clock? Okay, Donny-boy." He listened. "Okay now, cut the humor." But he chuckled again, shaking his head in mock disapproval.

Behind Gordon, at this angle, stood a tall grandfather clock with a sailing ship painted on its glass panel. The pendulum, a dull sun of brass, appeared and disappeared behind Gordon's crisply pressed chinos. The telephone table stood on delicate carved legs. Everything here was old, thin and carefully polished. The beige wallpaper was etched like brocade, all tiny flowers in vertical lines.

Gordon hung up and turned, reaching for his wallet. With his finger he examined its insides, fingering his money. Then he put it back in his pocket and looked up at Horace. He was badly startled, dead pale between his freckles. He squinted up into the dining room. "Who's that?" he said. "Is somebody standing there, for Christ's sake?" He took two steps forward, craning his neck. "Jesus Christ! Somebody *is* standing there! Say something!"

Horace had nothing to say.

"What do you want?" Gordon said. He reached for the wall switch and turned on the chandelier over the table. "Horace Whipple!" he said, and jumped back when he saw the gun. "What the hell!"

Horace pushed off the safety, and Gordon jumped again at that meaningful click. "Hey, wait a minute, Horace! What's with the gun?" He was so badly frightened his forehead began to glisten. He put his hand to his heart and took short, hard breaths. "Jesus, you gave me a start. Now, what's with the blunderbuss? Come on, Horace, what's the story?"

As if he really wanted to know. In Gordon's wary eye Horace

saw a flicker of plan. He had decided that he probably wouldn't get shot, that he would be dead already if he were going to be shot. "I mean, what's the matter, Horace?"

"Susie's dead." Horace spoke only out of politeness.

"Oh, yeah. Terrible! That's awful. Terrible thing. But you don't blame me for that, do you?"

"Yes."

"Aw, no, Horace. No you don't, not really. I mean I know how bad you feel and all. All upset, right? It's a terrible thing! Who could blame you?" Gordon's voice was kind and sad, his face serious, avuncular. He seemed to think he was doing pretty well.

"I don't want to hurt you," Horace said.

Gordon immediately misunderstood. "Of course not, Horace! I can see that! Come on in and let's sit down. Come on."

Horace despaired of their ever changing, the cold ones.

"At least put the safety back on, huh?" Gordon essayed a smile. "Okay, Horace?"

If only there was a chance for Gordon.

"Well, okay, Horace. We'll stand here and talk. You know, I feel terrible about Susie too. We were damned good friends, you know. Old friends, in spite of whatever you think might have happened way back in high school. Don't believe everything you hear, Horace. You know how everything gets exaggerated. Don't you?" The green-flecked eyes glittered uncomfortably as he looked for some sign. Then they peered straight into the barrel of the shotgun, flickering shut and open. "You know how that happens, don't you?" He tried to wave all that gossip away with his hand, to wave it off into utter insignificance.

The mind shifted, probing. Gordon turned fiercely sad. "You have no idea, Horace, how much I've suffered over an awful drunken mistake I once made. I was too young to drink, and just couldn't know what I was doing. I was absolutely pie-eyed, didn't know what was happening one night, when those drunken bastards found Susie and me and did that to her. Honest to God! I know somehow it was my fault—to get so drunk I couldn't protect her. God knows I tried, but they held me back. God, it was awful!" His mood changed to understanding, warmth, confiding warmth. "And don't think I don't know how upset you were when

493

you heard the rumors, either, Horace. Taking the money and all. A brave thing. I thought it was a brave thing to do!"

That strange quality of lies, how the open brain clicked and telegraphed its points.

He went on, speaking most plausibly to whatever he thought Horace Whipple was. Horace watched down the barrel of the shotgun as the bright face proclaimed its openness. The honest gestures flowed down the shoulders through the snowy broadcloth of the shirt toward the light square hands. He had to admire certain of those skills. The room around Gordon faded until he seemed to stand in a special light. Gordon explained with becoming modesty how he had fought in the war, gone through sheer hell in the service of his country. Then a modest shrug before he returned to the deep seriousness of the tragedy of Susie's death. Sorrow, shock. A moment of silence.

Gordon glanced at his wrist watch. Perhaps he still wanted to make that poker game. Yes, he probably did; he was thinking ahead. A self-deprecating slyness entered Gordon's expression, as though he were asking if it showed too much: "Hey, Horace? Is that gun really loaded? I never thought you were the hunting type. You know what I mean?"

Did the man think he was playing poker already? This man, Horace saw too clearly, would be successful in the world. His little talents would hurt many before he was through. Even afterward the poisonous lessons of his success would remain. The stupid gulling the stupider, the power of minor cunning. He hadn't Horace's education in evil, and was therefore hardly aware of his tools, of their origins. These were not the tools he had used on Susie, though he didn't know it. He had used her love. And of course they couldn't work on Horace. Gordon's fear was real, and gave him reason to scheme, but he was also depending upon Horace's reluctance to kill—an interesting card to hold.

Let him dig his grave.

"Why don't you say something, Horace?"

"I could never gamble," Horace said. Once David had tried to teach him how to play poker, but he could never lie about the cards he held, or understand why the other person enjoyed the necessity of lying. David had informed him that he was slightly

mad, slightly un-American. He moved the barrel up, so Gordon had to look straight down the hole.

"Horace, I think there's something else you ought to know about Susie." Horace watched him with curiosity because his method had changed again. Gordon was serious, rather manly, rather sad about what he had to say. "I suppose you don't know that . . . that time, you know, wasn't really the first time anything like that happened to poor Susie. Now don't get upset about what I have to say. But Susie was not—I'm sorry to say this—a virgin when that unfortunate thing happened." Gordon smiled them into a slight conspiracy of knowledge: men of the world, they could shrug sadly at human foibles. "Now, I know how you felt about her! Don't get me wrong. She was a sweet kid, one of the nicest persons there ever was, anywhere. She just . . . well, it had been that way with Susie for a long time. Horace?" He was gravely serious now. "Do you know what a nymphomaniac is?"

Gordon wasn't even aware of the nature of his crime, had no idea why he was being judged.

"Well, Susie had a kind of mental disease called nymphomania. I hate to say it, Horace, but that's the way it was. You won't get mad, now, if I explain what it is? Okay? By the way, if you decide to put that safety back on, be careful, huh? I mean don't pull the trigger by mistake? Okay? Well, nymphomaniacs just have to sleep with everybody that comes along. It's not their fault, now. Remember that! It's a disease. You know Susie's mother's in Concord. You knew that. Well, there's a history of mental illness in the family, you know." He shook his head sadly.

Gordon had been sweating, but now he was full of confidence, for some reason. It began to seem dangerous, just a little dangerous. Gordon peered carefully out of his head, seeming to see great results Horace couldn't see. His hair gleamed like red metal, and his big chest expanded with confidence. Freckles overlapped like plates upon his face and hands. It must have been that name for her that had generated such confidence. Horace raised the shotgun.

"Horace! What the hell? Are you *crazy?*"

Yes, he was mad. The man he knew to be Gordon Ward had become for an instant Zoster. Chitin slid, smooth sheaths along the jaws. The red was the blood of victims, the green eyes

495

were cold as absolute zero. Horace had never chosen to guard against them. He wanted to explain it all to Susie, how they would come to suck her warmth, how they liked torture. He had never told her about the flayed dog screaming for its skin. They were power, the ones who always had the power, didn't she understand? They could kill her any way they chose and never be made to suffer. He must warn her about them again. He saw her lying in her sleep, so frail, no lock on the door. Their grins, bloated parts, teeth, smirks, cold armor. It was almost too late. It was hard, what he had to do. He had almost died of fright at the unnaturalness when he ran at Leverah's window, staring with his open eyes. She fell, exploding in blood and her own terror. It was hard to do, wrong to do. Unnatural. But they made these rules, not he. Anticipating attack or flight, he quickly fired into the head of this one.

As the big body jackknifed, part of the head pushed off toward the wall. Long ropes and finer bells of blood painted the wallpaper, lay ribbonlike along the floor. He had expected power from Wood's shotgun, but the head! Pieces of scalp still grew orange hair. Pinkish-gray cereal gleamed on the carpet, crawled down a table leg.

In the silence of the gaudy hallway he remembered who he was and saw what he had done.

33

David stopped at Anna's Teach Your Dollars More Cents and bought five twelve-ounce bottles of beer. Anna made him show his driver's license before she'd believe he was twenty-one, in spite of his having bought beer there less than two weeks before. Though he suffered slightly from this insult, the redeeming thing

was that she had forgotten it was Sunday, when beer wasn't supposed to be sold. With a bottle of beer cooling his crotch, he resumed his meaningless patrol of the town.

He was pleased by his little truck. Its flathead V-8 purred along nicely. The only jarring thing was the one rattle in the body or bed somewhere he couldn't locate, but such a little imperfection made him more constantly aware of his machine's general well-being. And his nagging, wavelike concern about Horace—or more likely his awareness of responsibility for Horace—made his neat truck, his ride through the warm night with the big white instrument dial glowing, the crisp feel of shifting gears, more enjoyable too. Procrastination, a kind of hooky, but it was good to pass along the streets, the houses, under the tall trees.

He went down Water Street past the tenement. Window glass glittered where it had been pushed back from the sidewalk; the windows of Susie's kitchen were soft black holes. No Horace skulked between the old buildings, along the railroad tracks, behind the American Legion Hall. He cruised down Mechanic Street, crossed Poverty Street, then passed the mills, only night lights glowing deep in their huge rooms, floodlights on cinder parking lots empty now of all but a watchman's car or two. A whiff of tannery, a moonlit gleam of the river. Because he was pointing that way, he followed the Cascom River to the Connecticut and crossed the long covered bridge into Vermont, then turned and came back to Leah, to cruise the Town Square once again.

A few lights were on in the Wards' big brick house. Horace might blame Gordon in some way, and in spite of seeming foolishly dramatic, he thought of possibly warning Gordon. But there were many reasons for his not wanting to do this. Horace was not one to enter upon violence without being forced into it. They had always counted upon Horace's gentleness. It was himself he always hurt, unless by pure accident. He didn't want to betray Horace with that sort of bad judgment, either, especially to Gordon Ward. Horace had a queer enough reputation already. But the main reason for not seeing Gordon was what Kate had told him. He wouldn't be able to look Gordon in the eye. Perhaps he would never, on his own initiative, see Gordon again. Strange, because the facts of the matter were not that horrendous. Face it: when

girls liked boys, boys who liked girls did that to girls. Sometimes it took longer than at other times, but it happened. Then why couldn't he think of looking Gordon casually in the eye? Because he hated the son of a bitch. Because Kate Whipple was too beautiful and good for the likes of Gordon Ward. Gordon Ward should never have been allowed to play with her responses, even to touch her.

As he came around the square past the post office, the little round library, Trask's, the hotel, the Town Hall, people began to emerge from the first show at the Strand. He parked near the marquee and watched, doubting that Horace would have gone to the movies under these circumstances. But he doubted that he would find Horace anyway. He turned off the engine and leaned back.

Then strange things began to happen.

It was the beginning of an adventure he would always remember with a great deal of awe. Strange imperfections in timing and desire, childhood returning in force, with ironic lessons implied; he would begin to think of his whole life in terms of such timing. He would always seem destined to survive, to move on toward an ironic skewing of desire. He would remember the air-raid tower, when the little bullet born of a wishful yearning for action had missed his chest by the smallest hairline crack of timing. He had just missed, just been missed, how many times? He thought of Lucifer of the golden eye, the desperate screech of tires on asphalt, a short round in basic that demolished a nearby truck, a tree branch slowly giving way. There had been other times, and there would be more, but after this confrontation they would all fit together with a haunting, adhesive quality that would always cause him to dream upon his possibilities.

After most of the people had come out of the Strand and gone their way, Carol Oakes came out alone. She stood next to the coming-attractions display cases, striking as she always was, just slightly more a woman than other women. This quality could have been measured, he supposed, in tenths of inches, but slight though the measurements might have been, they were highly visible. She wore a light summer dress, chalky blue, and she struck him with all the force of high school. She seemed pale, worried, her large face translucent as marble. He sat within the sanctu-

ary of the cab staring avidly, letting all the guilt shocks, fantasies, the masturbation flashes of his adolescence come back as he examined her forbidden, always impossible excess of femaleness. Letty was smooth, possible, his likeness, friend and comrade. Carol Oakes was that somnolent goddess of breadth and burning, fragile and voluminous, wasp and cloud.

He was prepared to make these observations, to take these scorches upon his nerves and go, when she walked straight toward him with knowledge in her eyes. She put her long hand on the window sill of his truck.

"Davy?" she said. Her voice had always been throaty, with a small warble in it, as though she barely controlled some deep emotion.

"Hi, Carol," he said. Her eyes were a little older, which made them clearer, more distinct around the edges, the irises a more primary blue. Her unhappiness had a touch of rakishness about it—the way she tossed her head, her rich auburn hair swinging across her cheek. She seemed about to do something dramatic.

"Are you waiting for anybody?"

"I was looking around for Horace, but I don't expect to find him. You want a ride?"

"Yes!" She got in beside him and leaned back with an unhappy sigh.

"What's the matter?"

"Oh, it's Mike Spinelli. I'm through with him, absolutely *through!*" She took a Kleenex from a little cloth bag and blew her nose.

He started the truck and drove around the square to Summerslee Street, which led toward her house. When she saw where he was going she said, "Are you doing anything, Davy? Do you have a date or something?"

"No," he said, trembling like a freshman.

"Don't take me home, huh? I couldn't stand going home."

He drove on past her house and they entered the country. She accepted a beer. "God, that's what I need," she said. She leaned lightly against him—a lightness that was unbearably tender, as though she possessed magnificent reflexes toward a man. "Take me somewhere, Davy. Just take me anywhere." She held his beer so he could put his arm around her as he drove. It was all so

smooth, so charged it might have been the beginning of any of his thousand fantasies about her. He seemed a child again, dreaming of being a man, his hand for the first time actually touching her waist, her hip. When he came to Ralph Hill Road he turned east; this would take them back to the Cascom road, which led toward the lake and the cabin.

He could hardly believe any of it. Ladyfingers were going off in his knees. At the cabin she accepted a drink of whiskey, cried a little on his shoulder, cried a little more after they had come to rest on the couch on the screened porch. Moonlight bathed them in its cool light, and the wind died down to an occasional soft gust. As she told him her story about Mike Spinelli, how Mike was probably going to marry Jane Stevens, he took off her clothes. Hardly moving, she helped him. Pressures eased where his hands were. He could not believe what she seemed to be helping him to do. When they were naked her moans of pleasure were almost sobs; for a fraction of a moment he thought them exaggerated, as though she tried to prove her helplessness under his kisses—if she were helpless, stunned by passion, what she allowed him could not be her fault. Then his response obliterated any thought at all. That he could cause this goddess to thrash and whimper! They fell yet seemed weightless.

Afterwards she was so still he thought her actually unconscious until he gave the slightest indication—hardly a thought —that he might rise. Her fingernails pressed him back into her like threatening daggers, light needles of threat, and again he began to slide down toward falling—a strange slope, convex, all forbidden oil and soft color—toward the totality, the prickly hysterical pleasure of a child. She cried that she loved him. He was certain that he loved her. Nothing like this stirring of nerve and depth had ever happened to him. He was the cause of her rapture, and when the time came again he unraveled, froze; in his shut eyes constellations burned. And then, almost at once, her moist white body turned guiltily beneath him, freshly naked.

They had slept. Time had passed, leaving its echo. When he awoke she was kissing the nipples on his chest, but not as if to rouse him. "I love you," she said.

"I love you," he said. He did love her, though a warning, thin as a distant siren, told him he was dangerously convinced—

too dangerously convinced. But he didn't want to think, to endanger his love. He thought of marriage, of the nights, one long night turning her inside out, over and over.

"You're not like him at all," she said.

"Mike?"

"He's so *selfish*, Davy. I never realized it. I'm such a dumb bunny anyway." She stuck her little finger in his navel, and he sneezed. With a little giggle she did it again and he sneezed again. "I found your sneeze button," she said.

"You found all my buttons," he said, not wanting to make such a joke.

She laughed. "I shouldn't be so happy, I guess. I'm in no position to laugh. I was all fixed up for Mike and he stood me up again. It was just pure accident you came along, but I wouldn't of gone with anybody else because I always knew you had this thing about me."

"You did?"

"A girl knows. Whenever you looked at me you thought of something like what just happened. You even thought of the same thing in *grammar* school, for goodness' sakes."

"So did everybody."

"Yes, but I always wondered about you. Mike was the only boy who had the nerve to ask me. The others were such little children I'd of felt silly going out with them. Mike's so selfish, though. He never made me feel like you did. I never knew it could happen. I just wanted him more and more often. Then he made me go to Manchester and lie to the doctor so I could get the diaphragm and all, and pretty soon we never went out hardly at all. We just met for one single solitary purpose. Sometimes he'd call me and pick me up and I'd be back home by nine. He'd just squirt and go."

"Don't talk," he said. Her voice should form itself around better words. Its tremulous breath was too beautiful for those words. He must begin to change her.

"Again, Davy?" she said with wonder. Ah, that was better. She should only say words in groups of one or two, because he loved her. He couldn't think of letting her go. He didn't want to go back to Chicago anyway. They could live here at the cabin, and he could get a job, or transfer to Northlee College. Yes.

With her job at the Public Service Company and his GI Bill they could get along fine. He saw that future in mist, moon-colored, voluminous. She made him ache. A warm confusion of love and desire swirled around them—he could see its convolutions. All his problems, his aimless aspirations, were over.

"I never did it with anybody but Mike, Davy," she said.

"Shh. It's all right." He was turning to liquid, to rock, a smooth river broken in slow swirls by a still rock.

"I meant it when I said that, Davy. I'm wild for you."

"Shh, now." It was again utterly new, that shocking entrance.

At that moment real light flashed. Hugh branches printed themselves across the screens, leaves thrashing. Then the branches swerved and with incredible speed rushed across and out. A car had turned into the parking space. A car door slammed. He had just enough time to find his pants and pull them on before the screen door opened and the porch light came on with its harsh, tawdry brightness. Kate stood there, her hand still raised to the light chain. "Davy!" she said. He turned to Carol, who had found the old afghan at the foot of the couch. Her breasts gleamed before she got them covered.

As he had turned away from Kate he knew that something terrible was in her face, but he had to see the scene as it presented itself to her. Carol's big breasts, pink nipples standing, then her smooth glowing legs because the afghan had a perverse short fold in it. As he turned back, Kate's face was white, her eyes walleyed, her mouth a round hole. She bawled certain words he couldn't catch but knew were words. She stood as if bound to a stake, all the disintegration taking place in her mouth and eyes.

"Horace! Horace!" Kate cried.

"What? What?" He couldn't help imitating her voice because he felt her dread. She cried, still talking but not in recognizable words, shaking, choking on her breaths. He went to her, but as soon as her hands touched his skin she jumped back as though he'd frightened her. She looked over his shoulder, and he turned to see Carol slipping into her clothes.

"What about Horace?" he demanded. "What about him?"

She had gone all to pieces and couldn't begin to talk. Horrified, he forced her to sit down on the couch. Her keening was musical in its waverings, its slides into the minor. Sometimes she

seemed to be trying to laugh. Hysteria, he thought, so this is hysteria. He slapped her face lightly, but couldn't hit her hard enough to communicate the intent to shock. Finally he went to the kitchen, ran cold water on a dishtowel, came back and placed it on her face and neck. She shuddered and grew quiet. Carol sat on the other side of her and they held her and petted her until she could breathe normally again.

He knew something very bad had happened—again in his dishonorable absence. He knew he would have to hear it, but he was giddy, almost ready to faint, and he had the absurd desire to get some sleep before he was subjected to the news Kate brought. He must take care of Carol, get her out of this first.

"Horace killed Gordon! *God*, Davy!"

No, he couldn't believe that because . . .

"They're hunting him now, Davy! There're men with guns all around the house!"

"Oh, *Kate!*" Carol said.

David found his mind curiously traveling, an easy inward journey toward alternate possibilities. But Kate was here, and she didn't lie her way out of things the way he might. No hopeful theories came to light, so he came back to Kate. "All right," he said. "Let's go." He had the information straight enough, but soon would come the confrontation with his feelings. Horace. He heard him bawling, red-faced, too big to be comforted. The giant child.

Calmly he put on the rest of his clothes. His shorts he kicked surreptitiously under the couch to be recovered another time. What other time? He felt a bit like a kamikaze. Plan the next action and the next. Steer correctly. Kate shouldn't drive, so he would take them both in the Chevrolet. He was weak, cold in the mind. His fluids were low. He would take Carol home first, to be recovered another time.

They sat Kate between them in the car, Carol trying to comfort her, crooning gentle nonwords to her. "Poor Horsie," Kate said when her breath let her. David knew he needed more information. He had to have it but he didn't want it—he didn't want the information he already had. So Gordon Ward was dead; he couldn't yet begin to think of that enormous blank.

Carol's house was dark—it was one o'clock in the morning.

She patted Kate once more, said good night and got out of the car. David sat there for a moment, then was drawn to Carol. It seemed unlike him in these circumstances, even ominous, because he quickly got out of the car, ran up the walk and caught her on the front steps. When he kissed her she made a small noise of surprise and gratitude.

As he got back in the car Kate said in a small voice, "I'm sorry I had to interrupt you, Davy."

"Oh, hell, Katie," he said.

Kate said something he couldn't quite hear.

"What?"

"You weren't looking for Horsie," she barely managed to say.

"Katie, it was an accident! I was looking for him! I looked all over town for him!"

"You accidentally found Carol Oakes."

As they came to a streetlight he saw her pale, weepy face and was full of anger and pity. "I looked for him!" said one of his voices.

"You're always off somewhere."

"Yes! You're right!" he began angrily, but she put her hand on his arm. He said, "Katie, I'm sorry. You're right, as usual."

They passed the dark houses along Bank Street, past the high school, one red brick corner in the streetlight, the rest of the building set back in shadow. A light shone from deep in the basement somewhere. At the corner of High Street was a parked car, with two men leaning against it. As David slowed to make the turn, one of the men waved him down with a flashlight. Without a word the man shone the light in their faces, while the other's flashlight probed the back seat.

"Where you going?" the first man said. David hadn't seen his face.

"Home," David said. "Who are you, anyway?"

"There's a madman with a shotgun around here. Killed a man already. Where'd you say you lived?"

"Who'd you say you were?"

"Look, sonny, we're sheriff's deputies, if you have to know."

David could hardly speak through his anger. Kate had to hear this; his brother was their object, these strangers. Finally, his voice high and barely in control, he told them who he was and

where he was going. They became deferential when they heard who he was.

"There's a state cop up the hill. You'll see him."

Fifty yards from the house a state-police car was parked with two other cars. The police car's interior light was on, its front door standing open. A big state policeman sat in the front seat, one uniformed leg out the door. Several men stood around armed with rifles and shotguns. David stopped and explained himself again. The police radio crackled constantly. Occasional metallic voices came on the air, said cryptic words and snapped off abruptly as though cut off before they could possibly be finished.

"David Whipple," the state policeman said. David recognized him, though not by name. In his hard wide face and lounging bulk was the calculated absence of excitement of the man who had been there before. Though young, he had the mass solidity of middle age. Even his ears were huge, meaty in their simple folds. The other men watched his ominous deliberateness, his Olympian pauses between words, with the proper respect due such power. "David Whipple," the state policeman said again. The name became doubtful, slightly ridiculous, as though David were trying to pass a counterfeit.

Kate was crying quietly. Suddenly David realized that the man was having trouble understanding. He explained again who he was, where he lived, while the bland, dangerous calm of the state policeman continued, unsurprised, unimpressed.

"I'm taking my sister home now," David said, and let the car move slowly forward. The men moved aside for him and he proceeded down the street and into the driveway. Other cars were parked down past the house—one he recognized as a town-police car. Faces glowed faintly from the brush across the street, from behind trees.

"We're surrounded, all right," he said.

"Come in the house, Davy," Kate said, noticing his hesitation.

"You go on in, Katie." He unstrapped the flashlight from the steering column. An overwhelming revulsion had come over him, of being surrounded like this. He'd start shooting out of the

windows and battlements at them. He'd pick the sons of bitches off with accurate shots to the neck.

The moon had gone down, and the stars, so bright and thick they seemed to define a solid black cover over the night, pressed down over the hill. The maples rustled overhead like witnesses. He saw Kate into the house and walked back, his flashlight on, toward the police car—the command post. This street he'd always lived on, that he'd traveled night and day with no danger but the vaguely believed ogres of childhood, now seemed even less dangerous. Those fake Indians behind the trees couldn't touch him. He knew who they were, most of them.

The police radio crackled and muttered. Kenny Clark stood there, wearing an Ike jacket and dungarees. When he saw David he let his lever-action deer rifle lean closely against his leg, as if to hide it.

"Tell me what happened," David demanded. "I just got home and I don't know."

"Well, Dave, it was Horace . . ." The saying of the name seemed to scare Kenny into silence.

"Just tell me what you know, Kenny." Other men came up the hill to report, one speaking softly into a walkie-talkie, others among themselves. The state policeman lounged in his front seat.

What Kenny Clark had heard was that Horace had blown Gordon's head half off. He'd been seen and recognized by Mr. and Mrs. Ward, who caught him in their headlights as they came up their driveway. Mrs. Ward was in shock at Northlee Hospital. Horace had been seen once more, heading toward home.

"How come all the vigilantes, though?" David said. "How come the goddam army?"

"Well, Jeeze, Dave. We were all at the Legion Hall, you know. Atmon come in and told us what happened. Chief Tuttle was getting the state cops too. We just went home and got our guns, that's all." Kenny was nearly whining in apology. "He's armed, Dave. Hey, Dave? I know you must feel awful bad about it." Kenny began edging away, trying to look like duty. "Yeah, Dave. Gordon had a war record, you know. You know how the guys feel."

"Yeah," he said. He knew it too well. They'd all like a nice running shot, take a nice lead and squeeze, but it had little to

506

do with Gordon Ward. He stared at Kenny Clark, that semi-dim friend of high school, at this organization of men in the middle of the night. Up the street was his father's house, his home, the big house standing above the maples, windowlights fragmentary through branches and moving leaves. He and Horace had come home as babies to this street, that house.

Christ, he ought to know all these murderers because he was one himself. They all ought to be home with their wives, smoothing them down, making that mutual happy violence. But ah, the kill, the kill. Most of them considered their pricks to be guns, knives. Rape the bitch, feel the push. Candy Palmer's broad white ass in his hands.

He had to see Horace, to tell him something. He'd never told Horace what mattered. When he tried to teach him to drive he'd frozen with apprehension at what Horace might do to his precious truck. He must get to Horace before these men killed him. His little brother. In all his own fantasies he had been the one slipping stealthily through the bastards, the shits, knocking them off one by one. Never Horace, that poor gaumless child who always hurt himself. All Horace wanted was . . . sweet Susie Davis. Justice? He'd given it, and now he'd get it. Wood couldn't pay his fine this time. David turned to go back to the house. Unresolved surges of energy and resolve seemed to bloat his muscles, to convince him totally. Then those mirages of action boiled away, turned vague and impossible. If only he knew where Horace was, he could get through their lines and find him. First he would go to the house and get his gun. Which gun, and who would he use it on? He had no tools for this dilemma, no power.

Then came the shots, three shots from the hill above the house, quite far away through the trees and distance. It was a familiar sound to the hunters, though rarely heard in the dark of an August night.

"Holy Jesus, hear them shots!" The men listened, but heard only wind and the peepers in the underbrush.

"Come from up toward the reservoy!"

"Rifle. I can tell."

"Shotgun."

"Rifle—ain't so hollow, more of a crack, like."

"Dumb shits probably shooting at each other."

The one with the walkie-talkie, Keith Joubert, came running over to the state policeman. "They seen him! Atmon says they browned him a little!"

"Did they git him is what I want to know." The state policeman reached out his big hand, which was not to be denied, and Keith Joubert surrendered his walkie-talkie. The policeman got out and stood beside his car, his Sam Browne belt, the leather holders and boxes attached to it, gleaming black. "McManus here. What happened up there?" He listened. "Okay. Over and out." He handed the walkie-talkie to whoever was there to receive it and got back into his car.

"Did they git him?" someone asked.

"Think they nicked him a little." David had turned away, but he had to hear them. "Got a couple number-four buck in him, anyways. Don't believe he'll go too far."

"See? I told you I can tell a shotgun!"

David walked steadily away from them, toward the lights and towers of the surrounded house.

They thought they had heard shots from the hill. Henrietta jumped in her chair as if she had been touched by them, and Kate held her as hard as she could. They were all frozen into a terrible surmise. No one said anything about the shots, but Peggy left Wood's side and closed the casement window beside the shallow frame of the chapel. Wood's face was calm, unmoving. Harvey was pale and sick; he couldn't sit down, but stood teetering on his canes, taking a few steps toward the hall, then back toward his oak table. Several times he seemed to decide to sit down, even reached for the back of his tall chair, then changed his mind. David came in and looked at each of them in turn. With each look his mouth grew narrower and tighter. He stood in the dining room as if fixed there by what he gained from each of their faces.

Suddenly Henrietta cried to him, "What are they doing? What are they all doing?"

David shook his head, unable to speak. The room rose up around them, around their silence, its heavy wood and carved paneling, up to the false balcony and beyond. The chandelier came down from the dim heights of the ceiling on its brass pole

to light the oak table, the paper clips and adding machine, type-writer, pencils, ashtray, wire baskets full of papers. The business of the table was an unnatural island in the great space of the room. Its disarray seemed frivolous. The Whipples remained around the edges, almost in shadow, their stiff faces in control.

"I'm going to find him," David said.

"No! No! They might shoot you!" Henrietta said.

"It's Horace out there!" David cried.

"David." Wood's deep, whispery voice startled them. "Don't make your mother worry about you too."

"Me?" David shouted at Wood. "I'm the one nobody has to worry about! Right?" He grew red, unlike David, terribly angry. "I'm the one who's always off somewhere when anything happens, right? Screw you, Jack, I've got mine! That's my motto, right?"

"Wood! Don't let him go! Harvey!" Henrietta cried.

"I'm the only one in this fucking family who hasn't been hit! It's my turn, isn't it?"

"Oh, David!"

He turned and ran out through the dining room.

Harvey began to climb the stairs. He could do nothing, fat slob that he was, to save Horace from their bullets. They had the right, the boy was armed. It was too late, too late. Slowly, thinking before each step of canes, good leg, canes, bad leg, he climbed toward the first landing. What was he looking for? He used to run up and down these stairs the way David always ran up and down stairs. Something he must look for. He knew he should have been more patient with Horace. Every time he snapped at Horace he knew it wasn't necessary, it was a mistake, and he vowed to make it up next time. There always seemed to be so much time ahead in which he could make it up to Horace and undo all the other times. They could have a talk and he could explain to Horace that he loved him, that you didn't have to even things up with a shotgun.

He was going upstairs into his castle. He hadn't seen the upper reaches of his castle for a long time—that was why he climbed the stairs. Now he knew he would never find the secret room. His son had killed the only son of his friend. He stopped and had to grab the railing with his elbow as hard as he could because he couldn't stand it. His money was ashes, his castle a pile

of shit. He couldn't breathe, couldn't understand why his heart still beat. Nancy Ward lay drugged in the hospital, but she had to wake. What barren cold Gordon must contemplate, his only son gone.

Is it my fault? He heard his own querulous voice begin to ask. No, it wasn't his *fault!* He could prove that! But not to his insides, not now. His son's act was his own act. He couldn't stop that knowledge.

But there must be the ameliorating fact somewhere. He must clear his throat of this pain and look for it. He climbed the second flight to the upstairs hall, the high, distinguished mansion hallway that had made them all so important. Sweat dripped into his sore eyes, down his cheeks until he tasted salt. What could he tell Gordon of good import? How could he cheer him up? It was impossible that the world could be all ashes. He would have to talk to Gordon tomorrow and he had nothing good to tell him! He couldn't recite his own failures, could he? Would that make Gordon any happier?

He leaned against the brocade wallpaper and groaned. His pride in this wallpaper came back bitter in his mouth. Something broke inside his chest. Something must have ruptured, some tube or vein. He staggered and came down hard on his bad leg—that pain woke him up; he was still functioning. He couldn't live with nothing but unhappiness. He must have good news! Where was it? He had to have something to tell Gordon! God, he wasn't even a man: he'd almost blubbered for his mama. But there must be good news, there must be something! He sat down on a little maroon chair and put his face in his hands, feeling his soft cheeks. The only thing he could think of was that all the polls said Dewey would beat Truman.

Later, when Harvey began his slow descent of the stairs, Henrietta looked at him and away, having seen too much. He was too weak to have to go through this night. Playing at his games hadn't given him that kind of strength. She felt those guns at her heart, knowing how they might kill her. In her anguish she would wait, she would have to wait. She had waited before. But Harvey, the little boy, the bright show-off—he had to have some-

thing to look forward to. Kate let her go and she went to him.

He let her help him down the last few steps, then to a settee where she could sit beside him, her strong hands holding his soft white ones. Hers were darker, like weathered wood against snow. Horace was her child, hardly his at all. Horace's presence hovered like a giant above the house, over the towers and battlements. His brute strength and kind intentions—had they all so made themselves into monsters, nonpeople, that Horace could kill one of them? He could never hurt a warm living thing. It must have been a monster he had killed, one of his monsters. As if to prove him right they hunted him down with guns.

Harvey let his head fall on her shoulder. This weak man had once seemed so strong. His transparent hair let his scalp show through. Instead of getting gray his hair was losing all color, and as he aged, all of his colors grew bland and neutral. No one looked to him for strength any more, or consulted him. He played his little games of money, getting more and more money though he didn't work for it, or make anything, or do anything for people in return for it. No wonder he was secretive, and hinted at plots and deals, corruption and conspiracy. Poor Harvey, now he had no excuses. What was happening was happening.

But no one could help reaching for hope, any sort of hope. Gordon was dead. That was over; there was no hope there. Chief Tuttle had promised that they wouldn't shoot at Horace if Horace didn't shoot at them. Then why those shots? Was he hurt and bleeding now, her strange child? She shouldn't think of hope. She knew how to wait among the living; that was all a woman could do. She would not scream or cry. All of her children were strange, precariously balanced. They could break, and she must try to help them as long as she could. Bury the dead and help the living. She saw Horace dead and her heart shuddered. She saw the golden bristles along his jaw, the flesh beneath them bluish in death, his long wrists that were always chapped. All stone, distant as a photograph.

She had never been as close to Horace as she might have been. She loved him, but always with a certain other quality he must have recognized. Apprehension, maybe—some other emotion that got in between. He'd always been a little foreign to her, no matter how her heart claimed him. Not so much as he was to

Harvey, though; Horace was the type of person Harvey had always despised, no matter how hard he tried not to. How awful poor Harvey must be feeling now. To despise and love and be guilty. He vibrated, trembled against her. It had been years since he'd touched her in the presence of any of the children, and never because of this terrible need. Once they touched only in fun. All gone now.

Peggy and Kate were talking quietly, Wood listening, his face carved. Earlier Peggy had called Sally to tell her she was staying over, but told her nothing about Horace.

If Harvey trembled again she couldn't stand it. Her baby was out in the woods.

No, hold on. She was not weak. She might cry but she would not let go. There were the others. Something bad had happened to Kate, she didn't know what it was. Wood was eaten by something he carried in his head. And Horace . . .

She saw him dead, his skin still and cold as soap. Never again that brute push of need, dense and sensitive, or his spasmodic laughter. Clump, clump, and the crash of an accident, then his apology and sorrow, always clear and real. Primal—that was the word. Atavistic? The baby had had a tail, and he never joked at another's expense. A strange density there. But why must she, even now, coldly search for words? She always wanted the words precise, the prognosis complete. Not Susie Davis, who was warm and generous. Too warm and generous. No, you cold, cold person, you constant thinker. Are your tears real? Are they really and truly real? Yes, they hurt so much.

She hoped Susie had given Horace all of herself. Yes, she did hope that! She wanted them to have been happy, even if for moments.

The night went on into its darkness. The room grew cold and still. They were exhausted, impatient, afraid of what their impatience demanded. At two-thirty Chief Tuttle came back, his old face exhausted, and with his exhaustion for apology asked for a shirt or pants or something Horace had recently worn.

"Good God!" Harvey exclaimed. "Good God!"

But she went and got a T-shirt Horace had put in the laundry basket that morning.

"The hound won't hurt him," Chief Tuttle said to her. "The hound just smells, now. He don't bite at all."

Rather a dog than those men, she thought. Anything but those men.

When she handed the T-shirt to Chief Tuttle, Harvey jumped up. "No! No!" He found his canes and came staggering toward them. "No! No dogs! Don't give them anything!"

They all stared at him. His eyes were wilder, darker than they had been for a long time, and they had to remember his old energy. In the desperation of his headlong charge toward Chief Tuttle he staggered as though mortally wounded. The old policeman stood with his mouth open, the T-shirt dangling in his hand as if he hadn't quite received it yet.

"All right, now, Harvey," he said.

"Give me that goddam thing!" Harvey took the T-shirt and threw it on the carpet behind him. "Find him yourselves, you bastards! Play fair! Don't you know how to play fair?" He screamed the words, his cheeks quivering, spray in the air. His ears and lips had turned dark red. "God damn it, this is my house! This is my goddam land, don't you know that? Who asked *me* if all you bastards could come around here with your fucking guns? Hah?" He shoved his wild face up to Chief Tuttle's. The old man was grayer than before—gray as the color of his dentures.

"Dad," Wood said.

"And you have the goddam *nerve* to come in here and ask for a piece of his underwear! The fucking *nerve!*"

"I'm trying to git him back alive. Some different from them others, Harvey."

"Alive! Alive! Don't give me that *shit!*" Harvey took a step and fell down. Still cursing, he thrashed around trying to get a cane vertical. For a moment he tried to haul himself up on a cane as if climbing a pole, then fell back and began to crawl toward the wall. "Get my feet, you bastards! Wait! Wait! Get my guns, blow their fucking heads off! Clean out the goddam area!"

Wood had come slowly across the room to intercept him, and Harvey bumped into Wood's legs.

He looked up. "What? What?"

"We both feel the same. We all feel the same. Take it easy, now."

Harvey drew back. He seemed to grow smaller, to constrict like a snake. "Take it easy," he said slowly, carefully, as though tasting each word. "Take. It. Easy." His mouth writhed over his choices. Half-words began and were rejected. His hatred seemed to have absorbed all of his desperation. Finally, cold triumph glittering in his eyes, he said, "Go take some pills! Scrag yourself, why don't you?" He listened to what he'd said and then went into a fit that transcended mere emotion. Before their eyes he turned into planes of flesh and color, a strange mass of jerking protoplasm. The three women, instantly using their weight, their warmth, those qualities they didn't have to think before using, fell upon Harvey. They were afraid he'd bite his tongue or dislocate his back.

Wood and Chief Tuttle could only watch while the three women pinned Harvey to the floor. Peggy held his legs, Kate and Henrietta his arms and head. Soon he became very still, and his eyes opened, but they saw that Harvey's eyes hadn't opened upon this room, or their faces. His heart calmed and his breaths became regular and countable, but he stared at a world that was evidently more tolerable than theirs. Chief Tuttle helped get him to a couch, where his body relaxed comfortably. His eyes wouldn't close. The others watched him without having to diagnose his retreat.

"Harvey!" Henrietta said.

His eyes were empty.

"Harvey Whipple!" Henrietta said in anger. "Wake up! What do you think you're doing?" She pinched his soft cheek hard, jiggling his head, but the eyes didn't care.

They turned at a small noise from the dining room. David, new scratches and welts across his smooth cheeks, stared gravely at them all and got ready to speak. He cleared his throat. "Ahem," he said. "Horace." He cleared his throat again, but of course they all had received that message—all except, possibly, Harvey Whipple. "Horace," David began again, but before he could add the next word his mouth turned down at the corners into the irreversible spasm of a child and he began to bawl.

He turned away, then turned back to them in consternation, unable to control his sounds. When he managed to get his tongue

and throat under control it was only for the one word. "Dead!" he shouted, and ran past them and up the stairs.

34

The greatest temptation of the new day, David perceived, was to see himself as the dramatic center of this life. How young he was, how it proved him in the great world he had entered, to stand bowed before all this death yet be so vividly, so luxuriously strong and alive. The autumn air was sweet, the edges of clouds or of houses, telephone wires, whatever cut the blue, cut with such honed sharpness he wanted to cry out for the joy of seeing. In the clear air on the hills surrounding Leah, ledge and spruce, maple and birch were so fine in all their striations, their dapplings, he felt he might have seen a wasp land on a leaf three miles away.

And even his sorrow, when the eyes closed like lead and his throat burned because he could not undo time and make the young people alive, as he was . . . See? How kind, how full of sorrow he considered himself to be. Were his tears beautifully his tears for his own compassion? Alone in the woods, Horace had died slowly from the buckshot wounds.

In the dingy Baptist Church, at Susie's funeral, David sat with Wood and his mother upon the varnished benches. Nails had started from the lath racks that held the back-broken hymnals. The minister was an old man about to retire, and he spoke in a cracked, weepy voice one knew was his only voice—the same voice for breakfast or for baptism—to Susie's aunt and cousins. "Our dear one, called home to Thy mysterious will, Lord, in the bloom of youth, on the verge of life . . ." David felt the old man's weariness and fear. The relatives sat wooden-shouldered. Sam Davis was a prisoner between two husky cousins who were

not about to let the old drunk mess things up. The two-toned, brown-enameled coffin was closed, the flowers lush yet somehow minimal, penurious.

His eyes hurt from their avidity. The cut flowers were mashed together thick as cake; their perfume was the smell of death in Leah. Dead inside the eternal darkness of the coffin was a body he had made love to. David Whipple was now connected in deep ways to death itself. Her midnight-blue eyes were cold and closed, the cream of her flesh faded into clay. Yet he was alive and could remember her warmth. Then came, with the memory of her kind, quirky smile, sorrow he had to believe was real. Or almost could believe was real. No danger of her being knocked up now, was there? How could he stop his vile brain, its parade of freakish questions?

An old lady in a shiny black dress, rigid as a soldier, played the organ. From the rear of its jigsawed, varnished box came the rowing clunk of the bellows lever. Chords sighed and whined together with the remoteness of utter familiarity. When they were asked to pray, David looked from his slightly bowed head at Sam Davis' back. Sam was limp within his blue suit; the husky cousins were holding him up. They would have to carry Sam out like a pedestal clock.

David's mother wiped tears from her face. One hand held her glasses wrapped in tissue, the other stayed at her eyes and cheeks. Wood sat at her other side, the inorganic crease angular across his left knee at the hinge of his steel and plastic leg. David knew the funeral was over when Wood's hand made the cocking movement that locked his leg. He got up with the others then, and they walked out of the heaviness of the church into clear daylight, yellow and green. The relatives would go to the grave, and they would go home.

David drove. When they came to Bank Street Wood asked to be let off at Sally's, where Peggy was. Sally seemed to have taken the news well, but she was an old, old woman, and Peggy wanted to stay with her. Kate was at home with Harvey. He'd let them put him to bed, but hadn't spoken a word since his fit of the night before. He had retired. He was calm; he ate, he drank, he went to the bathroom. Dr. Winston's opinion was that he was taking a vacation.

When they reached home, David decided to have a drink. He couldn't go on vacation at the moment because he had something he had to do. The state had lost interest in the body of Horace Whipple, and also in Wood's shotgun. But before he began his round of errands he would have a drink. He went to the refrigerator and got ice cubes, amazed by their glimmer and sparkle, diamond-hard and blue. In the glass their refractions were miraculous, the tiny rainbows winking from the edges of prisms. The amber whiskey whispered down through the ice, then swirled ropily in the water before it joined that other liquid. If he was kidding himself, he was kidding himself, but . . . He spoke to the kitchen. "If I kid myself, why then I kid myself; a foolish rationality is the monster of small love." No, no, wait a minute, cat-killer, lover boy. He took a drink and immediately felt the alien presence in his brain—would it be good to him, or not? Would it help him go to Horace's room, where he must find the suit Horace would spend eternity in? Too late not to find out: he swigged the whiskey down and went up the narrow back stairs, wary as a thief.

Horace's door opened upon the room that was so uncluttered Horace might have moved into it yesterday. The room was a mirror image of David's own, and he saw himself in it removed, purified of his possessions. The bed was made, a little lumpy in places beneath the brown spread, but neither sloppy nor meticulous. The fireplace was never used. Dust was all it contained, a gray powder over the andirons and bricks. Old carbon, generations old, had turned silvery with dust. No books or papers were out of shelves or drawers; they were sealed by disuse into their places. Horace's alarm clock, on his bed table, still ticked. Strange, because Horace had been gone from this room for how many hours? That tick seemed all of Horace that was left here, because this had never really been Horace's room. He'd never had a room the way the rest of them had rooms. He'd slept here, or tried to sleep here. Now no more. Now he really slept. He was no more here than anywhere. *Even than in my memory*, David thought. Was that true? No, but the memory was inadequate, and couldn't stay. But Horace was a force, a needful push crowding him, shoving him off balance. He could even see himself resenting

that force as it slowly decayed. Light was dusty across the thread-bare rug, a lonely north light thin as whey.

The room was too silent. It was the clock. It had stopped! It nonticked, antiticked, pulled him with a force like vacuum toward it. *Say something!* The clock said 3:31. Its black face and green numerals stared without pulse like a dead animal. *Little Ben* was printed above the hand shaft. He wondered with dread and sorrow if Horace had ever read those words; it was, in small, the kind of question he had never asked Horace.

All this time he knew that Horace, if he had been the survivor, would have been adequate in his sorrow.

This room was ominous, as though it still contained the ghosts of Horace's fright. The yellow-browns of ceiling and panel-ing were different, colder than the other rooms—maybe because of the northern light coming down dimly through the thickest of the trees. He had to remember what a warm, bright day it was outside. He had never been alone in this room before. Horace had been here alive the few times he had ever come here. The wallpaper was the same pattern of small flowers as on his room's walls, but here it seemed to writhe, the thorns and stalks crowding the faded blossoms. No pictures hung across the wide spaces, only one oval mirror with silvery old glass like a passage of vision back through its fadings into the past.

He shivered, yet something reminiscent of duty kept him from hurrying out of here. It was too late to exorcise Horace's ghosts. Perhaps he had now inherited them. Perhaps Horace and Susie walked innocent and free in the Elysian Fields, hand in hand, without fear or degradation. Perhaps, shit.

He should not indulge himself in that tone, not here in this empty shrine. With panic a cool touch at the small of his back he went to the first of the two closets. It was the right one; he wouldn't have to open the door to the other. Horace's dark suit fell from the wire hanger into his hands, the hanger bending like a willow branch to let it fall. As he took the cloth from the deep closet it was as though he pulled it from hands, little fowl-cold claws that tried to keep it back. He shut the door quickly and went to the bureau to find a white shirt. He found a shirt all right, but now he had to find a necktie. The closets again. Why were the closets so hard to look into? If he opened that door would

there be a mouth as big as a wagon wheel waiting for his hand? Even so, he had to look, one door and then the other. The mouths were there, of course, but slyly invisible. He grabbed all three neckties from Horace's rack and walked, his mind crawling, from the room.

He took Horace's clothes to his truck. Kate had driven him out at noon to retrieve it and get some clothes appropriate for Susie's funeral. She had been subdued, thinking hard all the time. He wondered if she noticed, as he did, the sharpness of color and light.

"You knew Susie pretty well, didn't you?" she had said.

"You know I went out with her a few times."

"Yes," she said. "You must be very sad."

"I am, Katie."

"I don't know who I'm crying about. It's all so mixed up."

"Gordon too," he said.

"Yes, it's all horrible." She glanced at him and her eyes were glossy with tears. "Davy? Maybe we can begin talking about it sometime."

That was about all they said. He always felt good with Kate, and he thought of telling her that, but by then they had arrived at the cabin, where she let him off.

Now the little truck started at the touch of his foot, feeling like freedom. He fully intended to take Horace's clothes to Balchers' Funeral Home, and then on the way back stop at the police station and pick up Wood's shotgun. But he didn't drive toward Balchers' Funeral Home at all, he drove to the lake, made himself a drink and stood on the dock, watching the lively blue waves, feeling the slightly nippy wind across his face. "Essentially," he said to the lake, the blue sky, the lovely pulsing of the weather, "David Whipple is procrastinating. He chooses this nice place to be."

But it was not his right to choose, so he had another drink, his eyes becoming a little spastic, he noticed. The blue lake was too piercingly, beautifully blue. He must go back to Leah, to that mortician's lair. How many funerals a day were sufficient unto the Lord? Tomorrow would be Gordon Ward's, Wednesday Horace's. No mass ceremonies in Leah, at least for the time being. So he drove back toward the town, feeling the close embrace of Leah as though he drove toward a dense cloud, deeper and deeper into

519

it. Not a storm cloud, but a foglike miasma of knowledge and relationships. Even the clarity of vision dimmed in that direction, and he thought of it as a place, now, where one avoided eyes. At every crossroad he wanted to turn the little Ford's wheel and climb toward hills and freedom, stop maybe at a little store and buy a beer to sip. But he went on, because he had to.

Then he came to a gravel road leading off to the right. It was familiar in a startling way; he had passed it all summer with no twinge of recognition at all, as though time past were a different landscape altogether. It was the road to Dark Hill Farm he'd first climbed when he was sixteen. This sudden recognition seemed to be a sign, so he turned and began the long climb. It had been five years since he'd taken this road, and it seemed narrower, the trees larger. The way seemed too short, and he passed the old landmarks too quickly on his way—the millpond, Cilley's mailbox, unmarked lesser crossroads. Above the last, steepest hill the saplings had grown in diameter, and beyond the saplings the thick groves of spruce were still impenetrable, soft green cliffs imprisoning the road. Then he came to the clearing of the farm. His engine had heated up a little, so he stopped to let it idle as he looked around at the house and barns. His act of stopping declared him, as much as he wanted to be declared, a visitor to this place he had run from long ago.

A subtle feeling of unuse emanated from the barns and barnyard. The fields beyond had been hayed this summer, but something ragged about the edges of things, the earth not trodden enough where it should have been along the paths to chores, gave him some courage. Perhaps no one was here at all. He had no nostalgia about this place that he could detect; it had been one of the few times in his life when absolutely everything he'd done had been inadequate. Memory could usually salvage something or other from a time or place, but here all had been loss and frustration. Maybe he should carefully hold onto that time, and examine it well. He had played mooncalf to Tucker Cross; that should remain a warning. And he had run away after having come too close to murder. Did Lucifer still skulk about the gray barns, or had he died of internal ruptures? David could feel in his hands the sting of the two-by-four, and in his chest the deep, free breath of murder.

Soon he became convinced that no one lived in the red house beneath the pines, and the final proof was an empty windowpane in a downstairs window that was so soft a black, so furry and deep, it glowed its emptiness out at him across the pine needles. He drove on past the clearing, wondering why he hadn't merely turned around. It wasn't procrastination any more—he seemed to be looking for something up beyond, where the road went like an open door into the spruces again. It wasn't Diddleneck Pond. At least he didn't think it was. But some little manifestation or other drew him on until he remembered what it was, and the warm afternoon of late summer when he had seen it. Forneau's beer-can tree. Somehow he stopped at exactly the right place, walked a few yards through brush that was now solid leaves and stalks, and found the little maple tree. It was still small, now dead, and some of the rusted cans were immobile on the brittle branches. Most had fallen and begun to disappear into the rotten leaves of all those seasons. He shrugged and turned to go back, and it was then he remembered what he'd seen here—Joe Cilley bending Tucker's frail back as he French-kissed her, his brutal mouth over her delicate one. A beautiful stab of jealousy slid under his ribs, fresh as it had been then. "Ow!" he said happily.

The brilliant edges of leaves cut his eyes; suddenly his ears popped open, and the buzz and whine of all the woods insects assaulted him with the benevolent violence of an orchestra.

"Well!" he said. There was his little truck waiting faithfully, but with Horace's folded clothes on the front seat. He had to go back to Leah.

Balchers' Funeral Home was an old Victorian mansion nearly as large and ornate as the Whipples' house. Its smooth modern improvements of paint and siding, and of heavy, somnolent plantings, proved it no residence, however. The chaste sign hung by the walk on a miniature scaffold, lighted at night by small floodlights sunken into the turf.

He knew Phil Balcher, the son, pretty well. In high school Phil had been one of those quiet, solitary yet unlonesome people everyone knew were destined to grow up and become what they had always intended to become.

David parked among quite a few other cars in the carefully tended gravel parking lot next to the big house and walked, bearing Horace's clothes, toward what he took to be the side entrance. The weight of the whiskey had lodged in the back of his head, still working because he felt his imagination to be too free and dangerous, too eager for any new sights he might feed into it. He had to choose Horace's coffin, for one thing. Should he look at them all, he wondered, ponder this and that advantage, this color against that? Phil would be proud of his wares, he knew.

Last night he had been too late to see Horace. As he ran through the woods behind the dim beam of his flashlight, he missed a turn in the trail, lost the trail altogether and had to climb slowly toward the reservoir through the ten-year-old blowdown from the 1938 hurricane. When he got to the old air-raid tower, only a few of the vigilantes still hunkered around the place where Horace had died, talking it over, reliving their excitement. None of the men recognized him. They sat around a small fire, the huge pine columns of the tower looming up like a giant's legs, their rifles and shotguns, the tools of hunters and soldiers, familiar in their hands, in their laps or leaning against their necks. David's rifle, if he had been armed, would have lain as easily cradled against his own body. He stood at the periphery of the light. The stairs to the tower had rotted, he noticed, in the humidity of the woods. He soon learned that Horace's body had already been taken away.

Now Horace was in this building somewhere, embalmed, he supposed, or whatever they did now. It was not a subject that had ever before been of immediacy for him. The side entrance was rigged for deliveries, with a ramp. He opened the wide door and went into a hallway. Gray gun-metal coffins were stacked along one side on brackets made of ordinary galvanized plumbing pipe. He knew he was not in a place for visitors, yet a ghostlike push of momentum made him walk aggressively forward. He would go anywhere, open any door. At the end of the hall was a door with a window of frosted glass, the glass glowing with the antiseptic white of fluorescent light in the place beyond. He would always know that he had read that lucid, clinical light for what it was, known and chosen to enter in order to sear his eyes.

He pushed the door open and entered the bright room.

Color on his left, among whites and the busy chrome of table legs, tubes and faucets, made him turn toward lively reds and oranges. On a table lay a long body, on its back, legs slightly spread. It was Horace's face there, its crude bones beneath the silent skin, mouth gaped open like a retch so the broad upper teeth were visible. But the whole body was open, from crotch to neck, and the inside of that vessel gleamed as fresh as any meat on display. The insides of the ribs were silvery clean against the rare red meat, the wide columns arching upward toward the slit, tough binding of skin. The chemical reek was not from the body; it came from the walls or ceiling, so strong it seemed to disinfect vision itself. He could not stop the cataloguing, never thought of turning away. There was no heart in the splayed body, no liver or lights, no orts. The gaping mouth seemed to scream silently, the whole body protesting, as though the split chest itself were a toothed mouth. It had been cleaned like a beef, like a sheep, emptied to the neck. There was the pale esophagus cut off, a perfect O. There were the spine's knuckles, the hollow of belly, the bush of blond hair and the slack penis, the wormy bag of testicles dark as though bruised between the great gray thighs. But it was the red meat, the naked muscles glowing fresh red, that he would take with him like a treasure to ponder over. The scars on legs and arms, the old healed scars, were white basted seams. Below the bulge of brow the eyes were darkly sunken like dried puddles. It was all so silent, that meat. Horace's big hands, palms up, never closed. Away from the empty place, as they were, they still seemed capable, as did the feet with their working calluses, of human movement. But all was still as a photograph, now merely dead extensions of the red center.

Someone gasped. He turned to see Phil Balcher, pale, in a white apron stained pink, staring at him. Phil's lips moved as he tore the apron off. A string broke, David noticed, clearly understanding Phil's dismay. He felt his expression turn into the calm friendliness of meeting. A smile signaled itself to his eyes and cheeks—friendly, more than polite. Phil stared in awe.

"Hi, Phil," David's voice said. "I've brought the suit and shirt." He was aware of the meat there on the table, the nonwitness.

"Come!" Phil said, pointing to a door. "Come!"

Phil looked sick, and David wanted to reassure him. "I guess I came in the wrong door," he said, walking calmly toward the door Phil had pointed to.

"I've got to wash my hands!" Phil nearly cried. "Wait out there! Danger of disease, you know!"

Near the door, David noticed another table with chromed legs on casters as large as the wheels of a child's wagon. A sheet covered the obvious form of a body—the cliff of feet, the heavy mounds of torso and head.

"Who's that?" he asked.

"Wait outside!" Phil's dismayed voice cried. When David looked again, matter-of-factly, reassuringly, at Horace's table, Phil stared, horrified. How could he tell Phil it was all right? He himself was gravely calm, nonchalant.

"This door?" he enquired politely, taking the handle.

Phil grimaced as he nodded.

David entered an ordinary office furnished with desks and filing cabinets, calendar, clock, typewriter. He sat in a comfortable old swivel chair; the suit, shirt and ties in his lap. He had brought all three ties, thinking that Phil could choose the one he preferred. He wanted to be considerate of Phil, who was not a bad guy, really.

Phil came out, frowning. He'd combed his black hair smoothly away from his pale forehead, and he looked somehow lacquered, hair and skin. Even his white shirt and black necktie gleamed. That necktie could never be untied, David was certain. The glassy knot must have been molded into it.

Phil stared at him. "You were never very close?" he asked.

"Close?"

"You and Horace."

"You mean just now?" David asked.

"No, I mean . . . in life."

"Why?"

"He's not ready. They did a complete autopsy, you know. They always do in such cases." Phil was still horrified by what David had so calmly seen, and David observed this with wonder.

"I've seen dead bodies before," he said. He counted them: three soldiers lying beside the deuce-and-a-half that had been hit by the short round. One arm was several feet away, still looking

524

exactly like an arm and a hand, wrist watch and wedding ring attached. An old lady hit by a car in Seattle, her silver-rimmed glasses in her gray hair as though she had just pushed them up, her pocketbook strap still around her arm. The grammar-school janitor, the only Negro in Leah, lying in the satin sheets of his coffin. A million in the newsreels and movies, blown apart, shot, burned, starved to death. So why was Phil upset?

"Here are the clothes. You can pick the necktie you like best," he said.

Phil took the clothes and put them on a hanger, the shirt neatly over the suit coat. "You weren't very close to Horace, then?"

Phil evidently implied that the pile of meat in there was Horace. Why must he say that? Did the son of a bitch want to make him admit something?

"Are you going to sell me a coffin?"

"A casket," Phil said, correcting him. Phil put on his suit coat before he led David into the next room. Here were soft carpets, reddish warm lights, flowers, coffins—caskets—sedately elevated to chest level. Each had a discreet small price tag hanging on one of its handles.

"What's the cheapest one?" David asked. He smiled at Phil, the slightest edge of cruelty flickering like a knife in his mind. He thought of the possibilities. He wanted to laugh because Phil was all puckered up in distaste. The possibilities seemed enormously interesting.

"How about a plain old pine box, Phil? I always liked the shape of a good old coffin. Pardon me—casket. You know, the kind that's wider at the shoulders? I mean all these here are too round. They all look like Pullman cars—you know what I mean?"

"We've never carried anything like that. You want a metal interior lining to keep out—"

"To keep out what, Phil? Why do you want to keep anything out?"

"And a cement vault," Phil said with no apparent expression. "The vault keeps the turf from sinking. The vault only costs a hundred and fifty dollars, and it's a good investment."

Suddenly David was confused. The possibilities had come jumbling through his mind—all the old, sick undertaker jokes—

and he could no longer entertain any of them. It was too late, of course, for poor Phil's approval, but he would not continue. He would not discuss investment, the etymology of the word. He would invest Horace's body in a vault that was, or was not, vaulted. He would place his deciding hand upon one of these streamlined, pompously decorated caskets, all of which, upon closer examination, resembled new Buicks. He would not—could not—invest his guilt within the soft satin interiors that looked so comfortable until he felt his own butt cold and dead down in there. The logic of that comfort nauseated him. He would rather take Horace into the woods and dig him a good, deep hole. He and Kate and Peggy would lower him down on ropes, and Wood would say the proper words over his empty brother while Harvey and Henrietta Whipple stood with bowed heads and understanding hearts. Just the family, who would understand why it had been necessary for Horace to blow Gordon Ward's head into fragments. Sometimes such things were just. But what a gruesome weight of his own murderous failure pressed down upon this vision.

He grew dizzy, and under the pretext of looking along the bottom of a fat casket lowered his head so the blood could return to it. Mainly he had to get out of here.

Phil took his arm in a surprisingly strong hand. "I'll show you what we can do," he said, and led David out of the showroom, down a carpeted hallway and through a curtained arch. Soft organ music murmured from behind purple curtains, and on a dais in soft pastel lights was an open casket surrounded by cut flowers. The lights were peach-colored, warm as were all the colors of the room. Urns of pastel metal and pastel glass grew lush ferns in all the corners of the raised dais, and the sleeping head of a plump young man lay on a silken pillow at the very center of all the warmth. The still face, eyes closed and hair neatly combed, glowed as though lighted from within by real blood.

There were murmuring voices behind him, and Phil turned him toward the chairs at the rear of the little theater, where somberly dressed people stood muted or sat with heads bowed. The organ squeaked, high as the smallest mouse above the basal hum of its chords. The soft lights themselves, coming from hidden sources, seemed to press the sweet perfume into his nose and

mouth. He looked at his own hand, and it was peach-colored, glowing as warmly as the cheek of the dead young man.

Standing at the rear of the room, among the live people, was someone he recognized—Mr. Caswell, the mailman. And next to him was Mrs. Caswell, short and bundled by her flesh. She was the main person, the one the others came toward with formal, dipping steps, to touch her hand and move their lips above her. He looked back to the center of the lights. Was that Ben there in the casket, silently glowing? They all glowed in this heady light, everybody. Even Mr. Caswell's ordinarily pale, skinny face seemed to have fleshed out in the numinous light.

"See?" Phil said in his ear. "Doesn't he look well? Do you see how it comforts them to see him for the last time looking well?"

God, it was Ben, his friend, once the friend he used to fight practically to the death, whose bony strength used to frighten him—strength that came, he always believed, from the ice-sharp will in the skinny body. Maybe it was that will that had kept him alive all these years in the hospital. He turned to Phil, who wouldn't let him go or let him turn. "Oh," he said.

"Straighten your tie and go give your condolences to his mother," Phil ordered. "Ben was your friend."

David turned on him, suddenly furious beyond words. "Who the! How the!" he whispered, choking on the air in his throat. "Who the hell are you?"

"Shame," said the just, unctuous voice.

David tore his arm loose, or was at the last moment let loose, and walked in slow motion toward the quiet group, toward the toothy murmurs of the old man who now leaned over Mrs. Caswell. He waited in line, knowing none of these old people with their soft colors and brittle hair, the women all fat and stooped. When it was his turn, Mrs. Caswell looked up, surprised, and smiled sadly at him. "Why, it's David Whipple!" she said breathily. There were no tears in her wrinkled, powdery eyes, and suddenly David was on Ben's side, overcome with grief for Ben. The skinny enemy and friend rode his freakish giraffe of a bike down High Street on the way to school again. David squeezed her white-gloved hand, and she said, "Oh! My arthritis, David!" He let go her hand and saw her count, calculate his tears. "David was Ben's oldest friend," she said to the others. Which was probably

true. "Go up and see him, David," she said. "He looks so well. It's really a blessing. It's really a blessing. And David, tell your mother how sorry we are about her loss."

When he shook Mr. Caswell's bony hand, as if in shy agreement they avoided each other's eyes.

David approached the dais and cast his eyes upon the young waxen stranger. It was not the Ben who meant power and will, but an older, softer person who had somehow been corrupted by the compromising years. David was not moved; he would never let this soft, glowing imitation take Ben's place in his memory.

He went home. At supper, unaware, he took meat upon his plate and stared down at the pale red juices. His intent to eat of the murdered flesh twisted in his throat until he had to leave the table.

The Whipples survived the week of the funerals. Wood and David attended Gordon Ward's funeral at the Congregational Church. After the ceremony he was borne by the Legion to his grave, the Drum and Bugle Corps bravely executing the slow march in their blue and silver finery. Keith Joubert played taps in the bright, windy day, the silver echoes flying on the wind across the cemetery, around the white church and across the square. Mrs. Ward was either frozen or brave; her husband and her friends surrounded her whenever she had to stand. Harvey did not attend. That afternoon Wood spoke to Gordon, Sr., and later that evening Gordon, Sr., called Harvey on the telephone. They spoke for more than half an hour, and afterward Harvey found it possible to speak to his family again.

They all attended Horace's funeral, again at the Congregational Church, Reverend Bledsoe officiating. The pallbearers were David, Wood, John Cotter, Foster Greenwood, Robert Paquette, and Joseph Foss, friends of David's and Wood's. After the church ceremony they carried Horace past Gordon's fresh grave, the slit turf still clearly outlined, to the Whipple plot where people of other centuries, grandparents, great-aunts and -uncles were buried. Horace seemed a strange addition to that ancient company, none of whom he had ever known. Sally De Oestris

didn't walk the hundred yards to the grave, and when the last prayer was over, Peggy picked her up at the church.

They found themselves—Harvey, Henrietta, Wood, David, Kate, Peggy and Sally—in the great hall of the Whipples' house. They were all alive, dry-eyed, and in each was the tiny guilt-flutter of relief. Waves of sorrow, that ebb tide, would wash over each of them at unexpected moments. The mother's breast would suffer the ghost thumps of another's need. They would close their eyes and be imperiled by visions of Horace as a child crying in pain and embarrassment, such as the time he walked toward them holding his arm above the place where it should not have bent. Henrietta would see his red, roaring face in the hallway, at the cellar door. She would jump to keep his ghost from tearing off hinges. But the tide of memory could only recede.

The sunlight fell through the high, arched windows in sedate, rather misty columns. The parquet floor, the oriental rugs, the heavy furniture—everything seemed to proclaim its substantiality. Henrietta, feeling the sweet ache of tiredness in her legs, sat down with the rest of them for a moment before seeing to the kitchen. She had nothing to see to there, but it was her place to keep track of. They were all silent for a while.

"So," Harvey said at last, and they nodded, or at least breathed an easy breath of assent. They were all still alive. Though death might be the next welcome (Sally thought this, and looked at the young people for better news), all their own complications of fear and desire still operated on this bright September day. Already they had begun to look to themselves and to each other for signs and portents.

35

Ten years have passed. It is the day before Christmas, 1958, and again the survivors are returning to Whipple Castle. Henrietta has been busy for a week, opening and airing rooms, making beds, planning food and drink for the whole complicated operation. Sylvia Beaudette has been helping, but it is still quite a job, because the survivors have been multiplying. Cribs and bassinets have been brought from the various attics and set up in the old nursery, and in the process Henrietta has grown sad. Those dusty teeth marks in the enamel are messages from her youth, signals across time from her babies. Time passes. To the young it seems so right that old people are old, because the young want to grow up. But they will learn—are learning now, in fact. Wood is thirty-four, David thirty-two, Peggy and Kate both twenty-nine. She and Harvey are so old it doesn't matter any more. Imagine moaning that you aren't still in your twenties! In David's last letter he spent at least a page sighing about age and rot.

Sally died in her sleep last year, at the age of eighty-two.

Christmas comes around just the same, and somehow the lights of Christmas reawaken the child magic, if only for moments. When Henrietta takes the strings of light bulbs from the box, the little bulbs swing down and hit each other with hard *ticks*, and she remembers all the years of tiny fright they might break. The little wire question-mark hangers for the decorations —has it been a whole year since she's untangled them? A year is a moment, a blink of the eyes, and here you are again.

Outside it is gray, cold, with light veils of snow driven by the wind. She goes to stand in the parlor they never use, where it is chilly because the heat vents are nearly closed. It was from

here she used to look at Wood when he was in that period of retirement ten years ago, when he sat quietly on the porch, studying his abominations. Now the cold boards seem to move as the snow swirls across.

The mad powers have been at war again, strutting and posing like brainless cocks, and will go to war again. She sighs because, among other things, the most powerful man in the world is a general. But there will be this Christmas anyway. One takes the seasons as they come.

She hears running feet, and manages to brace herself before Billy grabs her around the leg. "Hey, Grandma!" he says. He is six, brown-haired, with bright black eyes. He gives the impression that he owns her, owns the house and everything in it. "I know where the presents are," he says.

She is about to tell him to stay out of the presents when she realizes the spirit in which he has confessed this knowledge. This will be their secret. His sister, who is eight, presumably doesn't know, nor do his baby cousins.

Peggy comes in after him, and he ignores her. His mother is as unremarkable to him as the sun. She takes his hand and pulls him toward the door. "Come on," she says, and he doesn't object.

"Don't tell anybody," he says to Henrietta, ignoring the indignity of his forced removal.

"You and your secrets," Peggy says, smiling wryly. She is seven months pregnant; Billy has explained this to Henrietta in remarkably technical terms. He is still a little confused about Daddy's seed, because he has a window-box garden at home and he knows about seeds. A thoughtful look crossed his face when he came to that term. He doesn't like vagueness, or secrets that aren't his, and soon he will demand clarification.

Henrietta follows them out of the chilly room and shuts the door. Here in the hall are warmth and voices. She remembers Peggy Mudd, the little woods waif who came to them so long ago, who has repaid them a thousand times for whatever they gave her then. It has been their luck. She knows why Harvey let Bertram Mudd live there in the sugarhouse (she can admit that knowledge to herself now), and it is all so ironic that Harvey's infidelity in some way brought Peggy to them—Peggy who took Wood from his limbo; they all saw it happen. Wood is now doing

his residency in internal medicine at Graduate Hospital in Phila-
delphia, studying, he has confessed to Henrietta, the coinage of
his obsessions. Because of the hospital's location he has also become
an authority on razor slashes, bottle cuts, stab wounds, contu-
sions and other symptoms of human intercourse. Reality has
substituted for his visions, and since it is only reality, he can
put it in its place.

It is when he looks at his wife that his face evens out,
smooths down, and he smiles.

Sally, who is eight, spies her in the hall and comes to take
her hand. Sally is blond, with dark brown eyes and something
of Wood's squareness in the bones of her face. "Come on, Gram,"
she says. "What are you standing here for?" Her level gaze and
general sophistication are marred by a missing front tooth, a late-
comer that has been much discussed, especially by Sally herself.
The tooth is known to be up there in the gum, growing, she
assures everyone.

She leads Henrietta down the hallway into the great room
where the tree rises nearly to the ceiling. Past the false balcony
it rises, glowing and twinkling, a perfect balsam fir. The room is
sweetly scented. The primary colors that never seem gaudy on
Christmas have warmed the heavy beams and panelings of
Harvey's great hall. At the top of the tree, small as a bird, the
silver angel holds its hymn book before its pure little ceramic
face. Written in the angel's book are the words "*Stille Nacht,
Helige Nacht,*" and Henrietta thinks how their tree has always
been more pagan than Christian, how little any of them have
ever mused upon their nominal religion. Christmas has always
been for *them,* for the Whipples. They have always had to come
home to strut and clash, to touch each other again in the Christmas light.

Horace loved it so when the tree was up. Sadness comes over
her, even among all this new life and laughter. David and Carol's
twins are sitting in their grandfather's lap—two girl babies so
pretty she is awed by their identicalness; how could such perfection be repeated? Gail, their three-year-old, is gentle and bright.

David's life took a turn after Horace's death. He went back
to Chicago and tried to decide in which direction his life would
go. Would he forget paint, words, those naïve aspirations toward

art and meaning, and go make money? He has told her about that first year, when just about all he did was play poker and drink. Letty spun off from the wastrel he had become; she is married, living in St. Paul. After that year, in which he nearly lost his GI Bill, he came back to Leah and married Carol Oakes, a nice girl who is lovely to her children, whose warmth seems to envelop and soften David's prickly edges. He kept going to school until he became part of the school; he is now an assistant professor of English, whose dissertation on the metaphysical poets will be published next year. He will then become an associate professor. He is working on a book of what he calls "radical homiletics," several parts of which have been published in the literary quarterlies. "What I want to do, Hanky," he once said to her, "is to change the world and tell the truth at the same time. Do you think that's possible?" In the parts of his book that she has read she hears strange echoes of her own thoughts; but he seems to want to change things she never thought of changing. He works at his craft with the intense optimism of the student he has decided always to be. Around him in his profession he sees men whose cynicism, so brilliant it seems to arc, to ionize the air in little sparks and flashes, signifies that they are dying of . . . sloth. In his wallet he keeps a plastic-protected photograph of Horace, who, he says, is trying to tell him something. "Aside from Carol and the children, who keep me irritated and alive, Horace's cryptic message keeps me serious."

Whatever that means. To Henrietta he seems happy enough. She senses that he is never flippant—perhaps that is Horace's message to him.

The laughter of children chimes in the room, blue, green, red, yellow, needle-silver—the colors of their voices. She stands among them being a grandma. The title will always startle her.

David has taken Harvey's new Cadillac to the station in Wentworth Junction to pick up Kate. She had intended to fly from New York to the new regional airport, but weather grounded her plane in Boston and she had to take the train the rest of the way. Kate is an editor again, this time in a small publishing house. She does well, for though she has become exotic to Leah, in New York she is considered to possess the mythical virtues of the New Hampshire hills and mountains, which perhaps in a

measure she does possess. She tests for what is felt. Wayne Facieux introduced her to that world, and they are still friends. He no longer writes poetry; his main occupation would seem to be to know everyone of importance in the literary world. His style has changed; he has been known to wear spats and a bowler hat. He is on the editorial staff of a small magazine known for its brilliantly cutting reviews. A strange, thorny bird, he seems to have many literary jobs, many projects going.

Kate's marriage, to a man she prefers not to talk about, ended without children or friendship, and it has left her with a certain brittleness and hesitation toward marriage itself. Her life, she says, is exciting.

The weather is closing in even more, now. The snow has thickened, and the wind has stilled, as though quieted by the heavy flakes. In the white dusk Kate and David arrive. The short walk from the garage has bedecked them with white flakes and jewels.

The children have been waiting for Aunt Kate, and they run to her, yelling her name as she comes in. David comes along behind with her suitcases—one filled with presents. She is beautiful to the children, with her golden hair and bright loving gasps of pleasure. Her eyes shine, her clothes are touched with mysterious hints of silver and gold. To them she is not exactly human, she is the glittering Queen of Winter, the Kind Witch of the North whose boreal power is the paradox of ice and Christmas. Gail, Billy and Sally take her to see the twins, and it becomes a ceremony that hushes them all. She shines down upon their symmetries and they stare brightly up at her, her glitter in their eyes. She embraces Carol, telling her with the power of prophecy what treasures she possesses. David, with an uncharacteristic, or perhaps seasonal, burst of emotion, embraces both Carol and Kate and tells them he does not deserve them, that they are his talismans, his cisalpine legions.

Everyone is here, and the tree, miraculous and silent, rises above them.

Later, after supper's microcosmic calamities, the babies are put to bed and the children settled before the television, where *A Christmas Carol* is to be performed. "Bah, humbug!" Harvey roars, but he decides to watch it with them even though he knows he'll cry like a baby over Scrooge's reformation.

The others settle around the tree. Sally De Oestris is not here, nor is Horace. They all remember the Christmas Peggy came to live with them, the Christmas Horace fell into the tree—balls, bulbs, bells and tinsel in mad confusion, the tree's stability shaken. David, with his propensity for ceremony, proposes a toast to those who are no longer with them. In sherry they drink to Sally and to Horace.

Wood puts down his sherry glass and looks at his wife. She smiles at the Whipples, and as he sees her smile in profile, her lips from this angle are totally new, a discovery to him. He must touch her, so he puts his hand on her belly to see if he can feel the baby move, or the beat of the little heart.

Peggy feels her husband's hand on the beat of the heart.

THOMAS WILLIAMS was born in Duluth, Minnesota, in 1926, went to New Hampshire when he entered high school and—except for Army service in Japan and graduate work at the Universities of Chicago, Iowa and Paris—has been living there ever since. His short stories have appeared in *Esquire, The New Yorker,* and *The Saturday Evening Post.* One was awarded an O. Henry Prize; others have been included in *Best American Short Stories.* His novel, *Town Burning,* was nominated for the National Book Award in 1960, and his volume of short stories, *A High New House,* received the Dial Fellowship for Fiction in 1963. He has also been a Guggenheim fellow and was recently awarded a Rockefeller grant for 1968–69. He now lives in Durham, New Hampshire, with his wife and two children and is at work on a new novel, *The Hair of Harold Roux.*